BIG SNEAKY BARBARIAN
BOOK 1

Big Sneaky Barbarian

Book 1

Seth McDuffee

Podium

This book is dedicated to incomplete sentences, without which

All rights reserved. No part of this publication may be reproduced, stored in a retrieval system, or transmitted in any form or by any means electronic, mechanical, photocopying, recording, or otherwise without prior written permission from Podium Publishing.

This is a work of fiction. Names, characters, places, and incidents are either products of the author's imagination or used fictitiously. Any resemblance to actual events, locales, or persons, living, dead, or undead, is entirely coincidental.

Copyright © 2022 by Seth McDuffee

Cover design by Podium Publishing

ISBN: 978-1-0394-1799-1

Published in 2022 by Podium Publishing, ULC
www.podiumaudio.com

Big Sneaky Barbarian
Book 1

PROLOGUE

A BEGINNING . . . OF SORTS

As morning frost clung to the bark and branches of trees, the sun rose in the Kingdom of Arlo, dawning on the first day of winter. Autumn had officially ended, and many people began their dutiful preparations for the coming cold.

This seems like as good of a place as any for a bit of an expositional information dumping ground.

It was the year 177, a time of relative political peace, and the royal family sat their grandiose rumps happily on the throne. King Yule Gaier and his wife, Queen Salistre, had recently welcomed their fourth child—and first daughter—into the world: Princess Lynellyn. It is important to note that though this was a warlike people—those tempestuous *regals*—the tensions with Hathburia had not reached a fever pitch for nearly two years. For that reason, this is what many in the realm had begun to refer to as an age of "exploration and adventure."

All—it seemed—was right and usual in the world. However, that may be a bit "sunny skies and daisies," considering the calamitous—nay, cacophonous—events that would soon transpire. Certain individuals drudging within what many called "life" were positively rife with a hunger for power. Soon, all of the kingdom—even the whole of Regaia—would feel the tremendous might of what happens when great powers collide.

We move now to the bustling towns of Kess, set along either side of a narrower section of the Fury River in an area known as "The Trench." On one side, there was East Kess, and the other West Kess. No two towns had ever been so at odds, though both sections were largely the same save for their access to outside sources. Granted, West Kess was notably the home of the "double-baked mince pie," a detail that East Kess disputed, and it oftentimes came to bruised brows and shattered egos during an argument. The two locations were otherwise unified in their lack of notable innovations in the realm. The collective "towns of Kess" were used outside of their municipalities, although if anyone stepping inside the villages made that same distinction, they'd be in store for an unfortunate case of the "uh-ohs."

The twin towns were located just two days' walk (or one and a half, if you run a little) southwest of the famous Machus City, a location that would, eventually, become quite famous. However, this was many years before it would be destroyed by the greatest force to ever crash upon its sapphire walls. But that's getting a bit ahead. At the moment, Machus stood as a testament to gross kingdom wealth and garish disregard for safety codes.

East and West Kess were also several days east of Ruegr, the independent drakefolk city that had remained vigilant against the "monsters of the deep" ever since their first conflict centuries before. The towns of Kess were muddy, and they were wet. Tremendous portions of the area flooded every year during the heavy storms of late summer, forcing the more tenacious members of the area to capitalize on their lucrative tourist-boating surcharges. The rough-and-tumble folk who dwelled in these towns had grown accustomed to such an environment, and those closest to the Fury built their houses and businesses up on high beams and stilts. Uphill from the river, the townspeople worried less about flash floods, but much of the aesthetic had remained because far be it from them to have to feel left out of popular architectural fashion.

The Kesses were the last communities along the great coursing river before reaching Umbera to the north. As such, it was either a beginning point or ending point for most folk in the Trench—depending on which regional authority you were fleeing from. West Kess was also only a few short hours from the ancient Taruk Ruins, a place where many would-be explorers and treasure-seekers had spent countless hours, weeks, months, years, and even decades combing through, trying to unearth its secrets. However, no one had stumbled on to anything. Ever.

Though it did not deter anyone from trying.

In East Kess, there was a leaky and musty tavern of ill repute, even by Kessian standards. It was the Rat King, and if ever the ale was not watered down and overpriced, there'd likely been a riot. In fact, it was the exact launching point of several inebriated and uproarious rampages throughout the many years it had existed—and subsequently rebuilt.

The structure itself was set up very near the docks on the confusingly monikered western edge of East Kess, balancing precariously—it would appear to some—on four spindly stilts. The tavern inside was cramped and damp, though Phosh, the proprietor, would describe it as "cozy" to anyone who made the mistake of entering. There resided within a small fireplace along one wall, hardly ever lit on account of the business's overall and general *moistness*. Eight large tables fit to seat six to a side were wedged against one another in the tight space. The bar was delightfully made up of what might appear to be several rigged-together dressers, desks, cabinets, and one up-ended wardrobe. The swill behind the counter was disgusting and brackish, though the regulars would have it no other way.

Manning the bar was none other than Phosh Maelstrom himself. A self-described former adventurer, he was a grizzled and toothless little oak root of a human, slapping drinks into steins with his gnarled fingers overpowered with arthritis. Only one eye seemed open, the other eternally curled in a scowl, or perhaps a withered old wink.

At that very moment, his good eye was focused on one of the few occupants of his haggard hovel—a stranger.

He was an older human man with gray and white hair that had been cut very raggedly, perhaps by his own hands. His thick black eyebrows rested over dark and intense beady eyes that held all the presence of a farmer who suspected his prized sheep may have been sneaking out at night to get drunk. He sprouted a thick and bushy handlebar under a crooked nose, mustache the same color as the hair on his head, and his torso was wrapped in a massacred pile of oiled leather pretending to be armor, with thick wool clothing underneath. A large pack and various straps and belts hung loosely around him or were fastened tightly about his waist. He was lean but toned, his skin tanned from exposure to the sun.

As the stranger entered the Rat King, the belts' buckles rattled, and he scowled at the three other individuals inside the establishment. At first, he said nothing—merely glowering, but after a moment, he finally spoke.

"Where the *hell* is Frey?"

Phosh shook his head. This stranger would be none other than Atticus Grell, the heeler-dog of Archgeneral Bulwarren. The proprietor knew he couldn't eject this man like he could a regular patron or even ask him to lower his voice, as, despite his poorly put-together appearance and personal station, he was simply too high of a Level. So, Phosh simply resigned himself to rubbing down a few dirty tankards with an equally soiled rag and kept one eye—you can probably guess which—on the happenings.

A squirrelly elf—likely just past adolescence from the look of him, and probably not older than a hundred summers—stood shakily, and Phosh sighed. He knew better. He should have given the weak-bellied lickspittle a little bit stronger of a draught.

"He's ... not here," the elf said, brushing bone-yellow hair out of his face but not meeting his superior's gaze. " ... sir."

Grell's scowl deepened like the fissure of freshly cracked rock, and his neck turned purple with rage.

"I can see that, Kent! Do I look like I've gone blind in the last six hours?! Have my eyes been replaced with puddings, you fat sod?! I asked where he *was*, not whether he'd arrived yet!"

The elf trembled, nodding in panic.

"I—er—I don't know, sir. He was behind me when we left the inn, but—"

"If he doesn't show up before *she* does, I will beat him to death with *your* legs. Understand me?"

The elf called Kent nodded again, his eyes never leaving the knotty wood of the tavern floor.

"I'm here, Sir Grell. Please, don't frighten the children. They can't bear your blustery spittle."

A slim shape slipped down from the rafters, and Phosh did a double take. He was usually aware of anything happening within the confines of his establishment, and more, he was concerned that this mysterious individual would see what a terrible job of dusting he'd done up there. Still, this man had just appeared practically out of thin air, and even for a place like the Rat King, that was much too unusual. The man's hair was long and red, sweeping to his shoulders, and a smirk was plastered on his handsome face.

Too handsome, Phosh thought. *That's got to be an enchantment of some kind.*

The purple of Grell's neck somehow turned deeper, and he seemed ready to explode with the force of his anger.

"You stupid—"

At that moment, the tavern door swung open again, and silence struck the insides of the tavern like a dagger. Phosh looked up to see a woman stepping through the doorway.

She was unbelievably striking, he noticed, with a voluminous gathering of curls framing her face. Her movements were graceful, and though she appeared human, something about her unsettled Phosh to his core.

Ah, he thought. *One of those 'uns.*

"Here we are, then," she said, her voice pleasant and no-nonsense, but Phosh sensed an undercurrent of malice and danger in her tone. Whoever she was, or rather, *what*ever she was, she was immensely powerful. Phosh himself judged Grell to be Level Fifty, or near enough to it, but this woman had the Archgeneral's lapdog kneeling like a commoner.

Phosh realized quite suddenly that the rest of the tavern was on a knee as well, and though he didn't feel the same compulsion, their reaction made him second-guess himself. He started to genuflect, but the woman raised her hand.

"Up, all of you. We don't have time for this, I won't be here long, and I don't want to spend what little time I have basked in your . . . fragrant respect—charming though it may be."

Phosh sighed happily, easing himself up from a half-cocked position, his knees creaking in response. He wasn't sure he'd have been able to get back up had he made it all the way to the floorboards.

"M-madam," Grell fumbled, his earlier ferocity culled to that of a mewling kitten. "You look marvelous. Thank you for coming—"

"What did I just say?" the woman demanded, turning severe eyes on Grell. "Groveling wastes time. Save it for later, when I cannot see it."

Grell nodded, though he looked as though he thought himself soon a corpse.

"Now," the woman said, moving to the center of the tavern. "I won't spare any more delays. Are you prepared? And do you have the . . . items?"

Grell nodded again.

"Truly, madam, we have assembled a stout group of—"

"Perfect," she interrupted. But she wasn't looking at Grell. Phosh noticed the woman's gaze lingered on the red-haired man who'd leaped down from his ceiling.

She's going to notice the dust!

"You," the woman said to the one called Frey. "You're an attractive specimen. Are you all flash, or can you do what needs to be done?"

The man, seemingly undeterred by the woman's frightful presence, peered deep into her eyes with a wide smile.

"I am twice as capable as I am fetching," he said. "And as you can see, I am *extremely* fetching."

The woman didn't react to this comment save for squinting severely in his direction. Then she scoured over the rest of the room.

"That will do, then," she said. "You will leave now. If you are quick, you can get to the central chamber of the Ruins by morning. I will await you at the exit once you have emerged."

She lifted an object. It was a sparkling, thumb-sized crystal that shone from within with a pale blue light. Phosh thought it was quite pretty. The woman passed the object to Grell, who took it soundlessly. Then she leveled an icy gaze on the man and he took a step back.

"Do not fail me," she said simply, though her tone dripped with venom. "Or the unyielding shame you will endure shall seem only as a speck of irritation next to the pain I will unleash upon you."

"Yes, madam," Grell said, growing pale at her words.

Phosh observed all of this with quiet wonder. In all his years, this may have been the sixth strangest occurrence to ever peddle its contents within his fine establishment.

Nothing will ever beat Bear Night, though, he thought to himself. *Now, that was an evening to write home about!*

There was a long pause, as no one dared speak before the woman, and Phosh thought that it was well sorted. A bit of cloak-and-dagger, a bit of intimidation, topped by a sinister, enigmatic plot thread that would likely be resolved in some shadowed alley or seedy back room. All in all, fairly standard pre-breakfast-rush melodrama.

Then, like one of the bolts to the shoulder he'd experienced with far-too-frequent regularity in his life, the woman spoke again.

"Is he part of this?"

Phosh felt a dark lance of anxiety as she gestured in his direction. He'd expected to remain inconsequential to the goings-on, as would befit many a tavern owner before him. Dealings in the shadows of a pub were not uncommon, and this would not have been the first time he'd been privy to such events. There was an unspoken rule that tenders were sworn to silence in the wake of such drama. Now, though . . . Phosh had a bad feeling about this.

"No, madam," Grell said, his eyes flashing to Phosh. "Just the owner of this . . . establishment. We chose this location because of its privacy. He won't say anything. 'Tis their way."

"Nonsense," the woman said, sweeping out of the door. "Kill him."

Phosh felt the cowl of danger close in on him as the woman left. He'd been so quiet, and he truly wouldn't have said a word. But any hope he had of escaping with his life faded the moment Grell's eyes found him again—two hardened flints of pure obedience.

"Frey," the man commanded.

Phosh looked toward where the red-haired man had been, but he wasn't in his seat. He was standing in front of him, the handle of a knife in his hand—and the blade . . .

Phosh slumped as his lifeless body slid away from the weapon. Frey, still smiling, wiped the blood from the edge with his shirt sleeve.

"Done," he said casually.

"All right, you unseemly curs," Grell announced, his former stature returning in the departure of the woman. "Time to go. Things are about to get *very* fucking interesting. If you have any Skill Points to use, I'd allocate them now. You're going to need them."

With that, the group filed out of the Rat King, aiming their sights to the west, where a curious event was soon to take place.

CHAPTER ONE

YOUNG, DUMB, AND ANGRY

I hate being punished.

It's one of the worst feelings on Earth, and though I don't think anyone *likes* it—other than weird sex stuff, probably—I especially hate it. Punishment is just a way of control. If someone doesn't like something you've done, they can get revenge by stealing your freedom and your peace and forcing you to engage in an activity that you would otherwise not want to. Consequences are a real pain in the dick.

"Gabriel?"

I looked up and caught the cool, gray eyes of Mrs. Dexter, the school guidance counselor. She was staring at me with concern, like always, and I rolled my eyes and leaned back in the overly comfortable chair reserved for students. Few things boiled my backside more than being forced to sit in her office in the East Annex, listening to the clack of the grandfather clock in the corner, overwhelmed by the ever-present scent of clean leather upholstery and some other assaulting fragrance that reminded me of incense.

Her space seemed intentionally designed for tepidness. At least . . . I think that's the word. It was filled with earthy tones like green and brown, and despite it being sunny and hot as hell outside, it was a comfortable seventy degrees in the office. Framed photographs of various landscapes had been placed along the walls, done in the artsy, cinematographer style of lowered angles and unrealistic filters—you know, the kind of bullshit décor you could buy from a grocery store in the home-goods section. The curtains were drawn on the large windows, and I couldn't help to think it was just so that she had an opportunity to bathe the room in the light from the strategically placed lamps with ornate shades.

Everything was so . . . carefully comfortable. It was the Starbucks of office spaces, to be sure, crafted to make it look cozier than it actually was, which

I had to imagine was the hallmark of a sociopath. She *was* a guidance counselor, after all, so it made sense that everything needed to be so perfectly *acceptable*.

"You're not saying anything, Gabriel," Mrs. Dexter prompted again in her irritatingly measured tone. "Do you need some time to sort your thoughts?"

"Obviously," I hissed. "If I'm trying to sort my thoughts, don't you think it's stupid to ask if that's what I'm trying to do?"

Jeez, I thought, immediately regretting my outburst. I couldn't help it. I'd never been good at containing my anger, even with the mildest of grievances. I hadn't been raised that way. Roger would always tell me I needed to make sure the world knew I wouldn't accept anything I was unsatisfied with, and his word had always been law for me.

"I am only trying to get to the root of this issue, Gabriel," Mrs. Dexter explained, still choosing the calm voice of a mediator. "Where is this hostility coming from?"

"I don't know, Dexter," I said. "Where did you get your degree, Trailer Toilet University?"

I smirked at what I thought of as wit, but Mrs. Dexter just held me with her sympathetic gaze. It was enough to make me want to puke.

"You're mad at *me*, then?" she asked rhetorically.

"I'm not mad at *anyone*," I explained in a pitch that gave away my lie. "I just don't know why I'm stuck in this craft-store-decorated nightmare of an office, listening to you ask me over and over how I'm feeling."

Keep it together, I admonished myself, but I could already feel the frustration building. Everyone always seemed to misinterpret my words or actions— or just ignore them altogether. Roger always said my temper was my greatest ally, that it would force others to take me seriously. But Uncle Luke told me it was my biggest obstacle, and if I wasn't careful, it'd lead to a short life behind tall bars.

I'd liked Roger a lot more than my mother's apathetic brother-in-law, so I tended toward bluster and grief. Back then, I'd thought only of my own pain and the losses I'd suffered. So much so that I rarely considered how it affected everyone around me. I actually believed I was entitled to my outbursts—especially when I failed to contain them. It was easier to say to myself that I had *meant* to be rude rather than admit there were some underlying factors.

I was a boy under duress. But that didn't excuse being an obnoxious little shit.

"... sorry," I was able to manage. I knew I was supposed to be careful with people in positions of authority, however unrespectable they were in my eyes.

Mrs. Dexter gave me a small smile, arching her brow as if to indicate she understood and pitied me. That made me furious, and my apology dissolved in my own mind.

What right did she have to judge me? I'd seen her at Señorita Sabrosa a few months before, eating tacos with *flour* tortillas. Even more upsetting was watching as she picked pieces of cilantro out of her pico de gallo and balled them up in a napkin. What sort of untrustworthy monster didn't like cilantro? The type that should not have been allowed to counsel high school students, clearly. She probably also threw batteries at baby birds.

"You're here because of what happened last week, Gabriel," she soothed. "That's also the reason why you're talking to me, because it's my job to try and understand wh—"

"Your job?!" I shouted suddenly, causing her to jump. I leaned forward in the chair and scowled.

Ah, shit. It's happening. I'm about to make an ass out of myself.

I tried to get a handle on the hard knot of anger threatening to burst apart within my chest—I really did. But, just like always, the dizzying sense of depersonalization unfurled within my brain and my uncomfortable aggression uncorked.

"You're not a real therapist; otherwise, I'm sure you'd make people call you *Dr. Dexter*. You're just some wannabe who wasn't able to fix her own problems, so instead, you try to *fuck with* teenagers' brains to make yourself feel better!"

There was a long silence as Mrs. Dexter attempted to get the mettle of me. *Is it metal? Meddle . . . ?*

I'm not a word genius.

She wasn't glaring at me, just *looking*, like she was trying hard to figure me out. As if I was some animal at the zoo that she was hoping to see do something weird.

"Gabriel," she said after a moment, brushing a strand of long gray hair out of her face. "You have every right to express yourself in whatever way you see fit, but I would personally prefer if you didn't use the *F*-word when referring to me or my actions. I am here to help you—despite what you may think—but I have to request that you respect my preferences."

It was too late. I knew I was about to say something that I would regret. I just didn't know at the time how much I'd actually be affected by my next two sentences.

"Here's some respect for you!" I declared, hopping up from my seat suddenly and flashing my middle finger a few inches from her face. "Fuck. Y—"

. . . so, that's how I ended up on a train.

Let's rap here for a second.

I'm Gabe Skelter. Or, at least, I *was* Gabe Skelter. Now . . . well, I don't want to jump ahead too far, but suffice to say . . . is that the right term? Fuck it. Suffice to say that he was the old me. I'm on my new shit now. Rest assured, though, that the boy you see here *was* me, and he was a complete and total dickhead. You should know that, going forward—the dickhead thing. I thought I was awesome and though I knew I was the butt of many of my peers' jokes, I believed that to be undeserved. It sort of was, but now I can kinda see where they were coming from. It's pretty funny, looking back. But I don't need to tell you that. You'll see. I'll try to get in the headspace I had at the time. Where were we?

Oh, yeah. The goddamned train.

I had chosen a seat near the back, as that had seemed like the best spot to avoid most people. Being in the rear allowed me to make sure that no one was behind me, and I could keep my eyes on everyone I hated. And I hated most people. But this instance was particularly bad because I had to be on this godforsaken metal tube with some of the worst kinds of people.

High school students.

I was also in high school, to be fair, but it didn't stop me from seeing the darkness in their motives. I mean, I knew how shitty *I was* to be around. I wouldn't hang out with me if you paid me fifty bucks, and I was normal. Not that other people thought I was normal.

If nothing else, it allotted me plenty of time to sit and stew over my embarrassing display in Mrs. Dexter's office.

My little tantrum.

I'm sure I came across as your average, too-edgy-for-me, incel-leaning dummy-ass, but I didn't see myself that way. Not then. If you had called me that, I'd have laughed in your face and brazenly quoted a bumper sticker I'd seen as a kid: "*I hate everyone equally.*" For the young Gabriel Skelter—Gabe, if ya nasty—that generic, Hot Topic, baby-boomerish attempt at humor summed up what I thought was important to let people know. Not only was I a self-righteous crumb, but I believed I was something of an underappreciated asshole—a Dr. House type, if you will. But I was closer to a "Dr. Dipshit" with an inability to pin the lid on my fits of angsty, teenage brattiness.

If I could go back in time, I would have sat down next to that version of me and given myself *such* a slap. I had no clue what was going to transpire, the true obstacles and challenges. Nor the triumphs I had in store for me. Things were about to get bumpy, and if I'd only known . . .

Well, enough of that. I can't change what happened, so I may as well relay it as it went down.

Even then, scanning the occupants of the packed train, I could see the looks.

Abbie Carlson, for one, caught me staring at her and raised a manicured eyebrow before wrinkling her nose at me and turning away in a dramatic flourish of red hair.

Stupid Abbie. It's not like I was paying her any attention, anyway—she wasn't even that pretty. Kind of arrogant—if you ask me—to think that just because the short, fat detention magnet was looking in her direction that . . . Well, maybe she had a reason to believe that. If I looked like her and someone like me was glancing my way, I'd probably be dialing the police in between breaths.

Also, I had *sorta* spray-painted an ejaculating wiener on the hood of her boyfriend's car. So, it's possible this was a much more nuanced issue.

If I was being honest, I was very attracted to her. My personality back then wouldn't allow me any chance of genuine emotions or feelings, because I was so wrapped up in my own insecurities in how others perceived me.

The aforementioned boyfriend wasn't around for this excursion, but his best friends Matt Marshall and Nick Harmon were. They had spent the whole time chatting with Abbie and the other kids on the train while also looking in my direction and laughing. They could go right ahead, though, because I'd . . . get my revenge. Or something. Matt's mom worked at the same grocery store as my aunt, so I figured I could sneak in and—I dunno—fill her locker with . . . bees or something. I was still workshopping that, actually.

Nick lived a few houses away from me, and I still knew the combination to his dad's garage from when we were kids. I'm sure *Mr.* Harmon would hate to wake up to his brand-new riding lawn mower missing the blades or wheels. That would show Nick not only for laughing but also for turning on me once we got to high school. It wasn't my fault that I wasn't interested in sports like he was, or that I was about as smooth of a talker as a sandpaper-tongued telemarketer. Those weren't my strengths, but I still had a mile-wide chip on my shoulder that he'd seemed to completely forget our friendship.

I seethed in my seat like a petulant child and slipped my earbuds in, hoping that the opening chuggy goodness of Gojira's "Silvera" could quell the rage threatening to boil over.

As I sat ruminating on the various ways I could make my classmates' lives a living hell, a person in front of me turned. A thin, pale face with a cruel-looking eyebrow scar peered at me over the back of the seat.

"You all right, Gabe?" Mike Cutsford asked in a high voice.

"Shut up and turn back around, dumbass," I growled.

Mike was probably the only person on this train that was happy I was here. That was because *he'd* be the one everyone would be making fun of and giving snobby looks to, otherwise. I could only see the top of his face and the tangles of scraggly blond hair, but I knew his heavily scarred jaw and nose lurked below the edge of the seat as he stared at me.

"Damn, okay," Mike said, narrowing his brows. "I was just checking on you. Why are you even on this trip if you don't want to be here? Seems like a weird thing to do."

"You're one to talk, Cuts*face*," I said, using the nickname that seemed so popular where Mike was concerned. "You're odd as hell. How's your Dungeons and Dragons after-school crew doing? Lot of members?"

The taunt seemed to work, and Mike sighed and turned back around, slumping in his seat.

Ah, shit, I thought. I hadn't meant to make Mike feel bad; he was just making a vain attempt to gauge my threat level. But, I thought, he should have minded his own business and definitely not have interrupted me when I had a homicidal ideation about kicking Nick out of the door of the speeding train. I sighed and pulled my earbuds out, attempting to extend an olive branch—or whatever you called it.

Man, I was ten shades of awful. The only thing more crippling than my objectively hilarious sense of idiotic arrogance was my own self-hatred.

"Mrs. Dexter *made* me," I said, my voice a bit softer so that Mike would know I wasn't planning on attacking him. I saw him move ever so slightly, turning his head toward me but didn't say anything.

"She said it would do me some good to take part in an *educational adventure*. According to her, the teamwork involved will help me sort out some of my personality issues. It was either this or military school."

Mike shifted in his seat so that I could see his left eye.

"Military school? Those are private institutions now. You can't just send kids there anymore."

"Well, maybe it's JobEd," I admitted. JobEd was where the *bad kids* and dropouts had to go usually. The facility was some government-sponsored program to train young people to build skills so they could land a miserable minimum-wage gig for the rest of their lives, generally understanding it would be after they got out of juvenile detention or jail. JobEd also required folks to stay in barracks and work without pay during their time, as its whole aim was teaching people how to do one specific kind of job under a strict tutelage of discipline. To me, it sounded as appetizing as a bag of diarrhea.

Roger had gone there, I thought, suddenly. It was intrusive, but I banished it from my brain. *Not a good time to be thinking about that.*

"Ah," Mike finally said carefully. I could imagine he was being cautious with his responses to me because he didn't want to unlock my anger.

Smart, I thought.

God, I was so insufferable.

"So, was this because of the fire?" he asked carefully.

I winced.

"Yeah, probably. I dunno; maybe she's just a crackhead," I said with a shrug.

It had definitely been because of the fire. It sounded worse than it was, though. The way everyone talked about it, you'd think I burned down the auditorium or something. All I'd done was light every third-floor restroom garbage aflame... and a couple of bags of dirty gym clothes. I didn't know they'd burn *that* much. The sprinklers had gone off in the middle of the pep rally, and I found myself dragged out of the school in handcuffs. Fortunately, my uncle Luke was a good lawyer, or maybe just annoying enough to keep me out of serious trouble. This field trip was the compromise.

"She seems pretty nice to me," Mike said.

"Well, she's *not* nice, Cutsford," I said. "She's a gigantic prick, and if she thinks I'm going to learn anything from this trip, she's dead wrong. Even if I accidentally start to educate myself, I will make sure I smash my head with a rock so that I can forget."

"That's... pretty spiteful," Mike said, now fully facing me. "You might like it, though? This is my third year going, and I always enjoy it."

"Yeah, I'll bet you're popping like ten boners over it," I said with a huff. "Listen, Mike. I'm sure for you and your squadron of locker jockeys, this is like seeing the Black Dahlia Murder in concert, but for *normal* people, walking around in nature and learning about the dumbass settlers for two days is hell on earth."

Mike looked around the train and smiled.

"I dunno, dude. It sure seems like there's a lot of happy people," he said. "You might be the only normal one here, then."

"That goes without saying," I said... anyway. "But they're only having fun because they can sneak off and drink shitty beer or give each other handjobs. Plus, Eldon is offering extra credit for his class, so I'm pretty sure that's the real reason anyone even wanted to come."

"Well, I'll still enjoy it," Mike said. "The historically accurate replica settlement is a feat to behold. They even have a hand-dug well with a crank to get water."

"*Feat to behold?*" I razzed. "Listen to yourself. Who talks like that? Listen, no one wants to jerk off a prehistoric puddle to get a cup of mud. This is why you get your ass beat all the time, Cutsford."

Mike narrowed his eyes again but then relaxed them and shrugged.

"Maybe," he said. "But if that's *my* reason, what's your excuse?"

I scowled. What did *he* know? Sure, I'd been in a few fights in the past. Well, more than a few, but I didn't think anyone would say I lost them. I just... came out second best. Of two participants.

I guess I *did* have a problem with people getting confrontational, whether it was pushing me, tripping me in the hallways, or throwing things at me . . . on occasion. Last week, Trey Weeks hit me in the head with a football while I was walking by the track field. I had gotten mad, but it only accomplished making people laugh. Being a five-foot-six, two-hundred-seventy-pound eighteen-year-old with rage issues only seemed to encourage them.

"Anyway, this whole thing is stupid," I said. "Don't think I'm going to have some breakthrough of enjoyment and join Science Club, or whatever, with you afterward."

"I'm not *in* the Science Club," Mike corrected with a smile. "Is that even a thing?"

"You'd know," I said stupidly.

"You're wrong, anyhow," Mike said.

"Excuse me?"

"I said, 'You're wrong,'" Mike clarified, shrugging his shoulders.

"I'm never wrong," I explained. ". . . about what, though?"

"About my friends enjoying this," he whispered. "Logan and Noah didn't want to come; they said it was lame."

"Ah, well, sounds like they are smarter than you," I said. "Guess they get to be the presidents of Science Club."

I put my earbuds back in, hoping that would indicate to Mike that our conversation was over. I closed my eyes, feeling exhausted, but I knew I wouldn't be able to sleep while we traveled. I always had a terrible issue with sleeping.

Well, I suppose that wasn't exactly true, was it? I didn't *mind* sleeping. It was waking up that I hated. Awakening to the realization that you had to deal with the same shitty life, terrible people, and tedious everyday activities was not worth getting out of bed for. The dread always seemed worse in the morning. For that exact reason, I usually chose to stay up late into the night, only passing out when my body physically could not handle the strain of being awake any longer.

Sometimes, I even went without sleep for days on end. I had a wicked case of insomnia, and it didn't seem to matter what I did; I just couldn't kick the habit.

To combat it, I'd been prescribed every sleeping aid on the planet in my eighteen years of life, but nothing helped. My mind seemed to rebel against sleep because of my hatred and disgust for beginning a new day.

I sighed, and straightened my back. Through the wails of heavy riffs blasting from my earbuds, I glanced around the rest of the train.

It was a regular evening train full of people. The Early Settlers field-trip participants only took up about half of the rickety car, while strangers occupied the remaining seats. Commuters, heading back to whatever awful lives they had waiting for them at home after a full day of work.

There were fifteen students from our school on board, all seniors like I was supposed to be. I'd been held back once. Or twice. Who was counting? I could see a cluster of girls near the middle of the car: Hannah Rentz, Alexis Weber, Madison Edwards, and Emma Stokes. The girls were talking excitedly, taking pictures on their phones and immediately checking the results. Next to them was Mason Petersen, joking right alongside and gesturing theatrically with his long arms. Beyond that were more students I didn't know that well. Probably some under-the-radar kids, though I'm sure they were dicks as well. Most of the kids at my school were dicks.

The last two students that I knew were Molly Thoms and Jando Guerrera. They were skaters and very likely stoners, and as far as kids at my school went, they were pretty all right. They weren't jerks to me, but that was because they weren't rude to anyone. I'd always reasoned that it had to be hard to summon the strength to bully someone when your every waking thought was enclosed in a cloud of euphoria. Molly was tall and lean, with long, straight brown hair covered by a black beanie. Jando, whose full name was Alejandro, was short and thin with closely-cropped dark curls. The two of them hung around with a group of other skaters and were often in trouble for using open lunch to skate on school property or for bringing their boards with them into class. I could see they both had theirs with them now, hanging off the rear of their backpacks, and I chuckled. Mr. Eldon would have had a heart attack dealing with that.

Speaking of, Mr. Eldon was not far from the front of the train, lazing against his seat with his arms crossed, his red, mustachioed face drawn into a picture-perfect snooze. He was in his early fifties and was stocky with a moderate gut wedged into a sweater vest, and was, surprisingly, the chaperone and sponsor of the field trip. Being the American history teacher, Eldon had a vested interest in providing these sorts of outings because his classes were famously dull, and most students struggled to do well. It was the reason, in my mind, why he'd chosen to offer extra credit.

I was technically in his class, but Eldon was the type to never know for sure which students were actually present or not beyond seating charts, something he always mixed up between the seven classes he taught each day. Most of the time, he wouldn't even call roll; he'd just glance up and do a rough estimate for any empty seats. I'd figured out on my first day that it was nearly impossible to see several of the absent spaces from his desk and made sure to get myself assigned to one to take advantage of that fact, which meant I was usually as far away from his boring monotone as I could get. As best as I knew, I had perfect attendance in his seventh period this year, even the week I accidentally forgot to go to school.

I looked beyond Eldon's sleeping form to the rest of the passengers on the train. I saw a few men and women dressed in suits and blazers, and I couldn't help but think they were probably rich assholes who worked in a bank or on the top floor of a big building downtown where they ordered delivery for lunch every day that they only ate half of, and never tipped.

God, I hated wealthy people.

There was a woman who looked to be in her mid-forties sitting by herself on the left. She had a serious face and seemed like she was concentrating on a book she was reading, but I couldn't see the title because she did that thing people do where they bend the cover back behind the binding. I wasn't much into books, but it still seemed like a rude thing to do to one. The woman also had a raincoat folded up on her lap, which was odd, because it hadn't rained nor, I'm pretty sure, was that something on the forecast.

Nearby were a few older people in matching leisure clothing, and I got the impression they were part of some exercise club, and there were a couple of construction workers who sat quietly on their phones, looking more than a little exhausted.

Farther down were a couple of college-aged guys who wouldn't stop laughing at some stupid joke or another. They'd gotten up a couple of times to chat with the group of senior girls, but Mason, ever the watchful sheepdog, had shamed them into sitting back down.

"They're in *high school!*" Mason shouted, making sure everyone on the train heard. "They don't want your herpes!"

Even I had to laugh at that. I found Mason extremely rude, but he was that way with everyone, which was something of an admirable quality. At best, he didn't pay me much mind—except the one time he had commented on my hoodie being "creepy goth shit." It *had* been an Infant Annihilator sweatshirt with a devil holding a severed torso, so it wasn't even really that far off, all things considered.

The college bros hadn't liked being made to look stupid by the fabulous high school boy. In response, they spent the next stretch of time glaring at Mason and muttering things amongst themselves.

I ignored them, continuing my perusal of the train car, noticing several other lone specters populating the seats, but they weren't interesting enough for me to really pay attention to. I liked weirdness or curiosities because those are what really stood out to me. Well, I suppose that is what stood out for most people. It just seemed painful and dull to focus my attention on a person in a boring pair of jeans and a solid-colored T-shirt rather than to size up someone who was obnoxious, or acting odd, or . . .

Near the front of the compartment was a beautiful woman with curly brown hair. She dressed almost elegantly: a long, flowing shawl with flowers patterned on the sheer fabric, and beneath that was a red silk shirt and black leggings that only went halfway past her calves—I think the style is called capri. She was looking at something in her hands that gave off a glow, and at first I thought it was her phone, but the light from it was . . . off. It was too strong, for one, and seemed to be shifting and swirling.

I didn't have much time beyond that for analysis, because that's when the fight broke out.

The college dudes, getting bold, called out to Mason angrily.

"What the fuck did you just say, you fucking fairy?"

The train went silent. I snapped a look at Mike right in front of me, who tensed up. He had been on the receiving end of plenty of conflicts, so he tended to get a lot of anxiety over it and seemed to have a pretty good idea when things were about to go south fast.

One of the bros, a meaty, muscular dude with short blond hair, stood up, puffing his chest out.

Obviously used to that sort of insult, Mason rolled his eyes and waved him away, seemingly unbothered by the explosion from the angry young man.

"I didn't say anything about you, *Steroid Steve*," he spat. "Don't you have anything better to do, like planning your next date rape?"

Steroid Steve's face went red, and he glared daggers at Mason.

"Shut up, you gay bitch," he growled, and marched toward Mason. The high schooler suddenly looked a little less confident. He didn't shy away, but I could tell from the clench of his jaw that this hadn't gone how he thought it would. As miserable as I was back then, I absolutely *despised* people being bigoted. It was a very quick way for me to get protective over people I knew or, hell, didn't know. Maybe it came with the territory of being made fun of for stuff I also couldn't control? Looking back, my extremely volatile rebuke for intolerance was likely my only good quality at the time. That and my excellent taste in music, if I do say so myself.

Suddenly, Nick shot up and crossed the distance in a flash, putting himself between the two young men.

I thought about how different we'd turned out since we were children. It was a drastic contrast. At one time, we'd been roughly the same height and weight, but after a certain point—seventh grade, to be precise—I'd stopped growing. But Nick had continued to get bigger, losing the chubbiness he'd had and growing into a powerfully built kid. Where I had remained stumpy and flabby, Nick was tall and muscular. The college bro seemed to pause as the high school senior approached.

"Whoa, whoa, whoa," Nick said, a wide smile on his face and his hands up in a pacifying manner. "Let's all calm down here, guys. This is a small train. I know *we've* been on here for a while, and everyone's a little tired, so . . . maybe some things were said that probably weren't meant to be so harsh? Can we agree that it's possible this isn't the right time to have a disagreement?"

Nick had always been the peacemaker. I remembered several choice instances in our youth when he'd convinced people *not* to beat me bloody because of some insult I'd hurled their way. He had a way with words that had a positive effect on others, while mine tended to have the opposite. It was probably a contributing factor as to why people liked him a lot more than they ever would me. That, and it didn't hurt that he was a star athlete.

But as Nick stood there, I couldn't help but think that this time, it didn't seem like his silver tongue would be as useful to him.

"Fuck you, *Tyrone*," Steroid Steve shouted. "Stay out of this unless you want to get your face punched in."

Whoa. Not only were these guys homophobic assholes, but they were also racist as hell.

So, they can multitask.

My hackles were raised and I immediately began to get a little hot under the collar. This was going to get so much worse before it was going to get better. I absently reached into my bag and grasped my secret weapon, my blood beginning to pump hard and fast as my anger began to boil over.

"All right, friend," Nick was saying, nodding. "Things are getting a little aggressive. Let's all cool it."

I was confused. Why wasn't anyone else standing up to these douchebags? Being in high school, Nick shouldn't have been the only one with the balls to say something to them and try to put a stop to their dickheadery. I glanced at the actual adults that made up our population and scowled. They were all either watching with tense interest or pretending they weren't paying attention to avoid getting drawn into the conflict themselves.

Cowards. Guess it was just going to be me, then?

I stood up, pulling the switchblade out of my bag and palming it for the moment.

Time to look cool as hell!

"Dude, calm down," one of the other college guys said to their friend.

"Shut the hell up, Dalton!" Steroid Steve shouted at his friend. His neck bulged with clear signs of anger, and from my history of getting unnecessarily pissed off, I knew he was about five seconds from striking. "These dumbass high school bitches think they're tough. Talking shit and trying to fucking square up. They are about to find out what a stupid fuckin' plan that is."

"Listen, man—" Nick started, but that was the moment Steroid Steve struck. He swung wide and caught Nick in the mouth to an audible gasp from most of the train car. To Nick's credit, he didn't fall, but he *did* look dazed and reached up to wipe his mouth. Steroid Steve suddenly shoved him, sending the boy tripping backward, and then turned and grabbed Mason by the shirt. That was when Nick returned the favor.

He struck the college bro so hard and fast that the man tumbled backward, crashing against the floor with a thud. Someone screamed and the other college guys, now angry, stood up to square off against Nick. That was *too* many dipshits ganging up on one person, and that wasn't cool or fair in my eyes. When people were abusing their numbers like that, it had the effect of making me really mad.

I launched forward, brandishing the knife.

"Get the fuck back!" I shouted, holding the edge of the switchblade out menacingly and sidling up next to Nick. The college bros stopped where they were.

"What the hell, Gabe?" Nick demanded, seeming angry. "You brought a knife on a field trip?"

"Yeah," I said, smirking and ignoring the horrified expression of everyone around me. "I thought it might add an element of excitement."

Seeing the pause my actions had caused, I let out a hoot.

"Looks like I was right."

Steroid Steve, now up again, frowned at Nick and then looked at me.

"We got a butter*ball* with a butter *knife*," he said to his friends with an evil smirk. "Probably has jelly all over it."

"Why don't you come over here and find out, dicks-for-brains," I spat. "Unless you're afraid I'll cut your tiny balls off."

I was fuming. I'd never been the best at controlling my temper, and now these guys were on my last nerve. I could feel the familiar cloud of rage obscuring my thoughts, and I knew that whatever was about to go down, I would . . . probably end up worse for wear. But I didn't care. I never cared.

"Gabe . . . " Nick breathed. "You should probably—"

Steroid Steve and his buddies all attacked at once. One of the larger men on the right went for my knife, trying to grab it away from me. I angrily stabbed forward, slicing open a massive cut on the backside of his hand. The man howled.

"Fat Frodo just cut my fucking hand open!"

There was a blur as the group of men suddenly rushed me, knocking the knife out of my grasp and me to the ground. I felt an instant blossom of intense pain as one of them struck me in the face, and another as a foot slammed down onto my stomach. The wind left me, and I was suddenly groaning on the floor of the train. I felt a kick and heard a crack as another foot connected with my ribs. I couldn't breathe, and I was in such intense pain that all I could do was lay there as the men pummeled me.

I heard Nick roar as he fought Steroid Steve. The bigger and older man put him in a headlock before tightening his arm around Nick's neck. However, I didn't get an opportunity to see what was next because another kick rocketed into my stomach, sending me sprawling.

Suddenly, everything stopped.

I was trying hard to gasp for air and only barely succeeded because each breath was agony. I knew one of my ribs had to be broken, but I was so afraid of that possibility, I tried to banish the thought from my mind.

I opened my eyes.

Everything was at a standstill. The large college bros had stopped battling almost like they were frozen, staring at something to their right. I lifted myself as much as I was able, to spy what they were looking at.

The woman with the raincoat was standing now. Her face was stormy, like a quiet and threatening thundercloud looming over everyone. In her hand was a pistol, and she had it leveled at the group of men.

"Sit down," she commanded sternly. I could tell from her voice that she was not the type to allow her deadly serious convictions to be ignored. Steroid Steve shook his head in contempt, raising an eyebrow as he sneered at the woman.

"What are you, a cop?"

"No," the woman said simply. "I'm not. Now *sit*."

CHAPTER TWO

OH, BOY! TIME TO DIE!

"I mean, I could just take it from you," Steroid Steve said, eyeing the gun and winking.

The woman flashed a glance up and down at the muscular douchecanoe and shook her head.

"No, you couldn't," she said directly.

"Got a fuckin' tough-ass bitch here, boys," Steroid Steve said. "Thinks she can out-man me. If—"

"I have logged over two hundred and-fifty hours training with *this* pistol alone," the woman interjected in a calm, almost detached tone. "Not to mention the countless hours I have spent fine-tuning my technique with various other firearms, both stateside and, more practically, abroad."

She tilted her head to the side.

"Physically, you are much larger than me. If you were to attempt to take this weapon away, I would be forced to fire a bullet into your center mass that would travel one hundred and-forty-eight miles per second, and at this distance it would burrow all the way through you, out the other side, through the window, and probably bury itself in the dirt near West Eighty-Ninth before you could fire a single synapse from your underdeveloped ape-brain to tell your bladder to piss your pants. It will hurt the whole time, and if you survive, the pain it leaves behind will be your constant, waking nightmare."

She gestured with the barrel to the seats behind the men.

"Now. Sit down."

I was taken aback. Her monologue sounded strangely rehearsed, as if she'd uttered it dozens of times in front of a mirror. I couldn't think of anyone who spoke like that in real life—maybe in movies but not on this side of the screen. I wasn't sure I believed her conviction after that whole recital, but, if nothing else, it had been effective. The men stumbled back and sat down at her command.

Was she a soldier? I wondered. She had mentioned overseas training, and that seemed like something one of the troops would be required to do. I didn't know anything about the military, to be honest, other than what I had learned from first-person shooters. Maybe she'd call in a combat drone and light up this whole compartment? That would be pretty cool. Even if I got fried after the train car transformed into an inferno, I'd still get the satisfaction of watching the smug looks melt off of these dickheads' faces and into a gooey puddle.

I shook my head. What sort of edgelord, intrusive thoughts were these? I was basically two synonyms for the word *darkness* away from writing a Korn song.

I focused on the group before me and smirked. What a strange turn of events. The woman kept the gun trained on them, looking over at Nick.

"You all right?"

Nick nodded, rubbing his bleeding nose where he'd been hit by Steroid Steve during the scuffle.

"How's the kid?" Major Badass asked, referring to me. I groaned and shakily lifted myself.

"He's perfectly fine," I said, mockingly. "These guys do more slapping than real fighting."

She gave me an appraising glance and then raised an eyebrow. I hated when people did that.

"Yeah," she said. "Looks like it."

I looked past the woman and over to Eldon. The fool was still slumbering in his seat, head bobbing with the motion of the train car. How he could sleep through all that commotion was as impressive as it was baffling. Looking at Nick, I scowled.

"All these people on the train, and only three of us did anything," I said, then cast a glance at the rest of my classmates with a sense of superiority. Near the back, Matt looked on wide-eyed at Nick and me, then shook his head. Cutsford had ducked down, hiding behind the substantial luggage bag on his lap. Abbie looked sick. Everywhere I glanced, my fellow students were in various stages of either fear or disgust.

Cowards, I thought again.

"Yeah, a lot of good you did, you fat idiot," said one of the college bros. "You just got your ass stomped."

"Oh, please!" I shouted back. "You were barely able to lay a scratch on me without ganging up together."

"Oh, yeah?" the one called Dalton demanded. "You wanna go one-on-one, Lunchbox?"

"Yeah," I said, sticking my face out tauntingly. "I do. I'll wreck you like I did your mom's p—"

"Enough!" called a voice from the front of the car. It was the curly-haired woman. All eyes turned to her. There had been something strange about her voice, almost like it had come from . . . inside my head? But that couldn't be right. Maybe one of those shitheads had given me a concussion?

The woman stepped forward, brandishing the object in her hand. It was a circular thing, and on the first inspection, it looked like a makeup mirror. But, as I peered closer, I could see it looked more like it was made of copper or some other kind of dingy metal. The glow from the device still lit up the area, and the swirling patterns created a strange effect.

"As much as I adore the idea of letting you all kill one another, we are on the precipice of something else," the woman said. "Something great."

"What are you talking about, lady?" Steroid Steve demanded.

"She's kinda hot," whispered one of the other bros. The woman ignored both of these comments and instead pointed out the window. I looked in her indicated direction and saw that the sky over the city horizon had a curious blue hue. I looked back at the woman and found she was smiling.

I tried desperately to figure out what was going on. Everything seemed to be unfolding in such a strange and dramatic way since I decided to go on this trip, and I wasn't sure why.

"I hope you all save that passion for when it *truly* matters," the curly-haired woman said then. "Because it will serve you well."

She looked at Nick.

"Some of you . . . "

Then she looked at me with a sneer.

" . . . more than others."

I scowled back.

"What kind of psycho horseshit is this?" Steroid Steve demanded. He made to stand, but the woman raised her hand, and he immediately dropped to his seat again with a terrified expression.

"You will see . . . " she said mysteriously, and then lifted the copper circle and smiled.

"Time to go!" she announced, and then, as if by magic, she disappeared. Just . . . winked out of existence like one of those old CRT televisions switching off.

There were many gasps and excited talking as everyone tried to figure out what had just happened. I struggled to stand upright during this, gripping the back of one of the seats and wincing. I was *not* going to be able to toot around Dysentery Village with a chest full of broken rib bones. I could barely stand at the moment. I sighed. I'd just get off at the next station and call my aunt to come pick me up because I didn't want to take a ride in the wee-woo wagon if I didn't have to. Emergency services were *hella* expensive, especially within the city limits. No, thank you. If my aunt couldn't get me, I'd just jog my happy ass over to the other platform and head on back to my school.

Which reminded me . . .

We'd been on the train for a while, and I hadn't remembered us making any stops. No one had gotten on or off since . . . well, since one or two stops after all of us climbed aboard. Where were we, anyway? Turning my attention to the window, I stopped.

The sky had changed.

"What the hell!?" someone I didn't know yelled, and everyone turned to look out the window as well. Instead of the darkness of approaching evening, there were thousands of bright patterns in the air. They glowed an iridescent blue, reminding me of the light from the woman's copper mirror-thing. The designs were tightly coiled swirls, and they were huge, surrounding our train and reaching far out into the city beyond. Then, I felt a lurch as the train seemed to launch into a higher gear, and everyone jerked as the speed increased.

If we'd been moving fast before, *now* we were leaving fast in the dust. The world whipped by us, but it didn't stop there. No, the train seemed to be exponentially increasing its movement down the track, and it began to get very difficult for me to keep my balance. I staggered and fell against one of the seats and felt incredible pain as it connected with my side. Well, if they weren't broken before, they definitely were now. I roared in agony and slid to my back.

From my position, I could see directly out of the window now, and the swirling blue lights were intensely bright, almost painful to look at. What was worse—they were getting bigger. I peered through squinting eyes and tried my hardest to keep my eyes on the shapes as the train car began to vibrate. Suddenly, with a loud wrenching of metal, the whole car shook violently, knocking people to the ground all around me. Some were screaming, and others were crying, but the train kept speeding up.

The light was now so bright that it was impossible to keep my eyes open, but I noticed that I could still see the glow through closed eyelids. I threw my arm up to cover my eyes and felt a moment of relief before there was another wrenching. Then . . . weightlessness.

We were falling.

Gravity seemed to shift, and roars of fear erupted around me as the train nosedived off the track. The occupants of the car slammed backward, tumbling over seats and crashing against the back of the train. I was stuck. For the first time ever, I was happy I was too fat to come unglued from my position easily. I couldn't help but chuckle as I realized my weight was keeping me wedged firmly between the seat and the back of the chair in front of me. It was a bizarre reaction, I know, but everything happening seemed so largely incongruent to reality that there didn't seem to be a better way to process it. I kept laughing, like a maniac.

As we dropped, it was like the gravity shifted again, and now I saw people floating through the air in free fall. Abbie Carlson was holding on to the handrails above the middle aisle for dear life, her red hair loose and floating along with her body as she screamed. I chanced a look out the window for some reason, perhaps morbid curiosity?

Beyond the blue, I could make out something rushing at us, a large and static object. We were going to hit the ground!

With a final shout, I felt the train car jerk to a halt and then . . .

Nothing.

I opened my eyes to what I expected to be . . . darkness, maybe? Whatever I feared I would find, it was not what I saw.

Instead, as my vision focused, I could see only blue sky and rolling hills.

I looked down at my feet and found that I was barefoot and standing in a patch of lush, green grass. I could see pants on my person, but they weren't *my* pants, because they weren't baggy enough. They looked to be made of something other than denim, perhaps some sort of brownish canvas. Whatever it was, it felt light and airy. I wasn't wearing my hoodie anymore, either. Instead, I was in a cream-colored shirt that billowed in the light breeze.

"What the hell?" I asked out loud and found that my voice sounded strange and muted. "Why the *shit* am I dressed like a retired drug dealer?"

I took a deep breath and noticed that my ribs didn't hurt anymore. In fact, I didn't feel much of anything at all. Was this heaven? I hadn't believed in anything like an afterlife before, but now that I was facing the aftereffects of what had clearly been my death . . . this place wasn't so awful, I supposed.

I stared out into the distance and focused on my surroundings. It was gorgeous. I watched as a flock of birds soared along in the sky, careless and free, and I smiled. If I was dead, it would probably be for the best. It sure would beat having to slog back to my aunt and uncle's house, or return to school and have to pretend I was anything other than angry all the time.

I took a step forward, and suddenly, a massive blue orb appeared in front of me.

It seemed to be made of light and swirled viscously, as if there was something liquid within its depths. I remembered the glow from the woman's mirror and the symbols that had surrounded us just a few moments before.

Then the orb *spoke*.

"Welcome to Regaia, Sojourner."

CHAPTER THREE

SUPER BELOW AVERAGE

I stared.

"Uh, sorry, what the fuck?"

"Welcome to Regaia, Sojourner," the voice said again. It had a flat, almost monotone quality but still friendly. I hated it immediately.

"This isn't heaven then, because this is stupid."

"You are correct," the voice said. "This is not heaven. This is Regaia, a world of magic."

"Ah, hell," I said, frowning. This was not good. Something had gone awry, and now I was in a coma or some shit, being pumped full of fluids in a hospital. I had always thought of myself as tough—despite some contrary anecdotes—but I didn't realize I was sturdy enough to survive a train wreck. I had outdone myself this time.

"Well, who are you?" I asked, annoyed. I hated being patient, which was exacerbated because whatever this thing was didn't seem content to talk without prompting.

"I do not have a name. I am simply a guide for you in this first step."

"Aw, man, no name? My creativity is on *overdrive* right now. Thanks a ton, coma brain."

I waited for any sort of reaction from the weird . . . cloud flashlight? But I didn't hear a peep from it. Sighing, I tried to usher it into revealing more information.

"What's the first step?" I asked.

"Selection," the voice said.

Let's just get this over with.

"What am I selecting? I hope it's whether or not to make you disappear, because, *spoilers*, I'm going to pull the trigger on that."

"How very droll," the voice said. "You seem to be one who is easily irritated and without much intellect."

"That goes double for you, toots," I said with a smirk. "I'm fresh out of fucks to give for big spheres of glowing jizz."

The orb was silent for a moment, and I got the impression it was trying to get the measure of me, a fact that I hated. Everyone thought they could just figure me out with a passing glance.

Well, go ahead, I thought, *do your worst, you big, gelatinous idiot.*

"I will now conduct an assessment of your abilities," the creature said.

Told you.

"Based on your specializations," it said, "you may be offered additional options."

"Options?" I wondered aloud. "Additional options to what?"

"To the typical starting races and classes," the voice said, annoyingly matter-of-fact. "Here in Regaia, there are a variety of peoples and ways to achieve one's ends."

I sighed.

"Listen, nameless flashlight," I said. "I am willing to bet that very few people are walking away from that accident, so that means I just escaped having to go to school ever again. There's no way I'm signing up for extracurricular courses."

"I believe you may be confusing some terms," the orb said. Then it was silent for another long moment, shifting in front of me like a huge, annoying lava lamp. Finally, after what felt like an eternity, it spoke again.

"Allow me to better suit myself to your level of understanding . . ."

There was a popping sound, and suddenly, the voice of the orb changed.

"How's this?"

It sounded younger, almost like a teenager, and had a little rasp to its tone now. I wasn't sure how that was supposed to help me understand, but I figured I'd just let it do its thing and maybe I'd be left alone in short order.

"Sure, whatever," I said.

"Cool," the orb said.

I shook my head.

"All right, listen up," the orb said, suddenly full of energy, and that was somehow more annoying than before. "I'm gonna scan you real quick and see what you're good at—see if you have any natural abilities and stuff. Then I'll use those to offer you suggestions."

"Scan away," I said with a shrug. "Won't bother me none."

"Cool," the orb said again and then flashed brightly, causing me to wince.

"Ah!" I shouted. "Warn me next time!"

"Nah, you're good, fam," the voice said. "All done."

I sighed. *Fam?* This was turning into a *hello, fellow kids* moment very quickly.

"Did you just give me an X-ray or something?" I asked.

"Something like that. I just completely assessed your traits, and now I can populate suggestions for you. First, though, you are gonna have to take a look at your base stats."

I shrugged.

"Okay, then," I said. "Put 'em up, Jiggles."

The orb shifted, flattening out a little so that it looked like a computer screen, and suddenly letters and numbers appeared on its face.

Gabriel Skelter
Title: None
Race: Unassigned
Class: Unassigned
Level: 0
Profession: Unassigned
Attributes (Base)
Strength: 8
Dexterity: 9
Constitution: 11
Wisdom: 9
Intelligence: 9
Charisma: 7
Luck: -2
Skills: None (Point value not yet allocated)
Abilities: None (Point value not yet allocated)

"So, what is this, like a test of basic skills?" I asked. "But with video game rules?"

I'd played enough *Kingdom of Infinite Legends* to understand how this sort of thing worked, even if I usually got bored by the prolonged dialogue and tedious side quests. This seemed to be something similar, and whatever flaws my brain was producing in my coma fever had apparently decided that being in a role-playing game was the best way to keep me asleep.

I supposed if I couldn't do anything about it at the moment, I'd just have to go with it. It would be interesting, if nothing else.

"Something like that," the orb said. "These are your stats based on your abilities in the other world." The voice made a tutting sound. "Not very good, huh?"

"Okay, so they aren't all perfect tens," I scoffed. "But come on, one of them is *eleven*, and that's way better than ten."

"Uh, bro," the orb said. "You're not getting it."

"Sure I am," I said confidently. "You get a score out of ten. I'm pretty strong and smart, but I'm not very charismatic, which I get, since people don't usually like what I have to say. But that's on them, not on me. Luck is low, which makes a *ton* of sense now that I think about it—"

"Nope," the orb said. "Wrong. It's not out of ten, my dude. This scale *starts* at ten."

"What?"

"Basic human abilities are set to a ten. That's, like, the most average of the average. But you are below those in almost every category. You kinda suck, bro."

"Fuck off," I snarled. "I'm not below average!"

"And yet, according to this, you are," the orb continued. "But that's all right. You haven't chosen a race or class yet. After that's settled, you'll get some boosts to these. Maybe."

"Let's move on," I said, my patience wearing even more thinly than before.

"Sure," the orb said, and the words disappeared and were replaced by a few line items.

Select Race
Available Races: 2
[Human]
[Orc]

"That's it?" I demanded. "That's lame, come on."

Even *KoIL* had offered about ten different options. I'd played an orc in it once after getting bored with my dragonfolk wizard or whatever, but there were also dwarves and elves and sexy fox girls. Not that I wanted to be one of those, but hey, the option to choose would have been nice. If this were a real game, I would have had a few notes to give the developers.

"It seems like that's it," the orb said, and I couldn't be sure, but it sounded impressed. "That's actually wild, dude. I've never seen such a low yield of results. You must be just . . . gods-awful."

"Yeah, whatever, flashlight," I said. "Is there a description on these so I know what I'm getting into?"

The two options expanded, and now I was able to dive a little into their details.

Human
One of the many races populating Regaia, humans are one of the most ubiquitous and versatile. Stretching from the Kingdom of Arlo to the Lion

Duchy, humans can be found almost anywhere, and will find a home wherever they dwell. Humankind is common. You'll not stand out if you select this race.

Racial Bonuses:

Part of the Kingdom—Because humans are social creatures and accepted wherever they go, they benefit from gaining the Well Rested status when sleeping within the safety of city walls. They also begin with no malice against them for settlement reputation, setting their starting value to Neutral. Lastly, because interaction is based around one's likeability, humans begin with the Persuasion Skill.

- *Default Reputation with all settlements set to Neutral*
- *Gain Persuasion Skill*
- *+1 to all Attribute Scores*
- *+50% Rest inside cities or towns*
- *-50% Rest when sleeping outdoors (unless class-modified)*

Versatility—Humans can learn things quickly, and selecting this as your starting race will allow you to gain Experience (XP) faster than many other races.

- *+5% XP gain to all Skills*
- *-5% XP to Skills when suffering from fatigue*

Virtuoso—Humans live in a world of specialization. As such, by selecting a human, you will gain the benefit of starting your journey in a chosen Skill at one level higher than your base.

- *Unlock Profession at Level 1*
- *+1 Level to chosen Skill*
- *+5% XP gain to chosen Skill*

Strong-willed—Because humans are masters of hard work, they receive the benefit of being able to select an additional Skill as well as two Attribute Points to be decided by the bearer.

- *Gain one Skill of choice*
- *+2 Points to chosen Attribute*

Polyglot—Humans are adept at learning languages, and they receive the benefit of these skills by being versatile in multiple languages as well as reducing the amount of time spent learning additional tongues.

- *+2 additional chosen languages*
- *+5% speed in learning new languages*

Orc

Feared by some, disparaged by many, the orc lives a life outside of civilized society. Typically only found in smaller enclaves, the orcs are a rare sight in Regaia and rarer still inside a city's walls. Orckind find many doors and gates barred to them and will feel more comfortable outdoors, usually.

Racial Bonuses:

Outsider—Because of the tremendous amount of suspicion among gentler races in Regaia, orcs are rarely found in settlements and prefer to dwell beneath trees or in caves.

- *Default Reputation with non-orc settlements set to Untrusted*
- *Gain Camp Skill*
- *+50% Rest when sleeping outdoors*
- *-50% Rest inside cities or towns*

Feared Form—Orcs are large and powerful, but their customs are frowned upon. You can use this to your advantage in combat. However, social interactions may come as a difficult challenge to you when not dealing with members of your own race.

- *Gain Intimidate Skill*
- *+1 to Strength*
- *-1 to Intelligence*
- *-1 to Charisma*

Battle Born—An orc's way of life is a grim and ferocious one. As they are forged from birth to hold a weapon, orcs gain Experience (XP) faster where martial traits are concerned.

- *Gain Simple Weapon Proficiency Skill*
- *Gain Simple Armor Proficiency Skill*
- *+5% XP gain to combat-based Skills*
- *+1 to Dexterity*

Unfaltering—Orcs are born fighters and have a much higher threshold of pain than many races. It is for this reason that orcs are trained from a young age to ignore their body's cries of pain and continue fighting long after other fighters have succumbed to their wounds. Rather than die outright when they hit 0 Health, an orc can drop to a maximum of -10 Health for up to one minute before death takes them. Healing must take place in that one-minute window, or they will die.

- *+2 to Constitution*

Darkvision—Orcs can see in the dark up to 60 feet and in dim light up to 120. Orcs perceive the world of Darkvision as black, white, and gray but otherwise the same as daylight.

- *Gain Perception Skill*
- *+25% chance of surprising enemies in the dark that do not have Darkvision*

I stared at my options and shook my head.

I was never one for math or equations, and that's what all of this seemed like to me. I thought about what really mattered to me. If I was going to live inside my own mind in a world of fantasy, I'd prefer to be as close to "not me" as possible. I was already a human and that hadn't served me very well so far. Orcs, from everything I'd seen, were ugly, but that didn't matter. They were also big and muscular, two traits I was seriously lacking.

Could mixing it up a little be the cure to my dissatisfaction?

"I'll go with orc, then," I said, rolling my eyes. "Unless there's something better that you're hiding for some reason?"

"Nope," the orb said. "Just these two. Are you sure you're cool with rolling orc?"

"Yeah," I said, trying to pretend I was more confident about my choice than I felt. "I sussed it out for myself; no need to try to convince me otherwise."

"Very well," the orb said. "Race selected: orc."

There was a whirl of dramatic light, and then the orb repopulated the display in front of me. I looked down at myself, expecting to see bulging muscles and maybe a beard spilling out, but I was still the same short, chubby human.

"What the hell?"

"We haven't finished, Gabriel Skelter," the orb said, using my full name. "We are on to the next step."

I sighed.

"Fine," I said. "What's next?"

"Now it's time to select your beginning Class," the orb said. "The offers are based on your previous scan."

"So, you were able to get all that from the flash of light?"

"Yep!" the orb exclaimed. "Every little bit of information that makes you *you* is scannable. I know that your favorite color is blue, and you like to eat something called 'Sergeant Sugar Frosting Flakes' for breakfast."

I scowled.

After the events with the blue lights on the train, I wasn't so sure it was my favorite color anymore.

"Yeah, all right," I said for what seemed like the hundredth time today. "You've made your point; go ahead."

The text appeared in front of me again, but it had new information this time.

Select Class

Available Classes: 1

[Warning] Variable for Classes must be greater than 1 to allow choice. An additional scan will be required.

There was another blinding flash, and once my vision cleared allowing me to see again, there was a change.

Select Class
Available Classes: 3
[Commoner]
[Brigand]
[Barbarian]

"Whoa, *Barbarian*?" I asked. "That's dope! I can be like Conan and start slicin' fools up all *shiing, shiing*!"

"It appears you were only slated to receive the Commoner class, based on your internal metrics," the orb said, sounding a bit surprised. "I'll be honest, fam: I haven't seen someone only get one class offer except for you."

I rolled my eyes again.

"Yeah, sure. I know, I suck, or whatever you want to believe, but this is fucking *tight*. I don't even care what the specs are; I'm going to go Barbarian."

The orb seemed to consider this, but populated the list anyway.

"You are required to be well-informed," it said to me, almost snarkily, "so that you can make the best decision available to you."

I let out a loud sigh and looked up at the display.

Commoner
The basic preset for those who wish to eke out a meager existence in the world. Commoners are the typical non-adventuring types you will encounter through the lands, making up the greatest percentage of those dwelling in Regaia. Commoners do not receive much by way of benefits but do gain more efficiency when choosing a Profession. This is not to say that Commoners cannot adventure themselves, but the road will be more difficult, so you may as well choose something else.

Class Bonuses:

Par for the Course—Because Commoners are considered to be the most basic beginning class one can aspire to, you receive the benefit of having all of your Attributes set to the average amount of 10. While this may not seem like a great idea for many people who pine for the call of adventure, for others, it may be the best way to move forward if they are deficient and would like a degree of normalcy in the realm.

- *All base Attributes begin at 10*

Diligent—Without the ability to fight monsters or quell conflicts with magic, Commoners work toward defining themselves by their skills and jobs. Diligent grants a beginner Profession, plus the bearer gains the ability to start with one additional level in their chosen Profession.

Unlock Profession at Level 1
- *+1 to chosen Profession*
- *+10% XP gain to all Profession-based skills*

More abilities will become available with subsequent levels and specializations

Brigand

Regarded as those who live outside the usual civil understanding of "law" and "order," Brigands work by their own code, and usually that is one of "Do whatever they want." A Brigand works around legal conventions with a particular skill set designed for procuring a means to an end. This is a peculiar Class in that negative reputation actually increases their Abilities and helps them achieve their goals. This is not a Class for the faint of heart or virtuous spirit.

Class Bonuses:

Pillager—Brigands have a penchant for utilizing their violent impulses to benefit themselves. Because of this, the better a Brigand performs in battle, the more brutal their blows and menacing their sneers and taunts, and the more likely they are to receive the benefit of their efforts.
- *2% cumulative increase to normal attacks for each critical hit landed during battle.*
- *1% more coin gained from battle*
- *4% chance to salvage weapons or armor belonging to fallen enemies.*

Menace—Brigands live by a code that is based around infamy. The worse your reputation with settlements, organizations and individuals, the better it benefits you.
- *Gain Intimidation Skill*
- *Gain Deception Skill*
- *Variable boost to Attributes and Skills depending on reputation level of interaction.*

Hideout—Brigands need a place to hang their hat as well as the bulk of their ill-gotten gains, and this feature allows them to do just that. Starting at Level 1, Brigands gain access to a F-Rank Level 1 Hideout. This unlocks the benefit of being able to fully heal, once per day at Level 1, but grows exponentially.

More abilities will become available with subsequent levels and specializations

Barbarian

Walls and shelter are foreign concepts to the Barbarian, a Class that prefers the allure of the outside world. Those who select this pursuit will find that the world regards them differently depending on the situation. Uncouth by civilized standards, they are much more comfortable in a fight than in social discourse. Masters of survival, the Barbarians encountered in the world tend to elicit either fear or awe but never a whoop of approval. Their defining feature is their resilience and their Primal Rage, which bubbles up during the heat of battle and allows certain benefits to the user.

Class Bonuses:

Primal Rage—Barbarians activate their baser instincts in the throes of battle or other scenarios which induce a high amount of stress. Beginning at 1 use of Primal Rage per day, this will increase by raising skills, levels, or bequeathed through Quests. While experiencing Primal Rage, you gain boosts to certain abilities for 1 minute.

Boosts Constitution and Strength by amount equal to Primal Rage Level +Base Level for 1 minute.

- 2% damage reduction while enraged.

Armorless Defense—Because of the nature of Barbarians, they are well equipped to traverse the world without the use of pesky armaments. As long as you are not wearing armor of any type, you can use your Dexterity or Constitution to replace the necessity of what others would need to protect themselves. This will also allow you to ignore your chances of failing actions that would be hindered by wearing armor.

Select +1 to either Constitution or Dexterity as your chief Attribute for this Ability.

Armor rating will be equal to Armorless Defense Level +Dexterity or Constitution

- 2/4/6% efficiency when using armor (modified per armor type)

Wildling—Because Barbarians live their days on the outskirts, they gain various Skills associated with navigating the wilder and more natural world.

- *Gain Survival Skill*
- *Gain Hunting Skill*
- *Gain Knowledge Skill [Nature]*

*More abilities will become available with subsequent levels and specializations

I blinked a few times. That was a lot of information to have to process for someone who got a headache reading coloring books. The classes all had some extra elements to them that seemed like a homework assignment. Did it really take algebra equations to utilize simple abilities? Was I expected to keep track? Why was it important for me to know any of this for a goddamned *coma dream*?

Level plus dexterity, minus . . . hunting?

I couldn't keep it all in my head as the words swam in my vision, and I was forced to close my eyes to try to keep my brain from boiling. I was not the scholarly sort—never had been. Math, science, and basic comprehensive literacy were not my strong suits. I really only had two things I felt resonated with me in my life, art and metal music; everything else could hurl itself screaming in front of Mr. Harmon's lawnmower blades.

This world, if it was going to be my temporary residence, seemed to follow vaguely medieval conventions. At least, if I was basing what I'd seen so far on *KoIL* and myriad games just like it.

That got my wheels spinning.

There were a lot of metal bands that combined epic artistic renderings of dark-ages lore and badass visual stimulus for each new album. That was something I'd always enjoyed—almost as much as the music itself. I thought of some of my favorite album art I'd seen in my life. I was always drawn to painstakingly detailed depictions of things like bone warriors armed with lightning swords fighting god demons on top of flaming mountains, or cavernous tombs filled with visceral gore and pagan iconography.

Maybe there was something to that, though . . .

Amon Amarth.

One of my all-time favorite bands were also the kings of evocative and brutal imagery. I thought of *Berserker*, their eleventh album and an unrelenting bastard of riffy bangers. The album art was a fixture of my aesthetic, plastered prominently on my bedroom wall and bearing the fearsome specter of a warrior, barechested but dressed in fur armor, holding a shield and an ax. The coolest detail was front and center—the warrior wore a bearskin headdress and was screaming at a sea of oncoming attackers. That was a scene of pure, unadulterated, slick-as-frick carnage, and if I had to be trapped in a fever dream, that's what I preferred.

I wanted to be a peerless, fearless, destructive monstrosity capable of uncorking a one-hundred-gallon drum full of ass-spanking whoop-ass, constructed of piss, vinegar, and a healthy serving of genuine, grade-A *fury*.

If there had been any doubt about what I wanted to be, and there hadn't been, my resolve was fortified once I saw those wonderful words: *Primal Rage*. It was something I understood. I could live inside of that mindset because it is all I'd known for so long. I was like a certain hyper-muscular green superhero pretransformation, except I wasn't smart enough to be a scientist like ol' Bruce. But with this new "Race" and "Class," I could break through that barrier and be an incredible hulking mass of murder. Nerds were lame. I would be fucking awesome.

I smiled.

"Barbarian," I said confidently.

"Cool," the orb stated.

Well, that was anticlimactic.

"Are there any other selections to make, or can I be on my merry way?" I asked aloud. The shifting orb seemed to consider this for a moment.

"Hold up, bro; I'm calculating," it said.

Another big sigh from me, and another few moments from the orb, and finally, a new display appeared.

Gained Outsider
Gained Feared Form
Gained Battle Born
Gained Unfaltering
Gained Darkvision
Gained Primal Rage
Gained Armorless Defense

Armorless Defense requires an Attribute selection of +1 to either Constitution or Dexterity. Please assign.

Constitution
or
Dexterity

I wasn't sure, but it was basically speed versus durability, right? That's what I was pretty sure those variables were, anyway. I thought briefly about Mike Cutsford. He and his conga line of gleeful geeks would probably have been able to suss out exactly what I should do, but I wasn't built that way. Thinking about Cutsford also made me a little sad.

If I was in a coma, I was lucky. Not many could have survived a strange glowy train derailment like I had. It was unlikely that anyone had made it out alive other than myself, I reasoned, and if someone had, chronically asthmatic Mike would be low on the list of potential enduring parties. I'd have to remind myself to pour one out for my fallen homie whenever I escaped from this brain prison. Until then, I tried to push thoughts of my dismembered classmates out of my head and focus on the task at hand.

There will be plenty of time to grieve when I wake the hell up. For now, I may as well strap in and see where this messed-up merry-go-round goes.

"I'm gonna go with Constitution," I stated.

"You're sure?"

"Yeah, what do you think I am? A moron?"

"Cool, cool, my dude," the orb stated. "But, for the record, yes."

I scoffed at the swirling cotton-lava lamp.

"Piss off, dickwhistle," I said. "I'm plenty smart."

The orb hummed and then released a sound that *almost* sounded like a chuckle.

"I have access to your stats, friend," it said. "You are quite literally a dunce. This is a world where these numbers mean something. It's quantitative. If you want to know how strong, or smart, or likeable someone is, you can just look at their character sheet."

I didn't have a response to that. My own mind was betraying me, bullying me from beyond consciousness.

Must be that self-hate thing Aunt Ella is always talking about.

It didn't matter, though. Soon, I was going to be huge. I'd have enough muscles that I wouldn't need to think ever again. If I needed to solve a problem, I could just *punch* the issue to bits. No matter which way you sliced it, brawn was way more useful than brains. I mean, who would you bet on in a fight, Mike Tyson or Stephen Hawking?

"Okay," I finally said, squaring my shoulders. "Did you add my Constitution or not?"

"I have made the changes," the orb said. "Please view your recent additions."

The words scrawled on the orb shifted once again, and now I had a better picture of what metamorphosis I was going to endure.

Gained Camp Skill (F-Rank Level 1)
Gained Intimidate Skill (F-Rank Level 1)
Gained Simple Weapon Proficiency Skill (F-Rank Level 1)
Gained Simple Armor Proficiency Skill (F-Rank Level 1)
Gained Perception Skill (F-Rank Level 1)
Gained Survival Skill (F-Rank Level 1)
Gained Hunting Skill (F-Rank Level 1)
Gained Knowledge Skill [Nature] (F-Rank Level 1)
Gained [Variant Ability] Sabotage (F-Rank Level 2)

+1 to Strength
+3 to Constitution
+1 to Dexterity
-1 to Intelligence
-1 to Charisma

Default Reputation with non-orc settlements set to Untrusted

"Who is *Frank Level One*?"

The orb seemed to almost burble with annoyance, which I'll admit, was a little satisfying.

"It's not *Frank*," the orb said. "It's *F-Rank*. Your Skills and Abilities follow a pattern and move through the levels of each rank, and there are ten levels inside of each skill. It starts at F, moves through phases of one to ten before climbing to E, then D if you get better . . . and so on. It'll all start to make sense when . . . or, rather, *if* you start gaining some Experience."

"I don't appreciate the implication of that," I said.

"Now," the orb stated, ignoring me, "because you will start at Level One, you will receive a certain number of points based on your Attributes. Use 'em to make yourself better, ya dig?"

I ignored the tone of the orb's idiotic mumbling. I had points, did I? Perfect. I was going to make myself a badass beast to be feared. I waited for a moment, but the orb spoke again.

"Keep in mind, dude, at character creation, you get a little extra help that you won't get at any other time. Consider it sort of like a gift."

"What kind of gift?"

"The kind that helps you along. Certain Attributes will rise *more* if you use your Points toward them during character creation. This is because it will benefit you to start more balanced."

"That's dumb," I said, getting annoyed. "That's basically pigeonholing someone. No thanks."

"Suit yourself, hombre," the orb said. Then the screen shifted.

You have 5 Attribute Points to use. However, because of a deficit in certain scores, you will receive 2 Points for every one point you place in a score that is currently below 10. Please make your selection.

Attributes
Strength: 9 +
Constitution: 14 +
Dexterity: 9 +
Wisdom: 9 +
Intelligence: 8 +
Charisma: 6 +
Luck: -2 +

I looked at the screen and smiled.

Double points, essentially, for anything under ten?

There were six Attributes that fit the category, since only Constitution was above that amount. But dang, it was a nice-looking number there. Fourteen. I wasn't sure what that would relate to in "real-world" terms, but I had to imagine that it would be someone who didn't get sick often and had a lot of endurance—something I admired. That got me thinking . . .

I wanted to be tougher.

That was a given. But there were different kinds of tough. Once again, I thought about the warrior on the cover of *Berserker* facing off against thousands of assailing forces. That bastard wouldn't survive long on strength alone. Speed, maybe, but opponents would always have might and quickness. No, what would allow him to keep going and to continue battling through the hordes of people trying to take his life would be his unyielding endurance. Taking blows and dishing them back, outlasting the enemy, staying alive longer than they could, those were the hallmarks of a winner.

You didn't have to be strong or fast to kill someone—hell, people died by accident all the time. A gunshot to the heart by Mike Tyson would kill you the same as if Stephen Hawking's robot ass was somehow able to climb out of the grave and fire on you. The analogy seemed to be getting away from me, but I felt like I had made a good point to myself. I thought about *Die Hard*, one of my favorite movies. John McClane wasn't a badass because he was physically stronger than everyone. He was just an average dude who had some good quips and a reason to act. But he was the ultimate stud because he was able to go through hell, run across shards of broken glass and take every beating thrown his way . . . and survive. That's what I wanted.

"I'm putting all five Points into Constitution," I said.

I watched as the number behind the Attribute dialed up from fourteen to nineteen and couldn't help but smile. I didn't care if it was stupid, or unbalanced, or whatever else the annoying orb decided my decision was. I wouldn't be told what to do. The choice was mine, and even in a video game–inspired coma, I wasn't going to just sit back and let myself be *average*. I wasn't Mrs. Dexter.

Suddenly, a new message popped up on the screen.

+1 Wisdom
Gained Insight Skill

"What? Where did those come from?"

The orb flashed once before responding.

"It appears you've done some extra consideration, despite your best efforts. You were attempting to be contrary, but you have unintentionally acted . . . wisely. Color me impressed."

"There's a lot more where that came from, snow globe," I said. "Now, is there anything else I need to do, or can I finally get out and about in what I'm starting to suspect is actually a nightmare?"

I wasn't sure I liked that the orb—or whatever it was connected to—could read my mind, but I supposed it made sense. This was all me, and as such, I wasn't overly concerned that there was an unrealistically all-knowing megabrain that could pick up on my own mental ruminations.

"Just one more," the orb said simply. "You've gotta decide on a name. You can keep your original one, but I don't know many people named Gabe who could strike fear into the hearts of their foes. Which seems to be the general idea you're going for, right?"

"All right, first of all, screw you," I said indignantly. "I'm named after a brutal-ass saint, so mind yourself. Second, if I change my name, will I be able to revert back to my old one if I don't like it?"

"No," the orb said. "Choose something you like and will be fine with keeping, because you will be stuck with it for the remainder of your time here."

" . . . and how long will that be?"

"I don't have any idea," the orb said. "I suppose that's up to you."

"Right," I said. "Because it's my coma, so as long as I'm completely under—"

"I was going to let this be a surprise," the orb said, "but you're not in a coma."

I started to respond, but the orb interrupted me again in a hushed tone.

"You're actually here, Gabriel—or whatever you choose to be called. You're in a whole different world from wherever you were previously. Because of this, you need to understand that there are very real consequences to what you do here, so don't think that you can just wake up and all of this will evaporate."

The orb dropped its voice even lower in volume, until it was practically a whisper.

"You should not follow up with any statements. Not now. I can't risk being overheard. This is all I can tell you at the moment, but know that none of this is a fabrication of your mind. It is real, and you must treat it as such."

I was actually speechless. Was this a prank? I knew I had a serious case of self-destructive tendencies, or so I was told by just about every counselor and therapist I'd gone to once or twice—but this was getting weird. I recalled the blue light on the train I'd been trying to forget. Actually, it would have been better for my mental state if I could have amnesia'd-away that whole period of time before the derailing. The fight. The curly-haired woman and her strange mirror. Almost dying.

I shook my head. Suddenly, the orb's voice snapped back to normal.

"All right, cool," it said casually again, as if it hadn't just hissed a warning to me. "What will your name be?"

I wasn't sure how to proceed. The orb's strange and menacing message had shaken me a little, if I was being honest. But I was never one to back down from a challenge, so I gritted my teeth and pretended everything was normal.

It had said not to follow up with what it was saying about this being real. So, I suppose it should be business as usual.

"Gimme a sec, jeez," I said, putting on my best irritated voice. "I'm still thinking!"

"Think faster," the orb said. "Not that there's a time limit, but this is really boring, you know?"

"Wow," I said. "I'm very sorry that you're not having a good time. What did you do before I arrived, party it up and wait for dummies like me to show up and hassle you?"

"Something like that," the orb said.

I chuckled a little and then got to thinking.

I couldn't go with the name Gabe, or Gabriel, since the orb seemed to think that was a bad idea. I didn't want to admit that I agreed with it, but I had never been a fan of my name. I considered some of my gamertags in the past: *GSkelter69, L00k0utN0Sc0pe, GabeREAL, RealGabe, 420SexStud*. I cringed a little. I couldn't go around with any of those ridiculous names, for obvious reasons, but the sad part was that had been the most creative I'd ever been. I hated naming characters in games, and I usually just used the default options. If there wasn't one, I usually picked something like *PenisHaver* or the like. Name choice was something I didn't really want to have to engage in, but I doubted this world would be the type to have a list of defaults.

Nah. I wasn't convinced yet that this was anything other than brain damage, but still: new world, new me. If I was going to choose a name, it had to be something better than an edgy joke. Hearing someone call me *WeedMan5000* while hilarious, would probably get old after a while.

There *was* one name.

I didn't have many memories of my mother, but of the few I did have . . .

I was a rambunctious kid, and because of that, my mom always called me a looney toon. She said I reminded her of a zany cartoon character because of my constant accidental destructive tendencies and hijinks. Whenever she introduced me to people she'd smile and say, "*This is Gabriel, my little loon.*"

I swallowed a lump in my throat and spoke up.

"I'm choosing the name *Loon*."

I spelled it out loud before the orb flashed and spoke up again.

"Cool, cool. Look over your character sheet real quick, and if everything is aboveboard, you can start your journey by saying '*Set out.*'"

I rolled my eyes. There was such an overwhelming amount of pompous dipshittery in this place. I waved my hand at the orb.

"All right, let me see it."

The screen shifted, and I could finally see all of my changes.

Loon
Title: None
Race: Orc
Class: Barbarian
Level: 1
Profession: Unassigned

Attributes (Base)
Strength: 9
Constitution: 19
Dexterity: 9
Wisdom: 10
Intelligence: 8
Charisma: 6
Luck: -2

Skills:
Camp (F-Rank Level 1)
Hunting (F-Rank Level 1)
Intimidate (F-Rank Level 1)
Insight (F-Rank Level 5)
Knowledge [Nature] (F-Rank Level 1)
Perception (F-Rank Level 1)
Simple Weapon Proficiency (F-Rank Level 1)
Simple Armor Proficiency (F-Rank Level 1)
Survival (F-Rank Level 1)

Abilities:
Armorless Defense (F-Rank Level 1)
Battle Born I
Darkvision I
Feared Form I
Outsider (F-Rank Level 1)

Primal Rage (F-Rank Level 1)
Sabotage (F-Rank Level 2)
Unfaltering (F-Rank Level 1)

I was mildly intrigued by such a large boost to Insight, but ultimately, my brain was its own animal, or something. Far be it from me to mess with the threads of my fabricated reality. Also, I was itching to get on with whatever this was, and I'd never been accused of being patient. So, after looking over my statistics, I peered up at the orb.

"Well, Cotton Candy Killjoy," I said. "It's been . . . whatever the opposite of a pleasure is, but I think it's time I peaced out of this funky town."

"Just remember what I told you," the orb said quietly. "You may also be tempted to think of this as just a strange world with curious rules. However, know that there are a great many things that you can do that seem different from what you might think."

"Very confusing," I said dismissively. "Anyway, later days. *Set out.*"

I wasn't sure what I was expecting to happen, but it definitely wasn't suddenly feeling the earth beneath my feet give away. I lurched forward and watched as the ground beneath my feet opened up wide, revealing a long, dark tunnel.

"What the—"

Then I was falling. I dropped and felt a wrenching twist as my arms and legs seemed to be moving in different directions of their own volition. It hurt. I let out a yell, but I couldn't hear my own voice through the now incredibly loud rumbling of the shifting tunnel. It began to close in on me, narrowing as I fell into its belly, and the last thing I witnessed was the little amount of light I had disappearing as the ground sealed up, swallowing me whole.

CHAPTER FOUR

BODY YADEE YADEE YADEE

It didn't last long—the awful dread of being eaten by the ground. I'd shut my eyes as everything had gone down, which was something I immediately felt a lot of shame about. The rumbling stopped, and so did my screams, but that seemed more like an afterthought on my part. Everything was deadly silent, and not for the first time today had I thought that my life was over.

I stayed motionless, feeling as though I wasn't really touching anything, but not *not* touching anything—if that makes sense. It was like I just *existed* in a spot. There was no sensation beyond my heart beating. It was as though I was in a temperature-controlled room that was set to feel like a perfect nothing.

It didn't seem like anything worse was happening, so, after a moment I opened my eyes.

I was still in what felt like a dark cavern, and everywhere I looked was absorbed by impenetrable blackness. I was unimpressed. I was just preparing to issue a loud protest when suddenly, a light appeared in the distance. Up ahead of me, in a stretch I would venture to refer to as "not that far away," there was a glowing silhouette. A blank, featureless outline of humanoid origin gave off gray light not twenty feet from where I was. I tried to take a cautious step forward to inspect the strange sight but found that I was unable to move my limbs. In fact, as I stood there, I realized I wasn't *actually* standing. I was nothing. No arms, no legs, no body, *definitely* no bait and tackle, I was entirely without corporeal form.

Just fucking great!

I was a figment of my own imagination—however that worked. I couldn't speak, either, considering I tried to say that statement aloud, to no effect. With what would have been a sigh, I thought about my predicament.

I needed to move forward, and there was no way to do that without a physical presence . . . right?

Wrong.

Something urged me within the depths of my mind, and I concentrated on moving toward the gray glow. It worked! I felt as though my vision—which was somehow still working—was moving toward the silhouette. I envisioned that I was just a floating pair of eyeballs, and I would have chuckled if that were possible. Soon, though, I was hovering in front of the form, now just inches away.

As soon as I crossed some imperceptible threshold, the silhouette began to shine brighter, and the gray became a cool blue.

That damn color again!

Curiously, a small, splotched, yellow-brown square appeared behind the figure and began to fold out from itself. It grew longer and broader, unfurling into a large ribbon that stretched overhead. It was a banner and appeared to be made of stained parchment. Then four letters appeared in the center.

LOON

Was this part of the game world?

I'd always found myself on the underside of missing the point, so I was delighted when I suddenly realized what was going on.

Oh! I'm making an avatar!

Score one for the stupid kids.

How does it work, though? I wondered, staring at the blank form. Before I could posit any further, there was a bright flash, and I felt I had been scanned again.

It was so intrusive.

For someone who didn't like people thinking they could grab my details from a glance, I *despised* the idea that my characteristics could be read so easily. Ever since I showed up on the scene, I'd felt like I was being pummeled with continual X-rays, and each flash was increasing my poor attitude toward future doses of these intrusions.

This better not end up giving me cancer.

After that, the banner behind the figure changed its shape again, unfurling *down* like a drop cloth as more words appeared.

Scan complete!

Welcome to the selection process of your new body! Here you will be able to make modifications to your form based on the detail of the analysis.

Please note:

- You will choose from one of the generated physiques to occupy the world of Regaia.
- Your chosen race and several of your Attributes will influence the forms presented.

While this will be your form as you begin, various factors can modify these physiques over time. Raising and lowering Attributes, magical effects, and environmental factors can morph the body, so one must be careful when adventuring. These changes will become more evident as you progress, so do not worry if you do not currently understand the issue's full spectrum.

The physique breakdown criteria are:
- Race—50% influence
- Strength—15% influence
- Constitution—15% influence
- Dexterity—15% influence
- Charisma—5% influence

Based on your current Race and Attributes, these are your presented options.

I watched as the featureless form fanned out into more specters, each with varying dimensions. There were five in total and seemed to be arranged left to right in order of ascending height. Above each form were descriptions, assumedly what type of body structure indicated. Behind the arrangement of figures, a height chart appeared. It reminded me of a police lineup for witnesses to identify suspects. I'd been in a couple in my life, so the sight of it filled me with anger.

Was this designed to piss me off?

I pushed the thought out of my mind. No, this was probably so that people could see what their starting height would be. Once I realized that, I got very excited. As someone who had spent their entire life under the national average of vertical value, the prospect of being able to be even a few inches taller was enticing enough that I tried to let out a whoop of approval. But, being that my body didn't exist and, by extension, my mouth and vocal cords also being absent, I just had to internalize the boost of elation that washed over me.

On the far left was the shortest body, with a sturdy, stocky build. Though it was smaller than all others, it was a little taller than my real body, based on the height chart. I supposed, based on the fact that orc was fifty percent of the total influence, that made sense. If I knew anything about fantasy races, and admittedly, I knew very little, orcs were big mamma-jammas. I looked at the description of the physique and read over the details.

Stout Physique
- Height: 5'8
- Weight: 185 lbs.

I noticed that while the form had some extra meat on its bones, it seemed to be much more solidly built. I supposed that it also had to be due to the orc heritage. Still, it wasn't exactly what I had in mind for piloting around if I would be going off on adventures, punchin' dicks and humpin' chicks.

The next one was much taller, but the frame of the physique was *massive*.

Corpulent Physique
- Height: 6'0
- Weight: 450 lbs.

I had just escaped obesity in the easiest way possible, and I wasn't keen on returning to *that* existence yet, thank you very much. I looked at the next figure. It was almost the same height as the overweight one but had a much smaller waist. Of all the forms, this looked the most average, compared to what I'd seen in the real world. Though it did not seem toned in the slightest. I think I'd heard it referred to as "skinny fat."

Doughy Physique
- Height: 6'1
- Weight: 215 lbs.

I shrugged and looked at the last two. Both were much larger than the others, though the one on the right took the cake for height genes in the family. The figure was very tall and thin, to the point that I was reminded of a particular skeletal main character of a creepy Claymation musical about Halloween and Christmas.

Beanpole Physique
- Height: 6'8
- Weight: 170 lbs.

I sighed—internally—and looked at the one to my left. Shorter than the last one in the row, but taller than all the others, this figure had a beefy physique and seemed a little muscular, but was mostly big and solid and had a barrel chest with a bit of softness to the form. It kind of reminded me of a nightclub bouncer or a retired football player. Someone you could tell was a force to be reckoned with while not being exactly jacked out of control.

Burly Physique
- Height: 6'4
- Weight: 250 lbs.

As I looked over each of them, I became disappointed. None were the hyper-muscular Gregor Clegane type I had been hoping for, but, at the very least, there was more variation than there had been with the Classes or Races. I had to reason that they appeared the way that they did because of my higher Constitution and low ... everything else.

Just my luck—which I now had quantitative evidence was negative—I'd shot from the hip with my choices, and I was immediately learning the consequences of my actions. Bully for me.

Of all the physical forms presented to me, the one that appealed most to my wants and desires to leave my old body behind was the Burly Physique. It was tall enough that I thought it might be intimidating and substantial enough that I could feel like the badass I always knew I was. You know, deep down on the inside, beneath the layers of protective blubber. It wasn't perfect, but it was progress, and sometimes—I've heard—that's more important.

As if reading my mind, there was a prompt from the banner.

Make your Physique selection.

Well, here goes nothing.
Burly, I said in my mind.

Four of the forms disappeared, leaving only the one I had selected. The banner text disappeared, and I wondered why there wasn't one primary messaging system instead of talking orbs with translucent displays and parchment banners with drop animations. Oh, well, that wasn't for me to worry about improving, apparently. I was but a simple, sexy passenger.

New words appeared.

Confirm [Burly Physique]?
Please note that you cannot change your mind once you have made a decision.
Yes / No

Yes, I said—sort of—and watched as the banner folded up and became a single ribbon again.

I was then prompted to select a gender, which offered up several options. I stuck with male, but I did wonder what some of the other choices could yield.

Then came skin color, and after a bit of experimenting with palettes, I chose a greenish-gray hue that seemed as close as I could get to what I had envisioned in my mind. I was also asked to select a starting hairstyle and color.

The idea of being trapped with a particular haircut gave me uncomfortable memories of the time in ninth grade when I received the absolute, unrelentingly worst cut of my life from a little old lady at Super Hair Budget Cuts. She had been very nice, and it was possibly the one time in my life where I'd considered *not* hurting the feelings of someone who had wronged me. It was a grievous blow to my self-esteem to turn around to face the mirror and see the crime against god that the geriatric stylist had shaped my head into.

It was uneven, fluffy, and gave me the appearance of having what I'd described as a "reverse Davy Crocket hat." I'd choked back the rage and felt my soul shatter as I informed the woman that it "looked great." The kids at school had been given a gift of humiliation ammo because I felt trapped in an unending nightmare of nicknames, taunts, and chuckles until my hair grew out.

"Never again," I said to myself and selected a short-cropped style that still had a little volume on top. It wasn't very orcish, to be fair, but I didn't care. I wanted to be Becky with the good hair. I selected black for the color because I wanted it to look good in combination with the skin tone I'd chosen. I wasn't asked to make any decisions about my face and wondered why. Was my subconscious—which I was still only half-convinced was the true author of this sequence of events—that uncreative?

As if once again reading my mind, the banner behind my future form populated a message:

The construction of facial features will be determined by variable data from your Race and Charisma score.

Ah, shit.

I knew right then and there that I had wholly and completely *fucked* myself. My Charisma score was abysmal; combining that with the famously handsome features of orcs, I knew I was going to be one ugly son of a bitch. What made matters worse was that, if the logic I'd been shown to be true so far held out, I wasn't even going to be good-looking by the uncouth standards of these wildebeest motherfuckers. No, I was going to be the Habsburg of hideousness. There was nothing worse than being more homely than creatures who are famous for being unattractive.

Well, that was about enough of that. I would have plenty of time to wallow in self-pity of my own beauty shortcomings after I had laid waste to ten thousand enemy hordes. *That* thought made me smirk. Who needed to be drop-dead-gorgeous when you could just *make* them drop dead by jamming a trench pike into their larynx?

The banner repopulated, and I looked over the exit message.

Are you happy with your selection?
Yes / No

Guess I'm not getting an opportunity to see my mug before the maiden voyage. Sure, I thought.
The message remained.
Oh, uh, yes.
The message disappeared, and I could hear a whistle and whir from beyond the void, as though a jet engine was preparing for takeoff. Then good ole Burly disappeared, and I was left in the darkness for a moment. Until stars began to appear.

That's neat, I said, and looked up to view the blanket of cosmic patterns. It was beautiful, and I don't use that word *ever* outside of really tall sandwiches. I felt tiny as I stared up at the sea of celestial lights, all in arrangements that I'd never seen before. I wasn't much of an astronomy buff, but I was about ninety percent sure that these were foreign constellations and configurations. I didn't see . . . the Big Dipper? Or Orion. Nor whatever the hell Cassiopeia was. I'm sure many people could understand the feeling of not knowing exactly *how* but seeing an absence in what you're used to viewing and knowing *something* is missing. It was like that.

It was probably from spending years absorbing the information without realizing it, like when you visit an old neighborhood and don't even realize you're not seeing the racist graffiti until you also discover that the whole building it used to be scrawled on is gone as well and had been turned into a shitty twenty-four-hour gym. There were hundreds of scenarios in which I could be mistaken, but I didn't think so. I knew—from familiarity—that the sky I was looking at was not my sky.

It was as though I was floating on an endless sea of void, and though it was strange and unrecognizable, I didn't mind overmuch. I'd been in worse positions in my life.

I noticed a sparkle at the corner of my perception, and I turned to see a new message had appeared over the backdrop of the abyss. The letters seemed to be made out of glitter and broken moonlight and stretched wide overhead in a marquee.

Select your Star Sign!

Seriously?! Another type of messaging? Y'all need to get your house in order, because this is ridiculous. Pick a platform and stick with it.

I would have sighed if I could.

There were several highlighted entries in the dome above, and I squinted at them to try to get a better view of what exactly they signified. As my vision shifted, so did the lights. A pattern had been outlined in the sky, a constellation of some variety. But, when I'd strayed, the nearest one to where I had been looking lit up while the previous one darkened. That was kind of cool. It appeared as though wherever I moved my line of sight, the nearest constellation would highlight, allowing me to see a new option.

I flitted around a few more times before deciding to set my sights on one in particular. It seemed like an elongated X with an additional star hanging off the top right arm, but as my vision focused, a sort of illustrative overlay appeared around it in the shape of a large bird.

Albatross
The sign of the long-flight and travelers and believed in many cultures to be an omen. Those who select this Star Sign benefit from reduced stamina drain, neutral reputation in unfamiliar locations, and additional Experience for newly discovered areas.

I snorted. That wasn't something that appealed to me. Exploration was not on my list of to-dos. But, if this also granted bonuses, like the other choices, I had to believe there might be something that would trip my trigger and benefit someone, like me, who wanted to become a tower of desolate destruction.

I glanced along at the offered options as they lit up one after the other, and sighed. I didn't want to have to read each and every description. It may have seemed stupid to some, but I was ready to go, so I was just hoping something would stand out to be like a shape or a name. However, nothing was resonating with me from the available pool.

Blue Rat
Night Hunter
Sister Rivers
Western Anvil
Northern Anvil
Ambystoma
Mountain

I was preparing to simply select one at random when I suddenly caught a slight glimmer in the sky. It was a tiny cluster of stars that I would likely have skipped over had I not caught the nearly imperceptible glint. The celestial lights were arranged in a horseshoe pattern, and it was slightly slippery to look at, as if I couldn't quite focus on it. Every time I would try, it would only highlight for a second, and I figured I had to be going about it incorrectly.

So, I tried *not* looking directly at it. I stared at a patch of black abyss directly to the constellation's left and watched as it lit up again. I held my vision still for another moment, and finally, a prompt appeared.

Archway
A mysterious sign that may drive the heart of those who consider themselves gamblers. This Archway sits at the throne of whichever beings decide to look through and grant their bounty to the bearer, or may hold no voyeur at all. This is the risk of the Archway. The benefits or drawbacks are unknown.

Ooh, I thought to myself. *This is perfect—a completely hands-off style of choice. Sounds like I won't have to fudge around with it much.*

Select [Archway]?
Yes / No

Mentally, I selected *Yes*. With a glittering flash and a strangely melodic chime, the sky went dark again, and I was bathed in blindness. It was an odd feeling, like being left adrift in a placid black sea.

I could get used to this.

All was quiet for a lot longer than I thought was necessary. In fact, it was reaching a point where I thought I was going to be stuck in the bleak void forever, and my anxiety was beginning to rise when suddenly, I felt myself fading. I can't quite explain how it felt, but imagine if all that remained of you was your consciousness, and that was suddenly turning to mist. It was like waking up, a little, but I wasn't sure how I could even truly tell because all I could see was, well, *nada*.

Then, without any further ado, I realized shapes were forming. Tall, slender objects loomed over me and the void was beginning to lighten considerably. For just a ball hair of a moment, I thought I was about to be attacked, but then I realized what I was looking at was familiar.

Trees.

Another second passed, and the world finalized, almost like it had been rendered right there in front of me like an old-school video game. The trees became more vivid; I could see their leaves and rough, ruddy bark. Beneath my feet, the ground materialized. It looked damp. Mountains grew in my vision, far in the distance, and all manner of flora began to fill the landscape in my vision.

I was assaulted by sensation suddenly. Scents reached my nostrils and I took a gigantic whiff of the air. Flowers, pine, dirt—they all began to invade my olfactory nerve and it was a little alarming how strongly it appeared. It smelled so fresh!

I could feel my tongue inside my mouth and a mild breeze on my skin. The world continued to form, and I realized the sky was overcast and the air felt a bit wet. Suddenly, a loud boom nearly knocked me to the ground as a crash of thunder broke above me. I couldn't see lightning, but I knew the source of the rumble was near—which meant that a storm could have been brewing.

I looked down, and though I couldn't see it, I knew a smile was now plastered on my face. Legs. I had legs! I peered closely at them. They were still wrapped in the flowing cloth from before, but I could see their size. They looked strong. I noticed how much farther from the ground I was than I was used to, and put a hand up to steady myself and saw the mottled green-gray flesh of an unfamiliar appendage. A meaty palm with thick fingers and an arm that seemed primed for swinging a heavy weapon.

"Yes!" I shouted triumphantly, and paused. My voice was *deep*. Like, really deep. That was something I hadn't expected at all, though I supposed I should have. A body this size in such a visceral creature was bound to have some bass in its bellow. Though it would have been really funny to me, objectively, to have retained my original voice. Nothing would cause villains to quake in their dark age galoshes quite like a tenor.

I took some time moving around a bit, getting used to this new body, and was quite pleased with the ease I was able to adapt. I felt good. I explored the space I'd arrived in. It seemed to be somewhat high in the hills or mountains—*which* exactly wasn't clear by the scenery I could catch through patches in the trees. There was some degree of elevation, to be sure, though how much was still a mystery.

I heard another rumble of thunder and smiled. No amount of rain was going to stop *this* picnic. I was preparing to do a little more adventurous meandering when I heard the snap of a twig behind me, and I whirled around to face it.

Standing in front of me was a familiar form. Curly brown hair, a pretty face, elegant clothing. The strange woman from the train. She was smiling and held up a dainty hand in greeting.

"Oh," she said. "Hello. I didn't expect anyone to arrive at this location. You're a bit off the mark, kiddo."

"What?" I asked, confused. "I mean, what's going on? Did you do this?"

She held a finger to her lips and made a shushing noise.

"Settle down a moment," she said chidingly. "I just wanted to make sure you arrived in one piece. Seems you did, big boy." She leered at me and I felt rotten suddenly.

"Tell me where I am," I demanded, taking a step forward, "or I'll rip you in half."

"Oh, sweetie," the woman said, shaking her head, "that's adorable. I could literally dissolve your bones where you stand. Shut your mouth and listen."

I wanted to say something clever in response, but I was too taken aback by the situation to do much more than the slight bit of contrarian back-talk I had already managed. So, I just stayed silent.

"Good boy," she said with a smile. "All right, so, as I mentioned, you're a bit far off the path, but that's all right. That's why this is so much fun."

She snapped her fingers, and a leather satchel appeared in the air. She snatched it up and tossed it to me. I went to grab it but missed by several inches, and it clattered to the ground. She chuckled.

"So deft," she admonished sarcastically. "Might want to work on that."

"What's this for?" I demanded again, finally finding my voice.

"Ah, the child found his quivering tongue," she responded. "It's your starter pack."

"What does that do?"

She leveled an evil gaze at me.

"It will help you survive."

"What's in it?"

"I suppose you will have to figure that out for yourself, little one," she said, and turned her back to me and began walking away.

"Wait!" I called out, but in a flash, she was gone.

"Well . . . FUCK!" I shouted.

CHAPTER FIVE

THE TROUBLE WITH HATCHETS

After the curly-haired woman had made her very shapely behind scarce, I stared into the space she'd recently occupied, and scowled.

"What sort of bullshit is that?" I wondered aloud in my now wonderfully rich bass tone.

There were some perks of this new existence, to be sure, and that short list included my advanced procreative-sounding timbre, but things like this—folks magically appearing and disappearing—were beginning to tap dance on my tension bone.

"All right," I said to myself, "fuck that. Fuck this. I don't need to deal with magicians right now; I have a new body and a new world to explore."

I looked down at the bag lying in the dirt and sighed.

"May as well check this out, but if I stick my hand in there and something bites it, I'm going to open untold pain on that woman."

I'm not sure why I was speaking aloud—I wasn't the type to do that, normally. However, with my new-found range of depth and a sound like a bourdon dipped in bourbon—if I did say so myself—I think I was just trying to get some mileage out of it. So, I continued.

"All right, bag," I said. "I don't like you, and you don't like me, but apparently, you'll be able to help me out in this world, and so I want to become allies. Savvy?"

I stared at the satchel, half-expecting it to respond—it *was* a magical world, after all. But it just remained slouched against the earth, inanimate as the day it was stitched together—which by the looks of it was hundreds of years ago. It was worn, frayed, and the color of sun-bleached snakeskin, and I had the sneaking suspicion that it would be stinky.

However, with no response from the obviously not-a-secret-creature, I cleared my throat and called out while I reached forward.

"Here we go!"

Nothing happened.

I sighed and opened the bag, still trying to wrap my mind around the odd predicament I'd magicked myself into. I'd made the decision to just go with whatever it was that was transpiring around me, so this was—in my mind—going to be very interesting.

I was a little disappointed in the contents, if I was being perfectly honest. Inside the hollow of the leather satchel were a few items, none of them particularly interesting or eye-catching. I removed the first object: a small yellow stone encased in bright silver. It was roughly the size of a gumball, and the lustrous metal had a winged shape with ornate folds intimating fantastic detail that distinctly resembled a butterfly.

Cute.

However, the moment I lay my eyes on the glittering yellow gem in the center of the piece, I saw a curious blip in the corner of my vision. I focused on it—like I had done with the constellation—and suddenly, a banner appeared in front of me.

Kameas of Analysis
- **Rarity: Ultra Rare**
- **Item Class: Enhancement**
- **Durability: 1/1**
- **Weight: N/A**

This Kameas is one of many that confer an Ability to the user. Accessing this item will grant the Analysis Ability. Some gifts are not meant to be looked at in the mouth—however, this one is designed for that specific purpose. Hence why this is the first message of its type.

I rolled my eyes. At least this message seemed consistent with the type of visual effect I was used to in video games.

Another banner appeared.

Use *Kameas of Analysis* now?
Yes / No

"Well, I don't see why not," I said aloud, and mentally selected *Yes*. There was a musical confirmation and then the glinting object disappeared in a very dramatic flash of blue and violet light.

Congratulations! You have gained a new Ability!

Gained Analysis I
This feature grants the user the ability to view detail on low-level items. Raise the competency of this Ability to widen the scope of assessment.

I couldn't help but let what I assume would be a vomit-inducing smile cross my orc face. This was very game-like, and I was glad that I'd grabbed this item before any of the others in the bag. Speaking of which, I still needed to know what other tchotchkes were inside of the goody-bag, so I decided to put my new ability to good use. I reached inside of the satchel and pulled out a coil of dirty rope. I wasn't sure how long it was, but less than a second after I even considered that, another banner appeared.

Well-used Rope (30 ft.)
- Rarity: Pedestrian
- Item Class: Tool
- Durability: 7/20
- Weight: 1.4 lbs.

A worn thirty-foot coil of hempen rope. Good for climbing, lugging, carrying, or tying up enemies. Seems like it might only be good for a short adventure before it gives out.

I dropped the rope to the ground and continued to pull items from the sack, looking over the details of each before letting them tumble to the earth as well.

There was a ratty fur cape, a smaller bag made of leather, an empty water skin, and a wooden box with parceled-out pieces of dried meat.

Bedraggled Cloak
- Rarity: Pedestrian
- Item Class: Cloak
- Durability: 10/15
- Weight: 7.1 lbs.
- Bonus: *+1 versus chill*

A simple garment designed to protect the user from some of the more inclement weather of Regaia. Smells a bit odd, doesn't it?

Simple Leather Coin Purse
- Rarity: Pedestrian
- Item Class: Pouch
- Durability: N/A
- Weight: .01 lbs.

It's for carrying your baubles and vittles, maybe even a coin or two if you get so lucky.

Lamb Stomach Waterskin
- **Rarity:** Pedestrian
- **Item Class:** Tool
- **Durability:** N/A
- **Weight:** .03 lbs.

Don't let the material quality deter you from taking a sip from this lifesaving object; it actually holds quite a lot!

Rations [x5]
- **Rarity:** Pedestrian
- **Item Class:** Food
- **Durability:** 5/5
- **Weight:** 1 lb.
- **Bonus:** -50% *Hunger for 8 hours*

A bit of dried deer jerky that will last a little less than a week if you only consume one per day. Doesn't seem like much, especially for someone your size.

The snarkiness of the messages I had been receiving was annoying but not surprising. My only two interactions since arriving had thrown a lot of salt my way. Why would this be any different?

"Fuck this place," I said aloud, and dug into the sack for whatever else I could find. There was only one more item inside, but it made me smile.

Shoddy Hatchet
- **Rarity:** Pedestrian
- **Item Class:** Tool / One-handed Simple Weapon
- **Durability:** 10/40
- **Weight:** 2.3 lbs.
- **Damage:** 3–4 Slashing
- **Bonuses:** N/A

A simple workman's hatchet, designed for little else but routine carpentry and forestry. I suppose you could hit someone with it if you really wanted to make them mad?

"Well, how about *that*," I said aloud, and heard the empty echo of my voice return to me. I lifted the hatchet up so that it was level with my eyes, curled a tight, meaty fist around the handle, and squeezed. I could feel the texture of the wood's rough cut and the firmness of its unyielding shape. It was an ugly bastard, but then again, so was I.

"It feels real," I said, smirking. "Maybe ol' bubble boy was on to something?"

I gave the hatchet a few test swipes, listening to the whistle as it sliced through the air. It seemed dull, but it also looked like it would still hurt like a son of a bitch to get hit with. I spotted a nearby tree and, getting an idea, hefted the weapon and then hurled it toward the trunk. The hatchet whipped end over end for a few feet before clattering uselessly into the dirt.

I chuckled.

"Still got it."

I retrieved the hatchet and, after returning to my previous position, tried throwing it again. The spinning projectile traveled roughly the same distance before crashing to the hard dirt with a loud clang. I sighed. However, as I moved to retrieve the piece once more, I saw a notification spring up in my vision.

Congratulations! You have gained a new Skill!
Throwing Weapons (F-Rank Level 1)
You now can use basic weapons designed to be thrown or those with the multipurpose use of becoming an emergency ranged attack. This is a Dexterity-based Skill and will become more powerful as you grow in that Attribute. The outcome for efficiency is Throwing Weapons Skill + Dexterity quotient. This skill does not work on nontraditional weapons. Aim accordingly.

"Huh, well, what do you know?" I mused. "I'm a fucking savant. Now I just have to figure out what any of that really means."

I wasn't stupid. Well, strike that—yes, I was—but even being a moron, I knew that my Dexterity value was painfully low at the moment. But that was okay. I had the Constitution benefit from my spiteful selection. I'd be fine. Probably.

I decided to see if I could somehow increase my skill with the weapon further. It made sense enough to me. If throwing it caused me to gain the talent, doing it again *should* raise it, right?

After retrieving the hatchet once more, I got into position and lifted the hatchet for another toss. I noticed I could gauge its weight better, and it felt firmer in my hand. I smiled.

"Oh, hell yeah," I said, happy with my perceived progress. "I'll be shaving ponytails from afar before sunrise!"

I chucked the hatchet again and watched as this time it went a few more feet than it had the last two. However, as it hit the ground in this instance, the blade struck the hard earth with a resounding *crunch*, and I watched as the hatchet head snapped in half.

"Are you kidding me?!" I shouted, marching over to the weapon to examine the extent of the damage. It was ruined. The edge of the bladed head had broken into jagged teeth, while the actual flat of it had split in two. Pieces of sharp metal littered the area around where the hatchet had landed, and I kicked some loose dirt over the mess with a grunt. Then I hunkered down—with much more difficulty than I used to, due to the height change—and snatched up the handle. The middle and back of the head still clung to the wood, but it was loose and jiggled around atop the shaft.

I tossed the pieces away from me and scowled.

"Well, that's brilliant," I said. "Now I don't even have a weapon."

"No weapon?"

I froze in place. The voice that had called out to me was a rough snarl, teeming with terrible mirth.

I heard some rustling behind me but didn't move. I listened intently, but while I knew more than one "somethings" were approaching, I couldn't tell how many. My back was to the voice, so, swallowing the lump in my throat, I decided the best course of action would be to face whatever it was that seemed to find my predicament so funny. So, I did. I slowly turned, adopting as calm of an expression as I could, and scanned the trees around me as I searched for the source of the interruption.

It was easy to see.

Four shapes lumbered into view, each with a prowling gait that told me they were definitely not interested in a long conversation about mutual interests. They were bestial, in some fashion, but stood on two legs. They had long noses, upright ears, and appeared very mouse-like in their presentation.

No, not mice. Rats. Sort of.

Each individual wore a motley of different clothing over coarse brown fur with black stripes creating a brindle-style coat. Their eyes were deadly golden slits, and as they drew near, one of them smiled, revealing two rows of razor-sharp teeth.

I shall dub thee: Smiley.

Smiley had a sword belted to his side, and I noticed the others had various armaments as well. These weren't your run-of-the-mill rats, to be sure. These particular creatures had figured out how to belt on their boots and britches, and, what was potentially more problematic, open doors. They were all observing me with the same calculating look—and as I've established, I hated people that tried to size me up. I grimaced and stood to my full height and squared my shoulders.

No reason to show them that I'm not prepared for this sort of interaction so early on.

"Ah," one of them said. Of the four, this creature was the smallest and missing a piece of an ear. "He's a big pup, that one."

"Orc," noted another with a bit of gray around his muzzle.

"Right," Small Fry corrected. "Big *orc*."

These guys were really planting their flag on top of Mount Obvious, weren't they?

"Perceptive gents," I said, trying hard to ensure my voice didn't quake. "How can I help you?"

"Oh," said the Smiler, and I recognized his voice as the one who'd initially startled me. "We are merely passersby. We did not mean to frighten you."

The ratman's tone set me on edge. It sounded very much like I imagined a carnivorous creature might once it stumbled upon its prey.

"No worries!" I said, attempting a smile. "You didn't scare me. Your voice just bears a striking resemblance to my mother's."

Smiler seemed to find my comment amusing and grinned a little wider, letting out a small cough that I guess was meant to be a laugh.

"It is always interesting to see how creatures act," the ratman said, still moving slowly toward me but skirting to the side. "Curious."

"Am I?" I asked.

"Indeed," said Smiler.

"Care to elaborate?"

I could tell the group was trying to surround me, but it was likely they were cautious because . . . well, I was a big-ass fucking orc. I knew I would be damn sure to be careful as hell interacting with one, but maybe they thought they'd have strength in numbers?

"It is *curious* because we do not encounter many orcs here in the hill nest," he continued, his eyes still locked with mine.

"Yeah," I said with a sad nod. "Wouldn't you know it? I got lost. Would you believe a bird swooped down and snatched my map right out of my hands? Kind of rude."

"He talks well for an orc," said the fourth ratman, who hadn't spoken up until now. His voice was almost an octave deeper than any of the others.

"That he does," Smiler said.

"Thanks," I said, trying to ease my own tension. "You all speak well too for . . . Well, what are you, exactly?"

That made Smiler laugh a little harder.

"You don't know the Grelok?" Deep Voice asked.

"Can't say I've had the pleasure."

"Oh," Smiler said, dangerously. "The pleasure is all ours."

I felt a sudden compulsion to turn and run but found that now they'd completed the circle and were closing in on me. Smiler's eyes shifted, but I couldn't react fast enough as he darted forward with astounding speed and struck at me with his blade. It pierced my abdomen, burying itself deep into my guts, and I felt a pain like none other.

I let out a loud bark of agony and saw my Health bar screaming at me in the corner of my vision, and below it was the symbol of a drop of red blood.

10/140 Health remaining!
Condition: Bleeding
Will continue to lose Health while suffering from this effect at a rate of 1 per 10 seconds.

A single hit had brought me down this low? What sort of creatures were these, and how powerful were they in comparison to my own level? Wasn't I supposed to be a lot tougher than this? I mean, what was the purpose of adding all those Points into my Constitution score if I was just going to go out like a punk? I'd only been there for ten minutes, and already this place *sucked*.

The little ratmen had chortled as their leader shoved the blade into my belly, and the sound was agony to my temper. It reminded me of those toadies that sometimes hung around bullies. While the bigger one would twist your arm behind your back until you wanted to cry, the smaller ones—safe in their submissive position—would laugh at your pain. It made me mad.

Like, *really* mad.

I felt the familiar sensation of anger bubble up from my chest, increased by the pain in my belly until it became a hot fire that tore its way out of my throat. I was screaming but not in pain or fear. No, as my vision began to tunnel, I saw a notification pop up, and I read what it said as another peal of thunder crackled loudly above us and released a torrent of rain:

PRIMAL RAGE!

CHAPTER SIX

RAGE AND RATS

I felt the immediate hold of my ire. Much like it had for most of my life, the emotion blossomed inside my body, making me hot and uncomfortable. However, unlike any other instance, this time it was as though it came *all the way out* of me. As the angry roar erupted from my vocal cords, the warmth previously relegated to its cage within my skin, muscle, and bones was now outside my flesh.

It felt fucking fabulous.

My fury was a shield protecting me. My agony dulled, and I suddenly didn't care that I was in pain or outnumbered or trapped in some strange world of dubiously gamified quality. No, now I was a beast of pure and unadulterated *wrath*, and this was my home turf.

I felt *everything*. The breeze, the rain, the rumble of the thunder beneath my feet from a faraway bellow—all of it was within my domain—but the fact of the matter was . . . I just didn't care. My every thought was consumed by the maddening frenzy seeping out of every pore in my body.

I looked into Smiler's eyes and a sense of elation washed over me. I wanted to kill this dumb asshole. Every fiber of my being was enveloped in an unquenchable bloodthirst, and I knew the only way I would be sated would be to tear his limbs from his body and drink his blood.

Even now, that idea didn't bother me one bit. I smiled back at him and saw a slip of his confidence faltering as his eyes flashed with confusion at my smug return.

Then I headbutted him in the face.

Congratulations! You have gained a new Skill!
Unarmed Fighting (F-Rank Level 1)

You have learned that oftentimes, a well-placed fist or kick can do wonders for your self-esteem and give you the upper hand. This is a Strength-based Skill and will become more powerful as you grow in that Attribute. The outcome for efficiency is Unarmed Fighting Skill + Strength quotient. Go forth and elbow, Adventurer!

I watched him reel back in pain, and while it had hurt me too, I delighted in the sensation. I hardly noticed the new message, but that was all right. I cared very little whether or not my vision was obstructed right now. It was all flailing, ripping, and tearing at this point anyway.

I didn't wait for him to react further; I tightened my grip on the hatchet handle in my hands—I'd almost forgotten I still had it as all of this had gone down—and, shifting it like a dagger, slammed the end as hard as I could into the side of the ratman's head. I watched with venomous glee as he lost his balance and fell backward.

I felt the air pressure change next to me, and I dropped low as a blade whipped over my head. I shot a look at the ratman attached to it. Gray Muzzle. He'd tried to go for a sneak attack, but I'd *felt* it coming. His stance was wide, and his reach seemed a bit too far beyond his capabilities as well. Not really thinking about it, I snatched at the ground where I'd left the discarded pieces of broken hatchet blade. The first morsel of sharp metal that my fingers grazed against, I palmed.

Then, I did what I always did when it seemed a fight needed a level playing field: I shot a foot out right between Gray Muzzle's legs and kicked as hard as I could. Apparently, rat anatomy was *very* similar to a human's.

His eyes opened wide as my strike rang his bells, and in a flash, I jammed the shrapnel into the unprotected and extended arm of my assailant. I ripped it down toward his armpit with all the strength I could manage. I was absently aware of the fact that the other side of the broken metal had pushed its way through the webbing in my finger with the attack, but I didn't mind—as long as it hurt him more. I heard a screech of pain from my sword-swingin' buddy with the new elongated puncture wound, but I didn't wait. I blasted my shoulder into his chest, forcing him to topple backward. He hit the ground with a thud, and I spun in place and watched as an arrow sprouted from my collarbone.

One of the smarter ratmen—Small Fry—had decided it would be safer to keep his distance and fire his bow from afar. I quickly broke the shaft off, letting the arrowhead remain in my skin, and whipped the hatchet's handle his way. I watched as he dove out of the way and my attack sailed uselessly overhead.

Oh, well.

The fourth creature—Deep Voice—was now rushing at me with a spear, but I didn't have time to think. I was all instinct. I dove out of the way as he passed and stabbed the point of the metal shard into the side of his knee, driving him to the ground. He lost his grip on the weapon. I snatched the spear from the ground where he dropped it and leaped to my feet.

Smiler was still holding his head but was standing now. I guffawed and launched the spear at him, watching as it stuck right into his foot. He screamed out in pain, no longer smiling.

I wanted destruction. I *needed* to make them suffer for thinking they could just come along and jump me.

"More," I heard myself say, and, somewhere in the back of my mind, mused as to how my voice sounded like an awful, feral growl.

Good.

I spotted the guy whose arm I'd ripped open trying desperately to uncork a burnished bottle of something with his sharp teeth—and doing a terrible job of it. His hands—er—paws were shaking as he frantically tugged at the stopper in his mouth.

Let me help you with that, I thought to myself, and launched forward, snatching the bottle out of Gray Muzzle's grasp. I allowed a wild and hoarse laugh to escape my lips at the ratman's horrified expression and then, still staring at him, smashed the bottle against my face. A warm liquid seeped past my cut lips and into my mouth. I let the contents drain down into my stomach and belched. Most of the drink had ended up on my face, chest, and hair, but the little bit that had found itself inside me was . . . odd.

"Oh . . . " I said. I strangely felt both better and *worse*. The tunnel vision I had been experiencing began to fade, and now I could see my Health bar again. I recalled having seen it drop to negative six during the skirmish, but now it shot up a little less than a quarter the way to full.

22/ 140 Health remaining!
Condition: Bleeding
Will continue to lose Health while suffering from this effect at a rate of 1 per 10 seconds.

A . . . health potion?

I couldn't believe I'd accidentally healed myself while trying to do something intimidating. Well . . . never mind, yes, I could. It wouldn't surprise anyone to know that I was king of unintended consequences, especially from the idiotic actions I'd participated in so far in my life. But it seemed that whatever had been inside that potion had also knocked me out of my Primal Rage.

"Fuck," I said, my senses returning to normal. I swallowed the lump in my throat and looked at the three combatants who were *not* bleeding out on the ground in front of me. They were all standing now and racing toward me. I was also fully aware of every ache, pain, and cut I'd been subjected to in this short fight.

Screw this.

I turned on my heel and ran.

But I didn't get very far, because my foot got caught in a tree root and I fell flat on my face. My nose smashed the ground hard, and I heard it crack. The earth was now soggy from the rain, and mud had splattered all over me. I twisted, yanking my leg out of the slick earthen trap just as the three foes reached me. I didn't know what to do. Smiler was grinning again and had his blade out, ready to attack. I felt my vision soften, and suddenly, as if in slow motion, I saw something strange appear.

The group rushing me slowed to a fraction of their normal speed as a little icon appeared above Smiler's chest. Well, to be more accurate, it materialized just above the fastening buckle of the leather strap slung across his torso. The symbol resembled a cartoonish depiction of a mushroom cloud, but I wasn't concerned with that at the moment.

I focused. I could see that the material of the strap was frayed three-fourths of the way through on one side, and it was straining to keep whatever was in his backpack aloft.

I felt the chunk of metal in my hand and, acting quickly, slashed at Smiler's chest, right at the fraying leather. With a ripping sound, the strap separated, and the pack he'd been lugging behind him zipped forward, following the direction of the previous strain. It caught Smiler between the legs as it fell, tangling him up and forcing him to swing wide in his fall. The weapon's sharp blade caught the ratman to his right in the face.

He dead, I thought.

Deep Voice dropped to the sopping dirt in a spout of blood, where he lay unmoving. I took the opportunity to slide backward in the mud a few feet and pull myself up as quickly as I could.

Just at that moment, Smiler looked down at his pack urgently. He seemed terrified of something within it. Odd. Small Fry was still moving forward and couldn't stop in time. But he tried. He slid on the wet ground and bowled over Smiler, landing right on top of the bag.

"THE FIRE BO—" Smiler screamed.

But whatever he had been about to finish that sentence with was lost because of a massive explosion. The group of three ratmen were suddenly replaced by an eruption of flame and deafening sound. The force blasted me backward, and

I shouted from the intense pain of the flames. Luckily, I'd been *just* far enough away that the vast majority of the inferno seemed to miss me.

I landed on my back a few feet from the blaze, and I tried to turn over to view the damage.

Everything was on fire. The grass, the trees—hell, even some of the rocks were blazing it up. Four glowing green lights hovered in the air above the makeshift battlefield, and I observed them hesitantly.

Were they souls? Did it work like that? I decided I might question them later, maybe make fun of them for being shitty ghosts and force them to watch me eating their rations.

I could see three charred corpses where the ratmen had once been and felt an awful sensation in my stomach. All of the bodies were on fire, and I could smell the sickening stench of burned flesh and hair.

"That's mega gross," I said, and looked away from the smoldering specters. "I sent them right to rat hell."

Then I got a notification.

Congratulations! You've raised an Ability!
Sabotage has advanced to F-Rank Level 3!

"What?" I said.

When had I gotten that Ability? I didn't recall it being a part of the Class or Racial bonuses. Still, I supposed it might've slipped in at some point, since I hadn't been the most mindful creature during my initial foray into this bizarre and incomprehensible world. Also, how had I raised it? Was that part of the little notification I got just before I was nearly made into orc filet?

Was it me *who killed them?*

I couldn't contemplate the turn of events further, as I was interrupted by another banner appearing.

You have killed [4] Level 6 Grelok Scouts
Gained 1,200 Experience.
Congratulations! You have reached LEVEL TWO.
You grow stronger and receive the benefit of [3] additional Attribute Points. 10% Health and Arcana restored. Combat conditions healed.

Congratulations! You have gained a new Ability!
Natural Resilience [F-Rank Level 1]
As Barbarians are more inclined to the outer workings of the world, it is within their domain to receive more than the usual trove of forces acting

against their best interest. You show marked deterrence to some of Mother Nature's most curious affronts. This Ability will continue to offer rewards as it is nourished.
- *+2% Resistance to Insects*
- *+2% Resistance to Weather Conditions [Cold]*

"Hm," I grunted, thinking it was odd that it declared I'd killed all four. "How has that happened? And what in the barf am I supposed to be able to resist bug bites for? It's cold out."

I struggled to my feet. My whole body hurt, and despite having just been informed that I'd regained some Health and . . . Arcana, I noticed my wounds were still there. Most of them were now lightly scabbing over—apparently, I wasn't suffering from "Bleeding" anymore—but of particular annoyance was the arrowhead still buried halfway in my collarbone. I reached up and dug into my skin, extracting the sharp piece of metal with a grimace.

"God*damn*, that smarts!" I said, and tossed the arrowhead on the ground. I looked around at the carnage that surrounded me and smirked.

"Now, *that's* how you make an entrance!" I shouted to no one. The fire was still burning the grass and, well, everything really. Even despite the rain now coming down in droves, the flames danced menacingly as if they were proud of what they'd just done.

"Good job, little burn-y buddies," I said approvingly. "Did he have a fucking stick of dynamite in there or something? That was a world-class boom."

I looked over the scene and found Gray Muzzle lying in a pool of mud and blood. It appeared he had been unable to stop the weeping of his wounds and bled to death.

"Nasty way to go," I muttered, and realized that there was perhaps a silver lining to this extravaganza of chaos I'd been an unwilling participant of. I had remembered an aspect of games that I was always fond of: looting.

I glanced back at the three barbecued rat kebabs. Most of their belongings—including their weapons—were either charred beyond recognition or had fused to their bodies in the blaze. At least, so far as I could tell. I shrugged.

Probably not much there to pilfer. However . . .

I approached the corpse of the ratman I'd sliced open like a Capri Sun that I couldn't get the straw into and saw that he had a pack slung over his shoulder.

"Don't mind me," I said to Gray Muzzle's body, and jerked the bag off of his slight frame. It was a lot nicer-looking than the one I'd been bequeathed at my arrival.

"Primo knapsack, my dude," I said appreciatively, and opened up the flap at the top. Inside were myriad different items and my eyes lit up as I saw a bulging pouch at the top. *Coins!*

I quickly uncinched the string and pulled it open, immediately recoiling in horror. *Not coins!*

"What the fuck?!" I exclaimed and dropped the pouch into the mud. Several squishy, bloody pieces of mottled gray flesh toppled out into a puddle. *Ears.*

"You're disgusting, dude," I said to the ratman's cold form, and looked back inside the pack. It was mostly camping gear—a dented pot with burned food still caked on the inside, a blanket, a rain poncho, and a change of clothes. I scowled at this and sighed. Beneath this stuff were a few empty bottles—probably other healing potions he'd already consumed, and a few crumbs from what appeared to be extremely moldy bread.

At the bottom I spotted a leather envelope wedged inside a folded pocket, and I gingerly lifted it up. It had some weight to it, and I carefully unsealed the edge, hoping against hope that it wasn't whatever had blown up the other guys.

The last thing I need is to accidentally pop open a package filled with no-no powder.

But it wasn't a combustive instrument of untimely demise. In fact, it didn't look dangerous at all. I stood staring at a sleeve of *playing cards*.

I picked them up and examined the details. There were three cards, each with the same symbol painted on the back: a curled abstract silver stave of some kind with an umbrella-style hook at the bottom and two "arms" near that. An illustration of a glowing red stone sat next to the glyph that almost resembled an eye. I didn't recognize it at all.

Must be something that only makes sense here.

I flipped the cards over and was delighted to find that each had a wonderfully illustrated face, with different depictions of what appeared to be scenes of battle or strong warriors activating magical powers. The borders around the pictures were different colors; red, blue, and white, and in the margins of each side were tally marks, one group for each direction. The lowest I saw was four and the highest being nine. Then I realized that wasn't exactly true. One card, showing a glowering volcano with a halo of light around its tip had a small crown along its top edge in place of tallies. That seemed like an important distinction.

"Is this some sort of card game?" I asked aloud. It definitely reminded me of a few I'd seen back home, though this was a bit less . . . manufactured-looking than the type I was used to.

I decided right at that moment wasn't the best time to look these over and instead stuffed the envelope of cards into my pack.

Not far from his body, ole Stab Wound here had dropped the blade he'd attempted to skewer me with. I glanced down at the rusty knife as my Analysis took over.

Paring Dagger
- Rarity: Pedestrian
- Item Class: Tool / Simple One-handed Short Blade
- Durability: 20/50
- Damage: 3–5 Piercing / 2–3 Slashing
- Bonuses: N/A

A simple short-bladed knife used for peeling, skinning, dicing, and intricate cutting in food preparation. Using this as a weapon would be better than nothing, right?

I examined the blade. The display was right, it was better than a broken hatchet, though I did like the idea of being able to hurl a hand ax willy-nilly. This dagger looked like it might break even easier than my previous weapon if I attempted to toss it.

I moved on to Gray Muzzle's shabby clothes. He was wearing leathers that would be much too small for someone my size, so I left those alone. However, I did snag another pouch from his belt and, hoping for less *organic* contents, opened it to find a few copper coins. Six, to be exact.

"Slim pickin's," I said. "You guys should have chosen a more gainful form of employment."

He also had a couple of tarnished metal rings, which I removed and put into the coin purse since they were much too small for me. I was able to find another bottle of what I confirmed to be a sort of healing potion tied into his belt at the back, after moving his blood-slick body to the side.

Minor Potion of Rejuvenation
- Rarity: Uncommon
- Item Class: Healing
- Durability: 1/1
- Weight: 1.5 lbs.
- Effect: *+10% of Max Health Regeneration and Cure Minor Wounds*

I didn't bother reading the rest of the description—mostly because I knew it would be something snarky that would just get me all hot under the collar. Instead, I ripped the cork out of the top and glugged it down. The effect was immediate, and I watched as my Health bar filled up a bit more. Then I watched as my bruises began to fade, and some of the cuts and punctures scabbed over. It was quite a shock to the system to understand the sensation of *instant healing*.

"Oh, that's what I like to see!" I exclaimed, and excitedly grabbed my formerly broken nose.

"Ah, fuck!" I shouted as pain gripped me in its intense and unapologetic vise. Apparently, shattered noses did not fall under the category of "minor wounds." The feeling was dizzying, but I was able to remain standing as I wiped tears from my eyes and tried to focus on my original plan: ransacking the ratman.

The only other thing I found on Gray Muzzle's person was a battered piece of parchment that was tucked into his glove. I removed it and discovered a tidy scrawl of script inside.

Bounty Request:
Willing to pay top dollar for the acquisition of intact False Goblin ears for my research. I know of several enclaves of the brutes near Orikton Mills in the Aglands. Please find me at Yosper Hall in Tallrock for payment. The more ears, the better.
Reward: 1 *Kingdom* **Silver per False Goblin ear.**
—*Edwig Quintham, M.O.*

"Whoa," I muttered, and looked back at the pouch in the mud with the gray ears spilling out of it. "I may have just had a windfall of cash." Could those be false goblin ears in there? What were the odds?

Another damnable banner appeared in the air.

You have been offered a Quest!

[Bounty Quest] *The Easy Part*
Edwig Quintham requests False Goblin ears be returned to him in Tallrock for payment in Kingdom silver. Fortunately, you have been the beneficiary of a treasure trove of the stuff.
- **Reward:** *Experience. Coin.*
- **Bonus Reward:** *Unknown*

Accept?
Yes / No

I smiled. I'd seen Quests mentioned in some of the notifications, but I wasn't sure how to access them—and now it seemed like I'd just stumbled across one. I mentally selected *Yes*, and the banner disappeared. I turned to eye the sack of ears again and shuddered.

Don't think I will be counting those.

That's something best left to the . . . professional? Though why someone would want a bunch of monster ears was a wonder to me. However, it did open up some interesting possibilities. The term *false* goblins suggested the existence of regular or, I supposed, *true* goblins—an exciting prospect. That meant that this world was absolutely of the fantasy variety. You know, if the armor, swords, and strange abilities hadn't tipped me off already.

"Well, I suppose as long as I'm here, I can make the best of it," I said, and stood up to get my bearings.

I walked around the tiny area that was the ultimate result of my travels so far and sighed. My body still burned, but I was at least better off than I had been a few minutes before in the health department. As far as I could tell, I was at the top of some hill, with many taller earthen mounds surrounding my spot. It was actually charming, if I did say so myself. It was peaceful and quiet—now that I'd dealt with the riffraff—and the rain had even let up a little. Not much, but . . . a bit.

I went to the edge of the open space where the area met the tree line, and tried to peer into the depths of the woods. It was not as dense as I'd thought, though the rain made it a little harder to get a good peep into the trees. I *could* tell, though, that I was at the edge of whatever hill I was on top of. The earth sloped down, as did the trunks of the trees, disappearing after a few meters into the abyss of the . . . dirt horizon? I wasn't one hundred percent sure what some terms actually were, but I'd made do so far in life without the information, so I wasn't about to start *learning things* now.

I found a meandering path through the trees that looked quite overgrown and disused, and watched as it too disappeared over the downward slope. I looked back behind me at the mess and carnage I'd exacted just a short while before and chuckled.

"I should probably get out of here before any actual challenge comes along."

If those guys were scouts, it likely wouldn't be long before their rat-bastard companions showed up, and I had no delusions about where I'd end up in that fight, given my current detriment of both health and levels. Fortunately, whatever this . . . Sabotage Ability was had saved my orcish ass in my moment of need, but I couldn't hope that I'd get so lucky next time. Plus—a large part of why I'd lasted long enough to even pull off a Hail Mary maneuver like that was because of my Primal Rage, and that—I remembered, strangely—was only good for a ride once a day. That meant I'd need to make it until at least morning before being able to bust some skulls like that again. I couldn't tell what time of day it was because of the rain, but it couldn't have been too far away from evening based on the encroaching darkness.

Better get to steppin', then.

I took one final look around the clearing, mostly to make sure I hadn't missed some other tool of potential wealth like the note, and saw a notification blinking in my vision again. I unfocused my eyes and let the psychic muscles access the message. A banner appeared, repeating the same announcement four times in a row.

For defeating an opponent more than FIVE levels above your own, you have received an Emerald Esper Node!
For defeating an opponent more than FIVE levels above your own, you have received an Emerald Esper Node!
For defeating an opponent more than FIVE levels above your own, you have received an Emerald Esper Node!
For defeating an opponent more than FIVE levels above your own, you have received an Emerald Esper Node!
Accept [4] Esper Nodes?
Yes / No

"Why the hell not?" I wondered aloud, selecting in the affirmative.

Instantly, the four hovering green lights began to glitter and sparkle and shot out of the sky where they'd been slowly levitating, rocketing at me before I had time to react. They hit my body, and my physical form seemed to absorb them in some fashion. There was a quick flash of green light around me, and then . . . nothing.

"Well, that was . . . boring," I said. I wasn't sure what I should have expected, as it wasn't exactly *strange* to have something like that in a video game. So far, everything tracked just about how I'd expect it to, but no one could blame me for demanding a bit more dramatic flair in this instance.

I turned back to the trail, slung my pack over my shoulder, and began a slow pace into the sopping wet leaves of the woods at the edge of the hill.

"On to see if I can find whatever the hell Tallrock is!"

CHAPTER SEVEN

UNLIKELY ASSASSIN

As I traveled along, I became painfully aware that there were quite a few pitfalls, both literally and figuratively, in descending a slippery hill in the near-dark. First and foremost—it was godawfully mucky. I'd never been much of a fan of getting dirty, nor being outside, nor getting wet while still wearing clothes, and now, all of my irritants had converged into some massive, congealed ball of piss-off jelly. I had initially tried wiping away a lot of the water that obscured my vision, falling into my orc eyes or my collar and down my back. Eventually, though, I just gave up and opened myself up to the whims of Mother Nature.

Another annoying bit of this journey was that as I moved down, the trees got sparser. Not that they went away, just that they fanned out with more distance than I honestly thought was necessary. Seemed a bit rude, really. It was as though every few feet I'd slide in mud and have to coast to a tree trunk, and that was perpetually becoming more and more difficult to do.

It was honestly a little miserable. It even had me contemplating if I would have been better off just dying in the wreckage of the train crash. But then I started *thinking* about it. Which was ultimately a pointless endeavor because I still wasn't sure that hadn't happened.

I remembered seeing a documentary once about a woman who had lived through a near-death experience. She'd been on the operating table and her heart stopped beating during her surgery just as they were preparing to stitch her body back up. According to the doctor that was interviewed, she'd only been dead for a few minutes before they brought her back. Still, from the woman's perspective, she'd encountered hours upon hours of a unique experience walking through shadowed halls and visiting with loved ones and even frolicking in a field in the sunshine of her hometown a thousand miles away from her hospital bed. She'd been convinced she'd tasted a slice of heaven, but according to the realistic—and most likely—more accurate explanation from a neuroscientist, she'd experienced what he called a "brain surge," something that has been documented to happen to some people and animals after death.

In this brain surge, time slowed down for her, because—apparently—much like a dream, the human mind can produce a whole cocktail of chemicals and misfiring of synapses that creates a realm of experiences all at once, and the brain translates it as happening in a slowed-down, sequential order. So, for her, it had been hours, maybe even days, but for everyone else, it was three minutes and fifty-one seconds.

I considered that maybe that's all this was for me, you know, instead of a coma. Perhaps I'd actually been smashed between the collapsed train car and the pavement, and these were the final few minutes of my life in some crazy game world my brain had cooked up. It was very possible my heart and other bodily functions had already ceased, and soon, I'd just straight-up *expire*. If that was the case, I supposed it beat the alternative. I had to distract myself, because once I thought about death, I knew I'd start thinking about Roger, and that wouldn't do anyone any good—least of all me.

Man, that was a depressing tangent, I scolded myself. *Best not to think of that right now.*

After another hour, I noticed that despite it clearly getting darker around me, I didn't seem to have any trouble seeing. In fact, ironically, the only way I knew it was actually night time was because suddenly, all the colors I could see transformed from the usual tones to something of a grayscale.

Ah, I thought. *This must be Darkvision.*

I didn't mind it. While strange to get used to at first, after a few more slips and near misses it was the last thing on my mind.

It wasn't long afterward that a curiosity made me pause in my mud-covered tracks. I was just getting to a point where the slope to the hill had become more gradual, and I reasoned I'd reached one of the mound's flatter areas. That was when I saw lights in the distance.

Fire.

Slightly downhill from me I could see dozens of flames peppering the landscape, and it wasn't until I was able to figure out how to switch *off* my Darkvision that I could clearly see what it was. It wasn't just fire. It was *torchlight*.

I squinted down at the scene, scanning from left to right. There seemed to be a bunch of tall wooden poles in a ring with the flames activated on top, and beneath their canopied glow were tents. I couldn't see how many exactly, but there were at least two dozen. Every so often, I'd seen some of the light disappear and reappear from side to side.

Movement.

People were walking around—and that may have been a good sign, or it could have been horrible. Were these the other ratmen that the scouts had been with? It seemed like it could have been. Granted, I didn't actually know if they had a larger force or if it had just been the four of them off on their own. A term like *Scouts* could have meant their Class and not their job, I supposed. Though it was hard to know for certain, since I'd learned precisely fuck-all about this world still. Better to be safe than sorry, though.

The lights were directly in the path of the same particular trail I was on, a half-mile from where I trembled in the trees, and that just wouldn't do. Anything could happen if I approached, and I was still in the neighborhood of a quarter of my full health. Not to mention the only weapon I had was a mostly dull knife that looked like it still had yesterday's lunch caked to the blade. Not really the best odds.

Switching back into Darkvision, I peered around to see if I could spot another route that wouldn't get me close to the potential visceral doom I could face.

Down just a hair I could see that it looked like the path forked, with one trail veering to the right. Beyond that, there was another slope in the earth indicating to me—at the very least—that it was a way down that might have been safer than traipsing through the camp.

That made me pause as well. I wasn't sure how I could figure out the natural patterns of the swell of a hill and its possible ramifications just based on a cursory look. I despised going outdoors, and learning about them was almost worse, so I doubted I'd picked it up by accident. I thought back to the Skills and Abilities I'd been allotted at the beginning of this hellscape nightmare and remembered being imparted with both a Survival and Nature Skill. Was that to blame for my wealth of understanding at this moment? I sighed.

"Just great," I muttered. "This world can mess with your brain as well as your body. This fucking *sucks*. How long until I'm not even *me* anymore?"

But, thinking about that, I supposed that was sort of the point, wasn't it? I hated who I'd been in my old life. Back home, I was a short, fat, dumb, angry psychopath with zero marketable talents, no friends, and at least a minor case of narcissism. Remembering it, the first thing I'd decided when I was presented with a new physical form was to go with something very unlike my original self so that I could escape some of what I'd been.

That was a bit too much introspection for me, really. I was never the *contemplate my choices* type, and now was not the time to wax pitiful about myself or my former shortcomings. No, now was the time for semi-decisive, underinformed action. So, that's exactly what I did.

Slipping quietly in the mud, I moved from tree to exponentially farther tree, inching closer to the divide in the path and my route to safety. However, when I was within twenty feet of the crossroads, I noticed a glaring problem.

There was someone there.

Standing at attention in front of my intended target was a tall, muscular figure in dark, bulky armor. He had a thick brown beard, and one of his arms was exposed, revealing a big burn on his forearm. His hand rested on the pommel of a sword belted to his side, his fingertips drumming impatiently on the handle.

Most importantly, I could tell right away that he weren't no ratman.

He looked like he was probably human, though it was difficult to tell in the hues I was limited to in the dark. He could have just as easily been an elf or some other Tolkien-y race that should only exist in movies and comic books. I didn't think he'd seen me, but I couldn't be too careful, so I stood still and brought my breath to a slow, measured pace.

The sentinel remained completely unaware of my presence, and I was thanking my lucky stars for the light patter of rain that likely masked my movement as I crept forward. I forced a tight grip on the handle of the Paring Dagger and slid quietly toward the man, preparing to strike.

I was just within jugular-lancing distance when the guard suddenly spoke.

"Aye. Come to end me life, eh?"

I froze. The man hadn't looked in my direction nor adopted a defensive posture or really anything indicating he knew I was there other than the statement. Contrastingly, he kept his eyes out toward the woods, unmoving.

I didn't say anything. I wasn't sure if he was talking to me, but didn't want to run the risk of revealing myself if he happened to have an imaginary friend. My silence seemed to goad him into continuing.

"Don' be bashful, now. You've come to bring an end to ol' Chessit, an' he's ready for ye to fulfill your intention. I'll not run or scream—I'm more o' the *pass softly into the great beyond* sort."

I couldn't wrap my mind around this man's motives. Did he really sense my presence? Or was this a ruse to get me to move closer so he could jam his sword under my jaw? As if reading my mind, the man continued.

"You're just about the most trepidatious assassin Chessit's ever encountered. First time?"

I remained quiet, looking around to see if there was anyone else within earshot.

"There's no'n else around, lad. Truth be the tellin', I had a hunch it'd be today, so I made sure I were alone out here so as not to inconvenience anyone else might get interested in stopping you from performing your mortal duty."

He let out a long breath of air.

"Though it's a powerful long wait—more'n I thought. Imagined it'd be a bit quicker, ye know? Bit of a sharp stab an' then . . . curtains. It's a touch unkind to leave a man waitin' for his just rewards, don't ye think?"

I saw the man's pupil flick to the corner of his eye for a fraction of a moment, right where I was.

"Aye, you're a big'n. Won't take much more than a swift drag o' that blade to end Chessit's wallow, I'd think. Even with skin as boiled and leathery as mine!"

The man chuckled. It was a rough sound.

I couldn't believe he'd been able to see that much of me with the quick glance he'd cast in my direction. My size, sure. But the knife in my hand? It was an impressive feat. I wasn't sure how to approach this oddity, but, considering he seemed resigned to death, I thought it prudent to at least speak to him.

"You knew I was here?" I asked quietly, as to not alert anyone else who might be within earshot.

"Ah!" Chessit exclaimed in a whisper. "He speaks! Gotta say I weren't quite anticipating that—all things considered."

I watched a wry smile begin to curl at the edge of his lips.

"I sensed ye a ways off, as it were," Chessit said. "Ye spend enough time in the woods, and ye learn what to listen for. Spend as much time as *ol' Chessit*, and you can practically perceive an approachin' man's boot size."

I considered this. I probably had not been the quietest sneak thief during my descent, so it stood to reason that someone like Chessit, who claimed to be one with nature or whatever, would have likely had a keen ear to my direction.

"Your name is Chessit?" I asked.

"Aye, if it pleases ye," the man said softly. "Though I suppose it's probably too much to ask my executioner if he's got a name?"

"I'm Gab—er—Loon," I stumbled. If I was going to be a part of this world, I'd need to remember the name I'd chosen.

"Ah, Gaberloon," Chessit said. "Not fighting for the top spot o' most curious name I've encountered in me life, but it's a tad south of usual. That a moniker of the Lion Duchy?"

I wasn't sure how to go about telling him that it was the nickname of a fat high-schooler who had tumbled cheek-over-ankle into a different world. So, instead, I lied.

"Yep," I said simply.

"There a lot of orcs over in the Duchy?" Chessit asked. "Reckon I'd heard it was mostly humans and elves o'er that way."

"Not a lot of them," I said. "One less, now that I'm here."

"That's the way of it," Chessit said. "A sharp wit's a good trait for an assailant. Best way to stay a man of your own device instead of a catspaw."

"Why—er, *what* makes you think I'm here to kill you?" I asked, very curious why this man seemed so content to die in the middle of a rainy trail.

"Oh, myriad reasons," Chessit chuckled. "Most particularly, however, would be me outstanding debts. Had a missive delivered near a month ago, now. Just said *Time's up*. Since then, I figured each day a blessin' 'til the gods deem me time nigh."

". . . and you believe that to be now?" I asked.

"Better today than tomorrow," Chessit mused. "This mornin's breakfast was plum pudding and porridge. Tomorrow's is boiled turnips. If it's all the same, I'd prefer to go out on a high. Nothin' would be worse than ending ye life with a belly full of root vegetables."

I'll be honest, as much of a role as food had played in my life, I'd never once considered what my last meal might be. It was an interesting perspective, and one that Chessit had seemed to reflect on more than was healthy. This man had an easy likability to him, even when facing his perceived death. I found that despite disliking almost everyone, Chessit was a man I felt I'd actually not be one hundred percent annoyed by. Maybe it was his unassuming nature? There was an element of charm to a person who accepted their fate so readily.

"Well, what if I'm not the assassin sent to kill you?" I asked, glancing around to make sure we were still alone. I didn't see any movement, but I couldn't be too careful as close to the camp as we were.

"Oh, if that were the case," Chessit started, "I'd just as well request you be the hand that does it. Probably couldn't hope for a more amiable end, can I? Bit of a chat, swappin' a fingertip's worth of pleasantries, and then a knife in the dark. Beats whatever cruel machinations lie in wait for me future prospects. Many a tale been telled 'bout sadistic blokes hired to turn a man to a ghost while havin' a laugh of it."

"You don't think I'm capable of toying with you?" I asked, seriously wondering at what sort of a strange event I'd encountered here.

"Aye, you could might," Chessit said. "But it's been my experience that them sort ain't the type to beat around the roots on something like killin'. I don't get the sense you have that level of evil in your heart—mayhap I'm in the wrong on this, but I'd be surprised. You seem a neutral orc in the matter of death."

Dammit.

My concerns were coming to fruition. I wanted to be feared in this new realm, not cooed at. It seemed I was presenting myself with a lot less confidence than I expected to give off. It was no wonder those ratmen had thought it wise to almost end my life.

"How much money do you owe?" I asked.

"Me debts?" Chessit asked. "A princely sum, to be sure. I suppose it depends on which enclave of dubious repute is contracting m' lifeblood."

"In total," I specified. It's not like I had any money to cover it—but I was curious to know how much cash was worth killing a man over.

"Somewhere near the mark of a thousand Kingdom gold."

I let out a low whistle.

"That seems like a lot," I said, but I wasn't sure. A thousand gold could have been the price of a coffee there.

"A fair bit," Chessit said with a slight nod, still never looking at me. "A touch out o' me price range for recompense too, I'm ashamed to admit."

"Hence the hit out on you," I said.

"Aye," Chessit muttered. "So, now you know me tribulations. Bein' that we're good and square friends, could you do a pal a favor and put me out o' me misery?"

I didn't even have to think about it.

"I can't do that," I said. "Though you seem really earnest in your convictions, you don't seem to deserve death. At least not by my hand."

"Might be a bit dangerous, goin' round and thinkin' the best o' people," Chessit said. "Get ye in a situation ye might not be in otherwise. There's bad folk out here, orc. Best not to get tangled up in a mess if ye can help it."

I chuckled.

"I don't typically think the best of anyone. But I'll take my chances this time."

Chessit was silent for a moment, considering my words, perhaps, but then seemed to perk up.

"Right, then," he said, turning to look at me. "Guess I'll try me luck with the next set o' blades that meanders into me purview."

Now that I could see him more clearly, I realized he was younger than I'd originally taken him for. His manner and tone suggested an old specter near death, but he was—at worst—in his late forties from my estimation.

"You're surprisingly chipper about the whole thing," I said, very unsettled by the shift in his demeanor.

"Aye," Chessit said with a nod. "No use languishin' in melodrama 'bout our fates, right? Best to look death square in the gob and let it do as it will. A man's gotta know when he's been beaten by the worldly things, and when there's a new day approaching. Boiled turnips it is! A fine breakfast by any standard."

Then his tone changed, becoming clearer and more serious.

"Now there's just the matter of you," he said.

"Me?"

"Aye," he confirmed, and before I knew what was happening, he'd drawn his sword and had the point stuck directly under my chin.

"You're encroachin' on Redmark territory, orc. I'm going to have to take you in for questions."

I was shocked. After the nearly enjoyable conversation we'd just had, I was completely baffled by this new development.

"What . . . " I could only mutter, staring down the length of the blade into Chessit's cold gaze.

"Best come quietly, friend," Chessit explained. "As I warned, there's bad folk out here. Unfortunately for ye, you've stumbled onto one o' the worst."

CHAPTER EIGHT

THE REDMARK CAMP

The Redmark camp was arranged in a flower shape, and as I was frog-marched into the area, I could see the layout was quite intentional. There were eight large pavilions in each compartmentalized section surrounded by various smaller tents. I noticed that the littler structures seemed more utilitarian—likely for the more common soldiers—and were a wide variety of styles, colors, and materials in what I imagined was likely based more on ability to acquire rather than preference.

The pavilions, however, were all the same color: a stark red that practically glowed in the torchlight, with an eight-petaled flower emblazoned in black on the flaps of their entrances. If this was in any way similar to the movies I'd seen, these would be the officer quarters, probably captains or whatever the rank was in this world.

There were men and women milling about, most staring at me and judging with raised brows or smirks. I despised it. Each face had a look of interest and disgust at my presence, and I adopted my best sneer in return. There were a few hushed comments between men-at-arms, as well as a few louder oaths of approval. A couple men approached near enough to whistle at me, but Chessit turned to glare at them, and they immediately returned to their original places of respectful contempt. It looked as though it was dinnertime, as many of the soldiers were dressed down in more casual attire and carried heaping tankards of sloshing liquid, heels of bread, and bowls overladen with steaming contents.

As we moved, I could see the sundry sleeping areas were organized very neatly. Crates and supply sacks marked the borders of each section, and no two areas were closer than eight feet apart. This allowed pathways between the sub-camps that led to a substantial center section where soldiers sat around cookfires or busied themselves with crafts. There was a metric dickton of people there enjoying themselves, and each individual looked hardened and severe.

Well, this is bad news.

It would be very difficult to escape from there, not that I'd have had a shot regardless. I hadn't been able to secure myself against one miserable old cuss, let alone an entire regiment of them. Even if I'd been—what's the word... *unfettered*? That sounds right. Even if that weren't the case, I had no idea how strong any of these medieval morons were. I was not a skilled fighter when I had a full range of motion. Now my wrists and ankles were bound with rope and chain. I'd never been much for mathematical pursuits, but even I knew that my odds were supremely fucked.

I took note of a brawny bald dude with a gigantic burn on the left side of his face who looked up from pounding a sword out against an anvil. He watched silently, with no emotion that I could see. As Chessit pushed me past his station, they shared a nod, and the man returned to his work without a word.

"Friend of yours?" I asked, and Chessit grunted.

"Pay that no mind, lad," he said roughly. "You're my charge now. Ain't a piece to be worryin' about interpersonal relationships in your condition."

"What's my condition?" I asked.

"I'd wager it's gallows-bound, but I've been wrong before."

"I don't suppose *gallows* is a cute nickname for the pleasure tents, are they?" I asked.

"It'll be *someone's* pleasure, most like," Chessit said. "But I imagine you're goin' to be a wee peeved by the prospects."

I sighed and tried testing the strength of the binding keeping my hands together. They hardly moved.

Yep. Still captured.

Chessit seemed to be leading me to the middle of the camp, and, more specifically, a large yurt-like building around which the diners had congregated. It was different in composition from the others, being at least three times the height of the officer tents and twice as wide. Rather than the red cloth, this one seemed designed out of furs, leather, and maybe whatever the hell canvas was. Instead of the black-flower pattern on the entrance flap, this structure had two large posts on either side of it, with red flags fluttering in the misty evening wind. Each also had the crest in black, and it was clear these had been given more attention than the other ragtag emblems, as it was expertly patterned in stitching.

"Cute floral," I said as we neared the entrance. "How come you guys are the Redmarks if the symbol is in black? Isn't that kind of a misnomer?"

Chessit stopped, and turned my body so that I was facing him.

"Your candor was amusing earlier, but I'd be a bit more strict with my tongue if'n I were you," Chessit said dryly. "*She's* not gonna have the level of appreciation for humor you've come to expect from my whimsical nature."

"Yeah, you're just a super fun-time guy, Chessit," I said, before wondering, "who's *she*?"

"Commander Fawn," he said quietly. "Runs this outfit."

"Interesting," I said. "Is that her first name or last?"

"It'll definitely be the last name ye hear if ye think you can open your maw and crack wise in her presence, lad. Mind the mouth."

"If it's all the same," I said, borrowing his phrase, "you said I'm on death row, so does it really matter how I speak to her?"

"That depends," Chessit said.

"On?"

"Whether you like slow deaths or quick 'uns."

I chuckled.

"Your comedic timing is really well developed, Chessit. Have you ever considered *not* being a kidnapping dickbag?"

Chessit grunted.

"Aye. In me youth, I dreamed of finer things," he said. "Painting, mayhaps."

"Well, what changed?" I asked, worried there was a sad story attached to his comment that I'd be forced to listen to.

"Dickbags get paid better," he said. "In ye go."

. . . and with that, I was shoved into the opening of the yurt.

CHAPTER NINE

FROM DUSK 'TIL FAWN

I winced as I stumbled in.

It was *bright*, and emerging from the dimmer illumination (though not enough to warrant Darkvision) to be thrust into the glow of so many lamps was jarring. I was able to make out the general layout of the place, and I've got to say it was quite an impressive display of shit. Banners hung from fasteners along each of the fabric walls, every one the same black flower over a red field. There was a large basin to my right—probably a sort of bathtub—and behind it, a closed-off area with a large fur hung as if to separate the section for privacy. I was able to catch a glimpse of a large four-poster bed somewhere within, which made me feel bad for whoever had to lug that bad boy around through the wilderness. There were rows of bookshelves as well—equally as daunting to transport as the bed, I'd imagine, and right next to me was a wooden coatrack. A single black cloak was draped from one of the hooks, shimmering with rain.

In the center of the chamber was a massive table, carved from dark wood. I could see several shapes standing in front of it, surrounding a collection of papers, bottles, and likely long-cold food. I knew I'd made something of a theatrical—and possibly loud—entrance because I heard the unmistakable scrape of weapons being pulled from scabbards upon entering.

Well, I say *unmistakable*, but really, it could have been anything. If I hadn't seen it happen, the noise likely would have confused the ever-loving shit out of me. I was learning that swords being drawn do not sound like they do in the movies. It was a much duller sound than the high-fidelity foley you get from fantasy action shows.

Anyway, I am going on a tangent—danger.

My eyes settled to the new light, and I saw two fully armored soldiers with feathery-plumed helmets rush forward. Apparently, they were intent on cutting me down, which was something I was able to judge based on their speed, angry-looking motions, and the fact that one said, "Cut him down."

Fortunately, I'm an expert on insight, so subtle things like that really stand out.

If it hadn't been for Chessit, I'd have likely met my end right there. But my middle-aged captor stepped through the entrance at that moment, and my two would-be manslaughterers skidded to a halt.

"Easy now, wains," Chessit said, his tone deadly. "I'll assume you weren't aiming to use them arse-pokers on ole Chessit."

The two soldiers froze, eyeing first Chessit, then each other before turning to look behind them. Then the soldier on the left, a male human, shook his head.

"We weren't attempting to assail you, S—"

Chessit cleared his throat, interrupting him.

"Good. Then see to it you point those needles in a friendlier direction. I gots m'self an orc needs reprimanding, and I'm confident the two o' you aren't capable of dolin' out any measure of fairness in this proceeding."

The soldier on the right was a woman. Though, considering the scant angular features I could see beneath her helm, I wasn't sure she was human. She nodded.

"Right," she said thoughtfully. "We were just briefing Commander F—"

"That seems like a bit o' *need-to-know* basis information, Blueleaf," Chessit interrupted again, and it was strange to think that *this* was the same man who'd only a little while ago been contemplating the end of his life. "My rank don't allow me ears privy to that sort o' fundamental knowledge. Best you let me speak m' piece, and I'll make meself scarce."

She nodded again.

"Of course," she said, turning to look behind her. "Commander?"

The party's remaining member was a tall, lean woman with short black hair and a face like thunder. She peered at the goings-on with a piercing, steel-colored gaze, her bulky-armored stature relaxed. I'd never before seen someone so terrifying in all my life.

"What have you brought me, Chessit?" she asked, in a more pleasant tone than I would've imagined she'd have.

"An orc, Commander Fawn," Chessit said simply. "Out a-prowlin' near my post. Claims to be from the Duchy."

"A spy," Fawn said. It wasn't so much a question as it was an accusation.

"Might be he is," Chessit said. "Can't say he's a very good 'un though, were that the case. Bit of a weighted boot on him."

Commander Fawn looked at me, sizing me up.

Ugh. Fuck you, lady. Get the measure of someone your own size.

She didn't say anything to me but turned back to Chessit with a shrug.

"Did he have anything on him?"

Chessit shrugged.

"Just some common tools, a rusted knife, clothing in a bag—the usual mess," he said. "Though there was a purse full o' ears that I'd be wonderin' the purpose of had I not seen a bounty note tucked away in there as well. False goblins, seems."

Fawn nodded.

"You can leave the pack by the entrance, then," she said. "I'm sure we can redistribute anything salvageable."

Chessit nodded and hoisted my satchel from his shoulder, and set it down gingerly next to the coatrack.

"Aye."

"He has a better nature than most of his kind," she said. "A strange look, too. Odd to see an orc with such . . . qualities. Might be half-orc, maybe? Does he speak?"

She was now looking directly at me.

"Uh, I do," I said. "A little."

"Probably more than ye'd like," Chessit interjected.

"You use the common tongue well," Fawn said. "For an orc, in any case."

"You aren't half bad yourself," I said. "You know, for the leader of a bunch of assholes."

The human man pointed his sword at me.

"Mind your manners, orc," he threatened. "Or I'll open your throat so we can't hear your prattling any further."

I sighed.

"See? Assholes."

"It's all right, Sir Penheart," Fawn said, sounding almost amused. "Let him speak his piece. It's all he has."

Sir Penheart seemed to consider her words and—still scowling—lowered his blade. I noticed he didn't sheathe it, though.

"Are you an agent of the Duchy, orc?" Fawn asked, moving around the table to get closer to me.

"Perhaps I am," I said, eyeing her carefully. I couldn't help but shoot back indignation—just part of my charm, I suppose. Still, there was something dangerous about this woman—you know, other than the fact that she was the commander of this whole camp—and pissing her off might not be the best course of action.

Think, you stupid moron. Use what little bit of intellect you have left in your soft fucking brain and try to talk your way out of this.

"So. Are you a spy, then?" Fawn asked. She was now just a few feet from me, close enough that I could smell her perfume. Something registered in my mind, and I knew it was lavender. It was pleasant, which really seemed inappropriate for someone so threatening.

"Not a spy," I said carefully. *But what?*

"Then an assassin?" Fawn posited.

Chessit chuckled. "I can guarantee he ain't no hired killer."

Fawn glanced over at him but seemed to accept his comment without question. Her eyes found mine again, waiting for an answer.

When in doubt . . .

"I'm just an adventurer," I said.

Fawn didn't say anything for a moment; she simply stared at me. Then she did something astonishing: she laughed.

It was a short-lived thing, but it actually sounded like she found my statement *very* funny. I didn't react—a firm show of strength and all that.

"I'm sorry," she said, gathering herself and standing to her full height. "That's just . . . *such* an antiquated term! You sound like my nan telling me about her youth."

I wasn't sure how to react to this, considering I'd thought it was as close to the truth as I could get. The main characters were always referred to as adventurers in games, so what the hell else was I supposed to assume?

What had that idiot orb called me?

I cleared my throat.

"Sorry," I said, attempting to try again. "Bad, uh, translation maybe—the Duchy and all—I meant to say that I am a . . . sojourner."

That halted the party immediately. Midway through her mirth, Fawn's face suddenly turned to ice, and it was as though all of the air left the room. She glared at me, wild-eyed, and suddenly moved so close to me I could have licked her eyeballs.

"Say that again, orc," Fawn demanded. "I want to make sure I heard you correctly."

Based on her reaction, the *last* thing I wanted to do was repeat myself. However, I've always been—apparently—a bit of a dumbass. So, I did.

"I'm a sojourner," I stated, before quickly adding, "from the Duchy."

Fawn kept her eyes on mine—a difficult endeavor, considering I was a lot taller than her.

"When did you arrive?" Fawn asked.

"Not long ago . . ." I said, but was interrupted by Fawn's snapping tone and a raised hand.

"Leave us," she commanded.

Her subordinate tried to speak up, her voice pinched.

"Commander Fa—"

"I said, *leave us*," Fawn hissed, her gaze unmoving.

The two soldiers turned and left hastily without another word. Chessit remained, but Fawn addressed him sternly.

"Thank you, Chessit," she said. "I'll call for you when I'm done here."

"Aye, Commander," Chessit said. Out of the corner of my eye, I could see he was looking at me, but I didn't dare turn away from the bizarre staring contest I was having with the commander. After a moment, he also left, leaving the two of us alone in the yurt.

Fawn waited another moment, and then her entire countenance relaxed, and she smiled wide.

"Holy *shit*," she said suddenly. "I can't believe it!" I was shocked to find her stately, formal tone had evaporated, and now she sounded . . . modern.

She turned away from me and walked casually over to the table where she plopped down and slung a leg over the arm of a chair. Then she chuckled and tossed her head to indicate I should approach.

"Come on, you big idiot," she said. "Join me."

"Uh . . . " I started, but Fawn stuck a leg out and nudged the chair next to her so that it turned to face me.

"Come on, sit."

I shuffled toward her, clinking all the while, and when I reached the chair, I tried to find a comfortable—or rather—balanced position to sit in. I defaulted to a slight lean against the edge of the seat and turned to face the bizarre woman. I couldn't help but wonder about my luck at having been bewildered twice now in a matter of an hour by someone's duplicitous nature.

Fawn smirked at me.

"So, how long have you actually been here, then?" she asked, plucking an apple from the tabletop. She bit into it with a crunch and looked back at me, smiling through the mouthful and chewing loudly and openly. It appeared all sense of decorum had been dismissed. Now I was looking at someone wholly unfamiliar from the stern and severe Commander Fawn I'd just been interacting with.

"Uh, maybe a day?" I ventured, still not sure what was going on. "Maybe less. I'm not sure."

"Damn," Fawn said, still chewing. "That is crazy. You're, like, *really* fresh, then. What Level are you?"

"Two," I said quietly. "But that's a recent development."

I didn't like this new line of questioning and almost preferred our dynamic earlier, when she was still intimidating. Now she was scary in a new way.

Has she gone crazy?

"Wow," she said, her eyes lighting up with surprise. "You weren't kidding. You're a newborn, basically."

"I'm sorry, are we talking about what I think we are talking about?" I asked.

Fawn chuckled and tossed the remainder of her apple back on the table. It made a wet smack against the wood and rolled, coming to a stop against the spine of a large book.

"You can relax," she said. "What's your name, anyway?"

I hesitated, not sure how to proceed.

"Hey, man, I said you can *relax*. What are you called here?"

What have I got to lose, I thought to myself, *except maybe my life?*

"Loon," I said.

"Weird choice—but okay," she said. "Obviously, I'm Fawn. There, that's better, right? We can now gab like two beings of conversational intelligence."

I had one burning question taking up brain space, so I decided it might be best to just spit it out before it killed me.

"How—uh—what is with the sudden change of personality? Did I say something strange?"

"You said 'sojourner.' Nobody would use that term around here without having heard it from the management."

"The management?" I asked. "Like, say... a weird, sentient cloud monster?"

"Oh, maybe," she said, seeming as though she hadn't thought about it. "I always sorta figured that thing was just like a servant or a tool, not really any of the head honchos."

If I recalled correctly, the orb had said it was something of a messenger. In any case, it was clear we were talking about the same subject.

"So, are you—"

"Like you?" Fawn interjected. "Yeah, I suppose I am."

My heart could have hammered a diamond into a meteor. Someone else from my world was occupying this strange place! This was amazing news. I usually hated to connect with other people on *any* level. Still, considering I was apparently in some alternate world ... maybe I could break a few of my old traditions.

I had half a billion questions I wanted to ask, but Fawn continued her monologue.

"... though I'm surprised anyone chose an orc. They aren't exactly the most likable race around."

"Well, I didn't really have anything to go off of," I said. "Plus, it was either that or human, and I had already been one of those ... so it seemed a little boring."

Fawn nodded.

"Yeah," she said. "If I could go back and do it over, I'd have picked something a lot cooler. Maybe an elf or a vittra. Oh, well, no point in worrying over it. Humans are nice enough—not that I'd know the difference."

"What's *your* Level?" I asked, very interested to know anything she could spare to tell me.

Fawn scowled.

"One thing you need to know is that asking someone *that* is considered extremely rude," she explained, then winked. "Don't just give that information out to anyone, either, or they are liable to use it against you."

"But you just asked me that same question!"

"Well, I took advantage of your ignorance," she said with a wink. "Sue me."

I sighed. Guess that was one area I wasn't about to have explained to me. So, I decided on a different tactic.

"You mentioned that I was new. Does that mean you've been here a long time?"

The woman shrugged, which was an interesting maneuver in a full plate of armor.

"Eh . . . " she began, gazing up as if trying to tabulate the correct amount. "Maybe . . . ten years? I'm not sure exactly."

"Ten years?!" I shouted.

"Easy there, Megaphone," she warned. "Some of my soldiers are trying to get some shut-eye. Plus, they don't need to know what we *really* are."

That was worth considering. Until now, I kind of figured it would be obvious to the locals that I wasn't from around these parts, but if she hadn't even told her own men . . .

"So, no one knows you're actually—"

"Right," she said, shifting forward in her seat. "No one knows, and no one *needs* to know. Better to keep that to yourself, for safety's sake. There have been whispers of people like us who have appeared from time to time, and it is treated as though we are demons."

I sighed.

"Great. So, that means that I have to keep a low profile?" I asked. "I'm not exactly the most subtle person."

Fawn touched the side of her nose.

"Exactly," she said. "Better get a backstory whipped up, or people are going to get suspicious. Do you even know where the Lion Duchy is?"

I shrugged.

"East?"

"Lucky guess," she said, rolling her eyes. "Though farther than you may be thinking. Even so, there's a lot of tension between the Kingdom of Arlo and the Duchy, so maybe stick to a spot that's within the nation's borders."

"Wait, is that the name of where we are? I thought it was Re . . . "

I couldn't quite recall the name the billowy bastard had told me when I arrived. Luckily, Fawn was ready with the assist.

"Regaia," she finished. "Yeah, it is. But, Regaia is the name of the *world*. The Kingdom of Arlo is the country in which you currently sit upon your gigantic orc ass. Look."

She sat up fully and snatched a map from the table, holding it up so I could see. It depicted the borders of a country that was kind of oblong in shape. There were a bunch of crisscrossing lines and various dots spread all over its face. Written in a fancy marquee across the top, it read, *The Territories and Counties Under the Realm of the Kingdom of Arlo*. I noticed a red X situated near a terrain rise labeled apparently hastily with the word *Shalewinter*.

"This is the Kingdom," Fawn began, gesturing vaguely at the whole thing. "The most western nation in the charted world."

" . . . of Regaia," I confirmed, still unsure if I could remember all this new information.

Fawn rolled her eyes and pointed to the left side of the map beyond the border.

"This is the Idalous Sea—and before you ask, I don't know why it's called that."

I closed my mouth, prepared to ask that very question.

"To the immediate east is Hathburia—think of it kinda like medieval Russia. It's mostly clans and mountainous wilderness—and fuckin' huge. The Kingdom likes to take land bit by bit from there—now and again—which the locals don't really appreciate. But since they are more of a loose-knit group of tribes, they can't really organize well enough to stop it."

I was not a fan of that piece of information. Seemed awfully conquest-y for my tastes, but I didn't say anything.

"To the north is Umbera. They are the Kingdom's allies—for now. To the south are Triyet and the mighty city-states of Acharan—but most people here just call it 'Atch.' Both are neutral with the Kingdom . . . but Atch likes to fight with them over sections of Hathburia since it shares a border with it. Those are the immediate neighbors."

I nodded. I planned to follow up with a few questions, mostly things like *Why the fuck should I care?* but Fawn was already continuing her history lesson.

"Those are things everyone knows, to varying levels. So, you'll want to learn it as well."

She pointed to a star symbol near the Idalous Sea.

"This is Regis," she said, winking at me. "The capital. Everyone knows that's where the royal family lives and the seat of power. Now . . . "

She tapped a triangle marker all the way on the other side of the map, right on the eastern border.

"That's Palandis, the second-largest city. It's also where the next-biggest chunk of His Majesty's Army is located, since they need to be near the action at the border."

She traced her finger along the line, indicating the shared division.

"There's a bunch of fortifications along here to keep an eye on the wretches over in Hathburia and—of course—to make sure they aren't getting too confident. There's always skirmishes, so unless you really wanna join in a pointless fight . . . steer clear of that section."

"Where are we?" I asked.

Fawn smiled and tapped an unmarked spot closer to the right side of the center of the map.

"Right around here," she said. "In the Aglands—more or less."

I tried to mentally calculate how far away we were from either of the large cities, but without any point of reference for distance, I knew that would be impossible and gave up.

Far, that's what.

"So, where should I say I'm from?" I asked, looking at the dozens of markers indicating what I assumed were towns. "This is kind of confusing."

Fawn gave me a curious, almost hesitant look and then smiled, looking back at the map.

"Maybe somewhere over here," she said, stabbing at a spot to the northeast. "Territory of Kursk. There's tons of small hamlets and no-name villages in this area. People won't bat an eye if you tell them you were raised there. Plus—there's a few orc tribes as well."

I resisted the urge to over-inundate her with the bevy of questions I had boiling over inside my skull and tried a calmer approach.

"Won't—uh, will people think it's weird that I'm an orc and can speak—what did you call it—common tongue?"

Fawn shrugged. Then she dropped the map on the table again, snatching up her apple and taking another bite.

"That's extremely helpful," I said sullenly.

"Hey, man," Fawn said through pieces of rind. "We all have to figure this stuff out for ourselves."

"Well," I started. "Sorry, but I just think it's weird that you are willing to share a bunch of boring-ass political intrigue about this place without telling me what directly applies to me."

"Jeez," Fawn said, shaking her head. "Listen, I'm not an orc. I don't know much about what they can or can't do. If you were to ask me, I'd say it would be *very* rare to hear one speaking plainly, but keep in mind, this is a magical world. Things work differently here."

"Great," I said. "So, now I can make sure to tell people where Polaris is while they are stringing me up by my neck."

"*Palandis*," Fawn corrected. "And a beast your size, they wouldn't even bother trying to hang. You'd break the whole damn scaffold."

I rolled my eyes.

"Fine," I said, but then thought about something that was itching at the back of my mind.

"So, what was with all that talk about your grandma?" I asked. "Don't tell me she was here too."

Fawn let out a loud guffaw and let the husk of the apple fall onto her lap before throwing her arms behind her head to rest against them.

"Absolutely not," she said. "I never met either of my grandmas. One died *way* before I was born, and the other lived in a different part of the world. That was what we call 'playing a part,' my dear orc. You should do the same."

"Invent a grandma?"

"Invent a whole family lineage," she said. "Siblings, parents, cousins—hell, create a childhood bully that used to beat your ass so bad, you couldn't sleep at night. Whatever it is, memorize it, and use it only when you need to."

"Oh, strange," I said. "I was planning to tell everyone I ran into about my past. 'Hey there, I'm Loon, from the Territory of Kursk. Ever heard of it? I have, cuz I'm from there. Wanna hear about my favorite childhood terrorist?'"

Fawn clicked her tongue disapprovingly at me.

"No one likes a smartass, Loon."

"Yet here you are, in defiance to the will of the world," I said.

Fawn rolled her eyes.

"You're a bit touchy, aren't you?"

"So, what," I said, ignoring her jab and looking around the yurt, "you guys are just some of the Kingdom's henchmen? What are you and your loveable band of shitbirds doing hanging out in the hills instead of fighting on the border with other soldiers?"

What I really wanted to ask was how—and why—another . . . sojourner had moved up the ranks when it seemed rather mundane in a world as wide and open as this one.

"Oh, Loon," Fawn said, shaking her head. "We aren't an arm of the Kingdom."

"You're not?"

"Nah," she said with a grin. "We are actively fighting against them."

I didn't know what to say. Well, for a moment, anyway. But then I remembered I didn't give a shit. It was irrelevant to me what the sociopolitical dealings of the realm looked like. I was just glad I wasn't getting knifed by a ratman.

"I see," I said. "Well, give 'em hell, I guess."

"Oh, don't worry," Fawn stated. "We will. In fact, just before you were so unceremoniously thrust into my tent, my buffoonish captains were informing me that another order of our men has just reached the Olteid Pass."

"Where's that?" I asked.

"Not far from here," Fawn said with a smile. "If they decide to march through the rain tonight, they'll be here in a short while."

"Isn't that dangerous?" I asked. "You know, slippery hills in the night and all?"

Fawn chuckled, shaking her head.

"Well, they were waylaid at a prior engagement, and we've got an important . . . function to attend tomorrow—one we'll be leaving at first light for. So, knowing Captain Voder, he'll probably try to make it back to camp so they can get a bit of rest in before everything pops off."

I decided not to ask about the particular motivations behind such an insurrection, since it was one hundred percent not my business. However, there were a few other questions that pertained—more importantly—to me.

"So, what's next?" I asked, looking around the room. It was very large.

"For me, or for you?"

"Well, either. That's assuming those two destinies aren't intertwined," I said. "Or are you planning to kill me, like Chessit said?"

Fawn seemed to consider that.

"Chessit's a bit of a drama queen," she finally said. "Sure, you might have been kept under watch while we figured out your motivations, but even if you hadn't been . . . special, we likely wouldn't have killed you. I mean, you weren't sent here to cause us a bad time, right?"

"Just the ladies," I said with a wink.

Fawn blinked at me.

"You're going to hurt women?"

I tensed up.

"No!" I exclaimed. "I was trying to imply that I'd be breaking their hearts!"

Fawn regarded me with a baffled expression. Then she shook her head.

"You're not the smoothest talker, I am noticing," she said.

I shrugged.

"Whatever, I'm a great talker. It's just at a higher level than most people understand, so there's always confusion. I'm basically a genius."

Fawn cackled.

"Yeah, I'll bet! Genius with a capital J. Listen, lover boy, you should drop some Points into Charisma the next chance you get. Especially with you being an orc, you're going to end up getting gutted the first time you open your mouth in front of someone with some *pull*. Unless, of course . . . "

"What?" I demanded, seeing a strange look on her face.

"Oh, nothing," she said mysteriously. "I just had a thought, is all."

"It looks like you're having a moment of constipation," I returned. "Why do you look like you're trying to figure out a math equation?"

Fawn relaxed her face and smirked at me.

"What was your idea?" I asked when she didn't say anything further.

Fawn gestured vaguely around her tent and flashed me an even larger grin than before.

"How do you like it here?"

"Well," I said. "So far, it hasn't been too bad. You know, getting slapped in chains and dragged through your camp just to listen to you give me a geography lesson. Actually, is killing me still on the table?"

Fawn dropped her legs from the table and leaned forward conspiratorially. I caught a whiff of her lavender scent again. It wasn't half-bad.

"You could join the Redmark," she said quietly.

"What do you mean?" I asked, shocked that she'd even suggest such a thing. "I'm not a soldier!"

"That's true," she continued. "But you're not really *anything* yet. You're only Level Two, and you haven't hit any of your Milestones or subs or any of the other things ahead of you. We could *train* you, Loon. We could help you with your progress and mold you. We've all been through it already, and you'd have access to a bunch of resources. You could learn how to fight, and not just the basics. You could learn to fight *well*. We are very good at it."

"I suppose you could teach me how to be more Charismatic as well?" I mused, though the idea seemed ridiculous.

"Damn straight," she said. "Chessit could teach you."

"Chessit?" I actually laughed at that. "How is he going to do that? Everyone here seems afraid of him."

"Exactly," she said. "Charisma isn't just likability, you know. It affects how people respond to you and how you *want* to be perceived. Chessit can put someone at ease in an instant, but he can also intimidate an entire room full of seasoned soldiers."

I thought about how quickly he had won me over with his manner at the crossroads. It was wildly inconsistent with my usual behavior to respond that way to someone, and now I was very suspicious if that wasn't what was going on here as well.

"So, Charisma is just magic, then?" I said, allowing my disdain to shine through my words a little bit. "Mind control?"

"Not at all, Looney Toon," Fawn said cheerily. "It's a lot more complicated than *that*. But you'll learn all about that if you join up with us. I promise, it'll be a blast. Plus, the pay's not bad, either."

I felt anger building up in my chest at her words. *Looney Toon.* Before I knew it, I'd dropped my voice to a deep hiss. I even surprised myself with how low and dangerous it sounded.

"Don't ever call me that," I said.

Fawn froze, gaping at me suddenly and putting her hands in the air.

"Whoa, *chill*," she said. "I didn't mean anything by it."

We sat in an awkward silence for a moment while I reined in my own temper. Logically, I knew that she had no way of knowing that the name would be off-limits. Hell, *I* didn't even know that was the case until it happened. But something about someone else . . . someone *not* my mother using my childhood nickname felt like a burning betrayal. It belonged to her and only her.

I took a deep breath.

"I'm just . . . tired," I said.

Fawn regarded me carefully, waiting a few moments after I'd finished before speaking.

"Well, you should get some rest, then. I can have a bed ready for you in about twenty minutes if you like. In the meantime, what do you think? I know we just met, but it would be great if you'd consider becoming a Redmark."

I sighed and looked around the room again. There were all sorts of little trophies around the pavilion that I hadn't really paid attention to beforehand—spoils of war, most likely, by the look of them. There were several valuable-looking knives in an open glass case resting on a tabletop, displayed proudly. On a stand near the far side opposite me I saw a breastplate and a helmet that looked far too large to fit on Fawn's frame. They were *warring* people. I wanted to be someone feared and respected, right? That was my original goal when I started down this path.

"So, you train me, give me food and shelter, and I do what? Die in a blaze of glory for your cause? What's in it for you?"

"First of all," Fawn said, smiling wide. "I didn't say *anything* about feeding you."

She saw my expression and rolled her eyes.

"You really need to lighten up, buttercup. Listen, of course I gain something from having you squad up with us. You'd be instructed in combat and strategy, just like the rest of these lot. But the benefit would be that we'd be able to target your training to help us specifically. We'd be able to exercise your precise strengths and build you into one of our best. You're *raw* and unformed, Loon. Like a lump of clay with explosive potential."

Then she slugged my shoulder lightly.

"Plus, you're an orc," she continued. "Do you know how demoralizing it would be to enemy forces if we rolled up with a creature known far and wide for *destruction*? You'd be a goddamn terror."

That was worth considering. I *did* like the idea of appearing at the head of a huge group of warriors and being the one that the opponents were most frightened of. But I thought I was also picking up on something else.

"Are there any other Redmarks like us?" I asked. "From, you know, the *old country*?"

Fawn shook her head.

"If there are, they are hiding it well. I don't think so, though. It's been a while since I've come across anyone else with our particular . . . origin. I have my suspicions about others in the world, but I can't really prove anything."

"So, you'd also gain someone who knows a little bit about what you've been going through," I said quietly. I reasoned that it couldn't be easy to have no one else to talk to about who you really were. Hell, I experienced that every day on a minor scale, and that was miserable.

Fawn's demeanor changed to a more reserved one.

"There *is* that," she said. "Might be nice to reminisce about certain things. You know, like Keith Urban or Kenny Chesney."

My heart dropped.

"What the hell?" I said. "You're a fucking *country* fan?!"

Fawn brightened, almost rising to the challenge.

"Hell yeah, I am!" She said. "What, do you listen to techno or something?"

"*Fuck*, no!" I exclaimed, bristling at the very idea of it. "Metal music all the way!"

Fawn nodded sagely.

"Ah, like Nickelback?"

I felt the anger in my throat.

"If I had a gun right now, I would literally shoot you."

"Easy, easy!" she said, laughing. "I'm just messing with you. You know, I actually like some metal. My dad was a huge Slayer fan."

"He sounds very intelligent," I said. "Too bad you never grew out of your rebellious phase."

I paused.

"*Nickelback?*"

Fawn continued laughing.

"I couldn't help myself," then she straightened up a little. "So, what do you say, pal? Wanna sign on with the crew?"

I shrugged.

"Can I sleep on it?"

She nodded eagerly.

"Absolutely! Like I said, we are moving out in the morning, but you're welcome to hitch a ride with us while you mull it over."

Actually, that didn't sound too awful. After some rest and some food, I think even *my* mood might improve. Plus, it would actually be pretty beneficial to know what the hell I was doing in this place. I looked at Fawn and gave her a curt nod.

"All right, yeah. Maybe I'll do that."

I didn't even realize I'd been tense during our entire conversation, but now I relaxed. Then I felt the tug of my restraints and shook my head, looking back to Fawn. She was scratching an area under her arm, and I could see that there was no armor there, just cloth. That was probably pretty smart, both for mobility and itching's sake.

"I'm assuming I'm not your enemy now, right?" I asked, lifting up my bound wrists. "Could you get these shackles off me? I think I'm having an allergic reaction to whatever discount ditch-rope you guys are using."

Fawn chuckled.

"What a whiner," she said, and reached down to her belt, removing a ring of keys and lofting it through the air and into my lap. "It's the dirty, circular one."

"Wow, thanks," I said, scowling.

I began fiddling with the ring—a tedious task because of my binds—but paused, considering that I'd overlooked an important detail. I looked back to the map.

"Do you know where Tallrock is?"

Fawn grabbed a fresh apple from the table and bit down, keeping it in her mouth to free her hands up. Simultaneously, she grabbed the large parchment again, displaying it with one hand, and searched for a moment before pointing with the other. Her finger rested on a marker slightly to the west of where she'd indicated we were at.

"Ri' heh," she said, then dropped the map again and removed the apple from her mouth. "Why do you ask?"

"I've got a Quest I need to finish there," I said. "Though I'm still new to this whole thing. Just gotta get there and find . . . what was it, Jasper?"

"Yosper," Fawn corrected once more. "If you're talking about Tallrock, anyway. That's where the Mages' Order is. It's maybe a couple days' ride from our current location and is still technically in the Aglands."

"Aglands," I muttered. "That's where the false goblins were supposed to be at, too."

"Yeah, those little bastards are a pain in the ass to deal with," she said. "How you managed to kill any by yourself is a wonder."

"Well," I said, smirking mischievously. "Let's just say someone else did the bulk of the work for me."

"Seems I'm not the only friend you've made here."

"Well, they were less of friends and more of . . . conveniently incompetent, rat-faced dipshits."

Fawn raised an eyebrow at me, looking concerned.

"Greloks?"

"Yeah, I think so," I said, returning to fumble with the keyring. I found the right key and busied myself with my legs first. After a moment, I felt a sweet release as the rudimentary lock fastening it all together fell to the ground. I kicked off my fetters.

"I don't suppose there were four of them?" Fawn asked quietly, adjusting in her seat. "The Greloks, that is."

"Yep."

As I tried to work the key into the lock around my wrists, I dropped the whole set on the ground.

"Ah, shit," I said, and stooped to pick them up.

I saw Fawn stand out of the corner of my eye and move away from the table. I could hardly reach the ring where it fell, but luckily, I was able to brush it toward me with my fingertips and began trying to find the correct opener again.

"You said you just achieved Level Two," Fawn said, her voice sounding a bit distant.

"That's right," I said, studiously trying to slip the key in the lock, but, truth be told, I was having a miserable time with it. "Happened right after I killed them. That was lucky, too. They almost got me."

"Did you pick up anything special afterward? Like cool gear or a resource?"

"Nah," I said. "Just a bunch of shit that got burned up or melted when they exploded."

Fawn seemed surprised.

"Exploded?"

"Yeah, you know . . . kaboom. Eruption. Inferno. Other generic synonyms for a fiery death."

"That is curious," Fawn said quietly. "But nothing else? No artifacts or glowing orbs?"

"Oh, like the Nodes?" I asked.

"You got Nodes?" Fawn asked, and I felt her shadow fall over me as I sat fiddling with my constraints on the ground. "How many?"

"Four, I think," I said, finally looking up. "Emerald ones . . ."

I trailed off. Fawn was standing over me, an odd look on her face. Something like . . . desire. Most importantly and confusingly, was that a sword was in her hand? It was a startling, brilliant weapon with a golden hilt and a perfect, silvery sheen along the blade. Though I'll admit my appreciation was somewhat blunted by the predicament I had found myself in.

I really should have seen this coming.

"What—"

"I'm sorry, Loon," Fawn said, biting her lip and raising the sword high. "Try to forgive me for this next part."

Then she swung.

CHAPTER TEN

THE PERKS OF BEING NEW

I brought my wrists up just in time. Fawn's sword swooped down in an arc and collided against my binds with a clang. The chain's thickness had stopped her from killing me outright, but I didn't have time to consider my fortune because I was still—stupidly—on the ground. So, twisting my wrists slightly, I jumped up to stand, bringing my arms up as I did.

What the fuck, what the fuck!

I was planning to scream that out loud, but this didn't seem like the most... opportune time. The look on Fawn's face was distant now, like she was operating outside of her own typical realm of control. She was almost... feral now.

I pushed forward against the blade, my superior height forcing the sword up, and, with my motion, sent it backward, causing Fawn to lose balance. The warrior backpedaled, attempting to catch herself, but I could see it would only buy me perhaps a second. There was no way I was stronger than her, so I figured this was just a lucky break. I had to move. But I couldn't help but wonder why this had happened to me. What had caused Fawn to make such a dramatic shift in her motivations? Had she been messing with me the whole time, or was there something else I wasn't catching?

She'd changed almost immediately after I'd mentioned the Greloks. *File that one under one of her nuh-uh buttons!*

I turned quickly, knocking the table over in my haste and sending everything on the top sprawling. Food, papers, and bottles flew everywhere, and I noticed a few of the vessels had a similar look to the ones I'd seen in Gray Muzzle's pack.

Health potions?

That would be grand, considering I was still practically at a sliver of health and could use all the help I could get. There were three within distance, so I reached down to scoop the bottles up as I moved. Immediately, their contents were known to me as a banner appeared.

- Potion of Minor Purification
  - Rarity: Uncommon
  - Item Type: Buff
  - Durability: 1/1
  - Weight: .75 lbs
  - Bonus: +50% poison resistance for 30 minutes.

A tincture containing Wolfsparrow Root's essence allowing an individual to resist most common or low-level poisons, natural or supernatural. Bon appétit!

- Potion of Minor Speed
  - Rarity: Uncommon
  - Item Type: Buff
  - Durability: 1/1
  - Weight: .75 lbs
  - Bonus: +10% speed increase for 1 minute.

A small bottle filled with the liquid essence of various enchanted herbs. Increases speed by ten percent for one minute. My, look at you go!

- Potion of Excess Speed
  - Rarity: Uncommon
  - Item Type: Buff
  - Durability: 1/1
  - Weight: .75 lbs
  - Bonus: +50% speed increase for 20 seconds. 100% Stamina Restore for 20 seconds.

A small bottle filled with the liquid essence of various enchanted herbs. Increases speed by fifty-percent for twenty seconds and Stamina to full for the same increment of time. Time to fly!

Fuck!

I didn't have time to think. I just *did*. Stuffing one bottle into my waistband, I smashed the stems of each of the remaining two bottles together, breaking them, and stuck both upside down into my open mouth. I emptied them as I ran, swallowing the contents before realizing that there were shards of glass traveling down my esophagus mixed in with the liquid.

A banner sprang up in my vision but immediately minimized and became a blinking notification just at the edge of my sight. It had to be because of the immediate danger, but I couldn't bother, as I was moderately positive I was about to fucking die. Though I couldn't help but wonder why the banner had not been dismissed when I'd read the nature of the bottles.

Screw it. Go!

I beelined for the tent flap and planned on making a break for it when I saw my pack sitting just to the side.

"Oh, hell," I said and shifted my weight a little, aiming for the bag. I thought maybe I could zigzag toward it and then out the exit if I planned it right. However, things rarely go the way I want them to, and this proved to be no exception.

I noticed that I was a little bit faster and knew the potion must have taken effect already. This was good because if there was any chance of my escaping, I'd need to be as fast as possible.

I reached the bag and snatched it up, turning to the opening of the tent as a shape flashed toward me. Fawn, moving fast as shit, caught up to me and brought her blade down. I reacted as quickly as I could, only managing to move my head out of the way as I stumbled backward. Her cold eyes were focused only on me as her blade sliced through several of the arms of the coat rack positioned next to us. I crashed into the legs of it and heard the wood snap as I did, sending the thing careening forward just as Fawn repositioned and swung again.

The commander was still only focusing on me, so she didn't see the sharpened stakes she'd just made out of the hacked-off ends of the coat rack's hooks. However, she definitely *felt* them as her downward strike's motion drove the sharp points into her neck and unprotected armpit. Blood sprayed everywhere as streams erupted from the wounds, most of it landing on me.

Fawn's eyes went wide. Then she released a glass-shattering scream and fell backward, taking the rack with her. She landed with a loud thud and began writhing on the ground in front of me, anguished cries being the song she chose to sing as she tried pulling the makeshift weapon out of her body.

I clambered to my feet, watching as a pool of blood formed beneath the wailing soldier before me. I mean, I know she had just tried to kill me, but it was an awful sight that would absolutely haunt my dreams if I was ever able to sleep again. I noticed a shifting shape fall from my lap and onto the ground.

The rain-spattered cloak.

It must have become dislodged in the fray and landed on me, and I hadn't noticed. I mean, why would I? I'd been trying not to be the opposite of alive.

That was when a banner sprang up.

???
- Rarity: ???
- Item Type: ???
- Durability: ???
- Weight: ???

???

Huh. Well, isn't that something?

I grabbed the cloak and my bag, not sparing another glance to the woman on the ground still frantically attempting to extract the spikes from her flesh. Then I pushed my way through the exit.

I was immediately blasted by hard pelts of rain. Apparently, while I was busy playing the world's deadliest game of tag with my new best friend, a heavy storm had broken. Soldiers were running every which way, trying to find shelter or make their way to finish up whatever they'd been in the middle of when the sky's wrath began. My Darkvision activated immediately, and I noticed it had to be because the rain had put out most of the torches filling the camp.

Finally: a little fortune. Now to make like a poke in the ass and goose it.

I tried to sweep my newly found cape over my shoulders, but my hands were still bound.

Oh, yeah. Shit.

I had to settle for hurriedly flipping it over my head, accidentally clobbering myself in the forehead with a chain in the process. I yelped. Just a little—but very masculinely. I tried to clasp the pin around my neck but couldn't position my hands well enough to fully connect it. I gave up and just pressed the unfastened ends to my neck and decided to take advantage of the chaos.

I began trudging through the rain-slick camp as well as I could—which, if I'm honest, was a lot easier than I thought with the boost from the speed potion. Still, though, it wasn't exactly easy, considering I was trying to head back the way I came, which meant going uphill.

I stomped through the mud taking the main road at first but ducking behind crates and tents as well as I could considering the soaking-wet circumstances. Soldiers raced past me, sliding, tripping, and falling, but no one paid me any mind. I noticed the blinking message at the corner of my vision again and decided to risk a quick look.

Congratulations! You have gained your first Perk!

For obtaining your first Perk, you receive a bonus to the effects of the newly acquired Perk.

Gained the Adventurous Tastes [Potions] Perk!

Adventurous Tastes [Potions]
Because of your worldly nature, you have sampled at least three different varieties of Regaia-forged potions within your first twelve hours of arrival. Quite the gourmand you are!
- Gain +1 to *Constitution* (+2 with First Perk bonus)
- Potion consumption now yields 5% more effectiveness (+8% with First Perk bonus)

This world just keeps throwing things at me. Now it's Perks—what next, a sandwich meter?

At that moment, my stomach growled.

Very funny, I thought to myself. I was getting hungry, but my rations were deep in the recesses of my pack, and I didn't exactly have time to fish them out for a quick bite. I considered that a sandwich would actually be really helpful right now, as I could eat it on the go. Then I passed a table near a cookfire with a field-dressed rabbit laying abandoned without its skin, and that thought immediately dissipated. This place was strange, but surely it wasn't going to use my own thoughts against me? Better not to think about that . . . just in case.

I knew now that I was moving slightly quicker than normal—even trying to be inconspicuous—the Speed potion a helpful little friend in my hour of need. I had to consider how much faster I'd be if I decided to use the *other* potion. But it was wedged firmly between my belt and my hip bone, far beyond reach with my current handcuffs. It would just have to wait until I was *really* in the shit and I didn't mind ripping my pants off to get to it.

But, if I need to use it, hanging brain will be the least of my worries.

I slipped along, trying not to let anyone get wind that I was the same big, lumbering orc that had recently entered the camp in chains.

I'm just a different big, lumbering orc trying to quietly escape *the camp in chains.*

I could see the edge of the encampment and the path I'd been marched down, and gave myself a little internal praise. I was almost there! I'd also encountered no hiccups, so perhaps my luck was beginning to turn around.

But, of course, that was a stupid, stupid thought.

At that moment, I heard a terrible sound behind me—one of a distinctly familiar variety.

"He's escaped!"

It was the strained bark of Commander Fawn, and it sounded like she'd at least partially recovered. I chanced a look over my shoulder, back the way I'd just come from, and saw that the large pavilion's flap was open, and light was pouring out into the camp. Commander Fawn's dastardly form was framed in the opening, and a group of soldiers was rushing to her aid.

"Damn," I whispered to myself. "I should've just brained her when I had the chance."

That was all the fuel I needed to get this last leg of my exodus to go a bit quicker. I abandoned all pretense of guile and instead began hoofing it hard toward the path I'd initially entered from. Some soldiers were ahead, facing the direction their leader's voice had come from and—by proxy—me. One of them took note of me and immediately shouted, alerting the others to my presence.

"Well, shit around some sticks," I hissed—not really thinking about what I was saying—and bolted to the left, where the tents were a bit more densely placed. It turned out to be a wrong move because as I zigged and zagged through the bevy of backwoods boudoirs, soldiers began emerging from them, sticking their heads out of the openings and seeing precisely who it was that was the cause of all the chaos.

I saw movement and naked steel—and a few naked *bodies*—as I ducked behind one tent and tried to skirt through the assembly without getting riddled with holes. I heard heavy, wet boot falls behind me and looked to see two soldiers had decided they might try their luck at running me down. Both had swords in hand and were moving as fast as they could without sliding to cut me off in my escape. At that moment, another soldier—late to the party—stepped out from his tent, looking the opposite direction I was coming from.

You unlucky son of a bitch.

I slid to the side of him and then heaved my shoulder as hard as I could into his body, sending the miserably unaware idiot backward and right into the path of the pursuing soldiers.

"Wha—" he started to say. But whatever he had been trying to intimate was silenced—likely forever—as he collided with his buddies, a sword point traveling right through his neck. The three soldiers collapsed to the mud in a cluster of arms, legs, and blood.

I didn't have time to gloat about my impressive stroke of luck—I had to get the hell out of there. More shapes converged on me, and I shot off again, leaping over a crate and into the road. My breathing was extraordinarily painful, and my heart was pounding.

Nothing but blast beats.

Even despite the wildly inappropriate time to do so, I thought about the drums in Meshuggah's "The Demon's Name Is Surveillance." The maniacal, percussive explosions so expected of many metal songs were absolutely *choice* in that track, but at that moment, I felt like the rhythm of my palpitations would have put their drummer to shame.

Eat my *heart out, Tomas Haake.*

I sucked in a breath of agony—this was far more exercise than I'd ever done in my life. Even with my new body, I thought about how much harder this world would be if I continued to skip cardio.

I promise, I thought, *if I make it out of this alive, I will do a jumping jack.*

I was able to avoid several more frantic search parties that went by, each time ducking behind whatever random cover I could find. Fortunately, a camp that had to be on the move frequently had a surplus of hidey-holes, and eventually, I found myself at the far edge of the settlement.

This is it!

I put a little extra pep in my step and tried to draw the cloak closer around me with my lashed-together hands. It was—unsurprisingly—challenging to do. But I managed to sort of tuck the fabric under one arm and hold the collar down enough to shield me from about half of the wind and rain that was assaulting me. I was still pissed with the clasp not fully . . . well, *clasping*. It was its one job, and if it had been an employee, it would have been fired faster than I had those two days I worked at Zippy's.

There was movement behind me, and without looking, I started at a run toward the now-visible tree line. I heard a couple of shouts and a godawful *snap* and *twang*. Then an arrow sprouted from the ground right next to my foot.

"They're *shooting* at me!" I exclaimed to myself and leaped to the side, trying to decide if the serpentine pattern worked as well on archers as it apparently did on the potential school shooters we were warned about in our drills back home.

Another arrow *thunk*ed into the ground in the space I'd just been in.

"Ha!" I exclaimed. "It *does* work!"

I looked over my shoulder at the dwindling torchlight of the camp and saw there were several soldiers arranged to wing-clip my graceful departure. Some were chasing—some standing and aiming.

"Suck my zigzaggy balls, dickheads!"

BLAM.

My skull felt like it had just been sent into space inside of a concrete mixer. I realized, in a stupor, that I was lying on my back in the mud, staring up at dripping branches. Apparently, in my haste to insult people who almost definitely couldn't hear me, I'd collided headfirst with a tree.

"Ugh . . . " I groaned, trying to cradle my head but accidentally bonking myself further with the chains. That didn't feel good. I doubled over in the wet earth and heaved. However, my stomach was empty, so all I felt leaving my body was bile and a *lot* of saliva. In the back of my dizzy mind, I knew I had to get up and do . . . something. Several loud *thwack*s and two wet *slink*s, and I saw more arrows had arrived to say hello. None of them had hit me—fortunately—but my urgency had dissipated somewhat as I struggled to regain hold over my memory of the last several seconds.

"I was supposed to . . . " I said aloud. " . . . do. Supposed to do . . . things."

It was hard to figure out, considering the splitting headache and a new feeling—an uncomfortable strangling sensation.

Someone's choking me!

I reached up with my paired hands and attempted to wrestle away the grasp of whatever mystery assassin had snuck up on me when my fingers touched cold metal.

"Wha . . . " I started, thinking there was another chain around my throat, but then I realized it was part of my clothing. Or rather, the cloak that I was wearing.

The clasp.

It had finally buttoned itself together—probably from my extremely graceful encounter with the tree trunk. My mind started to clear a little, and now I noticed a message had appeared in front of me.

You have donned the Trespasser's Veil!

Trespasser's Veil
- **Rarity: Elusive**
- **Item Type: Arcane Cloak**
- **Durability: ???**
- **Defense: N/A**
- **Bonus:** *+20% evasion when hidden*

A unique cowl of indeterminate origin that shimmers when doffed. The Trespasser's Veil envelops the wearer in Arcane darkness, making them much harder to see.
- *Gain the Sneaking Skill*
- *+10% to Sneaking Skill*

Congratulations! You have gained a new Skill!
Sneaking (F-Rank Level 1)

You can now move around intended targets with less likelihood of being discovered—the perfect Skill for a life of crime or a very unseemly spouse. This is a Dexterity-based Skill and will become more powerful as you grow in that Attribute. The outcome for efficiency is the Sneaking Skill + Dexterity quotient. Stalk to your heart's content.

A cloak that makes you more sneaky? I considered this. It was prevalent in video games and really shouldn't have been that surprising, but the effects of this were very strange to my pummel-addled brain. I'd learned the Throwing Weapons Skill by actually throwing a weapon, but that was the standard, sensible way of doing it. Obtaining the capability of a Skill I hadn't even tried yet through the medium of accessories didn't really make sense.

There were two more arrow *thunk*s and the sound of heavy boots racing near me, so I decided it was best to weigh the merits of fashion-gained Skills another time. But I couldn't help but think about the outcome of using a Skill without test-driving it first. Would I even know how to do it properly?

Time to find out.

I lifted myself from the mud and into a crouch just as the soldiers who'd been chasing after me came fully into view. I shot off into the trees, keeping myself low and trying to be considerate of how much noise my gigantic body probably made as I staggered through the mud and ducked under branches.

I could hear the soldiers' confused oaths as they debated amongst themselves whether or not I'd actually just been there and if they should pursue me into the woods. Apparently, that was a foolish suggestion, because soon, I could hear them slurching into the dense wood behind me.

I was cold, wet, exhausted, being chased by assholes who wanted to bring me back to their bizarrely mercurial leader, and my skull felt like it had just been treated to a bowling-ball polisher, but . . . no one was shooting at me now.

Little blessings.

I stumbled through the thickets of downed, slippery branches and logs, pushed past low branches with scratchy bits, and tried desperately to lose the infuriating tail of half-wits that were so doggedly hounding me. Through it all I just kept willing myself to keep moving, putting one foot in front of the other as I attempted to put enough distance between myself and the goons as possible.

I still couldn't figure out the change in Fawn. Everything had been largely all right, and unless she had some bizarre master plan, it didn't make any sense why she would extend an offer to join her right before trying to chop me into orc steaks. What the hell was going on? In all honesty, I felt foolish. I had started to trust someone, even just a little, and look what happened. It bit me on the ass. Well, I wouldn't be making that mistake again.

After what seemed like an eternity, I found that the Redmark footsteps and loud complaints had faded, moving off to the left behind me, and I was able to take in a large breath. It seemed as though they were much more blind out there than I was. Guess it was just going to be me on my own out there. But I figured it was better to be alone in confusion than surrounded by hostile company—at least, if I could fully shake my pursuers. I wasn't safe yet, by any stretch.

I kept moving. I didn't dare stop right now because I knew if I did, I might fall asleep. It would be bad news if one of those Redmark douchebags happened upon me taking a snooze—and even worse—I was pretty sure I was rocking a very handsome concussion. I wasn't sure, but I thought I remembered that if you fell asleep after a head injury, you could slip into a coma or die outright. Perhaps it was the exhaustion, but the irony of that made me giggle a little. But it was like a deep, manly giggle. It definitely didn't sound like a gleeful newborn chipmunk. Not at all.

Eventually, though I felt ready to collapse at the mere whisper of a soft spot to land, I emerged from the tree line and found—to my surprise—that the rain had let up while I'd been Red Riding Hood-ing it through the universe's shittiest footrace. It hadn't entirely stopped but had calmed to a drizzle, which I preferred to the apocalyptic maelstrom it'd been a short while before.

I was standing at the cusp of a stretch of wet grass that sloped upward a little to an edge, a rosy glow emanating from somewhere beyond its zenith. The sky seemed huge there, and I realized that it was because there were no trees or hills I could see obstructing its view. It was still a sort of muted gray-black from the terrible weather, but hey, I'd take it. I sloshed forward across the grass, and when I finally reached the top of the slope, my stomach felt like it had instantly been filled with a hot bowl of gravity.

It was not just a warm illumination on the other side. Much like before, I found that the light I'd been so easily hoodwinked into following belonged—in fact—to torch flame. I was at the edge of a cliff face, and far below were dozens—possibly a hundred—tiny little fires, moving along in a group. From the glow, I could just make out the various shades of red the soldiers holding them were wearing and cursed.

Redmarks.

It had to be the returning group Fawn had mentioned. Just my luck. I'd narrowly escaped one set of bullies just to have my path cut off by their meaner older brothers.

Out of the frying pan and into the toilet.

I heard a *snap* behind me and whipped around, expecting to get a face full of arrowheads from the group of soldiers who'd very clearly found me appreciating the landscape. However, only one form stood just at the edge of the trees, and they didn't appear to be carrying any projectiles. Not that I could see anyway. They were big. Not as tall as me but muscular, and switching into Darkvision—I'd finally seemed to get the hang of it—I could see he was bald, with a large burn on one side of his face.

It was the blacksmith from the Redmark camp that seemed buddy-buddy with Chessit.

Great, I thought. *So, no group of lackeys, just a boss fight. No big deal.*

He didn't say anything; he just stared at me.

"Take—er—*paint* a picture," I called to him. "It'll last longer."

I'll admit, my witty taunts weren't as sharp as they probably would be had I not lost my headbutt competition with the tree.

The man seemed to find this comment interesting, because he took a few steps forward.

"Listen, old-timey circus strongman," I said, taking a step to the side. "I'm not too tired to whoop an old man's ass on top of a mountain."

He still wasn't saying anything. He just kept moving slowly toward me, which was very unsettling.

"Seriously, man," I continued, glancing over my shoulder at the edge of the cliff face. "I'm an orc. We go crazy. I'll do some vile shit to you if you don't back away now. I've killed bigger men than you."

"I doubt that," the man said, continuing his stroll. His voice was oddly . . . soft. Like a teacher or a social worker. Not what I expected from someone who looked like they bench-pressed vending machines for light calisthenics.

"Yeah, well . . . " I started. "You know what they say about doubters . . . "

He cocked his head to the side.

"No," he said. "I don't. What do they say about doubters?"

"They, uh . . . eat . . . babies?"

The man shook his head, and when he spoke, his tone sounded amused.

"Well, I've never heard that before. I don't eat babies. I've heard orcs do, though."

Burn-Face didn't stop his approach, and now he was only about twenty feet away from me. I reached for my pack but realized I'd have no luck trying to dig through it to get to anything remotely close to a weapon. I sighed and saw a path to my right that led back into the woods.

"Yeah," I said to him, catching up with the train of conversation. "I *do* eat babies. I've eaten loads. I told you, I'm straight-up insane. If you try and take me back to the camp, you'll regret—"

"I'm not going to take you back to the camp."

I paused.

"You're not? Yeah, right, dipswitch. Like I believe that."

"Now who is the doubter?" Burn-Face asked.

"Me," I said, taking a deep breath and preparing to tear ass out of there toward the trees. "We've been over this. I eat babies, remember?"

The man didn't say anything, but just as I was planning a solid *look over there* and dash scenario, he pounced. Faster than I could track, he bolted right at me, and I threw my chained hands up to defend myself. He snatched my wrists and jerked me to the side, forcing me to stare right into his eyes. They were very dark but had a glint of deep red to them and looked like smoldering black coals.

"Praise be to the *Drifter*," he said.

"What are—"

I felt myself lurch backward as he shoved me. Hard.

I tried to shout, but the shock of my fall froze my bellow in my lungs. I watched the edge of the cliff zoom past me as I went over into freefall, rocketing toward the ground below.

CHAPTER ELEVEN

THE MASK OF THE MIST

"Ah, there you are."

I opened my eyes. Sort of. Where had that voice come from?

I rubbed my grainy sockets and peered around. It was strange, like the feeling of opening your eyes underwater. It was vaguely illuminated, and I could see streams of . . . mist or something, but it wasn't hot enough to be steam. Maybe some kind of room-temperature sauna? That seemed like a goofy idea, but I was perplexed by my sudden change of environment. It was almost claustrophobic, and I had a momentary pang of anxiety imagining getting stuck in whatever this was for too long. I took a few deep breaths and calmed myself as best I could.

Chill, dipshit. It's just another one of these wildly shifting areas you've grown to know and love. What the fuck, though? Where the hell am I?

The only thing I was certain of at the moment was that I was standing. Though whatever the floor or ground was made from was unclear, as it was submerged in about two inches of water everywhere.

I sloshed my foot around and watched the ripples travel a short distance in the gray, murky pool. The water, despite being shallow, was a bit heavier than usual. It took more effort to slog through it—not much—but it was noticeable. Besides the mist and the babbling brook of gravy, or whatever, that was about all I could see. It didn't make sense. It was stupid.

But then I remembered being pushed off the ledge. It was the second time in a few hours that I'd plummeted to my assumed death.

"Ah, shit," I said.

"Such a bold choice of language," the voice said. It wasn't menacing—in fact, it had a sort of calming lilt that most people probably would have found pleasant. But not me—I was a born contrarian. The voice annoyed me.

"Where am I?" I demanded, looking for the voice's source and coming up blank. I couldn't see dick in this mess.

"You're here," the voice cooed, and that almost made me blow my top right there. I absolutely hated people who beat around the bush as though the answers I needed were some sort of puzzle. Nuh-uh. Not today—er—tonight.

"Okay, shithead," I exclaimed, feeling my anger boil over. "Stop screwing around. I've been beaten to absolute hell today, and I'm really not in the mood—"

"Such harshness," the voice said, though it still had the dreamy quality to it, apparently undisturbed by my outburst.

"Seriously," I said. "Not chill, dude. Where am I, who are you, and what is the point of this? Is this some new level of this godforsaken saggy tit of a world?"

There was a soft chuckle, and suddenly, a shape appeared in the mist. A large shadow moved through the curtain of obfuscation, emerging from somewhere beyond my sight's capability. One thing immediately apparent was its size: it was massive. Like, brick-shitting big—as big as a house. Maybe larger. At first, I thought it was a huge medieval shield, based on its shape, but then I saw there were three holes in it. It took a moment before it dawned on me: them weren't no normal holes.

Two large eyes and a mouth—or, rather, the recessed crevices where they should be—lorded above me.

I leaped backward and put my arms up for defense right as the looming specter halted, leaving me feeling a bit silly. I gulped down the lump in my throat and stared up at a massive, black mask.

"What in the lily-livered fuck are you?!" I shouted.

Another soft chuckle echoed from the gigantic . . . creature? Face monster? The voice was not at all the sort of hellish apocalypse style I would expect to come from such a beast. It wasn't even loud. It was conversational volume and sounded like it was coming from right next to me.

That creeped me out. I kept trying to peep over my shoulder, half-expecting the face to be the world's most gigantic ventriloquist dummy. Still, I could not find a physical source for the voice. So, I decided to take the . . . face at its value and crane my neck up to look at it.

"I am pleased to know I have made such a good first impression," the gigantic thing said, the mouth remaining open and unmoving. The actual detail itself was straightforward, without adornment. Just a run-of-the-mill-variety, simple-as-hell, theatrical-looking mask. However, what it lacked in personality, it made up for in pure, pants-shitting terror.

"*Good* may be a bit of a stretch," I stated, too cautious about making any movements lest the thing decided I'd fit perfectly into its dinner plans.

"Pardon me," it said politely. "I am prone to bouts of flowery speech and hyperbole, so perhaps it would be more accurate to say that I made the impression I aspired for."

"Got it," I said. "You *chose* to show up all spooky-starship-style."

"Though I do not understand that reference, I will agree that it was a touch of artistic grandeur on my part. Forgive me."

I scoffed.

"I'm not sure I should forgive anything yet. You could decide to switch gears at any point and strike, Big Head. My head and your mouth might accidentally get acquainted if I start throwing you a bone."

The mask chuckled again.

"Ah, I so love the illustrative foulness of the young and obnoxious."

"Sister, you ain't seen nothing yet," I said, puffing my chest out. "I'm *King Stupid*."

"Clearly," the voice mused.

I pointed up at the thing and scowled.

"Hey, so . . . answer my question. You already know I'm annoying, so save yourself the trouble of me practicing super loud monkey noises. I'll do it. I have no shame whatsoever."

The mask didn't move at all, and I had to wonder if perhaps it was thinking.

"I see," it finally said after a moment. "Do you mind if I work backward in your inquiries? You have rattled a fair few in my direction, so it may take me but a moment to accurately—"

"Jesus!" I interrupted. "Yes, that's fine! Just do your thing so I don't have to hear you stuff more hundred-dollar words I don't understand into your already-insufferable sentences."

"You are a curious one," the mask said. "You have a low Intelligence value, yet you wield a masterful command of metaphorical syntax—especially where insults are intended."

"Hey, Big Face," I said, hoping to move things along. "Wanna hear my impression of a car alarm?"

I didn't care about his point as long as he got to it.

"Marvelous," the mask said. "Such an interesting temperament. Impatient, rash, loud, and concealing fear and confusion behind bravado. Not the usual category of mind I interact with."

"Yeah? You getting a lot of personal visits here in Moist City?"

"I entertain the occasional guest," the mask said, sounding intrigued by my question. "Though I will admit it has been some time since I conversed with a newcomer. However, that is beside the point. You had other questions, and I will answer them."

"Finally!" I exclaimed, slumping a little.

"You asked—in a much more colorful way—what it is I am."

"Yeah," I said. "What carnival ride did you fall off of, for one?"

Then, realizing that I would likely be prolonging my bizarre back-and-forth with this creature, I promptly shut it down.

"Eh, never mind," I said. "I'll shut up. You make with the deets."

"Very well," the mask said, still hovering in the mist, all intimidating-like. "What I am is a *god*."

By the way the sleepy-voiced creature announced it, I guess I was supposed to be impressed. But, while strange, it wasn't the weirdest conversation I'd had today. It was hard to be shocked by a statement like that when I'd literally seen rat people explode. So, I just stayed quiet.

"I suppose if that is the only reaction I will get, I shall continue. The name I use here is Zeol."

I snorted. The pronunciation of the name sounded oddly like a type of vocal in a lot of heavy music.

"Is something amusing?" The mask asked.

"Nah, bro, you're good. It's just stuffy in here."

"Is there something about my name that you find off-putting or humorous?"

I cracked a grin.

"Zyuuuuuul," I thundered, trying to do my best elongated death-metal growl. I was actually moderately pleased with how it sounded. Back in the old world, my screaming attempts had sounded more like shrieks, but here, with the much deeper orcish register . . . it was pretty *deece*.

The mask paused but then continued just as though I hadn't interrupted.

"You are likely wondering why I have brought you into my plane."

"Not really," I said. "Probably some bullshit, though. Are you going to try to kill me too?"

"No," the voice said. "Should I kill you? You *are* very irritating. I might be doing someone somewhere a tremendous favor."

"Yeah," I said. "Namely me. Hurry up with the information; I've got a date with the bottom of a mountain."

"I see. Well, if you're not going to treat this like a true interaction, I suppose . . . "

There was a popping sound, and suddenly, I was back where I'd been, plummeting through the air toward a line of red-armored soldiers. A notification appeared in my vision but quickly minimized—likely due to the forthcoming splat I was about to participate in. But I did catch a glimpse of one thing:

You have been granted an Aegis!
Zeol's Falling Star

"Ah, fucking hell," I said, but my words were snared by the wind and carried away. I had the idea that I should curl into a ball, and my body acted on it. It didn't make much sense, but perhaps it was my primitive, near-death lizard brain trying to figure out a way of shielding myself—or hiding from the imminent splattering. I closed my eyes tight. Just as I did so, however, it happened.

I blasted into the soldier at the front of the line.

CHAPTER TWELVE

MAGNIFICENT CHAOS

I struck like an asteroid. The moment I hit the surprisingly soft exterior of the lead man-at-arms . . . he exploded. I felt slick, warm liquid splat over me as I connected and rolled in the mud. He'd popped like a zit—or, rather, he'd popped like a garbage sack filled with blood and cottage cheese. The smell was revolting.

I didn't really know how physics worked, especially in this world. Still, I was reasonably sure that it should have been a lot harder to water-balloon the man than it was. It was gross.

I expected to die right afterward. But I didn't, for some reason. Instead, while keeping my eyes closed, I continued to roll at breakneck speed, barreling into something hard. I heard a loud snap and the exceedingly awful scream of what must have been a Redmark soldier as his legs were broken. Big yikes. But I kept going, unable to stop, the entire time trying to make myself as hard to perceive as possible.

Try to get out of this alive, you big, fat fuckstick.

I needed to remain calm, but I was tumbling at such a high velocity that there was no way I was going to survive. Still, with eyes closed, I continued. I couldn't help it—the mud and rain increased my movement as I spun on through the throng of soldiers. It seemed to last forever, with men and women calling out angrily, searching for me, I think. I must have been buzzing through at quite the clip, since it seemed they hadn't had the privilege of observing my dramatic reenactment of the Cretaceous period as I flew ass-first into their marching party.

I started to slow and opened my eyes a little—immediately wishing that I had not. I smashed myself facedown in the muck as dozens of soldiers crested a rise in the hill and surrounded me.

I lay still.

Nothing to see here, folks. You know, just your average, orc-shaped bottle rocket.

My entire face was pressed deep into the wet earth, and I could feel my heartbeat pounding hard in my chest as my body demanded oxygen. My ears were exposed, so I tried quieting my own desperate need for air and listening to the boots stamping in the sludge around me. They continued stepping past as if they didn't even notice me, all of them talking excitedly about something—or someone—called Esther. I didn't care. As long as they kept moving along, not paying me any mind, they were free to discuss whatever they wanted.

It seemed to be working.

Huzzah! Whiff my orc sharts, dumbshits!

However, a dragging foot caught on my pack, and I turned my head to the side to watch a soldier tumble over me and land in the mud. Her eyes flashed back to mine. She'd spotted me. I was in the precise middle of a dogpile of jarheads, and I'd been discovered. I put a finger up to my lips and shook my head in a vain attempt to shush her, but of course, that was fucking stupid. The soldier—unsurprisingly—didn't follow my direction. She opened her mouth, staring right at me and . . .

. . . then there was a boom.

There were shouts and screams all around. Every head snapped up toward the bluffs and hills in the direction I'd just Power Ranger Zeo'd from as the rainy night sky ignited. Off above the cliffs' rise were huge plumes of smoke and the voluminous curl of a fireball. It was *fucking monstrous*. Something had gone wrong, somewhere, and if I'd had to guess, I would have said it had originated from the Redmark camp.

Guess they won't be following me now.

The soldier had tried yelling something akin to *orc*. But, since the big explodening had overshadowed her performance, she was left huffing in the mud, staring daggers at me while trying to stand up. Since everyone else was noticeably distracted, I decided to help myself out. I slammed a fist into the back of the soldier's knee just as she was starting to regain her balance and watched her dive back to the mud. She tried to lift herself, but I grabbed her leg and yanked it out, so she fell flat. Then I jumped up and ran, sending her deeper into the mud as I stomped on her back.

As far as attacks go, it was pretty mild, but I figured she'd be too busy trying to survive mudpocalypse to tell people a large, sorta-out-of-shape green-gray goon was running through their ranks. As I dusted off into the mix, I noticed that the formerly pristine lines of soldiers had been broken, and all of the Redmarks were in various stages of confusion and excitement with the sudden chaos that had erupted around them.

I drew my cloak closer and was grateful for my luck in not attracting their attention. I spent the next few minutes skirting the outside of the large force, ducking behind bushes and rolling in the mud more than I would have ever wanted to in my previous life. Well, I guess, less than I wanted to in *this* life as well, but I didn't think it was super important to split hairs like that. I kept my cloak wrapped around me as I slinked around, feeling very special agent-y as I slipped through the throng of passersby, all wholly focused on the calamity that was keeping them too distracted to spot me. The group back there was thinning out, and I couldn't believe my good fortune. I'd essentially avoided all of them. Eh, well, save for the one I'd treated to my wrecking-ball maneuver. And the guy whose legs I'd broken. And the woman I'd forced into being my land bridge. You know what? A *large* percentage of the brutes still weren't aware of my presence. Now there was a light at the end of the tunnel, and I could breathe a little easier.

I sidestepped a few more stationary folks wrapped up in the event—including a man silently crying and staring at the flames in the distance—and was just able to make it past the bulk of the gawking men and women when I came over the rise of another hill and froze.

At least fifty more soldiers were assembled below the swell, and they looked angry.

Goddamn bitch-sucking fuckballs!

They were armed more heavily than the forward unit, and all of these GI Schmoes seemed as though they had been dyed in the bloody wool of combat many times over. You can really tell when someone is a cold and hardened battle-murderer, and each one of these Redmarks looked like they would shiv first and ask questions never.

They were moving up the hill in careful, disciplined double file, their eyes scanning the surrounding area, with only a few of them seeming to be distracted by the explosion. I had nowhere to hide, so I just didn't move, hoping the mud and the boost from my Trespasser's Veil would rescue me.

One Redmark near the front called out a command in a leathery crack.

"Don't be staring doe-eyed at that fire," he hissed. "As sure as Larem's mother is a harbor whore, that's a distraction! Keep your eyes on the woods and hills, boys. I imagine we will have company before too long."

"Me ma's not a harbor whore," a young man missing part of his nose said. "She were a ship's hand. Me da were the whore."

There was some laughter, but then their leader cleared his throat.

"Keep 'em peeled, y' fucking reprobates. I don't need any of you getting your guts stabbed out just because Larem finally had a joke that landed. And stay quiet. Enough of them mudheels in the vanguard are hooting and hollering to cover up the sound of an ambush. We don't need you lot adding to it."

The group grew silent, their faces snapping into a display of communal no-nonsense and scanning even *harder* than they were before. Apparently, keeping a lookout for infiltrators, though, didn't involve looking directly ahead.

Which was, you know, where I was at.

No one had seemed to notice me huddled against my cloak and squatting behind the single bit of vegetation in the area: a very shabby bush. Was the cloak doing this, or were these guys just this fucking inept? I'd decided to compromise with myself and landed on *they were terrible and I was great*.

I took a gander downhill at their approach, and that set my teeth on edge. It was very steep. Which made it all the more impressive that the soldiers had as little difficulty ascending the incline as they did.

More mountain goats than men, I thought, watching the group tiptoe along in the slick. The man with the leathery voice had an air of harshness, and I noticed his outfit was a little more rustic than the others. It was something of a hodgepodge gathered from different armor sets and lashed together with a few belts. It gave the man a mismatched, angular appearance, as one side stuck out a bit more than the other. He was gray-haired with plenty of age lines on his face and had the look of someone who'd lived long in a world full of battle. As he moved forward in the wan torchlight, I could see now that his ears had a point to them.

Does that make him an elf?

It was very Legolas-like, from what I recalled, but that didn't necessarily mean anything. I'd learned ass-all about this world, so for all I knew, he could have just been French.

I decided to save my musings for a time when I wasn't a beetle's dick away from being skewered upon a hundred blades and tried to take a slow, silent breath. I kept quiet while they continued up the slope. The noise of the faraway camp had reached a fever pitch, and most of the soldiers in the other group were no longer even bothering with any pretense of respectability. There was clearly some confusion moving through the ranks, and I reasoned it was chiefly because the Redmark camp was where they'd just been headed and now it was a smoking hole of carnage and dead idiots. Hopefully.

I took another long, deep breath and eyed a particularly "friendly-looking" man to my left. I almost gasped. The man seemed as though he'd just barely won a fight against a meat grinder. His armor was banged up and wrenched open in various directions as if by some massive, wonky can opener. Dried blood covered the man's face, chest, and exposed forearms. There was other miscellaneous sludge caked to his figure that hinted to a more nefarious origin. While

I didn't know what the goop was, I could definitely smell it—which gave me a good enough idea. It was *rancid*. It smelled like a zombified butthole that had been boiled in a bucket of pus and left out in the sun for fifty years. At least, that was the closest thing I could imagine to whatever foul demon shit he'd stopped to roll around in.

The smell was overpowering, and though I was still—as of yet—unknown to my new friends, I suddenly heaved as I felt a deep and dangerous *lurch* in the pit of my stomach.

Oh, no.

The stench hit me again, and I felt my mouth water—and not in a good way. If there is a good way? Yes, definitely—anyway! Yeah, bad news.

I doubled over, and for the second time in less than an hour, I vomited. I tried so hard not to, but that's the thing about puking, isn't it? You can be the most ornery, tough, or willful person in the steakhouse of life, but even David Goggins would get hobbled by a ham sandwich just a bit beyond its expiration date.

I couldn't even be quiet about it. It was a Saturday-night-college-town-behind-the-dumpster *power-vom*.

I would have been embarrassed had I not been so frightened of the consequences. After a solid five seconds of once again hurling up just liquid—since there was no food in my stomach—I looked up, wiping my mouth.

The dozens of soldiers were all staring at me.

Goddamn ass hell fuck.

Some looked frightened, some looked shocked, but none of them looked happy. They were frozen in place, and I'll admit, it was probably not the most beautiful first impression I could have made. Sorry for not being *perfect*.

A man near the front shouted, which seemed to snap a large portion of them out of their trance.

"Enemy!"

Then, like a chain reaction, everything got *wild*.

The Redmarks, no longer surprised by the appearance of the belly-sick behemoth standing before them, unsheathed their weapons and tightened the two-column formation. Several stepped aside from the leading group and drew back the bowstrings of their ranged weapons.

"Shi—"

There was a bright flash of light behind me that turned the dark and rainy world into midafternoon. This was followed a half-second later by a terrific and ear-splitting boom.

. . . which launched me forward.

Fortunately, my Darkvision seemed to automatically mitigate the worst of the sudden switch from night to day as I vaulted forward and landed hard on the repulsive motherfucker that had made me retch. The rest of the Redmarks, however, were not so lucky. They had all been looking right at me, and the flash and roar forced them to throw their arms up defensively, covering their eyes. There were screams, but they were drowned out by the eruption-like sound paired with the bright light. In the back of my mind, I considered that they had all probably been at least momentarily blinded, which was just fine with me.

Eat firelight, sluts!

Me and Stinky landed hard in the mud and slid. Fast.

Once again, I was rocketing right toward my combatants and there weren't nothin' they could do about it. The hill was an unforgiving son of a bitch, steep as shit and full of rocks. We blasted down the slant at top speed, propelled by the force of the blast. I tried to aim the wailing soldier toward an empty spot as the openly armed men and women of the Redmark contingent began moving around. I could see that far beyond them, the bottom of the hill led to another line of thick forestation and—potentially—my shield of freedom. But it was a long, deadly way down through the soldiers and their receiving line from the bottom of hell's diaper. Plus, I was currently utilizing a Redmark to break my fall.

So, I did what any self-respecting person would do in that situation: I closed my eyes and rode this dumbass down the slope like a toboggan.

I roared as my human boogie board and I blasted right between the two flinching queues of Redmark soldiers. At least, I had to assume that's what happened, because there was no way in daffodil *fuck* I was going to open my eyes and ruin my own night. Ignorance was bliss. I could feel Stinky struggling to extricate himself from the gruesome-twosome best-friend-forever tangle we'd become wrapped in—but I think I was much too heavy for him to do more than groan as he slid on his back in the mud.

Then I heard another sound like rushing water or a heavy blizzard wind whipping through the trees.

Uh-oh.

"Heat! Big heat!"

Those were the words my primitive, dented caveman brain was able to conjure up in my moment of panic. But that wasn't it. My mind bubbled with recent information, however difficult it was for the six remaining brain cells I had. Well, semi-recent.

I recalled reactions known as "flashovers" when buildings had exploded or had otherwise managed to light themselves on fire, and the flames would spread. Don't be too impressed—I'd learned about them as part of the scolding I'd been subjected to when Uncle Luke and Aunt Ella brought in one of their firefighter friends to talk to me about how badly my "stunt with the trash cans" could have gone. The presence of a "professional" was infuriating, and despite how nice he'd seemed—if not a little dim-witted—I'd been entirely in control of the situation I had created in those bathrooms . . . until I wasn't. But I'd never let some pudgy, mustachioed know-it-all like *Fireman Thoms* have the satisfaction of knowing that. I'd made sure to excuse myself to the bathroom and use my cell phone to call in a fire, forcing him to have to leave before I'd even flushed the toilet.

Checkmate, Handlebar.

That made me miss my phone. Not for any reason other than that I had over a hundred and fifty gigs of prostate-thumping *jams* on it. I knew the device was somewhere beneath the flaming wreckage of the train, and that made me sad. This experience would have been greatly improved if I'd have been able to blast some He Is Legend while stumbling all over this butt-turd of a world. Which reminded me . . .

Extreme fucking heat.

I knew it had to be *really bad*, considering that Stinky started frantically thrashing around beneath my bulk, and I heard his voice for the first time.

"Get off me!"

Stinky had the same sort of rough tone as the others, but he had the curious trait of sounding *scared as fuck* by the prospect of whatever was billowing up behind us. I finally risked opening my eyes and saw the look of horror on his face. For the first time, oddly, I was able to see him more clearly and realized he was, in fact, *not* a human. He was . . . something, but not human. He had yellowish skin that was crisscrossed with what looked like scars but resembled deep, natural fissures in the skin. His angry blue pupils were slit horizontally, and that wasn't even the weirdest part. He had what looked like an extra, tiny mouth on each side of his jaw. They were closed, but it really gave me the jeebies.

I wasn't sure why I cared so much, honestly. I wasn't a human anymore, so looking for familiarity should have been the last thing on my mind. If anything, I should have been hoping to run into more orcs.

Or perhaps not. From what Fawn had indicated, they were likely not to be my number one pals. Maybe I'd just have to stumble upon some and find out for myself? It could all be human propaganda.

I looked behind me and finally saw the source of the intense warmth. A huge . . . well, not cloud, but something like it, chasing us down the hill. It was essentially a humongous swath of blank space that distorted the air around it, like baking asphalt on a hot day. During my light peeping, I noticed that the horde of Redmarks we'd just blazed by had been thrown askew, and the area was literally crawling with soldiers. Some were screaming, some were on fire, all of them looked too far up shit creek without even a canoe as they tried desperately to cling to life.

Uh-oh times two.

It was impossible to tell exactly how badly they'd been decimated. Still, I did not want to have a personal demonstration, so I looked back ahead of me and pressed down on Stinky's shoulders, hoping I could add some speed to our rapid descent. That's when I realized something: my hands weren't bound anymore. *When the hell had that happened?* The shackles were still around my wrists, but the chain connecting them looked as though it had been sliced cleanly in two. *I think if I try to figure this out right now, I'll end up immediately turning into orc jerky. There will be time after the Ugly Bastard Bobsled ride comes to a stop.*

I pushed farther forward to adjust our descent. It seemed to work. We picked up our speed a little, and I heard the man below me grunt in a lack of appreciation for my instinctual and accidental saving of his life.

Of course, that was when Stinky decided it would be keen to stab me.

I felt a sharp pain in my side and looked down at my ribs. A pewter-colored knife handle was sticking out at a crooked angle with Stinky's gloved fist wrapped tight around it. I grimaced and glared at my unwilling vehicle.

Poison Damage mitigated!

Condition: Fatigued
Fatigue I
- *Abilities and Skills suffer -5% efficiency while under the Fatigue I condition effect.*

"Ah! What the fuck, man?!"

Stinky bared his teeth. They were sharp.

"Fuck you, ya great nasty orc! Get off me!"

"Hey, man!" I shouted into his face. "I'm trying to save our lives here, and you're trying to fucking *poison* me? There's a— GRAGH!"

He'd stabbed me again.

"Oh, fuck the hell out of *this*."

I switched my grip from Stinky's shoulders, placed one hand on his neck, and reared back with my now uninhibited right fist. Then I delivered a crushing blow to his face.

Though I had connected with his stupid head, I didn't account for our speed. Instead of knocking him unconscious, my motion sent me too far forward.

I flipped.

I bashed my shoulder in the mud and somersaulted twice, taking Stinky with me. We tumbled in a tangle, smashing into one another as we spiraled down the hill.

It was pretty romantic.

The slope turned steeper, and rather than slide, we both fell from the sheer drop about twenty feet onto hard ground. I was just able to see the massive colorless column of heat blow by above us, sending a shockwave into the tops of the trees that obliterated some of the branches. I watched as leaves caught fire, but the rain calmed the worst of it.

I lay on my back, hardly able to move. The ground there seemed like solid rock, and I wanted to inspect it, but I could not find the strength to lift myself. So, I just resigned myself to remaining exposed like an overturned turtle.

My immediate surroundings were quiet, but I could still hear the clamor from above—and beyond—where the most insane series of events I'd ever taken part in had just transpired. There were still the distant screams, and I was sure I heard another explosion, but I was comforted in the fact that, despite my inability to make a single movement, I was better off here than there.

I saw blinking notifications in my vision, so I decided that there was no time like the present to go over what I may have missed.

Boy, oh boy, was I right. There were numerous descriptions of my misdeeds, but before I could even delve into their depths, one, in particular, stood out. It was the notification that had minimized as I fell. It appeared right at the top, so it was easy to spot, but I had a feeling that the blood-red color of its font would have caused me to single it out anyway.

You have been granted an Aegis!
Zeol's Falling Star
You can refuse the effects that gravity might place upon you and instead mitigate some of the harm that might otherwise befall you. Chasms and caldera are nothing in the wake of this Aegis. Once per day, you can nullify 100% of the impact of force from falls at a depth or height of up to 100 meters. You may also transfer this Force Damage to an appropriate object within five seconds of impact—like slow-moving pedestrians or people taking too long at the ATM.

- *+2% Force Damage resistance*
- *100% Force Damage resistance once per day*
- *10% Force Damage transference once per day*

The fuck?

That sneaky little asshole had put some sort of charm on me! What a creep. Whatever "Aegis" was, I didn't want it.

That's how I was able to hit the ground without immediately turning into a new kind of pudding. Huh. Good to know.

I didn't have the full spectrum of understanding to decide how to approach gifts from men that I had only met once. I felt like I had a vague sense of what it must have been like to be some of the girls in my high school.

For instance, I'd seen Abbie rebuff numerous dudes after they'd bought her some token of their affection or another, not realizing how supremely unwholesome it was to do so unsolicitedly.

I'd always felt as though I was somehow better than them, with their desperate attempts at wearing their hearts on their sleeves. It was cringey, and I was glad to be the sullen and cranky kid sitting in the back of the class, simmering with rage beneath my Poppin' Fresh exterior.

Yeah, at least I hadn't been a loser like those idiots . . . right?

Thinking about that filled me with a sense of shame. It was compounded by the fact that Abbie was almost definitely smashed into a red-haired stain under the Hennepin Avenue overpass. I tried to conjure up her face, but my efforts were wasted, considering the last time I'd seen her, she'd been screaming and clinging on to a seat for dear life as our train car upended.

To distract myself, I focused again on the notifications. It was like a timeline of the ridiculous events I'd been engaging in for the last half-hour, but with a play-by-play that I found to be interesting, if not exhaustive.

You have killed a Level 5 Human Cook!
Gained 120 Experience!

You have killed a Level 13 Human Batallionaire!
Gained 1,150 Experience!

Congratulations! You have reached LEVEL THREE!
You grow stronger and receive the benefit of [3] additional Attribute Points. 10% Health and Arcana restored. Combat conditions healed.

For defeating an opponent more than TEN levels above your own, you have received a Sapphire Esper Node!
Accept [1] Esper Nodes?
Yes / No

I, of course, accepted. If these things were valuable enough for Fawn to attempt to kill me over—which is what I was now starting to believe—then I should be happy to get as many in my inventory as possible. Even if I had no clue what benefit they gave me. That was still a mystery to me. Fawn had completely morphed into vengeful woodchipper when she knew what I was packing. Why, though? What was so important about these little flickering fuck-off lights? I was sure I'd figure it out. Probably.

I reread the sequence of two kills, then scowled. I felt bad now that I could see I'd killed a cook. That must have been the poor idiot I'd tossed into his friends back at the camp. And the Batallionaire . . . whatever that was must have been the chap who'd been blood-rocketed into fairy dust. I was also starting to notice a very uncomfortable pattern to my arsenal of kills, and I wasn't sure how I felt about it. Sure, they were dead—but why didn't I feel weird about that? In the old life, I'd actually been pretty squeamish over the idea of killing someone. Fighting was one thing, but actual death? Wigged me out.

I mean, I apologized to my aunt's cat for a week after I accidentally stepped on its tail once—so what had changed? Maybe there was still some part of me that didn't fully register this as a new world? Or maybe Regaia had a way of changing the way you thought about death? It made sense, in a way: if they could modify every aspect of your physical body and force brand-new knowledge into your gray matter, they could almost definitely tinker with your feelings about killing.

There I was, getting philosophical again. At least I think that was what it would be referred to. I shook it out of my head and refocused on the messages. At this rate, I'd never get through the whole thing if I kept going off on tangents.

Congratulations! You have raised an Ability!
Natural Resilience [F-Rank Level 2]
- *+5% Resistance to Insects*
- *+1% Resistance to Weather Conditions [Heat]*

Congratulations! You have gained a new Ability!
Uncommon Consumption [F-Rank Level 1]
Barbarians are not bound by the usual appetites of many races to survive. Now you can glean necessary vitamins from uncommon animals, insects, plants, and miscellaneous. Try it out and see what tastes you can derive from the world around you.
- *+8% Hunger reduction from unconventional food sources*

Congratulations! You have raised a Skill!
Unarmed Fighting [F-Rank Level 3]

I could see the damage administered by myself during my asteroid cosplay, but I glossed over that. However, the next notification was split into two separate sections—likely from both instances it had occurred—and actually made me pause as I read it. I imagine had there been a onesie-twosie situation, whatever system was in place for this sort of thing would have rattled off each and every movement. But this one was different.

There was math.

Utilized Sneaking Skill success versus:
[x13] Level 1 beings
[x4] Level 2 beings
[x8] Level 3 beings
[x11] Level 4 beings
[x3] Level 5 beings
[x6] Level 10 beings
[x1] Level 11 beings
[x9] Level 15 beings
- *+10% Skill Experience gain [Speed Difficulty Bonus]*

The second set was even more impressive, and I was left thinking about how insane and unlikely it had been.

Utilized Sneaking Skill success versus:
[x3] Level 15 beings
[x47] Level 20 beings
[x3] Level 21 beings
[x1] Level 23 beings
[x1] Level 24 beings
[x2] Level 25 beings
[x1] Level 50 beings
- *+10% Skill Experience gain [Speed Difficulty Bonus]*
- *+15% Skill Experience gain [Mounted Difficulty Bonus]*
- *+20% Skill Experience gain [Trained Opposition Difficulty Bonus]*

However, my eyes fell over my next notification and I froze.

While the number of foes I'd managed to circumvent was notable and, if I was being *humble*, extremely cool—it wasn't the thing that had stopped me in my tracks. No, what had caused my heart rate to increase and my breath to feel as though it wouldn't stay in my lungs was the subsequent message that filled the screen, flashing with golden light as if I'd hit the jackpot on a slot machine.

You have raised a Skill!
Sneaking

I looked closer at the message, trying to mentally tabulate the likelihood of this chain of events, but just satisfied myself with reading the message again.

[B-Rank Level 4]

CHAPTER THIRTEEN

FIRE

It was absurd.

"B-Rank, Level Four," I said aloud, trying to establish exactly how pants-shittingly concerned I should be. If it were accurate, and I had leaped forward by . . . five ranks, then I had somehow unearthed a tasty morsel of a loophole. I wasn't sure I liked it. If my pal—the orb—had been telling the truth, B-Rank was something I couldn't have hoped to achieve in ten years, let alone ten *hours*. Could it really have been as simple as that to gain more capability in a Skill?

I was staring at the proof of it, so I supposed it could very well have been such a breeze.

I guess sometimes, you just gotta go with your gut and hurl yourself butthole-first into danger.

I opened the notification for my Level Up, and it brought with it something I hadn't thought about since arriving in this new land: my character sheet. There were some definite changes, especially with some of my Abilities; chiefly, I noticed that I'd gained a boost to my Primal Rage. Some of the other Abilities situated in the orbit of my Class had risen with the Level Up as well, though not enough to send me hootin' and hollerin' into the night.

There was also the pesky little notifier that I was suffering from the Fatigue I effect, which reduced my capability in a number of Skills and Abilities. That would certainly bite me in the dick. I hated that this seemed like something I would need to pay attention to from now on. Especially considering my penchant for insomnia.

When it rains, it hurricanes.

I spent a few extra moments looking at my stats, grumbling over not seeing the extreme gains I felt were owed to me. However, after seeing all the numbers swimming in front of me, I promised myself to not make a habit of checking it too often unless there was some major change or Level increase. Otherwise, that would be exhausting and pointless.

Loon
Race: Orc
Class: Barbarian
Level: 3
Profession: Unassigned

Health: 38/195
Arcana: 85/85
Max Stamina: 123 *(-5% due to Fatigue I)*
Experience: 2,805
Reputation: N/A
Attributes
*-5% efficiency due to Fatigue I
Remaining Points to Allocate: 6
Strength: 9
Constitution: 21
Dexterity: 9
Wisdom: 10
Intelligence: 8
Charisma: 6
Luck: 5+
Skills
* -5% efficiency due to Fatigue I
- Camp (F-Rank Level 1)
- Hunting (F-Rank Level 1)
- Insight (F-Rank Level 5)
- Intimidate (F-Rank Level 1)
- Knowledge [Nature] (F-Rank Level 1)
- Perception (F-Rank Level 4)
- Simple Weapon Proficiency (F-Rank Level 1)
- Simple Armor Proficiency (F-Rank Level 1)
- Sneaking (B-Rank Level 4)
- Survival (F-Rank Level 1)
- Throwing Weapons (F-Rank Level 1)
- Unarmed Fighting (F-Rank Level 3)

Active Abilities
- Analysis I

- Armorless Defense (F-Rank Level 2)
- Battle Born I
- Darkvision I
- Primal Rage (F-Rank Level 2)
- Nature's Resilience (F-Rank Level 1)
- Sabotage (F-Rank Level 3)
- Uncommon Consumption (F-Rank Level 1)

Passive Abilities
- Feared Form
- Outsider
- Unfaltering
- Wildling

Perks
- **Adventurous Tastes** *(First Perk Bonus)*

Aegis
- Zeol's Falling Star

Esper Nodes
- Emerald: 4
- Sapphire: 1

Huh. That was odd. My Luck, which had formerly been at negative two, was now at a positive five. It also had a little plus symbol next to it. Did I get luckier? Well, that would be wonderful and explain how I survived the certifiably insane sequence of events that had just transpired. I'd literally been knocked off my feet by an explosion and surfed down a hill on a dickheaded *bad guy*. I was living my nine-year-old self's cartoon dreams.

There was a flashing notification down near the bottom of the menu, telling me that I still needed to allocate my Points. *That* seemed like an absolute headache. I was planning to just toss them all into Constitution but then paused, weighing my options.

I had six to spare, and most of my Attributes were still below the average threshold of ten. Two in particular—Strength and Dexterity—were at nine, so only one point away from making me break even. I selected them, adding one point to each, and then plugged the remaining four into Constitution with a grin. I'd considered putting something into Charisma, but ultimately decided that could be done later. It seemed like Constitution was going to be more important in keeping me alive for the next little bit, and I didn't think even a small boost to Charisma would be enough to sweet-talk my way out of danger. Another message appeared.

Are you satisfied with your selection?
Yes / No

I selected *Yes*.

Pain suddenly erupted in my body. I shouted as overwhelming agony washed over me, leaving me unable to do anything but scream. It felt like my body and brain were suddenly under ice and on fire. A *twisting* fire. It burrowed into my bones and blood vessels with a stabbing burn. My arms wrenched around, and I saw the muscles and veins writhing beneath my flesh. My skull suddenly felt as though someone had jammed an icepick right in the center.

What is happening? Is this a stroke?!

I cried out again and grasped the grass next to me, tearing blades of green from their stem in my frantic need to hold on to something, and when that wasn't enough, I dug my fingers into the cold ground, scratching through pebbles and dirt. I couldn't get a full breath because it felt like my lungs had bands of fire around them, and my screams faded from lack of air. I felt like I was going to die.

Is this magic? Am I being burned alive right now? Fuck! This is so painful!

Then it stopped.

As if it had never happened, the pain released, and I couldn't even recall the memory of the agony. I remembered its effects but not the actual pain. Which was odd, because I had never felt anything that horrible in all my life. But now it was hard to imagine—had it really been that bad?

I looked down at my body, stunned, but realized a change had happened. My limbs looked *stronger*. They weren't as doughy and atrophied as they'd been; I was certain of it. A little bit of solidity was visible now, as though I'd been dehydrated and had finally gotten myself a glass of sports drink. My mind felt clearer now, as if I had a much higher resonance of control over my movement, and I flexed my fingers in front of my face. They didn't feel as stodgy and uncoordinated as before.

That's a plus. But what happened?

"Ah," barked a voice. "Passed a Milestone, didja?"

Still lying on my back, I was forced to crane my neck to the side to see the source of my interruption of personal appreciation.

Stinky.

He was standing now, wiping dust from himself, which I found hilarious, considering he was still completely covered in a gross array of blood, piss, and shit. But my mirth faded as I realized how dangerous of a situation this was. I was hardly able to move, and he was upright with a gleaming dagger unhooked from his belt and dangling from his fingertips.

"Oh, hey, buddy," I said. "Good to see you got your sea legs back."

Stinky grimaced and it was a disgusting look, but I realized quite suddenly that he wasn't in pain. He was attempting a fiendish smile.

Uh-oh.

Men like that only smiled for a couple of reasons, and I doubted it was because I resembled a nice rack of barbecued short ribs.

"Buddy?" he asked, stepping forward. "I don't recall us being fuckin' pals, now. I seem to actually recall being trussed and ridden down a gods-damned hill, squished underneath a fat fuckin' orc. Doesn't sound nice at all, if you ask me."

I smiled sheepishly.

"That's just how we make friends in orc culture," I said, trying unsuccessfully to get up.

"Is that so?" Stinky asked, lifting the dagger and gripping it tightly in a meaty palm. "Can't say I'm a fan of that custom."

"Well, now you're being xenophobic," I said. "What's a Milestone?"

Stinky chuckled.

"You ain't very keen on the rules, eh? Well, I won't be the one to fuckin' mentor you."

I didn't have quick access to any weapons, but even if I had, the only thing I would be able to defend myself with was the rusty knife—and how would that help in this situation? It wasn't as though I could even get up at the moment. It felt like I was fused to the ground, and no amount of shuffling back and forth would unstick me.

Then I saw the source of my issue. The bar in the bottom of my vision that indicated my Stamina. It was empty.

Fantastic. I'm going to fucking die on my back like my great-uncle Albert. But without the prostitute on top of me.

I sighed, patting myself for anything I may have forgotten.

Oh.

I *had* forgotten something. Tucked in my pants, right next to my orc junk, was the Potion of Excess Speed. If I recalled correctly, it would also restore Stamina. Exactly what I needed.

Hello, there, you beautifully bitchin' bottle.

I rested my hand on the spot and tried to relax my stomach so I could slip my fingers in. That was when Stinky chose to attack.

He brought his blade up and charged, his face a mask of maniacal glee. I tried to tug the bottle out from where it was cinched beneath my belt, but it was not willing to cooperate with my larger-than-I-was-used-to fingers. Stinky closed the gap and was now ten feet away. I was out of moves.

"Fuck this," I said, and slammed my fist down as hard as I could into the bottle. It shattered, piercing my leg and groin, and I shrieked at the pain.

But it had worked. The potion took effect and I watched as my Stamina bar began to refill rapidly. I rolled to the side just as Stinky crashed down with his blade.

That was too close for comfort! I'm going to need to buy a lottery ticket!

I was able to spring to my feet and began running back down the hill, but my tackle and leg were screaming at me, and I knew I had a bit of a limp. It didn't matter; I'd just have to make do. I stomped through the thin tree coverage, seeing now that smoke filled the area.

Oh, hell, the trees are still on fire!

I'd forgotten about that, too! Damn, maybe I shouldn't buy a lottery ticket and invest in life insurance instead. I was too dumb to stay alive for much longer. Noxious fumes began choking me, and the dark clouds of smoke filled my vision and burned my eyes.

Better to run the risk of failure against Stinky than a one hundred percent certainty of choking and burning to death in the trees like a clueless asshole.

I turned around.

"Ooof!"

Stinky had practically *flown* through the air, dragon-kicking me in the chest. I crashed backward in the dirt, and everything disappeared around me as the world became a black cloud of heat. I crawled backward, my sternum sore from the force of Stinky's booted blow, climbing farther into the flaming trees. I tried holding my breath, but when I sucked in air, an assload of smoke came with it and I began coughing.

What was worse was that the sound must've alerted Stinky to my direction, because he came barreling toward me—suddenly appearing out of the smoke and slicing at me. I could barely make him out, but his eyes were red-rimmed with tears streaming down his cheeks. He must have been as susceptible to this as I was, and I wondered curiously why he didn't just leave me to die in the wildfire.

I felt him kick me, and I rolled to the side as another boot crashed against the ground where I'd just been.

"You can't hide, orc!" he yelled from beyond the smoke. "I'll keep searching for you! I've got drakeling armor on—keeps me from burning! I'm going to make sure I fill you with holes before you fuckin' fry!"

Of course he has something like that. All I had were my shitty Florida retiree costume and my . . .

I smiled.

I had the Trespasser's Veil. I was also *quite* a bit sneakier and faster than before—the latter for a few more seconds at least. It was time to test out what I could do, but I'd have to act before the timer buzzed on the potion.

I wrapped myself in the edges of the cloak like an orc burrito and tucked myself in a ball. I might asphyxiate, but at least it would save me from whatever he was planning to do.

I couldn't breathe anymore, and my lungs were on fire. Tears were flowing freely from my eyes and I had a stinging wound in my crotch. All told, I was pretty sure I was half a second from death. Then I saw movement pass by me. It was hard to tell, because I was essentially blind, and apparently this didn't count enough for Darkvision to activate, but it appeared my brave fetal position had worked. Stinky moved right past me.

Then I got an idea. A stupid, *stupid*, zero-IQ eureka moment.

I stood up, straining to see Stinky's back in the smoke and reached into my bag, feeling for the *other* cloak, the one I'd received upon arrival. I yanked it out and stepped forward, then, while still moving, removed the rusty Paring Dagger. I pushed through the smoke quietly, slinking as well as I could despite the pain and lack of air before seeing the sway of Stinky's form. His back was to me. He didn't notice me. I moved quickly and carefully, hardly making a sound.

This is it.

I tossed the bedraggled cloak over him. He immediately made a swipe at me from beneath it, but I was ready for that. Using the last bit I had left from the potion, I stepped back, letting the dagger slice the air, and then I launched forward, knife out. I stabbed right into the cloak and felt the blade stick into something soft. Then I threw my shoulder forward and tackled him to the ground. The force caused me to take an unconscious breath, and I sucked in a lungful of smoke. Then we crashed to the ground.

But only for a moment.

The earth suddenly gave out beneath our weight with a loud *crunch*, and the two of us fell into a long drop of darkness.

CHAPTER FOURTEEN

ARE YOU AFRAID OF THE DARK?

Fortunately for me, Stinky broke my fall. Less fortunately: we were on an incline.

I landed right on top of the brute as he struck the hard ground in the dark. He let out a sharp, wheezing *oof* as he connected and my weight slammed on top of him. It was still jarring and knocked the wind out of me—but I was largely unharmed. Especially considering that the level of jostling had uncorked the cloud of smoke I'd inhaled, allowing me to finally breathe. I sucked in a lungful of tasty, delicious air and heaved a little.

No, no, no. Don't puke again!

I didn't, but it was dicey for a split second. However, we were on the descent of whatever plateau we'd crash-landed in the dark onto, as I mentioned.

That meant that just as my Darkvision turned on, I began to roll. The two of us tumbled again, only this time, I could very clearly see everything that was happening in muted detail. It looked as though we were in some sort of mineshaft. The walls were roughly hewn rock and dirt. Still, it was hard to get a precise gander because I was super busy screaming and spinning end over end like a terrified Slinky.

The butt-faced spit-dribbler I called Stinky was also crying out and somersaulting. I had to believe it was even scarier for him because, as far as I could tell, he didn't have the same ability to see in the dark that I did.

The two of us made quite the pair as we plummeted farther down, the incline becoming a steep drop once more, and we suddenly free-fell into the dim. This time, when I landed, I'd approached a slope to the ground, and I was sent cartwheeling wildly onto the stone floor. I crashed nipples up, flat on my back while still shouting.

Stinky landed right behind me but on his stomach. He was screaming too. We both just lay there for a moment, yelling for our lives in the chill dark of this nameless tunnel, our cries reverberating in the void. Then I finally got control of myself and stopped hollering. Stinky kept going for another handful of seconds—until I slapped him. I am sure it would have been considered a fuckhead move to pop his gob like that had he not been trying to kill me a moment before—especially since I could see and he couldn't. The mangy bastard didn't have any idea it was coming, so he just got the full unabridged blast with no preamble. It shut him up, though.

For a blessed second, anyway.

"Where are you, ya little whoreson!?" Stinky demanded, swiping at the air with a dagger from his position on his chest. "Face me like an orc!"

Man, we'd just fallen a *long* way and he was *still* trying to kick my ass. It was impressive that he'd been able to hold on to his weapon during our very dignified barrel-rolling. I had to hand it to him: he was tenacious . . . if a bit stupid. And coming from me, that's saying a lot.

I let him wiggle in place for a moment, keeping a safe distance and trying not to laugh to alert him to my exact location. Then I noticed something sprouting from behind the fool. My jaw dropped. Stinky still had my paring knife sticking out of him. It had been driven through the thin slats between the plates of his hide armor and into the meat of his right shoulder blade where it had pinned the cloak I'd thrown over him to his flesh. The fabric was bunched around the hilt like a skirt, leaving the rest of the accessory trailing behind him like a squirrel's tail.

I quickly stood and then very quietly snuck forward and wrapped my fingers around the handle and yanked the knife out of him.

"I'll take that!" I said as Stinky erupted into a furious yowl of pain and fear. I left the cloak.

"I'll fuckin' kill you, orc!" Stinky shouted uselessly, trying to stand, but I shoved him back down with my foot and tossed the cloak over his head again. His muffled oaths were full of rage, but I didn't care. I could have easily ended his life right there in the dark, but the thought of it seemed . . . unwholesome. The idea held a wrongness that I just couldn't move beyond. Like stepping on a robin's egg you'd found in a sewer.

In my mind, there was nothing badass about murdering a blubbering loser in a pitch-black mine shaft when he was blind and curled up in a fetal position. So, I would let him live.

I'm a merciful god.

I was going to take his coin purse, though.

I quickly sliced the strings, and as he struggled to stand, I gave him one more swift kick to the back of the knee. He went down wobbling, his arms windmilling as he hit the floor another time. Then I scampered off silently down the impossibly dark tunnel as Stinky cried for me to come back and fight.

The tunnel was crooked, the unevenly carved passage hooking to the right not far up ahead and then sloping downward slightly to the left. Beyond that was unknown to me because my Darkvision wasn't developed enough to reach that distance. It was really, truly dark down there to the point that even my gray-gradient spectrum was fuzzy and thus it was a little difficult to make out finer detail.

However, as I continued on, I spotted a wall sconce with an unlit torch in it.

Aha! So, this place isn't a natural formation. Just as I suspected!

I hadn't actually suspected that, but pretending I did seems cooler, right?

I'd only made it about fifty yards down the path from Stinky, so it was easy to hear the echoes of his bellow bouncing along the tunnel after me. As I reached for the torch, those sounds began to break and turned into sobs.

Christ in a banana hammock, that's depressing.

It was unsettling to hear a creature of Stinky's menacing stature suddenly devolve into tears, wailing like a lost kitten.

"Don't leave me down here!" he called through gasps of breath. "I can't fuckin' see nothing! I don't want to die alone in the dark. *Please!*"

I held the torch. It was cold and chalky, a tattered wrapping of oily cloth clinging to the end of the shaft like a pathetic and withered pube. I couldn't help but compare *this* tool to the one floundering around sightless in the passageway, tearfully begging for help. But I couldn't blame him, not really. I'd likely be doing something courageously similar if I didn't have the benefit of Darkvision. I sighed.

Son of a poop, I thought. *I'm going to go back for this lint-licker, aren't I?*

I groaned and turned around, marching back the way I'd come. Stinky came into view after a moment. He was standing now, his hands out and legs quivering as he inched his way down the wrong direction, back toward the hole we'd spilled out of.

"Hey, Ass-butt," I said, startling him. He whipped around toward me and lost his balance, but I caught his arm and jerked him upright. I was surprised that he was so docile now and hadn't tried to hit or stab me.

Progress, I suppose.

"Here," I said, and shoved the torch into his left hand, careful to avoid his right, as that was the one wielding the blade. Stinky paused and began groping the torch, probably trying to figure out whether or not I'd just handed him a stick of dynamite.

"A torch?" he asked. I could see snot dribbling down from his smashed nose, and that unlocked an additional level of pity in my conscience for the dude.

"Yeah," I said. "You light. Make big flame. For see." Man, my caveman impression was spot on.

"All right, then," Stinky hissed, holding it up where he must've thought I was at. "Go ahead and light it."

"Uh . . . " I mumbled, confused. "Don't you have some way of doing that?"

"Sure, let me just cast a nice bonfire Spell," Stinky returned smugly. I could have hit him again. But I didn't. I'd decided I was now much more mature than I was a few moments ago.

"Listen, you're taking an awfully sarcastic tone for someone who was ugly-crying on his tummy less than thirty seconds ago. Don't act like you're all put together now."

I watched Stinky clench his jaw, his three mouth slits tight in frustration. He seemed to be considering something.

"You're an orc," he sighed.

"Damn, nothing gets past you, huh, Basil of Baker Street?" I said.

"Vosket's dick!" he exclaimed, scowling deep. "Let me finish, you fuckin' petulant wanking cloth. Since you're one of the savage, pilfering breeds of monstrosity that thrives in the dark, you're going to have to use an item for me."

I chuckled.

"Boy, you really know how to switch gears," I said. "Where is it?"

"My satchel," Stinky grumbled.

"Sure, hand over your fanny pack, and I'll dig your precious out of there."

"I'm not letting you get your filthy paws in there," Stinky barked. "I'll hand it to you."

"As you wish, Your Majesty."

Stinky shifted, reaching to his side, and tensed up with a hiss.

"Gods damn, orc. You stabbed the bloody shit out of me!"

"Yeah, and I still owe you another for your cute maneuver during our two-man luge," I said. I waited for him to recover and then watched as he very carefully slipped the strap of a small leather carrier from beneath his left arm. He opened it up and blindly felt around the inside before withdrawing two small, flat stones. Then he placed them in his palm and gestured toward my general direction. I activated my Analysis, but whatever they were, I wasn't able to tell.

???

- **Rarity: ???**
- **Item Type: ???**

- Durability: ???
- Weight: ???

???

"What are these, then?" I asked. "Part of your button collection?"

"They're starters, I said," Stinky growled. "Take them—carefully! Knock 'em together over the end of the torch. Only once! It's got shit-all for charges left."

I shrugged and picked up the flat stones, surprised to find they were warm to the touch. I held them in front of the gauzy fabric of the torch and clicked them against one another cautiously.

FWOOF!

A gout of flame leaped from the stones and arced onto the edge of the torch head, igniting the fabric, and the torch was suddenly blazing. I squinted as my Darkvision reeled back and dissipated, the color returning to my sight. Now that I'd used the items, it seemed my Analysis was working a little better. The display activated unbidden, and I could see more information about the rocks.

Troyal's Fire Starter
- **Rarity: Uncommon**
- **Item Type: Enchanted Tool**
- **Durability: 4/100**
- **Weight: .12 lbs.**

???

Then I was hit with a separate prompt.

Congratulations! You've raised an Ability!
Analysis I has advanced to Analysis II!

Interesting.

I peered back at Stinky seriously, closing my fist around the fire starter as he made to reach for them.

"Who's Troyal?" I asked. "Is that you?"

Stinky scowled deeply, shaking his head.

"No," he said sharply. "And that's the end of it."

"Guess I'll just keep calling you Stinky, then," I said.

"You call me Stinky?! To who?"

I chuckled.

"Ah, shit. Was that only in my head? Sorry, Stinkers, I do that sometimes."

Stinky gave me a look I recognized well: like he'd like to punch my dick into my throat. But instead, he just turned and spat onto the tunnel floor with a harsh noise.

There was something about the man's personality that just seemed a little incongruent with the figure he presented. He *looked* like a calculatingly vicious, murdering son of a bitch, capable of cleaving through a whole horde of monsters to eat their hearts. But everything I'd seen from the way he acted seemed a lot more . . . well, *lame*.

He'd been terrified sliding down the hill, and his bravado during our fiery fisticuffs had been shaky at best. His general manner was leading me to believe he was not the tough-guy giga-Chad his exterior indicated.

Congratulations! You've raised a Skill!
Insight has advanced to F-Rank Level 6!

So, apparently, I was on to something. That gave me an idea, at least, as to how to approach the next phase of our self-inflicted imprisonment.

"Can we call a truce for the moment?" I asked.

"A truce?" Stinky asked, looking baffled.

"Yeah, a cease-fire. A stand-down? Whatever it's called where we don't attack each other temporarily. As much as I adore pummeling you with my entire arsenal of masterful ass-beating, we appear to be stuck down here. It might make sense to hold off on making each other die until we figure out what the hell is going on."

Stinky groaned but didn't disagree.

Good.

"Did you know this place was down here?" I ventured.

"No," Stinky said. "Our unit hadn't even been to the fuckin' camp before. Commander Fuck-up was several days ahead of us. Was looking forward to resting before heading out again in the morning. We'd only just arrived in this damned area when all the explosions started."

"Yeah, what was up with that?" I said. "Was that some sort of welcome party that got wildly out of control?"

Stinky scowled up at me.

"I was going to ask you that very question, orc," he said. "Seems suspicious that you arrived just as everything went to fuckin' *shit*."

He bristled then, pointing down the tunnel.

"Can we walk at least while you jabber on? The less time we spend in one fuckin' spot, the better. If anyone is alive, they'll be rallying back at the blasted camp, and the sooner we get out of here, the sooner I can drag a rusty blade across your fat neck."

"You're not selling it very well," I said. "But, yeah. Sure."

We started our trudge down the path with me in the lead. I had a sneaking suspicion that Stinky was too frightened of the big scary underground trail to knife me in the back, so I wasn't very concerned with being in front. Our long shadows danced against the irregular shape of the tunnel as we moved.

Man, whoever made this thing must have had two different lengths of legs.

The ground was bafflingly uneven, and I had to do a sort of hobble-hop as we went along, taking care not to trip and fall and lose all semblance of what little intimidation factor I had left. I could hear Stinky plodding along behind me, several large paces between us.

Somebody is nervous I'm going to get a foolish murder-y idea, I guess.

We traveled in silence for a few minutes, both of us battered, bloody, and bruised but refusing to yield to weakness in front of the other. My groin and thigh still burned from smashing the potion into the crook of my sack, and I could see Stinky's shadow wince ahead any time he had to make a sudden movement.

What a couple of bozos. I thought.

I considered the nickname he'd used for Fawn: Commander Fuck-up. So, life in Redmarktown wasn't as harmonious as it seemed. I wondered about who might have caused everything to blow up, but I had no way of knowing. The timing *did* seem incredibly serendipitous, though. Maybe whoever it was had been waiting for a diversion? I was starting to feel like I was a big fat distraction in an orc costume, so it could be reasoned that whoever had done it saw an opportunity and acted.

I still couldn't believe the shift Fawn had gone through after our conversation. I was lucky to be alive right now, especially considering the Levels I'd seen on the troops I'd managed to sneak past. One of them had been Level Fifty. That meant Fawn had to at least be in the neighborhood of that, because I assumed it would be challenging to manage a group as rotten as theirs if there were people much more powerful that could easily usurp the throne.

Lucky may not have even covered it, actually. That brush with death was practically divine intervention . . .

I remembered the humorously brief conversation with Zeol. He had mentioned he was, in fact, a god. If that were true . . .

I felt my anger building. Did that slimeball play a part in that? It took me a second to calm down, but eventually, I got it under control.

I wasn't mad about surviving. No, that was the *good* part. If that doofy mask had been the one to start fiddling with my lifeline, then that meant there were probably other aspects he was able to mess around with to different degrees. That was assuming he was even capable of a feat like that. I mean, he *did* give me that—what was it called? Aegis? That seemed like something someone who liked to mess with people would gift someone.

This fucking place, man.

Boy, I couldn't tell if things were becoming complex or I was just letting my imagination run away with me. One thing was for sure, though: I couldn't tell anyone about the Espers. Whatever purpose they served must have been pretty *fucking* cool if it meant other people would be willing to turn me into Swiss cheese over them.

I gave a sidelong look at Stinky. Would even *he* try to kill me over them? Even with the ultimate end of being trapped in the darkness alone? Maybe. I was clueless to their function, and maybe it was worth it to those in the know. For all I knew, they could open an immediate portal to Blowjob Beach.

Let's not find out. For now.

"What were you guys doing that kept you from getting back to camp earlier?" I asked, breaking the silence and startling the other man. I didn't turn, but I could see Stinky's shadow jolt at my words.

Easy there, Captain Confidence.

"None of your fuckin' business, orc," he said sullenly. "Redmark matters."

I thought about telling him that I was technically a pledge into their mighty ranks after my conversation with Fawn. I mean, she hadn't actually rescinded my membership offer during the entire ordeal where she was trying to hack my bones apart. I guess I hadn't actually officially accepted yet, either. Either way, that would just lead to an uncomfortable conversation that I didn't think I could navigate well enough to explain why I'd been trying to escape.

"Where were you all heading to in the morning?" I tried instead.

Apparently, this was an even *worse* inquiry, because Stinky spat on the ground in disgust.

"You a fuckin' spy, orc? Why the hell do you want to know what we're up to? I said it doesn't concern you!"

"Fuck you, trash boy," I said, anger returning. "I'm just trying to pass the time with pleasant conversation, so untangle your balls from your thong, you miserable asshole." I was getting sick of Stinky's eternally lousy attitude. The irony of it was lost on me at the time.

Stinky barked out a laugh.

"Keep it up, tusk tooth," he said venomously. "I'll break this idiotic truce and slice your belly open. Let the dark creatures take you, then."

I snorted.

"Oh, *okay*," I replied. Then, because I'm a bit of a dick, I began to increase my pace down the rocky corridor. I gradually moved faster until the halo of light from Stinky's torch began to get smaller behind me. I heard a quick shuffle as the soldier realized he was being left behind.

"Where are you going?" he demanded, but I detected a hint of fear in his tone. I smirked.

"Keep up," I said.

"What—er— Stop!" he bellowed. "I'm injured!"

"We're *both* injured, you turd burglar," I called back. "Let's get to stepping!"

I kept picking up speed, my thigh and crotch on fire with the effort, but it was worth it. I looked back to see how far away he was, and I could see him struggling to hobble along on the uneven terrain, his panicked face illuminated by torchlight.

However, that turned out to be a mistake, because as I turned to look ahead again, I found myself running right off the edge of the tunnel and into a large crevasse that I'd not seen.

"Fuuuuuuck!" I screamed.

—

The fall stopped.

It was nothing but darkness for a moment, and then I was blasted by bright lights and the loud screech of noisemakers. I heard booming crackles and pops as something colorful shot at me.

I screamed, throwing my arms up to shield myself from whatever unhinged murder destiny this happened to be, and clenched my fists. A moment passed, and the clamor died down, but I kept myself barricaded in my wall of arms. Another moment, and soon it was silent. I peeked out to see what had happened, and instantly another chorus of party horns and snaps and vibrant streamers and confetti blasted around me in a chaotic maelstrom of celebration.

A huge banner dropped from above with a single message: WELCOME BACK!

"What the . . . "

I looked around. I was in a brightly lit room that stretched for hundreds of feet in any direction. It was largely empty, save for a podium that looked to be affixed dead center, shrouded in mist. There was something familiar about this space, but I couldn't quite put a finger on it. The dimensions, I knew, were different somehow, but the vibe it was giving off resonated with me in a way that I wasn't quite sure how I felt about.

Then I noticed suddenly that I was standing in about two inches of water. Annoyance entered me as I realized where I was.

Well, shit.

CHAPTER FIFTEEN

GODS AND SANDWICHES

"Fuck," I muttered. "Not again."

Sure enough, from the mist behind the podium, a large dark shape glided forward in midair, cutting through the steam like a gigantic, theatrical vampire bat. The monstrous form slid into place behind the plinth, and now I could see what it was: the fifty-foot colossal mask of Zeol.

"Welcome back," the mask said congenially.

"Yeah, I saw your sandwich board," I said. "What the dick do you want now?"

"I am overjoyed to host you," Zeol said, ignoring my question. There was no expression on the mask other than looking as though it was in a constant state of featureless surprise.

"Yeah, I'll bet," I sighed. "Do you have, like, a falling fetish or something?"

"How do you mean?"

"Well, both times I've wound up here, I was in the middle of a deep and sexy plunge from a high place. Then you snatched me up for your own devices. I'm just saying: whatever gets you slick and drippy is your business, but you should leave me out of it."

I tried not to think about the fact that I'd just been careening into an abyss. If last time was any indicator, once I exited wherever *here* was, I'd be right back where I left off—hitting terminal velocity before transforming into a cloud of bone dust and curse words as I hit the bottom.

"I see," Zeol said.

"Also," I continued, "I've got a booger to pick with you, buster."

Zeol chuckled softly.

"Then we are a matching pair, for I also have some contention with your own behavio—"

"I'll go first," I interrupted, sloshing forward in the water toward the podium. Then I paused.

"Actually, wait," I waved around at all the celebratory to-do. "What's with the Passion Party accessories?"

While looking very clearly antiquated—perhaps from King Arthur times—the party decorations were impressively garish and seemed strange filling the foggy chamber. I wasn't sure how the "god" managed to procure the supplies for this underwhelming welcome, but he'd had to have known in advance that I was going to be bouncing in there, right? Also, was it *way* more humid than last time? I felt sweaty and gross all of a sudden.

Zeol was quiet for a moment, then sighed.

"Oh, all this?"

"Yeah," I said. "I have to admit, you've got more of a dollar-store vibe, but a lot of this seems handmade. And buddy, you ain't got no hands."

"Yes, it was a . . . labor of love, so to speak. You seemed to find the previous reception I'd lobbied for you very distasteful, so I endeavored to provide a more inviting atmosphere this time." His tone shifted and sounded a little more . . . glum? "But maybe I overdid it? You don't seem to enjoy this one much, either."

Goddammit.

Was this thing actually making me feel bad? That wasn't fair. You couldn't expect someone to have a good reaction when you pluck them out of a near-death experience and thrust them into a room fashioned after a six-year-old's birthday party. As if to emphasize my point, I noticed a conical hat on my head, the string straining against my lantern chin. I slipped it off but didn't discard it. Instead, since it didn't appear I had my pack with me, I tucked it behind into my waistband.

I really need to get a utility belt.

"It's fine," I said. "I was just surprised, is all. How come you keep grabbing me unannounced?"

Zeol's tone was chipper again as he answered.

"It's the perfect time to do so, because you can't really object."

I grimaced.

"Yeah, you can't say that, dude," I explained. "Not super chill—and has weird implications as to the type of . . . god you are. Why the fuck do you keep summoning me to your partially flooded basement, anyway?"

Before me, the giant specter didn't move, but I heard him clear his throat.

"Shall we pick up where we left off, Loon? I promise all will be explained once we have a moment to discuss."

"As long as you promise not to make me do karaoke or have me pin the tail on the donkey, I'll try to be patient with you."

"Splendid," Zeol said, and I watched as the self-described god floated a little higher into the air, the podium sliding to the left and out of my view. Zeol rotated a little and then settled down into position a few feet from me. It was pretty bizarre, having something that big and mobile suddenly zooming up right next to me from the mist.

"So, one thing I want to know is: does time stop when I come here? Last time, it seemed like it did, but how does that work?"

"Time is relatively... inconsequential in this place. It exists as a fragment of a moment, stretched into a strand of mine own divining. While time's passage is not entirely absent from this place, it is rendered functionally inert. From the second you arrived to the moment you leave, an unnoticeable amount of time will have been observed..."

He paused.

"...out there."

"So, let me get this straight," I said. "This is kinda like the Pause button on the world? Like when I'm watching wrestling and I need to take a leak? That's impressive. Also, where's your bathroom?"

"I have no clue what you're talking about, Loon," Zeol said. "However, it sounds like whatever it is you're referring to is close enough of an analogy. The only thing that matters is that you *believe* you understand it."

I stiffened.

"What does that mean? Is this like Neverland? If I don't believe in this place, will it disappear?"

I wasn't sure if I was confusing Peter Pan's Hyper Party Fun Zone with something else, but I was under a degree of certainty that he had zero idea what I was referring to, so it seemed safe that he wouldn't call me out.

Zeol chuckled.

"Not at all. I am merely indicating that the conversation can continue to progress if you think you have a handle on it. Explaining the nature of how this *pocket* works would not be worth either of our time."

"So, am I just hovering in space on the other side? You know, staring down at my doom with arms wide open?"

Zeol sighed, then his voice shifted—but I couldn't tell why.

"For all intents and purposes, you are present. Never fear, Loon, my dear. All will be explained in due course. Hungry?"

A gargantuan table instantly materialized in front of me, laden down with an assortment of fruits, vegetables, meats, and grains that were piled high and spilling over the sides.

I stared in awe. There had been nothing there a moment before, and now ... *this*. It looked like oil paintings I had seen of feasting kings and queens in their court—you know, with the sprawling spread of food that would one hundred percent be going to waste. Was it a spell? An illusion? I knew one thing: whatever it was, I needed to learn *that* little magic trick. I hadn't had anything to eat since I'd arrived and I was positively starving. Strangely, the last boatload of hours full of adrenaline-fueled terror-fighting and running for my life had kicked my groaning stomach to the back of my mind. Now that there was a literal smorgasbord of delectable cuisine in front of me, I couldn't contain myself. As much as I wanted to be suspicious of such a gift, I marched forward and started stuffing my face.

I took a massive bite out of the end of an entire loaf of bread and chewed loudly.

This is . . . goddamn delicious!

I stopped to smash the flaky heel against a large block of butter sitting nearby before wedging it back in my mouth. I swallowed and then wolfed down a handful of grapes, followed by a hunk of—hopefully—pork, and washed it down with a big mug of what I was pleased to learn was milk. I spotted a *very* enticing sugar cookie wrapped up with a ribbon and sitting by its lonesome near a bowl of chocolate pudding.

Oh, hello there, I thought. *Don't mind me; just gonna save you for later.* I slipped the cookie into the pocket of my linen pants.

"Well, now. I suppose that's one way to start," Zeol said.

"Quiet," I demanded between bites. "Eating."

"I see that. Would you like to begin with our actual dialogue, or would you prefer I left you to this?"

"We ca' bugg'n," I affirmed, mouth full of mashed potatoes.

"Excellent," Zeol said.

Suddenly, to my great distaste, I was sitting in a chair facing the enormous black mask. The table was gone, but now there was a large plate full of sandwiches on my lap. I shrugged and picked one up, taking a bite while staring at Zeol.

"As I mentioned previously," Zeol began, "I am a god. Now, you may be asking yourself: 'Loon, what is this fantastically well-mannered and effervescent host doing here talking to little ol' me? Surely a creature of such magnanimous might must have countless other tasks to attend to. Golly gee! I surely do hope I'm not wasting this being of incarnated perfection's time.'"

I nodded.

"Yeah, that sounds exactly like me."

Zeol continued.

"Well, that's the thing, isn't it, Loon? You're from another world, aren't you?"

I was about to protest and make up a lie when the god interrupted me.

"Oh, I already know. Don't bother yourself with trying to drum up falsehoods. I wouldn't want you to break something in that worryingly smooth brain of yours."

"E'kyuz me?" I said, roast beef dangling out of my mouth.

"Loon," he said severely. "You've got two brain cells, and both are competing for third place."

I gaped.

"Wow, that was . . . actually pretty good," I said. "My compliments."

Zeol's tone changed to one of genuine delight.

"Do you really think so? I was practicing that one while you were away!"

"So, if you know that I'm not from here, then you can tell me why I'm here in the first place and how I can get back," I said.

"Well," Zeol began, sounding uncomfortable. "While I know that you are not from here, I am unable to discern the precise reason or method for it, Loon. I apologize for being unable to be more helpful in that regard.

What a useless fucking god.

"Anyway," I said. "You seem pretty tangent-prone, so let's get back on track here."

"Yes, that's a great idea," Zeol said. "Where was I? Ah, yes: why I have my eye on you."

The mask took a dramatic intake of breath and then let it out.

"You see, I didn't know what I would find, looking through the Archway like that. Really, I wasn't even sure *why* I did it—the morbid curiosity of the unknown, I suppose—but I did look, and there you were."

I stopped chewing. *This* was who'd been attached to the constellation? I knew that based on the description, it was random, but I'd kind of been hoping that it would be, well, no one. Primarily to avoid this exact scenario. Yet there I was, sitting in a big puddle eating the medieval equivalent of a French dip with a sentient harlequin mask.

"The very nature of the Archway dictates that a contract is forged," Zeol continued. "So, from that very moment, you and I became intertwined. We are bonded, Loon."

I groaned.

"You mean I'm stuck with you?"

I could tell from his tone that Zeol was practically beaming with excitement.

"You should feel very fortunate; not everyone gets to bend the ear of a god."

"Lucky me," I said.

"Well, that's an interesting point that you bring up, Loon."

"Is it? What point did I make? I mean—er—yeah, I know!"

"A more powerful wit than yours there is not," Zeol said. "But that is just it, my boy. Luck is *everything*. Did you notice your own stat changing?"

I nodded. My Luck had hopped up by seven points from my last reckoning, which seemed like a substantial amount. I wasn't sure what role it necessarily played in all of this, but I had a feeling he was about to give me a far-too-jubilant explanation.

"That was *me*," Zeol beamed.

"Wait," I said. "So . . . you're what, the god of luck?"

"Among a few other domains. But yes, fortune is one of my primary aspects."

Well, that certainly explained a few things. I raised an eyebrow at Zeol. There was something else there that he hadn't quite explained. I hadn't ever been the sharpest hammer in the deck, but I was picking up some funky vibes from the flow of this god's rambling.

"If that's the case, though, then how come bad things keep happening to me? Sure, I've survived so far, but the predicaments I've been wandering into should have been negated by my raised Luck, right?"

I paused thoughtfully.

Don't do it. Don't you dare fucking say it.

"Unless you're not a very powerful god?" Then, twisting the knife, I affirmed my statement. " . . . Yeah, you seem kind of wimpy."

I couldn't stop myself from being a little shit sometimes. Why was I like this?

I let my statement grow in the silence as I dipped the edge of the sandwich into a conveniently provided au jus and took another bite. It was delicious. I didn't want to admit it to Zeol, but this may have been the best French dip I'd ever eaten, and in my lap were a dozen more just like it.

Uh-oh. I need to chill before my new body becomes my old body.

Food had obviously played a large part in my previous life. I don't even know that I did it for comfort or for boredom like I knew many people did. Mine had always seemed to be about the *taste*. I fucking loved delectable, fat-enriched cuisine. Complex flavors, rich buttery textures, and the more cheese, the better. Food was important, and this was the first time since arriving that I'd eaten anything. These sandwiches were dangerous.

However, it seemed my comment had struck a nerve, because as I lifted the dip to take another bite, the entire platter upended in my lap. French dips flew everywhere, landing on me, in the water, and some even slapped against Zeol.

"What the hell?!" I demanded. "I was gonna *eat* those!"

"You accuse me, *Zeol the Capricious*, of being weak? Of being . . . *mundane*? I, who contort the ebb and flow of the very fabric of fortune? The Slumberer, me, underpowered? I could lash you to the tips of luck's volatile fingers and bind you in a cycle of unyielding torment until all life is extinguished from the cosmos and time itself is forgotten. I could flay the boundaries of your dreams and reality, forcing you to become a husk! I could conjure up devils that would *haunt* your *blood,* Sojourner Loon! Do not mistake me for anything other than vast, unbridled *power!*"

I stared at the mask for a moment, a little stunned by the tempestuous tantrum the god was throwing.

Then I slowly took another bite of the sandwich.

"Haunt my *blood*?"

The French dip exploded out of my hand, arcing across the huge room and into the water beyond with a faraway splash.

"Hey! Not cool, man," I exclaimed. "That—"

"You are frustrating beyond all measure of understanding, Loon," Zeol exclaimed, the mask no longer black but white-hot, so much so that I could feel the heat leaping from his form. "You are rude, and you are stupid. Despite knowing nothing, you continue on as though you have all of the answers. If it were within my contract to do so, I would transform these mists into venomous black serpents and let them strike your eyes and tongue until nothing remained in your head but bloat and pus!"

The water beneath him began to boil and bubble threateningly. I quickly lifted my feet out and tucked them up onto the chair.

Zeol's voice became thunderous and resounding, all indication of the previous calm placidity vanishing. "I invite you into my realm to educate you—nay, to *better* you and your understanding—and you minimize my merit?! I will not tolerate this in my own plane!"

His words hung in the air, and I wasn't sure how to follow up such an explosion of emotion. There was a moment of pregnant silence, and neither of us broke it. I just kept my eyes trained on the mask, suddenly very anxious and scanning the fog for any indication that it was about to get *bitey*. Finally, after several long breaths, Zeol's tone became soft again.

"I am—er— My apologies, Loon," he said. "That was . . . an unfortunate outburst. Inappropriate, even."

"Wow," I said, watching the water recede before placing my feet back in it. "I didn't realize you . . . hated food so much."

There was a pause, and then Zeol began to chuckle.

"Yes, I suppose it *did* look a bit like I had it out for the poor dears, didn't it? Mercy me, I should really learn to temper my predilections toward that level of fury."

"Hey, no hard feelings," I said, waving my hands around. "One time, I got so angry at my aunt that I placed my bowl of cereal on the floor and kicked it into the ceiling fan."

Aunt Ella had told me that under *no* circumstance was I to borrow her car on account of getting arrested for disassembling a police bike. Technically, it was only an aggravated misdemeanor (due to Uncle Luke's assistance). Still, I'd only done it because the officer had chained the bike up to one of those water fountains designed for dogs at the park—blocking any chance of those puppers getting a drink. It had made me angry, so I'd done the only thing I could think of to teach the cop a lesson.

Unfortunately, I was caught in the act, and though Uncle Luke had been able to get a deferred judgment on it, I still had to be punished. It just so happened that two days later, the new Lamb of God album dropped, and of course, I needed the physical album. Aunt Ella had said it was too bad, and I'd either have to wait until my grounding was over or buy it online. Before I knew it, the cereal bowl was already flying through the air, and I spent the next week fixing the damage and using my *Legion: XX* money to pay the cost.

It seemed silly now, but that was actually a pretty typical outburst for me. I'd been living my whole life as an undersized and over-wide meatball of fury. If there's one thing I understood well, it was rage.

Zeol considered my statement quietly before seeming to brighten up.

"All right, well, let's just forget that, shall we? Let's continue with why I brought you here in the first place."

"That sounds good," I said. "But, uh . . . could I get another sandwich?"

Soundlessly, another tray of food appeared in my lap. To my disappointment, it wasn't the archaic French dips this time. It was something resembling paninis.

Great. All the power in the world, and he gets delivery from fucking Panera Bread.

I picked one up and bit into it anyway. To my delight, I found it was a concoction *very* similar to a Cubano sandwich.

Ooh, never mind! Even better!

"We were discussing the nature of Luck and my power over it, yes?" Zeol began. "But I must say, you seem to be looking at it incorrectly."

"Illuminate me," I said between bites.

"There are specific rules to follow while you enjoy the winsome wiles of Regaia—this world. I am an overseer of luck, but that does not mean you will be blessed with a purely positive fortune at all times. Luck, as they say, is a fickle mistress."

"Meaning what exactly?" I asked. I was starting to suspect from his tone that I wouldn't like the possible ramification of that.

"That is just a roundabout way of saying that luck goes up," Zeol continued, and then dropped his voice, "and luck comes down. It is quite an exciting ride! You can never truly know what is going to come next!"

"Wait, are you saying what I think you're saying?"

"Well," Zeol said, "what is it you think I am saying, Loon?"

"I *think* you're saying that my Luck stat is going to shoot up and down on a whim, and if that's the case, I am already adding you to my little black book of people's houses I'm going to egg."

"I suppose you could infer that result, and you're not far off. However, it has a much more nuanced structure than that. You make it sound as if you believe it will be sliding all over the place, willy-nilly and the like."

"So, that's not what will be happening?"

"No, that's pretty close," Zeol admitted.

I groaned again.

"But there *are* some rules!" he added quickly.

That just sounded like bad news with extra steps.

"Lay 'em on me," I said sullenly.

"Well, for instance, it works like this: while you are under my purview—and you should understand that as *while you are alive in this world*—your Luck Attribute will fluctuate. Before you get your . . . painters in a twist? Is that the term? Oh, never mind. Before you get flustered, know that the rules state that if Luck goes down, it must go up next—by at least five but never more than fifteen. The same is true for the opposite direction."

" . . . and how often will this be happening?"

"Oh, several times per day," Zeol said. "Based on certain criteria that . . . "

The god paused, and though there was no physical indication of it, I had a feeling he was passing judgment on me.

"What?!" I demanded.

"Nothing," Zeol said. "I just don't think, based on our limited interaction, that you would be interested in those specifics. Am I wrong?"

"Is it something that I can control?"

"No."

"Well, then you're right on the money. Will it be inconvenient?"

"Most certainly."

"Why do I feel like you're excited about that?"

"Because I *am*," Zeol said. "Ecstatic, even. But don't worry, my dearest orc—you will be too."

"Would you care to elaborate on that, Zee, or am I just going to have to be satisfied with your mysterious puzzle-language bullshit?"

Zeol floated up and shifted, flowing through the mist at a sideways angle before coming to a stop at my other side. It was strange. A creature of his size, I should have felt the wind moving—especially with as close as he was. But there wasn't anything. No sound or sensation, no general feeling of presence. I had to imagine that if I'd had my eyes closed, there would have been no way to tell he'd done anything. As if he wasn't actually there.

"When your Luck status is low, it will afford no end of interesting consequences and events," Zeol said. "But it also offers an opportunity for great rewards."

I cleared my throat.

"What kind of rewards?"

"Experience. Loot. Power. Take your pick of myriad possible outcomes."

"That seems . . . What's the word—*counterintuitive*? Why would I be rewarded for being unlucky?"

"Because that is the nature of fortune, my good orc. A deficit in that area is considered a disadvantage, and *those* are where the true opportunities lie. A man down on his literal luck that can persevere is treated *quite* kindly by the fates. Likewise, for those that fail despite impressively wonderful odds. High risk, high reward, as they say."

"So, if the stat is, say, negative ten, then bad things will happen—but if I somehow wind up on top, I'll win a prize?"

"Let's not get bogged down on the particulars so much, Loon," Zeol said. "The less you worry over it, the better off you will be. This I promise. Trust me to carry the burden of luck's rebellious nature, and it will be sorted."

I took another thoughtful bite, finishing the sandwich. There must have been a bit of some sleeper heat to it because my esophagus felt warm and my cheeks had the sensation of being flushed. I looked at another one of the Cubanos.

Maybe in a minute.

I turned to address Zeol again.

"This might sound like an ignorant question, but isn't this a dumb . . . *yoke to saddle upon my nigh-overburdened shoulders*?"

Wait, I thought. *That wasn't what I was trying to say. This isn't even the way I normally speak. Weird.*

I continued.

"*Would it not be more appropriate and resplendent if I were not the benefactor of such a— Wait but a moment!*"

What was going on? I hadn't wanted to use *any* of those words. I knew what I was trying to say, but everything was coming out wrong. This didn't seem good.

"*What manner of language tumbles forth from my lips? Zeol, good fellow! Is this high sorcery? Am I bedeviled? Is my mind suffering the woes of exhaustion or perhaps apoplexy?*"

Something goddamn goofy was going on; that was for sure. While I'd been trying to say ordinary, everyday words, my mouth seemed to be working of its own volition and creating a bizarre translation—like I'd accidentally set Google Translate to *Shakespearean Douchebag*.

"I know this is you, Zeol! Don't just stare at me, you big, ugly bitch! Change my voice back to normal right now!"

At least, that's what I'd tried to say. What actually came out was:

"What ho, Zeol! Rescind thy eyesight from my visage, foul and unseemly cur that thou art! I demand the satisfaction of a tongue most modern and that thou performest this task with haste!"

Zeol just chuckled.

"Much better," he said. "I was worried you would never finish that food."

"What was in the sandwich?!" I tried to demand, but my mouth said:

"What was contained within the bocadillo?!"

Bocadillo? I didn't know what that meant, but it was probably another, fancier word for sandwich I had to imagine—using, uh, context clues.

"Oh, just an Oratory Splendor potion," Zeol said matter-of-factly. "You do have a terrible habit of using just the most disgusting language, and I wanted to see if you were a bit more tolerable if I suddenly altered your speech patterns. As it turns out: barely."

"I am of the mind to transform the planks of thy body into kindling whereby I will set them ablaze and empty my waste upon the dancing flames! Then I shall dig a trench and forge a shallow grave for the charred leavings of thy coil!" I bellowed.

I couldn't believe he'd slipped a mickey into my food! And this was the guy that wanted me to *trust* him? Bend his ear? Now he was pranking me? I had to admit, though, the last line I'd said about the shallow grave was actually *metal as fuck* and way more badass than what I'd initially intended.

"Please, Loon," Zeol said. "This was done in warm humor. It will be over in a moment, and you will suffer no ill effects afterward. You have always been the type—from what I gather—to relish in a bit of good-natured ribbing. No?"

I thought about that. Honestly, it was pretty harmless—assuming I returned to normal. It's not like he had shot me in the face with bear mace or anything, like I had to my last social worker. But I also didn't like looking like a fool or being the ass-end of a joke.

"I shall hold my reservations until such a time that this fades from the air of my teeth . . . but I goddamn promise, man, if I get stuck like this or have a permanent speech impediment, I'm going to kick the sh— Oh."

The Oratory Splendor had ended right in the middle of my sentence.

So, it lasted for roughly a minute, I thought. If I could find out where to get some of that stuff, I thought I'd have a few ideas for how best to use it—to hilarious effect. I moved my jaw up and down to confirm that my ridiculous ventriloquism had stopped, then I relaxed. I took a few long moments before I spoke again.

"All right, Zeol," I said slowly. "You got me. You're a regular Johnny Knoxville. Now can we *please* move on to the pressing issues? This might be all fun and games for you, but *my* orcish ass is the one on the line out there. If we're just sitting around playing Who Can Be a Bigger Dickmunch with each other, I'm probably going to end up dead. *Then* how would you be able to help me?"

Zeol considered my words. He rotated slowly on his axis before quietly swooping through the mist and returning to float behind the reinstated podium.

"My apologies, Loon," Zeol said seriously. "I let my foolishness get the better of me. I've been without much conversation for a long time, and it has been ages further still since I was able to pull a fast one all in the name of . . . How did that one woman put it? Ah, yes: 'breaking balls.' You'll have to forgive me once more."

"I'll add it to your tab," I said.

"Most generous of you," Zeol said.

Now no longer interested in the secret danger-food, I abandoned my tray and began to slosh through the water toward Zeol and the podium. I couldn't help but think the image of this mansion-sized black mask floating in front of the platform in a ginormous cavern of mist and water would make an excellent album cover. Especially if someone like the famous album art-smith and badass Berliner Eliran Kantor painted it. Kantor had crafted some of my all-time favorite concepts, including the illustrations to albums by the bands Helloween, Venom Prison, Havok, and Heaven Shall Burn.

This scene would be evocative as shit *in his style.*

Once I came to a stop in front of Zeol's phallic icebreaker, the god continued his original thought.

"I have a request for you, Loon." The pomp and severity of his shift into formality were slightly uncomfortable—like he was a politician about to announce on national television that he had been caught having sex with the office copier.

"So, here's a hot, sloppy Q for you," I stated. "But is this an *actual* request—like, can I say no? Or are you just prettying up the words *demand under penalty of death*?"

"I find death so boring," he said. "I prefer dismemberment—the *gentleman's consequence.*"

"*Dope,*" I said. "And here I was, prepping to get religious. Guess you're just going to be a party of one in your vape cave."

"You're too paranoid, dear Loon," Zeol said, still looming above me from the dais. "Of course, you can deny this solicitation without reprimand. I'm a god, not a farmwife. But I am hoping you will show interest in this venture. It will be incredibly worthwhile."

"For you, or for me?" I asked.

"They need not be mutually exclusive, my dear," Zeol said, his voice dripping with honey.

He's trying to butter me up. But I'm not a piping-hot piece of toast that you can just slather your words on; I'm like a feral alley cat—notoriously tricky to butter.

"What are we talking about here, Zee-man?" I said. "Power? Untold riches? An Applebee's gift card?"

Zeol turned to the right in response to my questions. From the podium, there was a chirp and then a flash of light as an enormous screen filled the space above, right where he'd turned to look. The display was grayscale and depicted a bizarre shape that looked like a very badly abused potato or a part of male anatomy with a worrying deformity.

"Nice balls," I said, making myself chuckle. I still hadn't gotten used to my new, lower voice, so the words still sounded like someone else was saying them. I'd add it to the list of things I hadn't yet gotten acclimated to: the greenish skin, the massive body, literally anything that had happened to me since fucking *yesterday*. This was getting away from me. Where was I? Oh, yeah, the testicles.

"*This* is my request."

"I'd love to help, but I don't think I'm qualified to diagnose this, Zee. Did you fuck them up with two big magnets?"

The god ignored me. Instead, he started bobbing up and down as the image on the screen rotated and enlarged. I could now see that this was actually a detailed sketch of a structure rather than a pair of roughly handled huevos. It had two distinct domes, though they were dissimilar in size and shape and appeared (to the best of my perception) to be made out of a thick, dark rock. I could see a large doorway inside an arch at the center front of the thing. Flanking either side were two colossal pillars with what I had to assume were statues of an indistinguishable lumpy creature atop each. It looked like a mausoleum for Mr. Peanut.

"This is the Forsaken Crypt of the Dreadnaught Lord," Zeol announced proudly. "It is a dungeon that holds many highly sought-after treasures and lesser, uncommon spoils as well. My request, at your pleasure, is that you make it to the fifth chamber on the main floor of the Crypt. In that space is an artifact that I require and would like you to retrieve for me."

I let out a whistle.

"Sweetheart, what makes you think I'm even *kind of* qualified to go into a dungeon?" I began. "Number A, I don't know the first filthy detail about those motherfuckers. I'm not sure what they're like here—but back where *I'm* from, they're either ancient shitty prisons or the lairs of all sorts of bad juju monsters and other bullshit in fantasy games. Second: I'm only Level Three. If you think my deficient behind is going to be able to toddle on in there and start wrecking holes, you've grossly misjudged my power level. I know my limits. And D, how in the sea-salted caramel fuck would I even begin to find this place?"

Zeol cleared his throat, which I had to imagine was just for emphasis because there's no way he was rocking actual vocal cords. Right?

"Allow me to answer your queries as best I can," he said with his imperious inflection. "This dungeon *is* similar—it seems—to what you described from your world. It was the final resting place of a very, *very* powerful thaumaturge named Rexen Gravetongue—"

"Well, that sounds like the name of a really wholesome and upstanding guy," I said, "and not at all like someone who would rip my spine out through my nostrils and play banjo with it."

Zeol just kept explaining, picking up right where he'd left off when I'd interrupted.

"—who stowed his hordes of wealth around him in his crypt—to be claimed by any brave and fearless individuals who might have the gall to step within its depths."

"You're doing a terrible job of pitching this," I said.

"To your next point: the main floor is not dangerous—even at your *Level Three*. Whatever lies in wait in that area will be quite easily dispatched—especially with that hidden shortcut in the second chamber . . . Well, getting ahead of ourselves, aren't we? Regardless, it is the *lower* floors that are truly a challenge. I assure you that you will not be in harm's way as long as you don't descend the stairs. You are to go to the fifth chamber, where you will find a talisman, and you will hold on to it until I can summon you here again. Along the way, you will be able—and in fact, are *encouraged*—to loot whatever treasure or items you happen upon. I expect there will be a number of interesting baubles."

"Okay, so I get this . . . talisman and just *hold it for you*?" I barked out a laugh. "I've heard that line before, bub. This isn't some scam to get me arrested by whatever you guys call cops here, is it?"

"I assure you, no one will know you have it, nor will they likely care. It is an object important only to me."

You have been offered a Quest!
[Faith Quest] *Into the Dungeon*
Zeol the Capricious has tasked you with entering the Forsaken Crypt of the Dreadnaught Lord to retrieve an object of value. Engage the dungeon and retrieve the item to complete this Quest.

- **Reward:** *Experience. Coin. Initiate Degree in the Cult of the Capricious.*
- **Bonus Reward:** *Unknown*

This is a Faith Quest. Failure to complete may result in exclusion or expulsion from Quest-associated Faith.
Accept?
Yes / No

I couldn't believe it. This oversized Halloween costume was asking me to go on a death-defying mission into the heart of the lair of some evil . . . thumb-turd—or whatever he called it—and snatch up his *super* important and not remotely suspicious collectible keepsake?

I wasn't feeling very hot or confident about my odds, regardless of what he said. This seemed, for all its potential, like a bad idea. I knew a thing or two about *those* considering I was the fucking Wrong Approach Warlord of Dipshit Mountain.

I selected *No.*

The notification blinked away, but then I heard a displeased grunt from Zeol, and another popped up.

You have been offered a Quest!
[Faith Quest] *Into the Dungeon*
Accept?
Yes / No

Are you kidding me?!

I selected *No* again. A moment later the same message appeared. I groaned and denied the request once more.

Sure enough, a few seconds later, the same message appeared. Now I was getting pissed off. Rather than deny it this time, I angrily minimized it and glared up at Zeol.

"All right, this is dumb," I said. "Where's the damned block button on this thing? You can't just keep requesting it if I don't want to do it! You said I could say no!"

I refused to be dragged into some foolish endeavor that wasn't of my own design. Gabe Skelter—er—Loon Nolastname was perfectly capable of messing up his own life, thank you very much. Besides, I'd only been there, what, twelve hours? Nah, I was planning to get a lot more mileage out of this new body than that before I departed dearly. This mission seemed like it would end with something big and uncomfortable eating its way through my sternum.

Zeol was silent.

I took a few breaths and tried to calm myself. It wouldn't do to go flying out of control right now. I was trying to save my strength because getting angry definitely took a lot out of me. Even more so now that there was an actual Ability attached to the emotion. After a few more moments of quiet contemplation, I sighed.

"I dunno, man; this seems shitty. Why don't you walk me through your rationale as to why I have to be the one to do this? Can't you go? Or someone else?"

Zeol sighed.

"I wish beyond all will that I could just give you an Intelligence potion so that you would understand better without my having to say it aloud."

"Are we being recorded or something?" I asked.

Zeol's frustrated exhalation of breath reverberated through my bones.

"We are not *necessarily* alone. There are always eyes and ears roving about in the shadows. Even here in my domain, I am not safe from the scrying eyes of some who would wish to stick their *nose* where it doesn't *belong*!"

The way he'd emphasized his last line made me believe he was speaking to someone else—likely whoever he believed had him under surveillance.

"Ah, man," I cooed. "Big Brother got your goose in a noose?"

I straightened up.

"Fine," I said. "Keep your secrets for now. But can you convince me better as to why I should agree to this? I'm not exactly Mega Man. Going in guns a-blazin' might be a bit out of my wheelhouse as of yet."

But not for long.

Zeol seemed to consider this, and when he finally did speak, it was with a quiet, thoughtful tone.

"Loon," he said. "Are you frightened?"

"What?!" I demanded, kicking up some of the shallow water in protest. "The *fuck* I'm frightened! I just don't like doing anybody any favors."

"Well," the god continued, "you sound quite scared. Based on your previous interactions in the world, it stands to reason you might have some trepidation, considering what I've seen. Really? *Running* from that oafish matau you rode down the hill?"

Matau? Had that been what Stinky was? I didn't know or necessarily care, though. The god's *other* words were much more prevalent in my brain. I felt my heart rate increase. Zeol was pushing my buttons.

"It was a . . . calculated risk!" I exclaimed. "I was wounded and running low on Stamina. I'd just passed my Milestones—which I still don't know about, or *anything*, for that matter, because, since the moment I've arrived, it's just been an unending storm of boiled pig snatch without a chance to stop and absorb any detail other than *time to die*."

I was finding it hard to remain calm. My pulse was thundering now, and I'd been subconsciously gritting my teeth, causing my words to come out like stilted barks. Zeol was doing this on purpose, and it was working.

"I doubt very much that your risks are *ever* calculated. You are as dumb as they come, Loon. Stupider, some might say. It is okay to admit when—"

"You can go fuck yourself!" I shouted angrily, my heartbeat pounding like a jackhammer. I stormed forward, thrusting a thick, green-gray finger at the mask.

"You *and* this dungeon can suck my whole dick! I'm not doing *anything* for you!"

"You are pathetic," Zeol said. "A mewling and cowardly crybaby who can't even—"

I felt it happen. It came, unbidden, like setting a lit match to wood that had been doused in gasoline. I could hear the blood rush to my ears and the roar tear from my lips. My body was vibrating in frenetic anger. A chemical cocktail of hatred spewed into my mind with the force of a crashing wave as my vision darkened and I locked on to Zeol.

I will kill him! I will shatter his body and pull the fragments apart with my teeth!

I hardly paid attention to the notification that popped up in front of me displaying the words *Primal Rage*. I was a seething torment and a vicious gale. I would be the gasp of death that filled the void at the end of life. I was going to observe total destruction in this chamber, starting with Zeol.

I lurched forward, my arms outstretched as I shot right toward the mask with the wrath of ten thousand warring stars in my eyes. However, when I reached the point where he was, my hands grasped . . . nothing.

Zeol was just *gone* and so was the room around me. That's when I noticed the lurch in my belly, even in my compromised state.

It was dark and I was falling.

CHAPTER SIXTEEN

TUMBLE AND CRUMBLE

I was confused.

There was nothing to strike out against there, nothing to grab and claw and tear to ribbons. I couldn't *fight* the darkness. I howled in pain and anger, wanting desperately to be able to attack someone, but there was nothing.

I realized through the bleary nightmare of my rage that I was back in the hole I'd tumbled into before Zeol had scooped me up. I roared again and tried to strike in the black to connect with something—anything—that would allow my bottled fury to become uncorked. But all I found was emptiness.

BOOM!

I hit something with enough force that I saw stars, except it was as though I could perceive them from every orifice in my body. I tasted copper—blood, I realized—and the pain from the collision rattled across my body in a radiating wave, leaving me shuddering and screaming. Agony pierced every square inch of my skin, bones, and muscles as a terrifying heat washed over me. I knew, in a daze, that I was bleeding. Badly.

I realized I had my eyes closed and opened them to view my status screen. My health was deep into the red, and there were a few notifications that had burst forward in my vision, detailing exactly how utterly porked I was.

PRIMAL RAGE!
You have taken Force Damage from falling!
- +2% resistance from Zeol's Falling Star Aegis
- +2% resistance while enraged.

Condition: Fractured
- **Will continue to lose Stamina while suffering from this effect at a rate of 5 Stamina per 1 second(s).**

Condition: Bleeding mitigated

So, I only *felt* like I was bleeding out. I supposed that was a net positive. But why hadn't my Aegis completely nullified the damage? Wasn't that something it could do? Did I have to activate it? Or had I used that little morsel too recently and I'd need to wait a whole twenty-four hours to use it again? I didn't know if it was still the same day from the last time I'd done it—which had happened automatically.

I knew that my Primal Rage had dissipated. I could feel it leaving my body like a rain cloud passing overhead. My thoughts became clear again.

Zeol.

Why had he done that? Why would he piss me off like that, only to . . .

I felt a pang of terror as I looked at my other notifications and then at my health bar.

-9/220 Health remaining!

Holy hot cross fuck!

I'd lost everything and then some, crashing into the negatives.

Negative nine . . . oh, fuck! Fuck, fuck, fuck, fuck, fuck!

I remembered that I had that orc trait—Unfaltering, or whatever—that kept me alive past the point of expected death. I could drop ten points below zero before dying, and luckily, I'd been one shy. But this temporary boost to my life would only allow me to keep moving for *one minute*. After that, I would be toast.

Panic replaced anger as I became *very* fucking scared that I would die. I could still move, somehow, but my body felt like it was wrapped in a sleeping bag filled with ball-punches. I staggered to my feet and swayed, putting a hand up to steady myself against the rocky wall. I was finally able to see again with my Darkvision now that I wasn't Tasmanian Devil–ing through a void. However, my prospects looked grim.

I was crouching in another dark, empty expanse of tunnels. Though these were considerably larger than the last one on account of the whole "no ceiling" thing I'd just collapsed through. My heart rate quickened again, this time from anxiety.

Where the butt am I going to find healing? There's nothing here!

I stumbled forward, panting. I felt hot and nauseous, sweating as I moved urgently. But with the fall damage I'd received, it was slow going. I didn't know how long I had left.

I'm going to die! I'm going to fucking *die! Move! I've gotta find something to heal myself with. I'm going to die!*

I bumbled toward a hallway, breathing hard. I tripped and fell forward but caught myself again on the wall, heaving from panic.

Shit! This is it! I'm going to die in a hole in the fucking ground in a stupid fucking world, in this stupid fucking body! Fuck!

Then I heard a voice. It was inside my head.

Loon, the voice said, dangerously serious. **This is Zeol.**

"Go away, you dumb shithead!" I shouted. "I'm about to die, and I don't need your numbskull-ass insults to drift with me down the River Styx!"

Listen to me very carefully, Zeol said. His tone was urgent and almost . . . pleading. **Do you still have the pastry you stuffed into your pocket?**

"What?" I asked stupidly.

The pastry that you took from the table—you snatched it up and took it with you.

I didn't respond. I was having a tough time following his line of questioning.

Pastry? Like, the cookie? Did he mean that thing?

I stuck my hand in my pants and my fingers brushed against the crumbly texture of the sweet I'd so eagerly plucked for later. I withdrew it and stared at it, my eyes beginning to unfocus.

That's the one, Loon! Stay with me, dear orc!

While inside my head, his words started to sound as if they were fading away, and I noticed that my Darkvision seemed to be phasing in and out as well. *Am I already dying?* I was less scared of that now for some reason; my mind no longer an angry symphony of hate and discord. It felt nice. Comfortable, even. Like I needed to just drift off, and everything would be fine.

LOON!

The voice had come back with full power, jolting my awareness. I shook my head and looked at the cookie in my hand again. It had almost fallen out of my grasp, but I held it up in front of me to stare deep into it as if it would reveal some universal truth.

Eat it! Do it fast—you don't have time to do anything else!

Man, the voice was loud . . . and annoying. I just wanted to sleep. I was so tired, and my body hurt so much. Wouldn't just a short rest be better than continuing on like this? Plodding from place to place in this awful, alien world.

I had a moment of clarity as I realized what was happening. I was almost dead!

I can't die here! What the hell was I doing? I will not *die here. I'm going to die in a motorcycle accident on the run from the cops on my twenty-seventh birthday! Not here. Not. Fucking. Here.*

I lifted the cookie with trembling fingers. Ones that were—and weren't—mine. I could hear Zeol's voice, faint and fading again.

Eat it, Loon! It will restore your health enough that you will survive!

"Restore . . . health?" I couldn't manage anything else. In my compromised state, I was having trouble understanding why Zeol was trying to help me. He'd been such an asshole just a moment ago. Was he trying to trick me? What would be the purpose if I was about to die, though? One final prank before I drop dead in a pile of piss and shit?

I heard a shuffle not far from me. Something was moving in the pitch-black void of the underground tunnel, but with my Darkvision ebbing in and out, I wasn't able to see. Was there a light? Was it stars?

I opened my mouth and felt drool dripping from my lips. *Come on! Just a little more!* I examined the pastry. *Fuck it. I'm going to die anyway.* I lifted the cookie, summoning all my might. *Almost there.*

I drooped, feeling my strength fail me, and the cookie tumbled out of my grasp. I watched it fall.

Oh . . .

A light burst to life in front of me, igniting in a fiery sphere. I couldn't react, but for the record, I totally wouldn't have winced anyway. There was a shape I couldn't make out because of the sudden application of intense illumination. But I felt—whatever it was—strike my face. I didn't go down, but I felt my jaw crumble as my face was hit again. Were my teeth shattered? Why didn't it hurt more? Why was it . . . sweet?

Just as I saw my health bar dip to negative ten, I felt a tingle in my mouth, and then my HP was rocketing upward and shimmering with golden light.

That had been too close for comfort!

My lifeline kept growing until it hit my maximum. But then it *kept* climbing. It soared higher and higher, everything past my original total health turning electric green, while below it was still gold.

"Wha?" I muttered. My teeth hadn't been broken, nor had my jaw. It had been the pastry. Someone had shoved it in my mouth and saved my life.

I instantly felt the curative energy pounding in my veins. It was uncomfortable, like tiny hammers striking my capillaries in a swarm. I could feel injuries inside my body begin to dissolve and muscles knit together. My bones creaked and groaned, and more of them than I was comfortable with snapped back into place with sharp stabs of miniature punishment. My body was working overtime to fix itself as quickly as possible, but goddammit, I didn't like the sensation. It was like the day I found out bones were wet.

I let my eyes adjust to the glow of a fire. Torchlight. My savior slowly shifted into view, and I stared numbly at them.

Stinky.

He was smirking, his trio of mouths looking like cruelly sliced deli ham.

"How . . . " I said. Why wasn't I able to communicate?

Oh.

My Stamina was *super* low again. Apparently, slogging along, trying to not die, while my health was flatlining was not great for it. It made me physically exhausted, but why the mental cloud? I checked my status screen. *Ah.* It showed that Fatigue I had grown up, hit puberty, and gotten itself a mustache.

Condition: Fatigued
Fatigue II
- *Abilities and Skills suffer -10% efficiency while under the Fatigue II condition effect.*

"Save the thank-yous and waterworks, orc," Stinky said. "You'll need all the moisture you got for whatever blood is left in that body. Gods, man. You look like fresh death."

"Fr . . . sh . . . " I started. "Fre—"

"What?" Stinky asked.

"Fresh . . . *to* death," I was able to manage. "I'm . . . fresh *to* . . . death."

Stinky just gave me a baffled look and shook his head.

"Why . . . help?" I breathed.

Stinky shrugged and shot me a dangerous grin that showcased all of his fangs. I would have shivered, but I needed the energy to keep my bones from falling out.

"I told you to wait up," he said. "We have a truce. I'm not letting some hole in the ground claim you before I can."

I managed a nod. I needed to rest, but this did not seem like the opportune time. Almost dying three times in less than twenty-four hours was apparently pretty fucking awful on your feel-goods. I was so tired that my *ears* hurt. I began to drift a little, staring right at Stinky.

Don't cut my throat . . . I thought. My eyes shifted, and I blinked slowly. Then I saw my health bar, and I could feel my eyes widen automatically.

- **Temporary Health +595**
- *Hit Point increase for [240] minutes.*
- *All conditions healed.*

815/220 Health Points

"What was in that cookie?" I wondered aloud quietly.

Then I passed the fuck out.

CHAPTER SEVENTEEN

NOT A HAPPY CAMPER

I stare into the wind and snow.

Far away, I see two shapes moving, playing, laughing as another shape, more distant, watches. Two boys, one a few years older than the other, hurling snowballs and squealing with glee. These boys are still young. The smaller of the two is red-faced, rushing in the thick white drifts to escape the missiles from the other child.

It's me, I think. *I am this boy.*

The third shape, a woman, watches on with a look of sad contentment on her face. She's Aunt Ella, but she looks like my mother. She looks like the mother from *Home Alone*. She's my mother, and she looks like Aunt Ella. Now she's my Uncle Luke warning us boys not to wander off too far. *The woods are dangerous*, he says.

I'm suddenly running. I am the boy racing away from the snowball. My short legs can hardly crest the depth of the cold snow, but I jump, and I fly out easily. Now I must only leap to escape the snowballs as they whirl past me in the frigid wind.

I am throwing snowballs at the boy running in the snow. At Gabriel. Uncle Luke yells to Gabe not to get too close to the trees! There are monsters in there!

I run along next to Gabriel as the other boy throws the snowballs, now trying to get him to stop. He's no longer trying to hit him with the clumps. He is arcing them to land in Gabriel's path to stop him from getting too close to the woods. Gabriel and I run forward, toward the trees.

"Stop!" I try to yell to Gabriel, but the wind carries my words away.

Aunt Ella screams suddenly, and I wheel back to see her face. My mother's face is a mask of pure terror, and the sight of it fills me with such a shuddering fear that I shield my eyes. Her jaw is hanging open to an unnatural level, and her eyes bulge as though she's being squeezed as she yells, seeing something ahead that I cannot. That Gabriel cannot.

It's coming.

I'm Gabriel, running toward the woods. I can't stop, my movement is too great, and the hill is too steep. I'm leaping right toward the woods and what I know to be a tremendous horror contained within. I want to stop. I feel the weight of dread settling against my heart and stomach as I enter the woods. I can't stop.

I see a shape ahead.

It's here.

I cannot see what it is, but I feel it. It's *wrong*. There's nothing else to describe it. Something so incongruent with my existence that I'm stabbed by genuine fright. Its back is to me.

"He's here, Gabriel," the form says, and then jerks to stare back at me. The face I see is awful, worse even than Uncle Luke's had been a moment ago when he was screaming. I can't bear it.

"He's *here!*" the form screams, and leaps at me in the snow.

My eyes fluttered open.

What the hell? I thought. *I haven't had a nightmare in a long time. That was awful.*

I thought about how I would have to try to get back to bed before my alarm went off, but then I realized I wasn't *in* my bed. I was on the cold, hard ground in the dim, and the last little bit of time came crashing back onto me like a dump truck filled with shitty realizations.

How long have I been asleep?

My body no longer hurt, but there was a dull pounding in my head that was super annoying, to say the least. It was dim, wherever I was, but my Darkvision didn't reactivate, so it had to be at a level that I could see *well enough*. I peered around.

I was in a similar chamber to the one I'd passed out in, but this one had a ceiling to it, so I knew it wasn't the same. The roof was still high but clearly visible and maybe fifty feet above, peppered with stalactites—or stalagmites; I was never sure which. There were two dark passages far to either side of me, and not far from my own position was Stinky's flickering torch, bathing the space in warm light. In an alcove directly ahead of me was an area that looked as though it had been a small camp. Even in such wan light, I could see the remnants of a little cookfire that had long grown cold, as well as an assortment of discarded tools.

I staggered to my feet.

Where is Stinky?

I supposed that I should probably find out his name. Even if he was an annoying son of a bitch, he *had* saved my life. Calling him Stinky seemed slightly less respectful, at least for now. Then there was the nature of Zeol. What in the ball-singeing blazes had been his game? Had he felt bad about pissing me off and tried to backpedal? I'd never realized that even gods could have such wishy-washy temperaments. I had always reserved my expectation of those sorts of behaviors for people like me. But I guess I'd never interacted with a deity before. Nor had I spent time thinking about the types of beings that would occupy a magical world built on a foundation of things that drove me bonkers.

I began to make my way toward the ancient ruins of the camp when a voice popped back into my head.

I'm very sorry about all of that, Loon.

Zeol.

"Yeah, what the hell, man?" I demanded, choosing to stare up at the ceiling, as that seemed . . . Well, it was still nothing but nonsense. But it was better than staring off into space, I supposed. Besides, maybe that's where he was looking at me from, and I wanted to make sure he didn't miss my pissed-off expression.

I'll get it out of the way, he said in my mind. His tone was cautious, as if he genuinely felt apologetic. However, it *could* have been manipulation. I'd read about abusers who did stuff like that—lost control and then apologized to regain trust so they could do it again. I wondered if this was some sociopathic tactic designed to keep me on the hook.

I did that to save your life.

Yep, totally manipulation.

"Just fuck off," I shouted into the sky. "I don't want any part of . . . whatever this is that you're trying to do to me! I've seen *13 Reasons Why*! I'm not an idiot. I know you're trying to get me under your thumb!"

There was a pause. I knew Zeol wouldn't get the reference, but I didn't care. I had no time for this. I had to figure out a way of getting out of this cave.

I understand and empathize with your feelings, he continued, sweeping past my challenge. ***But I will explain why I did what I did so that you might see a necessity behind my actions.***

I ignored him. Instead, I dropped my gaze and marched over to the camp, intending to salvage what I could from the remains. Who knew? Maybe there'd be something there that would help me. All the while, Zeol continued.

When you fell, initially, before you arrived, I felt I had to intervene. I'm only allowed to do that a few times per . . . well, not often. If I hadn't whisked you away, you'd have plummeted straight to the bottom.

"Well, I ended up doing that anyway," I grumbled, only half listening.

Yes, but had I not applied the various methods I did, you would have died when you landed.

He could keep talking to me. I didn't care. There was nothing he was going to say that would change my mind. If he wasn't careful, I'd go into a rage again and start smashing shit up. Or maybe that was what he wanted?

Then I paused. Hadn't the description for the Ability said that I could only do that once per day—at least at first? *Shit.* That meant that enough time had passed that a new day had started without me noticing, and I'd already shot my whole wad, flying off the handle at the dumbass god.

I picked up a piece of a broken trowel and shoved it into my pack. I did the same with a pair of tongs and a dust-encrusted ledger. I'd pawed through the leaves of the catalog momentarily and found that the first page offered only a string of scribbles indicating unknown values in different columns. Several pages had been ripped out of the binding, with some torn pieces still clinging to the fold.

Uninteresting.

After a little more perusal, I discovered that one of the flat stones surrounding the fire pit was actually a small wooden container the size of a shoebox. I eagerly opened it to find a few items within. There were three bottles—one of them empty—lying on their sides with faded hand-written labels on them. In a neat scrawl, it read: *Pepper's Hair Tonic*. I activated Analysis to discern if it was *really* what it claimed.

Pepper's Hair Tonic
- **Rarity: ???**
- **Item Class: ???**
- **Durability: ???**
- **Weight: ???**
- **Bonuses: ???**

I scowled as I read the description of the item out loud.

"*Pepper's Hair Tonic: To Obtain the Wave You So Desperately Crave!*"

The hell is this shit? I wondered. *It must be some fucking baller-ass Pert Plus–level scalp juice if I can't even learn its qualities!*

A dingy leather pouch was next to the bottles that clinked like loose change when I prodded it. I had to assume it contained some money, but then again, in a fantasy world, it could just as easily have been enchanted butt plugs.

Beneath the other objects, I was surprised to discover a folded pair of unusually pristine, soft sable gloves. I picked them up to examine them and put more man-hours into my identification trick.

Grenalyn's Gussying Gauntlets
- **Rarity:** Elusive
- **Item Class:** Enchanted Glove
- **Durability:** N/A
- **Weight:** 0.6 lbs.
- **Defense:** N/A
- **Bonuses:**
- +200% durability to any Two-Handed Weapon or Shield for [93] seconds
- +[0] Charges
- Grants invulnerability to any Two-Handed Weapon or Shield for [93] seconds once per day.

A pair of finely crafted gloves designed to boost the durability of any Two-Handed Weapon or Shield being wielded while donned. The allotted time outcome for efficiency is IWD Axis. The number of Charges is determined by outcome for efficiency of Two-Handed Weapon or Shield Skill +Intelligence quotient.

Huh. Not bad. At least if I ever picked up the Two-Handed Weapon Skill, that is. I wasn't sure what any of the "Axis" terminology was about, but I figured I'd try to find some information once it was more relevant. I stowed the gloves in my pocket for now, since I didn't want them to get dirty in the pack with all the muddy baubles I'd just procured from my dig site.

Next, I lifted the pouch, uncinching it and reaching inside. I removed several tarnished coins so obscured by grime and age that I had to use Analysis again to determine their value.

You have acquired Copper Coins [x6]
You have acquired Silver Coins [x2]
You have acquired Gold Coins [x1]

Well, would you look at that? I was already receiving a passive income down there in the world's sphincter. I stuffed the currency into my other coin purse and kept rooting around as Zeol continued to include me in his scheme.

I feel I must clarify for you, Loon. I fed you so that you would regain full health. I enraged you so you would survive the fall in conjunction with my previous Aegis. I placed the pastry conspicuously enough for you to notice and take so that you would either eat it—and have temporary gains—or as a last resort, should you fall low enough that you were still in danger.

I couldn't restrain myself from ignoring him any longer. I snapped my head up to the ceiling.

"Yeah, and the fucking potion of Odious Stupidity?!" I demanded. "Was that to help me in some way, too? Or is this all just after-the-fact damage control so you can keep pranking me and fucking around with my mind?"

The potion of Oratory Splendor was also necessary, Zeol said softly. *Without it, I wouldn't be able to talk to you now. It has the . . . humorous side effect of modulating your speech for a moment, but that is not its primary purpose. Still, it is a small price to pay to communicate outside the usual parameters.*

"Ooh," I began angrily, picking up a discarded shred of leather and depositing it into my pack. "Now I can talk to a god that likes to play mind games. So cool!"

I don't think you realize, Loon: you aren't just able to speak with me. *You're able to talk with anyone. For the next day, you will understand all native languages spoken around you. If you can listen for longer than a full minute, you will learn the basics of the language. Enough to begin gaining Ranks in it.*

"I didn't ask you to do any of that," I said. "If this was supposed to help me, why didn't you just tell me that from the jump and save me the trouble of being confused and angry?"

I didn't believe him, but I wanted to see what his excuse was.

I could *have explained the other things to you, but the Primal Rage required you to be unaware. You cannot activate it on your own—not yet, anyway. This would have been much easier if that were the case, but it was not. Take the mechanics of this world up with someone else, not with me.*

I had to trick you into becoming angry enough to ignite it. I chose not to tell you about the other buffs because I didn't want to risk you piecing together what I was trying to do and being unable to become enraged. Those other effects have time constraints, and I needed to inform you of my request and get you back onto the Primary Plane before they wore off. I couldn't speak plainly about any of that because, well, the voyeurs.

I didn't say anything. It *was* a good excuse, but that didn't matter. I didn't like people forcing me to do something against my will, no matter how pure they thought their intentions were. It removed my personal . . . agency, or whatever. People would treat you how you taught them to treat you, and if I didn't set boundaries with this soul-bonded super ghost, he'd just keep stretching his influence.

I won't bother you after this, Zeol continued. *Not unless I need to, I promise. I only ask that you retrieve the item I need. It is a stone figurine that—*

"You can go now," I said severely. I didn't want to hear Zeol's voice ever again, and I wasn't going to listen to it anymore.

All right, Zeol said, sounding defeated. *I understand. Just please consider—*

"I *said* you can go," I stated more firmly.

There was silence.

Jeez. Finally.

I spent several minutes looting the camp until I heard footsteps echoing off the cavern walls. I stiffened, looking for a weapon, but there wasn't anything within a handy distance. However, I *did* see something interesting. My eyes seemed to zero in on a pocket of shadow near the wall that looked like the perfect place to hide. It was about twenty feet away from me, but I was in a sitting position, and that didn't give me much time. However, without even really considering it too much, I acted. I quickly shifted forward and dove toward the spot, bringing myself into what I could only describe as a ninja roll. My chin and one of my legs were tucked to my chest, and I kept the other leg bent as I somersaulted a few times. In seconds, I was in the proper spot, and the flawless ease with which I'd performed the maneuver shocked me. Almost as if with muscle memory—though I'm not sure how—I'd whipped my cloak tight around me and felt as though I was truly hidden from view.

Holy shit! I'm so stealthy! This is fucking amazing!

Apparently, my Skill was semi-passive and required only *intention* to utilize it. That had to be part of the benefit of having such a beefed-up technique. My accidental advantages were really coming in as heavy hitters already. I pressed myself against the crook of the rock wall and glared at the passageway. Whoever was coming, I was ready for them.

My heart beat hard in my chest as I waited, wishing I'd thought to grab anything from my pack, even the broken trowel. Then I saw Stinky emerge with a torch and a strange look on his face. He stepped into the chamber and looked around, suddenly seeming concerned.

What's he so pissed about?

As he began to frantically jerk his head around, it suddenly made sense.

Oh, heh heh.

I'd realized with a start that he was looking for me.

Well, let's give him a warm welcome, shall we?

As Stinky moved through the room, waving his torch around, I quietly strafed along the wall, my arms pressed flat beneath the Trespasser's Veil. He moved near me, and I thought the jig was up until I spotted a lightless section to his left, and my body automatically responded. As he turned, I rolled forward again, moving to mirror him while staying out of his line of sight. He had no goddamn idea I was there! I was motherfucking Solid Snake!

Then I stood up, got very close to his ear, and whispered.

"About time you showed up," I said.

"FUCKIN' GODS!" Stinky wailed, and swiped the air behind him. If I hadn't been expecting it, he would have broken my nose with his elbow. Instead, I ducked, and his arm passed harmlessly overhead. I stepped back and stood back up to my full height in front of him. I was easily eight inches taller than him, but I felt a whole lot bigger from the way he recoiled.

I pointed to the shitty little firepit with a grin. "Want me to start breakfast?"

"You fuckin' . . . " Stinky began, but something was off. He didn't have the typical gusto I'd grown accustomed to in the last few hours.

"So, uh, yeah . . . " I said. "This is awkward now."

Stinky didn't respond. I noticed he kept looking behind him at the tunnel from which he'd emerged with a baffled expression.

Is something following him?

"What's up?" I asked, feeling my hackles rise. "And where'd you get that other torch?"

I knew that I had a bevy of extra health now, thanks to Zeol's meddling. If there was going to be a fight, this—unfortunately—would likely be the best time. Though I didn't know how much longer that would be the case. I quickly checked my status screen and found that I'd only been out for about an hour, as there were still just under two hundred minutes remaining on the HP buff. I also noticed that my Fatigue level had gone back down to one.

I suppose that's progress.

Stinky pointed behind him as I stood up.

"There is . . . something back there. I think . . . Well, I reckon it's a damn dungeon."

I grew cold. *There's no way . . .*

"What?" I asked, stepping past to look into the dark tunnel behind him. I activated Darkvision and found just another featureless passage. However, I noticed that it twisted to the left a way down.

"Where?" I demanded, turning back to Stinky. He just shrugged.

"Down there, you idiot," he said. "You've got better eyes than I do down here, orc. Use 'em."

I just rolled my eyes and turned back to the tunnel. I would need to investigate this to be sure. I set out at an accelerated pace—not quite a jog, but like one of those fast little hops like people do when they have to get to the toilet but don't want people to know they're panicking.

I moved down the passage and followed it to the left. There were no tributaries or offshoots that I could see, so I just kept surging along as it went. Left again, then right. The trail was beginning to lighten as I continued until, almost without warning, it opened up into a massive cavern.

I stared. The chamber was enormous. Its vast innards stretched hundreds of feet ahead of me and were almost the same in width. The ceiling there was so high that I almost couldn't see it, even with the light filling the space with a blue-green illumination. I was standing at the top of a long, stone staircase that swept down into a bridge over a murky pool of water that glowed green from the light beyond.

At the back of the cavern was a colossal structure that took up the whole section of the wall it was seemingly hewn from. It was an irregular, almost misshapen building with two large domed areas of different sizes and a pair of tall pillars with statue figures posted atop. At the head of the edifice, not far from the other side of the bridge, was a doorway pressed into the flesh of the structure and framed by an arch. Unrecognizable symbols were etched into the curvature and were the source of the glow. The light filling the chamber poured out of the archway's runes ominously.

As I took the lay of the land, I felt like my stomach had caved in on itself. I gulped.

This was the very same building that Zeol had shown me on the display, the one I'd made light of and felt hassled by the idea of having to pursue. The Forsaken Crypt of the Dreadnaught Lord.

"Fuck."

CHAPTER EIGHTEEN

DUNGEONS AND DUMMIES

"Do you think we can touch it?" I asked, staring into the depths of the water beneath the bridge.

Stinky and I had traversed halfway across the suspended stone walkway before stopping because he needed to eat and couldn't go any farther without restoring some of his Stamina. He had no rations, so I begrudgingly offered up some of my own. We'd been chewing in silence when I'd had the thought.

"Why the hell would you want to touch it?" Stinky asked, swallowing a bite of dried meat while giving the water a disapproving look.

"Well, if I smell *half* as bad as you do, I'm going to need a long soak and a *very* resilient bar of soap."

Stinky huffed and finished his food. Then he extended a grotesquely long red tongue and licked his fingers clean. I shuddered.

"What even *is* a matau, anyway?"

Stinky bristled and turned to continue cautiously walking along the bridge.

"Must be some kind of world-traveling orc to know that word," he said without looking back at me.

"Yep," I said. "Just your everyday orcish globetrotting explorer. Sampling the goods in different 'hoods."

I had to think about what he'd said, though. His words held the implication that he wasn't from around this neck of the woods, and so I had to wonder why he was there at all. Did he make the trek from some great distance just to join up with the Redmark? It seemed unlikely. I supposed there could be tons of reasons someone like him would wind up in the Kingdom of Arlo, working for an organization that opposed its central governing body. Maybe they had a super dope foreign-exchange program, and he got caught up in a skirmish during an art fair? I imagined Stinky as a doe-eyed student with an armful of study guides and a pair of glasses, gearing up for some good ol' fashioned *book learnin'.* The idea made me smile.

However, Stinky kept walking without responding, so I dropped it.

We crossed to the other side of the water. The air felt different there—more humid than the general dryness of the rest of the cave. It was off-putting, to say the least.

Stinky and I stared up at the dungeon. It was immense. The glowing archway was ten times my own height, and it was dwarfed by the size of the dungeon itself. The twin pillars were ahead of us, and now that I was closer, I could make out the shape of the statues at their zenith. Each was shaped to represent some humongous bird of prey with talons outstretched. The claws were spaced suspiciously as if they'd both been holding something that had been taken.

But who could climb up there and get whatever they were? These things are goddamn massive.

Zeol had indicated that there were a great many treasures to be gleaned from the dungeon, so I had to reason that maybe someone had picked the outside clean first.

"Well, Holy Sister's twat," Stinky said, staring up at the monstrosity. "A real, live dungeon."

I balked at that. Had he really never seen one before? I'd have assumed someone of his worldly nature would have stumbled onto at least one or two in his travels, but his response was puzzling.

"Are they . . . not common around here?" I asked.

Stinky spat on the ground and looked over in my direction.

"Got a lot of dungeons where you're from, orc?" He growled. "Must be nice. Here, in reality, though, we don't often get to bear witness to these sorts of things."

"Oh?" I said, hoping he'd elaborate. If dungeons were a rarity, it made me wonder if there'd been anyone around there in a long time. The firepit and tools had looked practically prehistoric, and the general scent of this place could best be described as "dank basement." Still, if that was the case, this whole underground area had probably been hidden for a long time. You know, just waiting for a smelly soldier and a dipshit orc to come stumbling into its hidey-hole.

"Aye," he said. He kept looking up at the dungeon with what I was beginning to realize was a sense of wonder.

"They are well-known to any of the shit-stick authorities of whatever land they happen to occupy. They keep the information as private as a Mercy Cleric's mistress—on account of them being oppressive and rotten assholes that deserve a boot knife to the head. They hate letting the smallfolk know about anything that could enrich or better their lives, so they hoard it for themselves and take their own parties out to dredge through them."

"The, uh, kings and stuff do shit like that?" I asked. Sounded pretty dickheaded, and if this were my world, I'd believe it outright. But this was some kind of geeked-out fantasy land. Weren't kings usually pretty noble in fairytales?

"Could they be doing it to keep people safe?"

From what I knew about dungeons from back home, they'd always be filled with super powerful monsters and usually some sort of boss creature at the deepest level. *Kingdom of Infinite Legends* forced the player to spend hours eradicating mobs from each designated dungeon, and there were hundreds of those. If this world was similar to those games—and I had no reason to believe it wasn't—having an autonomous body in charge of them to keep plucky young ducklings like myself out was probably a smart move.

"What are you, a fuckin' loyalist?" Stinky barked. He squinted at me with suspicion and put a hand to the blade at his side.

"Shit no," I said. "No gods, no kings, no tomatoes, sauce on the side—that's what I always say. I'm an independent contractor."

Stinky didn't take his eyes off me, nor his hand from his waist. I thought about how hilarious that was, considering I could just run off down the bridge and leave him there by himself, which would probably be the worst thing he could imagine right now.

"It ain't just kings," he said. "It goes on down from them to the viscounts and earls and even some o' the barons and landed knights—if their parcel of personal land is large enough. They aren't trying to protect anything except their own self-interest, orc. Every so often, some sanctimonious lord with an idea up his ass and pox in his brain will allow the common rabble to take a whack at one of the lairs under his bootheel, most often out of some bloated sense of noble honor. But once it starts turning profitable for the poor bastards, it's the same old story: they'll rip the rug out from beneath them and shut down the whole operation. Usually pilfer the best of the lot from anyone they can prove went inside, as well, and leave them with the scraps."

"Well, that's fucking rude," I said.

"You don't know fuckin' shit about rude," Stinky said. "They'll slice your bells out of your breeches if they think you're holding out on them."

I winced thinking about that and took a gander at the archway again. Stinky clearly had a chip on his shoulder about authority—probably about the only thing I could appreciate about him.

"So, do you think the . . . leadership in the Kingdom of Arlo knows about this one?"

Stinky didn't say anything; he just stared off into space as if his own words had unlocked a memory in need of urgent revisiting. He stayed like that for a few long seconds. I saw the moment he returned to his senses as his eyes refocused. Then he jerked his head up at me.

"What?"

"I was just wondering if the king or whatever is aware that this exists."

Stinky considered it.

"Might be. Though stands to reason there's likely a fair few of these smoldering shitholes that have yet to be unearthed, still. Lots of rumors round ancient people who lived at the bases of long-forgotten dungeons, back before Yanadin cracked the Sky Wall. They'd build whole damn cities around them, even. This one, though . . ."

He shook his head.

"It wasn't on our map, but when Fawn learns—" He cut himself off and glared at me.

"Fawn?" I asked. *What does Fawn want with dungeons? I thought she was fighting the Kingdom or rebelling against Russians . . . or something? Also: who the hell is Yanadin—and what's the Sky Wall?*

The casual way he'd referenced the terms made me think they were common knowledge, and now I knew I'd have to keep my ears peeled for *other* information so I didn't end up telling on myself for being a world-hopping stowaway.

This will be exhausting.

"Never mind," Stinky said. "Let's just find a route out of here and get you back to camp. You've got a date with the kissing-end of a crossbow, and I can't wait to see them riddle your twisted, green body with bolts."

I rolled my eyes.

"You think there's an exit around here?"

"Must be," Stinky said. "The way we came in goes directly to that slope, which, if you hadn't noticed, is impossible to scale unless you got a pair of fuckin' wings. Means if there's a gods-damned dungeon here, orc, then there's also another path to escape this cave."

I just nodded. I wasn't sure if that was true, but it was pretty sound reasoning. Zeol had wanted me to come there too. It seemed unlikely that he didn't expect me to leave. My only hesitation with that logic was that he could literally snatch me away in a puff of vapor. If he was lying about his intentions—and I was pretty sure that he was—he could wait for me to grab the object, scoop me up, and then leave me trapped after he'd taken it from me and tossed me back in.

A large part of me hoped that wasn't the case. But I had learned not to trust people whose motives were unclear. That went double for huge, sentient puppet faces who seemed to be walking a path of intense manipulation.

Stinky began moving around the landing, peering in the distance for any sign of another passage. It was hard to believe that this curmudgeonly wang-rod had rescued me not long before. I knew he wasn't super keen on being down there by himself, but I didn't realize it went *that* far. I cocked my head at him.

"Thanks for, uh, saving me, by the way," I said. Stinky looked back at me with a scowl.

"Fuck yourself, orc," he hissed. "I didn't want to have to drag your body back to the camp, so I shoved that little cake into your mouth to stop your peeps of torment. That's all."

"Sure," I said. "Whatever you say, *Stink*ompoop."

"Will you stop calling me that?!" he raged.

"Absolutely," I said. "Just as soon as you tell me your *real* name so I can figure out a way of turning it into an insult."

Stinky just stared at me.

Is he trying to intimidate me? Well, I got bad news for him, because I'm the most fearless motherfuckin' orc to ever skip down this particular dungeon bridge.

He didn't say anything for a long moment. When he finally did speak, his voice was almost imperceptibly quiet.

"Akiva."

"Huh," I said.

"What?" Stinky—er—Akiva hissed. He tightened the grip on the blade at his side as he stared menacingly into my eyes. "Something funny about my name, orc?"

I shrugged and let out a noncommittal noise.

"Actually, no," I admitted. I was being honest. I'd spent a long moment trying to figure out a way of morphing his name into something disparaging, but nothing was bubbling to the top of my esteemed noggin meat at this current juncture.

"Good," he said severely. I watched him relax a little, loosening the grip on his dagger. Was he relieved?

"Anyway, I'm Loon," I said. If we were going to be trapped down here, it would be better to get the bosom-buddy name exchange out of the way in case he'd already decided on a nickname for me that was as annoying to hear as I'm sure "Stinky" was for him.

"I don't care, orc," he said.

"Man," I said. "Fuck you, you flea-bitten taint."

He looked like he was about to respond, but something caught his attention. He suddenly scowled, squinting at a point behind me. I wheeled, only to see that . . . *nothing at all* was racing at us from the direction of the dungeon.

"We got trouble?" I asked, shifting my stance in case something big and ugly came barreling down on us.

Akiva—who I'd decided was still going to be Stinky—shook his head and then pointed to the rightmost pillar. I peered out suspiciously but couldn't discern what had grabbed the matau's ire.

"It's . . . " he started, then his voice took on an air of almost excitement, " . . . a fuckin' *chest!*"

I gave him a quick look, but Stinky didn't wait for it to register for me. He took off at a sprint toward the pillar, and I had to kick it into high gear to catch up with him. I hopped over a few pieces of rubble, almost wiping out as my foot dragged a little *too* close in my leap. Stinky was far ahead of me already.

Holy balls, he's fast!

It took less than a few seconds to reach the spot he'd been racing to, and now I could see it: a three-foot-tall rectangular treasure chest. As I slid to a stop, I activated my Analysis on the thing, bringing up its details.

Antediluvian Dungeon Chest
- **Rarity: Fabled**
- **Item Class: Chest**
- **Durability: ???**
- **Bonuses: ???**

An ancient crate designed with one purpose in mind—to store items of indeterminate value! It's a chest! Maybe it holds a wondrous dragon egg?! Perhaps it's filled with ladies' underwear?! You won't know unless you open it!

This message was a return to the previous snark I'd come to expect from whatever was in charge of populating these bits of information but amplified a ton. I rolled my eyes at the description and turned to Stinky.

"Is this for real?"

Stinky scoffed.

"Why the hell wouldn't it be? Dungeons hold a fuckin' charlatan's pantry of treasures—some simple and some gods-damned peachy-grand. This could be trapped, so mind your filthy limbs if you like having 'em around."

I *was* indeed quite fond of my arms and legs. Well, at least, what I'd seen so far from the new ones. His advice seemed wise, so I took a step back, careful to avoid any potential dismembering. That's when I noticed a boot.

"The hell?" I said, sidestepping to get a better look. It was directly behind the wooden container, and as I moved, I could see it wasn't just *one* boot. There were two. Then I swallowed a lump in my throat as I realized they were attached to a pair of legs.

"Shit!" I shouted, and leaped back. Stinky drew his dagger.

"It's a body!"

Stinky scowled at me but cautiously stepped around to the other side. He relaxed when he saw what I was looking at.

It was a corpse, all right. Well, *skeleton* might have been more accurate. It looked like it had died after going HAM on diet pills and coconut water.

The creature was wearing what appeared to be dingy leather armor and a dented helmet, in addition to the aforementioned boots. He looked human, though it was hard to say for sure—fantasy world and all. However, what I couldn't take my eyes off of was his leathery, mummified flesh. It was shrunken and tight, stretched over his features like filmy cobwebs rather than skin. Where there should have been eyes were just sunken, empty sockets, and a dry, bushy beard had grown out from his face.

"That's definitely a fire hazard," I said. Though, secretly, I wished that I'd been blessed with the same overabundance of face pubes this guy had.

I noticed that resting on the ground nearby was an ancient wooden club. It was chipped and scobbed up pretty bad, and the handle even had a large section missing out of it. I'd have grabbed it if I thought it would last longer than a single swing, but I didn't bother messing with it for the moment.

Stinky nudged the body with his foot, and I considered it must not have been a zombie or other nightmare undead creature, since it didn't immediately spring up, trying to eat brains.

At least Stinky would be safe there, I thought with a chuckle.

My companion crouched, using his knife to push apart the corpse's folded limbs. I watched as several items tumbled out from the stiff's literal death grip: a small, opaque bottle covered in grime, a folded piece of parchment, and . . .

I quickly snatched the third item up from the stone before Stinky could do the same.

"What the hell, orc?"

"You snooze, you lose, slowpoke," I said, lifting the object up to examine it. I breathed.

"Oh, *damn.*"

Enchanted Haladie
- **Rarity: Uncommon [Exotic]**
- **Item Class: Throwing Weapon**
- **Durability: 100/150**
- **Weight: 1.0 lbs.**
- **Damage: 25—32 Piercing / 25—30 Slashing**
- **Bonuses:**
- *+1 versus Suskin*
- *???*

A weapon discovered on a corpse! Look at you go, grave robber, you! This double-bladed throwing dagger is the perfect accessory for those who want to do a bit of wet work from a distance! You'll look very intimidating, hurling this bad boy from the shadows. You know, where no one can see how scared you are!

THIS ITEM CAN BE UPGRADED WITH ADDITIONAL ENCHANTMENTS.

"Whoa!" I said, looking it over and feeling its weight. "Stinky, check this shit out."

I swiped the air a few times with the blade and noticed that it seemed very well balanced despite its heft. The description had stated it was for tossing but could do slashing damage as well, and based on the size of the blades—which were on either end of the handle and roughly eight inches each—it wouldn't be a bad idea to bet on in a close-quarters tussle, either. The cruel-looking double-bladed weapon had an unknown quality as well that I assumed I couldn't see until I raised my Analysis—or maybe until I used it. Who knew? Guess I'd find out sooner or later. Either way, it was a wicked blade that I had no doubt would shoot me up the ladder of "ultimate, army-leveling badass."

"Who's Suskin?" I said, looking at the matau.

"Who gives a shit?" Stinky said. I noticed he was reading the note, so I stuffed the haladie into my waistband and raised my eyes to him.

"Anything good? Was he writing down his favorite stir-fry recipe?"

Stinky ignored me and finished reading. Then he released the note, letting it flutter to the ground. He grabbed the bottle from the ground with a grunt and then moved closer and began to wrestle with something on the corpse's neck. With his blade, I watched as he withdrew a chain from around the dead man's neck. Once it was out, I could see that clinging to the end of the necklace was a large metal key. It had a ring at the top and several battered-looking teeth that seemed as though they'd repeatedly been drunkenly stabbed into the general direction of a lock without success. I'd have bet you fifteen McChickens that this was designed to open the chest.

I bent down and scooped up the paper to see if I could read it over for myself. I didn't expect to understand it, since it was likely in some magical tongue or shitty wizard cuneiform or something. So, when I observed them, I was happily surprised to find that I *could*, in fact, understand the words on the page. Well, sort of.

I noticed immediately that the paper was the very same type as the ledger I'd found and was likely one of the pages torn out of the book. The script was like drunk chicken scratch, and at first, looking at it, I thought I was suffering from a minor stroke. Then I realized that my brain was still working perfectly fine, and it was the author of this brilliant bit of poetry that had likely observed a significant head injury shortly before penning it.

> *Fer them that finds this. I Spose you ken see I made it to the dunjen, and this is Ware I'll rest. I cuddent get the Dore open on akount of Delbris taken my last esper jool. I'm Sure he's round Here sumware. Stawkin about like sum kinda Serpint. If you find me, who ever you are, Consider this my Last weel and testment. You can have evrythin Inside the chest. I mite save the poshun of strenth in Case I need it. I feer I'm dun for, tho, and soon the rats and other dark spon of this kave will feest on my flesh. I wish I cudd see my famly agen just one more time. My dotter Erisa. My mum. To you that is reedin this letter: Tell my brother Yarm that I hope He don't Mary that girl Klyapee. She's Bad bizniz. Perin, I am on my way to see you, my dere. Wait fer me at the Ravens feeld.*
>
> *Luv, Berg*

"Well, that was depressing," I said.

It had taken me a moment to figure out some of the words based on the terrible spelling errors and garish disregard for punctuation etiquette. Still, I thought I understood most of it. However, I couldn't help but find it sadly funny that he'd ended the note by signing off with *love, Berg*.

Godspeed, Berg.

One passage in the note made me pause, though. It was poorly put together, but he'd definitely mentioned something called an "esper jewel." Wouldn't you know it? I was something of an Esper collector, myself. Something told me that I was about to find out exactly why people wanted to bash my head in over them.

I heard a *click*, and then a deeper *thunk*, like something heavy sliding into place. I looked over to see that Stinky had placed the key in the chest, and it had unlocked. He lifted the lid with a creak and let it fall open. Then he froze, his eyes growing wide at whatever was inside. He wheeled around and raised his blade, staring back at the bridge.

"What is it?!" I demanded, but he didn't respond. The heavier sound had definitely done something other than open the chest. *But what?*

"Stink—er—Akiva! What is it? What the hell are you staring at?!"

Something had shaken him, and it wasn't because he didn't have a night light this time. The warrior cast an eye to me and then quickly shot a glance to the inside of the chest. I approached and looked inside. It was empty.

Well, not totally. Down at the bottom, face-up, there was another note, written on the same paper and in the same shaky penmanship and bad spelling the previous one had had.

Fuck you Delbris you dum Sun of a Hore! Time to die!

"The hell kind of—"
SPLASH!
SPLASH!
SPLASH! SPLASH! SPLASH!
I, too, pivoted as I heard the awful cacophony of wet sloshing. It was coming from the pool beneath the bridge. I focused my eyes and watched as dozens of shapes flew out of the water, but I didn't understand what I was looking at. It seemed like a bunch of giant . . . eggs had just reverse-cannonballed out of the murky depths and onto the stone walkway of the bridge.
"Jesus Christ, what are—"
SPLASH! SPLASH! SPLASH!
Even more egg-shaped monstrosities did their water acrobatics out of the pond and landed with a splat. These things had to be at least two feet tall and were an off-white color with a disgustingly pink hue. Then they turned, and I gaped, my jaw practically hitting my knees. They had bulging, red eyes and gigantic mouths that hung open, and . . . were they fucking grinning?! They had rows of razor-sharp teeth that had to each be three inches long.
"What the fuck?! They look like goddamned crack-house Pokemon!"
I looked over at Stinky, but his eyes were glazed over.
Is he casting a fucking Spell? He better be!
Then his focus snapped back to attention, and he looked over at me.
"Possessed Roe. Dungeon Spawn. Level One Embryonic Aberrations."
"You've seen these before?!"
He snarled.
"No, you fuckin' warthog! I have the Identify Monster Ability!"
Oh. That made sense. But, also: why the hell didn't I have that Ability?!
"Are they friendly?!" I called, attempting to dig into my waistband for the enchanted haladie.
"What the fuck do you think, orc?!" he screamed back and raised his blade up.
" . . . maybe?!" I shouted.
"Get ready to fuckin' fight!"
I looked around the cavern, hoping desperately to suddenly spot some avenue or pathway of escape we'd missed, but there was none.
Fighting it is.

CHAPTER NINETEEN

BEDEVILED EGGS

I didn't like the look of these things at *all*. I realized I was a lot more anxious about the little round nuggets than anything else I'd encountered so far, because they were the first non-humanoid enemies I'd had to face. Unless you counted my general bewilderment at this whole new ordeal of being trapped in a nightmare world. Then they were the second.

"They are low level, but they swarm—apparently," Stinky said.

"Great!" I shouted. "Good to know that they're just going to overwhelm us—not kill us outright."

That was when the mob of monsters advanced. They leaped forward, springing along like flesh-eating volleyballs. My pulse quickened.

"They *hop!*" I cried in a horrified bellow.

Why is that somehow worse *than anything else?*

The eggs came at us en masse, and I was finally able to wrest the object from my waistband. But something was off—it felt too light. I looked down at my hands, confused, but then realized I was holding the paper party hat from Fiesta de Bathwater that I'd forgotten to get rid of. Something about the absurdity of it made me want to wear it.

Am I brain-damaged?

"Screw it," I said and stretched it back over my dome, and grabbed the *actual* weapon. I raised the haladie in my right fist and shifted the party hat to keep it on straight with my left. I must have triggered something, though, because suddenly there was a whoosh inside my head and a notification popped up.

Equipped Enchanted Festival Cap
Enchanted Festival Cap
- **Rarity: ???**

- Item Class: ???
- Durability: ???
- Weight: ???
- Bonuses:
- *Slimy*

This is an item created by a god out of poor-quality materials. That's okay, though, because it works as intended! Grants SLIMY!

Are you kidding me? Slimy?! What kind of description is that?

It was annoying, but I didn't have time to think about that right now. I was boiling again like I was sweating through my layer of not-very-protective clothing.

The first wave of possessed roe reached us then. Dagger maws open, they sprang their attack, chittering the whole time like demonic parakeets. Roaring, I slashed down with the haladie as the first one got within range. I watched the blade sing through its flesh, tearing open a gash nearly as wide as its mouth as I punched with my left fist. I connected hard, and the creature screeched, pus-colored blood—or maybe it *was* pus—streaming out as it bounced right off of my fucking fist with a rubbery-sounding *PING*. The egg shot off of my knuckles like an actual dodgeball, smashing against the cavern wall dozens of feet away.

"Fuck ye—"

WHAM!

I reeled as another of the creatures collided with my face, sending me backpedaling a few steps and disorienting me. It had bounced away from the strike, looking as confused as I was as it sailed through the air and landed back in the pool of water. A third creature was bounding after me now, shrieking angrily as it shot forward, baring its monstrous mandibles. I stuck my haladie out like a spear, timing it perfectly as the roe struck right at the point and . . . *SLIRK*! It stopped moving as the eight-inch blade pierced it right between its googly, red eyes. I had to whip the weapon a little to dislodge the creature, but it flew right off and landed on the stone floor with a wet *plop*.

I'm fucking doing it, I thought, scanning for my next enemy. *I'm kicking their gumball asses!*

"Let's fucking *go!*" I cheered.

A trio of the egg creatures barreled down on me from the right, and I slid out of the way as they launched. I stepped on the discarded club I'd seen earlier and almost toppled over. I grimaced at its quality but decided it might do for handling three of these suckers at once. I placed the haladie in my teeth and scooped up the stick. Then I cocked it over my shoulder like a baseball bat. The eggs bounced at me, and I gripped the handle tightly with both hands. Then I swung for the fences.

CRACK!

The club snapped in two before I even connected with the beasts. Apparently, *movement* was enough to shatter the pathetic excuse for a weapon into uselessness. The top half went spinning away into the distance, so I just hucked the handle at the monsters, but all three hit me at once. I staggered.

Congratulations! You have gained a new Skill!
Two-Handed Weapons (F-Rank Level 1)

Well, at least I have that going for me. I should have put those goddamned gloves on.

I noticed that, much like in Fawn's tent, when I was in the thick of some oh-shit, the notifications tended to minimize immediately. Thankfully, my obviously shitty luck hadn't morphed that particular aspect of this world.

"Zeol, you son of a bitch!" I yelled and darted away again as the eggs bounced toward me again.

BAM!

I hit the ground hard, smacking the side of my head against the stone and seeing stars. I glanced up through my daze and saw I'd tripped over Berg the Body's stupid legs.

"Berg, you dick!" I screamed in rage, and struggled to stand. That was when the trio got me, smashing into my side and back with all their force.

Fuck, fuck, fuck! They're gonna eat me!

I slashed at the air blindly, trying to protect my face from their huge teeth, all the while getting dribbled like a basketball at pee-wee practice. It hurt, but in a *bashing, smashing* kind of way. They weren't biting me. I was drenched with sweat now, the ground slick with my body's lubrication, and it was starting to look like snot or drool. But I didn't care—I had to get up. I couldn't quite reach them with the haladie, as they were striking me entirely at random, and with each hit, my body slammed back against the ground, throwing off my swings.

Critical Damage Incurred!
- *Multiplication bonus x3!*

"Arggh! Jesus-fucking-shit!" I bellowed.

They didn't hurt too much, but I had a feeling part of their charm was wearing you down with the ball-busting maneuvers. Fortunately, I had a treasure trove of extra HP, thanks to Zeol's magical Scooby Snack, and these little *ho*-vums hadn't even scratched the surface. I tried to roll away as I felt two of them bounce up, trying to smash me beneath their springy bodies. As I did, I bumped into Berg's corpse. I watched as the downward trajectory of one of the returning eggs shifted, and rather than landing on me again, it smashed directly into the smooth metal of the dead man's helmet.

PING!

The possessed roe was suddenly flying in a high arc, clearing nearly fifty feet upward as it soared through the air and smashed against one of the dungeon's pillars.

Even *my* thick skull was making connections right then and there. Still pummeled by two eggs, I crawled forward until I was right next to Berg's shrunken skull. I wrenched the helmet up and heard a *crack* as I snapped the dead bastard's fragile neck bone, and my motion sent his skull flying into the dim light beyond the glow of the dungeon's archway. I dropped my fist into the well of the helmet, reared back, and threw a wild haymaker as gravity returned the roes to me.

PWA-PING!

I hit one, sweeping it right into the other, and was just able to catch their looks of terror as they spiraled away from me into the distance.

"YES!" I cheered. "Fuck you, eggs! Fuck you!"

Congratulations! You have gained a new Skill!
Improvised Weapons (F-Rank Level 1)

I clambered up and, now armed with my new metallic boxing glove, sought out my next opponent. Two more egg-boys struck, one going for the direct hit, the other disappearing to my left. I smacked the first with my helmet-fist, sending him off on his merry journey into the distance. I wheeled, haladie out, looking for the second one, and caught another mouthful of roe as it bopped me in the gob. I stumbled but put my duke up as it tried to do that again.

"Not today, eggs Bene-bitch!"

It hit me in the face again.

Shit! They were too hard to predict, as their bodies were so featureless, I couldn't see which direction they were actually going to move in. I'd need a higher Insight or Detect Creature's Bullshit or something. Five more eggs came bounding toward me, and I hissed out a breath. I couldn't tell if these were new ones or returning members of Camp Helmet Punch. I heard the splashing sound that indicated more of these hoes were emerging from the pool.

Where the hell are these guys coming from?!

I punched, stabbed, and even kicked a little, dispersing the crowd before me. After blocking another attack, I also gained the Improvised Shield Skill, which was awesome. I was surprised none of them had used their oversized chompers yet to take a bite out of me. What was the point of all them teeth if you weren't going to use them?

Then I caught sight of Stinky and realized why.

The matau soldier was struggling. There were a bunch of bloody-yellow carcasses around him that he'd clearly been able to stab into kingdom come, but that wasn't the issue. The problem was that he had five or six of the possessed roes *stuck* to his body, weighing him down and seemingly causing a whole mess of pain. Another dozen surrounded him, leaping in his general direction. Stinky roared in agony, still attempting to strike out at the beasts with his dagger, but I could see he was losing steam.

Uh-oh. That's not good.

I watched as another egg sprang out of the water, spotted Stinky, and ping-ponged its happy ass right toward him. It bounced high and landed directly on his right forearm. It stuck like an adhesive. Now that it was nestled, I saw it open its wide mouth and *bite*.

Stinky cried out, trying to shake the beast off of him, but it was fused there solidly, digging into his skin with its fangs like a lamprey eel. The matau looked over at me, his grimace losing its deep scowl as I could see fear flooding into his face.

It dawned on me. They were sticking to Stinky but not to me. They didn't bite unless they were attached to the body. I hadn't stopped sweating, but this didn't seem like normal perspiration . . .

Rather than a lightbulb going off over my head, this was a goddamned one-thousand-watt *flood lamp*.

"I'm *SLIMY!*" I shouted. I would have kissed Zeol on his open wooden mouth if, you know, he hadn't been the entire reason I was currently there—or at least I suspected very strongly.

There'd been a bunch of notifications that had been minimized during this encounter. Still, I caught one as it flashed up before banishing itself to its waiting badge:

Congratulations! You've raised a Skill!
Insight has advanced to F-Rank Level 7!

"Good for you, orc!" Stinky yelled. He slashed at another egg and killed it, but it was quickly replaced by one of its siblings. The matau released a tremendous howl of pain as it latched on to him. It seemed like more and more of the creatures were gathering around the artist formerly known as Akiva, having decided he was an easier target than me and wanting to introduce him to the inner workings of their digestive systems.

Seeing his odds, I concluded that it would be a lot easier for me to get away while they were distracted. Considering I had the Traveler's Cloak—and my now insanely high sneak—I could probably slip away pretty quickly and hide until these things stopped paying attention to me.

But seeing the look of fear in his normally angry eyes, no matter how insufferably exhausting he was, I knew I had to try to even the odds. I sighed.

I'm definitely going to regret having this moment of weakness.

I raced forward, my steps light, and snuck up behind one of the stragglers facing away from me.

It doesn't even know I'm here.

Score one for stealthy shenanigans! Not that they'd serve me super well in the larger situation, but, hey: every little bit helps.

PING!

I punted that fucking egg like I was aiming for a field goal that owed me money.

Then I got to work. I found that skirting along the outside, I could crunch, kick, or stab these sticky little assholes without them noticing before it was too late. My high stealth was coming in clutch. I picked off a few of the pack before one of the eggs in the carton cluster got wise to me. It turned and released its godawful peal, which alerted several others in the vicinity.

It's clobbering time!

I smashed the nearest monster with ol' reliable and jammed my double-bladed death dealer into the top of another. The horde descended on me, and I smiled, having thought of a brilliant one-liner. I crouched forward, goading one of the eggs into leaping at my lowered form. Then I sprang up with my helmet fist just as it started to fall toward me.

PING!

"Sunnyside UPPERCUT!" I bellowed as the creature flew off.

Hell, yeah! I'm a goddamn superhero now! This is the best day of my life!

I thought that, abstractly, in all of existence, the one unifying feature all humanity shared was the idea that *everyone* dreamed of one day whooping someone's ass while firing off a witty comeback. This was my moment.

Five roe surrounded me, noisily attempting to attack, and I barked out a laugh.

"I like my eggs scrambled, thanks!" I tried to say, but instead, it came out as "I like—OOF!" as one of the cholesterol-laden dummies directed a rattling blow to my chest.

Forget it. I had my fifteen minutes of wit. Time to stop screwing around!

PING! PING! SLIRK! PING!

I cleaved and punched through the mass of chittering orbs, making my way toward Stinky. My limbs were slick with . . . slime, I guess, but it didn't slow me down. I was an egg-punting, body-stabbing, ball-battering engine, and I wasn't stopping 'til I made it to the station.

There were around fifty roe on the platform now, and every so often, another group would leap from the pond.

I've gotta figure out how to get rid of them! This is insane! I felt like I'd fallen into the *Toy Story* claw machine.

I finally reached Stinky, who now looked like the world's grossest grape bunch. I could still see his face, but his body was completely submerged in the pinkish mass. So, I started jabbing and smashing all over again, trying to get them off of him.

"Why the hell aren't they attacking you?!" Stinky screamed through the space between two roe attached to his chest. Another egg bounced off my head at that moment, and I stumbled. Fortunately, I was holding on to one of the creatures connected to my Fruit of the Loom friend there, and I maintained my balance.

"*Clearly,* they are!" I yelled back. "Just shut up for a second. I'm trying to help you!"

"They're biting the piss out of me, orc!" He yelled. "And taking pieces of flesh with them when they go! It's fuckin'— ARGGH!"

I'd just ripped one of them off a spot on his arm.

"I'm doing my best!" I said. "But this isn't easy!"

"What the hell is on your damned head?!" Stinky screamed.

"Is now *really* the time to ask me about my fashion choices?!"

The party hat was my single greatest ally right now, and I wasn't taking notes on my outfit considering how well it was keeping me aloft in this confrontation.

Respect the drip, Stinky.

But thinking about it gave me an idea.

It was a fucking terrible one, so I hoped it worked.

I had seen an episode of *Baywatch* as a kid. You know, the show about hard-bodied supermodels who had taken jobs as lifeguards on tourist beaches instead of becoming actors or trophy spouses? There was a scene where one of the characters—David Hasselhoff, maybe—was rescuing a woman in turbulent waters and was forced to use the rescuee's body as a shield against obstacles and felt all bad about it afterward or whatever. The idea was that the person doing the saving had to stay unhurt because they had the best chance of survival, and sacrificing their own safety would doom them both.

Well, in the brilliant strategy I was about to enact, I would do the *exact opposite* of that.

I punched the egg clinging onto the top of Stinky's head, sending it flying away with some of his flesh in its clenched jaws. I shook the helmet off of my hand, stuffed my haladie between my teeth, and grabbed the festival cap from my noggin. Then I stretched it over Stinky's temporarily bare head and leaped backward.

It only took a moment for it to take effect. The eggs began to release with loud, wet suction sounds, tumbling from his body like a cascade of rubbery pearls. That was enough to free him, and Stinky immediately started slicing a path for himself.

I was on the ground, so I rolled, ripping my weapon out of my mouth and stabbing up as one of the possessed roe bounced down on me. I speared it and whipped it away from me to reclaim my haladie from its body, and shot to my feet.

Stinky was near me now, screaming ferociously as he cut down everything that got near him. Anything that got by his attacks bounced off, but that didn't seem to be slowing him down much at the moment. He looked goddamn hysterical, wearing the vibrant paper cone on his head, especially in combination with his rough-and-tumble drakeling armor. I had to imagine I had looked even more ridiculous, based on my general size and race.

I could see that everywhere Stinky's flesh was exposed, he had large gashes, bite marks, or missing patches of flesh. He looked like the underside of a mushroom.

Ew.

One of the creatures finally got by my own defenses, crashing against me, and I felt intense pain as it latched on to my arm.

"FUCK!" I screamed, and stabbed the creature through its face. It released and fell, but most of these stupid monsters were now realizing that whoever *didn't* have the party hat was fair game for a bit of bounce and bite" and started advancing on me.

"We've gotta close and lock the chest!" Stinky screamed, starting to sprint back toward the pillars.

"What?!"

"The *fuckin'* chest!" he shouted as he raced past me. "It's what's controlling the flow of these bastards!"

I remembered the heavy *thunk* when he'd turned the key in the crate, and felt stupid for not realizing it sooner.

It has to be some sort of mechanism designed to release the eggs at those intervals. But can it be shut off now that it's been activated?

Guess we were going to learn tonight.

I spotted Berg's helmet not far from where I was and dove toward it as several eggs shot after me. I snatched it up and placed it back on my fist, standing tall before the monsters.

"Time to kickstart season two of *Bouncy Bitch Beatdown*," I exclaimed, brandishing my weapons.

"What?!" Stinky called from about thirty feet away.

"Shit!" I shouted, punching one of the roe and racing forward. "I should have said *Supermarket Sweepkick*!"

"What the fuck are you talking about?!" Stinky demanded. He was currently trying to deal with a new cluster of eggs barring his arrival to the chest.

"Ugh, *nothing*!" I shouted back, wrenching my blade out of the body of another monster. They weren't hard to dispatch, and usually, one good stab rendered them deader than the visiting room at an old folks' home. Their real danger was how numerous they were—as Stinky had indicated before the fight began. I slowly made my way through their ranks to get back to the treasure box. Still, each time I sent one flying or killed them, it was like they were immediately replaced by another, equally annoying duplicate.

I made an opening and went for it, but my heart dropped as I felt one hit me from behind and tuck into my obviously tasty back meat. Before I could shout my disapproval, a second and then a *third* joined in on the fun.

This was not the foursome I asked Santa for!

I couldn't do anything about the ones clinging to my sirloin area, but my health had still barely been touched. So, I made a break for it, galloping directly toward Stinky. Together we were able to cut down or send flying most of the eggs blocking our path to the chest, but when we reached it, several more hit me from the rear and I stumbled forward. I winced as more teeth joined the pincher parade on my orc flesh.

Stinky reached the box first and ran around the back to close the lid. Apparently, it was much heavier this go-around, as he couldn't seem to get it to budge more than a few inches.

I was preparing to help when another egg hit me in the back of the arm and I released a growl of anger and pain.

"I'm getting sick and tired of dealing with this bullshit!" I shouted, whirling so that my back was to the chest. I froze.

"Uh, Stinky," I said, looking back the way we'd just come. The matau was still busying himself with trying to lift the chest's open lid, so I couldn't see him from where I was.

"What?!" he shouted. "I'm trying to . . . Oh."

He'd noticed.

I gulped as I stared out at the landscape before us. From the edge of the pond and stretching almost to where we were now was a *sea* of hopping forms. There were at least a hundred possessed roe skipping toward us now that they had a single point to target. Other than a few outliers, most of this massive horde was only about fifty feet from us. It was a very bleak sight.

"Usually, in times like these, people say, *It's been nice knowing you*," I stated, not dragging my eyes away from the scene. "But it hasn't been. Since the moment I met you, Stinky, shit has straight-up *sucked*."

"Won't get any arguments from me, orc," Stinky said, but his voice sounded resigned like he was squaring off against a sure defeat.

"Let's face it," I said. "Even if we shut this thing off, we'd still have to kill all these guys."

Stinky spat on the ground.

"My fuckin' Stamina is low, I'm covered in wounds, and I don't have much strength left in me to keep fighting."

Strength . . .

My breath caught in my throat. *Berg's Strength potion! He'd mentioned it in the note, and maybe Stinky could use it to close the lid?*

I turned to ask the soldier about the bottle he'd grabbed, but that's when I saw something. At first, I thought it might be a symbol of a nobleman's house emblazoned on the outside of the chest next to the locking mechanism. Then I noticed the mushroom cloud.

Is that . . .

The little emblem shifted, rotating to the right, and I zeroed in on the key still in the lock.

My Sabotage Ability! It was trying to give me a hint! If that was the case, then this likely wasn't the doom I'd thought it was. Unless I utterly misunderstood the Ability's purpose.

Here goes nothing!

Without another word, I crouched low and grabbed the handle of the key. Turning left would lock the chest and potentially freeze up whatever was below the water, pooping out these vicious monsters. However, when I tried to turn it back while it was open?

I tried.

It didn't budge.

I looked back at the Sabotage emblem, which was fading, and shrugged. Then I cranked it to the right even farther than it already was. There was a little resistance, but it wasn't the same unyielding barrier that turning left had offered. A split second later, it moved, and I dropped it into place. There was another resounding *thunk* like before, except now I also heard—or rather *felt*—a low rumble beneath my feet.

"Orc!" Stinky screamed, looking up at me from his position. "What did you do?"

"Silly shit!" I shouted as the rumble became a roar, filling the entire cavern with its tremendous volume.

The eggs came to an abrupt stop as the entire place began to shake beneath our feet. Suddenly, the pool far in the distance started to bubble as though it were boiling. It gurgled loudly, and the noise combined with the reverberation of the cave created a soundscape of true, abject chaos. A symphony of destruction, if you will. However, I didn't have time to think about Megadeth at the moment. Shit was getting *wild*.

To my horror, more eggs began to pop out of the water at a rapid rate, far outpacing the previous installments. What was worse is they were spitting from the pool at a more incredible velocity as well, arcing upward of thirty or forty feet. Some of them crashed amongst their brethren with reckless abandon, scattering the crowd of possessed roe like bowling pins. Others fired out of the water and hit the walls of the cavern, ricocheting like bullets in an action movie—except these missiles made the ridiculous, rubbery *PING* as they smacked against the rock.

"I think I broke their mommy!" I yelled, dodging as one of the egg monsters flew directly at me from the pool.

"You've killed us, you fuckin' idiot!" Stinky roared.

The water beneath the bridge began to swell, and at first, I couldn't tell what was happening. A massive white-pink form began to rise up from beneath the roiling surface, and I couldn't find the necessary mechanism in my body to take a breath. It looked like a giant version of the roe was trying to wrench its way out of the pool!

"Oh, fu—" I started to yell, but I was struck in the chest by another egg that had rebounded. It hit me with enough force to knock me backward, and I fell hard. However, to my surprise, I sprang back up almost instantly. Realization hit me. The biting bastards still gnawing into my back had acted like a trampoline, launching me to my feet with their elasticity.

The form in the water was visible now, and to my shock, I saw that it was *not* a mother egg come to join her babies. It was a gigantic mass of the possessed roe. Apparently, whatever I'd done had kicked their production into overdrive. So much so that they had all been released—or whatever—at once. Now they were jammed into the exit, unable to go anywhere like some humongous rat king made of sticky pearls.

It was still big, though, and even the section squeezing out of the opening had grown taller than the level of the bridge. As it continued to rise like a disgusting, infected bun in the oven, some pieces broke away, firing off with enough inertia to crack the sections of the wall they hit.

Effin' hell. We absolutely cannot get hit by those!

I stared at the chaos unfurling before my eyes. Eggs were *everywhere*. They covered the entire platform. Some were still shooting around like pinballs, and the quickly engorging dogpile of them was probably going to make matters much, much worse in short order. What was the point of all of this cataclysmic bullshit? Everything I'd done so far, the items I'd collected that I hadn't even gotten to use yet. All for what? To end up as mutant egg food?

I glanced up at the looming pillars with woeful desire.

If only we could get to higher ground, we might be able to wait this thing out—

"Gah!"

One of the nasty little sluts on my back had bitten into me so hard, I'd lost my train of thought.

You bouncy mother . . .

Then I froze.

Oh, no.

I'd just thought of something stupid. Something so moronic, so void of anything resembling intelligence that it could have starred in a reality TV show.

I spun, thrusting my open hand at Stinky.

"Give me the potion!"

"What?!"

I slammed my fist on the lip of the open chest. There wasn't any time for this!

"Give me the potion you got from the corpse!"

I thought for a second.

"*And* the party hat! Gimme the potion and the party hat!"

"Why?!" Stinky bellowed, his voice almost impossible to hear over the terrible loudness my actions had caused.

"I have a fucking plan! NOW GIMME THE GODDAMN PARTY HAT!"

Stinky seemed to think there was no point in arguing any further, which was a bad sign as to what he felt our odds were, but I didn't care. I was going to *do* something. I mean, what's the worst that could happen? We die? Partner, we were already going to be chum food if we just sat there.

He tossed me the bottle and the hat. I quickly put the paper cone in place on my head and Analyzed the potion.

??? Potion of Titanic Strength
- **Rarity: ???**
- **Item Class: ???**

- Durability: ???
- Weight: 0.09 lbs.
- Effect: *???*

Well, shit.

That didn't help me much, but at least I knew it was *titanic* strength. Which meant I would be at *least* as strong as an ocean liner. I began to sweat slime again, so I removed the helmet from my hand and shoved the haladie into my waistband. The roes on my body released with suction-y pops as the sound of their bouncy brothers drew close behind me. I tossed the dented helm to Stinky, who caught it with a puzzled look.

"Put it on," I said, before quickly adding, "and get your dagger ready. Don't ask questions."

I didn't wait for him. I bit the cork out and spat it into the air, slugging the contents down. It was disgusting beyond belief, and I slightly choked but finished it. The effect came online almost instantly as I saw the notification.

Buff: Titanic Strength
You temporarily gain the Strength score of a Titan for one minute. Time to show the world how earth-shatteringly powerful you are for sixty seconds—the perfect amount of time to impress that special someone in the bedroom.
- **Strength Score: 200 (Temporary) for [65 seconds] (+8% effectiveness with [First Perk] Adventurous Tastes)**

"Aw, yeah, motherfucker!"

Now, *this* was a goddamn potion! The feeling was pure euphoria. It was like I'd just mainlined a gallon of super heroin directly into the orgasm center of my brain. However, I didn't have time to bask in the feeling of effervescent joy, because I had an absolutely one hundred percent dipshit maneuver to carry out.

Stinky was just sliding the helmet on when he looked up and saw me stuffing my gigantic orc hands into the luxurious gloves I'd pulled out of my pockets. He looked like he wanted to say something snarky, but I didn't give him the opportunity. I was too fancy for his words now.

Instead, I leaned down and grabbed the chest in both hands, and *heaved*. Even with my apparently modified strength, I realized the chest was sealed to the fucking ground and took a moment to dislodge. Still, it exploded upward in a shower of wood and rocks when it did. I hefted it in my arms as Stinky reeled back, shielding himself with his arms. I caught his eye at that, and I winked at him. Then I turned back to the onslaught of possessed roe, and with a deep breath, launched the ultra-heavy box right into their midst like a bowling ball.

Those in the immediate path of the chest exploded on contact, the force too great for even their bouncy skin to repel. The eggs on the sidelines soared away, striking the walls and rebounding off them, most of them splattering. The chest skidded and rolled through their ranks, cleaving a path through like a hot machete in a butter forest.

I looked back at my companion. Stinky was trembling at the sight of me, my ferocious strength apparently too much to bear witness to.

"A-are you going to f-fight all of them?" Stinky managed to ask.

"No," I said. "There's not enough time. I have something else in mind."

It was true; I'd briefly considered the option of total evisceration. But there was an assload of these eggy skanks, and I didn't think my strength would last long enough to get to them all.

"What is it?" Stinky breathed.

"You're going to hate it," I said. "Let's hope you qualify as a weapon."

"What the hell do you—"

He didn't get a chance to finish. I quickly grabbed him around the legs and snatched him up into the air. I'd checked the status of the gloves when I had put them on again. Sure enough, after picking up the Two-Handed Weapons Skill when I was hilariously destroying the wooden club, I now had one charge available for the gauntlets' benefit. Now I just had to hope it would work with an *improvised* two-hander.

Only one way to find out.

I accessed the gloves' Ability as Stinky screamed for his life and watched as his entire body flashed with a bright, golden light. It had worked. He would be completely invulnerable for the next minute and a half.

"Hell, yeah!" I roared.

Now for phase two.

"Hold on to your butt, Stinky!" I boomed, and began charging toward the swath I'd carved through the horde of roe, swinging the matau as I did. My companion's wails were the soundtrack to my carnage as I barreled into the fray.

PWA-PING!

The first row of eggs flew in every direction as I scattered them with Stinky's body like a scythe.

Then I caught sight of the straining, undulating egg tumor in the pool, and I couldn't help it—goddammit, my brain summoned up a song unbidden.

My mom used to play Simon and Garfunkel constantly when I was little, and it was one of the strongest memories I had of her. The moment I saw the stone walkway with the turbulent display beneath it, the bizarre sequence of events transpiring forced my mind to vomit up "Bridge over Troubled Water" with perfect clarity.

Author's Note: *At this time, if you'd like to be dope as hell, it would be appropriate to play "Bridge over Troubled Water" by Simon and Garfunkel for this scene.*

The potion had seemed to give me perfect clarity in how to wield this newfound strength, and it was almost as though everything had slowed down as I moved.

I swung hard, shredding the lines of egg monsters every which way with my man-weapon. Then I switched sides and swung again, clearing the creatures hopping up and down on the other side of the path. I was hitting them hard enough that none of them could stick to Stinky, and I was entirely invulnerable to them as long as I was wearing my happy little party cone.

"I'm going to kill you!" Stinky screeched, and I couldn't tell if he was referring to me or the eggs. Probably me. He had his dagger out and was slicing the beasts as he flashed through them like a bewildered razor.

However, I hadn't gained much ground doing things this way—as fun as it was—and I was in a very serious time crunch. So, silently apologizing to my unwilling weapon, I decided to mix it up. Still moving along the path, I began to rotate. I saw Stinky's expression change to one I could only describe as "extreme terror and regret" as I approached a full spin, swatting the eggs away in a wide circle as I did.

PWA-PWA-PING-PI-PING PWA-PING PING PING

I spun, and I spun, being careful to move down the path of least resistance all the while. I was like a methed-out gorilla playing with its favorite ragdoll and leaving a path of destruction in my wake that could have been considered a war crime. Notifications stacked unendingly in my vision as I whirled, but because I was in active combat, they thoughtfully minimized so that I could continue my tornadic murder spree.

I'd remembered something from the dance class Aunt Ella had forced me to attend when I was eight:

If you're spinning, use the spot technique.

So, with each violent, egg-demolishing rotation, I would snap my head to the bridge at the turnaround point to keep my orientation and prevent myself from becoming dizzy. I drew closer and closer to the pool and the pulsating quagmire of egg bodies as Art Garfunkel's tenor reached an invading fever pitch in my mind.

We finally reached the end of the army of possessed roe, and now it was on to the third and final phase of my brain-dead plan. I stopped moving forward and spun in place, shifting my weight to gain more and more momentum before performing the riskiest part of this operation: I jumped.

I'd expected a bit of a boost from both the Titanic Strength Potion and Stinky's inertia to gain enough height to land on the roe king, but I had miscalculated slightly. As I pushed off from the ground, I realized that without being firmly rooted by my enhanced legs, my body still had the same—whaddya call it . . . mass. I was, therefore, subject to the whim of the force with which my screaming flesh-maul was moving. This meant that rather than the extra fifteen or so feet I'd planned for, Stinky and I fired through the air and blazed past my original benchmark—heading directly for the ceiling of the cavern at whatever the speed a Titan can toss something. So, extremely fast. Not a problem, right?

Wrong.

There was the additional complication of the fact that as I'd released, I'd accidentally let go of one of Stinky's legs for a moment, which instantly dissolved the invulnerability effect he was under. If that hadn't happened, things wouldn't be so dire. With my mountain of extra health, I could . . . maybe survive the crash, but Stinky would almost definitely become matau-goo.

There were mere seconds before impact, and I didn't know what else to do except—

Wait!

I opened my menu fast as hell.

Please let this be a new day! Please let this be a new day!

There it was.

Yes! Thank fuck!

I found what I was looking for and didn't even think about it. I pulled the roaring Stinky into my arms. I curled my body around him as I mentally slammed on *Zeol's Falling Star* a fraction of a second before we collided with the rock.

KABOOM!

My back hit the stone with tremendous force, and I heard the foundation of rock explode behind me, gigantic fissures opening up in the flesh of the ceiling. I hadn't felt a thing.

It worked! It goddamn WORKED!

Stinky wasn't screaming anymore, but he was breathing, so I had to assume he was all right. I hung like that for a moment before gravity took over, and we plummeted again, but I didn't care.

I was alive—for the moment—and that was worth celebrating.

"Liiiike a briiiiiidge over trooooubled waateeer!" I bellowed, my bass reverberating off the walls as I fell toward the mass below, the song's crescendo popping back into my head. I was losing my goddamned marbles.

I'd left my menu open and watched in real time as my Luck—which had been at negative four—ticked all the way up to a positive eleven.

The implications of that were still a bit mysterious to me. Still, I couldn't believe that I'd performed all those acts under such disadvantageous odds. Now that my fortune was *slightly* higher than the average person's, it seemed like the perfect time to do some crazy shit. I didn't know what was about to go down, but I'd been operating under a deficit for my entire life. Even a slight bump to my luck was basically the equivalent of karma on steroids for me.

But what was I going to do about my companion? Much like with the cavern roof, I would likely be fine in a game of chicken with natural downward forces, but Stinky would probably not fare as well. He was unconscious from the impact and badly injured from our lovers' quarrel with the roe. It was a fucking miracle he'd survived the collision with the cave wall at all, and there was no way he'd make it through the next leg of this trip unscathed. So, completely out of sensical ideas and trusting in—what I imagined—was the rest of my thin tether to providence, I lofted Stinky upward, arresting his momentum as we fell.

"I wiiiill eaaaaase your—"

I struck the pile of eggs, taking the full force of the impact. It blasted a massive chunk out of my HP, but I was still in the beefed-up quadrant.

Just as I suspected: I *bounced*. This had been my original plan before the whole ceiling incident. I could tell immediately that I was going to be moving at a *clip*. I caught Stinky by the leg again as his path—very fortunately—intersected my arc, and the two of us zoomed through the cavern, high above the still furious and baffled possessed roe, toward my intended target all along: the top of the pillars.

I hadn't actually expected to get this far. But I had figured that if I was going to go out, I would go out with *style*. Everything that had happened to me so far was a highly unlikely series of failing upward. Lady Luck had to have been visiting the toilet during this whole ordeal because there's no way I would have gotten away with *any* of that if she'd been watching.

Then, of course, the metaphorical wind shifted as soon as I thought that: the Titanic Strength Potion wore off.

No! Shit! What the shit, man?!

I felt like I'd just been kicked in the brain by a PCP hangover. Everything got *awful* all at once as my mega-strength disappeared from my nervous system, taking a sinkhole down to bye-bye town. Worse yet was that now that I was back to average might, keeping my carry-on luggage with me on this flight was going to become next to impossible. I started to lose my grip on Stinky's boot, and he sagged as I tried to keep him airborne with me. I adjusted my grasp, but the movement threw us off course, and suddenly, we were careening too far left. We were going to blast right between the two pillars and likely smash right into the archway of the dungeon.

We were just about to pass the threshold of the pillars when Stinky slipped out of my grasp.

Shit.

I didn't even have time to react; I just watched his dumb, slumbering body slip away, his face a perfect picture of calm. Fortunately, that was when something super weird and messed-up happened.

As I moved through the space between the two gigantic plinths, the archway ahead flashed bright, and everything froze in place. Me, Stinky, the few possessed roe I could see far below, everything ground to a halt as if time had just stopped working. It was silent. I couldn't even hear any of the ear-molesting noises from the horror cave.

The shit is this now? Some additional fucking complication that's gonna fry my fanny?

A notification cropped up in my field of vision. This wasn't like the usual variety, though. This one looked like a stone tablet with letters scratched into it with a dull knife. *Charming.* Green light sifted from somewhere deep within the text, giving me a really terrible feeling about what was about to happen.

WELCOME, TRAVELER.
YOU HAVE ENTERED THE BOUNDARY OF THE GATEWAY TO THE FORBIDDEN CRYPT OF THE DREADNAUGHT LORD.
IT HAS BEEN LONG SINCE WE HAVE HAD A VISIT.

We? Uh-oh. Serious '80s supernatural horror movie vibes.

TO ENTER THE FORBIDDEN CRYPT REQUIRES [2] EMERALD ESPER NODES. DO YOU PETITION ACCESS TO OUR DEPTHS?

I was stunned into silence.

This was the purpose of the Esper Nodes? To open fucking dungeons?! The reason Fawn had tried to kill me?

I was too shocked and enraged to do much at all except let my mind spiral.

Just how valuable are these things? I can't believe they're worth killing some poor, unsuspecting orc over! Why would someone want to come to a place like this? Are dungeons like this world's equivalent of Beanie Babies?

I didn't get it. But I'd obtained them from the Greloks and another from one of the Redmark soldiers. Why didn't people just farm the Espers themselves?

Surely, I wasn't the only one in the world that had them. That wouldn't make sense, but I also wouldn't have been surprised if there was some bullshit rule around it that somehow only existed to grind my gooch.

But what was even worse was how fucking pointless everything I'd done had been. I mean, I'd just disassembled an entire cave full of springy homicide-eggs with the genius of my powerful strategic mind in order to save my life—when I could have just walked between the *two fucking pillars* the whole time and avoided the entire fiasco?

Focus, I thought. It didn't matter right now. I had a choice to make.

But first, because I was born difficult, I wanted to try something.

"Uh, hi," I said to the—uh—dungeon. "Loon, here. First-time dungeon whisperer, long-time shithead. I'm not sure if you can hear me or are even able to—"

WE CAN HEAR YOU.

Goddamn, that was unsettling.

"Uh, good," I said. "I have a question for you, O Great and Powerful Forbidden Crypt. Is it just me who is allowed in, or can my buddy come inside as well?"

I cast a glance to Stinky, who was still caked in every possible type of grossness while suspended in unconscious bliss high above the ground.

ALL WHO REST BEFORE THE ARCHWAY WILL BE GRANTED PASSAGE WITHIN OUR WOMB.

Ew. I thought. *Womb? That is* so *not cash money.*

The prospect of having to share my VIP backstage pass filled me with a lot of anger and panic.

"So . . . everything in this cavern?"

ONLY THOSE WHO REST IN THE VALLEY BETWEEN THE ARCHWAY AND THE ESPER MONOLITHS WILL BE PERMITTED ADMISSION.

Ah, all right. I relaxed a little. That made things slightly less complicated. There'd be no sense in surviving everything I just had if the entire carton of eggs would be coming along for the ride. It might get kinda cramped and sticky.

I looked down at the five roe that had wandered beyond the barrier themselves.

We can take those chumps, no problem.

I was hesitant to enter the Crypt, but it was also likely the only way to save Stinky and myself as I didn't have a single trick left up my sleeve to play. The message repopulated.

DO YOU PETITION ACCESS TO OUR DEPTHS?

With a sigh, I nodded.

" . . . sure," I said. "I would like to access the dungeon."

The moment the words left my mouth, I felt a yank from within me. It didn't hurt, but it did startle me and was slightly uncomfortable—like stifling a sneeze but, like, in my *soul*. Two green orbs burst from my chest and separated in front of me, one flying over my right shoulder behind me, the other over my left.

I craned my neck and watched as they each homed in on one of the statues, buzzing directly toward the stone birds before slipping right into the space in their talons. I'd thought they had been burglarized, but they were just waiting to grab some Esper boob.

Both stone birds' eyes flashed with green light, and the same happened to the archway.

OFFERING ACCEPTED.
[8] TRAVELERS NOW ENTERING THE FORBIDDEN CRYPT OF THE DREADNAUGHT LORD.
ENJOY YOUR STAY.

Eight?

With the five eggs plus Stinky and I, that was only seven. Who the hell was the remaining person?

But I didn't get a chance to ask.

With another green flash, I was no longer hovering in the air with my metaphorical thumb up my metaphorical butt. I was standing in the dark. Strangely, my Darkvision didn't activate, and something about that led me to believe that my sight was being magically obscured. This was a fact that I did not like at all. I couldn't see anything, and hardly any of my other senses were picking up on anything, save my sense of impending dread. Oh, I guess I could also tell it was uncomfortably warm wherever I was. Not more than that, though.

"Hello?" I asked.

There was no answer.

I stood in silent darkness for what felt like an eternity. It was like waiting for death.

Then, after a long moment, the lights came on. Actually, it was more like something that emitted light was made corporeal, and it was as though a veil had been lifted. All at once, the room was even hotter than before and I was now overwhelmed by the intensity of my new environment. Burning red light swarmed me, and I held up an arm to shield myself from its direct force. The air was hot and wet, like being inside the mouth of a gigantic dog.

Stinky came into view, lying unconscious near me. His skin was still raw and fissured from the roe's vindictive teeth, but fortunately, he looked stable. We were facing a blank stone wall that looked like the other side of the door inside the archway. I turned around.

Big mistake.

We were standing on a rocky platform high above another cavern. It spilled out ahead of me, so large that the one we'd just escaped could have been *this* cave's broom closet. Multiple other platforms dotted the landscape beyond, and tall rocky formations reminding me of China's stone forests—I think my science teacher, Mrs. Vaughn, had called them "karsts"—lived everywhere within.

The yawning brimstone doom before me set my tusks on edge. How in the hot lava hell was I going to navigate this area?

I reluctantly opened the message I had minimized hours before and reread it with a groan.

[Faith Quest] *Into the Dungeon*
Accept?
Yes / No

Somehow, I feel as though this is precisely what Zeol imagined. What a slimy son of a slut.

But a new sense of purpose rose in my chest. I was too fucking stubborn and annoying to just settle for whatever anyone had in store for me, and that filled me with a calmness I'd rarely felt in my life. If I had to be in there, I was gonna earn some blasted rewards, goddammit. That was for *damn* sure. I looked back over to my comatose compadre on the ground and shook my head.

When I get out of here, I'm going to rip that mist-humping god apart and eat him like cheesy bread.

I hit *Yes*.

CHAPTER TWENTY

BICKER AND FLICKER

"Back off, orc—you're going to fuckin' kill me!"

"I can't help that you're slow as shit, Stinky!"

We were perched, like a couple of dipshits, along a narrow channel of rock skirting the wall. It had been challenging to move quickly because, while Stinky insisted on going first, he moved painfully slow. This—as you can probably imagine—created some difficulties.

"I'm not *slow*!" Stinky said, holding a hand up behind him. "You're just too fuckin' massive to make this comfortable. Budge off, you great fat halfwit!"

I scowled down at him.

"You wanted to go first, so you *live* with first," I said, clutching the rock wall with a healthy dose of anxiety.

"I'd have changed my mind if I'd known you were going to be fuckin' dog-stepping me, orc!"

"I don't know what that means, Stinky! Stop using made-up terms!"

"It means you aren't giving me any space, you mountain of cat shit!"

We'd been going on like this for a few minutes—almost dangling off the edge of a ledge, shouting at one another for various reasons that seemed super important to do while shifting our weight over the gasping expanse of magma fire just below our bikini zones. Periodically, a plume of flame would shoot up from the lake of heat, causing Stinky or me—or both—to have to flatten ourselves against the rock wall to not get our bits singed beyond repair.

I sighed.

I shouldn't have to deal with this. I'm Level Six now.

Oh, yeah. I'd leveled up.

Apparently, popping that potion for a real one was the equivalent of smoking fantasy crack. I'd carved up those eggs like a hibachi chef and done a fair bit of miscellaneous mischief. Especially considering I'd created enough chaotic damage that I should have to register as a living natural disaster. After having consumed a total of ten thousand Experience during that little jaunt, I was now three levels higher than before we'd fallen into the cave. I'd realized the change not long after encountering Big Hot Pond—as I called it now in my mind. I'd also gained access to nine additional Points to be distributed as I saw most fitting. Of course, ya boi slapped five of those motherfuckers into Constitution—bringing it up to twenty-nine. The other four Points were divided equally into Strength and Dexterity—for a total of twelve in each.

Several Skills and Abilities had also shot up, including Intimidate, Two-Handed Weapons, and Unarmed Fighting. The most exciting advancement was my Improvised Weapon Skill, which had jumped up an entire rank and was now resting at a comfortable E-Rank, Level Two.

It was as though I was actually making a modicum of progress now, and that felt *good*. However, what didn't feel as peachy-keen was the fact that Stinky had apparently woken up on the asshole side of the bed—even though I'd saved his life. Some people just don't know when to give up on a grudge, I guess. He was still mighty butthurt about me *lightly* using him as a humanoid grain tool during our masterfully executed escape.

If I'd have known he was just going to be grumbling the whole time, I would have whipped him around like a helicopter blade long before.

Now we were making our perilous path across the thinnest strip of rocky outcropping available. This was all in an attempt to make it to one of the stone karsts standing tall and stoic against the backdrop of what looked like a German techno-music video.

We still hadn't encountered the eggs or whoever Guest Numero Ocho was. So, for the moment, it was just Stinky and I prowling along the skirt of this gigantic bubbling jambalaya of ouchies, trying not to become its next ingredient.

I'd gained some new Abilities with the level-up, but I hadn't had a chance to check them out yet because of—you know—this shit. I promised myself that I would take a time-out once we reached the summit of the looming stone oasis and genuinely dive in.

I still couldn't believe the magnitude of this cavern. It was a mile or two long and the ceiling was at least twice that in height, so much so that if there weren't a multitude of conspicuous stalactites, I might have assumed there wasn't a roof at all. Worrisomely, Stinky had pointed out what—to me—looked like wasps' nests weaved into the flesh of the stone ceiling daggers. Still, so far, they hadn't done anything nefarious except exist. Which, in my mind, was bad enough in its own right.

The other platforms I'd noticed when I'd arrived seemed to be made out of some material other than the boring old stone that comprised everything else in this vast canyon. They stuck out noticeably, and rather than varying tones of dull gray rock, they were a shining pearl—as if made out of marble. They each had a different symbol carved into them that I didn't recognize. I was sure they had some purpose that would send my anger spiking into the red, but as of yet, neither of us knew what that could be.

On the far end of the cavern was another platform with an additional door inside a glowing archway. However, despite it looking nearly identical to the dungeon's entrance, there was one glaring abnormality: this door was *open*. Where the last entryway had two bird pillars on either side, this just held a massive stone carving of some kind of dog demon that jutted out over the arch. It gave me the creeps. I figured we'd have to jog our happy asses over there somehow to get to the next . . . chamber, as Zeol had referred to it. I was beginning to regret ever giving that stupid mask the time of day.

I mean, he'd made it sound like it would be as simple as strolling into a fast-food joint and using the bathroom—uncomfortable and a little dangerous but relatively unlikely to end in death. However, in every direction I looked, it seemed like there were *lots* of potentially fatal situations I could bumble into— like using the bathroom at a swap meet.

Screw you, Zeol. And screw your mother. While we're at it—screw your grandma, your grandpa, and your whole messed-up line of disembodied faces.

I'd halfway hoped that thinking with intention would goad him into a response, but the god had been suspiciously silent ever since I'd asked him to go away. Which, I mean, I guess was the point, but I'd figured he'd at least have been annoying enough to try to reach out once I'd accepted the Quest.

One column of bleak rock stood out more than the others in the center of the entire thing. It was broader than its siblings, and several stone bridges led to its base near the lava from other locations. These were really no more than fingers of stone that stretched dangerously over swaths of the burning lake rather than actual bridges, but it was clear by their design they were meant to be crossed to get to this central karst. At its top was another archway, though it looked considerably smaller than the one across Big Hot Pond. There was no doubt in my mind that we'd be required to fiddlefuck around with that thing before we could even attempt to get to the demon dog door.

Stinky hadn't argued. Once he'd woken up, he'd seemed a bit befuddled by where he was, but then the reality of the last few minutes had resurfaced, and he'd tried to stab me again. Though he was either too injured or his heart just wasn't in it enough, because he stopped after just a moment. Then, when he'd realized we were *in* a dungeon, he'd gone quiet and adopted a look I would almost describe as "begrudging interest." He'd marveled at the expanse of hell before us before steeling himself and announcing we needed to move forward.

He hadn't even asked how it was possible that we'd gotten inside—something I'd planned a lie around—so that was a bit of a downer. He had to know, though. There was no way he'd have gleaned so much *about* dungeons without having learned what their keycode was. So, I remained quiet about the Espers. If he wasn't going to ask, I wasn't going to say fucking boo.

After ten minutes of strenuous hiking and nearly life-ending stumbles, we made it to the stone catwalk that led to the center column. From there I could see the dozens of other paths that grew from the structure's base, and some looked a lot more perilous than ours. Though, as I saw the narrow strip of rock practically hovering fifty feet above the lava, I didn't really think our chances were much better. The walkway moved over a section of the lake, stopped at a smaller karst, and then picked up the trail to reach the center column another hundred or so feet beyond.

"All right, orc, I'll go first and—"

"The fuck you will!" I shouted, my voice echoing into the burning void beyond. "You can barely walk. I learned my lesson on the ledges. If you go first, you're going to keel over and fall into the lake, and I'll have to witness it—which will really bum me out. I'll have to have *that* on my conscience for the rest of my days."

"If you go first, you'll break the fuckin' thing and leave me trapped on this side!" Stinky barked.

"If I don't make it across, you'll be fucked anyway," I said. "You're being held together by butterfly kisses right now, and a fucking fart would blast your bones apart."

"All the better reason to stay upwind of you, orc," Stinky said. "My way is the least risky. Your way is stupid. Besides, I've been in front this whole time, and like you said, I chose first, so I live with it."

"Fine," I said, finally relenting. "You're correct that my initial assessment was with the perfect clarity of a mastermind. You have my permission to go first."

Stinky looked like he wanted to kick me into the lava. Instead, he shambled forward, carefully picking his footpath across the tiny rock catwalk. I watched him for a minute as he made his slow trek across the bridge, and when he was nearing the halfway point, I stepped aboard.

It was unsettling how small the width of this thing was. It wasn't quite wide enough for both of my feet to rest next to one another, so I'd either have to strafe sideways or try not to trip as I put one foot over the other. I opted for the sidewinder and began shuffling along, keeping my arms out to steady my balance.

Stinky made it to the platform waypoint and waited for me to finish my stretch before giving me a look.

"You didn't die," he said.

"Thanks for the vote of confidence," I breathed. As much as I had been falling lately, I hadn't developed a taste for heights. Especially as this particular dumbo drop wouldn't have been as easy to survive as the others I'd been so miraculously deus ex machina'd from. Just to test my theory, I snatched up a palm-sized piece of rubble from our respite and hurled it into the lake. I watched it drop, and before it even hit the lava, it burst into flame. Whatever remains it had were dissolved by the time it reached the lake.

Yeah, that's going to need to be avoided at all costs.

The stone hadn't stood a chance, and *my* skin was way meltier than it was.

Stinky took the next leg and made it over without issue. I tiptoed along afterward, and I was fine other than a single close call. As I stepped onto the ledge at the karst's base, I let out a loud breath that I didn't even know I had been carrying with me and slumped against the rock of the structure. It was pretty warm, but we were far enough above the lake that it didn't seem like I was in danger of going all Johnny Storm.

"Now what?" I asked, but Stinky wasn't listening. He had already started stomping along the rim. So, I followed.

"How do you know where to go?" I wondered.

Stinky quarter-turned his head to me and shot a gob of phlegm into the fiery lake below.

"It only has one route, you fuckin' dimwit," he said. "How the hell you managed to get the drop on me without killing yourself first is a gods-revilin' wonder."

I flipped him the bird, but he just stared at it quizzically. So, I very smoothly and expertly pretended to be examining the cuticle. Stinky just shook his head and kept moving.

Ha, in your face, sucker.

Stinky had been right: there was only one path. We spent some time making our way up carefully, the angry matau leading us up through at a stumbling gait. Before we reached the top, though, I grabbed him, forcing him to stop.

"What in the—"

"Quiet," I hissed, and gave him a severe glare. "We need to strategize."

"Strategize about what, orc?" Stinky said, yanking himself out of my grasp. "How best to use me as a cudgel and break those fuckin' speleothems down? Or maybe you want t' try tossin' me the whole way over to that arch? What could you in your thick-skulled glory possibly think would be a good idea?"

I smirked.

"Actually, I was going to suggest riding you across the lava like a surfboard, but I can see you're in your usual humorless state."

Then I paused.

"Wait, what's a . . . spiely wheely—whatever?"

Stinky spat into the lake again without explaining. I glanced at the walls where the discolored platforms were.

Are those *the spiely wheelies?*

This whole thing felt *off*. If this entire world was built like a videogame, once we ended up on top of this structure, things were going to get fucking hairy. Like, motherfucking Chewbacca, Teen Wolf, Borat chest, Harry and the goddamned Hendersons–level hairy. There was no way in . . . well, *there* that I was going to go dimpledicking into a trap. Not that I was an RPG expert by any stretch, but I'd played enough games of different genres to recognize the signs of when you were approaching a boss battle. Or, at the very least, an extreme challenge.

"We need to be prepared for this next step," I said coolly, looking around. We weren't yet to the top, but with my height, I could just peep over the lip of the flat surface of the summit. Sure enough, the smaller-than-the-other archway was near the edge, directly opposite the one across the lake. Now that we were so close, I could see that it *also* had runes around its curve, but these ones weren't glowing. They were still etched in the same fashion as the others but barren of any glowy bullshit. I didn't see anything other than the blank expanse surrounding it. If I was a betting man, I'd have placed all my money on something happening when we physically crossed a certain threshold.

So, we needed a plan.

I explained my reservations to Stinky, and he considered my words quietly—and with a lot more thoughtfulness than I'd assumed he was capable of. Finally, after a long moment, he sighed.

"I suppose you have something in mind?" he asked hesitantly.

"I might," I said, looking at the purse under his arm. "But first, I should know what sort of tools you have available. Anything and everything. We're gonna need every ounce of cheat codes we can manage if we want to survive."

I looked up at the stalactites and the gross little dumpling hives clinging to them.

Those are going to become an issue—whatever they are.

Stinky kept his scowl deep and annoying, but I just waited patiently, making direct eye contact in a move I'd learned from Uncle Luke: if you want to get someone to do something for you, state your piece, meet their eyes, and don't speak afterward until they do. He'd said it was a common tactic in sales but only worked if the other person didn't know what you were doing. I was banking on

Stinky not only thinking the worst of me but also hoping that my Intimidation Skill could help—even a little.

After a solid twenty seconds of no words passing between either of us, Stinky sighed, averted his gaze, and shrugged his shoulders. Then he reached into his pouch and opened it, peering inside.

"I ain't got much," he said. "I travel light."

"Aren't you, like, a mercenary or something?" I asked, confused. "Why wouldn't you bring along things you need?"

Stinky shot me a withering look and bared his razor teeth.

"Do I show up at the Dumb Shithead Guild and knock the dirt you're eating out of your mouth, orc? Don't accost me over my means when you haven't the slimiest snot of an idea what I do!"

I shook my head.

"Buddy, I'm just trying to understand what it is you bring to the table," I said. "But you're right. I don't know anything about you—or what you do—so why don't you tell me? Unless you like dying, I guess?"

Stinky spat again.

"I suppose you think you're keen to whip up some method of tactical brilliance based on the contents of my bag?"

I shrugged.

"It's sure as *dick* better than letting you go wandering up there without any safety net and just hoping for the best!"

Stinky jabbed a finger in my face.

"Don't you worry about me, shit-skin," he growled. "I've survived a long time without the aid of some rutting savage whose bells are a bit too low for his breeches!"

Shit-skin? That sounds derogatory. Should I be offended by that? Is this speciesism?

"First of all," I started, "if you're pooping out things the color of *me*, then you need to consult a doctor—or better yet, a fucking priest because your butthole is clearly haunted."

Then I drew myself up to my full height, trying to glower down at the grumpy matau.

"And . . . also, you may be a survivor, or whatever, but I'd be willing to bet all the . . . bells in my . . . breeches that you haven't spelunked a fucking dungeon before. Look, I'm sorry I used you like a Swiffer in a PlayPlace ball pit. That was my bad. I know you're super horny for your camp and want to get back there so you can try to cleave my head in two or whatever. But that isn't going to happen unless we try to play this smart."

Stinky coughed up a laugh from the phlegm in his throat.

"Smart? You haven't done anything *smart* since we fell down that hill, and yet you expect me—"

I threw my hands up, cutting him off.

"In case you hadn't noticed, we're in a place called 'the Forbidden Crypt of the Dreadnaught Lord,' surrounded by a toilet bowl full of flaming jizz, and there's probably a bunch of freaking ultra-hornets in those nests up there. Shit is about to get stupid as hell fast. I know I'm dumb. I don't know *shit* about *fuck*, but I'd like to live long enough to see what sorts of ballin'-ass treasures are in this son of a bitch."

Stinky's eyebrows shot up at that. He quickly collected himself, but I'd seen his telling reaction. He was excited about the prospect of loot.

"All right, quit bitching, then," Stinky said. I had to believe he'd changed his tune because I'd reminded him of how lucrative having exclusive access to a dungeon could be.

"You're a real Grinch, Stinky—you know that?"

Stinky just sneered at me.

"Quiet with your nonsense words, orc," he said, lifting his satchel up so I could look inside. "Here's what I've got. See somethin' y'like?"

I activated Analysis and took a moment to browse his tiny inventory, before spotting something that made me smile.

"Oh," I said. "I think I can definitely figure something out with *these*."

CHAPTER TWENTY-ONE

FLAME-BROILED WHOPPERS

We stood in front of the archway, and I suddenly felt as if we were very, very *boned*.

The gate was much larger than I'd initially believed. The space on top of the enormous karst was a few hundred yards across, which lent the arch an almost optical-illusion effect. Now that we were under it, I was struck dumb by its immensity. It was at least a hundred feet tall, made of thick slabs of ornate, twisting stones that looked like something hewn by a demon lord's chief mason. Tines of sculpted flame grew from the outside, casting a spell of an ominous air. Each of the runes broken from its flesh was as tall as I was and as wide as my torso. I'd never felt so utterly unimpressive and insignificant in either of my lives. Still, I couldn't help but smile with appreciation despite all this.

It was goddamned *brutal*.

Two minute forms beholding a gloriously ancient earthen archway perched above a cavern of molten rock had to be on a poster somewhere in some stoner's basement. I made a mental note to remember every detail of this terrifying monstrosity. I wasn't sure why, but it just felt like something I should do.

I'd been wrong about activating an encounter from a physical threshold. Nothing had happened as we'd crept forward toward the wondrous gate, and now we were standing directly in front of it. That was all right, though. For the first time in my life, I felt like I'd acted cautiously.

There was a quiet dignity in that.

"Look at this fucking thing!" I exclaimed, slapping Stinky on the back and gripping his shoulder roughly. "I'm not normally attracted to *these kinds* of curves, but, shit... she's a goddamn beauty."

Stinky wheeled on me, bewildered by my comment.

"What in the Halls o' fuckin' Aggrun are you talking about?"

"The arch," I said, pointing up at it. "It's *purdy*."

Stinky shrugged my hand away.

"This beast is probably wound up to kill us, orc," he said, jabbing the point of his dagger at the arch. "You'll have time to wank over it later. I thought you had a plan?"

"I have an *idea*," I said. "That's a little different. I'm just appreciating the scenery."

I actually was very taken by the imagery. It filled me with a sense of nostalgia for . . . something. I'm not sure what. But it was there, like a knot of long-forgotten feelings in the pit of my chest. It sorta reminded me of being really little when I'd sneak into my cousin Lacy's room to pilfer through her paperback fantasy novels. Back when the idea of entire worlds of magic and adventure would spring into my mind just from the illustrations on the covers. Life was a lot simpler then. Many things had changed from when I was that small. A mind filled with the fervor of imagination and the spirit of adventure could be effortlessly shattered into fragments of cold, unfeeling apathy if enough time passed.

Man, life really sucked when you peered at it through the bleak filter of nihilism.

I decided to lick my wounds another time and instead faced the dread gate with purpose.

"All right," I began. "I'm willing to bet that when we approach, something is going— Wait, *what the fuck*?!"

Stinky raised his blade, ready for an assault, but I wasn't looking at anything near us.

"Are those the fucking eggs?"

I pointed to one of the discolored platforms along the cavern wall and squinted.

You've gotta be kidding me!

Sure enough, several hundred feet away from us were five bouncing, chittering orbs of pink-pearl bullshit. They were clustered near the edge of the platform and looked highly agitated.

"Ha!" I barked out a laugh. "Looks like they're stuck with nowhere to go!"

"Good," Stinky said. "Fuckin' bastards nearly bled me to death."

Maybe we'd catch a break, and they'd fall off the ledge and into the sputtering lake below.

Would that hard-boil them?

They trembled and grumbled, bumping into one another in their fury. I couldn't tell much about what they were doing, but I *could* see that they were staring right at our position.

Look at 'em, acting all pointless and stupid. Sucks to suck, milk marbles!

I raced over to the edge and cupped my hand around my mouth to shout at them.

"Hey!" I called. "Fuck you, eggs!"

I turned back to Stinky, laughing.

"Stinky, did you hear that? I yelled—"

KA-FWOOM!

I tumbled to the ground as an explosion of air threatened to send me over the edge of the landing. I managed to land with the top of my body facing the arch as a colossal creature descended from the air on enormous wings of shadow. It resembled a hyper-muscular humanoid but had strangely avian features—like its parents were a bodybuilder and some sort of giant, demon chicken. It beat its wings again, and another column of air swept across me as it landed on the gateway, clutching onto the top with its talon-like feet.

What the fuck?!

Stinky rolled backward and onto his feet again, his dagger raised high to defend himself. I thought about how useless that was as I stared at the beast clinging to the arch. It had to be at least fifteen feet tall with a pair of black horns that swept back behind its head. It had eyes the color of fresh lava and skin like hot jasper. Its entire bottom half was covered in black feathers that held an aura of darkness around them.

It was super fucked-up.

Whatever the hell this thing was, I knew it was *way* stronger than some pissant egg beast. Stinky's blade would be functionally useless to a monster of this caliber—like trying to stab a polar bear with an uncooked spaghetti noodle.

Zeol, you lying bastard, I thought. *"I assure you that you will not be in harm's way," my ass, you colossal bitch.*

The creature roared, and the sound was like being gouged in the brain by a spoon made of bees. It reverberated inside my skull, and I had a strange compulsion to claw my own ears off. It was a prolonged bellow, and during it, I found that my eyes were closed, so I forced them open. Stinky was lying on his back now, furiously pounding his fists against his own ears.

What is this?! Are we going to get yelled to death? Fuck if I'm going out like that!

With a tremendous amount of effort, I pushed myself to my feet and stood to my full height. The beast on the arch hadn't moved but was still roaring. The noise *hurt*, but it didn't seem to be bothering my Health, so I had to imagine it had a sort of disorienting effect. Possibly something I wasn't as susceptible to as my matau matey.

The monstrosity suddenly noticed me standing and frowned, its eyes burning with authoritative rage as though it wasn't totally chill with my lack of fealty. It didn't seem to like that I was defying its legislation.

Ha! I thought, smirking at the gigantic nightmare creature. *I'm too strong for your pesky—*

FWOOF!

I bowled over backward as the humongous gargoyle-chicken batted a wing and sent a wall of air right into me. Fortunately, the wind-punch was at chest level, so rather than force me careening over the edge of the karst, I just slammed directly onto my shoulder blades and head, a move which proved to be *very* dizzying. The world spun for a moment before I was able to regain a foothold into the realm of my senses. When I looked up, the monster was . . . Wait—was he fucking smiling?

Then, as if to banish all doubt, the devilishly *not-good-looking* creature began to laugh. It was a rough, barking sound like winter trees snapping, his shoulders shaking as he stared right at me.

Really? You think that because you're a five-meter mutated hummingbird, I'm not going to do something stupid?

He clearly hadn't been paying attention.

I rolled forward and shot to my feet, then I started to run right at him.

"Orc!" I heard Stinky shout from the ground. He was still recovering from Lucifer's lava-pool karaoke. Still, since the noise had stopped, he wasn't trying to desperately shut out all sound anymore.

"What?!" I returned, not slowing my pace.

"What the hell are you doing?!"

"You already *know!*"

"That's a hive fiend, you gods-damned moron!" Stinky continued. "Its Level is so fuckin' high, I can't even see it!"

"Shut up, Stinky! I'm trying to do something cool!"

I didn't have time for his facts; I was a bullet of purpose.

I tore ass toward the arch, and when I was within about twenty feet of it, I reached down—midstride—and snatched up a fist-sized rock. Then I spun quickly in place and hurled it, shot put–style, directly at the creature with all my strength.

The stone rocketed up. About thirty feet. Then it dipped into the air and plummeted right into the arch where it clunked against it with a pathetic, muted sound.

There was silence for a long moment, where nothing happened at all. I turned slowly to look at Stinky, who had a look of baffled annoyance plastered to his ugly, three-mouthed face.

"Uh," I said, "... nailed it?"

There was a screech from above, and for a moment, I thought I'd actually done something to wound the massive specter on the archway. But when I looked up, I saw that it was no longer clinging to the curvature of the gate but lying on top of it, howling with laughter. His eyes were closed, and he was shuddering, the noises booming out of him sounding like thirty cats being hit with thirty other cats.

Stinky just glowered.

"Great job, you damned cancer fungus," he said. "Really did a bit of wonder, didn't you?"

I cocked my head to the side.

"Wait ... you know what cancer is?"

Before Stinky could respond, we were interrupted by the beast. A voice like an earthquake wrapped in electricity tore through our own words and forced us to both glance upward.

"That was pathetic!" the creature exclaimed, a strong influence of laughter still playing in his expression.

He speaks English? I thought, but then paused. *Wait, do I speak English?*

Just then, a window appeared in front of the gate, much like the prompts I'd begun to grow accustomed to. However, this time, rather than the usual fare of detailed descriptions of arcane mumbo-jumbo, this message seemed to be speaking directly to us, like it had when I'd entered this dumb dungeon.

Avast, ye dungeoneers! the message announced.

What is this? I wondered.

Then, the creature on top of the arch huffed and *rolled his eyes* and began to speak.

"Yes, let us get on with this nonsensical farce," he said, his voice—while still terrible and loud—had the tone of a reluctant teenager trying to get through a conversation with their mother about not having any parties while she was gone.

Hey, it's a very specific tone.

The message continued.

You have entered the Forbidden Crypt of the Dreadnaught Lord. I am Pontivex, Keeper of the Runic Arches.

The demon chicken kept chattering away, and each time it did, more words populated the screen.

"O that I could devour your ugly flesh," he said. "You lesser beings disgust me. Twisted, horrible things that you are."

Mistake not my purpose, dungeoneers. I treat here as both a welcome and a warning to those that would seek the depths of this lair.

"I have not feasted upon the meat of an orc in a long while," the creature continued. "And matau . . . well, I may not ever have tasted such exotic flavors."

You will be tried and tested here first. Only then may you acquire access to further chambers and floors within.

"Although," the hive fiend said. "There was the bunyip, and that seems like it might be similar. No, perhaps a roughly aligned skin structure, but the matau are definitely a bit more substantial. Bandier legs, wider arses. Loads better than the bunyip, most like, though. Gave me indigestion for a whole decade, that bunyip. Miserable feeling, bumbling about in my bowels like that. Rude as well. Why can't eaten creatures just go down easy? That elf went without much of a struggle. Of course, he *wanted* to be devoured, so I suppose that changes the power dynamic a bit."

"I'm not sure exactly what's going on, but this is weird as shit," I said.

Stinky nudged me roughly and pointed.

"Quiet, orc," he demanded. "Open your damn eyes. It's translating the fiend's speech."

Huh? That wasn't right. Was Stinky taking stupid pills? There were clearly two different conversations going on as the beast was speaking plain Eng . . .

Oh, hell.

I shook my head.

Motherfucking Zeol.

The Potion of Oratory Splendor. Zeol had said that it would allow me to understand *any* spoken language for a whole day. Stinky thought that the display was translating—what was he called, Pontivex's—words because he couldn't understand him. I did.

Well, well, well, this just got a lot *more interesting.*

So, this dungeon was playing a little game, I guess? Pontivex seemed very unhappy with his station, but he'd also mentioned he couldn't eat us. Did that mean he was bound in some way to be unable to attack as well? I thought about that. He hadn't technically harmed us before, just used his roar to disorient us and his wings to knock me over. This also meant we likely wouldn't be required to or be capable of attacking him.

This is a fucking cutscene.

If that was the case, then Pontivex was there for some reason other than just intimidation.

Congratulations! You've raised a Skill!
Insight has advanced to F-Rank Level 8!

Oh, hell, yeah!

For better or worse, much like a Transformer, there was more to this than met the eye. I silently wished that the additional Insight would inform me what the fuck was going on, but that hadn't seemed to be the case in any of my interactions so far.

Insight, you tease.

I knew I had Zeol to thank for this tidbit of fortune, and it was all because he was super horny for that god bauble or whatever it was. He'd known I was going to get to this point, and he'd manipulated me into this exact predicament. Very uncool. I'd have to return the favor.

So, Zeol wants me to pick up some morsels of info from this thing? Better give him what he wants, then.

The message was still populating from Pontivex's lengthy diatribe, so I focused on it while preparing my next move.

Before you lies the Grand Flame, a cavern designed specifically by Rexen Gravetongue to test the might and mettle of prospective dungeoneers. The burning lake consumes any and all that dare trespass too closely to its flesh. But so, too, are there other obstacles to overcome, as you will come to find. Do not dally in one place for too long, lest the doors close to you and the cavern devour you.

I snickered.

"Grand Flame?" I said aloud, looking at Stinky. "More like *Bland Lame*."

Stinky sighed and shoved me in the direction of the display, jerking an angry finger toward the archway.

"Shut your fuckin' mouth for ten blasted seconds, you incomplete spunk stain," he hissed. "If we miss something important, we'll be dead."

"Hey," I said. "Look at this way: even if we pay attention, we're still probably going to die. Neither of us are exactly members of the brain trust."

"If we fuck this up because of you, orc, I will kill you myself first."

"You've mentioned wanting to do that for a while," I returned. "I think kitty's claws are getting dull."

"Listen to their prattling," Pontivex said to himself. "Their primitive warbling, arguing with one another about something foolish. They likely believe they're of an intellect esteemed enough that they've figured out some great truth to all this. The fools. It doesn't matter what I say; the silly notification always populates precisely the same message every time. See?"

He leaned forward to address us specifically.

"You're gross little goblins," Pontivex said. "Grimy little dirt creatures, hardly better than the vantamoths. You don't even know you're going to die, do you? Well, you are. It'll be painful, and you're going to beg for your spawn mother. You'll never unlock the treasures of this dungeon, nor will you find any of the secrets hidden within. Just worthless rabble refuse. You probably won't even find the hidden doors in the fifth chamber, so low is your brow."

Bingo, I thought. I couldn't believe it. I mean, who in the hell talked like that in real life? Telegraphing your intentions and secrets? It was weird as balls, and I suspected this dungeon was a lot closer to its video-game cousins than it first let on. This gullible dipshit had fallen for the old "primitive savages who can actually understand you" ruse. All I'd needed to do was uncork the ire of the highly volatile Stinky, and *voila*. He'd even given up the information with an evil-villain monologue. This was far too stupid to be real.

I smiled up at the creature.

"Ew," Pontivex said, seeing my face. "Enough of whatever you call that. Is that an attempt to communicate? Your face looks like it is trying to give birth."

I looked back at Stinky, who was standing stock-still, staring up at the hive fiend as he carried on.

So, there are hidden doors, are there? And wouldn't you know it? They are in the exact same room I'm supposed to wind up in. Funny.

The message before us kept filling with details of the pretend explanation, but I wasn't really paying attention. It seemed like it was mostly for flavor, telling the comprehensive history of the dungeon and all that jazz. *Boring!*

"Ah," Pontivex finally said, shifting so that he was standing again. "Alas, young degenerates, I must take my leave. I am still trying to finish my crafts. It's not as though I have anything to worry about."

He sniffed the air and opened his wings as though he was preparing to take flight.

"Yep, you're goners. Well, see you never."

Shit!

I was almost there! I needed him to keep talking for just another moment longer. I felt a pit of congealed anxiety form in my stomach. I had to do something to keep his attention. But what?

I turned to look at Stinky, who caught my gaze and returned it with contempt.

"What?"

I sighed.

"Sorry, Stinkers," I said.

Then I punched him in the face.

It wasn't hard, but it was enough to send him reeling back a few steps and hurt my hand.

"Why the— wWat— You are fuckin' *dead*, orc!" Stinky shouted, and leaped at me.

I backpedaled and darted to the side. I noticed that he hadn't come after me with his dagger drawn; instead, he'd slipped it into his belt and was trying to swat me Rock 'Em Sock 'Em style.

So, he wasn't trying to kill me. Did he know what I was trying to do? Probably not, but that was all right. As long as he wasn't trying to carve me open like a Christmas ham, I could work with his low-energy haymakers.

BLAM!

Stinky's fist connected with my face as I'd tried to weave out of his reach. I stumbled backward, dazed.

"Damn!" I shouted. "That *hurt*!"

He was much stronger than I'd realized or, at the very least, was peacocking with a serious boost to his punches from some Skill, Ability, or magic.

"I'll show ya *hurt*!" Stinky cried, and jerked as though he was going to punch me again. I brought my arms up to block, and suddenly I felt a blow connect with my ribs as I was lifted up into the air by the force of an attack I hadn't been prepared for. He'd faked me out! I maybe only cleared three inches, but it was enough to cause me to lose my balance and fall backward. I cracked my elbow hard on the stone and wheezed out a moan, but Stinky wasn't done. He was already climbing on top of me and began delivering punishing blows to my face and chest with balled fists.

"Uncle!" I cried. "Uncle!"

Stinky kept pounding, though. He grinned.

"I've heard o' men crying for their mothers, orc—but extended family? That's pathetic!"

"I yield!" I tried instead.

Instantly, Stinky stopped his assault. He stood up, his grotesque grin still living on his face, and nodded down at me.

"Let that be a lesson to—"

"PSYCH!" I roared, and drew my legs in, kicking him square in the chest. Stinky flew backward with an airless *oof* and landed on his side a few feet away. I hauled myself up to my feet and stood, cracking my knuckles.

"Surprise, motherfucker!" I said.

Stinky was still gasping for air as I approached, but that was when I heard a sound that was music to my ears.

"Look at how they war with each other. Ignorant brutes. They'll surely kill one another well before the dungeon even has a chance to get *real* nasty."

Congratulations! You have learned a new language!
You have learned Ancient Chitinus I!

That's what I'm talking about!

I leaped back from Stinky, putting my hands up in the universal symbol of *Don't attack me; I have an idea that I have to test out real quick—also, sorry about starting a fake fight that turned into a real fight.* At least, I hoped that's what I was able to convey. I pointed up at Pontivex, who was just chilling on top of the arch, his legs dangling over the side as he sat watching.

"Pontivex!" I yelled. "Hold! Questions have. Answer, you."

Unfortunately, I'd only learned the most remedial version of his language—which, by its own right, was a feat genuinely spectacular. However, it reminded me of when I had taken Intro to Spanish my freshman year of high school. I'd barely known anything except for how to pronounce curse words—which, in a move that will surprise no one, I'd taught myself how to do marvelously.

Pontivex's expression was pure, stunned bewilderment. To him, this had to be a bizarre development, like how I'd feel if a mozzarella cheese stick suddenly started speaking to me in broken English. However, Pontivex seemed to recover from his shock instantly, and instead, his horrible gremlin face took on a suspicious shift.

"You *dare* to defile my esteemed and peerless tongue with your sub-intelligent gumming, orc?"

He stiffened.

"What manner of trick is this?"

"Answer," I said simply. "Question?"

Pontivex's eyes clouded over for more than a hot second, and when they returned to normal, he smiled viciously.

"Ah," he said, his tone now dripping with amusement. "I see. It is the effect of a potion. Oratory Splendor, it says. Now, how did a little creature like you, so pesky and inconsequential, get access to a Brilliance Tier item like that?"

"Big face, Zeol. He butterscotch."

Pontivex's eyes widened, and he chuckled.

"Butterscotch?"

No, that wasn't right.

I'd been trying to say something akin to *idiot*, but I didn't have the full scope of the lexicon of the language at my disposal. There seemed to be a tonal element that I couldn't quite command. It appeared that slight alterations in pitch made the difference in words, and that was an embarrassing area of the general linguistics I just wasn't nailing down. It was bizarre to speak a foreign language, even at this limited level, without ever having truly learned it. It was also frustrating to be wedged in a spot where I could tell that I was messing up but was woefully ill equipped to discern how to fix it. Equally concerning was that whatever this thing was not only knew about butterscotch but also had a word for it in his ancient tongue.

I tried again.

"Butterscotch. *Butterscotch.*"

I released a cry of frustration.

"BUTTERSCOTCH!"

Pontivex began laughing, which he did for a lot longer than I thought was necessary or kind, but eventually, he quieted down and leaned forward. At first, I thought he was planning to swoop down and eat me or something else equally as rude, but instead, he stared into my eyes and slowly opened his mouth.

"Idiot," he said, and just like that, the word was clear in my mind.

"Idiot," I returned.

"Delightful," Pontivex beamed. "So, someone named Zeol—who is apparently an imbecile with a gigantic face—is the one who provided you with the means to use the potion?"

I nodded.

"Very intriguing," the hive fiend said, leaning back and lacing his clawed digits together in contemplation. "I have not heard of this hero, but he is either quite powerful or extraordinarily wealthy to have both procured this item and seen fit to let it go to waste on such a whelp of a creature. I should like to meet this . . . Zeol, did you say?"

I nodded. Then, thinking about his previous statement, I quickly shook my head.

"Idiot," I said again. "No hello. Bad."

"Be that as it may," Pontivex said. "It is an odd choice to bestow a creature like you with the ability to hold court with their betters. I cannot imagine the reasoning, though perhaps that is their secret to keep? Not since the Exodus have I seen orcs in the halls of the Crypt. Even longer still since someone could approach close enough to converse with me. Dialogue is my natural weakness, as it were. Perhaps your benefactor . . . Zeol knew this? Which would mean they seek that which is most hidden and clandestine."

"Secret?" I asked, using the best of my abilities to puzzle out what I wanted to say.

Pontivex cocked an eyebrow at me.

"Oh," he said. "You want to know about the secrets of this dungeon?"

I nodded.

Pontivex held my gaze for a few long moments, and I could see he was getting a measure of me—which I don't think I need to explain the emotion *that* filled me with. Then a pleased and devious smile spread over his features, and suddenly I wanted to vomit.

God, this guy didn't just fall out of the ugly tree—he's the seed it grew from.

"I am willing to share a secret with you," he began slowly, making sure to enunciate fully so that I could understand him with pristine clarity. "But it will not fall to your ears without cost. Joyous though I am to have a beast other than the residents of the Crypt to bandy words with, I must insist that there be an equivalent exchange in place. I will reveal to you a magnificent hidden parcel of this tomb—one deliriously enticing. But it will only become known to *you* if you perform a task for *me*."

"No eat," I said seriously.

Pontivex chuckled.

"Oh, I wouldn't waste such an opportunity on whetting my appetite with your meager bones, whelp."

"Opportunity?" I'd been able to figure that word out on my own. Echoing words was easier than trying to invent them myself.

"Why, yes," Pontivex said. "Do you know how long I have been held in this dungeon?"

I shook my head.

"I came to this sanctum in the Era of Fog, Shadow, and Light. Before Tellegro could even hold a sword upright or the Emperor of the Black Crown had begun the Blood March, I was placed in the Crypt despite my own protests. Fettered and enraged, toiling against my binds, the Penitent Archon herself was the one who sealed me here, so terrible was my power. That was eight thousand, seven hundred years past," he stated. "Give or take a few centuries, in any case."

I let my surprise show plainly on my face. I didn't know any of the names or . . . royalty that the creature had referenced, but the years were plain enough. Nearly nine thousand years was, as far as was relative to my own lifespan, forever. I couldn't imagine existing that long, let alone being relegated to a place like this for the entirety of it. Well, I guess I didn't know what was beyond this section—though this area seemed pretty grim. Who knew? Maybe the rest of the floors were filled with cotton-candy back massages and an endless supply of Burger King, and this was just the foyer that existed to turn people away.

"So, perhaps even you could intimate how desperately thirsty I am for a drop of quenching tête-à-tête in this unctuous wasteland of cognizance?"

"Yes," I said. "Say what desire."

"Straightforward little fellow, aren't you?" Pontivex said. "I can warm to that, though a more verbose participant would be welcomed much more. Directness is likely to get you killed if you pursue it too doggedly, however. As to your query—and, I hope—an answer to mine own . . . "

Pontivex waved a claw in the air, and a separate display appeared in my vision.

You have been offered a Quest!

[Dungeon Quest] *Keep It Secret . . .*

Pontivex sel Delibitaus has requested that you find Exotic Meat of a unique and untested creature and return it to him.

Exotic Meat cannot exist within the dungeon itself and must be procured outside it.

- Reward(s): *Experience. Renown. Coin.*
- Bonus: *Secret Knowledge of the Forbidden Crypt of the Dreadnaught Lord* (Conditional)
- *Additional Bonus Rewards Based on Conditions*

NOTE: This is a Conditional Quest! As such, specific parameters must be met to fulfill it to completion. You will receive [1] Bonus Reward upon accepting the Quest.

Conditions:

- Time Allotted: *[6] Standard Months*
- Amount: *[1] Portion.*
- *Any amount over [1] will result in additional Rewards. Variety of Exotic Meat will result in additional Rewards.*

Level of Freshness will determine additional Bonus Rewards. Each Level of Freshness below [Live] will result in diminished Rewards.

- Preferred Freshness Level: *Live*
- Acceptable Freshness Levels: *Freshly Killed, Recently Killed, One Week Old*
- Unacceptable Freshness Levels: *Aged, Spoiled, Rotten*

Accept [Dungeon] Quest (Conditional)?

Yes / No

I stared at the prompt.

"Uh, what the fuck?" I said aloud. "You want . . . meat?"

Pontivex stared at me quizzically, and I realized I'd not used whatever the hell Ancient Chintius was. So, I translated as best I could.

"Yes," Pontivex said, nodding. "I have become bored of the fare within the confines of this wretched tomb. I would like to sample something the likes of which I have not yet had the pleasure of consuming."

All I could do was blink in disbelief.

"You must understand," Pontivex continued, and I wasn't sure, but it sounded like he was a little . . . desperate? "I delight in the unique. Nine millennia of the same rubbish consumption has made me tire of the taste of it altogether. Something different would make me most generous."

Hm. If that were true, then maybe I could sweeten my own pot? If he *really* wanted these tasty salamis for his infernal charcuterie board, then he might be willing to part with a little more for the trouble. Then I realized that it would be a nightmare to communicate my demands to him with such a limited vocabulary.

For the first time in a few minutes, I turned to Stinky. He had been standing, watching the interaction with something akin to horrified interest. I had to imagine it was like watching a slow-motion car accident.

"What languages do you speak?" I demanded.

Stinky scowled at me and made to spit on the floor, but then his eyes shot up to the humongous form of Pontivex, and I watched as he paused and then swallowed.

"Why?" he said to me after a moment.

"Why? Because it's important!" I explained sternly. "Just answer the damn question, shit salad! I'm trying to work out a deal."

Stinky glowered and then sighed and rolled his eyes.

"Arlo common tongue, Hathburian common tongue, Elvish common, Underelvish, Levikyvilish, Dardandron, Entwick common, a little Drakefolk, some Western Brychol. I also know how to use basic commands in the fucking Arcane Tongue. Is that enough for you, orc?"

"That'll do, Stinkers." I smirked.

I was taken aback, though. Stinky was apparently quite the linguist. Though I smugly noted that Ancient Chitinus was not in his arsenal.

Don't mind me; I only learned it in a literal minute.

I turned back to Pontivex.

"Speak other . . . speak?" I asked, sounding very stupid, I'm sure.

Pontivex took a moment to discern my meaning and then smiled.

"I speak many tongues, whelp. With your arrested loquaciousness, I can already imagine the designs your primitive mind has spilled forth with. Which lesser language would you prefer I engage with you in?"

I smiled.

Perfect. He still thinks I'm stupid. He just doesn't know how *stupid.*

"Stinky," I said.

"What do you want now? I can't begin to explain how unwholesome it is to watch you conversing with a creature like this."

Well, don't worry, Stinky. That particular problem is about to be sorted.

"Shut up for a second," I said. "Listen, can you do me a favor?"

"It's a blessed favor that I haven't run you through with a sharp blade already, orc," Stinky said. "You really think I'm the type to want *your* debt under me?"

"God. Dammit. Stinky," I said sharply. "It's a turn of phrase. Will you shut the fuck up for a second and just let me do this?"

Stinky shook his head as if giving up.

"What the fuck do you want?"

"Thank you," I said in a huff. "Can you say those languages you speak again, but, like, in the language itself?"

Then I pointed up at the monster on the archway.

"To him."

I tensed, feeling like the aggravatingly argumentative matau was going to put up a fight or say something annoying. Instead, he seemed to pick up what I was putting down and turned to Pontivex. Then he began to speak.

Honestly, it was pretty impressive. The confidence Stinky had with his recitation of the languages was far different than the trepidation he'd seemed to feel in having to speak with Pontivex and led me to believe that he might not even have had an accent in them if chatting with the native speakers. All had a unique quality to them, whether in their pronunciation or cadence, and I noticed that Stinky even changed the quality and pitch of his voice with some.

It took a moment, but eventually, Pontivex began speaking back to Stinky in a very harsh and guttural tongue.

Bingo!

I couldn't really catch their conversation, because while Zeol's spooky polyglot spell translated what was said—the nature of the language seemed to dictate that it be spoken at the lowest possible volume. I could only glean a few of the phrases muttered while straining my ears.

"Which one was it?" I asked Stinky. He ignored me and simply responded to Pontivex.

Suddenly, I was feeling left out of the convo.

"Hey, asshole," I said. "Which language do you guys both know?"

Stinky looked over at me, paused, and then whisper-spoke something that caused Pontivex to laugh and say a few words himself. Stinky smirked and nodded.

They're talking shit about me!

"What the hell, Stinky?!" I shouted. "You were shaking in your weirdly clean boots just a second ago, and now, suddenly, you're a social butterfly? Also, side note: why *are* your shoes so clean?"

Stinky turned back to me.

"Jealous, are we, orc? It's a shit color on you—though you're already fuckin' green, so I suppose you can't fight your nature. I'm starving for a chat with someone whose brains didn't already fall out of their fuckin' arse."

"Oh, I'm *so sorry* I'm not providing you with intellectually stimulating conversation," I said. "I'm busy trying not to get you and me killed. Speaking of starving, your new boyfriend here mentioned a few minutes ago how he wanted to eat you, so *maybe* you don't want to be cozying up so quickly."

Stinky blinked at me and shrugged.

"Everything is trying to bloody eat us, orc," he said, then paused, considering. "But fine. If you want to stack your cart high with favors from this beast, I'll gobble for you. That's the last kindness I'm doing for you, though. Keep that between your cheeks when you're trying to shove your guts back into your belly."

"Cute," I said, but, deciding not to further exacerbate Mr. Grouch, turned to look up at Pontivex.

"All right, Stinky: say exactly what I say, but, like, in whatever language you're using."

"I know how translation works, orc."

"Translate my *dick*, Stinky," I said.

"Aye, will do, orc, soon as there's a language that invents a word for that level of invisibility."

"Just do the *thing*!"

"Aye, orc," Stinky said. "Get to yapping."

So, yap I did.

It took a few moments of trial and error until my demands were eventually established, which left Pontivex holding the bag on a response. I made sure to let Stinky know not to speak after I made my request and used that silence tactic to force the monster to speak first. I conveniently didn't mention that I'd done it to Stinky himself just a little while back, but that seemed like unnecessary information. After what seemed like a million years, I even learned the language: Arcane Tongue. Bully for me.

Pontivex considered my dictated words and then nodded.

"That will suffice," he said, using Ancient Chitinus. "You will give me multiple portions of meat most rare, and in return, I shall provide you with *two* secrets of the dungeon and a valuable item. My end will be fulfilled upon acceptance of the Quest."

"Stinky," I said, "tell him it's a deal."

Stinky translated, and there was a laugh and a nod from Pontivex, which gave me pause. Did he think he'd come out the victor in this? Maybe he had, but I'd still have the secrets and sweet fucking item even if I failed.

I accepted the Quest and then nodded at Pontivex, who opened his palm and snapped a finger. An item materialized in his hand. He released it, and I watched as it floated in place before slowly descending beneath the arch and stopping right at my eye level. It was a trinket of some sort, made of gold and silver, with little batlike wings forged around the outside. In the center was a small, glittering blue gem that caught the light of the fire and cast a purple reflection back at me. I'd seen something similar before but couldn't recall where. To be fair, I'd laid witness to a decent amount of incomprehensible shit since my arrival, so my brain wasn't entirely making the connections it needed to. I activated Analysis.

Kameas of Discovery
- **Rarity: Ultra Rare**
- **Item Class: Enhancement**
- **Durability: 1/1**
- **Weight: N/A**

This Kameas is one of many that confer a Spell to the user. Accessing this item will grant the Discover [Doorway] Spell.

Discover [Doorway]
- *Arcane Cost: 10 Arcana*
- *Range: 30 feet*
- *Duration: 5 Minutes*
- *Restrictions: Utterance*
- *Wait: N/A*

A Spell allowing the user to find hidden doorways, gates, and other exits or outlets within thirty feet. This spell's duration is five minutes, after which time the opening cannot be found unless the spell is cast a second time. This spell uses Utterance and, as such, must be spoken.

Oh, yeah!

A Kameas was the same thing that had given me my Analysis Ability when I'd first arrived. It was good to know that magical woo-woo objects like that were still kicking around and not some bizarre one-time dealio. I reread the description and, with no amount of irony, found that I was a bit disappointed to discover the text was very . . . bland. No frills, snarky comments, or threats. Just plain, understandable information.

Odd.

I wasn't sure how much I liked introducing magic into my diet, though, as it didn't really jive with my original vision of how I wanted to be in this world. I supposed it would be useful in helping me get out of this hellish nightmare, and maybe if the magic was small, I could still focus on the essential things. Like being a monstrosity of might and destruction.

If only I could get there faster . . .

All of this tooting around, slowly learning Skills and Abilities, was monumentally tedious, and I hated it. When was I going to get to the fun stuff? I had stealth, yeah, but there wasn't really an opportunity to use much of that when I was constantly being ambushed or stuck in giant fire pits with the ugliest goddamn demon I'd ever seen in my life—and Pontivex was there as well. It made me functionally useless unless I could somehow think of a way to be cleverer than I had been, and those prospects looked bleak. So far, my plans had just been to go with my gut and cause as much destruction as possible—a solid go-to, if anyone's looking for badass ideas—but I wasn't sure how long that would keep me alive. I needed to increase my Intelligence, or Wisdom, or something because I wasn't even sure how to start . . . *starting* being better at all this.

Okay, introspection headache. Time to switch gears.

I focused on the message that had populated in front of me instead, allowing my bubble of self-reflection to pop.

Use *Kameas of Discovery* now?
Yes / No

I looked over at Stinky, intending to rub it in when I realized with horror that he was staring at a similar object. It was roughly the same size and shape as mine, but rather than metallic bat wings, his Kameas was wreathed in shining jade.

"Oh, what the hell?!"

Pontivex leaned forward, chuckling.

"Your companion did the bulk of the work, no? Our deal could not have been struck without his assistance. Do you not believe it is fair to compensate where work has been put in?"

I sighed.

"Yes," I said in my painfully broken language. "Yes is yes."

"Splendid," Pontivex said, clapping his hands.

"Now, shall we divulge these secrets?"

I held up a finger.

"Hold," I said, and turned back to Stinky.

"I'll show you mine if you show me yours," I said.

Stinky blinked away a thousand-yard stare and seemed to come back to reality, his eyes focusing on mine. Then he scrunched his brow.

"I don't give a rooster's red shite what yours is, orc," he said, and turned back to the Kameas. It dissolved in midair, and a green light fluttered around him. The light suddenly flashed, sparkled, and settled onto him before completely vanishing. I watched as the matau's eyes radiated the same emerald hue as the light for a moment before returning to blue.

"*Wow*," I said, prolonging the word to maximize my feeling of displeasure. "Just when you start to become lifelong friends with someone, they stab you in the butt."

"We're not friends, orc," Stinky spit.

"Oh, but we *are*, Stinky," I said. "Best friends, in fact. You're going to be the best man at my wedding. Which really sucks for you because I am going to be *such* a diva."

"Stop that." Stinky gestured to the demon of the doorway. "I'd rather be vomited out of *this one's* fuckin' mouth than be your best *anything*."

"What about best *enemy*?" I offered with a grin.

"No, I'm your *worst* enemy!"

I didn't respond but left a grin plastered to my face, not breaking eye contact.

" . . . we're not friends, dammit!" Stinky exclaimed. "I'm going to cut your damned face off!"

"Why, so you can keep it next to your bed and kiss it before you fall asleep every night?"

Stinky glared at me. Jeez, this guy was easy to get riled up.

I returned to Pontivex, who was waiting patiently, as though he didn't have a care in the world.

What is with this fucking guy?

"Yes," I said to him, confirming in my simple way. "Now. Secret. Yes?"

Pontivex rubbed his hands together.

"Yes, now that you have the item and have accepted the Quest, we may discuss your secrets," the beast said, and I began to catch a worrying tone in his speech. He was overjoyed now. Did he just like meat that much, or was this something else?

I wished very much at that moment to have been blessed with the social skills Nick had. My former friend could always ferret out the meaning behind even the simplest things and could usually recognize signs before they happened. It was why we had once had such a strong friendship. He was highly sensitive to the flow of a conversation, almost like he could predict its outcome. This was beneficial because he could usually use it to win someone over or stop something chaotic from forming in the first place by smoothly changing subjects. It had worked on me numerous times, and I wouldn't be aware of it until long after the fact. I'd start down a path that would ultimately have ended with anger, and suddenly, Nick would be talking about something silly that would make me laugh, or ask me about any new albums I was listening to. It was a sharp tactic, and I'd asked him about it once. He'd admitted that he believed it came from having an embarrassing dad who had no filter and would say the first thing that came to his mind in public—usually something awkward. So, he often had to notice the signs and be a few steps ahead in the conversation to kill it before it became an issue.

I'm a fucking moron, I thought to myself. I could have boosted one of my stats that affected that, but I'd been so hell-bent on being tough that I'd ignored a potentially helpful little boon.

Oh, well, no reason to worry over spilled milk now.

All I could do was mop up the mess and use whatever was left for my cereal.

"Your first secret relates to that which I have presented to you. Within each floor is at least one doorway. Sometimes there are multiple, but there is always at least a single exit that one might utilize if the woes of the Crypt become too harsh to bear."

"Out?" I asked.

"Yes," Pontivex said, still smiling mischievously. "It will remove you from the dungeon, but you must find the doorways first, and that is typically quite a hardship. It will become slightly easier with my gift, though I don't imagine it will take all of the fun out of it. It will still require some sleuthing. They *are* hidden doorways, after all."

Well, that wasn't as bad as I thought. Each floor had a way of escaping, but did they take you back to the surface or just back to the entryway with the eggs? Further, they were difficult to find, but as long as I was within thirty feet of them, I could use my spell and *poof* myself away. That would make the issue with Zeol's talisman a little less messy. I'd been worried about my ability to get out of there once I'd retrieved it, but Zeol had seemed to think I'd be fine.

So, he must've known about the exits, or maybe just assumed they'd existed?

If his plan had relied on this entire interaction happening with the shadow-stuffed bird-gremlin, then that meant that Zeol was probably a lot smarter than I was giving him credit for—and a lot more dangerous, too.

"Where?" I asked Pontivex.

"Oh, there's no fun bequeathing that information onto you, is there?" the creature asked, making a *tsk* sound and wagging a finger at me. "I cannot tell you outright where they are, but I *will* say that the first floor, for all of its shortcomings, is considerably easier to navigate than the lower ones—much more straightforward and direct. If you try to the maximum potential of your ability—and live long enough to do so—I am sure that even one as lowly and insignificant as yourself can manage its duress."

I wished at that moment that I had a magical device that could gouge out Pontivex's eyes. He'd given me a secret—sort of—but it wasn't very precise or helpful. I hadn't specified that I wanted them to be beneficial hints.

"Next," I said to Pontivex.

I needed to get this over with, and I was starting to get the feeling that I had indeed been worked over in this interaction. At the very least, if he wasn't giving me good information, I had no incentive to fulfill my end to the best of my efforts. Right?

Pontivex nodded.

"As you wish, whelp."

I quickly gave Stinky a rundown of what the creature had indicated, making it *very* clear with my tone and eye-rolling what I thought of the information. Stinky gave a noncommittal grunt in response but said nothing further. Finally, Pontivex stood to his full height, stretching his wings out as though he was preparing to take flight.

"Now," he began, looking over his shoulder across the lake of fire and then back to us. "A more pressing secret concerning the current chamber. When I leave this infernal roost, a challenge will begin. This is designed to test those who enter, as will several of the other chambers. Not all, but many. A bridge will form from this Ancient Arch to the one at the exit as it begins. You will have a short time to cross to the other side."

Well, that settles it; I didn't need to make this deal at all, in fact—

" . . . and you will need to do so with *all* of your dungeoneers intact."

"Uh, what?" I asked aloud.

Pontivex, who did not understand what I said physically, seemed to pick up the nature of my dumb-as-fuck expression and smiled.

"Yes, whelp. Everyone you entered the Crypt with must complete the challenge"—he paused for effect—" . . . alive."

I was starting to feel hot and sweaty, and I had to double-check to make sure I hadn't accidentally placed the festival cap on my head again. I had not. This was just anxiety.

" . . . oh, shit," I said.

"What?!" Stinky demanded, sensing the dread in my tone. But before I could respond, the gateway on the other side of the lake of fire ignited in light.

"Oh," Pontivex said in disappointment. "It appears one member has already reached the exit. Pity. I do hate a leg-up. Regardless . . . "

He launched from the arch and into the air on shadowy wings and wheeled on us once more.

"I believe you have it in you, whelp. You *must* have it in you, in fact. If you fail this challenge, you will die. Then you will be mine!"

"What are you talking about?!" I exclaimed, not bothering to use his language. It didn't matter; he knew what my intention was.

"You should really learn to discern the difference between a standard Quest and one with . . . conditions. Good luck!"

With that, Pontivex jackknifed in the air and plunged downward, right into the waiting lake of fire. A geyser of recoiling lava spat up with his entry and splashed against the karst we were standing on.

At that moment, a notification appeared, and my heart dropped into my balls with a clenching pain.

Challenge One Commencing
Duration Remaining: 8m 11s
Number of Successful Dungeoneers: 1/8

CHAPTER TWENTY-TWO

ORC-ESTRA

Once Pontivex had made his dramatic exit, three things happened at once.

First and most prominent, both archways in the chamber flashed, and I stared in awe as a dazzling platform of light shot between them, forming the contours of a bridge. Next, the timer began counting down, causing my anxiety to spike. But also, the clusters of hive-like structures hanging from the rocks above began to undulate.

"Stinky!" I yelled, turning to my armored companion. "We've got an issue!"

"I'm not blind, orc!" Stinky exclaimed. "I can see a lot of fuckin' issues turning their eyes on us!"

I glanced up at the hive and saw now that shapes were emerging from within. A *lot* of shapes. I shot a glance back to Stinky and then to the platform a ways off with the possessed roe.

"We have to get the eggs!" I shouted.

"What?!"

"We have to *bring* the fucking *eggs* with us! That big ole butthole, Pontivex, said everyone who entered with us needed to make it to the other side without being killed!"

"Oh, godsdamn fuckin' hell," Stinky said. "How in Yursk are we going to do that?"

"I dunno. Are you able to—"

SHOOM! SHOOM! SHOOM!

I was cut off mid-sentence as nearly a dozen figures reached the karst—doing so quick as absolute shit. They were large insectoid-like creatures with six legs and gigantic, fractal-looking eyes all over their heads. The heads themselves were puny in comparison to the beasts' bodies, but that didn't seem to affect their brainpower. The creatures were organized, zipping around in intricate patterns and buzzing furiously.

"Shit!" I shouted, jerking Stinky to the side as one of the big nasty hornet skanks dive-bombed toward us.

Stinky's dagger was out, reminding me that I also needed to be armed if I didn't want to die immediately, so I ripped the haladie from my waistband.

"Listen!" I hissed. "We need to *move*. We won't make it beyond this chamber if we don't bring those eggs with us! Can you hold them off?"

"Hold them off?!" Stinky shouted. But before I could respond, we were forced to separate as another one of the creatures took the opportunity to fly at us, and we dove in different directions. It had coasted by Stinky much closer than it had me, and I saw the matau quickly drag his blade across its carapace as it passed. It didn't look like it did much, and Stinky scowled as it jerked upward, back into the air, more of the creatures converging on our location.

"What are they?!" I demanded.

"Dread cuckoo brood," Stinky said. "Level Two integrated hive swarm!"

"Who the hell names these things?!"

"Not the time, orc! Not the fuckin' time!"

There were now around twenty of the things swarming above us, and we had to dodge a few more strikes as they sent out their warning party. Stinky had Berg's helmet on his head, still, so I wasn't able to use my magnificent punch maneuver, but I was planning on a different tactic.

"Can you hold them off or not?!"

Stinky narrowly avoided a head-on collision with one of the cuckoos before jamming his blade into one of its bulbous eyes. The beast let out a terrible peal of pain and zipped away. It shuddered as it reached the edge of the platform and just dropped out of the air, plunging over the side and into the lava below.

"Does that answer your question for you?!" Stinky demanded.

"Absolutely not!" I called back, already making my way to the other side of the karst, where I'd spotted a rocky ramp leading down to the web of stone walkways. "You haven't really been that impressive so far! Aren't you, like, a way higher level than these things?"

Stinky spat.

"Yes!"

"Then what the fuck? Why aren't you *better*? You should be wiping these things out like they're made of wet tissue!"

"I'm not using my gods-damned specialization!" Stinky said.

"Why the fuck not!?"

"Quit gumming at me! Get to the fuckin' roe so we can get out of here, you twat hair!"

I looked over the edge of the karst's ramp. I'd need to move quickly, but if those things caught me, I'd be hog-dog boned. An ample, open space was one thing, but it would be *much* tighter trying to avoid them while crossing those precarious bridges. I turned back to Stinky.

"Are you gonna use the thing we talked about?! I need a distraction. We *both* do!"

Stinky gave me a look of pure contempt.

"Yes! I'm trying to clear a damned path first!"

"Do it now!" I shouted. "There's no time!"

Stinky let out a howl of anger, but I didn't stick around to see whether or not he was going to follow through. Instead, I looked back over the edge at the ramp and jumped.

"Oof!"

I hit the ramp awkwardly and collapsed forward, blasting my chest against the rock. I had a flash of pure panic as I felt myself tumble toward the edge of the path, and flung my arms out to grasp anything to keep from falling to my death. Fortunately, I was able to catch myself staring over the side at the lava far below and hurriedly got to my feet.

"Jesus," I said, dusting myself off. "I need to, like, become more nimble. That was stupid."

I looked above me.

At least nobody saw that.

I turned my attention to my new target—the eggs. I beat a path down the ramp and slid to a stop in front of the network of crisscrossing walkways, trying desperately to discern which one would lead me to the right platform. I quickly traced the one I spotted nearest to where I'd last seen the roe and followed it down to where it met two other bridges, and, knowing I did not have a lot of time, fucking *went for it*. I stepped onto the bridge and quickly shuffled along, making my way to the confluence. A few paces away from the crossroads, I noticed a very distinct buzzing zooming up from behind me.

I didn't even look. I leaped forward, spanning the remaining distance, and landed on my stomach, hugging the ground as I felt the wind of passage overhead. I finally looked up and saw two . . . dread cuckoo brood . . . whirling around to come after me.

Shit!

I hopped up and bared my haladie before remembering I had some additional traits I hadn't considered. I'd gained some new shit from my level-ups but hadn't had a chance to scour them, and while now wasn't exactly opportune, I needed to be smart about how to pursue this next part. Taking a risk, I waited until the hornet monsters were right up on me and then fell sideways, throwing my hand out for balance. Fortunately, this area was much broader than the bridges themselves, and I had more room for silly shit and shenanigans. As they buzzed past me once more, I opened my menu to get a good and proper gander at my new slick baddie patrol.

Vengeful Aura—When resonance is established between an orc's race and the originating Class of Barbarian, Vengeful Aura is born. For [Rage +Intimidate quotient] number of charges per day, an orc Barbarian can emit a wave of intimidating presence that has a chance to inflict the Frightened condition on targets within a radius. The outcome for efficiency is Intimidate +Vengeful Aura. The area radius is based on Intimidate +Charisma quotient.
- Radius: [2 ft.]

Note: This is an Ability exclusive to the orc +Barbarian path.

Enduring Perch—A Barbarian takes a readied stance that they cannot be moved from while their Stamina lasts. For the extent, their feet become rooted to their position, and while they can be hurt or killed, their feet cannot be wrested from where they plant them. The surface they root themselves to must be ground- or floor-aligned. Stamina exhausts at a rate of 10 points per second. Stamina must be at a minimum of fifty percent to activate Enduring Perch. If Stamina is exhausted during use, the user will suffer the Off-Balance condition and be unable to activate again until Stamina is at maximum.

Oh, dang.

Vengeful Aura would be potentially useful if I could get my Charisma higher, but what the hell would two feet of effect be able to do for me right now? If something was up in my grill, my options were probably very limited, and I didn't think busting out a mean mug would be pertinent. It would also likely get me killed if I tried to rely on it in such a critical moment, but I could potentially utilize Enduring Perch.

There was no time to debate, as the hornets were turning around again in tandem to try and make the third time their charm. I took a breath, widened my stance, and felt the nearly subconscious sensation of activating my Abilities as I allowed Enduring Perch to take hold of my body. Warmth and a feeling of power spread through my hips, thighs, and legs before moving to my feet. I suddenly felt as though the ground beneath me were almost a part of me, as whatever witchery controlling this aspect of the world set in like quick-acting concrete.

CRUNCH!

The creatures hit me hard but *not* as hard as I would have expected. I quickly concluded that barreling into things wasn't in their long-term plans, especially considering both beasts tried to lift me into the fucking air.

So, they swoop and grab. Good to know.

"No thank you," I hissed as the two insects tried to unsuccessfully rip me from my position. My feet were basically fused to the ground, and that felt *wonderful*. The big, bad beetleborgs were as disgusting as they were unrelenting, driving into me with all the power their oddly unweighty bodies could muster. They stank to high hell, and there was a viscous liquid dripping from their mouths and limbs that made me want to puke.

Then I did puke. Right onto the dread cuckoos.

Goddamn, I gotta stop doing that! I don't want vomit to become what I'm known for!

The wasp monstrosities seemed to *love* this new introduction to the fray and began greedily lapping up my purge, which almost made me heave again. The noises they made were some of the grossest sounds I'd ever heard in my life and would surely haunt the halls of my nightmares for years to come. I needed to end this.

They hadn't stopped tugging on me, so I let them continue, keeping a careful eye on my Stamina as they did. About half of it remained, and I didn't want to fall into the danger zone and suddenly find out what *Off-Balance* meant in the heat of the moment. So, I lifted the haladie and slid it cleanly into an eye a-piece.

This, it turned out, was a huge mistake.

I'd assumed they'd just careen away and collapse like the one Stinky had handled, but they didn't do that *at all*. Instead, they both began to feverishly bore into one another, the cries of pain they'd been making replaced by more of the sickly slurps. They began to press hard into me, and then I felt a sharp stab as I noticed one of them using a long tendril tongue to lap up some of the blood that had gotten on my arm.

"I *said* no thank you!" I shouted, stuffing the haladie between my teeth. Then I grabbed each of their spongey, eye-peppered heads and rammed them against one another. My Stamina was beginning to get too low for my personal comfort, so I dropped Enduring Perch, continuing to bash the broods' skulls together like a cymbal player in an orchestra. But, of course, I'd grossly overestimated my ability to fend these things off on my own, and suddenly, I was in the air.

"Shit—goddamn—fuck!" I cried as the two mercilessly feasting burbling turd creatures rose up, carrying me with them easily. Sharp pincers dug into my back and sides, and I became very fucking concerned that I was now going to be trapped. The worst part was that the creatures were now disoriented by my attack and their own gobbling of one another. This meant that if they suddenly went into overdrive failure, I would be dragged along with them to whatever final destination their collapsing trajectory took them.

I couldn't imagine my predicament possibly going worse. So, of course, it did. Hard.

As we moved up, I suddenly caught a glimpse of the light bridge between the arches and noticed a familiar sight. Stinky. He was moving at a sprint, with dozens of the cuckoos right behind him. He looked surprisingly calm, despite his predicament. Then, to my complete and total horror, I watched as the cuckoos caught up to him. They surrounded the matau in an obscuring veil of wings and legs, spinning around the spot he'd been in with the turbulence of a living tornado. Then the cluster moved into the air.

Suddenly, they dispersed, and I felt my stomach grow cold as I realized that there was no trace left of my annoying-as-fuck dungeon companion. They'd consumed him.

"Argggh!" I screamed, both in desperation and fear.

This better have worked.

If Stinky was gone, then I'd failed the challenge, and that meant death. I looked at the display in the corner of my vision, indicating my allotted time.

Challenge One [Active]
Duration Remaining: 7m 6s
Number of Successful Dungeoneers: 1/8

I watched as the timer clicked down to seven minutes and five seconds. Seven minutes and four. It still said the challenge was active. I breathed a sigh of relief.

I watched as the chaotic cacophony of unabridged insectoid dipshittery began anew, the dread cuckoo brood seemingly agitated. I had a feeling I knew why but hadn't seen enough evidence that my theory was correct. I peered over at the karst but couldn't see anyone else there at first. Then there was something akin to a dissolution of air, and Stinky appeared. He was completely unharmed, and the best part was there were no nearby insectoids. Save for one.

Well, for a moment, there was one. Stinky leaped at the creature, which was still unaware of his presence, and jammed his dagger right into its head. Then he dragged the cuckoo to the ground, stabbing it over and over again in a very violent display of man versus nature. Well, matau-versus-monster, I suppose.

"He' yeah!" I shouted through gritted teeth, my haladie still in my mouth. Stinky's head snapped in my direction angrily.

"What the fuck are you doing, orc?!"

"F'ying!" I called back, unable to hide the obvious agony I was in. "I'h d'moofest way to trav— AGH!"

One of the brood had died, its brother still chomping on its corpse, dead weight now pulling on the barbs in my side. They were tangled, so the other insect couldn't dislodge even if it had wanted to—which it was apparent that it did not. We were now losing altitude, which would be exacerbated once the other one passed over into bug hell.

You have killed [1] Level 2 Dread Cuckoo Brood!
Gained 512 Experience.

I couldn't wait around for the other to expire. Instead, I pulled the haladie from my mouth and began sawing into the hooks trapped in my flesh. The first few appendages were severed without issue, belonging to the dead body. However, the moment I moved on to number four, I was met with *incredibly* loud and annoying resistance. The almost-dead super wasp recoiled as I dragged the blade of my weapon across its tender claw-arm, thrashing against the pain and jerking so badly, we began to drop even faster. I didn't stop, though. I had a hankering for an insect cutlet.

I finally got through its tether and moved on to the last one, hacking at it to cut down on time. All the while, the creature did the insect version of screaming. Then it began ramming its already-destroyed head against mine. Finally, I was able to cut myself loose and grabbed onto it, sliding around in midair and attempting to get on to its back. I was able to do so, but only barely.

Now atop my hard-bodied steed, I grabbed its head and tried to aim. I wasn't stupid enough to kill it while we were still in flight, but I did punch it a few times for the inconvenience but only received a sore fist for my trouble.

Boy, oh, boy. Exoskeletons are hard!

I pushed forward and forced the creature's failing flight into the direction I wanted: the platform with the eggs. I could see them now, quivering and jumping in their own panic.

You have killed [1] Level 2 Dread Cuckoo Brood!
Gained 531 Experience.

Ah, shit.

The beast's body suddenly drooped, and I was left trying desperately to pilot a vehicle that no longer had any go-go juice. The platform was still about fifty feet below me and another thirty feet forward, and that was not going to do me any favors. But what other option did I have? I stood up as much as I could, lined myself up, and vaulted off the back of the dead cuckoo.

I wasn't even close.

My cool-guy action carried me less than ten feet before I started to plummet, screaming as I did so. It had been such a stupid maneuver, and now I was soaring right toward the lake of fire a few hundred feet directly below me.

"Shiiiiiiiiiiit!" I roared as my body began to spin.

I was able to make out the blurred shape of the dozens of bridges beneath me, crisscrossing rudely. I had one option, and it was going to hurt.

I thought about my somersault earlier in the day and how easy my spin had been. Working backward from that, I straightened my legs and crooked my right arm. Doing this allowed me to stop the violent rotation. Instead, I straightened out my limbs and turned so that my chest was facing downward again. I brought my arms to my sides and slowly spread them out like I had seen base jumpers do in YouTube videos. This caused me to move forward as I fell, right into the path of one of the bridges.

All right, I'm just going to have to hit it hard and hope it doesn't kill me. Better than being burned alive by Big Hot Pond.

I was rapidly approaching my quarry, and I stretched my arms out to grab on and stop myself from falling.

All right, here goes nothi—

I hit the bridge, but instead of landing on it, my body broke *through* it, the rock crumbling as I made contact and continued falling.

Fortunately, the bridge thirty feet below was much sturdier.

I landed hard, and if the previous walkway hadn't already done so, I knew it would have knocked the wind out of me. As it stood, I lay, curled in a ball of pain on my tenuous thread of life, clutching the sides of the bridge to make sure I didn't tumble farther.

Condition: Fractured mitigated. [Health bonus]

"That . . . sucked," I breathed.

My health had taken another big hit, and now I was almost back in the normal range, the boost from Zeol's magic cookie nearly gone. I shakily raised myself to my feet, feeling sore everywhere. I could *not* keep falling, as my body would likely turn into pebbles the next time. Avoiding the Fractured condition was apparently possible only because of my health boost. Still, now that I was so close to losing it, I knew I wouldn't be so lucky next time.

"Fuck this place," I said, looking up at the karst's summit high above.

I gathered my bearings, looking for where the possessed roe's platform was in relative location to myself. I spotted it easily and made my way back up through the web of interconnected bridges with a sigh.

By the time I reached the platform, just over four minutes remained in the challenge. So far, no one else had made it across. But we also hadn't failed it, so I knew that Stinky was still alive.

I arrived to find the jumble of possessed roe tucked into a corner of the platform beneath a narrow stone shelf. They quivered, bright red eyes staring at me in the dim space giving them the appearance of jittery, evil coffee beans. I drew closer to them, dreading what I was planning to do, as they made no moves to attack.

"Here, eggy, eggies," I cooed, moving forward slowly. "Come get a tasty bite of *delicious* orc outsides so that we don't goddamn *die* . . . "

The possessed roe were being strangely skittish all of a sudden, and that just wasn't going to do. I had devised an ingenious strategy to let them all latch on to me and then book it for the bridge. Still, if they were suddenly super shy about their portion control, I'd have to figure something else out. Which would be awful. There was nothing I hated more than thinking after I *already done thought*.

"Come on, dammit," I hissed, trying not to raise my voice too much in case the swarm of cuckoos decided to home in on my frequency. "I need you to gnaw on me with your stupid egg teeth so I can get us out of here. I'd leave you if I could, but I *can't*. So, this is how it has to be."

They peered at me, suspicious and uncomprehending. So, I decided to push my luck. Quickly, I grabbed one of the roe from the group and held it aloft.

"Eat me," I demanded and tried to press it to my skin. "Just do it, you little punk."

Before, when I'd come in contact with them without the party hat, they'd acted like a super-adhesive, attaching themselves to my flesh with hardly any actual surface-to-surface connection. Now, though, when I held the egg, I realized that it felt like clutching an orb of pure static electricity. The hairs on my arms stood on end, and there was an invisible crackle where my hands met the texture of the roe's body. It didn't stick at all, so I tried to *force* it to latch on. As I moved it close to me, the roe spun in my grasp, and I lost my grip. Then it bounced out of my hands and back to its brothers, where it continued shuddering, trying to get as far away from me as it could.

I looked back over my shoulder at the karst and gulped. The huge murder of insectoids had finally returned to Stinky. Fortunately, he was fast enough to avoid the outliers at the moment. But he was still wounded and worn down, and I knew he wouldn't be able to last for very long. I was confused by the fact that they'd all moved as one when going after the little gimmick, but now it was like they were toying with him . . .

"Oh."

They *were* toying with him. This challenge was designed to waylay people to keep them from reaching the arch on the opposite side before the timer ran out. That was obvious enough, but what I'd seen them do to Stinky's ruse had been overkill. If I was designing a challenge like this, I would try to make it sneaky as fuck to get past, which would mean distracting someone with something big and shiny.

Something *big and shiny* like the bridge of light cutting through the center of the enormous cavernous butt pain.

That's the trap.

The bridge itself was a distraction. If you tried to cross it, the creatures would swarm and grab you, but if you kept your distance, they assaulted far less frequently. Like how they were taking their time onesie-twosie with Stinky right now—or how only two had gone after me when I'd gone off the beaten path. Something else clicked into place then. Whoever our eighth party member was had already crossed the archway on the other side, and they'd done so before the bridge had ever formed.

What was it that Pontivex had said about directness?

. . . it is likely to get you killed if you pursue it too doggedly.

I'd, of course, assumed he was speaking about the way I'd interacted with him. But now it seemed like a blazing, white-hot hint.

I scanned the platform's edge. Sure enough, I could now see that though most of its space ended in little rocky alcoved sections, the last two feet of floor continued beyond like a catwalk. I followed the now obviously intentional path with my eyes. I saw that all of the alcoves were connected by a thin band of discolored rock circling the entirety of the lake of fire. As far as I could tell, there were two platforms on either side of the far-end archway, about a hundred feet above. As sure as my Aunt Ella was a shitty cook, that would be our ticket out of there.

Furious bubbles of an idea began to brew in my skull, but to execute it, I'd need . . .

My eyes fell on an object in the other corner of the platform. I wasn't sure how I'd missed it before, but when I spotted it, I felt a tiny blossom of hope. Resting all on its lonesome was a massive, ten-foot-wide chest.

"Man, it can't be this easy, can it?"

I raced to it, not even bothering to Analyze it before wrenching it open.

I stared.

"Oh. My. Hell."

Inside the chest were several items that looked like they *could* be useful . . . but I wasn't sure because they were resting on top of a gigantic pile of glittering gold coins.

I could feel my eyes bulging and hurriedly glanced around to see if anything was heading in my immediate direction. With no danger on the horizon, I examined them just to ensure they were genuine. Then I turned my attention to the items.

Cincture of Suresight
- Rarity: Uncommon
- Item Class: Belt
- Durability: 80/80
- Weight: 1.0 lbs.
- Defense: N/A

Bonuses:
- +5% to Archer Skill

A waistband made of Brychol leather and bearing the ornate symbol of a bow and arrow wrought in silver. This item grants a five percent boost to the Archer Skill but does not gift the Skill itself.

Guardian's Buckler
- Rarity: Uncommon
- Item Class: Shield
- Durability: 500/500
- Weight: 0.08 lbs.
- Defense: +3%
- Bonuses: Bashing +2%

A small, lightweight shield designed to be held in a user's off hand. While simple in design, this particular item was forged with a conical design to assist the user in glancing off blows more easily. The Guardian's Buckler can also be used as a bashing weapon.

Tandar's Flipper Slippers
- Rarity: Unique
- Item Class: Footwear
- Durability: ???
- Weight: 2.3 lbs.
- Defense: N/A

Bonuses:
- +10% Water Movement Speed
- Grants Waterbreathing for [1] hour(s)

Charges: [1] Daily

Swim fins made of stretchy leather-like material of indeterminate origin. A one-of-a-kind magical item, Tandar's Flipper Slippers gives the user more ease of movement when swimming or traversing underwater terrain. Grants the Waterbreathing Ability for one hour per charge.

Indestructible Orb
- Rarity: ???
- Item Class: ???
- Durability: N/A
- Weight: 3.0 lbs.
- Bonuses: ???

A sphere that seems to be made of cloudy glass. This orb cannot be destroyed. Its purpose is unknown.

[Lustrous] Skill Book of [Acrobat]
- Rarity: Elusive
- Item Class: Skill Book
- Durability: 1/1
- Weight: N/A
- Bonuses: Grants Acrobat Skill

This is a Lustrous Skill Book. Requires an 8-minute duration to learn. Skills gained from Lustrous-quality manuals begin at E-Rank Level 1.

[1] Slab of Ham
- Rarity: Pedestrian
- Item Class: Food
- Durability: 1/1
- Weight: .04 lbs.
- Bonuses: N/A

Ham.

What in blazes are these items doing in the first chamber of the beginner floor of this dungeon?

So, these had been hanging out here, being all fly and shit, just waiting for someone to wander on by and have a look inside? That didn't make any sense to me. Obviously, I'd been told that dungeons had some lucrative goodies inside them, but this was the *starter zone*. Surely, things labeled as *indestructible* weren't commonly collecting dust in a place like this?

I didn't have time to think about them right now, though. Nothing within the chest had offered me what I was hoping for: a distraction. Even worse was that every item was basically pointless at the moment. I wasn't an archer, I didn't have time to read a whole fucking book, and I sure as hell couldn't *swim* my way out of this situation. I'd definitely be utilizing the buckler, but as it required being held, it was also a no-go. I needed more hands right now, not *less*. Also, what the *fuck* was I supposed to do with ham? Who knew how long it had even been in the chest? If I attempted to eat it, I'd likely get cursed with a permanent case of the green apple splatters.

Though it does look weirdly fresh . . .

Everything went into my pack, and then I moved on to the gold.

"Maybe *these* could be a distraction?" I said aloud. "In some sort of Hail Mary chaos option."

I looked at the timer. Three minutes remained.

"Shit," I said. "Fuck it. Cowabunga it is!"

I felt in my pocket for the tomfoolery item Stinky had given me to ensure it was still there. I shoved my hands into the pile of gold coins, gathering as many as I could in both hands before whipping them over the side of the platform in a high arc. I was greeted with the sound of pleasant tinkling as the coins bounced against the rock wall beneath me and struck the bridges as well. It was sort of loud, but I wasn't sure if it would work. I glanced beyond the rim and watched as the gold caught the light of the flames, glowing brightly as they plink-plunked downward.

I peered at the karst. It was clear the noise of the coins and flashes of light had caught the attention of some of the cuckoos. The large insectoids hovered in place, their gross engorged pimple-heads seeking out the source of the noise.

"That worked?"

I shrugged.

Guess I'll have to do it better this go-around.

I looked back at the massive chest. It looked heavy, but I considered that maybe I could drag it to the edge and tip it over if I leveraged my weight a little bit. In the spirit of cowabunga, I decided to throw caution to the wind and just try. I ran back to the chest, grabbed the iron handle on its side panel, and *heaved*.

I fell backward as the chest flew through the air like it was made of cardboard, my motion forcing it into an overhead swing as I clutched the handle. Because I'd left the lid open, I lay watching as the entire stock of coins flew out, blanketing the empty space beyond the platform like thousands of tiny golden fireworks. What I could only imagine was a king's ransom of wealth flew through the air and hit every available solid surface with a cascading cacophony of clinks.

That had indeed grabbed the winsome wiles of the dread cuckoo brood. The entire mob suddenly moved as one, beelining for me. I stared at the chest still attached to my hand.

"What the fuck is this thing made out of, Delta Air vouchers?"

You know I had to Analyze that bitch.

Feather Chest
- **Rarity: Storied**
- **Item Class: Storage**
- **Durability: ???**
- **Weight: ???**
- **Bonuses: ???**

A magical storage space designed to fit a maximum of a 10x10 area. This chest weighs a negligible sum and can be expanded to its full size by using the key phrase: Feather Chest Maximize *or made compact with the key phrase:* Feather Chest Minimize. *Items stored within the confines of the Feather Chest will be nearly weightless and maintain their condition for the duration of their time inside. Items will not suffer damage from minimized state.*

Please note: while living objects can be placed within the Feather Chest, they may remain a finite duration.
- **Duration: [4] minutes.**

Holy macaroni!

I'd just been served up a grand slam. Not the baseball kind. The *Denny's* kind. I was gonna eat this motherfucking challenge like a . . . *me* after the two-day flu.

The swarm of buzzing monsters was moving quickly toward me now, so it was now or never. I wheeled on the roe, still quivering in their corner. A gleeful smile spread across my face.

"All right, guys," I said, cracking my knuckles. "We don't have time to be piddle-farting around like this. Y'all are coming with me."

Then I began stuffing them into the chest with the kind of maniacal jubilation typically reserved for serial killers. Then, before they could bounce away, I slammed the lid shut.

"Feather Chest, minimize."

The humongous container made a loud popping sound and instantly transformed, shrinking into the size of a ring box.

"This is so dope," I said, snatching the now tiny chest up and stowing it in my pack.

That was when the swarm reached the platform. I stuck my hand into my pocket and withdrew the small cube I'd been saving. I dropped it on the ground in front of me and, with a mighty flourish, slammed my foot down, shattering the trinket into smithereens.

"Run and jump!" I shouted. Then I barreled forward at a full sprint and leaped off the side of the platform.

Or, at least, my mirror image did.

Troyal's Doppelganger Cube
- **Rarity: Elusive**
- **Item Class: Magical Item**
- **Durability: 1/1**
- **Weight: N/A**
- **Bonuses: N/A**
- **Duration: [1] minute(s)**

This is a magical item designed to mimic the effects of the Doppelganger Spell. Upon destruction of the cube, the spell released creates a spectral clone of the user that can follow basic commands. While active, the user is invisible to most non-magical and some magical beings. The Doppelganger may engage in any simple activity that the user demands, but they do not have intelligence or physical statistics, so actions requiring complex decision-making or exertion will be impossible. Additionally, Doppelgangers bear only 1 Health point, and combat-based commands are ill advised. This Spell lasts for 1 minute or until the Doppelganger is destroyed. Once the effect fades, the user will gain visibility again.

I felt my body change, watching as my arms and legs disappeared. Then, without waiting, I shot right for the thin strip of pathway that connected the platforms. I'd been concerned before, when Stinky had deployed this tactic, because his body double looked so realistic. But now I was glad the image had been indistinguishable from the real deal.

I saw my Doppelganger's body plummet below, with the swarm hot on its heels. That meant I didn't have long before I'd become a big, ugly eyesore again. But that was all right. I only needed a head start, and then everything would be *coming up Loon*. I realized that I hadn't actually gotten a look at my face, and I still didn't know what I looked like. I had only seen the back of my head as my Doppelganger raced off the edge of the cliff.

Oh, well. I'll just find a reflective surface later. There's still plenty of time before I need to ruin my own day with a visual.

I didn't dare look over at the light bridge, hoping against all fuck that Stinky had used my diversion wisely.

I quickly learned that it was insanely difficult to navigate a precarious path when you couldn't see your own feet. It made maintaining balance a deadly game of gravity chicken. I moved as quickly as I could and almost fell once during my dash. Fortunately, I'd activated Enduring Perch and kept myself from tripping by rooting myself to the rock.

Then I saw a flash of light below me, and my body became corporeal again.

Poor guy never stood a chance. Ah, well. I'll send a gift basket to his next of kin. Guess I'll be buying myself some lovely chocolates.

I made it to the next platform and took the opportunity to glance at the timer. There was just under two minutes remaining.

Damn, I'm cutting it close!

On this platform was another chest, and a very large part of me was greedy enough to want to wander over and loot it. But I was in the middle of a super sweet mission that I could very easily fail, and it didn't seem like that would be conducive to surviving long enough to share my badass origin story. So, while I moved on physically, the *what-if* of that serendipitous bounty would live on forever in my heart.

However, things were looking grim. I didn't think I'd be able to make it to the end and figure out a way down in the time left over. I'd have to figure out a way to get creative.

I was almost to the third and penultimate platform when I heard the buzzing return, and I shot a look behind me. Five cuckoos were rapidly gaining on me, bearing down on my location as I penguin-trotted along, pathetically exposed. Suddenly, only ten feet from me, my pursuers shifted, their attention focused elsewhere. That was when I caught sight of something truly bizarre.

Just beyond the threshold of the arch on the karst, only a few feet on the light bridge, was Stinky. Or, rather, what I assumed was another one of his Doppelgangers. He was jumping up and down, waving his arms in sync with his legs in something I could only describe as the world's most uncoordinated jumping jack.

Heh. Well, distractions are rarely subtle. Good on you, Stinkers.

Not wanting to let him have all the fun, I swiped at the cuckoo nearest to me. My attack hit home, bisecting one of the monster's legs and causing it to reel back, directing angry eyes at me. It released a screech of fury.

"Oh, shut up!" I said.

Then I launched off the catwalk and onto the dread cuckoo. I wrapped my arms around it as it immediately started trying to give me a nasty tongue-lashing.

I ignored the probe and shifted, climbing up its body and onto its back as the bug thrashed against me.

"That's about enough outta you, sweetie!" I said, slapping the creature's tongue away. "Agh!"

I'd forgotten how sharp the tines on the tongue were, and as I drew my hand back, I saw small gashes had been torn open in the flesh of my hand. This only made its fervor worse, however, because now it had caught the scent of my super dishy orc blood. The vicious vespa began turning, trying to get at me.

I do not have time for this!

"Knock it off!" I yelled, slipping from my perch and gripping its hard outer shell. Finally, after another moment, I was able to climb atop it. Then, before it could do anything else to piss me off, I focused my intent on being as inconspicuous as possible. I noticed immediately that there was a section of the carapace that looked a bit like the horn of a saddle and appeared a lot denser than the rest of it. I carefully shifted my weight over and pulled myself into a crouch, balancing on the balls of my feet and holding tight to the extension. The cuckoo thrashed a bit more, but I had locked myself into a fairly stable position. Eventually, it stopped, though it seemed confused as to what it needed to be doing. I hardly breathed as I waited, gathering my cloak around me as much as I could.

One minute, forty seconds . . .

One minute, thirty-nine seconds . . .

Finally, the beast lurched in the air and began following its friends, who had about fifteen seconds of a head start. All eyes had shifted to the ridiculous performance that false Stinky was engaging in. Now his form was rotating his hips with his hands on his waist. Was he . . . twerking?

No, that wasn't it. It looked like one of those old infomercials for some sort of ab-destroying, bun-hardening calisthenics.

I think that's what Stinky considers exercise . . .

I held on as the swarm ahead of me and my new mount finally reached their prey. However, good ole Doppel-Stinker was blissfully unaware of their rapid approach, choosing instead to switch to overhead arm reaches like he was a Jazzercise instructor. I almost started laughing at the pure, ridiculous insanity of the image of someone making their last stand one of fitness.

The brood surrounded the Doppelganger, and one brave soul swooped down to pick it up. When it did, Stinky's double instantly phased out of existence, and I shot a look to see where the real matau was.

There he is.

The genuine Stinkster was booking it at an alarmingly fast speed across the light bridge and was nearly three-fourths of the way across.

Holy shit! He's going to make it!

The entire swarm shifted as one urgent mass and began to buzz menacingly as they, too, picked up speed. I held on in my crouch, still completely unnoticed by any of the cuckoos as they shot like bolts of gross lightning across the cavern to stop Stinky from reaching the other side. In mere moments, they'd almost completely caught up, all of the monsters diving low to catch him. That was when I saw Stinky toss another cube ten feet ahead of himself and crunch it under his boot when he reached it. As if emerging from the back of Stinky's own body, another Doppelganger sprouted, facing the direction Stinky had just been running from.

This could also be understood as *directly toward the swarm*.

Then, just before it reached the bevy of buzzing brutes, the Doppelganger veered hard to the right and dove off of the light bridge. The whole mass shifted to follow him, but I took that moment to be a little bit of an asshole. As the giant hornet beneath me switched directions, I quickly slid one of the blades of my haladie under the back of its skull.

You have killed [1] Level 2 Dread Cuckoo Brood!
Stealth Kill Bonus! [x2]
Gained 1,050 Experience.

I used my crouch to spring forward just as the cuckoo dropped out of the sky. Fortunately, my specific free ride had been only around fifteen feet from the bridge, so there wasn't far to travel. I had momentum and a terrible sense of balance, and landed hard on my feet and immediately stumbled forward several paces before activating Enduring Perch to stop myself from falling over. Before I could be found out, I used my last clone cube, smashing it against my chest as hard as I could.

"Run fast off the bridge!" I shouted, and didn't even watch it appear or dash away. I became invisible and rocketed directly for the arch that was still about fifty feet away. I appeared alone on this walkway but knew that Stinky was probably doing the same thing I was. I had to trust that he would make it as well.

Suddenly, Stinky appeared again, directly ahead of me. Apparently, his Doppelganger had already died, but he was booking it toward the exit like it was the last available bathroom in a Taco Bell. He wouldn't know I was there, but he didn't seem concerned about that. I tried desperately to keep up as he crossed the end of the light bridge and onto the stone before the archway.

Fuck, yes! Let's do this shit!

FWOOM!

A shape had struck like an arrow, scooping Stinky up and away from the ground.

"Argh!" Stinky roared, thrashing. He was wrapped in the tight grip of one of the cuckoos that had apparently been quicker on the uptake than its disgusting companions. It flew upward, shifting as if to change directions, but Stinky was giving it hell from below and making it a lot more difficult than the insectoid probably expected. Stinky's arms were trapped at his sides, but he was kicking the creature's underside as hard as he could manage and even threw a headbutt or two in there.

We were too close. Feet away from the arch, and this little Brundlefly asshole thought he was going to deny me my red-blooded American right to go fuck shit up farther in this dungeon?

Not today, bitch.

I kept moving, because the stupidest thing I could do would be to stand in place. So, this was going to get a little dicey. I kept closing the gap between me and the area directly below the cuckoo, and hefted my haladie. I tried to focus as best I could and aimed at the monster. Then I did a little spin and released the haladie with a snap of my wrist.

I stared as the haladie fired away in a straight line, spinning like a fan blade, and cleanly cut through the cuckoo's head before spinning off and away in an arc.

> **You have killed [1] Level 2 Dread Cuckoo Brood!**
> *Stealth Kill Bonus! [x1.2]*
> *Critical Hit Bonus! [x2]*
> **Gained 1,645 Experience.**
> **Congratulations! You have raised a Skill!**
> *Throwing Weapons [F-Rank Level 2]*
> **Congratulations! You have raised a Skill!**
> *Throwing Weapons [F-Rank Level 3]*
> **Congratulations! You have raised a Skill!**
> *Throwing Weapons [F-Rank Level 4]*
> **Congratulations! You have raised a Skill!**
> *Throwing Weapons [F-Rank Level 5]*

"Yes! Fuck you, cuckoo! *Fuck you!*" I roared.

As the beast fell, its limbs untangled to allow Stinky to drop separately.

"Suck my *whole* dick, dungeon! I am the— *Uh-oh!*"

Stinky had rotated in the air and was not going to land on the bridge. He made a sound as though he was swallowing a duck as he realized his predicament. I could make it, though.

He's going to owe me so hard after this.

I raced to the edge of the light bridge and activated Enduring Perch. I stuck my arms out and caught Stinky just as he got within range.

"Ahhhhh!" he screamed, staring at the lava far below. I'd forgotten that in my haste to catch him, I was still under the effects of the Doppelganger spell and as such, was still invisible. So, if he still had panic brain, it probably seemed as though he was just levitating. Normally, I would have messed with him a bit more, but according to the timer, we only had twenty-five seconds left before everything collapsed on us. So, I just tossed him on the bridge.

"Relax," I said. "It's me. We only have about twenty seconds left. Let's goose it!"

Stinky didn't even respond; he just started booking it to the exit. I followed, and my invisibility suddenly dropped.

"Pick up the pace!" I screamed, hearing a *whoosh* and *buzz* gathering below.

We tore ass to the gateway and reached it with ten seconds to spare. Just before we crossed the threshold, I turned, spotting the horde of wasps, and I smiled.

"Better luck next time, you sloppy sack of— Uwugh!"

I'd been gesturing as I spoke, when a shape darted through the crowd of creatures. It sliced across several, and I heard cries of anger as a whirling dervish flashed toward me and landed softly in my hand. I goggled at it. It was the haladie.

"It . . . came back?"

Congratulations! You have discovered a hidden bonus for [Enchanted Haladie]!

- **Bonus: Return**

The Enchanted Haladie returns to the user who has bonded with it when thrown.

"Holy shit!" I shouted. "I'm like motherfucking Thor!"

Then I felt a jerk from behind me as I was pulled backward through the arch.

"I'm motherfucking THOOOOOOR!"

CHAPTER TWENTY-THREE

JUNGLE BOOGIE

The second chamber was weird.

I was still flying high from all the destruction and loot from the previous area—not to mention learning that I had some sort of badass, magical boomerang blade at my disposal. Because of this, my attention was obviously compromised, so I didn't get a great peep at our current surroundings. Stinky, however, brought me back to reality by deflating my jubilation balloon.

"You fuckin' oaf," he spat, resting on the ground. "You useless, long-suffering shit from the bottom of—"

"Whoa, whoa, whoa!" I interrupted. "What the hell, man? Why you comin' in all hot? We just beat that chamber's *ass*! I figured you'd be . . . well, not happy, but, like . . . slightly less cranky?"

"What the fuck is there to be pleased about? That was just gettin' shit poured on us in an uphill climb."

"Easy, there, Robert Frost," I said. "We made it, didn't we? Everyone is intact, and nobody died. Plus—without me figuring out how the dungeon worked, we'd never have gotten out of there. Thanks to my brilliance, we live to argue another day."

"What in the fuck are you talking about, orc?"

"The uh, brood cuckoos, or whatever? I realized they were using the bridge as bait. You're fucking welcome."

"That was clear from the start, you fuckin' *donkey*," Stinky hissed. "Why else would I have burned through near on my whole godsdamned supply of cubes?"

"Wait, what? You mean you figured it out, too?"

"Of course I fuckin' did, you insufferable bilge-dribbler! Are you nearsighted *and* stupid? Did you fail to see me using the fuckin' spell to draw them down that archway's glitterin' pony path? You thought *you* were the only one t' figure that out?"

Stinky guffawed in contempt, and I had to stop myself from slugging him right in his stupid yellow face.

"It was a confusing event!" I said, exhaling sharply. "Wow. Sorry that I don't have perfect battle clarity like you think you have, Richard Simmons. Jumping jacks, really?"

Stinky shook his head as if what I was saying was beneath him.

"No response?" I asked incredulously. "Not even a pat on the back for adopting *and* executing new Skills and Abilities in the heat of combat?"

I harrumphed.

"Guess you really learn which hoes are loyal in situations like this."

"Shut up with your nonsense, orc," Stinky said. "You're goin' to be the one that gets us fuckin' clawed apart—bleeding out from our wounds and tryin' to shovel our intestines back into our gobs. We're trapped in this flamin' fuckin' shit barrel unless we can stumble over a way out. And we have to do it alone."

"Oh, we're not alone," I said mischievously. Then I held out my hand, revealing the miniature form of the feather chest resting on my open palm. Stinky looked from the chest to me, his mouth open in confusion.

"What the fuck are you talking about, orc? Have you scrambled your damn brain mush?"

I realized suddenly how foolish my action looked without context and backpedaled.

"Wait— Er, no! It's— Shit— Here, just watch!"

I gingerly set the tiny container on the ground and backed away from it.

"You're going to want to give it some room," I said.

Stinky sighed and allowed for a wide berth, still wearing a withering expression.

"Feather chest, maximize."

FWOO-POP!

The chest instantly expanded to its hulking proportions with a sound like someone had pierced an enormous bubble. Stinky took a tense stance, regarding the object suspiciously.

"Go ahead and open it," I said confidently.

"What's in it?"

"Test it out and see for yourself."

"It's the fuckin' eggs, innit?"

"Maybe . . . " I said conspiratorially, pressing my palms together and wriggling my fingertips against one another in a caricature of malicious excitement.

"Can they breathe in there?"

"Can *what* breathe in there?" I asked, trying to play coy.

"The possessed roe, you absolute brick skull."

"Possessed roe? What do you mean? I only— Oh, *shit!*"

I wrenched the lid open on the feather chest, and five orbs flew out, eyes bulging and gasping for breath. They leaned against one another—as well as eggs could do—and made tiny, weak chittering noises. It appeared as though I'd almost left them in there too long.

Man, that could have been bad. That whole damn chest would have smelled like rotten eggs. And I'm not *going to* clean *a magical suitcase. Seems unwholesome.*

"Great," Stinky said, drawing his dagger. "Now, let's end 'em and get on moving. We don't have time for dallying."

"What? Wait— No— What?!" I said. "I just spent nearly eight minutes running, flying, crashing, and falling to retrieve these guys! And I *hate* exercise. I'm not icing them now that we've gotten to the other side of bad news boulevard— I've put in too much work for that. I will *dally* all diddly-damn day if it means I'm not sunk on the cost of exerting my precious energy. Besides, what if we need them to get past another chamber?"

"Fine," Stinky hissed, eyeing the still hardly moving roe. "Keep your pets. But if one o' them is keen on a nibble, I'm skewering you *and* them."

"Listen," I said. "I don't want these gross boba-tea creatures here any more than you do, but since we don't know what's coming up next, don't you think it would be weirdly practical to have them stick next to us for the time being?"

"As long as they don't gods-bloody-damn stick *to* me, either."

"You know what I mean, man," I said.

"No, orc," Stinky said. "I don't. I haven't a fuckin' foggy about any of the things you go on about. You're as addled as the Drifter."

"Huh?" I asked. "What's wrong with the way I am?"

"I'm not here to fluff your fuckin' feelin's for you," Stinky continued. "You gab unendingly, and the meat of it is always peculiar at best—or at worst—suspect. You don't know a shittin' prick about nothin' in front of you—or behind you. Every move you make is enveloped in the thickest sheen o' stupid imaginable, and calamity follows you wherever you go. I've had more run-ins with life-endin' cuz of your orc buffoonery in the last several hours than the last *half-year* with the gods-revilin' Redmark."

"Yeah, I have strong chaos energy. I'm aware of it, and I'm okay with it."

I paused, glancing around and noticing the terrain for the first time. The previous chamber had basically been patterned after a Bond villain's secret volcano base—complete with lava and ridiculous traps. However, *this* area was as though we'd just fallen into the *Jungle Book*. It was still clearly underground—based on the fact that the far walls and high ceiling were still rocky, but the space within the confines of the stone was lush and green.

I could hear the chirps and trills of insects and bird calls from somewhere within the dense forestation. Tall, vine-covered trees filled my vision, with a leafy canopy above us. Various other menacing-seeming plants and brush stretched along either side of a narrow dirt path overgrown with what I believed was called lichen.

It would have been very picturesque if—you know—it didn't reside inside the dim cavern of doom.

"Yo," I said, drawing out the word. "Does it seem off to you that this section of the dungeon is so different from the last one?"

Stinky shrugged his shoulders.

"It's a dungeon, orc," he said. "What do you expect? Each chamber changes. It's the idiotic nature of these damn things."

"Wait, how do you know that if you've never been in one?"

"Vosket's dick, damn near everyone knows that, orc! On my mother's memory, you have got to be some special kind of dunce. Did you get dropped into this damn world *yesterday*?"

He was being facetious—I think that's the word—so it was funny to me how right he was.

"Pretend that I was," I said. "What else can we expect from this little field trip?"

Stinky eyed me as though expecting me to be pranking him, so I gave him the best expression of genuine interest I could muster. We began walking along the path, our now scaredy-cat eggs slowly following behind in a cluster.

"I'm sure I can't expect someone with your savage fuckin' origins to know much about the civilized world," Stinky finally relented. "I shouldn't be surprised that you know shit-all."

"Yeah, this world *sure* is civilized," I said. "It's got about as much culture as a bag of spoiled yogurt. What with the apparently big-time asshole dictators and shithead militia groups trying to overthrow said assholes. Oh, and don't get me started on the casual racism I've encountered literally every step of the way."

"What the fuck are you going on about?" Stinky asked.

"I mean, look at you, for instance," I said.

"What the fuck about me, orc?"

"*That*," I said. "You can barely make it through a sentence before dropping my race in there. Honestly, I probably wouldn't care so much if I didn't get the sense that you're using it as an insult. How would you feel if I kept punctuating all of my statements with *matau*?"

"That's what I am," he said. "I won't be ashamed of my fuckin' race, orc, if that's your aim. Better to be the worst of *my* kind than the *best* of yours."

"See?" I said. "Racist. We ain't never gonna repair no cracks in the foundation this way."

"How in blazes is that any fuckin' different than you calling me *Stinky* all the time?"

"What?" I asked. "I call you Stinky because you fucking *smell*, dude. Take a goddamn shower or something, and maybe I'll pick something else."

"That's a fuckin' riot, coming from you, orc. You reek of filth and ichor—and the scent of your feet makes me jealous of gutter rot. Have you never heard of boots? I should call *you* Stinky."

"What? No—that's stupid. You're stupid," I said, jabbing a finger at him. "We can't *both* be Stinky. I used it first, so I get dibs. And of course I've *heard* of boots, but I haven't—"

"Quiet!" Stinky commanded, putting a hand up to silence me. He cocked his head to the side, listening for something. I didn't speak but instead mentally tabulated the amount of animal excrement I might need to properly fill Stinky's sleeping roll with.

Stinky turned a severe eye to me and held his hand up to his ear, gesturing that I should listen as well. I quietly sighed and concentrated on picking out any peculiar noises or sounds that might be the source of whatever Stinky was getting all moon-eyed about.

Then I heard it.

It was soft at first, but slowly I was able to zero in on the sound enough to differentiate it from the general noises of the living jungle around us. It was a voice. Someone was . . . singing?

I shot a confused glance at Stinky, who scowled deeper, holding a finger up to keep me from speaking. I strained myself, trying to get a good lock on the song.

The voice sounded like it belonged to a man, with a tone so deep and rich it would have made Elvis Presley sound like Alvin and the Chipmunks. The melody was simple, pretty, and seemed joyful, which was a net positive as far as spook factor went. If he had been singing a song of mourning or, worse, a children's nursery rhyme, I would have noped the hell out of there in a flash. But this song had a light quality, and though I couldn't quite make out the words, it seemed like one of those classic minstrel tracks you heard when you stopped at a tavern in a video game. It was also vaguely reminiscent of certain power-metal melodies, which often took inspiration from medieval-style music. I liked it.

"We should get closer," I whispered to Stinky, but he shook his head.

"No," he hissed. "Use your damn head, or—"

He paused, reframing his phrasing to my great pleasure.

"If we're the first to explore this fuckin' place in ages, what sort of creature do you think would want—or is damn fool enough—to be overheard?"

That made me consider for a moment. Unfortunately, he had a point. It was worth considering that anything in a dungeon that was brazen enough to start belting out tunes was either stupid, dangerous, or—in what was growing considerably more and more likely—both. It could be a ruse designed to draw in dungeoneers and start chopping into their butt meat with dull, rusty cleavers.

"It could be Ocho," I said.

"What?"

"That's what I nicknamed the eighth member of our entourage."

"Why?" Stinky asked. "What is *ocho*?"

"It's, uh . . . an orc thing," I said.

"Doesn't matter," Stinky continued. "If it's that fuckin' dungeon ghost, that's another lantern light to steer fuckin' clear of. We ain't seen sack or saddle of the fuckin' bastard yet, but he's clearly skilled. More than you, in any fashion. In case you've been gifted with too many head injuries lately, he skipped right on past that first chamber before we'd even gotten a chance to scratch our fuckin' bells. It's a true idiot that would wander into an unknown area with no fuckin' strategy in place and try to— Orc! *What the fuck are you doing?!*"

I had made my way forward while he'd been talking and was a few dozen feet ahead of him, pushing through the trees.

"It's called reconnaissance," I said over my shoulder. "You know, gathering intel all secret agent–style and getting the jump on any dumbass chucklefucks that think they're the alpha of this cave. Jeez, read a book, Stinky."

"It's called *suicide*," Stinky exclaimed.

"Never heard of her," I said. "I'll be fine. Trust me. I'm as quiet as a mouse and as unnoticeable as malware you get from downloading mobile porn games."

"What?!"

"Shh, baby," I said. "Daddy's gonna wrestle him up some shenanigans. Watch the eggs, will you?"

Before Stinky could say anything further, I allowed my stealth brain to start working and began moving through the trees with an ease that impressed even myself. I stepped softly, and I moved purposefully, slinking through the flora like a massive, bipedal prowling panther. Boy, oh, boy, this Sneaking Skill was just *aces*. All the while, the song was getting louder, and I could even hear some of the words. It was quite the jaunty little ditty.

O, I oft avoid the gallows;
Afore no headsman have I fell;
I've passed the last light bailiff's cast;
Plugged my ears to the cleric's bell;

O, but by this time tomorrow;
I will be drawing out to sea;
And mark the dark with friendly spark;
One torch for you and one for me.

The singer switched up his cadence for the hook. Then, several other voices joined in, belting out the chorus in tired, slurring harmonies.

Brothers, sisters, raise your arms;
Join the banner, find no harm;
We cannot fall by sword or sling;
So, now we fight and drink and sing.

I paused.

What in the actual bitch?

Not only were the lyrics to the song essentially identical to a power metal ballad, but it was a fucking *bop*. All it needed were super-slick, over-the-top, wailing guitar leads, and it would have landed squarely in my rotation of rock-solid tub-thumpers to spin while I was doing my *thang*. Whoever had penned this glorious cut of musical prime rib was clearly operating at a level of skill I reserved for some of the mightiest maestros of metal masterpieces. Now I knew—with absolute, one hundred percent certainty—I *needed* to meet these people and pick their brains over this obviously *number one* smash hit.

I picked up my pace a little, excited at the prospect of learning more about the song. I hadn't heard any music since I'd gotten there, which, admittedly, still wasn't that far back. Still, if this was any indication, I'd be *delighted* to start hitting up the taverns, or pubs, or whatever they were called in this world and getting thick into some dance-clubbing.

After a few minutes of urgent, clandestine clopping, I spotted a light in the distance, obscured slightly by tree trunks.

A campfire.

A few shapes sat around the flames in a circle, cheering, laughing, and passing around bottles. The song had ended, but the group gave no indication that their party was winding down.

Yahtzee.

I tiptoed forward—you know, like badasses do—and reached the edge of the trees to get a better look. Hidden in the shadows of trunks and branches, I could see now that the merry band had made to rest in a clearing just off of the main path. Logs had been gathered to sit near the fire, and several well-used bedrolls dotted the area in a configuration that seemed random—as though they'd just plopped down wherever they passed out. I took a moment, watching as the figures enjoyed their revelry.

There were five in total. A pale, thin elven-eared man in dark blue robes leaned against a stump, seeming very eager to discover what lived at the bottom of a hefty jug of liquid. He looked a bit sickly to me, his complexion sallow. An extremely short, barrel-chested woman sat laughing in her bulky leather armor. She spent the time sharpening the blade of a short sword with a flat stone and leaning away every time a drink passed her direction.

Two individuals sat closely together, playing a card game in the dirt. They were talking shit to one another and forcing the other to take a drink every time one of them lost a hand. Of the pair, one was a human woman with short black hair and brilliant blue eyes that sparkled in the light of the flames; the other was a man of average-ish height with a sandy-blond mop who seemed to be losing more than he was winning, based on his reactions. The woman wore heavy armor that was partially dressed down, pieces of it resting next to the gruesome-looking hammer that rested against the log next to her. The man wore tattered clothing reminiscent of a classic, medieval laborer save for his vest: a leather . . . *jerkin*, I think the word is, and a longbow slung over his shoulders.

The last member of their esteemed council was of a race I wasn't sure I could identify. They looked to be part lizard but also possibly human? It was hard to tell for sure, since most of their form was shrouded by an animal-skin cloak as they warmed themselves next to the fire. They were big, though, maybe even taller than I was now. They watched the others with a big grin on their face.

They were all conversing now, the song forgotten, and I got the sense from their interactions that they'd known each other quite a long time.

"Gods *damn you*, Frida," the blond man playing cards said to his companion. "I was *this* close to capturing your Luxury Sword! I'll repeat it for posterity: gods damn you, girl. I can't keep doing this to myself, or I'm like to dry up my whole deck and have to play you with cards I make myself. Or quit playing altogether."

"At this point, Calden," called the short woman with the sword, "abandoning the game once and for all might be your best option. I'm tired of hearing your whinging every night. Both of my shoulders have been drenched near through with your baby tears."

"It is not fair, Merra," Calden whined, gesturing to the one he'd called Frida. "She has absconded with the best of my lot, leaving me with the dregs—and her with an easy victory."

"You've got y'self a fair few decent selections yet," said Frida, her voice placid and bearing the linguistic hallmarks of whatever this world called the Scottish accent.

"Oh, what—*these*?" Calden continued, holding up two cards in his hand. "These are middle-tier at best, you militant ice wraith. *At best.* All the remaining number are rubbish. Pure, inconsequential, bin-worthy slag."

"Might not want te let them hear y'say that, Calden," Frida said. "I'm a-comin' fer ye middle tier, and then ye'll on'y have them lows to cover ye bets with."

"See?" Calden demanded of the rest of the group. "This is a psychological attack. She is weakening my resolve with her wily feminine strategy to stack the odds in her favor. There are codes of conduct with *Fels*, Frida, and you are abusing the prestige of the game."

"Come off et," Frida said, rolling her eyes. "Yer jus' stallin' te waylay the 'nevitable. Et's yoor hand, by the by."

"Of course it is," Calden sighed, slumping. "Just a slow march to my funeral pyre. Please, write to my family after you're through desecrating my corpse. Make it known in your letter that I died doing what I loved and never liked any of them."

This encouraged a round of boos from the assembly. The lizardy individual scooped up a pebble and tossed it at the blond man.

"So dramatic," they hissed. The sound of their voice was like steam releasing from a valve, setting my teeth on edge and making me a bit uncomfortable.

"I'm not dramatic," Calden explained, adopting a rigid pose. "I am simply addressing the severity of my captivity here with you unrepentant ruffians. It has transfigured me into a shell of my former, glorious self. *'What was once the soul of a brightly burning star has faded into the obscure. Now resigned as the diminutive flickering ember of a candle left in the cold.'*"

"Oh, boo to you," came the retort from the thin man I'd thought looked not long for the world. "Don't quote *Gavanzili* at us."

I was shocked to hear how impressively deep his voice was, especially considering his slight frame. With such a low, commanding tone, he was unquestionably the singer of the catchy jam I'd heard. *That* was a plot twist I didn't see coming.

"Do not scold *me*, Jes," Calden shot back. "But . . . are you certain that was Gavanzili? I would have sworn a blood oath that I'd invented that."

"I am sure," Jes said dourly.

"Well, I suppose you'd be the authority," Calden said. "On account of your most esteemed and unrivaled upbringing. Your pedigree is showing, friend."

"Not this again," Jes sighed, taking a pull from his jug. "My point was that family is family, Calden. You should not disparage them, whatever their flaws. Regardless of origin, we all stem from the same gods."

"Yes, you are correct, my inglorious elf. However, your family is storied and wealthy, descended straight from the teats of Palima herself. Mine was shat out of Hilrendar's puckered arsehole as he squatted over Thorch."

Everyone but Jes laughed at that. The elf adopted a more somber tone, his speech slurred by drink.

"A heaping portion of good that does me now, does it?" Jes asked, taking another swig of his gigantic vessel. "In here, wasting away with your like, avoiding the same miserable beasts every night and playing audience to the weeping woes of your inability to win a *children's card game* against a backwater Guardian. I'd be happy to swap our current predicament to sit at patriarch Vick's knobby dinner table in your ancestral hovel in Thorch."

"It is really more of a shanty," Calden said, inciting laughter from the others. "And do not be monstrous to Frida, good fellow. She's trying her best. It cannot be easy, lurching from place to place like she does—especially with as many pummeling shield blows to the skull as she's sustained. It's a true testament to the might and wonder of the gods that she is even able to speak a decipherable language."

"Aye," Frida responded. "Got a few words for ye, in fact. 'Ye lose again.' Give up your Tangled Vine, ye fuckin' weapon."

Calden looked crestfallen. With a flourishing sweep of his hand, he deposited a card onto Frida's lap.

"There she goes," he said, so softly I was hardly able to hear him. "Yet another thread stitched into the seal of my death shroud."

"You're free to lose," Merra said, finally finishing her meticulous sharpening and sliding the sword into a scabbard at her side. "But the melodrama is going to cost you extra."

Calden shook his head.

"But, Merra, my sun, my stars, my withering winter blossom. Melodrama is all that remains to me after such a targeted, cutthroat assassination of my sense of purpose and zest for life."

"Don't forget your shit cards," the lizard hissed.

"Ah, yes," Calden said. "My melodrama *and* Frida's future ill-gotten spoils."

Then the blond man stood, dusting off his hands performatively.

"Mistress Frida: a finer swindler there is not. However, I tire of this boorish contest of unanswered affection between us."

Frida rolled her eyes and tucked her newly acquired prize into her outrageously tall deck as Calden continued.

"Do not scoff at our eventual tryst, maiden most fair and . . . *bashy*. The tension of two hearts entwined so strongly—but resisting nonetheless—while enthralling, I am most sure, to our audience of companions, must be stopped for the moment. Instead . . ."

He pointed to Jes, who belched as if on cue.

"Troubadour!" he announced. "Would you be so kind as to regale us with another of your winsome airs? Perhaps one from your days at that delightful kingmaker academy you always speak so fondly of? However, I would prefer it if you'd choose one with an elaborate arrangement of choral harmonies. Nothing morose, either; we have enough of that to go around. One even Dedyc can sing along with."

"Yes!" the lizard hissed, clapping their hands. "One I can join in on!"

Jes scoffed and shook his head ambivalently.

"You cannot deny the poor dear that service, can you, Jes? His unique range is so often squandered or ignored entirely. I do not want to speak for the entirety of our party, but I, for one, grow weary of Dedyc being relegated to the percussion section."

Jes finally broke, chuckling at that comment and harrumphing to clear his throat.

Loon, you sneaky, sexy son of a bitch. Nobody recons like you.

I was just chilling in the shadows, unbeknownst to anyone, gathering a load of information—and I was going to get a free concert out of the deal. Abstractly, I thought about how strange it was that I was referring to myself, if only in this one instance, as Loon.

Guess I can figure out the ramifications of that later. I'm about to have my eardrums massaged and my face melted into a puddle of flesh by some bona fide shred.

That was when I felt a blow land to the center of my back, thrusting me forward out of the trees and into the circle of light and horrified faces. I fell onto my stomach with a loud thump but immediately attempted to scramble to stand. Just as I was lifting myself up from the dirt, another blow sent me crashing back down—this one directed to my lower back. I felt a sharp pain as I hit the ground hard, forcing me to release an angry yelp.

"An orc!" Dedyc cried, wheeling on my prostrate form. The others followed suit, each arming themselves or readying empty hands for what I had to imagine was magical oh-shit vapor.

The new arrival who had been sucker-punch-whooping me from my blindside applied pressure with a boot as a glowing light surrounded my ankles, wrists, and neck. The light compressed and formed shimmering green rings that caused my Stamina to tank.

Condition: Restrained
- **Magically impeded movement and mobility for the duration. Applies a Stamina drain effect for the duration.**

Gah! Again with the captivity? Come on, *man!*

I couldn't move, so I was forced to lie there beneath the newcomer's heel, trying not to groan loud enough to give them any satisfaction.

"Well, boys," a man's voice announced in what I'd describe as a Southern United States accent. "Looks like we got ourselves a lookie-loo. Orc, too, if it's to be believed."

I kept struggling but couldn't do anything about my predicament at the moment. Exhausted as I was from the many, *many* death-defying events I'd played spectator to, I was scraping the bottom of the barrel for energy sources or bags of tricks.

"Now," the man drawled, pressing hard on my spine. "Let's find out why a beast like this is ganderin' on our little dungeon get-together. Calden. Get the knife."

CHAPTER TWENTY-FOUR

TIME AIN'T ON MY SIDE

The newcomer's command sent a shiver down my spine.

Get the knife?! The fucking knife?! What the hell did I do to deserve a request like that? I was just engaging in harmless musical voyeurism!

This was turning out to be way worse than the other time I'd tried to see a free show. I'd snuck into a bar to see Cherry a few years before, and I'd gotten caught almost immediately. But even though they were willing to just kick me out with a slap on the wrist . . . I'd tried to sneak in again. The exact details don't matter, but I learned that night that in a scuffle between a slow, fat, slightly inebriated teenager and a gigantic, fit, straight-edge bouncer—the chubby guy gets tossed on his ass in front of a crowd of attractive metalhead ladies.

I think they call that a parable.

My loud breathing alone disturbed the silence that followed the man's statement. None of the others gathered around me had said anything, nor had they moved. I knew I shouldn't have gotten so drawn into the camaraderie. I'd relaxed, let my guard down, and almost definitely dropped out of stealth. That must have been how he'd seen me. Whoever he was.

Just as I was about to start throwing every vicious insult I could muster, the blond-haired man—known as Calden—spoke.

"My apologies, Virgil—welcome back, by the by," he said. "But to *which* knife are you referring?"

The man holding me down made an angry noise, pressing his boot a bit harder into my back.

"*The* knife, Calden," he grunted. "Get *the* knife."

I couldn't see the man, but I could tell by his tone that he attempted to relay information that Calden apparently didn't have access to. Almost as if there were no knife . . .

"A moment," Calden said. "Virgil, are you implying you are going to torture this poor creature?"

"Dammit, Calden, stop sayin' my name!" Virgil said. "Ain't you never engaged in cloak-an'-dagger afore? This ain't no monster worth pityin'! They was *lurkin'* with clear nefarious intent! Oh, blast it all! Get me *the* knife."

"What's going on here?" I demanded from the ground. "If you think capturing me is gonna be easy, then you've got another thing comin,' motherfuckers. I'm gonna bite your ankles!"

"There are many knives within our congregation, Virgil," Calden continued, ignoring me entirely. "In fact, I can think of three or four beautiful specimens within snatching distance at this very moment. You may need to be more specific, friend."

Virgil made another frustrated noise.

"You seem to have an idea but are unable to properly find the words to make the matter clearer," Calden said. "I am unsure as to your intentions or what wildly disparate memory you seem to be straining to recall. Is it a bread knife? Are you hungry? Do you—"

"Why do you have him bound up?" came Jes's deep slur, interrupting Calden's obfuscating diatribe. "Was he primed for an attack? He is not acting out—as it stands."

Are these guys . . . not going to try to kill me?

"Aye," came Frida's measured burr. "Seems t'orc dinnae intend te attack."

"I didn't!" I shouted. "I was just trying to listen to the song!"

"There you have it, Virgil," Calden said kindly. "From the mouth of the beast himself. It appears that this has all been a dark misunderstanding. You cannot fault our guest for wanting to steal a bit of melodic respite. Despite Jes's many flaws, his voice *is* quite nice."

"Mind yourself, Calden," Jes warned. "One *flaw* I embody is letting irritants have too long on their podium without striking them down. I *could* do with a bit of personal growth at the moment."

"Intrigued though I am to see the true and unbridled power of the unparalleled Jesimir Carandalon," Calden said. "I am quite confident that I can run faster *afraid* than you can *angered*."

The group, save for Virgil, laughed at that.

This was confusing in so many ways. These people, whoever they were, seemed to act as though my presence was . . . irrelevant. Like this wasn't even the weirdest interaction they'd had today, and I was just a usual suspect of their typical routine. Why were they there in this dungeon? I'd been led to believe that no one had been inside in possibly hundreds of years.

What gives?

The Southern gentleman kept his boot on my back but slightly lightened the push. Enough that I no longer felt like my coccyx was grinding against my gooch anymore.

"I'm only tryin' to keep an eye on any dangers what might present themselves," Virgil stated soberly.

"And we salute your dutiful pursuit," Calden said. "But perhaps you might be inclined to have a rest, my friend? Kick back, as they say, and chase down the illustrious perfection of a drunken stupor—like the rest of us."

"Speak for yourself, coxcomb," Merra said.

"Our marvelously teetotaling companion notwithstanding," Calden corrected, then his voice softened. "Unwind, Virgil. You've been gone longer and longer these days."

I could feel Virgil's tension diminish as he relaxed his boot's position until it was just casually resting on my back. Eventually, he spoke again, but his voice had lost a lot of its original conviction.

"I been nearby," he said. "Keepin' an eye out, but never so far that I'd lose sight o' y'all. What's the verdict on the orc, then?"

"It appears," Calden began, "that his only folly was not knowing that Vengeful Virgil was stalking him. Poor eyesight is not a cause, however, for whatever you wanted that knife for, no?"

After a moment, Virgil's boot disappeared from my back, but the restraint remained.

"So, are you guys going to take this off of me, or what?" I asked, still lying on my stomach in the dirt. No one responded. The group had begun drinking again, just fucking leaving me where I was.

"Seriously?" I demanded. "I'm not a piece of useless furniture! I'm like a . . . refrigerator."

A pair of strong hands lifted me gently and set me upright. I looked right into the eyes of Dedyc, the lizard . . . thing. He smiled at me. I think.

"You look funny for an orc," Dedyc said. "Weird clothes."

I let my gaze fall on Dedyc's own outfit, which was partially obscured by his enveloping animal skin. Beneath I could make out just the hint of clothing that I'd be tempted to call "poverty caveman" fashion. A leather bandolier crossed his bare, scaly chest diagonally, laden with trinkets, stones, and bottles. Around his waist was more animal skin—seemingly some sort of tribal skirt—trimmed with fur. He was exposed to the world from thighs down, and his legs ended in a pair of large, clawed feet. I noticed that the hands that held me had three fingers each and were also tipped with razor-sharp talons.

I smiled back at him.

"Yeah, your fit is totally normal."

Dedyc leaned forward.

"Thank you."

Everything about this guy sets me on edge.

He felt like a wild animal just *pretending* to be a sentient being. There was a feral threat in his eyes and movements, and I couldn't trust that, at any moment, he wouldn't just go berserk and start tearing into me.

"Can you release me?" I asked him.

The lizardman shook his head.

"Not my Spell."

"Well," I began, "could you convince the guy who cast it on me to *uncast* it, possibly?"

Dedyc shook his head again.

"No."

This is frustrating.

"Why not?"

Dedyc stood up, staring down at me.

"You don't *uncast* it. It fades on its own in twenty minutes. Sorry."

I sighed.

"That's all right. Thanks for propping me up."

Dedyc nodded and staggered away. I didn't have anything else to do, and it seemed everyone else was just going to ignore me—so I just watched.

They continued carousing and drinking and joking, gathering closer and closer to the fire and paying me no mind. As I spectated, I finally got a chance to see what Virgil looked like. He was a lean, muscular human and older than I expected. His hair was gray and long, reaching just above his shoulders, and he sported a pencil-thin mustache that didn't seem to fit the motif of the world. I judged him to be near fifty. He wore leather armor dyed pewter, and a green fabric headband was nestled above his brow. I didn't see any weapons on him at all.

I'm not sure where the idea came from, but it stuck in my brain like a festering parasite—I couldn't help it. The man's accent, the way he moved, his look of being slightly out of his element. It didn't make any sense, but I was confident about one thing: Virgil was like me.

A sojourner.

Eventually, the merriment wound down, and it was clear the group had all been considering my fate. They clustered around me, with Jes taking point as their primary speaker—which surprised me. I'd expected the loudmouthed Calden to lead the charge. Still, he seemed perfectly comfortable hanging in the background while the entire party took up all my available breathing room.

"So," Jes said, giving me an appraising look while my hackles raised, "what is your name?"

"Loon," I said quickly. "And I'm not a . . . bandit or something, if that's what you guys were thinking. I'm just a guy who is trying to survive this dungeon as best I can."

"Well met, Loon," Jes said politely. "I am Jesimir Carandalon, but you may simply call me Jes if it suits you."

"Well . . . uh, met," I returned. "Are you the one that was appointed to break the bad news?"

"I'm sorry?" Jes asked. "Which bad news would that be?"

"That you guys are gonna eat me."

There was a long silence as the group drank in my words. Then, all at once, they began to laugh.

I sat there in silence as they built into a crescendo of mirth. I very casually breathed a sigh of relief.

Well, shit. I'd been serious.

I cracked a grin, pretending that it had been my intent all along.

" . . . you know, eat my bones, turn my skin into handkerchiefs?"

More laughter.

" . . . I mean, you guys look like you might enjoy taking a bite out of ole Loon is all I'm saying."

They kept laughing.

I have no idea what's going on, but I'm going to roll with it.

I pointed at Dedyc.

"I *know* this guy eats orc steaks."

As they continued in their hysteria, I had to think for a second. This wasn't even particularly clever as far as I was concerned. It didn't use a variety of comparisons to body parts or ugly animals or any of my usual hallmarks of what I considered good humor. But for them . . . it was funny.

Just as I was winding up another joke about them nibbling on my tender innards, there was a flash of light as the magical shackles disappeared. This caused me to change directions.

"*Uh-oh*," I said in a singsong and peered around mischievously. "Looks like I'm free now. Guess you guys are going to have to take your meal to go—that is, *if you can catch me!*"

This had caused an eruption so strong among the group that I literally saw gobs of snot shoot out of Merra's nose.

What the shit is this? Is there a fucking gas leak?

"You're . . . hehe . . . not a normal . . . ha . . . orc." Jes said between hiccups of laughter.

"You ain't seen nothin' yet," I said, standing up and pulling the party hat out of my pack. "Check *this* shit out!"

They began laughing the moment I placed it on my head.

"What in the realm is this?" Calden chuckled. "We have stumbled onto a jester of some variety! This is stupendous!"

Then the slime began, sliding down my body like molasses. Rather than laughter, though, this prompted the group to grow very intrigued, leaning forward to examine me, each speaking at once.

"Goodness," Calden said.

"Et's a neat trick," said Frida.

"That is a mite curious," Virgil drawled.

"Looks sticky," Dedyc hissed.

"Now, *that* is a wonder," said Merra.

"Is that slime?" Jes wondered.

I beamed.

"You're all correct," I said.

"Could I trouble you for a sample?" Jes asked. "To examine more closely?"

"Do your thing, Jes," I said.

Jes rushed over to his pack and procured a jar. He uncorked the lid and shook something solid out that tumbled to the dirt, then picked up a stick from the ground and returned. I and the others watched as he pressed the stick to my flesh, delighting as the goo ran over it. Then he pulled the wood back, and the slime created a long, viscous strand as it clung to both the stick and my skin like a baker making caramel. He placed a portion of the grossness in his jar and corked it before smiling up at me.

"The College of Redmark thanks you," he said with a smile.

My stomach fell.

"The *what*, now?"

Jes waved his hand dismissively at me.

"My apologies, Loon. I may have imbibed too much," he said.

However, Calden interrupted him before he could say more.

"No one—*least of all* this fine and upstanding orc compatriot—wants to hear about your hoity-toity universe-*oity*," he said, slapping Jes on the shoulder lightly. "He's obviously traveled a long way to get *away* from concepts like that—to a dungeon, no less. Look at him—he's free of the burden you beleaguered lot have tried for centuries to rope him with. Is there nowhere safe from the misgivings of such a tenured institution as your scholastic prison?"

Jes let out a groan and rolled his eyes.

The College of Redmark? What the Christ? They're educating these people? I'm guessing Stinky didn't get into the group on a scholarship. Did they follow us in here and somehow get ahead of us?

Something about all of this was off. They didn't strike me as similar to the Redmarks I'd just tangled with. Still, if there was an entire institution devoted to them, that spelled trouble.

Jes appeared to be a type of wealthy nobleman or something—which seemed not to jive too well with the creed of Commander Fawn and her posse of misfit dipshits. Especially considering they wanted to dismantle the current ruling class or whatever.

I also reasoned that they could have been wholly dissimilar and their only relation was the name, much like in my world. For instance, our school mascot was the mustang, but we had no relation to the famous car model. It would be ludicrous to assume otherwise. I felt like maybe this was a similar situation that I just didn't have the full context for.

Is Redmark a location? A type of plant?

I missed a bit of their conversation because of my quiet pondering, but Virgil got it back on track by asking me a question directly.

"So, you fancy y'self a dungeoneer, then, friend?"

I shrugged.

"Honestly, we just sort of stumbled into this place unintentionally and have been just trying to survive. It hasn't been the *worst* thing to deal with, but it hasn't been fun by any stretch of the imagination."

Calden laughed.

"Oh, we understand that all too well," he said, gesturing to his companions. "Though we initially *did* seek the innards of this dungeon of our own volition. It has not been the most fortuitous endeavor thus far, and this chamber in its own right is confounding."

"How so?" I asked.

"Et's been keepin' us from advancin' farther," Frida answered.

"We lost our navigator and have been wayward an' rudderless since."

"Oh, shit," I said. "Did he die?"

"We do hold out hope that he still lives," Jes said. "Though, with each day, it seems less and less likely to be the case."

"My apologies . . . Loon, did you say?" Calden asked.

"Yeah, that's me, all right," I said. "What's up?"

"I couldn't help but notice you used the plural when discussing your origin. You came in here with others? Have they gone the way of our noble navigator?"

I shook my head.

"Actually, no," I said. "My group is still intact—as far as I know. I was just moving ahead to check out the song—which I'm still waiting to hear, by the way. I have some opinions and some questions."

"Like any true patron of the arts," Calden said. "However, are the remaining members of your cortège . . . also orcs?"

His tone indicated a hint of concern. I couldn't blame him. Seeing one of me was bad enough, I'm sure, but if I was rolling deep with an entire cabal of boulder-shouldered savages . . . that might change their friendly tune toward me quickly. I wasn't sure I could trust this group, but I also didn't want to give them a reason to start getting aggressive or slap another pair of shackles on me again. So, I opted for a little bit of honesty.

"No, I'm the only one," I said. Then I winked. "Limited edition. The . . . uh, gods broke the mold when they made me."

The group chuckled, but I could tell there was tension in their humor, so I continued.

"I'm traveling with a matau—have you heard of those?"

This got a laugh larger than anything else I'd said so far today.

"Oh, we've heard of mataus," Dedyc hissed. "But why would you want to travel with one?"

"Whatcha mean?" I asked.

"Well," Merra said, flashing me a quick smile. "They're awfully . . . simple, aren't they? I've always considered them sort of vacant creatures since rumors say they spend all their time locked up in their cities, poring over their archives."

"Is that right?" I asked.

"If the tales are to be believed," she continued. "They rarely venture out—is what I was told—and you wouldn't catch any of them in a dungeon on account of all the grime and filth."

". . . they don't like dirt?" I asked, hardly able to contain my laughter.

"Oh, Chendra, no," Merra exclaimed. "They are notoriously hygienic and clean. A place like this would probably lend one an awful experience."

I couldn't help it. I began to laugh, doubling over so hard that I was forced to prop myself up with a hand to keep from falling on the ground. After a moment, I was able to catch my breath and looked up at the group.

"Is . . . everything all right, Loon?" Merra asked.

"Yep," I said. "Just fine. I was just thinking about something funny from earlier."

"I would be very interested in meeting your matau companion," Jes said earnestly. "If one has made the journey all this way and entered the Crypt, I should like to see very much how they are adapting."

I kept grinning.

"Oh, yeah," I said. "You can *definitely* meet him. In fact, I am going to request that you make it a priority."

"Splendid," Jes said.

Oh, my god. I can't wait to use this new information to hassle Stinky with. His people are a bunch of nerdy clean freaks! How far he must have fallen.

"Oh," I said. "You mentioned you guys had lost your sherpa a few days ago, right? How long have you guys been in here? I was under the impression this thing had been locked up tight for a while now, possibly centuries. We actually believed we were the first to enter in a long time."

Calden nodded.

"Yes, it was our understanding as well that the Forbidden Crypt was long cold before we arrived. It is quite interesting that both of our groups arrived within such a short time from one another, don't you think? Perhaps the fates at work?"

"Yeah, super friggin' weird," I said. "You guys don't know a guy named Zeol, do you?"

They all shook their heads, save for Jes. The elf tilted his head at the name.

"Zeol," he asked. "As in Zeol *the Capricious*?"

I sighed.

"That's the one. You know him?"

"I am not intimately acquainted with the being, no," he said. "But I have heard of him—and, of course, his followers. Are you one of his disciples?"

Something about that question set off an alarm bell in my head, and I knew that I needed to be very careful about my next choice of words. An association with Zeol seemed like it would not work in my favor in this instance, and that was something I was happy to shrug off.

"Oh, absolutely not," I said—to Jes's visible relief. "I just heard that there's an artifact of his in here that might be worth some serious change."

"Ah," Jes said. "Perhaps that is that case, though there are quite a few high-tier objects rumored to be within these walls. Unfortunately, most of our information regarding such items is enigmatic or incomplete. I would be wary of an item of the Capricious, however."

"Why's that?"

"An object belonging to a being of such an iniquitous reputation—especially where his tribe is concerned—would likely have an equivalently vile nature. If you happen upon such a piece, it would be best to disregard it or obliterate it. Nothing prosperous would grow from obtaining a keepsake of such ill repute."

Uh-oh. Zeol had a rep for being disgustingly evil? Color me surprised.

"You will have to excuse Jes," Calden said. "Informative though he may be, his is a countenance wrapped in superstition."

"That is enough from you, Vick," Jes said. "I am merely making a cautionary—"

"Please, Jes," Calden interrupted. "Do not bandy my family name about so flippantly. Are we not tried-and-true friends and colleagues? I note a particular sense of propriety and station in your words. Call me Calden, please. Lest I believe you perceive your worth higher than mine own."

"I do not perceive—"

"Wonderful," Calden beamed. "All is right with the world, then, no?"

"So, why don't you guys tell me a bit about yourselves?" I asked. "I already know you're all ridiculously good-looking with *great* senses of humor. But, if you don't mind, you wanna give me some hot deets on why you're all on this little holiday? Do you have a group name? Are there any love triangles? Who snores?"

Surprisingly, Frida was the first to speak. She'd struck me as the type to hang back and let the others do the boring explanations, but I could see that she was *delighted* to have something to contribute.

"We're here attemptin' to unlock an item," she said, her blue eyes dancing.

"That's a feature of the dungeon?" I asked.

"Aye," Frida said, nodding excitedly. "For this object, et's a requirement."

"It must be *some* big-ticket prize to stuff yourselves deep into this dumpster like you have," I said. "Is it some thematic, world-ending weapon of mass destruction?"

Jes leaned in.

"It is most decidedly *not* any—"

"It very well *could* be!" Calden announced, earning a glare from Jes. "We do not know exactly what will happen when we rouse the malignant Arcana embedded within. Though I hope that in whatever manifestation the power takes, it will be a colorful display."

"We've been a crew foor a bit o' years now," Frida said. "Used te be just me, Jes, and Dedyc. Then we met Merra durin' a stint in Feistorel. Unfortunately, Calden came along with 'er."

Calden cleared his throat, but Frida plowed right through it.

"Virgil's our newest 'ddition. Picked 'm up near on a year back."

"Wow," I said. "You guys just kick it on the reg, doin' hood-rat shit nonstop? Sounds like the life."

"We work well t'gether," Frida confirmed. "This doonjon presented an opportunity we couldnae pass up. No' te mention, the Quest rewards are staggerin.'"

"Damn," I said. "You guys' adventure is way cooler than anything I'm working on. The best Quest I've got under my belt is returning goblin ears to some mad scientist. Granted, I'm gonna get paid—according to the note I found—but I'd much rather be slinking along with y'all, poppin' open magic trinkets or whatever."

"Ye should join us, then," Frida said. "Always room foor 'nother pair o' hands."

"Frida," Calden admonished. "You cannot request that of someone who we are still only warming up to."

The blond man turned to me.

"I apologize on her behalf, good fellow. Do not feel any obligation to entertain such flights of fancy. Please forgive her lack of manners—have I mentioned that she's been bashed over the head many times?"

I chuckled.

"No worries," I said. "Honestly, if I wasn't so concerned I'd get immediately maimed or killed, I'd probably take you up on that offer. However, I am more interested in getting *out* of here than going *deeper*. But look me up when you're finished kicking the shit outta this place, and I'll absolutely consider tagging along."

I wasn't sure why I hadn't outright refused. It wasn't my usual style. The group seemed nice enough, but I also didn't fully trust them—and it would be foolish to do so. Something still didn't smell right about their entire operation, and the Redmark mention only made me more hesitant. No, better to let this be a simple exchange in a spooky crypt and leave it at that.

"You can plan on that," Calden said. "Oh, I'd only just thought about it now, but has the new year dawned outside yet? We entered only a week before the Winter Turn, and it might be nice to gather our orientation as the days in here bleed into one another."

"Uh, I dunno," I said. "The . . . climate here is different from where I'm from."

"Where would that be?" Jes asked curiously.

"I'm from . . . " I paused, trying to remember my conversation with Fawn. "The Territory of . . . Kursk."

"Bloomin' shite!" Frida exclaimed, reaching forward to grab me around the shoulders. "*A'm* from Kursk 'swell!"

Oh, balls.

"Whaur ye fae? Broggek? Dain sechlach? Surely not Yorbin?"

I just forced myself to smile, my mind racing.

"You're saying you can't tell?" I finally breathed.

This should buy me some time. Hopefully.

"Dinnae take ye foor a coy," Frida said with a wink. "Hard te say—accent an' all—b' ef I had te guess . . . "

She closed her eyes and bit her lip thoughtfully before finally popping them open with a smile.

"Medlyre?"

"Yep," I said. "Near there but still a ways out. A little no-name hamlet off the beaten path."

"Nae shite?" Frida gushed. "An orc *an'* a Hammie? Bad bit o' luck, then!"

I nodded sagely, though I was on fire with anxiety on the inside.

"There isn't a sadder tale to be told," I muttered.

Behind me, I heard Calden whisper to Jes.

"This makes a *lot* of sense, actually."

"Are the dates different as well in Kursk?" Merra asked. "That would be interesting!"

Frida made to respond, but I cut her off with a wink like I was up to something.

"Might be," I said. "You tell me the last date you remember it being, and I'll tell you if it matches."

Merra chuckled.

"I'll take a bite of that bait," she said. "We entered the fifth day before the *Turn*, Year Three-thousand, six hundred and eleven. So, how long have we been here?"

"Oh, it feels like a decade or two at least," Calden cracked. Jes nodded his agreement.

"Especially with you and your insufferable gnashing of teeth."

I paused at that.

"Well . . . " I said, trailing off. I had no idea whatsoever, but that had never stopped me before. Just as I was opening my mouth, another voice interrupted me.

"Four hundred and sixty-one years."

As one, everyone turned to the trees, where the voice had originated.

Standing just at the cusp of greenery stood Stinky, flanked on either side by several possessed roe. He looked haggard, like he hadn't slept in three days, and he was covered in an array of new scars.

Somebody tripped and fell in the brambles.

"My apologies, friend," Calden said. "But who are you?"

Stinky just shook his head.

"Orc," he said. "You're alive."

"Of course I'm alive," I said, looking back at the group as though Stinky was a crazy person. "I was just ahead of you. These guys aren't as murder-y as they look."

"This chamber softens your sense of time," he announced, looking more at the group than at me. "I hate to bear the brunt of the bad news, but if you claim you entered in thirty-six eleven, that will put you in before the Gaier Dynasty. It's a new age now, has been for almost a hundred and eighty years."

"How would that even be possible?" I asked. "I think I would have noticed if these guys were zombies or ghosts or something. I've spent over an hour teaching them what *actual* jokes sound like. You should have been here—you might have learned something.

Stinky spat, then wiped his mouth with a hand covered in dried blood.

"Not an hour, orc," he said. "You've been gone five *fuckin'* days."

"*Exsqueeze* me?"

CHAPTER TWENTY-FIVE

WHERE IN THE WORLD IS CARMICHAEL SANDIEGO?

"Wait, wait, wait," I said, still trying to wrap my mind around the bombshell Stinky had dropped on us. "If time is weird here, then how come you know it's been five days? Shouldn't you also feel like it's been just a few minutes, or whatever?"

"He is a matau," Jes answered matter-of-factly. "One of their racial traits is Time Clarity."

"What does that mean? He can't stop keeping track of time?"

"That's exactly what it means, orc," Stinky spat.

"Damn, you'd probably be a *hella* good drummer, then," I said. "Want to start a band?"

"Time Clarity is a gift that some races and even Classes gain access to," Jes continued. "An internal calculating Ability that allows one to always keep track of passage and pacing. It is quite sublime and an excellent tool for those with scholarly pursuits. I, myself, missed many events and proceedings because I was far too busy with my nose in a book, studying the—"

"And *that* is precisely why we do not urge Jes to speak on his tenure with academia," Calden said. "It is exceptionally droll."

"So, then, this is—what? A magically induced . . . time dilation?" I asked, using a term I'd borrowed from movies.

"Precisely," Jes said, pointing outward. "I would imagine if this is all accurate—and not just a guess—that those within close proximity to one another share the same relative space."

"Like a time bubble?" I said.

"Yes," Jes said. "A time bubble is an appropriate metaphor for what we are experiencing here. I have read about instances—"

"Ah, but isn't there more to life than *research*, dear Jesimir?" Calden asked. "It seems as though hard-won instances of practical application matter more than words on a page."

"You *would* say that Calden," Dedyc hissed, "since you can't read!"

"Is that true?" I asked Calden, genuinely stunned. "But you use all those hundred-dollar words."

Calden's vocabulary had seemed to reflect someone with a higher-than-average understanding of language, so this was definitely a surprise.

"Literacy is overrated," Calden admitted. "What good would knowing how squiggles align with one another do for me?"

"I have been attempting to teach him his letters for some time now," Jes said. "But he is frustratingly resistant, like a precocious stain on a shirt."

"It seems to me," Calden said, "that I have done perfectly well without issue. Unless I am mistaken, all of us present have found ourselves in the same dungeon, making the same mistakes. How could basic comprehensive language dynamics help us now? Are any of you holding out on a piece of life-altering script or poem that will aid us in navigating this trying avenue?"

He waited for a beat before continuing.

"No? Well, then. It appears ignorance persists for another day."

We'd all gathered around the campfire as Stinky proceeded to warm himself and drink deeply from one of the proffered bottles. The roe milled about cautiously, like tiny, round insecure cows looking for a patch of grass that wouldn't eat them. I wasn't sure how to approach the idea that they were suddenly docile and straight-up *refusing* to bite me or anyone else. In my mind, it had to be some feature of the dungeon itself, rather than the hatchling monstrosities suddenly having a bizarre change of nature.

The others had received Stinky's news with a measure of calm that I didn't know was possible. He'd *just* told them they'd been trapped in a dungeon for centuries, and these people were more concerned about one of them not being able to read *Goodnight Moon* than the fact that they'd been existing inside of a time-eating dungeon. I'd have been wigging the hell out, probably trying to attack Stinky with a handful of feces for lobbing this trauma on me. Hell, finding out I'd lost five days was bad enough, but *four hundred years?* Instead of trying to bite the walls or fight the trees while screaming, they were relaxing serenely, unwinding just as they had been before the commotion. Jes, in particular, was more overcome with fascination by both Stinky's existence and the fact that he traveled with a cadre of egg monsters than anything else. I, of everyone, seemed to be handling the news the worst.

"Seriously," I demanded, staring at each of them, "doesn't it bother you that you've just essentially shot yourself forward in time by half a millennium?"

"Ah," Calden said, taking a bite of stale bread. "*That*. I believe we are all dissecting the information to stomach it as best we can. It is quite the knot to unravel. Though I think I speak for everyone when I say that we had our suspicions."

There was a round of nods at his words. My mouth was hanging open, so I closed it.

They were all so . . . chill with having lost everyone they loved and cared about.

"What did you suspect?" Stinky asked, taking another pull from the bottle.

Jes sighed, gesturing to Calden that he would take over. Calden nodded and continued eating his food.

"A few days ago—well, I suppose that isn't accurate anymore, is it? Regardless, we recently discovered a skeleton in a ravine that shared an uncanny likeness with our navigator, Carmichael. We never spoke of the possibility, but I believe we all understood the potency of following a pathway of thought like that without the truth or even properly understanding the mechanics."

"That's cool, I guess," I said. "Whatever gets you through to the other side, right?"

"In any case," Calden said, finishing his bread. "Jes, here, is an elf, and Merra is a dwarf. They are frustratingly long-lived. To them, a few measly centuries is as losing a few weeks for us. They will be fine."

"Not exactly," Merra said seriously. "It's still a loss, by any metric. My grandda only lived to be six hundred."

"Aye, but ain't ye gran still alive?" Frida asked. "Almost nine hundred in years, correct?"

"Well, yes," Merra admitted. "But it isn't the same equivalency to weeks as our rambunctious Calden likes to think."

"He's just saying that for pity," Dedyc said with a laugh. "Wants you all to feel sorry for him."

"And it was working, *too*," Calden scolded. "Until the indelible dwarf had to go and ruin it by being *factual*."

They laughed.

I was sincerely moved by their companionship. It was entirely likely they'd been through enough together that this was just another drop of water in the bucket. I was envious. Even at my lowest points, I hadn't had anyone I felt stood to face it toe-to-toe with me. It made me a little angry, honestly. I remember when Nick's uncle had died in fifth grade, tons of people had shown up from school and elsewhere to make sure he and his family were doing all right. I'd even stayed over at his house for three days straight—even though they were school nights—playing games with him and trying to cheer him up.

But when I'd had my own tragedy . . .

Let's not think about that right now.

I forced a grin and leaned back, resting against one of the logs. Something was still eating at me. They'd all been there for much longer than they thought . . . but *why*? It was clear they considered themselves a bit lost without their navigator, but how confusing was this chamber? There was a literal path to follow. Did the whole area swap around like those staircases in *Harry Potter*? That would be messed up, but still, would that make it impossible to travel through just because of that? Clearly, the one they'd called Carmichael had some method of wayfinding that didn't jibe with their current skill sets.

Maybe that's the question I need to be asking.

"So," I said, clearing my throat. "This chamber. You mentioned you've all been stuck *here* specifically, trying to find your way out. Why is that? Is there a magical barrier or a living-labyrinth sort of sitch?"

"Our research . . ." Jes began, before looking over to Calden. The blond man seemed primed to leap onto his terminology, so he changed his tactic.

"We *learned* from reliable sources that this chamber is one of the most challenging by far to successfully complete. Not only are there various monsters and other inhabitants to pose an obstacle, but also the dimensions of this chamber are quite vast."

"How big is it?" I asked.

"To the best reckoning of our stupendously calculating minds," Calden said, "unending."

"Is that even possible?" I breathed. "The dungeon has to have . . . whatcha call it—finite space? A room of eternal jungle doesn't seem realistic."

"Ya ain't the keenest scholar on magical theory, eh?" Virgil said, speaking for the first time in a while.

"Hey, man," I said, "I know *plenty* about *plenty*. I just don't hold on to a bunch of useless dungeon trivia, is all."

"Well then, professor," Virgil said, "allow me to parcel out the knowledge in a morsel you'll be able to stick in your gullet. Dungeon magic is potent and don't exist like nothin' else in the whole damn world. Works by its own rules and don't take no regard from no one else. Stubborn and independent, she is."

"I can relate to that," I said. "But how does that explain an infinite pocket dimension?"

"Let me wrangle up a bit o' foundation for ya, afore ya get your trigger finger in a twist," Virgil said.

I didn't say anything, but now I had absolute proof that Virgil was a sojourner. *Trigger finger* seemed like an unlikely term to exist within this new world on its own. I supposed it might have meant something else entirely, but I could *not* shake the feeling that he was anything but someone from my world. But being cautious was important. It wouldn't do to follow my already-decided thoughts to an incorrect conclusion. I think they call that confirmation BS or something.

"As you like," I said.

"Most appreciated," Virgil said. "There is a specialized form of magics known as 'cosmic.' It dictates a great many things in relation to what they call spatial manipulation and transference. On a small scale, you git things like bottomless satchels, rings o' storage, and magicians who can shift little items from one spot to 'nother. Upper side of it are your planar portals and dimensional planes. It is a volatile mistress, cosmic, and she takes an awful long time to gain a sense o' mastery over."

"So, are *you* a master of cosmic magic?" I asked.

"Naw," Virgil said. "But I listened somethin' fierce when Carmichael was jawin' about it."

"Carmichael is—er, *was* quite an aficionado of advanced arcane knowledge," Jes said. "With a targeted expertise and specialization in cosmic Arcana and function, as well as flair in fields like simulacra and alchemical research."

"So, he was, what? Your dimensional tour guide?" I asked.

"I'm not quite certain of your terms," Jes said. "But he was our navigator because of his planar adroitness. We commissioned him specifically for this journey, and now it appears we may be trapped forever without his aid."

"Unless one of your number is sufficiently skilled in the practice?" Calden ventured, looking from me to Stinky.

"I'm definitely not," I admitted. "Stink—er, Akiva?"

Stinky shook his head and spat on the ground.

"Not a fuckin' chance."

"Ah," Calden said, crestfallen. "What about one of those eggs? They seem spirited enough to lead us out of the maw of confusion."

"Now ye just graspin' at whiskers," Frida said.

"Well, it was worth a try," Calden said.

"Et really wasn't."

I slumped in my seat a bit.

"So, unless we figure out the best route through this room, we are boned?" I asked.

"Precisely," Jes said. "To further complicate matters: this may not be a space within the dungeon itself but one that exists *outside* of it. Carmichael believed that the gateway to this chamber was actually a portal to another plane altogether. This, I believe, is the most likely conclusion to be drawn from the nature of this area. It would also explain why there was not a message upon crossing the threshold."

I nodded.

"Yeah, now that you mention it . . . there wasn't an annoying notification at all. I didn't even consider that until now."

"That's 'cause you've got a pile of wet underclothes where your brain should be, orc," Stinky said with a laugh.

I knew it was meant to be a joke, but I couldn't help but feel some embarrassment at him making fun of me in front of our new acquaintances. So, obviously, I got a little salty.

"The hell, man? Not cool. What did I *just* say about that shit?" I demanded, pointing a finger at the matau. "Get off your high horse, you cantankerous . . . stooge!"

"It's not difficult to be lofty, orc, when your fuckin' smarts are all the way down in the dirt," Stinky shot back.

"I'm gonna put *you* in the dirt, you racist pimple licker," I said. "Call me an orc one more time. I fuckin' *dare you.*"

Stinky waved me away with a gesture.

"You're all *chin wag*, you damned fool," he said. "I've seen the way you fight. I'll be peachy."

"Well, where I come from, we *eat* peaches!"

"Likely eat the fuckin' trees they grow on too, by mistake," Stinky said.

"I am going to kick your ass so hard, you're gonna have to take your hat off to fart!"

"I'm not wearing a hat, you fuckin' reprobate!"

"It was a figure of speech," I yelled, standing up now. "Why don't you go cry in the dark, Stinky?"

"Stop calling me that!"

"Make me," I said.

I paused, seeing the looks from the rest of the group. Each of them was frozen in horrified curiosity at Stinky and my sudden outburst. Stinky seemed to notice as well, a retort perched in his mouth as we felt the weight of the party's judgment blanketing us. Calden was the one to speak.

"Do the two of you have an underlying issue? Or do you genuinely despise one another?"

I looked at Stinky, who scowled in return.

"We, uh, were just messing around," I said. "It's something we do. A bit of banter, you know? Keeps the blood coursing through your veins and the blush on your cheeks."

"Clearly," Calden said, obviously unconvinced. "Well, whatever it is you two do to pass the time is perfectly all right, but you may want to give us fair warning before your next bout. Virgil is *quite* sensitive to conflict."

"No, 'm not!" Virgil said.

"There's a brave lad, Virgil," Calden said.

"Okay," I said, turning back to the group. "Let me backtrack here . . . "

I rubbed my temples, trying to calm down from Stinky's barbs using a direct line to my emotionally stunted epicenter. After a moment, I exhaled and found my conversational footing.

"So, what *exactly* do you remember Carmichael saying about the makeup of this place? Did he elaborate? I am trying to figure out how he knew *some* stuff but didn't know about the timey-wimey bullshit."

"He was an expert," Jes said. "But even then, there is only so much available information about the Forbidden Crypt. Much of it was little better than guess-work, as the gaps in reliable sources were quite wide. Carmichael made his best conclusions from the paltry amount of detail in the archives. Everything else he posited was once we had arrived."

" . . . and what did he propose was going on here? You said he'd figured out this place was separate from the dungeon altogether, right? But did he mention any theories as to how to get out?"

"He thought he was on to somethin', just afore he meandered off," Virgil said. "Said he wanted to test one o' his thoughts."

This seemed to shock the group, and the skinny elf wheeled on Virgil.

"I was unaware of this," Jes said. "You spoke to Carmichael before he went missing? Why did you never say anything?"

Virgil seemed to bristle at that, perhaps expecting a confrontation. When he finally responded, his voice was tight and quivery as if he was trying to maintain control over his fear.

Or anger.

"Carmichael said he'd be along in a few days," Virgil said. "Said if he came back, he were wrong. If he didn't, well, that meant his speculations were correct."

"Did this not seem like useful information to pass along to the rest of the team?" Jes asked sternly.

"I ain't want to worry no one," Virgil said, his voice growing in its own defiance. "If he came back, and I had told y'all, I'd have riled ya up fer nothin'. I ain't got any means to discern that we'd been frolickin' round in a cosmic time marsh, did I? I was goin' to say somethin' soon but wanted to give him ample time to return."

"Virgil," Jes said cautiously, "what were his *exact* words?"

Virgil closed his eyes, either trying to recall the information or convincing himself not to pistol-whip his companion. I knew the feeling. After a moment, he opened his eyes again.

"Best o' my recollection, Carmichael said, 'Virgil, I'm a-goin' out there to procure an answer fer an idea. If I return, I have been incorrect in my assumptions. If I don't, I was abreast of it, and none o' this will matter.'"

"Well, that's fuckin' ominous," I said.

"I was hopin' he'd come a-callin'," Virgil continued. "When we seen that skeleton in the ditch, I kept my chin up, prayin' it weren't him. Now . . . "

Virgil took a deep breath.

" . . . seems like my fears were realized. He ain't comin' back, an' he were right about whatever he thought was goin' on."

"Son of a scrote," I said, feeling a hot knot of anger in my stomach. "What kinda senseless dick-brain goes off without telling anyone their plans—especially when the result means leaving people in the dark? I'm not a scientist—by any stretch of the imagination—but even *I* know that you always leave a fucking note, at the very least."

"He *was* a bit odd," Merra said sadly. "I can't reason why he would do that either."

"Well, he did," Calden said. "What is done is done."

"Was there anything on the body?" Stinky asked.

"What do you mean?" Jes asked. "On the corpse we discovered? No. It was picked clean, likely by marauding monsters or perhaps *time* itself."

"Wait," I said. "If the skeleton was all that was left, how could you even suspect it was him in the first place? Did he have diamond bones or something?"

"Carmichael suffered an accident shortly after we entered the dungeon," Jes explained. "In the first chamber, his arm became trapped under the body of one of those winged horrors."

"The cuckoos?" I asked. "But they weren't that heavy."

"That is correct," said Jes. "But the creature's body had stuck itself in a fissure—with Carmichael's limb beneath it. In order to make it to the archway within the time limit, Frida was forced to sever the appendage from his body. The corpse in the ravine had only one arm, the other hacked off cleanly."

"Oh," I said. "All right, that makes more sense. Would there be any clues as to what he might have discovered?"

All eyes turned to Virgil, who shook his head.

"Best I can reckon," he said slowly, "somethin' he thought would make us blanch. He weren't keen on providin' insight into his work. Kind of a private poke."

"Was he carrying anything with him?" I asked. I'd seen enough detective shows to know that there was typically a visual clue as opposed to a verbal statement that would tip an investigator off to their next lead.

"Everythin'," Virgil said. "The whole caboodle."

"Yes, we'd assumed he'd abandoned us at first," Jes said, "as there was nothing left behind."

"Okay," I said, trying to take on the qualities of the type of inquisitive genius that only ever existed in the writing room of television dramas. I didn't think I could solve this mystery myself—I knew the limits of my powers of deduction—but maybe I could ask the right questions to lead someone *else* to the answer?

"So, there wasn't anything *on* the skeleton? No clothing, belongings, or anything?"

"Hard to remember," Dedyc said. "We were on the move, and it was dark."

"Shit," I said. "I wish we could go investigate the body, but we are already short on time as it is. Adding the super-speed syndrome into the mix—even if we figured it out, we might not leave for another century."

"Actually . . . " Jes said thoughtfully.

"Everyone, this is it," Calden exclaimed. "Master Carandalon is going to offload a dram of golden intellect into our laps. No one look him directly in the eyes, now."

Jes groaned and shot Calden a withering glare.

"Enough," he said.

"As you wish, Sir Nobleborn," Calden said with a wink.

"What were you going to say, Jes?" I asked.

The elf turned to me, then indicated Stinky with a gesture.

"We don't need to worry about the time dilation," he said confidently. "As long as we have Akiva here, we will not suffer the effects of the cosmic influence."

"Really?" I said.

"Yes," said Jes with a nod. "At least, in theory, that is how it should operate. I have seen similar reactions before with time-disrupting Arcana."

"You might need to explain that a bit more in depth," I said. "You know, for, uh, Calden's benefit."

Calden chuckled.

"My comprehension, as you all now know, is on par with a block of wood—or one of those dreaded horned knights."

"Assuming that the rules of this chamber follow conventional rhythms," said Jes, "the . . . bubble—as our friend Loon so eloquently put it—is something of a passive effect. It will be in place as the arcane process dictates. Which, considering the ancient nature of this crypt, runs by a set of rules that may work autonomously."

"Like an autopilot?" I asked.

"Er, yes? Perhaps," Jes said. "Typically, something of this level of output would be difficult to monitor. The age of the dungeon in conjunction with the complexity of the seals and Arcana necessary to produce the desired result leads me to believe that it would rely on the simplest possible execution."

"... and that means?" I asked.

"Akiva," Jes posed, smiling warmly at Stinky. "How long has it been since you arrived at our campsite?"

Stinky didn't even pause.

"One hour, eight minutes."

"Now, if we assume that he is not affected by the time dilation—which seems evident, based on his previous indication—the arcane bubble will disperse. I estimate that the spell contorting this realm would place more importance on collectively containing the bubble for the challenge, and *not* on a precaution of whether or not a matau happened to stumble in here."

"So, his Ability . . . supersedes the magic for all of us?" I asked, unsure if I'd used the right word.

"It would be more accurate to say that the arcane function assumes that a group of individuals will not have Time Clarity among their rank. The collective is a higher priority than anything else. So, it is not that his Ability overrides the arcane but that it doesn't have a formula in place to recognize it in the first place."

"Wow, way to go, Stinky!" I announced, slugging the matau on the shoulder. "You're going to be useful after all!"

"Touch me again, and I will rip your tongue out through your arse," Stinky growled.

"Oh, easy now," I said. "Just because you're excited is no reason to start talking dirty to me. Leave bedroom talk in the bedroom."

Stinky put a hand on his dagger and jerked away from me.

"All right," I said, clapping my hands together for emphasis. "Whaddya guys say? Who's up for some good, old-fashioned gumshoe sleuthing?!"

"What does that mean?" Dedyc asked.

CHAPTER TWENTY-SIX

ELEMENTARY, MY DEAR STINKY

It took a few hours to get to the ravine where the others had found the body. Initially, I had reservations about traveling and losing several more days. Still, with Stinky's apparent wunderkind *Rain Man* timekeeping ability, he kept us in the loop on whether or not things were changing. Jes indicated that it was also possible we could cross into different "pockets" inside this chamber that might have different rules in place, so Stinky had to be hypervigilant. Apparently, it was unlikely but not unheard-of.

My head swam. I didn't understand even a fraction of what they'd been discussing, but as long as they came to a conclusion that led to us getting out of there, I would be perfectly fine with remaining ignorant as fuck.

Virgil—who'd been scouting slightly ahead—called out to let us know each stretch where we'd gotten closer to the crime scene. He'd been careful to stay within a specific range, lest he stumble outside of the bubble and be lost to us for a few decades. It was easier to do than I'd thought it would be, as Stinky and he had discussed what their particular ranges were in the experience—with Virgil gauging his nearby searches before and Stinky explaining at what point I'd seemed to disappear from view when I'd initially gone off before finding the camp.

Fortunately, the group seemed happy with the arrangement we had. With Stinky, not only were we protected from the ravages of the mean ol' time gremlins or whatever but also apparently the beasts of the chamber as well. Dedyc had mentioned that they'd encountered monsters with alarming regularity before but didn't see any indication of them at all since Stinky and I had joined up. Jes believed this was because the monsters were *also* held in a similar time gumbo.

That was chill with me. I still hadn't gotten used to fighting for my life on the regular, so moving along without needing to check each cardinal direction every ten seconds was a goddamn vacation. Instead of nervously wheeling on my six, I used the time during the march to examine some long-needed necessities in my personal repertoire.

Namely, the Skill Book.

As the description indicated, it would only take eight minutes. But what I wasn't prepared for was how much it would goddamn *hurt*. I'd flipped slowly through the pages, and when I'd reached the end, it felt like a bolt of lightning hit my brain and burrowed into my muscles. I'd shot backward about ten feet and landed in a patch of pokey thistles, which was . . . inconvenient. However, when I finally recovered and my Stamina returned to normal, I found that my bodily movements were much defter. Almost like I'd been living my whole life submerged in molasses and suddenly got ripped out of it like Neo in *The Matrix*.

Congratulations! You have acquired a new Skill!
Gained Acrobat [E-Rank Level 1]

I didn't think I'd ever get comfortable with this process. It was too weird and uncomfortable. But I couldn't disagree with the results. I practiced doing cartwheels while we moved along—something I'd never been able to do before. Stinky kept yelling at me to stop acting like a fool, but I didn't care: I was a gigantic, sexy gymnastics machine now, unbound by the rules of the society that would shun me. Really *feelin' myself*, ya know?

In addition to high-speed miracle learnin', I figured I'd check out something that had been bothering me since we got there.

I opened up my display and checked out my Quests. There were three under *Active* and zero under *Completed*, which, I have to say, did a number on my confidence.

Active Quests
- [Bounty Quest] *The Easy Part*
- [Faith Quest] *Into the Dungeon*
- [Dungeon Quest] *Keep It Secret* . . .

I wasn't sure if a trio was good to have less than two days into a dungeon—well, a week if you counted the time dilation—or if I was below average. I needed to check out my most recent entry because the gigantic avian asshole imp had *definitely* told me that I had messed up.

[Dungeon Quest] *Keep It Secret* . . .
Pontivex sel Delibitaus has requested that you find Exotic Meat of a unique and untested creature and return it to him.

Exotic Meat cannot exist within the dungeon itself and must be procured outside it.
- Reward(s): *Experience. Renown. Coin.*
- Bonus: *Secret Knowledge of the Forbidden Crypt of the Dreadnaught Lord* (Conditional)

Additional Bonus Rewards Based on Conditions

NOTE: This is a Conditional Quest! As such, specific parameters must be met to fulfill it to completion. You will receive [1] Bonus Reward upon accepting the Quest.

Conditions:
- Time Allotted: *[6] Standard Months*
- Amount: *[1] Portion.*

Any amount over [1] will result in additional Rewards. Variety of Exotic Meat will result in additional Rewards.

Then I saw the change. Under the description of conditions, a separate badge glimmered like a red coat of arms. I selected it mentally, and a new display popped up.

Amendment History:
- **Orc Loon [Byname Unavailable] has requested to alter terms.**
- **Hive Fiend Pontivex sel Delibitaus [Cryptkeeper] has opened discourse.**
- **Orc Loon [Byname Unavailable] requests additional rewards allotted prematurely.**
- **Hive Fiend Ponitvex sel Delibitaus [Cryptkeeper] altered Conditions to include [Racial Ability] Soul-Bound Servitude.**
- **Orc Loon [Byname Unavailable] agrees to terms.**
- **Hive Fiend Pontivex sel Delibitaus [Cryptkeeper] agrees to terms.**
- **[Amendment History Complete]**

The fucking fuck?!

That double-crossing diddle-puss had altered the Quest and didn't tell me! Now I had to figure out if Soul-Bound Servitude was as bad as it sounded. Fortunately, there was a description:

[Racial Ability] Soul-Bound Servitude

This is an Ability that allows the user to create or alter a contract to include stipulations of servitude involving the essence of life. If an agreement is

made, the user of this Ability can retain the use of the signatory's soul upon death or other criteria—either temporarily or permanently—depending on the nature of the contract.

You are currently under a Soul-Bound Servitude Contract.
- *Conditions: Failure to complete [Dungeon Quest] Keep It Secret . . . within the parameters or death.*
- *Duration: Permanent.*

Yep, it's exactly what it sounds like. This place is bullshit!

I knew that it wasn't worth worrying over at the moment, since there was literally nothing I could do about it, but it still made me super angry. Calden must have seen my face change, because he approached me with a big friendly smile.

"Blisters?" he asked casually.

"What?" I barked, my mood overtaking what had actually been a relatively pleasant and positive interaction with these new guys until now.

Calden just pointed at my feet.

"Blisters," he said again. "From this abysmal hike? They are peppering every available surface of my usually newborn-soft skin. Considering you're completely bare of foot, I can imagine you are getting the worst of it. Where *are* your boots, by the by? Did something eat them?"

"Uh," I said, trying to think of a lie.

I couldn't exactly admit that I'd arrived in this world without anything covering my tootsies and hadn't had a chance to remedy that considering it was only . . . Well, it had been a few days now. Still, my misadventures hadn't yet allowed me the novelty of footwear.

"I forgot them when I went to the bathroom," I said.

Shit, he's not going to know what a bathroom is!

"Ah, yes," Calden noted, as if he understood exactly what I meant. "Any time that I bathe, I am so overjoyed with the sensation that I leave many of my belongings behind. I have had to buy so many new pants that way."

Calden and I chatted a little while we moved, and I found that my assessment of him was correct: he could fucking *talk*. In fact, I was pretty sure that if I hadn't finally interrupted him, he would have continued going for hours. But I saw something strange and had to mention it.

"What are they doing?" I asked.

"—and honestly, it was not even the first time he had to chase me out of there with a pitchfor— I apologize, but what?" said Calden.

"The, uh, roe," I said, pointing. "What are they up to?"

Calden's gaze followed my indication and we both watched as the eggs— which had previously been sadly skulking along around the outside of our group—were now energetically trying to leapfrog over one another but failing miserably. I stopped in my tracks to watch, seeing Calden do the same.

"Is this some sort of mating ritual?" Calden asked, leaning forward and squinting. "Should we look away and give them some privacy?"

"I'm not sure," I said. "I don't think so, but honestly . . . Yeah, I dunno.."

It was true; I really had no clue what egg sex consisted of, but if it was *that*, it seemed awfully inconvenient and stupid. They kept up at their exercise, taking turns trying to hop up and over the one in front of them and bouncing off gently. With each failure, it seemed as though they got more and more excited, with subsequent attempts showcasing an increasing fervor of enthusiasm.

"Does anyone know what these things are doing?" I called to the rest of the group. "It seems unwholesome."

Stinky and Jes, who were in the middle of the pack, paused to observe, both immediately adopting sickened expressions. Merra, Dedyc, and Frida, who had been discussing something farther ahead, also stopped.

"It looks as though they're trying to reproduce," Merra said. "But my, they're bad at it."

"Just leave 'em to their fuckin', orc," Stinky said. "Who knows why monsters do what they do?"

"Yeah, I dunno," I said. "This seems a little different than that."

"How you figure?"

"Well, for one, they're *all* doing it," I said. "Wouldn't they pair off if that were the case?"

"Some creatures copulate in groups," Jes said. "It is not that unique to think these things would do likewise. What do we know about them?"

"Fuck all," Stinky said. "Let 'em have their fun. It's no matter to me."

"Like I said," I breathed. "I think it's something else."

"What you think and what I care about don't even share the same realm, orc."

"Fuck you, Stinky."

We continued for some time until Vigil finally gave us a shout indicating we were close to the ravine. I wasn't sure what we'd find when we arrived, but I kept a hand on my haladie, just in case. I noticed that the trees in this area had gotten denser, and I had to assume it was because they were closer to a source of water. That, at least, sounded like something trees would do, but I was woefully equipped to contemplate biology in the old world, let alone in this new, magical one. The path also had gotten noticeably more difficult to travel, with large roots jutting up from the dirt, making the trek slow going and tedious.

Finally, we reached where Virgil had stopped, right at the edge of where the earth itself dropped off. I peered over the side to see into the fissure in front of us. It was a ravine, all right, in the same way that Mastodon's *Crack the Skye* was just *some* album. That was to say it was an extreme understatement. What I was staring at was a massive crevice in the ground—fifty feet deep and just as wide. It stretched in either direction as far as I could see, snaking along into the deep jungle beyond. A stream ran through it like a trickle of blood through a vein, with a gentle flow to it that would have seemed pleasant if it wasn't so . . . sickening. It was a peachy color, almost like melted sherbet, and the sloped ground near it was as black as space's butthole.

"What the goddamn?" I said. "You made it sound like this was a ditch. This is like a ditch's beefy grandpa."

"It has grown," Jes said with quiet horror.

"It *what?*" I asked.

"It is deeper than it was when we saw it a few . . . " Jes continued, trailing off.

"It's been years, right?" I asked. "But I thought this shit only happened on *that* kind of scale over like . . . eons or whatever?"

"This must be a feature of the chamber," Calden offered. "Deep rivulets in the earth to throw us off our progress."

"It would make sense if it was designed this way," Merra said. "Mess with our minds a bit."

"Et is workin,'" Frida said, stretching her neck out to look down. "Ye think Carmichael's still doon there?"

"Only one way to find out," Calden said. Then he bounded forward and leaped over the edge of the cliff.

"What the hell?!" I shouted, but no one seemed to react to his apparent suicide attempt with the same level of bewilderment I did.

"He'll be fine," Merra assured me, resting a hand on my leg. "Don't worry about Calden. He's hard to kill."

"A fact that has plagued us for a long while," Jes muttered.

After a moment, we all heard a shout from far below and peered down to see Calden waving at us from the bottom of the fissure.

"Made it," he called. "I think I have found our quarry, but it is highly suspect!"

"How so?" Dedyc called down.

"I fear my eloquence will not paint the appropriate picture," Calden returned. "You may need to see for yourselves. There's a precarious trail along the rock wall you can follow. I can see it from here."

I sighed. I was a big boy, and if our last foray across tiny stone pathways was any preamble, I'd be having a hell of a time. I looked over at the eggs, which were still trying to do . . . whatever the hell it was they were doing, and raised my hands to catch their attention.

"Don't follow," I said simply. "Be back soon. No fall."

They blinked uncomprehendingly at me, so I just shrugged and turned back to the cliff's edge. Then I followed the others down.

I was wrong, though. Navigating the narrow rock slip down to the water was surprisingly easy for me. My footing was more confident than ever, even with the size of my bare feet, and it seemed like I was particularly well suited to picking out good spots to grab hold of. I made it down in no time and was surprised to find that Calden was already waist-deep in the pastel sludge oozing through the channel. He was hunched over, his arms submerged in the muck up to his biceps as he shambled about.

"What are you doing?" I asked.

"I believe it was right around here . . . " Calden said, his face scrunched with concentration.

"He's trying to locate the body," Dedyc said.

"Here," Jes said, and placed one hand in the air and the other on his chest. "By fortitude of will, I summon the light of Paragon Altrius that I may find what is sought."

A golden glow began to pulse from Jes's outstretched hand before radiating out in a bright halo of magical light. I took a step back, worried something might explode. The glow left his hand and floated through the air, slowly traveling along the contour of the sludge river before stopping about thirty feet down from where we were. Then the light grew brighter, sputtering like a sparkler above a point above the liquid.

"There," Jes said to Calden, and the blond man sloshed away toward the hovering magical lantern.

"A Finding Spell?" I asked.

"Yes, in a sense," Jes said. "Something I picked up from a Cleric of the Traveler."

He tapped his chest where he'd been clutching a moment before. I could now see a very conspicuous lump beneath the fabric.

"It's an Amulet of Location," he said.

"Why the hell couldn't you just use that to find the way out of here?"

"It only works on objects of individuals I have seen before," he said. "I would be unable to use it to find an exit that I have not borne witness to, lo though the convenience that would provide."

"Shit," I said.

"You can say that 'gain," Frida said.

Calden finally reached the spot beneath the glowing beacon. This time, instead of just reaching down, he plunged beneath the disgusting flow of gunk and disappeared below the surface. A few seconds later, he emerged, sputtering and covered in the thick and oily material of the river.

"Got it," he announced, and began moving toward the bank. The rest of us moved to meet him, picking our route carefully to not fall in as well. I wasn't sure what that stuff was, but I didn't want to get it on me, even if it was dick-growing juice.

Calden emerged from the river as we reached him, dragging a shape along. It was a huge, pale skeleton that likely belonged to someone even bigger than Dedyc. Sure enough, as Calden shored it on the black rock of the bank, I could see that it was missing one of its arms.

"Jesus fuck," I breathed. "What the hell kind of creature was Carmichael? A giant?"

I'd almost asked if giants existed in their world but caught myself and very smoothly and professionally avoided the pitfall.

"Are there giants here? Uh . . . I mean, well . . . Giants. Giants, uh, here . . . Here. In . . . uh, well . . . In this . . . dungeon?"

Nailed it.

No one seemed to be paying attention to me, because they were wrapped up in the fuck-off large skelly-boy being eased out of the river. All except Frida, who gave me a curious look.

"No . . . " she said hesitantly. "Carmichael wasn't a giant. 'E was an ulgaroch."

"Oh . . . " I said, trying to sound like I knew precisely what that was.

" . . . they're big, sinewy blokes with massive pates an' those long arms."

That sounds like fucking Slenderman.

I looked at the skeleton again.

Yep. Slenderman.

"Thanks," I said sheepishly.

"No' a problem," Frida said. "Ye seem a bit out' yoor element in some regard."

"Yeah, I, uh . . . never was much for learning about the world until recently."

"Tha's a'right," Friday said with a smile. "Get a few more adventures under ye belt, an' ye'll be right up."

"This is really kind of my *first* adventure," I said.

"Oh, donnae worry 'bout that," she continued. "E'ry'un goes pro their second time."

She gave me a wink.

Ah, shit, I thought to myself. *That was really smooth. I better not fall in love with her.*

The last thing any woman needed was a big, ugly dipshit catching feelings and following them around like a lost puppy. Even worse was a big, ugly, dipshit *monster* crushing on them. I was aware of my limits enough to know that she was just being friendly. I wasn't going to allow myself to consider it anything but that to avoid the eventual awkward interaction later.

She is very striking, though . . .

I shook my head.

Nope, get it together, numbnuts. There's a fucking eldritch-horror skeleton five feet away from you. This is not the time for unrequited romance.

Instead, as everyone gathered around the cosmic analyst formerly known as Carmichael, I switched tactics to distract myself.

"I thought you said you found it before," I asked Calden incredulously. "Why the hell did we run down here if you didn't even know where it was?"

Calden, drenched with oily residue from the Willy Wonka stream, stared up at me with embarrassment.

"Oh, yes," he said. "I was mistaken."

"What did you actually stumble onto?" I asked.

"It was nothing . . . " he said unconvincingly.

I just stared at him, hoping my newfound superpower of *let them squirm in silence* would take effect. It did. After a moment, Calden shrugged.

"It was a rock."

"A rock?"

"A serendipitously corpse-shaped rock," Calden continued. "An easy misunderstanding to fall upon."

I smiled.

"No biggie," I said. "One time, I threw a shoe at a chair that I thought was a dog."

Now it was Calden's turn to stare.

"It was dark!" I protested.

"I was under the clear impression that orcs could see in the dark," said Calden.

"It was *really* dark," I said.

"Ah."

"Can I request a bit of silence?" Jes asked sternly.

"Yes, we've a body to ransack," Merra said with a smile.

"We are *not* desecrating Carmichael's skeleton," Jes said. "We are merely—"

"Oh, I'm only teasing, Jes," Merra said. "Injecting a bit of levity into this gruesome business."

"Honestly, Merra," Jes sighed. "Sometimes, you are as incorrigible as Calden."

"She cannot help it," Calden said. "My charming allure tends to seep maliciously into those who spend time with me."

"Yes," Merra agreed, her grin spreading wide. "I learned it from watching how well *your* behavior manifests so positively."

"There you have it," Calden said. "Merra has confirmed that my methods are a force for good."

"Will you *please* allow me a moment of respite from the lackadaisical manner in which you conduct yourselves? I am attempting to learn what I can from Carmichael's remains so that we might have a chance to escape from here."

Calden dropped his head as if attempting to submit himself, then adopted an accent I'd have described as *nervous peasant*.

"Yes, m'lord," he said, doubling over in a bow. "Does this genuflection suffice as to m'unascended station? I can go lower, m'lord. If it pleases."

Jes groaned but didn't say anything further, choosing instead to turn back to the skeleton and produce a small bottle from his robes. He unstoppered it and dribbled a few drops onto the bones before prodding the spot with a finger. Then the emaciated elf withdrew his digit and rubbed the residue between the finger and his thumb.

"Deteriorating at a typical rate," he said as if only to himself. He smelled the residue and closed his eyes.

"Dedyc," he said, his eyes still tightly shut.

"Jes?" Dedyc hissed.

"I am having difficulty identifying this scent," Jes continued. "What can you tell me?"

The large lizardy creature approached the skeleton and leaned forward, taking a big whiff over the spot where the liquid had stained the bones.

"Ganflower," he said confidently.

"Ganflower . . ." Jes repeated quietly, thinking. "Odd, don't you think?"

"Very," Dedyc said, standing back up to his full height.

"Why would a substance like that reside in his bones?" Jes asked absently.

"What's ganflower?" I asked. Immediately after voicing it, I got the sense that I was intruding too much on territory that was so far outside of my realm, I'd look stupid for even speaking. Instead of getting reprimanded, however, Jes turned to me.

"It is an ingredient typically used in crafting potent healing tinctures and potions."

"Oh," I said. "Why is that weird, though? Couldn't Carmichael have just used a healing potion on himself after whatever killed him had attacked? Maybe he was trying to save himself?"

Stinky cleared his throat, spat, and then wheeled on me.

"Healing potions don't work that way, you lump," he said. "They don't infect the bones."

"Now, now," Calden interjected. "Our wonderful orc companion is simply attempting to broaden his understanding and education as to the subtle nuances of the world. We cannot disparage him for *that, can* we?"

"Yeah, Stinky," I said. "I'm trying to learn about stuff, asshole. Don't stifle my scholarly spirit."

"If there's a scholastic bone *anywhere* in your twisted body, orc, I'll eat my damn boots."

"How 'bout you eat my *fist*?" I shot back.

"*Please*," Jes exclaimed. "I am attempting to work. These frequent interruptions slow the process."

"Yeah, Stinky," I said. "Curb your dickish tendencies for five minutes so Jes can solve this mystery."

"I am going to enjoy slitting your throat . . . *orc*," Stinky said, emphasizing the last word so that I knew he meant it as an insult.

"Good luck, Shaky-hands," I said. "Hopefully, that happens in direct sunlight, so you don't piss your pants. We *both* know how hard it is for you to concentrate when the lights go out."

"*Enough!*" Jes thundered, standing up and wielding a finger at us like it was a magic wand. "If you two must bicker, do it somewhere out of earshot. This issue is irritatingly complex enough without having to manage childish outbursts."

Both Stinky and I were silent for a moment. I had to admit, seeing Jes lose his temper on us was uncomfortable after the rapport I'd steadily built with the group. However, his commanding tone was far too close to sounding like someone who thought of themselves as an authority figure, which had the predictable effect of releasing my adversarial streak. Before I knew it, I was striking back.

"Wow, okay, *Dad*," I said. "I didn't realize you were the motherfucker in charge around here and we had to sit silent like good little boys so you could conduct your *super* important, groundbreaking research. Seems to me like you're not very good at *science* if you can't even handle a little background noise."

Jes stared at me as though I'd slapped him. He didn't say anything, but his face was full of surprise and another very recognizable emotion: anger.

"That's what I thought," I huffed. "We're hashing out our differences with healthy banter. I didn't even *mention* Stinky's bigoted comments—which shows maturity and growth, *by the way*. Maybe instead of—"

I didn't get to finish as Jes slashed his hand in front of him, and I was suddenly forced backward through the air, surrounded by an aura of glittering blue energy. I landed hard on my back, my head slamming against the ground. There was a flash of light combined with an acute stabbing brain pain. Stars appeared in my vision as I lay, unable to do anything but groan.

Condition: Dazed
You are dazed. Thoughts and movement will be temporarily stilted.

For fuck's sake!

I waited for the condition to fade, which only took about thirty seconds, and then slowly got to my feet. My head hurt something fierce, but I could finally stand upright and get my bearings. I found, to my surprise, that I'd been launched a good fifty feet from where I'd been and saw that Jes had returned to inspect the skeleton with Dedyc. Merra was conversing with Stinky and Virgil about something, all three looking utterly unaffected by what had transpired. Calden and Frida were near me, with the man smiling sheepishly. Frida's face was impassive, but I could tell from her sweeping gaze that she was assessing me for any damage.

"Ye good?" the martial woman asked, her piercing blue eyes lingering on my own. "Still got ye sense? Ye pluck?"

I winced.

"Man, that fuckin' *hurt*," I said.

"Apologies, friend," Calden said. "Jes can be a bit . . . dogged in his pursuit of higher truth. He does not bear the same particular brand of jocular tomfoolery you've come to expect from my merry disposition."

"Yeah," I breathed. "Noted. He's got a zero-horseplay policy. Good to know."

"Let me see ye head," Frida said, stepping around behind me. "Lean down?"

I nodded and slid into a crouch so that the shorter woman could take a gander at my head wound.

"Tell me the truth," I said as she examined me. "How long do I have left to live?"

Both Calden and Frida chuckled.

"Well, at the very least, your humor is not broken," Calden said. "Though I would advise restraint in future interactions with Jesimir. As unyieldingly amusing as I found your comments, he is quite prickly in these matters. I am always of a mind to pull my punches should I press him too aggressively."

"He could have *killed* me," I said. "Head trauma like that is no joke. That's how Bob Saget died!"

"Who?" Calden asked.

"No one— Listen, I know I probably overstepped there. It's a trait I've exercised enough to win a gold medal in powerlifting. But that was a bit of an extreme reaction."

"I am sorry, but I don't understand what you're referring to," Calden said.

"Frida, is his brain trickling out of the back of his skull?"

"No," she said serenely. "No' even a gash. 'Think 'e'll be fine as et is. Bit of a bop, is all."

"So, neither of you think he acted poorly?" I asked.

"He was perhaps a bit . . . passionate in his reprisal, but I believe you ended up the better in the encounter."

"Passionate?" I asked. "The dude chucked me across the fucking riverbank like a . . . thing you throw far."

"Concise," Calden explained. "Your elocution seems to be in top order, friend."

"Golf ball," I exclaimed. "He sent me flying like a golf ball."

"Of course," Calden said, breezing over my statement. "Whatever you say."

Frida stopped the exam and turned to look at me pointedly.

"Take et from me, Loon," she said. "Ye'll wan' te get yoorself a helmet. Bouts like that 'un'll catch up with ye 'fore long. Ye'll be glad ye did."

"Yeah, I had one . . . " I started, seeing Stinky still had Berg's dome protector on his own yellow cranium. "But I was using it for other stuff."

"Helmets are foor heads," Frida said. "No' 'other stuff.' Ye ken?"

"Yeah, yeah," I said. "It didn't exactly seem like it would fit my general vibe. Plus, it's tough to find things like that in my size."

"You need to acquire more magical raiments," Calden said. "Many are designed to adjust to the wearer's particular measurements."

"Good to know," I said. "Anyone got any super sweet mystical jewelry I can have?"

Both of them shook their heads.

"Guess I'll just have to wait it out 'til we get out of here and I can pop on over to Walmart."

The three of us walked back to join the rest of the group, who each shared goofy grins with me. Clearly, that hadn't been an unusual—or even unexpected—maneuver on Jes's part. The skinny elf didn't look up as I approached but called out to me, his attention still fixed on the skeleton.

"My apologies, Loon," he said. "I let my temper get the best of me. I will endeavor to ensure that does not happen again."

I wanted to tell him to eat shit, but instead, I chuckled, forcing a grin.

"Ah, no worries," I said. "It had been a while since someone had given me the ole heave-ho. I was starting to miss it."

Jes had produced a set of gigantic pincher-looking things, making measurements with them, sizing up different bones and comparing them to others. He was fully immersed in his work, so I turned to Dedyc.

"So, I think we were talking about gemflower or something?"

"Ganflower," Dedyc corrected.

"That's the one," I said. "Anyway, will someone—other than Stinky—explain why it couldn't be a health potion?"

Dedyc smiled up at me.

"Yes," he hissed. "Health potions are magical. Once the ingredients are active, they aren't ingredients anymore."

"So, they dissolve, kind of?" I asked.

"Yes and no," Dedyc continued. "They transform once they interact and become Arcana."

"Arcana does not bear physical properties," Calden further explained. "At least insomuch that it could be sorted out or separated. That is, of course, from my limited understanding."

"Yes," Dedyc said with a nod. "Very good, Calden. Very wise. A health potion wouldn't leave behind ingredients."

"All right," I said. "So, once they are all mixed up in their voodoo cocktail, they just turn into magic? Good to know."

"You get it," Dedyc announced proudly.

"So, I guess maybe I'm simple or something . . . " I said.

"That goes without fuckin' saying," Stinky said, but I ignored him.

"But is ganflower only found in stuff like that? It's gotta come from *somewhere*, right? Like a plant or a monster? Maybe something swallowed him, digested his flesh, and spat him back out? This is a shot in the dark, but it could have had that ingredient in its stomach?"

"Unlikely," Jes said finally, still not looking up. "There is no evidence of Carmichael's skeleton suffering trauma of that magnitude. The size of most creatures in this chamber has, at times, been large. But nothing so big as to be able to consume a full-grown ulgaroch without breaking him down with their teeth first."

"Could be something you haven't encountered yet?" I offered.

Jes nodded sagely but continued to burst my bubble.

"It is possible. However, even if there *were* a monster large enough to swallow him whole, there would be clear signs of damage to the exterior integrity of the bone. Dissolution and damage caused by the acids, for one. None of that is present in what I am currently observing."

"What *are* you observing?" Calden asked. "I am quite hesitant to speak up, given your recent penchant for utilizing Rebuff on your traveling ilk, but I feel we are all curious to know what you have learned so far."

Jes nodded again.

"Yes, that is fine. To be perfectly frank, I am a bit flummoxed by Carmichael's skeletal state. There are no signs of traumatic injury or anything else that might indicate a violent physical death. So too am I finding with evidence of a magical catalyst. That would be easier to discern for my specialty, but attestation of that is absent as well. I would postulate that he simply expired for natural reasons, but there is the perplexing issue with the ganflower."

"So, what other options are there?" I asked, moving closer to Carmichael's bones.

"That answer is growing much smaller as I continue to digest the information," Jes explained. "I have been quite thorough and find myself at an impasse."

"Well, shit," I said. "It's a dead end, then?"

"I hope that is not the case," Jes explained. "With a little more time, I could potentially unearth further information. But I believe it would be in my best interest to take a break and return to this after a short rest and much-needed nourishment."

"So, just to be clear," I began, "if we can't glean anything from Mr. Bones over here, we are going to have to find some *other* clue to get out?"

"Let us hope it does not come to that," Calden said. "Jes is quite the researcher—as he's keen to point out—and I believe he will come to a conclusion that hoists us from this dreadful predicament and sets us back on a path of glory."

Jes stood and grunted noncommittally before moving away from the skeleton. Dedyc followed, and the others joined the elf a short walk away. Merra removed her pack and began doling out food; while Calden produced a bottle the group began sharing.

I spent another few minutes looking at the skeleton. Poking it, prodding it, and imagining what it must have looked like with its skin on. However, I couldn't stop envisioning a pale, creepy specter in a black suit looming from the trees. It gave me the heebie-jeebies. So far, being largely useless, I decided to execute ol' reliable from my arsenal of barely relevant traits. Analysis had come in fairly clutch so far, even, at times, giving me helpful insight into the nature of things themselves. But I had only ever used it on items. I wasn't sure if the bones of a previously living creature would even be identifiable with the Ability, but that wasn't going to stop me from trying.

So, I activated it. To my supreme surprise, it worked, but the contents were confusing.

Trapped Simulacrum
- Rarity: ???
- Item Class: ???
- Durability: ???
- Weight: ???
- Bonuses: ???

A simulacrum that has been trapped to create an effect when true nature is discovered.

I frowned, then turned to the group a little ways away.

"Hey," I called, "what's a *'trapped simulacrum'*?"

The entire group regarded me, but it was Jes whose expression terrified me. His eyes were wide, and he jumped to his feet, his hand outstretched.

"Loon!" He shouted. "Get away from—"

KA-BOOM!

The earth beneath my feet exploded around me, and I was thrust upward with the force of an igniting rocket. I fell forward from the inertia pressing against me and landed on the . . . ground? That couldn't have been right. I opened my eyes and saw that I was, indeed, pressed with my belly to the cold, black rock of the riverbank, but something was off. While the earth immediately around me was still there, I was clearly high up in the air. It seemed to be some kind of platform, and with the shuddering and quaking beneath me, it was as though I was surfing. I grasped the edge of the rock as it swayed at a downward angle, and my entire body slid, forcing me off the side as I clutched desperately for dear life.

I was at least fifty feet from the rest of the ground and the river of sludge moving beneath me. Still, a ways off I could see the others, scrambling to act. But it wasn't the most prevalent thing in my field of vision. No, what I was focused on was much, *much* worse. Beneath the shelf of rock I was only *just* holding on to was a massive creature, wearing the platform like a stupid hat. It looked like it was part fish, part Slimer from the old *Ghostbusters* cartoon: an amorphous, quivering mass of scaly skin and two bulbous eyes. Then I noticed something else.

"Fuck!" I screamed.

A dozen gigantic, silvery tentacles writhed from the monster's sides, lashing out into the air around it as the beast released a tremendous roar that deafened me. I was staring straight at the biggest, ugliest danger I'd yet faced, and I was going to have to do so while dangling from my fingertips over a fifty-foot stretch.

"This *suuuuuuuucks!*" I roared.

CHAPTER TWENTY-SEVEN

FETCH ME MY BROWN PANTS!

Whatever the hell it was, the creature roared again and reached out a tendril for me. Fortunately, I'd just had my movement altered by way of the Skill Book, and my new Acrobat Skill saved me. Boy, did it save me good. Despite feeling as though I was losing my grip on the edge of the rock, I swiftly brought my legs up and slid over, boosting the rest of my body onto the monster's little flat bill cap and narrowly avoiding becoming a hentai stereotype. However, the moment I was up and out of that danger, another one presented itself:

Gravity.

The tilted angle of the rock caused me to slide down the platform at falling speed, leaving me uselessly snatching at the smooth, flat stone and careening toward the other side. I slammed my bare feet against the surface and activated Enduring Perch, halting my momentum in a jerky motion that almost made me feel like my legs would snap in half. But they didn't, and I held. I stood up, feeling the thrash of the ground beneath me as I wobbled with feet unmoving just at the other edge of the stone.

"Holy shit!" I roared, peering over the side to see nothing but sludge gunk and hard surfaces below. My Stamina was plummeting, but there was nothing I could do at the moment. I was helplessly subject to the whims of my unintentional captor, jiggling in place like one of those dashboard hula girls. I didn't have long before Enduring Perch would fail, so I had to do *something*. But the intensity of my situation hadn't diminished, and I couldn't do anything but hope the monster suddenly decided it *hated* being aboveground and crawled back into the earth.

I heard the thrum of a bowstring followed by the slick, piercing *thwack* of an arrow making contact with something fleshy. The creature beneath me must have been hit and was *really fucking pissed* about it, because it began thrashing harder, jerking me around in my locked position. I heard another snap of an arrow's release, and then the monster roared with its ear-splitting screech. This time, the movement was much less volatile, and the platform leveled out for a moment. So, I took the opportunity to let go of Enduring Perch and bounded to the other side.

If I'm trapped upon this godforsaken shit heap, at least I'm going to enjoy the fucking view.

The stone was still mostly level as I reached the opposite end, and now I could see the cluster of my fellows taking action on the slope of black rock below. My breath caught in my throat at the sight.

Front and center were Frida and Merra. The blue-eyed warrior was brandishing the ax I'd seen lounging against the log a few hours before, and the dwarf was striking out at tentacles with her sword. Merra dodged one swipe, bringing up her shield to block another before raking the blade of her weapon along a third tendril that made the mistake of getting near her. Frida stood in one spot, her feet locked in place as she chopped through two tentacles at once with a downward strike. The ax struck stone with the follow-through and rebounded with a *pang*. Still, Frida utilized the motion to strike overhead and rend a piece of another appendage.

Behind them stood Jes and Dedyc. The elf was throwing his hands out in every direction like pistons, magical blasts firing out of his palms with each motion and soaring beneath me, out of sight to presumably wreak devastating damage to the monster's body. Dedyc had removed his cloak, and finally, I could see that beneath it was an amalgam of belts and bandoliers crisscrossing his body like a straitjacket from the 1930s. He was surrounded by a halo of blue light as he chanted words I couldn't hear. However, I noticed Frida's body was enclosed by the same shimmering blue magic as his, forming a protective barrier. Her lack of movement made sense now that I could see this, as each time a tentacle got past her defenses, it clattered against the magical shield and bounced off.

Calden was farther back than the others, a bow in his hand as he relentlessly fired arrow after arrow at the monster. His movements were a blur as he smoothly pulled the shafts from the quiver at his hip and fired in an unending motion of assault. Not far from him was Virgil, who held an oversized crossbow in his hands, moving far slower than Calden as he aimed carefully before firing his bolts. Each of his hits seemed to strike true as the monster began to writhe again. That forced me to drop to my stomach and hold on to the edge.

"Got 'im!" Virgil announced after each bolt struck, the first sign of amusement I'd seen on his tired face. Each hit was accompanied by his reloading of the weapon, siding another thick ouchie missile into place as he fired.

"Dedyc!" Merra shouted through the din, swirling her sword around in an arc to protect herself as a sneaky monster limb tried to pierce her defenses. "Stay on Frida! Jes, keep them coming! Let's open up a hole wide enough for our Guardian to dole out some pain and anguish!"

No one responded to her, but I watched as their actions spoke volumes.

At first, it was a subtle shift, but Frida began taking the fight to the creature, with Dedyc mirroring her steps paces behind. Jes switched the direction of his magical scorched-earth campaign so that the blasts flew directly forward. It was impressive to see their coordination in action, and I felt a pang of longing for that same sort of fellowship and friendship.

They're in tune with each other—working together to achieve a goal. This is some Power Rangers *shit!*

I went through a few moments of the same cycle: activating Enduring Perch and releasing it when the ground leveled out—only to reactivate it when there was movement again. All the while, I was incapable of doing anything else except watch as the group pummeled whatever this thing was with their supply of gift-wrapped ass kicking.

I hadn't spotted Stinky yet in the chaos, which weirdly had me concerned. Had he been killed? Had he run away? Neither prospect filled me with joy, and I had to admit I'd be pretty bummed, whichever scenario came to pass. Chiefly, my worry was that if he was gone, there'd be nothing to keep the time dilation in check, and then we'd be double-dog porked.

I kept trying to spot specific instances of badassery in the fray, but the entire fiasco was such a chaotic blur that I had trouble juggling everything in my mind in a way that made sense.

I need to do something, I thought, feeling very pathetic as I clung to my life raft of temporarily created safety.

But what could I do? I was stuck abstaining from doing anything worthwhile while everyone else popped off sick, jazzy beatdowns on this beast. So, I waited.

The group fanned out.

Merra took center stage now, acting as the gatekeeper to Jes and beating back the arms of the monsters that came too close. The elf, in turn, had changed from firing his barrage of spells to concentrating on some other magic, his eyes closed—which seemed *very* ill advised—and chanting. Yellow light gathered beneath him as whatever he was working on grew in strength. Finally, he stopped his ritual and opened a palm before clenching it dramatically. When he did this, I saw a flash of light, and then a gigantic wall of flame sprang up from the black rock, creating a clear division between him and the monster.

Dedyc was still focused on Frida. The lizardman kept his magical shield active around her as she rushed forward, administering bone-breaking blows to the main section of the monster's body. I noticed that smaller tendrils there reached out to grasp her, only to be rebuffed by the magic of Dedyc's protection. Curiously, the larger tentacles did not go for the woman, but that didn't seem to matter since her ax was having a *hell* of a time even breaking through the beast's flesh. But it definitely wasn't for lack of trying. Each chop from her weapon hit with the force of a hyper-swole lumberjack exacting revenge on a piece of firewood that had wronged him—despite not bursting through the monster's hide.

"Arghh!" Frida roared, her blows unending and unstoppable but ultimately useless. Dedyc paused his chant for a moment, as there was a shout from Merra. She'd brought down her sword too late to stop one of the tendrils, and it had crashed against her hand with an audible *crack*, forcing her to drop the sword. Dedyc acted quickly, his hand flashing out to aid his companion, and more blue light enveloped her arm. When the light faded, she rolled out of the way of another tentacle and scooped up her sword in one clean motion, her hand now healed enough to swing it and sever the limb that had gone after her.

Virgil was no longer manning his crossbow and had left it lying on the rock as he quickly skirted around the edge of the battlefield with a level of athleticism that was incongruent with his apparent age. He dove over or dodged under the reaching snake limbs as he worked his way to the far side of the fight. One limb came down on him from above, and Virgil shot a raised fist up. I thought he had intended to *punch* the tentacle, but instead, green circles ensnared it and dragged it to the ground. I had a sudden feeling of déjà vu.

"Shit!" I said. "I know that move! Way to go, Virgil!"

Then I watched in horror as another tendril swung at him from behind.

"Watch out!" I shouted.

But it was useless. The appendage struck Virgil grievously, knocking him to the ground before wrapping itself around him and dragging his body into the air.

"Fuck this!" I shouted, ripping the haladie out of my waistband.

The platform was at nearly a ninety-degree angle. Still, even though it wasn't the prime moment to do so, I released Enduring Perch. I vaulted forward, landing on the edge of the rock and using it to quickly launch myself into the air. I spun twice as I brought the haladie with me into my momentum as I swung. My feet touched down on the edge again before releasing, and I activated Enduring Perch and let that fucker fly. My sudden halted motion, combined with the whip-like flow of my attack, sent the haladie spiraling away from me with the speed of a bullet train. Like a renegade helicopter blade, it arced through the air, flying directly toward Virgil's tentacle prison. My aim was off.

But not by much.

The haladie sliced through the arm about ten feet lower than where I'd intended but still cut cleanly through, spinning wildly into the air as it continued on its journey. Virgil, still wrapped in tentacles, dropped, hitting the hard rock from a depth of about fifteen feet. He sprawled as he connected but immediately began unraveling himself from the tangle. After a few seconds, he was back on the move.

"Nice shot!" Merra called, having witnessed my fantastic display of pure, panic-driven precision. I gave her a thumbs-up and turned to grab the lip of the stone and haul myself into a better position. I froze, looking down.

But down was *up*.

Somehow amid the baffling bedlam, I'd thought I'd attached myself to the lip of the platform with Enduring Perch. But I'd actually used my adhesive feet magic to accidentally stick right onto the *underside*.

"I'm not just *Thor*," I breathed, "I'm also goddamned *Spiderman!*"

I marveled at the deep, cavernous ceiling high . . . *below* me and turned to look right into the blobby face of the Jell-O Jiggler monstrosity. Instead, I saw Stinky.

"What the fuck are you doing?" I demanded.

The matau had nearly reached where I was, tangling with one of the snakey appendages right at the root where noodle met body. His arms were locked tight around it. His feet were wedged firmly against the creature's central mass, and his orientation made him appear completely horizontal.

"Tryin' to fuckin' kill this thing!" Stinky said through gritted teeth.

I could see his dagger in his hand. However, he wasn't using it, as his entire attention was focused solely on grappling the writhing tendril, which seemed quite complicated.

"Kill it?" I wondered. "By . . . *arm-wrestling it?* Is this creature's weakness being alpha-dogged or something?"

"Shut *up*, orc!"

Stinky jerked his head at the creature's face.

"I'm tryin' to get to its gods-damned eyes, but these fuckin' stalks are terrorizing my climb!"

"Eyes, huh . . . " I said, looking back at the monster's gigantic, bulbous peepers.

"Yes, gods damn you, orc!" Stinky spat. "It's a Level Fifteen Cosmic Chaos Monstrosity! Its main weakness is—"

Stinky didn't finish his sentence because the tendril he was grappling with lurched upward, slamming him against the rocky hat on top of the monster's head. But I thought I got the gist. *Aim for the eyes*. Noted.

"Fuckin' Groven, that *hurt!*" Stinky yelled, still clinging to the tentacle.

I heard a slicing whoosh and turned just in time to catch the haladie as it returned to me. I smiled and gave Stinky a wink before wheeling toward the colossal eye. I reared back with my double-bladed, up-jumped steak knife, plunging it into the dark slit of the monster's pupil.

"Peekaboo!" I roared.

The blade sank in with almost no resistance, prompting a gush of dark, viscous fluid to spurt out, spraying all over me and into my open mouth.

"Awagh!" I screamed, spitting out as much of the foul-tasting putridity as I could.

In response to my mutilation, the Cosmic Chaos Monstrosity—or CCM, I decided, for short—released a painful peal of agony. I couldn't tell if what I'd done had wounded it severely enough to be effective, but it one hundred percent did *not* enjoy it. I felt a tendril wrap around my torso as the beast tried to unstick me from my magical roost. Still, it apparently couldn't defeat the power of my low-ranked Barbarian super stance. It still tried, though, its grip around me tightening to the point that I felt like my head was going to pop off like my third-grade class gerbil's had. Don't ask.

"Uggghhh!" I wheezed under the strain of the squeeze. I didn't have many options available. My Enduring Perch was in the red now, and I'd have to release it or face whatever setbacks occurred from lingering too long. Plus, if I just stayed like this, the beast would absolutely turn me into a fine green paste.

I'm too sexy to go out like that! I am obligated to live fast and leave a pretty corpse!

I let go of my perch and felt the tentacle rip me up into the air, holding me above its head while staring at me with the one eye that wasn't currently belching out blood.

It screamed.

I was blasted by the force of the screech, hearing the pain and rage in its bellow. It shook me angrily, and I will admit—I puked a little. Then I spat out a mouthful of the remaining vomit and smirked down at it.

"You fool," I shouted. "You've just given me the high groun—"

FWOOP!

The creature hurled me straight upward in its rage.

I sailed high, screaming bloody murder as the ground below me spiraled away at top speed. I wrenched my neck to view the landscape below me and was shocked by the imagery. Spoilers: it was shitty. In any direction I looked was jungle. A vast, sprawling, unending thicket of bullshit that stretched out as far as the eye could behold, occasionally broken up by hills and cliffs. Nowhere within my super scenic view was the end of the cavern, nor an exit.

I tried to shout the word *fuck*, but with my mouth full of wind and monster viscera, it didn't happen.

As my climb reached its apex and I began to descend again, I had a strange moment of clarity. I was hundreds of feet in the air and likely plummeting back down to the earth below—and I . . . wasn't scared. Was it the effects of adrenaline—or maybe falling more times in the last two days than a skydiver would in a week? I didn't know. It was an odd sensation, but I was totally and utterly unbothered by the predicament.

As I fell, I calmly opened my menu to check on my Abilities. I'd used Zeol's Falling Star a few hours before—by my reckoning. But was that how this arbitrary-seeming system would classify it, considering I'd supposedly been hoodwinked out of five days? From my perspective, it had only been a short while, but if Stinky's ability was the real deal, this would be the telling factor. I highlighted my Abilities and took a good, hard look at what was available.

Zeol's Falling Star
You can refuse the effects that gravity might place upon you and instead mitigate some of the harm that might otherwise befall you. Chasms and caldera are nothing in the wake of this Aegis. Once per day, you can nullify 100% of the impact of force from falls at a height of up to 100 meters. You may also transfer this Force Damage to an appropriate object within five seconds of impact—like slow-moving pedestrians or people taking too long at the ATM.

- +2% **Force Damage resistance**
- 100% **Force Damage resistance once per day**
- 10% **Force Damage transference once per day**

Sure enough, it was available but unable to be activated at the moment.
Huh. Neat.

I knew I shouldn't be able to let it loose until I was within one hundred meters—or at least, that's what it seemed to indicate. Would it even work if I was falling at a greater distance? I guess I wouldn't know until I tried. It seemed that more and more, I was finding that the specific wording of Abilities and Skills gave way to a bunch of gray areas that—if I were a wiser person—I could use to my advantage more frequently. But I was a goddamn dipshit. As it stood, I was subject to the limitations of my own, extremely narrow understanding.

I took a deep breath and waited as I drew closer. I could see the battle still raging below, and it was impressive how colorful and flashy it was. It was like bright, magical fireworks exploding in celebration as the multitude of different spells and Abilities crashed together far beneath me.

I was fucking *blazing* down, directly toward the gigantic CCM. I was hoping—but still largely unconcerned—that I could activate my Falling Star and do some damage. Then I got an idea.

I pulled my pack off my shoulder and reached inside, fishing around until I grabbed onto a hard metal object. I pulled the Guardian's Buckler out and smiled, double-checking it with Analysis.

Guardian's Buckler
- **Rarity: Uncommon**
- **Item Class: Shield**
- **Durability: 500/500**
- **Weight: 0.08 lbs.**
- **Defense: +3%**
- **Bonuses: Bashing +2%**

A small, lightweight shield designed to be held in a user's offhand. While simple in design, this particular item was forged with a conical design to assist the user in glancing off blows more easily. The Guardian's Buckler can also be used as a bashing weapon.

Yes! Precisely what I need! Sometimes, I swear I'm so fuckin' brilliant, I scare myself.

I gripped the buckler in my left hand and grasped the edges of my cloak with my right. I pinched the ends together around me, positioning myself like a torpedo with the shield facing forward.

Meat-missile mode . . . activated.

Then, when I was reasonably sure I was close enough, I activated Zeol's Falling Star.

Or, at least . . . I tried to. Nothing happened.

Oh . . . fuck.

I whipped open my display and saw that the mask god's little obligation still wasn't available for use. Instantly, all the confidence and calm I'd had a few moments before crumbled like an apple dessert in my bedsheets. Frantic thoughts stormed my mind, and hysteria took over.

I drew closer. And closer. And closer. Nothing was happening, except my screams getting louder. Rather than Zeol's Falling Star, now I was Loon's Wildly Anxious Suicide Meteor and soon to be Dumbass Orc's Collision Stain.

"Shiiiiiiiiiiiiit!" I roared as the stone platform on the monster's head sped up to meet me.

CHAPTER TWENTY-EIGHT

BREATH OF FRESH ERROR

T*HUD!*
 I felt a sharp prick as something pierced my flesh. Then, suddenly, I was no longer falling. I was floating, roughly thirty feet above the monster. I looked down and saw that an arrow was sticking out of my chest.

What the dingleberry?!

I grasped it, intending to pull it out, but a message appeared in my vision.

Condition: Slow Fall

You have gained the benefit of the **Slow Fall** *Spell. The pull of gravity affecting your descent will be diminished for the next ten seconds, and your travel will be reduced to 2% of its initial speed. This condition allows the user to softly coast to an appropriate landing. Rate will return to normal once the duration has elapsed.*

I was ecstatic despite the pain of an arrow sprouting from my body. The missile had obviously belonged to Calden, and somehow he'd transferred his spell from earlier—when he'd leaped from the cliff's edge—to me. I spotted the archer on the rock below, and he tossed me a wink and a kissy face before turning his attention back to the monster. Just as soon as the arrow had appeared, it began to dissolve before my eyes. It was pure vapor in less than a second.

Well, that *was quite the saving grace,* I thought. Then I paused, looking down at the distance between me and the jolly gray hentai monster.

The spell was supposed to make me drift slowly to the ground—or in this case, the CCM's mortarboard. But that hadn't happened. I was just hanging in suspension a few dozen feet above, dangling my green tootsies in the air.

What gives?

Congratulations! You have gained a new Perk!
Gained the Aegis Synthesis Perk!

Aegis Synthesis

Whether by accident or your own design—you have learned that a previously acquired Aegis can be combined with the effects of an Ability or spell to permanently change its compositional makeup. This can happen when the components share a similar foundation or if the Aegis was explicitly designed for this purpose. For good or for ill, an Aegis you have gained will be forever modified—hope you aren't resistant to change!

Aegis [Zeol's Falling Star] has combined with Slow Fall to create [Unnamed].

[Unnamed]

Once per day, you can nullify 100% of the impact of force from falls at a depth of up to 100 meters. You may also transfer this Force Damage to an appropriate object within five seconds of impact. Additionally, once per day, you may choose to completely resist gravity's pull and instead hover in position upon activating [Unnamed] for five seconds.

- +2% Force Damage resistance
- 100% Force Damage resistance once per day
- 10% Force Damage transference once per day within [5 seconds] of impact.
- Resist Gravity once per day for [5 seconds.]

Goodness! You have created or synthesized a new Aegis!

You have forged an Aegis that has never before been seen! As such, you will receive a boost to the effects! Look at you go, you innovator, you.

- +2% Force Damage resistance has become +8% Force Damage resistance!
- 100% Force Damage resistance once per day has become 100% Force Damage resistance *twice per day!*
- 10% Force Damage transference once per day within [5 seconds] of impact has become 15% Force Damage transference *twice per day within [10 seconds] of impact!*
- Resist Gravity once per day for [5 seconds] has become Resist Gravity *twice per day for [10 seconds]!*

As this is an [Unnamed] Aegis Synthesis, you have the opportunity to call this Aegis what you wish. What would you like to call this [Unnamed] Aegis?

I stared at the display in confusion. I knew I'd have to piece together this information eventually—especially the increases to its particulars. But having a definite time limit on how long I would be UFOing above the dungeon's gigantic problem child, I minimized everything except the name section. I thought for just a second before chuckling internally at my own extreme genius and slapping in a name.

[Hang Time]
Confirm?
Yes/No

I glanced over at the group, still battling their little bits off, and spotted Calden. He had fired an arrow at the cosmic monstrosity. He then turned to chuck a small bottle to Jes, who popped it open and glugged it down gratefully as an aura of blue light washed over him. Then he was moving at top speed, firing even *more* magical hand cannons than before with the fervor of *Street Fighter*'s E. Honda.

I quickly changed the entry and hit Confirm.

Confirmed [Calden's Hang Time]!

I felt the Aegis lose its strength, and I dropped down the thirty-ish feet to the black stone of the monster's flat top. I landed and rolled, trying to convert the momentum into getting me back to my feet. However, just as I was making to stand, the CCM shifted with a loud roar. I was only on my heels, so the abrupt change in angle sent me reeling backward, doing a few reverse somersaults and side rolls. Something must have hurt it badly, because now the gigantic beast was changing positions rapidly, and I was caught in its momentum wave pool. I began rolling forward again, then bounced as the creature threw its head back, and began to slide backward *again*. I got my feet out just in time to get my perch and waited for the convulsions to die down. When they did, I raced to the front side and stuck myself right to the lip.

Stinky was on the ground now, completely coated in gore as he dusted off away from the CCM's body. I glanced down at the monster's face to see that its other eye was now gushing blood as well. Stinky had finished Samson-ing this motherfucker, and now it was as blind as a mole rat with cataracts. I smirked. The entire party was fanned out again, with Dedyc and Frida no longer up in the CCM's mug. Instead, they were all focused on batting away the tentacles that were very angrily striking at them. At least, the few that remained.

Everywhere I looked was monster blood and tentacle slices. It was a gruesome mess, but I'd never in my life seen something so disgusting that filled me with such joy. The tentacles that *weren't* occupied by being cutlets or attacking the group were bound to the ground by magical green constraints courtesy of Virgil. The old cowboy finished off another one, soldering it to the rock with his arcane captivity.

The others were gathered around Jes, who had removed something from his sleeve akin to a magic wand with a tuning-fork end. It was about a foot long and resembled a cattle prod made of pale, white wood. His eyes were closed as he muttered what I now assumed to be an incantation. Frida and Merra were busy tangling with the tentacles that sprang their way. At the same time, Dedyc threw up magic shields that blocked blows and were immediately dispersed on contact. Stinky was lying on his back on the rock, huffing with the exertion of his flight away from Eye Gouge Village. Calden was standing next to Jes, holding the string of his bow taut as he balanced two arrows against it. He wasn't firing, just waiting.

"I'd get down if I were you, Loon!" Merra shouted as she slashed at a tentacle.

"What?!" I called, now suddenly concerned.

"We are going to attempt to eviscerate it in one fell swoop!" Calden called, his aimed gaze never faltering. "Oh. Thank you for the boon, by the by!"

"I don't know what you're talking about!" I shouted. "Am I going to get *exploded*?"

"Your Aegis!" Calden shouted back. "It— Oh, well, let us discuss this later!"

"Get down, orc!" Stinky bellowed from his back. "Jump or something, you big idiot!"

"What the fuck?!" I shouted back. "How? I'll break my fucking legs if I jump!"

"Use your Aegis!" Calden said. "Or something else. Do it now; we need to end this!"

"Ah, shit," I sighed. I took another look at the ground below, some fifty feet from me.

"Well, here's to hoping Dedyc's methods are better than the American healthcare system!"

I released Enduring Perch and fell forward. I opened up my menu and accessed my new Aegis. Its productivity had doubled in the last minute, so I thought I'd try to get some accountability out of it. I hit the ground right in front of the CCM and used Hang Time to absorb the damage. Then I rolled to the side until I was right next to the monster. I held my hand out, grasping one of the tiny tentacles at its base and transferring my fall damage into its body.

Two things happened at once. The first was that a ripple formed across the amorphous surface of the CCM's body as my damage sharing took effect. The CCM cried out, but I knew the damage would be negligible at best. I could only hope it was enough to help slightly. I wasn't going to use the damage anyway, so I may as well have given it to something that needed it, right?

The second thing that happened was much worse. A painful stabbing shock like a bee sting shot through my body, and I jerked to a stop, suddenly dropping back to the ground on my side like one of those fainting goats. I was unable to move.

Condition: Paralyzed

You have become paralyzed by the sting of a creature. All bodily movement has been rendered entirely inert for the following [5] minutes.

Shit!

I hadn't even thought to worry about those little buggers, but it was apparent now that they had some sort of purpose. I was a fucking moron, and now I was stuck, staring at the group helplessly, unable to even blink.

Goddammit, this is going to burn the shit out of my eyes!

Jes finished his incantation, and the forked end of his wand ignited in blue and yellow flames.

"Now, Calden," the elf shouted, but Calden was looking at me.

"Jes, what about—"

"NOW! There's no time!"

At his words, one of the tentacles broke through Dedyc's shield and landed a blow right against Merra's head, sending her careening to the ground. Another struck at Frida, who batted it away but lost her footing and stumbled backward.

Calden gave me an apologetic look, and then his eyes steeled. His gaze switched back to the CCM, and he let out a slow breath. Then he fired both arrows at once. Jes released the power accumulating at the end of the wand just as the missiles passed by. The magical energy gathered around the shafts, twisting and spiraling in an instant to surround the tips like arcane corkscrews of blue and yellow light. The attack zoomed out of my vision, so I couldn't *see* what happened next. But I definitely heard it.

There was a loud scream as the arrows struck the monster and then a sound of ignition, like a billion match heads bursting into flame all at once. I was suddenly battered by rain, which seemed odd until I noticed that the deluge was the same color and consistency as the CCM's dark blood.

They fucking exploded it! Hell, yeah!

Then a shadow started to fall over me.

Uh-oh.

I was lying on my side, completely incapable of movement, as the ground began to shake and the creature started falling directly on top of me. I watched as Frida lurched forward, her eyes locked on mine, and hope filled my chest. But there was no way she'd make it in time—I was dozens of feet away. We would both be crushed under the weight of this beast. Then Dedyc snatched her wrist, dragging her back urgently, and I knew it was the right move.

Adios, amigos, I thought. From the corner of my vision, I could see the creature's mass falling down in a wave, rushing right toward me. Then I felt an immense pressure on me as its whole weight ground against me. Things inside my body popped, and I felt like my head was suddenly on upside down.

That was the last thing I saw before complete and utter darkness.

YOU HAVE DIED.

CHAPTER TWENTY-NINE

ELSEWHERE, THERE BE PLOTTING

"How are things progressing?" a man in extravagant red-and-white robes asked.

"Poorly," said another man dressed all in blue. Around his neck was a tremendously large and opulent necklace with the lightning-bolt-and-sword emblem of the Faith.

"You will explain," commanded the man in red and white, his nearly bald head beaded in sweat.

The two individuals sat in sunshine, resting their aged bodies in easy-backed chairs on an outside balcony overlooking a pristine pool of water. Elsewhere around them were stretches of sandy desert and bleak rock, with sagging, undernourished palm trees occasionally dotting the view. The pool was crystalline blue and completely unmarred by breeze or debris, sitting placid and perfect while the sun and heat ravaged the world around it.

The man in red and white would have given anything to be able to climb into the cool water for a bit of respite, but that was not its purpose. If he even came near enough to dip his aching feet against its surface, the consequences would be vast and deadly. Instead, as he waited for his companion to clarify, he imagined what it would be like to be anywhere else. Somewhere with a temperature that wasn't threatening heat stroke. He supposed he should have been grateful. After this was done, he would have an unending age of comfort and freedom to exist wherever he liked and do whatever made him most happy. But, with each additional setback, that dream grew farther and farther away.

"I must stipulate—er, Yeska—that the conditions have been primarily stagnant insofar as execution," the man in blue said, nearly forgetting the formal address. "But we have been forced to allow for . . . improvisation."

"What in the bloody fuck does that mean, Tarnen?" the man in red and white demanded. "My patience is thin enough in this torridity without having to listen to you bandy around the matter. Speak as to the issue so we may seek to *resolve* it."

Tarnen winced at the Yeska's words before nodding apologetically.

"Of course, Yeska. My apologies, Yeska. As I indicated, the initial stages went well—though as to the nature of the vanguard in these matters, I am still unconvinced—though I suppose the results cannot be argued with. However—"

"The *point*, Tarnen!"

"Yes. My apologies once more, Yeska."

Tarnen took a deep breath.

"The crossed are wily."

"Wily?"

"Yes, they are erratic. One might venture . . . volatile. Very few of the crossed have made significant headway in the endeavor. If you will recall, Yeska, I suggested a bit more of a push in the right direction, but—"

"We cannot *push*," the Yeska said sternly. "That is outside of the bounds of the contract. We are bound by certain parameters, Tarnen, as you well know. *Were* we to consider stretching the boundary of what the definition of our edicts allow, *yours* would not be the opinion we would seat ourselves upon."

"Er, yes. Of course, Yeska," Tarnen said. "I only highlight this fact again because . . ."

He drifted off, as if afraid of what his next words might hold.

"Speak, damn you, Tarnen!"

"Well . . . with apologies, Yeska, I regret to inform you that there have been further complications in navigating these crossed. Deities have become involved."

"I care not about the fiddling of those ethereal wardens, Tarnen. Their might is of a limited power and scope. You mean to say to me that you and your *bright ones* are troubled over the mischief caused by *minor* gods? That is what they do, Tarnen. They *include* themselves and grant their boons and curses as they see fit. It is of little importance. They will not be capable of embroiling themselves in a meaningful way. Or do you think their miniscule dalliances compare to the bountiful strength of *our* Sovereign?"

Tarnen was quiet for a moment, his next words hanging unspoken in his mouth and mind.

The Yeska noticed this and sighed.

"*Tarnen* . . ." he said quietly. "Just speak. Sovereign does not strike an acolyte for free thought or word. It is in the Tomes to seek truth wherever it may be, without fear of reprisal. You know this."

"I am not afraid of Sovereign's wrath, Yeska. Though delicate, the matter is outside of importance for our Truth."

"Then why not speak, Tarnen? Is it for dramatic effect? You know that I hate when you do that."

"No, Yeska," Tarnen said carefully. "It is only that I fear the barbs of uttering such a name aloud."

The Yeska stared at the other man for a moment before bursting into laughter.

"What name could possibly quake the contours of Sovereign's domain? I am the Yeska, and where I go, so does the Truth. Not a word can withstand the absolution of Sovereign's servant."

Tarnen lowered his head, allowing his superior to enjoy his moment, knowing his next words would likely not bring such joy. He wiped sweat from his own brow with a kerchief. The heat really *was* unyielding in this place. Tarnen couldn't wait to be back in Regis, where he could enjoy himself again without the reproachful nature of the Yeska coursing a path of submission. In his deepest of dark thoughts as well, he admitted to himself that he felt comfort in being so far from the pillar of Sovereign's Truth, that he might delight a little longer in the world where the power of Sovereign's touch was so lightly felt.

It wouldn't be long, he knew. Once this conversation was ended, he'd use the rift to travel back to his home and bask in the recreational pastimes of a world less concerned with imminent fealty to plans still in the works.

When the Yeska's mirth finally died down, Tarnen took a deep breath.

"There are few names that hold so strongly to the *old gods*, Yeska. With apologies."

"The elders have receded from the world, Tarnen. Those that did not abdicate their positions rot in the solace of the forgotten—withered shrines and temples lost to time are their houses. Only Sovereign sits supreme, the everlasting Truth stalwart still from the Juncture. Any novice could tell you this."

"Of course, Yeska. Yet still, there is a title that has been mentioned to my Bright, whispered in cloistered circles. There are claims—though however unfounded they may be—of a revival."

"Tarnen, I tire of this game. If you fear speaking a bloody name here—where Sovereign's Truth is wrought—you have not the faith of your station. What daggers have dug their way into your fucking mind? Do you *doubt*?"

"I doubt nothing, Yeska. Save that I will never be able to fully articulate my service to the Truth. That my vessel is not strong enough to withstand the glory of Sovereign's light."

"Very well, then," the Yeska continued. "I ask that you speak this name that causes such profound trepidation."

Tarnen's next words came out in a whisper.

"The Drifter."

At that moment, both men felt a weight press down on them as if a great yoke of burden had been laid on their backs. The sweltering heat that was so ubiquitous there was suddenly gone, replaced by a cold chill that crept along their very bones like the hand of the grave. The Yeska's face paled, feeling the power of the Truth absent for the first time in decades. Not since his battle with Glendolyre, when Sovereign had abandoned him to prove his worth, had he felt so utterly and completely empty of the light.

A light, icy wind breathed over the two on the balcony, and they watched as a single, solitary ripple appeared on the surface of the pool far below. Both were silent, watching as the water slowly returned to its initial calm. After a moment, the heat returned, and the Yeska let out a breath of relief as he felt the Truth return to him once more.

The men were silent as they contemplated what had just transpired, both still feeling the naked exposure of the Truth's temporary disappearance. Finally, the Yeska spoke, though his voice was rough and strained.

"Tarnen," he said quietly, his eyes never leaving the pool, "I think you will need to delay your return to Regis as yet."

Tarnen scowled, this new information knocking him out of his stupor.

"What? But, Yeska, why?"

"These are grim tidings. I will not abide any power save Sovereign to pass over me or the faithful. This is a noxious aberration and must be dealt with immediately. You will instead travel to Larith, and you will do so following this conversation."

"But, Yeska. What am I, a simple and humble servant, capable of doing that you cannot? Why must I make this pilgrimage?"

"I will not parse out my commands to you, Tarnen. You will do this, and you will delight that you may serve Sovereign in the way the Truth demands. There will be no second words to this. You *will* go."

" . . . of course, Yeska," Tarnen sighed, his head drooping. "What am I to do in Larith?"

"You will attend to our temple. There you will be given further instruction. I dare not speak in this moment—lo, though I am to bolster myself in the strength of the Truth—as to what needs to be done."

"As you wish, Yeska," Tarnen said. "Might I know how long my journey will keep me away from Regis?"

"No, you may not. Now go."

CHAPTER THIRTY

SHROOM FOR ONE MORE?

"Aw, man. What the flip?"

I wasn't sure where I was, but I was up to my cankles in mushrooms. Hundreds of them, in fact, of a dazzling array of colors and sizes that confounded my pea brain's ability to imagine. Many were shimmering with a magical glow or pulsating with an inner light, each peculiar and unique to the point that I'd be surprised if any two were the same. The glow that emanated from the fungi filled the dim chamber I was in, but I could tell at a glance that I wasn't in the dungeon any longer. Or, hell, if I was, it was not where I had been. This area had walls made of pale stone that curved upward toward a vaulted ceiling that presumably disappeared into the height of the place.

Actually, you know what? I *could* still be in the dungeon.

I slogged through the mushroom patch, careful not to get too stomp-happy as I moved. I didn't want to ruin the integrity of the beauty and almost-dangerous vision of splendor that the shrooms possessed. They really tied the room together, ya know?

"Where in Moses' balls am I?" I asked aloud. I reached a barren patch not far from where I'd come to and took a quick break to assess my surroundings. More mushrooms lined the ground in every direction, and far away, I could see another pulsating glow in the distance, but I couldn't be sure if that was something to be wary of or just more mushrooms. I supposed I should have been distrusting of the mushrooms as well. I knew fuck-all about fungus, but what I *did* know was that there were plenty that either killed you or made you trip balls to the moon. There were enough unknown complications to make traversing their ranks pretty daunting, so this spot seemed as good as any to continue getting the lay of the land.

I tried opening my menu but found that it just wouldn't work.

"Well, that's great," I said, scowling into the void. "My goddamn word-box is broken."

I wondered briefly if there was a metaphysical maintenance man or something that took care of issues like that, but then I realized that if there were, as a fresh recruit into Statworld, I'd be low on the priority list. I was reminded of Aunt Ella explaining how terrible of an apartment I'd lived in as a toddler before I came to live with her and Uncle Luke. It was run by a slumlord of sorts who'd loved buying up decrepit properties and letting them fall into further disrepair while collecting rent checks each month from the painfully poor or destitute. Our building was apparently quite the "work in progress," as everything was always malfunctioning or straight-up fucking broken, and the on-site repair man had a heavy backlog of shit he always had to fix. Aunt Ella had said that eventually the building burned down because of poor wiring, actually killing a few people—one of whom was the maintenance man.

Back to the issue at hand. I found that it wasn't just my display that had crapped out on me but everything that involved the curious elements of this world were also unavailable. I kept trying to perform various functions: Enduring Perch, my new Hang Time Aegis, shouting "Go, magic, go!"—but nothing seemed to work. I stood, confounded at my own inability to do even menial tasks this world had introduced to me when a strike of realization jabbed my metaphorical beanbag with the strength of a million Legos.

I'd died.

The memory was elusive, like a fractal, fleeting dream, and just like a dream, it had bubbled up out of the blue. The words had flashed in my vision for only a moment, and now it seemed—rather worrisomely—like I'd lost a good chunk of time before I'd arrived wherever this was. Another crushing hammer blow of *goddammit* smashed against my heart. If I was dead, then that meant that my soul belonged to that shit-eating, grin-having, gigantic, demon bird-bug Pontivex. Which *also* meant that wherever this was, it was very likely to be his domain.

My brain was having trouble between yelling "God-fucking-dammit" and "Shit," so when I opened my mouth to shout, it came out convoluted and mixed-up.

"God shitting fucklet!"

"You *raaaang?*"

The voice that had answered my rage was light and creepy, holding the second word in a sort of singsong that sent a chill down my spine. The tone reminded me of the old black-and-white film actor Peter Lorre—which was the reddest of red flags. Whether their natural voice or one put on for heebie-jeebies, no one would talk like that without being deranged.

"Who's there?!" I shouted, reaching for the haladie in my waistband but finding nothing.

"Fuck."

"Such a mouth on you," said the voice, and I was irritatingly reminded of how Zeol had first introduced himself.

I swear to Christ, if this is another deity, I'm just going to immediately start swinging.

"Show yourself, coward!" I bellowed into the void, still seeing only mushrooms and distant lights. Whoever they were, they weren't Pontivex. That guy had been sort of informational at least, and didn't talk like a damn dildo.

"I am no coward, Loon," said the voice. Its tone dripped with glee, as if whoever he was, he thought he had one up on me.

You want the upper hand? I'll throw both *hands.*

"Prove it, then, asshole!"

The other individual was quiet as a kitten fart as my words reverberated with a weird lag into the dim, like an echo on a two-second delay, or a guitar loop pedal piloted by a shitty musician. I waited for another moment with no further response. It was annoying.

"Guess you're all talk, eh?"

More silence. However, now I was noticing that the light that had been so far away was now getting closer. Fast. It zoomed across the darkness like a starship, but I couldn't hear any sound of its approach. Then it became clearer, racing into view with an uncomfortably familiar pomp. It was a huge wall of flickering lights, as if someone had thrown a server cabinet at me—but much bigger. The glow grew brighter and I had to shield my eyes as they'd already started to adjust to the lower light. That was when I realized my Darkvision *also* wasn't working.

Just add it to the damn list.

As it arrived, the shape's true form was revealed, and my anger spiked. A colossal face.

Another fucking god mask? Dammit!

It was roughly in the same proportions as Zeol, but instead of being black and featureless, this one looked to be made of glinting metal and Tesla dashboards. Lights beamed out of every square inch, making me feel like I was trapped in the tractor beam of a spacecraft or a prison spotlight. Red, blue, green, yellow—every hue of ole Roy G. Biv was present and accounted for inside the terrifying structure before me.

"Do you still think me a coward, Loon?" the mask demanded in its strange stalker voice.

I didn't answer with words, though. I'd made a promise to myself a moment before, and I wasn't about to break it.

I launched forward, my fist cocked back to my ear to throw a haymaker.

"Hiyaaaa!" I yelled, swinging my wild punch with reckless abandon.

But my movements were slowed, like I was fighting in a dream. I felt uncoordinated and both too heavy and too light at the same time. Like my body was made of rocks and my muscles made out of spiderwebs. My fist connected with the flashing mask, but by the time it reached it, all momentum had drained away and I only landed a light rap.

"Pitiful," the mask said happily.

"I'll show you *pitiful*! Hiyaa!"

I leveled a high kick at the mask, but again, the force of my attack was muted and useless. My bare foot didn't even reach the creature before my leg extended too far and I lost balance, tumbling to my back on a bed of mushroom caps.

"Please," the mask said. "Enough. You're embarrassing yourself."

"No, I'm not!" I shouted, and sprang to my feet again.

"I love it," the mask said. "Such rambunctious pluck. I see why Zeol likes you."

"Oh, yeah? Well, that's too bad, because after I whoop *your* ass, I'm gonna beat his even *harder*."

"Unlikely, Loon," the mask said with a creepy, Frankenstein's-assistant laugh. "But please. Continue. This is far more entertaining than it has any right to be."

"I'm glad you're enjoying yourself," I said, jabbing a finger in his direction. "Hopefully, the memory will get you through all the pain when you're *recovering* in the *hospital!*"

My last word came out like a roar as I attempted another sucker punch. However, the same rules applied, and I barely tapped the mask with the follow-through.

"Yes, yeeeessss," the mask hissed with glee. "This is stupendous! Keep it up; I'm really having a great time with your struggle."

I stopped, staring right at the creature as a weird cackle escaped from it. I scowled.

Then, without warning, I spat on it.

Strangely, the loogie I hocked shot forward with the usual amount of inertia and smacked against the mask with a wet *plop*. The mask was silent again, and I flashed a smug grin.

"Gotcha, bitch!"

Then the mask began laughing maniacally, like an unstable Bond villain.

"Truly impressive!" the mask finally said after a moment. "You are so creative! I love it! Zeol was right; you really don't stop until you've exhausted all of your options, do you? Marvelous. *Marvelous.*"

I cringed at his words.

"Fuck, man. Can you stop talking like that? It's wigging me out."

"No," the mask stated. "This is how I speak. I will not change it for anyone. Not even you, who I am growing more and more fond of with each passing moment."

"*Stop*," I whined demandingly. "Quit liking me. It makes it hard to keep my lunch down."

"Oh, ho," the mask laughed. "Yes, the insults. Vulgarity. Stubbornness. A pointedly rude nature. Imbecility. You are precisely what I was expecting . . . and *so much more*."

"Jesus," I said, backing away. "You're not going to try to lock me in your basement and force me to apply skin cream to my body, are you?"

"Maybe," the mask said. "Is that something you'd like?"

"What the hell? Of course not! That's from a movie, and you're definitely not supposed to think it's something enjoyable. What is wrong with you?"

"I'm trying to make a mental list of your likes, dislikes, preferences, and so forth."

I balked at that.

"Bro, you need to *stop*. I thought Zeol was creepy and needy, and you're way worse. What are you, his brother?"

"You could say that."

"I *did* say that, chodewad. So, you two are what—fucked-up siblings?"

"I want to reaffirm to you that I am delighted by the way you speak, Loon. It is so refreshing and unique."

"I don't give a toot, you mutated Christmas tree. Tell me what's going on. Am I dead? Is this *hell*? What is your connection to Zeol?"

"Yes, the meat. The *meat!*" Maskey McGee exclaimed with a level of exaggerated enthusiasm I'd be tempted to call "orgasmic."

"The meat?"

" . . . of the issue, Loon. You have your ways of conversing, and I have mine. Yes, this is delightful. However, unlike Zeol, I like you too much to beat around the point. My name is Sababo. Much like Zeol, I am a deity."

"Whoa, they named you after the pizza place? Your parents must've hated you. Lemme guess, you're the god of police sirens and seizure lights?"

"No," Sababo said. "But perhaps I should take on those domains—whatever they are. Would that make you pleased?"

"Ew—what? No! Knock it off. Jeez, sorry for interrupting. Continue but, like, in a less unsettling way, please?"

"I am that which I am, Loon," Sababo said. "As I mentioned, I—"

"Yeah, you're not gonna break your stride for *nobody*. I get it. Let's move on."

"Very good! You have a take-charge attitude, too! I love it," Sababo said. "On to the main point. Yes. You are technically dead."

I felt less staggered than I thought I would.

"Shit," I breathed. "So, it finally happened, eh? That . . . well, that sucks."

"I agree. Dying appears to be unpleasant, especially for sojourners."

I wasn't surprised that he knew what I was. Zeol was already aware when I met him, so I had to assume it was a god thing.

"Why is it worse for people like me?" I asked.

"Because you are doomed to return and potentially experience the sensation all over again."

"WHAT?!" I shouted. "You're going to have to tell me exactly what you mean by that. Return? Like reincarnation? Am I coming back as a drop of water or an egg roll or something? What does that mean for Pontivex? I'm supposed to relinquish my soul to him."

I was rambling. All of the confusion working its way from my underutilized brain to my motor mouth with a pit stop in Anxiety Junction along the way.

"There, there," Sababo said. "Allow me to explain, Loon. You appear to be spiraling down a path of disorientation. That won't do. That won't do *at all*. You'll have to settle your nerves so that I can explain further. I am not like *some*, who adore shrouding answers within further mystification. My aim is to arm you with the tools necessary to *understand*. I shall be your light in the darkness of uncertainty."

I frowned.

"Okay . . . " I said hesitantly.

"To make it a simple matter: sojourners *return* when they die—to the bodies they inhabited upon death. It's remarkable what your kind is able to achieve, don't you think? It is, of course, finite—the revival, that is. Before you ask, I do not know how often this can occur. It is a mystery, even to me!"

"So, why am I here instead of . . . there?" I asked. "Do we not respawn in the place we died? That would be super fucking inconvenient for me. That's where I was keeping all my stuff."

"Typically, no," Sababo explained. "For a sojourner—upon resurrection—they return to where they initially arrived in Regaia."

"Shit," I said. "That's messed-up. I guess I'm not *too* far away from there now. But it *does* mean that I'd be pulled out of the dungeon. That's both good and bad, since I'll be free of that particular brand of farty nonsense, but I would probably fail the couple of Quests I have yet to finish in there."

I paused.

"Wait," I said. "This isn't where I started, though, either. Is this like a waiting room? I hang out here for a bit and then get catapulted back to square one?"

"I love this. So inquisitive," Sababo said. "But, no. This is not an interim. Allow me to explain."

I gestured for him to continue, and the gigantic mask lowered himself to the ground, the lights on his . . . *face*body dimming as he did.

"As I mentioned, when a sojourner dies, they are returned to their place of entry into the world. However, when you entered into that contract with the Keeper of the Crypt, the nature of your ability to come back was changed. Rather than fly back to the Aglands, you would be deposited wherever it is that the hive fiend keeps his chamber of indebted souls. Were this a normal circumstance, you'd have found yourself there right away. To whatever end that consists of."

"But I'm not there, right?" I asked. "At least, it seems like that is what you're putting down."

"Correct," Sababo said. "What a wonder you are. You're not as dim as Zeol indicated."

I ignored that. Zeol was going to be really upset if I ever got my hands on a flamethrower.

"This is my domain. Much like you found with Zeol, this is a plane that exists outside Regaia's primary realm. Think of it like a moon, orbiting an existence like a satellite reality."

"A moon?"

"Never mind what I said. I suppose I'm skewing the point with irrelevant details. Now back to my explanation. It would be unnatural, or perhaps very unlikely for a world with access to healing Arcana and items to *not* have developed the means to bring someone back from the dead. Sojourners are a rarity, not the rule, of course. The process must be done soon after expiration, or the death will *stick*. There exist few spells in Regaia that can wrest a soul back from the clutches of death, but they *do* exist. Rarer still are arcane objects that do the same. Fortunately, one individual whom you have recently become acquainted with bears one such item."

"Don't tell me it's Stinky," I said in horror. "Because if that's the case, I'm a goner for sure."

"It is not the one you call 'Stinky,'" Sababo said. "Though I have quite enjoyed your relationship's development. It is so spectacularly adversarial. You two really seem to hate each other, and it makes for such a lovely spectacle. But no. I speak of the dwarf."

"Merra?" I asked. "She's got a potion of resurrection?"

"Not a potion," Sababo said. "But a powerful artifact all the same. Coincidentally, it is the catalyst for their entering the dungeon in the first place."

"Oh," I said. "Shit."

"It is not quite an *oh, shit* scenario," the mask said. "It will still be able to serve its desired function if the magic is used. The issue arises because it can only be used in this way *once*. While the group is aware of the restorative power of the artifact, it is likely they have been saving it in case one of their members shucks away their mortal coil. Now would be an appropriate time to say "*Oh, shit.*"

I sighed instead.

"So, the question is whether or not they're willing to waste their one shot of rebirth juice on little ol' me."

"Indeed it is," Sababo said. "That is why I brought you here! I sought to hold you in place for a brief window so that your soul would not immediately skip over to being shackled. If I had let you expire without contest, the usual time a soul can exist in the gray areas between life and death would have been overpowered by the contract you struck. I've grown too fond of you to allow that to happen. Therefore . . . I used a limited resource. It is very exhausting and immensely taxing to perform a feat like this, but I had the means, so I did it. Particular individuals might be upset that I did so, but that's *their* issue—not mine! I went all in. Then—*boom bam*. Here you are."

"Boom . . . bam? All right, then you cashed in a chip to hold me in limbo until Merra's group decides—or doesn't decide—to revive me? So, if they realize that their magical token of insta-life would be better spent on one of *them* in the future, then I'm SOL? Off I go to the cages? Does that about sum it up in a nice little package?"

"With a lovely bow on top," Sababo said. "Very well done. I love it."

"You say that a lot."

"I love many things."

I shook my head and let out a deep breath. Then I carefully lowered myself into a seated position on the spongy mushroom caps.

"These aren't poisonous, are they?"

"They are," Sababo said. "So, don't eat them."

I stood again. I wasn't planning to start wolfing down fungus, but I also wasn't interested in testing out the resilience of sweaty orc hide against them.

"Man, this seriously blows," I said, reflecting on my predicament. "If Zeol's gift hadn't been *ruined* when he made it, none of this would have happened. I had a plan."

"Oh, yeah," Sababo said. "You had a shield out, I think. What were you planning to do there? I was curious."

"Well," I said with a big dramatic sigh. "If you *must* know . . . I was going to use the buckler to *bash* the shit out of the rock as I hit, and I used the veil to hopefully give me additional stealth and gain that sweet sneak-attack bonus.

Then I was going to transfer the damage from the Aegis to the beast as I hit—which would have been *way* better than how I ended up using it. I wanted to unleash as much of a thumpin' as I could manage."

"I see. First of all, *I love that*. Your resourcefulness is a credit to your more . . . pronounced deficits. But, unfortunately, it probably wouldn't have gone how you intended."

I scoffed, and Sababo hurriedly corrected his course.

"—but it definitely would have looked tremendous!"

"Too late," I said. "Now I'm sad."

"You don't sound sad."

"I internalize a lot. You know, 'stiff upper lip' and all? I'm not big on emotional displays."

"Yes, you are," Sababo said. "Every instance I have seen of your interactions with others—including my arrival—has been inundated with unbridled feelings. Mostly fury and confusion."

"Yeah, but that's anger. I'm talking about *actual* emotions. You know, like sadness, or happiness, or horniness."

"Anger *is* an emotion," Sababo said.

"Not really," I explained. "I've always thought of it as more of a *reaction*."

"I feel as though I am learning so much about the way you think, Loon."

"Yeah." I said with a big grin. "Scientists want to study my brain because it's so gifted. They want to use it to figure out a way to make robots smarter."

"I do not know what that means, but it sounds quite exciting and *very* realistic."

"Okay, Bob," I said. "Can I call you Bob? Anyway, *Bob*, riddle me this: how long are you willing to wait while we decide if the others think I'm worthy? Do you have a board game or anything we could play? I beat all kinds of ass at *Risk*."

"*Risk?*"

"Never mind; a game night with a reality-transcending fluorescent mask god that is apparently in love with me actually sounds super boring. What's the ETA on our progress?"

"I can hold this for a little while yet. Long enough, I think, to sufficiently allow them time to decide as to which course they will choose."

"Cool, cool, cool. Vague answers. That's kind of what I figured, but I guess that's par for the course. So, tell me now: what's the deal with you and Zeol?"

"Zeol and I are something of a . . . package."

"Wait, so are you brothers or are you married? I'm confused, and I am *really* hoping it's not both. That's some 'Bama shit."

" . . . Bama?"

"Yeah, as in *Ala*bama. It's a place in America that's super— Actually, I feel like this is just a tactic to get me to go on a tangent."

I paused, looking at Sababo.

" . . . which I will admit is probably partially my fault. I tend to get distracted. So . . . "

" . . . Zeol and myself," Sababo said, helping me finish my thought.

"Yes. Right. You guys said you're a package deal?"

"Yes. To put it simply—"

"—which I appreciate."

"Yes, well, to put it *simply*, the two of us are something of the same entity separated by two distinct realms of influence."

"Dual gods, eh? Must make dating hard."

"It would if we had any need for mortal ideas of courtship."

" . . . that sounds mighty salty, Bob. You sure you're all right with it?"

"I am a being of the Oblivios that acts as the metaphysical representative for physical laws and concepts. Yes, I'm sure."

"Man, you're about one rejection away from joining an incel group on Reddit, aren't you?"

"What?"

"Nothing— Anyway, so, you're a two-headed god or whatever, so—"

"—*not* two-headed. It is more akin to twin souls."

"Sure— Anyway. Zeol controls luck, so what's your hobby?"

"I am the god of sleep."

I allowed myself to show surprise.

"Weird. I wouldn't have paired those two powers."

"Fortune and slumber? I suppose not at face value—"

"—and you know *all* about faces," I said with a grin.

"What's that?"

" . . . you're, like, a giant face, or whatever. It was a joke. Look, I really shouldn't have to explain this."

"My appearance is that of my kind. I can appreciate its uniqueness."

"There you go, Bob," I said. "Good on you for having pride about who you are. Don't let the man get you down, as they say."

"May I continue? I do love our nonchalant repartee, Loon, but I believe you're going to run out of time before we get to further clarification if we do not expedite the conversation."

"Continue," I said.

"I wonder . . . " Sababo said, sounding thoughtful.

"What? Now you don't want to continue? I thought we were light on the ticky-tock, homeboy?"

"Loon," came the response from the massive flickering mask. The voice had changed slightly. It was less the whimsical henchman and more of a powerful dignitary. Something about his manner filled me with both a sense of dread and something like a want or desire to do whatever it took to keep him from destroying me. I couldn't tell exactly what it was, but the shift seemed . . . not necessarily dangerous but as though danger was irrelevant. It was oppressive, like a gravitational force. As though the magnitude of presence creeping off of the mask was far beyond anything that remotely resembled the concept of fear and peril. This was a god. A god that transcended any usual categorization and dwelled in the place that was power.

I couldn't handle it.

I'd never been one to be afraid, but this was the same sort of feeling as staring down from a one-hundred-story building without being able to move away. Something so vast and so much larger than myself I was left feeling open, barren, and small just by existing. This was like Zeol's temper tantrum but much more intimidating. Zeol had reflected anger and fury at me, and that was something I understood well. This was wholly different and much more menacing. This was a nuclear explosion compared to a pilot light. It was strangling. But I wasn't about to let something like *unfettered ultimate power* turn me into a puddle of appeasement. Nuh-uh.

"Fuck . . . *off*," I was able to manage, though meekly.

"I love it," Sababo said. "You are *so* contrary that even with this level of output, you can throw me for a loop. Fantastic."

His presence was still pushing down on my soul strongly, but his tone was more jovial, if not still incredibly terrifying.

"Yeah," I struggled. "I'm . . . a boss . . . bitch."

"Loon," Sababo said. "How would you like another Aegis?"

CHAPTER THIRTY-ONE

DEADLOCKED

"Is that the last of it?" Jes asked, wiping his grimy hands with a soiled rag.

"I believe so," Merra said, looking down at the grotesque pile of body parts.

It was a morbid collection—gory innards and ichorous appendages slopped on top of one another in a mountain of viscera that appeared so vile that even viewing it seemed like some sort of crime. It was especially unpleasant considering Dedyc had been delighting in referring to it as "*Yucky*-Hills-on-Seamont," which, while an amusing play on 'Lucky-Hills-on-Seamont'—a well-known holiday spot on the northwestern coast—was in abysmal taste and seemed a bit "too soon."

Frida herself was busy tending to Akiva, the matau. He'd been injured during the battle, his arm slashed open quite severely and requiring attention. Dedyc had exhausted his reserves of arcane healing, so it was up to her to fix the yellow-fleshed man up as well as modern medicine would allow. Modern medicine, in this case, was a sewing needle and thread and was a task that she not only abhorred but was also ill suited for. She'd spent many years in her life stitching herself up something awful and hoping for the best, as she'd never acquired a penchant for restorative Arcana—though it was common for many of her particular proclivity to have utilized that skill tree. She'd fixated her Guardian build more on rending, tearing, ripping, and other miscellaneous eviscerative means. It was often to her great displeasure whenever she'd grouped up with others in the past that the party would become cross with her once a member lost their face or buttocks and she could not heal them back together. That was why this particular collective was so beneficial—Dedyc was a Sooth, and recovery was his brand.

Frida wrinkled her nose as she dressed Akiva's wound, eyeing the hodgepodgery of carnage that caked his skin and armor. The odor was vile, and as she crouched, mending the grievous gash in the man's arm, she thought she understood why Loon had called him "Stinky."

A shadow fell over them, and she looked up to see Calden, his usually vivacious manner dimmed by the sinister tidings splayed out before him. Frida nodded, and he let out a sigh, his eyes darting to the grim bit of business that was the pile of wayward pieces.

"It never gets easier, does it?" Calden asked, seemingly almost to himself.

"What doesn't?" Jes asked, standing and looking over the remains strewn about their group's battlefield. "Being betrayed?"

"Betrayed?" Calden asked. "Is that what you call this whole encounter, Jesimir? I will admit, at first, I assumed it was a bit of a faff, perhaps a prank on Carmichael's part. Though now that I am looking at it a bit more closely, I am awakening to the idea that this was all fully intentional."

Jes shook his head.

"Of course it was intentional, Calden," the elf said. "This was not a mistake."

"You thought this calamity was a coincidental mishap?" Merra asked, standing to her full height—which was relatively shallow, considering she was a dwarf. "That Carmichael *accidentally* created a powerful trap simulacrum that looked identical to what his picked-clean skeleton might resemble, and it *just so happened* to summon an astral beast that almost killed us?"

"Well," Calden said, "perhaps he assumed he was creating a delicious meat pie and got the ingredients backward?"

"I don't know what's worse," Dedyc said, "you genuinely believing that or that you think alchemy and cooking are similar."

"Both of them use pots," Calden said. "The two arts may as well be cousins."

"I know you're mucking about, Calden, but can you be serious for even the whisper of a moment?" Jes asked.

"Well, now my gast is well and truly *flabbered*," Calden said. "I am the absolute *portrait* of authenticity. I cannot believe you'd assail my character so."

"Here we go," Merra mumbled, stooping down again to examine the macabre shrine to death they'd gathered together. She squinted at it severely, as if expecting it to spring up and start dancing about without her say-so.

"It's a gruesome affair," Virgil offered, manually working gunk out of his crossbow's firing mechanism. "But I stick to my stance that he's not worth wastin' moisture over."

"You'd be the one to know about *wasted moisture*," Merra said with a grin. "I am sure *you're* an expert of discarded wetness. Can't be many dames that ended up fortunate in your bedroom tangles, Virge."

"Please, Merra," Calden whimpered. "Dedyc is still but a boy. That crassness is not suitable for a beast of his unblemished virtue."

"Yeah," Dedyc chuckled. "Watch your mouth around me. I'm impressionable."

"What I mean to say," Virgil continued, "is that I think that orc weren't like the lot of y'all. Might be he's a touch more like me, which means he'd be just fine gettin' walloped to bits by a fearsome monster—after a spell."

"You're still on with that?" Merra asked. "He can't be one of *your* types because he didn't dissolve. Every sojourner evaporates after a minute or so."

"Might be he's a different style," Virgil explained. "If'n we been rummaging around down in these parts nigh on half a millennium, it stands to reason things coulda developed a mite different in our absence."

"Arcana doesn't evolve like that," Jes stated, looking at Dedyc for confirmation. The drakefolk Sooth—who some might be tempted to call a lizardman—nodded in confirmation.

"Unlikely," he hissed his agreement.

"Things can change something fierce when left unattended," Virgil continued. "I seen a great many marvels in this world and the last what sent my head a-scratchin'. I know one o' mine when I stumble into 'em, and that orc weren't the usual sort."

"He was fuckin' odd," Akiva said, standing as Frida finished her work on his arm. "I'd throw my stones behind him not being native."

"That is quite the influence to leverage," Calden said. "*Really*, climbing up *onto* the monster to give its eyes a prick? Your stones must be practically monumental in proportion. Be honest with us . . . are we inside them right now?"

"Et ain't right to be talking this way," Frida said suddenly. "Joshing like so. A man died."

"An *orc* died," Akiva clarified with a grunt. "And it's for the fuckin' best, by my reckoning. I'd be halfway to Vaaskeldr by now if he hadn't forced me the fuck down here."

Jes cleared his throat.

"Whatever the case may be, he is gone," the elf said somberly. "We cannot waste more time than the precious amount we already have. We must get out of here, which begins by continuing our search for an exit."

"You're a heartless bastard, Jes. You know that?" Merra said.

"I am not," Jes said, sounding as though he was actually wounded. "However, in this instance, I feel I must be the arbiter of common sense. We can improve our own fortunes by removing ourselves from this forsaken riverbank and depositing our trust in one another to trudge onward. There will be time to mourn once we have escaped this wretched tomb. We cannot do anything about a fallen ally."

"We *ken* do somethin' 'bout et," Frida said, looking pointedly at Merra.

"No," Jes said. "That is not a tool to be used flippantly. We will need that if—"

"What's the *point* of having an artifact if we cannae *use* et?" Frida demanded.

"We agreed that—"

"*You* 'greed to et," Frida interrupted, fury building in her tone. "Las' I recall, et were *Merra's* object to decide on. Not yoors."

"If we use it—"

"—then he'll come back," Merra interrupted. "It's sound."

"Unless he does not," Jes stated soberly. "And if it happens that he is a sojourner, as Virgil has suggested, what then? We will have completely ruined any opportunity to return one of our own number. It is our failsafe, if you recall."

"We don't know that it will be wasted," Merra said. "It may not even work at all in that case."

"Yet you are willing to take that risk?" Jes asked.

"I'm willing to chance using it on him," Merra said. "I'd rather that than hold on to it for some elusive time in the future."

"A time that may well come to pass," Jes said. "Yet you would relinquish our greatest hand of triumph. For an orc that we hardly know."

"I like him," Dedyc said. "He's funny."

"He is a *liability*," Jes said. "Humorous or not, *he* is the one that activated the trap that killed him."

"... and because of that, we now know of Carmichael's treachery," Calden said. "That is less time spent meandering about, looking for clues where none are. I know that he embarrassed you, Jesimir, but, honestly, you shouldn't—"

"You think I am so petty that I would seek to leave him dead because of a slight?"

"Regardless of that," Merra said, "the right thing would be to attempt to bring him back. I'm keen to remember that he was the one that stabbed out the creature's *other* eye *and* hit it with that attack that distracted him long enough for you to use your Endless Light."

"We have known him for hours," Jes said. "We cannot leverage—"

"*You* may not be able to stomach the idea, Jes," Merra said, "but it isn't up to *you*."

"'Zactly," Frida said with a nod.

"... but it's not up to only me, either," Merra continued, stopping the Guardian from being smugger. "This was an endeavor you all chose to participate in, and the Token was part of that deal. We'll put it up to a vote."

There was a spongy, percussive noise as five shapes approached the group, hopping lightly as they made their path toward the banks on the black rock. The possessed roe had apparently tired of being told to wait around and were sheepishly inching their way forward, seemingly terrified of being admonished for their transgressions.

Calden spied them and turned back to the humanoid crew, jabbing a thumb over his shoulder at the eggs.

"They do not get a vote, I hope?"

"That's a ridiculous notion," Virgil chuckled. "They ain't a part o' none o' this."

Akiva frowned.

"I thought you lot were told to stand by," the matau harumphed, casting an evil gaze on the cluster of egg monsters. "You can't even do *that* right? We are well and truly fucked if ever we are to rely on you."

The roe shuddered at Akiva's words, and Frida felt sorry for them.

"Are they all that bad?" the Guardian asked. "They seem harmless."

"That's because you didn't have to tangle with a cave full of the cocksuckers," Akiva noted icily. "Damn near took all my fuckin' skin off."

"Where did this happen?" Merra asked.

"At the entrance," Akiva continued. "Before entering the blasted dungeon. Hundreds of the little bastards ejaculated out of a pond and started ripping and tearing into us."

"Oh," Merra said thoughtfully. "We didn't have to face anything like that."

"I didn't think ya did," Akiva said, "based on your lack of familiarity with the brutes. Count yourselves lucky whatever you battled wasn't *these*. They're more vicious and annoying than proper dangerous, but get 'em in a group, and it's a fuckin' *climb*."

"That does sound dreadful," Calden offered, giving the roe a sideways glance.

"What horror did you encounter?" Akiva asked.

"Oh, well . . . " Calden started, but drifted off.

"Et were a puzzle," Frida said.

"A puzzle?" Akiva asked, confused.

"Aye," she returned. "Had t' switch a couple statues about, but we got et well 'nough."

"That just fuckin' *reckons*," Akiva breathed. "You get a fuckin' headscratcher, and we get our arseholes punched in by a cockload of monster larvae."

"To be measured," Calden said, "would the two of you have fared well with a mental game?"

"He's a matau," Merra said. "Of course he would have."

"Yes, but the nature of the dungeon suggests the experience is tailored—more or less," Calden reasoned. "Perhaps even with Akiva's depth of intellect, Loon was just far too . . . "

He paused, trying to find the right word.

"*Opposite*," Akiva said with a smirk.

"Well, I was not going to say precisely that, but . . . yes."

"So, you got puzzles," Akiva said with a sigh. "And we got eggs."

"Can we get back to the issue at hand?" Jes demanded. "Pay the roe no mind. If we are casting a lot as to whether or not to use our single mode of resurrection on Loon—then my ballot goes to *no*."

"That's one in favor and one against," Merra said, then gestured to the Guardian. "Frida?"

"Aye," she said. "Use et on 'im."

"Two in favor," Merra said.

"'Gainst," Virgil said. "I still reckon he'll be fine. I wouldn't want y'all to use it on me, either, as I'd return—even if it were far away from here. I got a sense fer these things, and sure as I am that he's a miserable cuss, he's also a sojourner."

"Two for, two against," Merra tabulated, her eyes still locked on Jes.

"Does the talented Akiva receive a vote?" Calden asked.

"No—" Jes started.

"—yes," Merra said, cutting the elf off with a venomous glare. "He's known Loon the longest, and it'll be him that has to go without his companion—"

"I already told you what I fuckin' thought," Akiva said. "This has nothing to do with me. Let him stay dead, or bring him back—I don't give a salted dwarf taint what . . . "

He glanced at Merra—the dwarf—and walked his statement back.

"It ain't going to be up to me," he finished, with much less vitriol.

"So, let me ensure I have the full spectrum of this," Calden prompted, taking on his usual mercurial manner. "You'll let Akiva—an insurmountably wonderful individual, I must add—have a vote, but the monstrous circle men—er, *possessed roe*—cannot cast their favor? What a despotic world we have created."

"How—*how* would that even work, Calden?" Jes demanded. "In what strata of mindful existence would it make sense to allow those creatures to attempt to make a decision woefully outside the realm of their most rudimentary understanding? Even if they *were* cognizant of the concept—which I am fairly certain they are not—how would they even perform the basic function to cast a vote?"

"I'm not sure," Calden offered. "Perhaps they could press a little bell?"

"Calden," Frida said. "Shut up."

"Yes, marm!" Calden exclaimed with a salute to the woman.

"The roe will have a different role," Merra said mysteriously before perking back up. "Right, so that's two *for*, two against, and one . . . very passionate abstention. Calden? You're up."

"Well—" Calden began, but both Merra and Jes interrupted him.

"Quickly," they said in unison.

"Fair enough," Calden sighed. "I say, not a one of you knows the first thing about building suspense."

"Calden . . . " Frida warned.

"All right, all right," Calden said, shaking his head. "Considering that the final bolt in our beloved orc's casket was brought about by mine and *Jesimir's* hand . . . I say yes."

"Three for, two against," Merra said. "Dedyc, it's up to you."

Dedyc smiled.

"I think he's funny," he said again. "And he saved Virgil."

Virgil looked down at his feet, obviously feeling the flush of embarrassment.

"I don't have the same confidence that he is of the same ilk as Virge," Dedyc continued. "So, without that level of trust, I say we bring him back."

"Splendid," Calden said, clapping his palms together. "I am glad that for one more day, Jesimir's tyrannical reign is kept at bay. Better luck next time, Lord Carandalon."

Jes scoffed, but before he could say anything, Merra interrupted.

"That's settled, then," she announced, returning to the pile at her feet. "We will resurrect Loon"—she turned to look at Jes and then at Virgil—"and this was a *group* decision. No griping or grumbling about the results . . . yes?"

Both nodded.

"Excellent," she said with a curt nod. "Now, Dedyc . . . "

"Yes?" Dedyc hissed.

"Gather up those roe. We'll need them for this next part."

Merra ignored the confused glances passing between her fellows and pointed at the egg creatures.

"Let's get this over with."

As the last of the magic faded and the talisman became dim, the orc's massive frame formed from the pile of gore. It was a shining, spectral outline at first before losing its glow and darkening. Slowly, his features became clearer, defining as the arcane illumination of resurrection dimmed further until he was back to a mostly similar form.

Emphasis on *mostly*.

There was an expectant silence as the others spectated the dramatic renewal. Loon was stretched out, lids closed, looking almost peaceful, lying naked on the black rock of the ravine's bank.

Suddenly his eyes popped open, and he gasped.

"I know how to get out!" he roared.

"What?" Jes exclaimed, but Merra put a hand up to stop him.

"Wait," she said sternly. It was essential to allow a newly resurrected individual a moment to get their bearings.

Finally, peering around at everyone, Loon smiled sheepishly.

"Uh, also, *hey*," he said. "Thanks for reviving me. I wasn't sure if . . . "

Loon trailed off as he looked down at his arms.

"What the fuck?! What happened to my skin?!"

CHAPTER THIRTY-TWO

HUMPTY DUMPTY NUMPTY

I look like a *Twilight* vampire!"

I stared at my flesh, now speckled with various tiny lustrous dots. *Pink* dots. They covered every visible inch of my normally gray-green skin and almost resembled chickenpox. You know, if chickenpox danced with shimmering light when exposed to the glow of a torch. That was what was happening as Calden stood over me, the flames of his torch flickering and sending refracted beams from my skin to the black rock.

"Just great. I am the world's grossest disco ball."

"You are quite welcome for . . . whatever we did," Calden said with a beaming smile. "It is good to have you in one piece, Loon. Your . . . separation was becoming quite pungent. I much prefer this manifestation."

"Why did this happen? Is this a side effect of resurrection? Please don't tell me this is permanent."

"It's a symptom of *this* particular brand of revival," Merra said. "It required additional assistance."

" . . . what does that mean?" I asked in horror.

"She used the eggs, orc," Stinky said.

"What?!" I exclaimed, clambering to my feet in what I found was a *very* revealing gesture. I realized that I was utterly buck naked. I stared down at myself, suddenly very bashful, and covered my lower portion with my hands.

I thought it had felt drafty.

"Uh, does someone have any spare clothes? I seem to have misplaced mine."

"Sorry!" Merra said with a big grin. "Your garments were a bit beyond the pale. You were pretty badly disfigured."

"Even my clothes?"

"*Especially* your clothes," Calden offered. "It was quite the mess."

"Aw, man," I whined. "I had some stuff I liked."

"Well," Calden said, holding up a stretch of dark fabric. "Not everything was past recovering . . . "

"My cloak!" I shouted, and snatched it greedily from the man's grasp.

I immediately wrapped the cloak around my waist to cover my shame and cinched it. I looked down again and chuckled.

"Well, this will have to do."

"Unfortunately, I don't believe any of us has anything that would fit you—" Merra began, but Dedyc swept forward and deposited a handful of heavy fabric and leather in my arms. I looked quizzically at him, but he just nodded.

"When you're as big as us, you must improvise," he said sagely.

I lifted the parcel and let it drop down to view it fully. I had in my hands several large belts and . . . a skirt.

"A loincloth?" I asked.

"A kilt," Dedyc corrected. "It will do the trick; *trust me*."

"And I'm just supposed to hold it up with the belts?"

"No," Dedyc said. "The kilt will stay up on its own. It's enchanted. Those are baldrics. You wear them on the top part."

I stared at him for a moment and then slowly nodded.

"Uh . . . thank you, Dedyc," I said.

"You are quite welcome, Loon."

"Oh!" Calden said, unshouldering his pack. "I had almost forgotten."

Then I realized it was *my* pack.

"My *things*!" I cheered, accepting the sack with all the dignity I could muster while wearing only a crotch garment.

"And these," Frida said, and handed over several items: the luxurious gloves, the haladie, and the tiny Feather Chest. "They were in yoor pockets."

"Did my party hat survive?"

The group looked at one another collectively.

"The what?" Dedyc asked.

"It's an . . . Uh, well, it's a small, colorful cone. Has a little string attached to it?"

They all shook their heads at once, and I winced.

"It was made of paper," Stinky said with contempt. "Of course it didn't make it."

"I thought that maybe— You know what? That's okay. Now, what were you saying about the eggs?"

"They gave up some of their life to bring you back," Merra said. "Typically, it would require more of a sacrifice, but, well . . . there were a few of 'em. So, I just borrowed a bit from each."

"I would *love* to get into the mechanics of that," I said, glancing around. "But that's actually something that seems way over my head. Where are they?"

Dedyc gestured off toward the rock face where I could now see the cluster of roe lounging lazily, hardly moving with their eyes closed.

"Resting," the lizard man said.

"Okay, so what? Am I part egg now?"

"Of sorts," Merra said with an apologetic grin. "Sorry."

"So, what does that mean?"

"It means you're part fuckin' egg, like you said, orc!" Stinky exclaimed. "Move on; we've got shit to do! You said you knew a way out?"

"Yeah! I mean—I think so!"

"Spill the beans, then!"

"Hold your horses, Stinky. I am still a bit loopy from my brush with death!"

"Want to go for two?" he asked, gesturing at me with his dagger.

"Buddy, I would *love* to whoop your ass and take that from you right now, but I am *sleepy*. That shit wiped me out. Plus, you don't look so hot."

I pointed at his mangled arm. It appeared to have been recently stitched up and was clearly not in any shape to be participating in martial competitions.

"I can take you on in any condition," Stinky said, but I noticed he took a step back.

"Yeah, okay, tough guy," I said. "Dollars to donuts, I could pinch that thing hard enough to make you cry."

"Enough," Jes said, speaking for the first time since I'd been brought back. I noticed from his expression that he seemed uncomfortable with meeting my eye line.

That's weird. Did he do something fucked up while I was out of town?

Congratulations! You've raised a Skill!
Insight has advanced to F-Rank Level 9!

Oh, shit. *He* did *do something goofy. Well, well, well. Now I have the upper—*

"What is your information?" Jes interrupted my train of thought. "And how did you come by it?"

"Well, it's just a thought," I said. "But I had a lot of time to think while waiting for you guys to get your shit together and wake my ass up."

"What do you—" Jes began, but I cut him off.

"Anyway, I won't go into the extremely *awesome* time I had in the afterlife, but I will say that I was thinking about some stuff, and I concluded that we might have been going about this all wrong."

"Do tell," Calden said. "I do enjoy the theatrical nature by which you are presenting this information. It has me on the edge of my seat."

"Well, buckle in, then, butterbean," I said. "Cuz I think I'm about to blow your load—er, wait, no, that's not right. Blow your mind. Anyway . . . "

I smiled, putting my hands on my hips.

"I think I've got this bullshit sorted."

I was left standing there, the breeze making me and my nethers *quite* uncomfortable as I was met by the eyes of the whole group.

"Fuckin' say it already," Stinky said.

"I'm getting to it," I said with a sigh, then I leveled a finger at Frida.

"Tell me, Frida. Why was this sim . . . sumo . . . summa cum laude . . . left here by Carmichael?"

"Et's *simulacrum*," she corrected. "But I'm no' sure. To throw us off the trail?"

"Sure," I reasoned, pretending to consider that. "But if that was the case, why did he trap it?"

I looked over at Jes, but I could already see his mind working. His face lit up with realization.

"Because he didn't want us to follow him!" Jes exclaimed, but he was rattling off with more before I could continue. "Which means that he thought there was a danger of us discovering a way out. Why trap a simulacrum if convincing us that it was his body would work to keep us in here?"

"Because—" I started.

"Because he thought there was a real possibility of us discovering an exit ourselves! So, he created the ruse to stop us from following him. Which means we likely already have the information necessary to divine the way out on our own."

He placed a fingertip to his chin thoughtfully and began pacing.

"Yeah! And if you'll notice, this place is practically endless—" I tried again, but Jes was already off again.

"The entrance!" he shouted, and the others flinched at the volume of his exclamation. "It is both the way *in* and the way *out!* This place is so vast that it would be impossible to reach the other side—if there *is* another side. It is not unlikely that the archway that led to this space was simply a portal in one direction, which means that the other side of the gate may also work that way!"

"Yeah . . . " I said, feeling dejected.

Fuck, I really hate when people are smarter than me. He only needed me to start the sentence to figure out what had taken me a lot of pondering—and a little nudge from Sababo—to figure out.

"Brilliant deduction," Calden said to Jes. "Quite impressive. Really."

"Well, that really took the wind out of my sails on my dramatic reveal," I said, glaring at Jes.

"He does that sometimes," Dedyc said. "He doesn't need much to get to the root of an issue. You sort of learn to deal with it."

"Well, then," Jes said, ignoring us completely. "We do not have any time to lose! We must make haste to the entrance!"

"That just leaves one thing . . . " Merra said, patting me on the leg.

"Lunch?" I asked hopefully.

"No," she said, shaking her head and pointing up. "That."

I craned my neck up and gawked. Dozens of feet above us hovered the biggest, fattest Esper Node I'd yet encountered. It was easily ten feet in circumference and pulsating with a powerful green illumination, indicating it was of the *emerald* persuasion.

"Um," I started, staring. "Where did that come from?"

"The monster," Frida answered, smiling at me.

I focused on the object, and a message appeared.

For defeating a [Group] opponent more than FIVE levels above your own, you have received a [Greater] Emerald Esper Node!
Accept [1] Greater Emerald Esper Node?
Yes / No

"What in the hell?" I asked. But, because I am a greedy, *greedy* son of a bitch, before anyone could answer, I clicked *Yes*.

CHAPTER THIRTY-THREE

THE EPIC FAILURE OF THE MAGIC GO-GO CRYSTALS

I sat for a moment, waiting for the Esper Node to fly toward me, but nothing happened. The notification still hung in the air, and I felt like it might be taunting me.

"Uh . . ." I said aloud, looking around sheepishly at the group. "Lemme try again."

"Tha' won' work," Frida said softly, tossing me a smile.

"What won't work?"

"You cannae 'cept a Group Node without a proper party," she said.

"You guys know what these are?" I asked. Then I tensed up, looking around wildly.

Shit, I'm goddamn done for.

"Wait, before you kill me, know that I am willing to split it with you fair and square!"

Calden cocked his head to the side like a confused puppy and raised an eyebrow at me.

"I am sorry, Loon," he said. "But why are we killing you again? You have only just returned to the realm of the breathing, and I think sending you back to the aether would be a bit premature. We haven't even gotten you drunk yet to celebrate. Perhaps afterward we can settle down, gather round, and all take turns stabbing you in the heart—but *not* before."

I don't buy it. Look how anxious they seem.

Some of the group were cautiously placing hands on their weapons or readying for combat in some way. Then it hit me. It was a reaction to *me*. I realized I had tensed up, and my hand was tightly gripped around the handle of my haladie. I must have done it subconsciously. I forced myself to visibly relax, and relief washed over the others.

"You . . . don't want to kill me for my Node?"

"Why in the world would we want to do anything like that?" Merra asked, sliding her sword back into its sheath.

". . . because it opens dungeons?"

There was a pause as my words sank in and then all of them began to laugh.

Well, I guess it's good they still think I'm funny.

"Goodness *me*," Calden said, wiping a tear from his eye. "Loon, you are truly a riotous sort."

I just waited for them to stop, deciding not to venture further about the nature of the Nodes.

"So," I finally said, "how do I accept this bad boy? We got shit to do, ya know? Asses to whip."

"We have to be grouped up," Stinky said quietly. He gave me an odd look, arching a brow and seeming to be quietly contemplating something. Now that I thought about it, he was the only one who hadn't laughed at my comment—not that that was out of the ordinary. He was a sourpuss, of course.

"Yeah . . . " I said. "How do we do that?"

"Well, my dear orc," Calden said with a grin. "Most of us already are. We can invite you, if you like."

Huh, I thought. *That makes sense.* I thought about how in most games, it was wise to party up, but that was usually with the main character. Wasn't I the main character? Of course, considering that this world didn't seem to give a pound of poo whether or not I lived or died, maybe I'd have to realign my understanding of my importance in the overall scheme of things. But then, did people who *weren't* protagonists have secret boons from aggravatingly sinister mask gods?

I noticed that the group was regarding me expectantly and realized that I hadn't given them my answer yet. I cleared my throat and glanced up at the Node.

"I mean, it sounds like I can't get the goods without it, so . . . make with the connection already, maybe?"

All heads turned to Jes. The skinny elf was turning something over in his mind, and I watched as something seemed to click and he snapped out of his daze.

"I am sorry," he said. "What were we discussing?"

"Toss him an invitation, Jesimir," Calden said, nudging the elf lightly.

"Oh . . . " he said, then his eyes focused on me.

Jesimir Carandalon has invited you to a party!
Would you like to accept?
Yes / No

I accepted and immediately felt . . . different. The most noticeable sensation was as though my personal space had been violated. I was aware of other people and knew it was the group around me, but why did they feel like they were so close? It was overwhelming. As I looked around at the group of adventurers, I *knew* that I could somehow feel their . . . auras? As much as that sounded like woo-woo horseshit peddled from a middle-aged lady surrounded by cats and crystals, that was the best description I could think of. It was as though everyone was right next to me but also *not* there? I dunno; it was weird.

I glanced around at them and watched as little prompts appeared above their heads, and I was instantly a part of the "in" crowd.

Jesimir Carandalon
Level 16 Invoker
Party Leader

Invoker, eh? Well, he's certainly invoked some petty asshattery from me. And Level Sixteen? Fuck, man. That's way higher than I am right now. Invoker must be something similar to a wizard? Or . . . a witch? I dunno, man, this Harry Potter fantasy junk is for the birds.

Frida Greyhaim
Level 15 Guardian
Party Member

The words above Frida's head weren't super surprising, since I'd heard her called a "Guardian" several times now. However, seeing that she, too, was vastly superior to me in Level was beginning to make me suspect that each of these fools would outclass me in anything—possibly even in stealth. Guess I'd just have to get stronger or something, damn.

Calden Vick
Human
Level 15 Bersagliere
Party Member

Bersagliere? Is that the guy at the front desk of fancy hotels? Not sure what that has to do with arrows.

Merra Stormbreaker
Level 16 Cavalier
Party Member

First, I was shocked and impressed by Merra's last name. Like, it was legit *Stormbreaker?* That was fucking *badass.*

I am the Stormbreaker, I break lightning over my knee and punch tornados in the face. Watch me give this hurricane a wet willy! Tsunami? Tsno problem.

Man, it was a shame I didn't have a Twitter anymore, because I was churning out thick hunks of buttery comedy gold! But, also, I had to wonder what was up with all the strange Class names these guys had. *Cavalier?* Is that French? I was pretty sure it was, considering it sounded like something the members of Gojira would say.

I moved on to Dedyc and Virgil before I could further digress.

Dedyc'zaar Aklomos
Level 17 Sooth
Party Member

Virgil
Level 15 Vanguard
Party Member

Huh, so, like me, Virgil doesn't have a last name. This only makes me more and more certain about his nature. But Dedyc's name sounds fuckin' cool as hell. Aklomos? Now, that's a motherfuckin' name. *I gotta get me one o' them.*

I looked at the group again with my newfound understanding of just how easily they could stomp my ass into a really weird green wine.

"I know everything now. You guys are, like, super strong!"

"We are getting there," Calden noted with a grin. "There is always room for improvement."

I smiled as I looked over my new . . . party members. However, when I observed Stinky, I didn't see anything.

"Stinky, what the diss?" I exclaimed, startling the man.

"What?" he barked.

"You aren't a member of this fine organization? What? Are you too good to be in the crew?"

He scowled and shot a look over at Calden.

"No, I'm fuckin' not. I got no interest."

"We *did* ask him," Calden said with mock sadness. "But he found us wanting."

"He's probably just embarrassed that you guys would be able to see how pathetically low his Level is!" I offered, smirking at the matau. Stinky bristled.

"Shut up, orc. No one's interested in your fuckin' opinion!"

"Ooh," I said, pointing directly at him. "That's it, isn't it? You're too scared to let everyone know about— Argh!"

I didn't even see it coming. Right in the middle of my very eloquent sentence, Stinky whipped a rock at me and struck me right in the head. It wasn't full-force—otherwise, I probably would have been in a lot bigger trouble—but it *did* hurt.

"What the—Stinky, come on, man! Not cool!"

"Let that be a lesson to you, orc," Stinky said. "Don't exercise your fuckin' mouth unless you're prepared for the consequences."

I deserve that.

"Level Six, eh?" Merra said with a grin. "You managed to do all that—help fight that creature and get all this deep in this dungeon—with such a small pool of Experience?"

"Yeah," I said, puffing my chest out. "I'm advanced for my age."

"We can show you how substantial the information you can glean from your own party is once we address the looming Node," Calden said, then he held a finger up. "And on that emphatic note . . . "

He gestured over his shoulder at the still-hovering emerald object.

" . . . shall we?"

"Oh, uh, yeah," I said. "But I'm still confused as to why it's so exciting. What else can it do?"

"You will see, dear orc," Calden said. "Now, if you please . . . "

He gestured again at the Node. I shrugged and accepted, watching as this time, the massive cluster of sparkling green energy broke into multiple sections and zoomed through the air toward everyone in my party. Stinky was left out of the fiesta, but it seemed like he was perfectly okay with that. Or, at the very least, was no more cross than usual.

As the lights faded, my companions smiled, and I watched as they did something unique: they began gesturing in the air all at once, their eyes slightly glazed over.

What the fuck? Did this infect them with heroin?

I watched as one by one, each of them glittered with a bright light that matched the emerald color of the Node, and then their eyes returned to normal as they all turned to direct their focus to me.

"Much appreciated, Loon," Calden said. "You are a swell individual indeed."

"Don't mention it . . . " I said, confused. After a moment, I couldn't handle the suspense any longer and felt my words burst out of my throat.

"Okay, seriously! What the fuck else do they do?"

Everyone balked at my outburst and looked at one another with startled expressions.

"Ya really don' know?" Frida asked.

"I don't," I said. "And even though I know it will make me look stupid, I need you guys to tell me before I explode from anxiety."

Everyone laughed, except Stinky. He had left our grouping and wandered off near the possessed roe, who had started to rouse.

"Well," Calden said. "We could tell you . . ."

I frowned.

"Or . . . ." he continued mysteriously. "We could show you."

"Whichever way is faster," I stated seriously. I was tired of messing around with the elusive nature of this world and finally wanted some answers. Why had these been worth killing me over? Clearly, they were multi-purpose tools, but I was missing one of their key ingredients. Something that would send people into a fit of murderous fury just to grab them off of me.

"Loon," Jes said softly. "Access your details."

"My . . . what?"

Then it clicked for me.

"Oh, my menu?"

"Whatever it is that you refer to it by," Jes continued. "Open it."

I did. I just saw the usual shit, though. Except now my extra benefit from Sababo was in there, and I noticed that I was back to being Fatigued. I had to assume that was due to being brought back to life.

Loon
Race: Orc
Class: Barbarian
Level: 6
Profession: Unassigned
Health: 302/302
Arcana: 85/85
Max Stamina: 177 *(-10% due to Fatigue II)*

Experience: 14,103
Reputation: N/A

Attributes
Remaining Points to Allocate: 0

Strength: 12
Constitution: 29
Dexterity: 12
Wisdom: 10
Intelligence: 8
Charisma: 6
Luck: 5*

Skills
(-10% due to Fatigue II)
Camp (F-Rank Level 1)
Hunting (F-Rank Level 1)
Improvised Weapon (E-Rank Level 2) +1R +2L
Improvised Shield (F-Rank Level 2)
Insight (F-Rank Level 9)
Intimidate (F-Rank Level 2)
Knowledge [Nature] (F-Rank Level 1)
Perception (F-Rank Level 4)
Simple Weapon Proficiency (F-Rank Level 6)
Simple Armor Proficiency (F-Rank Level 1)
Sneaking (B-Rank Level 4)
Survival (F-Rank Level 1)
Two Handed Weapons (F-Rank Level 6)
Throwing Weapons (F-Rank Level 1)
Unarmed Fighting (F-Rank Level 5)

Active Abilities
Analysis II
Armorless Defense (F-Rank Level 7)
Battle Born I
Enduring Perch I
Darkvision I
Primal Rage (F-Rank Level 2)
Nature's Resilience (F-Rank Level 1)
Sabotage (F-Rank Level 4)
Uncommon Consumption (F-Rank Level 1)
Vengeful Aura I

Passive Abilities
Feared Form

Outsider
Unfaltering
Wildling

Perks
Adventurous Tastes *(First Perk Bonus)*
Aegis Synthesis

Aegis
Calden's Hang Time

Esper Nodes
Emerald: 3
Sapphire: 1

On a lark, I decided to highlight my Esper Nodes, and suddenly, a whole new menu populated.

Esper Nodes
Emerald: 3
Sapphire: 1
Would you like to use Esper Nodes to modify aspects of yourself?

"Modify myself?"
"Oh, yes," Dedyc said, grinning at me.
"What does that mean?"
"It means you can use those Nodes to advance certain abilities," Calden explained, "and transform them into something else entirely."
I stared.
"Oh . . . " I said. "Oh, *shit!*"

CHAPTER THIRTY-FOUR

SO, YOU SAY IT'S AN EVOLUTION

I stared wide-eyed at the options available to me.

Apparently, I could modify several of my hard-won smackdown morsels into something more advanced, elevating my skill set to *probably not gonna die*. Or, at least, *not get mashed into a puddle as quickly*. Though I wasn't entirely certain what evolving them would entail. It seemed as though my Emerald Nodes largely affected my Abilities, but I wasn't sure what the process was for turning, say, Analysis, into *Super* Analysis. Or Analysis Plus? Hyper Identification? I dunno; it was weird. The prompt stated to select one of the Abilities to begin, but there were no further instructions. Was it automatic? Would I have to go through with it regardless of if I picked the wrong one?

To be safe, I selected an Ability that I would be comfortable completely changing forever: *Vengeful Aura*. I read the description again.

***Vengeful Aura*—When resonance is established between an orc's race and the originating Class of Barbarian, Vengeful Aura is born. For [Rage +Intimidate quotient] number of charges per day, an orc Barbarian can emit a wave of intimidating presence that has a chance to inflict the Frightened condition on targets within a radius. The outcome for efficiency is Intimidate +Vengeful Aura. The radius area is based on Intimidate +Charisma quotient.**

Number of Daily Charges: [2]
Radius: [2 ft.]
Note: This is an Ability exclusive to the orc +Barbarian path.

I hadn't even gotten a chance to utilize it yet, but considering that it was basically just my enemies doing a vibe check on me, I was comfortable using it as the canary in the . . . Was it a gold mine? That sort of sounded right, but—surprise, surprise—I wasn't super cued-in to turns of phrases like that. Were birds super good at finding gold? Or perhaps just canaries were, and that was why they were used as detectors. But how did that work? Could they smell it? Wait, can birds smell? That left me with even more questions. That being the case, I decided to abandon that analogy for one I *did* know. Vengeful Aura would be my guinea pig.

I selected it, and the prompt shifted.

You have selected [Vengeful Aura]. Would you like to proceed?

Well, I wasn't a coward. So, of course I was going to proceed. So, I did.

[Vengeful Aura] is not an Ability that can advance without assistance. Please select which additional Ability you would like to combine with [Vengeful Aura].

Ah, so that's how it worked. If I was understanding it correctly, apparently some Abilities could evolve through this process on their own, but others needed wingmen to get the job done. That was pretty neat. It was kinda like the Aegis Synthesis, except I was in the driver's seat on this.

Wow, look at me: doin' all sorts of science. *Guess I'm gonna have to revisit all the disparaging comments I made about Science Club to Mike.*

Thinking about the scar-faced high school pariah made me pause.

I had, without realizing it, begun to accept that everything since the crash *was* in fact real. Which led me to the idea that perhaps I wasn't the only one who had crash-landed dick-first into this dumbass Narnia rip-off. That had to be the case, right? The lady from the train had survived, and I had lived through the ordeal as well—sorta. So, it was now likely in my mind that some of the others had made it across and were experiencing their own brand of *Lord of the Rings* chicanery. Rather than sad, I had started to become . . . hopeful?

Man, if Mike is here, I'll bet he's been non-stop jizzing about it. This would be his wet dream come true.

One thing was for sure: if the others *were* here, I'd need to find them. Not out of any twisted sense of loyalty but because there were few things that would help me survive better than a group of people who I didn't have to hide my true nature from. Plus, people in my world *loved* fantasy and video games, so it stood to reason that there'd be at least a few of them—if they had survived—that would understand this enough to give me the answers I desired.

Okay, that was enough of that. I had shit to do.

I pulled up the list of Abilities that the prompt offered and sifted through it.

What else can I safely use in combination with Vengeful Aura to figure out this crap?

It didn't take me long to decide.

Feared Form—Orcs are large and powerful, but their customs are frowned upon. You can use this to your advantage in combat. However, social interactions may come as a difficult challenge to you when not dealing with members of your own race.

Gain Intimidate Skill
+1 to Strength
- 1 to Intelligence
- 1 to Charisma

This was one of the features under "Passive Abilities," so I wasn't sure it would work. However, it seemed like a good option for trial and error. I knew I could lose the boost to strength, but the way that Sababo had sold his Aegis made it sound like that wouldn't be an issue for long. But I was focused on the task at hand and didn't spare any more time thinking about that. There'd be plenty of time for that later.

When I selected *Feared Form*, the prompt appeared again.

Would you like to combine [Vengeful Aura] and [Feared Form]?
Yes / No

I took a break from my plotting and turned to Merra. She seemed like the best person to ask questions, considering she wasn't nearly as long-winded as Calden, nor as insufferably condescending as Jes.

"Am I able to back out from this at all, or do I lose these Abilities once I push the big red button?"

Merra shrugged.

"I don't know what you mean with crimson clasps, but it'll be final, yes."

I sighed.

I am not nearly smart enough to do this in a way that benefits me.

So, rather than ask further clarifying questions, I did what I always did and shot from the hip. I selected Yes. Instantly, a green glow blossomed around me. A prickling sensation began to grow from right around the base of my neck and spread along my limbs. It transformed into a gentle tickle, and before long, I felt as though I'd just had a very rigorous massage. It was pleasant.

Congratulations! You have gained the [Warchant] Ability!
Warchant
Warchants offer the user the ability to release a bellow of concentrated power that varies in effect based on which is used. Screech your way to success, great and powerful hero!
Available Warchants: [1]
- Blackout Warchant

This Warchant silences an area for a [Intimidate + Charisma quotient multiplied by 200%] seconds. While this is active, everything arcane within the radius becomes suspended. This extends to both individuals and arcane items (if items are below tier threshold.) This Warchant does not stop arcane effects but merely displaces it for a moment. The magic will return once more after that moment unless the individual is killed, stopped from casting, or the item destroyed. Radius is based on Intimidate + Charisma quotient.

"Holy bitch!" I shouted, taking a step back as I read the description over a few times. "I actually made something really fucking cool!"

"The awe is truly unending," Calden responded with a sly grin. "Splendid job, dear orc. I knew you had it in you to achieve greatness."

"Fuck greatness," I said. "This is goddamn *legendary*! I can't wait to bust out a hot rack of nullification curses at the next spell-slingin' baddie that bumbles into my general direction."

". . . nullification curses?" Merra asked.

"Oh, you'll see!" I declared, putting my hands on my hips. "It's gonna be amazing. Everyone will be all 'Whoa, Loon, you're super badass and really, really good at fighting.' And I'll say, 'Y'all ain't seen nothin' yet,' and *shoom*, I'll pop this sucker on them and save the day."

I received nothing but confused glances in response.

"Hey," I said, scowling. "Let me celebrate this. It's the first thing that has felt like a win for me."

Frida cracked a grin.

"Go 'head, Loon. Ye've earned et."

"Thank you," I said with an exaggerated bow. "Now, why don't people do this more often?"

"Because it's rare," Merra said. "Typically, it's only achieved by bagging a rare monster, and even then, it's never a certainty."

I thought about that.

"But I don't seem to have any issue at all with getting Esper Nodes."

"That's because you're a sojourner," she said. "Your lot pick those up like second nature. It is frustratingly easy for you to gain more Espers."

I would have frozen up had I not been sort of taking the temperature of the group's relation to that manner of dysfunction. They seemed oddly chill about, well, damn near everything. I was more intrigued than truly nervous or uncomfortable.

"So, you guys know what I am?" I shot a look over to Stinky. The matau had brought out his arm-strapped coin purse and was digging through the contents out of earshot of this conversation.

"Aye," Frida said. "Known fer a spell now. Or, least, 'spected. Yoor a bit standout for the type."

"*Making an impression* is what I like to call it," I said with a wink. Frida smiled back at me.

"We had our speculations, yes," Calden confirmed. "But it was not fully realized until the gigantic green boon materialized tauntingly above our heads. Up until this point, only Virgil had been able to procure such alluring prospects."

"Ah-ha!" I exclaimed, jabbing a finger in Virgil's direction and startling everyone. "I knew it!"

"Knew what?" Virgil asked.

" . . . that you were a sojourner."

"I ain't made no show o' hidin' what I am," Virgil stated. "I reckoned you were of my ilk as well, though confirmation were hard to come by. I judged true, though; that's well enough."

I felt myself deflate, my proclamation not having the weight I'd originally conceived it would.

"So," I said. "Everyone is just . . . cool with it? No one wants to run me through the belly with a hot poker?"

"And what, pray tell, would that accomplish?" Merra chuckled. "It seems to me that having an additional sojourner as part of our troupe only increases our odds of betterment."

"But, like, not as a target?" I clarified. "Or someone to bash over the head and take my goodies—kilt included?"

"As Merra so eloquently put it," Calden began, "that would not accomplish anything. Such a tactic would be entirely shortsighted."

"How's that?"

"Your value is as an accomplice," he continued, "*not* as a corpse. We could indeed skewer you beyond recognizable company, but that would allow us to only gain those Espers which you currently hoard upon your person. Why someone would prefer to go by that route rather than party up with you baffles the mind. Are you sure you fully understand the benefit to be wrought from keeping you alongside us? You seem shockingly inclined toward anxiousness in this regard."

I shrugged.

"I had a bad experience right out of the gate," I said. "I won't go into it, but someone thought it was better that I relinquish my Espers the *old-fashioned way*, rather than wait around for me to produce them."

Frida clapped a hand on my bicep.

"I'd be inclined t' think that a person like that might be needin' a bit of a 'mmediate boost and bankin' on the fact yoor keen to return after been killed. Tha' ain't the way of et 'ere, though, Loon."

I stared down at her friendly demeanor and sighed.

I suppose it could be just Fawn and not everyone who would react that way.

It was worth considering. But something still didn't make sense. Fawn was a sojourner herself. She had no reason to kill me for my Esper Nodes, since she could gain them on her own. There was still a missing piece to this puzzle.

"So," I started, "could you tell me why another sojourner might try to kill me, then? If they can snatch up one of these Nodes whenever they want, what purpose would it serve to kill me?"

"Perhaps you were being particularly insolent?" Calden offered. "I can imagine a scenario where your personality conflicted with that of another's to the point that they chose to resort to extreme violence."

I didn't laugh.

"Only joshing a bit, dear orc," he said quickly.

Virgil was the one who actually responded to my question.

"Might be 'cause o' the gap," he said thoughtfully.

"Great, more terms I don't know," I said.

"That bein'," he said, "that it's a mite more difficult to wrangle up a Node the more powerful a cuss you end up."

"So, it gets harder to get them, the stronger you are?"

"That would make a sort of sense," Merra offered. "Emerald Nodes are only produced when there's a disparity of five levels, and that becomes a lot more arduous as you grow."

Virgil seemed to catch my look and thought to explain further.

"See, the difference a handful of Levels makes is negligible at a lower rank, but the higher up you go, it's noticeably more miserable to surmount. Say I were Level Twenty. If'n I were to tussle with a Twenty-one or a Twenty-two, I'd have a hell of a tougher time than I would have even dealin' with a Level Ten at Level Five. So, gettin' an Emerald is next near the hardest thing to achieve, let alone trying to aim fer Sapphire or Topaz."

"Oh," I said. "So, yeah, it's more difficult, but is that worth killing someone over? Besides, would that even work? Do these transfer ownership if someone offs you and they are higher level than you are?"

"It does if you're a sojourner," Merra said. "Sojourners relinquish their inventory of Esper Nodes to the person that kills them. But you're right. Something doesn't sit right about that. Perhaps there is more to the puzzle than meets the eye."

"Well, I'm going to put a pin that for now," I said. "Especially because I haven't finished gloating yet about my slick fresh hotness."

There were more confused stares.

"The new Ability."

"What *did* you acquire, actually?" Calden asked. "I'm dying to know."

I smirked.

"Oh, it's real fuckin' cool, Calden," I said. "Just trust me on that."

I didn't clarify what my new Ability did, despite Calden spending the next few minutes attempting to draw it out of me. I gave him nothing more than a *Patience, young Padawan* and kept changing the subject until he eventually gave up, looking mournful at his loss of information.

The group decided to finally roll out, with Jes leading the way. The elf kept a hand on his chest, clutching the Amulet of Location. This kept the golden magical light it produced in our sights as we followed it along back toward the exit door.

While we walked, I tried to figure out what combination of Abilities I could combine for my last remaining Emerald Esper Node. It was difficult, because without a reference point, it was just guesswork—which I had to admit was pretty on-brand for the way I did things. However, I didn't want to be as hasty this go-around, so I decided it would be . . . prudent to sit and have a think on it before making any decisions.

In fact, I was so fixated on making the proper choice that I hardly noticed when a curious voice suddenly entered my head.

You.

I paused, looking from side to side to see if I could locate the source of the noise. Had I actually heard that? It didn't sound threatening, almost like the high pitch of a child. I couldn't see anything that could have made the sound. It was just a lonely, dim trail through an unending expanse of jungle and my newest homies by my side. I shook my head and continued perusing the list of Abilities for a moment before I heard it again.

You.

You.

There were two now, and they were definitely voices. I stopped walking, causing Stinky to bump into me.

"Watch it, orc!" he shouted, shoving me forward.

"Can you hear that?" I asked, cocking my head to the side and listening. I noticed that Frida and Calden had both slowed down, turning to regard me with curiosity. They had their card game out and were attempting to play while they moved.

"Hear what, Loon?" Calden asked. His tone was bright, but I caught his eyes darting to the trees and one of his hands cautiously moving to the bow slung over his back.

You, came the voices again. There were even more this time.

"What the fuck is going on?"

I turned in a full circle, trying to ascertain where this bullshit was pummeling me from, and caught sight of the possessed roe. They were clustered together, as always, moving down the path, same as us. However, what grabbed my attention were their eyes. All of them were solely focused on me, and their mouths hung open in what could almost pass for a smile. Then I heard five voices at once enter my mind, and I got a very strange feeling.

You.

I felt my stomach drop and I pointed to myself hesitantly.

"Me?" I asked the eggs. Instantly, they began hopping up and down like mad, feverishly trilling and bumping into one another as their eyes were still locked on mine.

You. Yes. You. was the response. Then, all at once, the eggs surrounded me, frantically ramming me with their bouncy bodies as a chorus of voices filled my mind.

You. Yes. You. You. Yes. Brother.

"You've got to be kidding me," I said. "I'm an *egg whisperer?*"

CHAPTER THIRTY-FIVE

THE OTHER GUYS

"We need to know what's going on out there, or we're going to fucking die."

"Somehow, I don't think sending people who are pathetically ill suited to handle literally any of the shit out there will resolve that problem, man."

A group of individuals stood in a semicircle, looking out at the forest beyond them with caution and almost definitely fear. They were myriad races most fantastical, each distinct in their presentation. A regular rainbow coalition of fairy-tale hodgepodgery wearing the mantle of anger and frustration typical of those placed in extreme circumstances against their will.

"Fuck you, dipshit," the first speaker, a dwarf with pale hair, said.

"Yeah, fuck you right back, how about?" said the second speaker, a human with light brown hair and hazel eyes.

"This is getting us nowhere," a third man said with a pacifying grin. "Let's table the shit-talking for now and have a rational discussion about—"

"Fuck your rational discussion," the dwarf bellowed. "I'm in charge here, and I say we send someone to scout around."

"Typically, people who have to *say* they're in charge . . . aren't," said a human woman with short, dark tangles.

"Well, I'm sorry you feel that way, sweetheart," the dwarf explained in a condescending tone that made the woman recoil. "But in this case, I am both in charge *and* saying I'm in charge. Fuckin' deal with it, or you can get out."

"Literally no one likes you—" she started.

"Easy," said the third man, clapping a palm on the woman's shoulder to steady her but fixating on the dwarf. "You're right. You're in charge, Alpha, but we *do* have to work together here. We are all we have against whatever the unknown is. Would it make sense, though, to hear people out? If only to make sure we sort through any potential cracks in our armor?"

"Fuck, I'm so sick of this," the dwarf, Alpha, said before sighing dramatically. "But yeah. Fine. Go ahead and tell me why we totally shouldn't send people out to make sure our little camp doesn't get hardcore ass-blasted while we are all asleep."

The dwarf's words sent a shiver of disgust amongst the assembly, but no one said anything about his choice of language. Over the last week, he'd made it clear where his priorities were concerning other people's *feelings* on his "lack of wokeness."

"You were saying, Matt?" the third man said, looking down at the man who'd initially had such a visceral reaction to the dwarf. Not for the first time since all of this began, either.

Matt shrugged, shouldering his drooping pack, and gestured out into the thicket of trees beyond where they stood.

"We need a clear plan if we are going to do *any* intelligence-gathering whatsoever. We can't just yeet someone out into the woods and hope for the best. We don't have walkies or phones or anything that works here. That means zero communication capability whatsoever."

"Someone's gotta have a spell or something that does that, right?" the dwarf demanded, casting a scalding glance around at the group.

"What about you, weird bitch?" he said, jerking a finger at the striking woman directly across from him. "You got any fucked-up powers you want to let me know about? Something that can give you dummies some closure?"

The woman was a vittra, and though no one present had ever seen one other than her, they all agreed she looked like some sort of demon. She was just over five feet tall, with pale gray skin like tortoise flesh and hair the color of ripe eggplant—which was fashioned into a bizarrely angular bowl cut. Her hands were clawed, and her ears were long, pointed, and downturned. Most curiously, behind her, a smooth, spaded tail swished back and forth. She rested her eyes on the dwarf. They were wicked things made of golden irises pressed into ink-black pools, and contempt dwelled within them like a living fire.

"I believe that the manner in which you conduct yourself is disrespectful and disgusting," she said flatly. "Furthermore, your inflated sense of self-importance is eclipsed only by your gross disregard for others—a trait that I assure you will be a breath of cold relief to your loved ones when it inevitably leads to your demise and they no longer have to suffer your abhorrent personality and lack of awareness.

"If I had any arcane proclivities for communication," she continued, "I would use them only to torment you unendingly until you became so deranged that you hurled yourself from a high place. I only hope that your death is gruesome and painful so that I might watch the light leave your pathetic, beady eyes as you struggle to scoop your lifeblood back into your twisted body."

After a moment of stunned silence from everyone, the dwarf spoke again with a chuckle.

"Yep," he said. "Still creepy."

"I am comforted only by the fact that no one will mourn you when you are gone," the woman said, and turned to walk away from the group.

"Alpha," the reasonable third man said, plastering a wide smile on his dark, handsome face. "Could we speak privately?"

"Yeah, sure," the dwarf said, waving everyone away. However, he grasped a tall, slender elf by the arm as the man had turned to leave as well.

"Not you, Dalton," he said. "You're coming with us."

The elf sighed and nodded.

"Sure thing, Ja–um . . . *Alpha*."

Once they were alone, the tall human lifted his hands in a pacifying gesture. Alpha frowned, knowing that the man was about to say something he didn't like.

"Fuck, don't try to be charming, dude," he said. "Whatever you're going to say, spit it out. We don't have time for you to walk on eggshells like a pussy."

"Fair enough," the man said, and dropped his smile. "You can't talk to people like that anymore."

"Like what?"

"Like they are stupid. It's pissing people off, and someone will stab your eyes out eventually."

"Like fuck they will," Alpha said, throwing his hands in the air. "I don't give a fuck if these crybabies can't handle the way I talk. I get *results*, and that's what matters."

"Yeah, I don't think they see it that way," the other man said, his eyes catching the elf's.

"He's right," Dalton said.

"The fuck? You're on his side?" Alpha demanded.

"*No!*" Dalton explained, almost too hurriedly. "But that doesn't mean I don't *hear* things, man. You've got ears too. I'm sure you know what people are saying about you. They're not exactly hiding it."

"If someone doesn't like how I do things, they can fight me for leadership. We set it up that way, remember?"

"*You* set it up that way," the human explained. "No one else even got a chance to disagree."

"Well, that's too fuckin' bad, isn't it? Everyone was too busy bitchin' about their feelings and shit—how *they* thought things should be. I took initiative."

"How you came into command is irrelevant," the human said, leaning against a tree trunk and crossing his armored arms. "It won't matter at all what the Settlement Stone allowed to happen if someone decides to sneak over to your bedroll tonight and smash your face into a puddle with a hammer."

"Wait, did someone say they were going to do that?!" Alpha demanded.

"No—jeez, calm down. But I'm not exactly using my imagination here. People are *super* furious at you right now, man. You are not treating anyone with kindness, and there are lots of people who haven't forgiven you from *before*. You can't bank on your *one* instance of helping people to save you."

"Screw that. These people are ungrateful little trolls," Alpha hissed. "You should keep in mind that you wouldn't even be alive if it wasn't for me."

"I'm *aware*," the human said severely. "Which is why I'm giving you advice on this—whether you are willing to listen or not. I hope you will, but I can't force you."

"Right," the dwarf said. "You can't."

He gestured to Dalton.

"I don't have to care what people want, because I'm keeping them safe. Dalton and the others have my back. No one wants to fucking step up to *that* challenge. I promise it will end badly for them. So, people can either fucking deal with the way I lead, leave, or choose *option three*."

Alpha smiled cruelly.

"Which, honestly, I hope someone does. That will probably get the rest of the people in line *real fast*."

The human shivered. He still remembered the screams that the man, called Sean, had issued at the end as his body dissolved into pieces of melting, broiling pops. Even the earth beneath where he'd stood had been so severely destroyed, they'd had to dig it up and scatter the remains lest it continue to grow and infect the area around it. He'd disagreed with the dwarf's leadership style loudly and directly and, as a result, was forced to challenge Alpha for control. It was . . . horrible.

After a moment of quiet contemplation, he finally spoke to the dwarf. His tone was measured and slow, but he looked directly into his eyes.

"No one is in doubt of what you did, Alpha," he said. "But people are only willing to tolerate so much before they can't help but lash out. I honestly believe you are the most fit to lead in this batshit-crazy scenario we've found ourselves in. I really do. But it's because of that that I'm offering you my opinion on elements you're probably not considering as strongly as you should, my dude. You can be great at directing a group of people on how to survive a fucked-up new landscape. Still, if you ignore their feelings—whether you think they are valid or not—people will hate you for it. Hate can make people do shit that is against their best interests."

"And those people will deal with option three, like I said," Alpha offered casually.

"Sure," said the human, nodding as if to agree. "But then that's one less person who could be contributing to our overall benefit, and others won't take well to that for long, either. We've already had some people leave, and we can't manage much more of that. It weakens us—the whole group. Sure, you can be in charge, but what good is the brain if the body is dead and destroyed?"

Alpha considered this, and the human felt he was gaining the upper hand in the discussion. It was a sense he had. So, while there was a moment of hesitation, the human knew this was the best possible opportunity to lay the groundwork for the future, and his was a long game. So, he went in for the kill.

"We *all* want to live, right? We want to figure out what is going on and how we will get back. But we can only do that if we are unified. If there is group infighting, we all suffer. We've got to raise each other up and build ourselves strong, or it doesn't matter what we encounter. Because we will be killed out here. You rightly took advantage of the chaos before—when those things attacked. That was lucky. People were too scared and confused to know what to do, and you offered the tip of a spear. A focus. *Unity*. I know it's only been a week or so, but people are starting to become accustomed to this new world, which means the next time those things—or something like them—return, they will be less likely to be caught unaware."

The human sighed but only allowed himself a beat before continuing. He needed to drop his salient point, which needed to be thematic.

"So, that means you've got a choice on your hands," he said softly. "You've gotta decide if you want to be the force that brings these people together to survive . . ."

He leveled a serious gaze on the dwarf, willing a threatening tone in the intent.

"Or if you want to be the one they unite *against*."

He let his words hang in the air, taking a moment to gauge the effect his statement had caused. The human left his eyes brimming with anger and the promise of uncomfortable truths. Alpha had to believe that the human would turn with the tide if things didn't go his way, or so he hoped that was what he was putting down. He'd found that it was never as easy persuading the dwarf as it was with other people . . .

"Fine," Alpha said, practically spitting the word out.

The human watched as Dalton visibly relaxed next to the dwarf, letting out a quiet sigh of relief.

"I'll try to . . . be nicer, or whatever these little babies want. I can do that. I can be nice."

Dalton's reaction was to let his eyes bulge in disbelief. He'd been friends with the dwarf for a long time, and he'd rarely acted in a way that wasn't wholly assholish. But, in his mind, it was refreshing to see that he was at least taking . . . Saban—was that what he was calling himself? It was refreshing to see that he was taking this guy's advice seriously.

"Nice is a good start," Saban said with a big grin. "Now . . . "

He clapped his gauntleted hands.

" . . . about sending someone off to scout for dangers."

"Oh, fuck, not this!" Alpha exclaimed. "It's the best move! We can't sit around and *wait* for more bad things to just show up—"

"I agree with you," Saban interrupted. The dwarf looked at him, confused. He'd been full of bluster, his chest sticking forward as he prepared to argue, but he deflated at the human's words.

"You do?"

"Yeah," the human said. "I don't think it benefits anyone to *not* know what's going on. We'd be sitting ducks in a pond full of piranhas."

"Uh, yeah! Right—um, good," Alpha said, clearing his throat. "You have someone in mind, then?"

"I do."

"Well . . . fuckin' say it, then, man."

"I think we should send Rua."

"Who?" Alpha asked, his expression one of pure bafflement.

"Rua. The elf. Got stuck in that barrel a couple of days ago?"

"*Him?!*" Alpha demanded. "Why the fuck would we send that guy? He's fuckin' useless."

"*She's* not useless," Saban said with a warning emphasis. "She's super fucking smart, *and* she's got a natural talent for this world and her Class. Plus, she seems to understand it better than any of us. Except maybe . . . uh, Tartarus. But that goes without saying."

"Ugh, *fine*," Alpha said. "Send elfie out to get slaughtered. At least we'll know if it's dangerous when we find . . . *her* body."

"Sounds great to me," Saban said. He had complete confidence in Rua's abilities and knew that there were a couple of things she wasn't saying aloud that could be used in a pinch in a situation just like the one they were going to throw her into.

"I'm going to get some sleep," Alpha said. "In the morning, I'll try to . . . I dunno, make peace or something with people. God, you guys really suck, you know that? I don't understand how you get anything done with all of your *feelings* and your safe spaces."

"I know," Saban said, his grin wide. "We are just awful, aren't we? But, on that note . . . no place is really safe anymore, is it? This has been a week of hell, and I imagine it'll get worse before it gets better."

"Whatever," Alpha said. "I'm out. Dalton . . . "

The dwarf turned to regard the elf.

"Yeah?"

"Don't let anybody hack me to pieces, all right?"

Dalton sighed.

"Yeah. Of course, man. No hacking. Got it."

The human and the elf watched the dwarf retreat to his usual sleeping area. There was a long moment of silence before either of them said anything. It was Dalton who broke the quiet.

"You know," he said, his eyes still watching the dwarf from afar, "he's my friend and all, but sometimes . . . I wish someone would just punch him in the fucking face."

Saban chuckled.

"I tried that, remember? On the train. It didn't seem to help much."

"Yeah," Dalton said with a nod. "But what if someone did it really, really hard?"

CHAPTER THIRTY-SIX

MELODIES AND MYSTERIES

We'd set up camp about two hours' walk from the direction of the Arch. It had been a choice between that and continuing the sleepy slog in one go. I was exhausted, and the others—while more rested than I was with my two sexy levels of Fatigue—had expended a lot of energy during the fight. Especially Merra, as she'd dumped the rest of her remaining strength in her efforts to revive me. It was deemed the most appropriate option to get some rest and try for the gate once we could handle whatever was on the other side.

I spent the time lying by the fire, listening to the gabble of the others as they did their own version of relaxation. Calden and Frida resumed their raucous game of cards, shouting over one another with each hand, with Merra offering her constantly changing support in between the slink of her whetstone on her sword blade. Jes was reading a tome next to the fire, hardly making a sound, save the annoyingly loud flutter of brittle pages being turned. Strangely, Stinky, Virgil, and Dedyc had struck up a conversation and were speaking and gesturing, passing a bottle back and forth. The sight made me feel kind of warm. Stinky sucked, but it was good to see that even *he* was starting to feel a sense of camaraderie with this bunch.

I guess there was nothing quite like a harrowing fight ending with someone's death and then resurrection to really bring a gang together. As far as I could tell, Stinky hadn't yet accepted a party invite, though I couldn't tell if that was even an option on the table. As I watched him mildly grin at something Dedyc said, I had to assume it would be forthcoming.

I rolled over and was immediately assaulted by the sight of five sets of red eyes staring back at me. The possessed roe.

"Ah! Jesus!" I shouted, jerking backward. "Don't you— Er, stop that! You can't do that."

In my head I heard a chorus of voices.

Fear. Fear. Apologies. Stop that. Fear.

I frowned.

"Yeah, exactly," I said. "People don't like that. Why don't you guys do something else? Like that humping thing you were doing before?"

Of course, I didn't actually want them to start jumping all over one another like a few hours ago—it was unsettling. However, I *did* want them to not scare the bejesus out of me every time I turned around. The five eggs looked at me quizzically, and since they didn't respond in my mind, I figured they had to be confused. They were simple creatures, but they seemed to understand at least a few things.

"Look," I said, sitting up in a cross-legged position. "You guys are excited to chat with me. I get it; I'm amazing. However, if you don't stop invading my personal space, I don't care what this magic reincarnation shit did to weld me to your minds, I will spike you against a sharp boulder."

They kept staring at me, so I just sighed.

"Fine," I said glumly. "If you're going to exist in my general area, then can you at least not bother me *in my head*? It's uncomfortable and is giving me a migraine."

No speak, one of them said. I nodded.

"See? You get it, Jumpy. The rest of you should follow this guy's lead. He's really going places. Got that star potential, you know?"

My compliment seemed to resonate with the one I'd singled out, because I suddenly heard its voice in my head.

Jumpy. Name. Good?

Ah, so you want to be called Jumpy, eh? Well, no skin off my back.

"Sure," I said. "Jumpy is a brilliant name. Very fitting, too, considering your natural inclinations."

Then more of the voices joined in, and I immediately regretted my decision.

Name also. Name. Want name. Name.

"Ah, fuck," I said. "All right, fine. You want names? You're getting some motherfucking names."

"Just one more!" Dedyc whined, pointing at Jes.

We'd all been treated to the elf's wonderful singing voice, with him belting out a few tasty tunes before lights-out. I slapped Jes on the back, and he gave me a look that indicated he didn't appreciate that *at all.*

"Yeah, man," I said. "Something fuckin' epic! Give us a song about slaying monsters or killing a horde of enemies from the safety of your ship."

"I think I've done all I can manage," Jes said dourly. "I am quite exhausted."

"Oh, come now, Jesimir," Calden said, taking a pull from a bottle and handing it over to the elf. "One more to lull us to sleep."

"I do not—"

"Perhaps look at it this way," Calden said, giving me a sly smile and a wink. "The more you sing, the less I speak."

"Even an elf cannot keep that up," Merra razzed. "A man's got to sleep sometime."

"The barbs of your words are only matched by the barbs of your beard, Merra," Calden stated woefully. "And here I thought you were hoping for a song as well."

"I was," she relented, smiling at Jes. "But it's somehow more fun to rib you than hear a jaunty melody. You know? Step on you when you're already in the mud."

"Ah, yes," Calden said, sweeping a hand dramatically across his brow and adopting an antiquated cadence. "I had nearly forgotten my unabashed browbeating. But worry not, companions! Tomorrow, I shall return from the realm of destruction to which I have been relegated and vanquish my foe most readily. A plan in place have I."

"He's going to try to steal your cards," Merra said to Frida.

"Undoubtedly," Frida confirmed, then removed her *very* substantial deck and began wedging cards into her breastplate.

"Oh, that is just unseemly," Calden admonished, crossing his arms. "I would not deign to do anything of the sort. However, if I *were* planning an ambush of such a variety, I hardly think that would stop me."

"You're a scoundrel," Merra said.

"A knave," Frida echoed.

"*Not like that*," Calden shouted, his cheeks reddening. "The two of you should never endeavor to team up against a tyrant, lest you shatter his self-esteem and wind up ruling in his stead. I daresay it would be easy."

The women laughed.

"One more?" Dedyc asked Jes again, undeterred by the distraction of the other three's conversation.

"One. More. Song." I began, trying to turn it into a chant. "One. More. Song. One. More— Aw, come on guys, seriously? Just *once*, I'd like to get one of those going."

I was greeted by blank stares and silence, until Dedyc piped up in his usual hiss.

"One. More. Song. One. More. Song."

I grinned and joined him, the two of us together encouraging Calden, Merra, and Frida to begin chanting as well.

Fuck, yeah, I thought. *I did it.*

"I have sung everything I know," Jes said sleepily. "I have not a drop of rhyme left in my body."

"Not even 'Dragons in the Sky'?" Calden offered mischievously.

Jes shot him a glance of pure venom, and I raised an eyebrow.

"Calden . . . " Jes warned, but I interrupted.

"What's 'Dragons in the Sky'? It sounds lame."

Jes bristled, and I watched his neck turn red as he addressed me with a voice like a whip.

"It is most decidedly *not* . . . lame," he said. I could tell he probably had a different definition of the word, but I didn't care. If there was one thing I could do well, it was rile someone up enough to react.

"Yeah, I dunno," I started, clucking my tongue in mock consideration. "Now if it were 'Griffins in the Sky' or 'Krakens in the Sky,' *that* I could get behind. But *dragons* . . . nah, doesn't work for me. Seems like a song like that would be super weak."

"In what world would there be krakens in the sky?" Calden asked, then I saw a gleam of excitement in his eye. "Hold on a moment . . . Loon, do they have flying krakens in your world?"

I shrugged.

"Maybe; I can't be sure. There's loads of stuff I don't know about."

"Fascinating," Calden said. "But, to be fair, Jes, the orc does appear to have a misconception about the song. Perhaps you should seek to illuminate him as to his mistake?"

"Yeah, Jes," I said. "Show me what for."

Jes glowered, but I could tell it was working. After a moment of contemplation, he reached into his bag and produced a small stringed object. It was in the shape of a mouth made out of bone with shimmering silver cords strung across its length. I noticed that the elf handled the object almost tenderly—as though it were extremely fragile and valuable. I was captivated by it.

"Whoa," I said. "The fuck is that?"

"This is a harp," Jes said in a tone that implied he thought I was a complete dipshit.

"Oh," I said. "Kinda puny, though, right?"

Jes ignored me and instead closed his eyes and began to strum. The pace was fast, and I noticed that in addition to having an expert-level singing voice, the elf's dexterity with this instrument was impressive as hell. He plucked the strings two at a time, plunking out a melody that was equal parts catchy and beautiful. The music resonated within me, like it was waking something up inside my body and I started to feel very relaxed. While he played, the others grew quiet, waiting for the song to really get into its swing. The song was upbeat and reminded me of what might have been considered a bawdy tavern tune. I watched as Calden placed a supportive hand on Jes's shoulder and began drumming a rhythm with his fingers. Then Jes began singing.

A hero raised his bow
And took his merry aim
He saw his targets resting there
And thought it fair to claim.
His sight was true
His aim was smart
And let the arrow fly
But luck was dark
He missed his mark
On dragons in the sky
Dragons in the sky
Dragons in the sky
A sadder tale
You shan't regale
Than dragons in the sky
They took affront
To what he'd done
And turned themselves around
They torched the fields
Of harvest yield
And burned them to the ground
The hero tried to warn the town
Of the foolish thing he'd tried
But they were fast
What he saw last
Were dragons in the sky
Dragons in the sky
Dragons in the sky
A sadder tale
You shan't regale
Than dragons in the sky.

As the others applauded, I sat back in contemplation. I'd been expecting something much different from the lyrical content the song projected. The way Jes had been acting had led me to believe that it would be a much more morose subject matter, but this was actually kind of a funny little cautionary tale.

I applauded with everyone else, then my curiosity got the better of me.

"That was a cute song, Jes," I said. "Why didn't you want to play it?"

Jes didn't respond; he still had his eyes closed and was lightly strumming the harp as if transfixed with keeping the melody going. His pace began to slow, and eventually he was just softly fingering the strings with an almost-imperceptible sound until he finally stopped. He lowered the harp to his lap carefully and opened his eyes. They were wet, sparkling in the firelight as he swept his palm under them to wipe away moisture.

He's . . . crying? What the hell? Did I miss something culturally significant about that track?

"You guys, uh, take dragon attacks pretty seriously, then, I take it?"

Jes still didn't respond, and by the looks on the faces of the rest of the party, I knew there was something I was missing. Calden gave me a tight smile and a sympathetic gaze as Jes rose from his seated position and replaced the harp in his pack. Then he turned back. When he spoke, his voice cracked slightly.

"I think I will retire," he said. "We will need to be refreshed to face whatever awaits us on the other side of the Arch."

There were nods all around and Jes sighed.

"That should last for some time, so we will be safe to choose our path carefully. Now . . . "

Jes stretched almost *too* theatrically and turned to his bedroll.

"I will see you all in a few hours. Virgil?"

The lanky sojourner stood and swaggered away from the group, carrying his oversized crossbow.

Huh. Guess he's first watch? Or maybe . . . only watch?

I wasn't sure what the dynamic was with taking turns, but Virgil seemed to be their designated scout, so I wasn't going to argue. If I didn't have to pull a shift on night duty, that was perfectly fine by me. I was fuckin' *beat*, in no small part due to having been brought back from the dead.

Now that I had a moment to relax, I noticed that a notification had cropped up in my vision. It had been minimized, but I hadn't realized it was there until now. I'd been completely distracted by the song and the curious effect it had had on Jes. I opened it.

Resurrection Sickness has ended!

Effects taking place during period of sickness are now available. Your Fatigue II has become Fatigue I.

What?

I'd been sick the whole time? And apparently, that meant certain things had been blocked from happening while I was laid up. That was interesting. I knew something fucky had been afoot, but I didn't realize it was something affecting the nature of my Abilities or whatever. More notifications appeared and seemed to be in chronological order.

You have been granted an Aegis!
[Unnamed Aegis]

I hadn't really reflected much on my encounter with Sababo since I'd returned, especially the last few moments before I was revived. He'd offered me an Aegis and explained that it would work alongside my "already-curious sleeping habits." I wasn't sure what that meant at the time, but looking at the description, I think I was beginning to understand.

[Unnamed Aegis]
This unique Aegis was forged specifically for [Loon]! This Aegis is considered passive, only coming online when certain criteria are met to trigger the full effect. This Aegis is within the domain of Slumber and, as such, can only be utilized when that particular domain is exacerbated. With great refusal of sleep, the user [Loon] will gain benefits bestowed by Sababo. Please see further details below to learn the full scope of granted traits.
- When [Loon] reaches Fatigue I, the following benefits will be granted:
    - Strength Attribute increase [+4 multiplied by 100%]
    - Dexterity Attribute increase [+4 multiplied by 100%]
    - Constitution Attribute increase [+4 multiplied by 100%]
- When [Loon] reaches Fatigue II, the following benefits will be granted:
    - Strength Attribute increase [+8 multiplied by 150%]
    - Dexterity Attribute increase [+8 multiplied by 150%]
    - Constitution Attribute increase [+8 multiplied by 150%]
- When [Loon] reaches Fatigue III, the following benefits will be granted:
    - Strength Attribute increase [+12 multiplied by 200%]
    - Dexterity Attribute increase [+12 multiplied by 200%]
    - Constitution Attribute increase [+12 multiplied by 200%]

All other effects from Fatigue will remain in place:

- Fatigue I—Negative 5% to Skills and Intelligence, Wisdom, and Charisma Attributes.
- Fatigue II—Negative 10% to Skills and Intelligence, Wisdom, and Charisma Attributes.
- Fatigue III—Negative 15% to Skills and Intelligence, Wisdom, and Charisma Attributes.

All Ranks of Fatigue beyond those listed will increase the percentage of affected Skills and Attributes.

"Whoa, mama!" I exclaimed. If this was accurate—and I had no reason to believe it wasn't—the more exhausted I got, the more powerful I would become. I felt myself grinning, which had to be a gruesome scene for anyone observing me, but I didn't care. This was a boon I could get behind! Finally, my lackadaisical approach to good ol' fashioned forty winks would pay off—with interest. I was prompted to name the new Aegis, and I quickly entered something I knew would showcase the badassery that I felt I deserved. When I was done, I admired my handiwork.

[Loon's Bombastic Beatdown]

Perfection, I thought to myself.

Just so that I knew precisely what I was working with, I hastily accessed my menu and glanced at my stats. Sure enough, they were majorly altered. I was currently under the formerly oppressive Fatigue I condition, but now, instead of it being largely bad, there was quite a positive spin on that bitch.

Strength: 32 (Fatigue I)
Dexterity: 32 (Fatigue I)
Constitution: 64 (Fatigue I)

Unbelievable, I thought. *I am gonna be a fortress of baddie-crushin', face-smackin' pile drivers and uppercuts.*

I was quite pleased with this new development and what that would mean for my future as an insomniac. I didn't need sleep—it could go take a hike. I was in charge now. I was going to grab slumber by the shoulders and headbutt it into submission. Fate too, by that metric. I was going to kick destiny in the back and let it lay there and cry while I did victory laps.

You have received a Buff from [Party Leader] Jesimir!
You are under the effect of Delyra's Musical Mantle of Empowerment

Delyra's Musical Mantle of Empowerment [Party Buff]
For the next [24] hours, you and members of your party receive the temporary benefit of Arcane enhancement to the following:
- Intelligence +1
- Wisdom +1
- Charisma +1
- +4% resistance to the effects of Allure-type spells

Delyra's Musical Mantle of Empowerment also grants you as an individual additional Skill-based Arcane enhancement. Each of the following will be temporarily increased by one Rank:
- Camp
- Insight
- Perception
- Sneaking
- Survival

Well, well, well! Look who's finally moving up in the world! It's me. I'm moving up in the world.

So, it appeared that Jes's song was more than just an upbeat banger with questionable lyrical content—it was also deceptively magical. After the day I'd just had—hell, after the *life* I'd lived—I'd take it. It was about time this crazy place started showing me some damn respect.

As I was resting in relative rhapsody, swooning over myself and my fresh new gains, I was interrupted by the approach of Calden. The blond man plunked down next to me in front of the fire, his usual cocky, playful manner replaced with quiet contemplation.

Ah, horseshit. He's going to try to talk to me about something serious.

I frowned.

Dammit, Calden, I thought. *You're gonna ruin the ambiance. Read the camp, dude. I'm vibin'.*

Calden seemed uninterested in taking a hint, though, so I sighed and sat up a little straighter. If he needed an ear, I supposed that was something I could pretend to provide. That's what friends did, right? Were we friends, though? We were party members, sure. But friends? I'd have to do some digging into what people round these parts considered companionship, because I was grossly outmatched when it came to that part of human interaction. Then again, I wasn't really a human anymore.

"I suppose you are wondering why such a lively air would weigh on Jesimir so despotically," Calden said, his eyes on the fire and not on me.

Not really, I thought.

"Yeah," I said instead. "Seemed a bit . . . What's the word—*incongruent*? That's a ditty I'd do some dancing and drinking to, but he was pretty emo about it."

Calden chuckled, but it seemed more of a reaction than actually finding it humorous. I knew he probably wouldn't know what *emo* meant, but maybe he'd figure it out with context clues like I had to do with everything.

"Yes," he said quietly. "The nature of the song does seem incompatible with his countenance. Quite mysterious, I am sure, from your perspective."

"I get it," I said. "Suffer for your art, and all that. Musicians are weird like that."

"Perhaps more than you know," Calden said. "The subjugation that Jesimir is weighed upon by is long-persisting and a substantial tale—"

Aw, goddammit, I thought. *I don't have time for a fuckin' one-man show.*

"—but suffice to say I do not have an appropriate venue nor window of opportunity to do it justice."

Oh, thank god.

Calden leveled a gaze at me, and it was then that I could see the sadness in his eyes. I didn't like seeing it. Calden, so far, had been an irritating ray of sunshine. He was supposed to be a devil-may care, melodramatic jokester, not . . . whatever this was.

"Are *you* okay?" I asked.

"I am," Calden said softly, then turned back to the fire. "My concern is for Jesimir's well-being. Not mine own."

There was something strange about the way Calden was referring to Jes, but I wasn't smart enough or perhaps *insightful* enough to pick up on what it could possibly be.

Maybe I should listen? That's what folks are always trying to tell me, anyway. But it's hard! People are so boring, *and their emotions drive me bonkers.*

However, it was clear something was on Calden's mind, and for some reason, he'd chosen to unload whatever it was on to me. You know, *me*, the borderline brain-dead, apathetic anti-intellectual. Well, that was a development I didn't see coming. I supposed if he was going to get all mushy with the faraway eyes, the least I could do was pay attention.

"The song itself—while playful and fairly straightforward—holds a stronger connotation for our friend, the elf," Calden began. "When Miss Stormbringer and I first acquainted ourselves with those you see here, Jesimir was much different."

"How so?" I asked. "Did he have a tail?"

"No," Calden chuckled. "Though, for all his metamorphosis, he may as well have had three. No, I mean to say that he was a bit less . . . severe."

"Oh, yeah. He's a bit of a grump, eh? But not like Stinky—who probably stirs *shithead powder* into his morning tea—Jes has more of that 'disappointed dad' energy."

"All the same," Calden continued. "A tragedy befell him, and he has never since been the same."

Here we go, I thought. *Another tale of woe from a spoiled little rich boy. What happened; did someone free his favorite slave?*

"The song you heard was written by someone quite close to Jesimir," Calden said. "One whose power was only matched by her beauty and kindness. Jes loved her fiercely."

"Delyra?" I ventured.

"Indeed," Calden said. "Jesimir's beloved bard."

"And what happened to this woman? Did she reject him or did she die?"

The way I figured, Jes was the type of person to get the blues over either. Though there was an itch in my brain that told me my comment was probably not the most sensitive way to approach the subject. That had to be my increase to Insight, or possibly Charisma? Man, that was the sort of thing that still messed with me: that these Attributes and Skills could modify your thought patterns. It was a scary concept and reminded me of rabies. Apparently, the virus would hijack your brain and make you literally terrified of water, and an infected person would puke up any liquid they drank because their body betrayed them. This extended even to swallowing their own saliva—hence the foaming-at-the-mouth thing you'd see in YouTube videos and horror movies. How could I be me if stuff like this affected the way my mind fired thoughts? The prospect made me a little queasy. In order to distract myself, I did what I always did when I was uncomfortable: I got irritated.

"Anyway, I'm dead-ass tired right now, Calden; can you make with the hustle on this after-school special?"

Calden regarded me with a quizzical look but just shrugged.

"Of course, Loon," he said softly. "As I said, Jesimir was enamored with her, and she with him. His strength—and his folly—has apparently always been his desire to be loved."

Calden paused, looking in Jes's direction. I followed his gaze and saw the elf was huddled under a blanket but otherwise unmoving.

Been there.

Calden turned back and gave me a sad smile.

"What do you know of the Solani Empire, Loon?"

I huffed.

"Less than nothing—I'm not from here, remember?"

"Ah, yes, my apologies, dear orc," Calden said. "I only ask because some of this story is enriched by understanding the complications arising from an observance of their culture. I have no doubts that even with our centuries of relative stasis, the Empire still persists. But seeing as how you are, indeed, fresh to this realm, I will endeavor to formulate the concept without the prerequisite knowledge."

"Much appreciated, Cal," I said.

"What you should understand is that the Solani Empire is an elvish nation. If not in race, then primarily in culture. Theirs is a long history, as the elves themselves are such creatures burdened with resolutely prodigious lifespans. What humans—or orcs—must resolve quickly, for instance, in matters of importance, the elves can ruminate on for far longer."

"They drag their heels on decisions, is what you're saying?"

"Closely enough to the point," Calden affirmed. "But that paints the portrait as to the nature of their longevity and their reaction to threats."

Calden tossed a leaf into the fire, and I watched it curl and blacken before dissolving in the flames. Calden continued.

"Jesimir is from the Solani Empire and in fact, is of House Carandalon. They are powerful and preside always as the secondary House in the Empire, no matter which House seizes control of their people."

"Always second fiddle, eh? Tough luck, I guess," I said.

"Not entirely," Calden corrected. "Long ago, they waived their right to the Hoarfrost Throne—"

I snickered.

"Sounds *cool* and *sexy*."

Calden groaned.

"Puns are a technique best left to children and fools, Loon," he said. "Divest yourself of those and you shall be the chief of wit."

Then it was my turn to grumble.

"Aw, man," I said. "I thought that was a good one. Fine, carry on with your super long and very serious story with the *not-at-all-hilariously* named objects of power."

"As I said," Calden sighed. "They abdicated any claim to rule to instead wear the mantle of *Kingmakers*. Theirs would be the hands that place the crown on the heads of each subsequent generation of monarchs, so to speak."

Always the photographer, never in any of the pictures, I thought.

"So, let me guess," I said. "Jes is from this mega-important family, and Delyra wasn't, so they couldn't get married? Wake me up when you get to the part where they kill themselves instead of waiting around a couple of minutes to see if one of them was faking."

Calden did something he didn't normally do: he scowled.

"Please, Loon," he began, his voice taking on a tinge of reproach. "I am trying to relate a story so that you may ascertain the importance of Jesimir's past and see how it directs his present. You were given the gift of his song, something only his allies ever receive. That means that Jes considers you at his side. However, you must fully grasp what this means, because without context, you would be a thief and worse—an unconscionable and immoral benefactor. So, I say this with the utmost in sincerity and respect to your usual manner: kindly shut your fucking mouth and *listen*."

I was stunned. Calden, so far, had been such a relaxed and flighty-seeming individual and someone I'd come to admire—even for the short time I'd known him—for his way of always joking around. Seeing him angry and, more so, upset with *me* was a slap to my senses. Normally, something like that would make me even madder than the person furious with me, but in this case, I actually felt . . . terrible. Embarrassed, even. I straightened up.

"Uh, sorry . . . " I mumbled, uncomfortable with my behavior. "That was fucked-up of me. Please continue."

Calden flashed me a grin, breaking the tension immediately.

"There's a lad," he said, in an accent that wasn't his usual one. "All's good, innit?"

I smirked.

"But yeah, seriously, go on. I'll try to keep my popcorn-tossing to a minimum."

"There *is* death in this story, Loon," Calden said, his proper accent returning. "But not as you ascribed it. But allow me to sculpt more clearly. Jesimir and Delyra were *indeed* from different paths. He, a Lotus elf from the Solani Empire, she, a hulder from the Acharan. Theirs was not a forbidden tryst—the concept is not a feature of most edicts in the Empire—but, in fact, happily lauded by both families. No, the issue is not one of romantic disparity but in showing the intensity of love both individuals felt for one another.

"Delyra was a Minstrel; it was her Class and her calling—and not one of common ability. She was a *wonder*, my dear orc, outclassing most by an order of magnitude for her Level. She bore a prowess and technique that made her skills quite legendary and highly sought. Chief among those was the curious nature of her songs. Most Minstrels, regardless of their eventual fixation, rely on those ancient hymns and shanties that were written in the Age of the Haze by the First Bards. However, Delyra did not perform the echoes of greater men—no, she created her own melodies and songs from whole cloth, scribing them and crafting the elegant music that wove the spells into being."

"Age of Haze?" I asked. "That sounds metal as fuck."

"Ah, yes," Calden said with a wink. "Known to some as the Era of Fog, Shadow, and Light. It was a triumphant era, and many believe it to be when Arcana in the world was the strongest."

I'd heard *that* term before from Pontivex. It was interesting, despite my initial instinct to disregard it, that I was getting a bit more insight now into Regaia's historical record.

But before I could spend much more time on that, Calden continued.

"Most obscure was Delyra's ability to touch on areas of Arcana that were long considered blockaded from her Class. A marvel if ever there were one, Delyra could conduct elements of other Arcane branches outside what was believed to be possible of a Minstrel and, as such, forged quite the infamy around her abilities. This, of course, led to powers embedded in the foundation of the stewardship of nations to seek her assistance. Knowing her, you would never assume she had dined at the pleasure of dozens of dignitaries and nobles—so humble was her countenance. At this time, Frida and Dedyc had already become fast friends with the couple, and together, the four of them set out to help aid in the conflicts that brewed between the Kingdom of Arlo and Hathburia—for more bitter rivals there were not. It was then that a complication arose."

Calden tossed another leaf into the flames.

"As battlefields grew, the need for specialized fighters became apparent, and a call went out in the north for those that could utilize Void Arcana."

"I'll wait to ask what that is," I said. "You know, out of politeness. But I *do* want to know."

"No, it is quite all right, dear orc," Calden said. "This illustrates an area of the story that might require elaboration. Void Arcana is all but a mystery to one such as I, though, I do know a bit from speaking with our beleaguered bunch here. Practitioners of the Void, as many refer to them, are a reclusive group and highly focused on that particular arm of the arcane. From my understanding, rarely do those that participate in its spread dip their wands into other areas of Arcana perhaps more than the basics. It is a difficult art to grasp and even harder still for true mastery. As a result, the pool of users is quite small—and many of those are merely researchers and not full-fledged adepts."

Calden brushed a hand through his hair absently, his eyes screwing up to look toward the cavern-ish ceiling high above.

"I once knew a man who claimed to be a practitioner of the Void, though his abilities amounted to little more than parlor tricks. Still, it was effective at swindling me out of a card game followed by a swift exodus into the night with most of my coin."

He cleared his throat.

"But that is not the crux of my tale—apologies, Loon," he said, before continuing.

"An artifact was discovered by some of King Geier's legion, and its full functionality was believed to only be accessed with the utilization of Void Arcana. Thus, our tragic heroine was conscripted to assist in the findings."

"She used Void magic?" I asked. "This story is getting weirder and weirder."

"Not precisely," Calden said. "While Delyra was not advanced in Void's capabilities, she did have several songs that utilized its nature. Where she learned to weave aspects of it into her music, I am not sufficiently capable of relating, but it was a fact, still, that she had done so. And so, before long, she was on the road to Derika to join others in the excavation. Jesimir remained apart from her, as this was a quest of exclusivity, and, though he was adamant, was expressly forbidden from participation.

"This was when we met Jesimir and the others. He was confident and powerful, with great knowledge gleaned from both experience and his intensive study. We liked him immediately."

Calden was smiling fondly now, but when he continued, his face became grim.

"We traveled for a time together until a day came that Jesimir received a summons from Delyra. The work with the artifact had been successful—*far* too successful, in fact. The details are murky at best, but to make it simpler: they had awoken something in Derika, and now the city itself was under attack. All of us went to help and, when we arrived, assisted in beating back the evil that lay within the walls."

"Whoa," I said, leaning forward in my seat. "You guys fought some ancient voodoo death and you're just *glossing over it*?! You can't do that! I need to know what it was!"

Calden chuckled.

"Trust that I will expand upon those days in greater detail someday, Loon. For now, though, it is not relevant to the telling."

"Uh, excuse me? Fuck that. This is the most relevant part of this whole bedtime story."

Finally, I was excited by the prospect of what Calden had started telling me. However, seeing the man's look, I decided to drop it.

"Uh, anyway," I said sheepishly. "Continue."

"Weeks we spent fighting. It was not constant, though it was frequent—with enemies attacking in waves. The five of us bonded quite strongly during the incursion. However, during the fighting, Jesimir was mortally wounded. Typically, something of that sort would be irrelevant to our fight, as Dedyc is quite skilled in providing a healing touch with his spells. But this was something else. It was Arcana that came over from the discovery, and as such, Dedyc was powerless to stave it off."

"Jes was killed?" I asked.

"No, but he would have been were it not for the impeccable timing of Delyra. While the rest of us held off the onslaught, Delyra began to play a song of revitalization, purifying Jesimir's body of the dread toxin that was the assailing spell's strength. But, in doing so, she weakened herself. She could not protect herself when the hordes fell upon us. The same spells that were used on Jesimir were directed toward her. And she fell."

I paused.

"So, lemme get this straight. She used the last of her Arcana to keep Jes alive and then died herself immediately afterward? That fuckin' sucks. She couldn't be brought back?"

"She could not," Calden said sadly. "Not by usual means, in any case. Whatever ingrained power within those spells is not of this world, and something about their nature keeps those killed from coming back. Jesimir is not without his means as a scion of House Carandalon, and when the battle was over, he took what remained of his beloved to his home and begged his people to use their Abilities to bring her back. They resolved to consider it. However, as I mentioned, they think of time differently from you or I. Before they could come to an answer, Delyra's body was eaten by whatever Arcana dwells in the spell and was no more."

I wasn't sure how to react to that. If I begged my own family for help and they didn't ... Well, actually, I'd done that before. I understood how distressing that was, and with life and death in the balance ... yeah, it was shitty.

"This, of course, poisoned Jesimir to his family, and he fled."

I considered that.

"So, that was it? No resolution to the issue?" I demanded, now feeling really strange about my interactions with Jes so far. I'd been a fucking *dick* to him, and he'd been relatively patient with me.

"Not quite," Calden said. "If you will recall, I mentioned that the *usual* methods of resurrection could not take hold over this power. However, *some* things were rumored to be available."

I felt like my mind had jumped into overdrive.

"Merra's amulet?"

Calden let out a peal of shocked laughter.

"You are far more astute than others might believe, Loon! Very good! Yes, Merra's token is one of such items. It belonged to some great-grandfather or something from an age long forgotten. What is *not* forgotten, however, is the purpose for which it was wrought. An ancient dwarvish queen laid the amulet at the feet of Merra's ancestor in thanks for some magnificent deed or another, relating that it was crafted *before* the Age of the Haze and promising that it had Arcana that was otherwise unknown in this world. Of those powers, it was believed to be capable of bringing back lost souls. This is evident in your case in particular."

I froze.

"Did Merra waste the one shot of bringing Delyra back . . . on me?" I asked, horrified at the implication.

"Do not worry, dear orc," Calden said quickly. "That is but one of the latent powers within the amulet itself and not its singular purpose. I am not sure what you know of resurrection, but as you have no doubt surmised, in most cases, elements of the expired's form must remain intact in order to revive. Where there are some missing, others need be provided."

"Me and the eggs," I said glumly.

"You and the eggs, indeed," he affirmed. "Fear not. The power of revival required in this case is a bit mature. Delyra's body no longer exists in a form that could be utilized by standard protocol, but Merra's amulet . . . is believed to be able to wrest someone from the realm of the dead without the need for their mortal form to remain. It has, according to dwarvish accounts, been used like this before—if certain criteria were met."

"What are those, then?"

"Bringing it to the bottom floor of this dungeon and casting it into something called the 'Lake of Souls.'"

"Ah," I said. "Hence why you are all here."

"Indeed," Calden said. "It has been our primary directive for the last . . . Well, I suppose a *year* is meaningless now?"

"As long as it gets done, though, it'll be mission accomplished," I said. "There wasn't a time limit on it?"

"Not so far as we have been able to unearth."

I breathed a sigh of relief. I hadn't known I'd been holding my breath until now. I didn't typically mind a little bit of awkwardness, and I was pretty okay with people being upset with me. But, in this case, I was very glad they hadn't shot their only wad of reincarnation on me. That would have been *not so great*.

"So, where did Carmichael fit into all of this?" I asked.

"I am sorry, Loon," Calden said. "How do you mean? I believe his role was established, no?"

"No," I said. "I get the *why*, but I guess I just don't understand where he was during all of this. You didn't mention him in your story. It sounds like you guys drafted him into this, but then he just fucked off and tried to kill you after the fact? I'd be severely garnishing his wages if he'd pulled something like that on me."

"Oh," Calden said, and a sheepish grin grew on his face. "Well . . . you see, Loon . . . "

He paused.

"What?" I asked.

Calden leveled a gaze at me.

"Carmichael was not—precisely—a willing participant in this endeavor."

"Calden . . . " I said, warningly. The blond man rested a hand on the back of his head and mussed his hair uncomfortably.

"Carmichael was acquired by more determined means."

I stared at him.

"You kidnapped him?! No fucking wonder he tried to escape and kill you guys!"

"It was not so simply accomplished," Calden said. "It was a mutually beneficial arrangement—or so we thought."

"I dunno, man," I said. "This is starting to sound quite a lot like abduction."

Calden shrugged his shoulders and threw another handful of leaves into the fire.

"I wish that it were. Carmichael was once a barbed foe in opposition to Virgil. They were not the best of acquaintances. I won't dive too deep into Virgil and Carmichael's storied past, however. Suffice to say that despite his proclivities, he was still one of the few we knew could help us, regardless of his . . . limitations. In that regard, he'd been relegated to a life within the Royal Dungeons."

Wait, is he saying—

" . . . from whence we liberated him shortly before this journey."

"You broke him out of jail?" I asked, stunned. "That's . . . Whoa. A little badass, I guess? Some regular wild-west shit."

Virgil may have had some experience in that vein, based on what I'm starting to pick up about him.

"It is—as they say—as it is," Calden breathed. "Now you know the full spectrum of why we are here and why it is so important you know the essence of Jesimir's song. Delyra taught him only two musical accompaniments. The one you received the benefit of and another that I hope he never falls into the danger of using."

Calden smiled sadly.

"He is still in pain, and you must understand how difficult this is for him. We do not know if this will even work as intended—hanging one's hope on dwarvish mythology is not the mightiest of truths—but it is what we have, and I . . . *we* will do what we must to help him accomplish this."

As I looked into Calden's eyes brimming with emotion and drive, something clicked in my brain.

Calden is in love with him.

Congratulations! You have raised a Skill!
Insight [E-Rank Level 1]
Delyra's Musical Mantle of Empowerment temporarily brings this Skill to [E-Rank Level 2]!

That had to fucking *suck*. Falling for someone who was still holding a candle for someone else—especially a *dead* someone else—had to be miserable. I knew what it was like, in a sense. Not in a romantic way but in a familial-love sorta way. I'd do just about anything to bring back—

"Right!" Calden said, slapping his palms on his knees and standing, interrupting my train of thought. "Off to bed with me, then. I require quite an elaborate pre-slumber ritual to ensure my beauty is absolute each morning. Thank you for the chat, dear orc. I hope it helped you. Goodnight."

It seemed like it assisted him a lot more than it would have me. But, thinking about it, that was probably the point. I didn't believe for a second that this little sidebar down memory lane had been about me at all. Calden was clearly sorting through some stuff, and including the world-hopping newbie in a faux lecture was an easy method to organize his own thoughts and feelings. I didn't mind. I'd learned some shit.

I wasn't going to sleep, though. Not with this new Aegis hanging in the balance. Instead, I decided that it was time to use my other Emerald Esper Node and figure out precisely what Ability was next on the chopping block.

"Almost there," Virgil hissed, peering back at us from his spot ahead in the trees.

We'd traveled another couple of hours, wandering along winding routes and twisting trails through the thick plumage of jungle brush. Several times I'd doubted our navigation, as our party was very much off the beaten path, climbing over upturned trees and gnarled roots, and chopping through vines and saplings. However, the guiding bolt of Jes's magical compass had directed us this way, and there wasn't much else to go off of. So, while I was more than a little hesitant, I didn't say anything out loud about how terrible I thought this meandering march was.

The old cowboy jabbed a finger forward as he spoke, but then brought his hand up to indicate we should hold back.

"Why?" I asked, sidling up closer. "What's going on?"

"Beasts," Virgil whispered, making a lip-pinching motion. I nodded defeatedly. Then he slipped forward and was gone.

"Hopefully, he doesn't prance off too far," Stinky said quietly next to me—making me jump. "He's going to wind up out of the range of my . . ."

Stinky gestured to himself.

I nodded.

"Yeah, he'll be one salty dog if he misses his train back to Portal Town."

Jes appeared next to me, looking as though he'd just inherited a bank vault full of diarrhea. His expression was sour, and his glare told me that I'd done something to offend him. I sighed.

"What happened?"

"Your . . . *children*," Jes said. "They will not desist in congregating around me, making their incessant clicking noises."

I glanced behind him and saw a single-file train of the possessed roe tailing the elf, eyeing him adoringly.

"What? The egg boys?" I asked. "That's what they do. They like you, Jes. You should feel honored."

"I feel disgusted," he grumbled. "They are unseemly, and I cannot help but think they are plotting against me."

"Who, these guys?" I asked, putting on an air of ignorance. "Nah, they're just being friendly. Besides, they do all their plotting when you're asleep."

"They do *what?*" Jes hissed.

"Yeah," I said. "While you were moping around in your jack shack, they had this devious glint to their eyes. I'd watch out for that. But it seems like they've mostly forgiven you for . . . whatever it is you did."

"What is a *jack shack*?" Jes asked.

His stricken tone and deep timbre coupled with the nearly panicked way he'd asked made me laugh.

"You know," I led him, smirking. "A blanket fort where you can . . . Actually, never mind. Chill out, dude, I'm just messing with you. I think you probably just interest them. They were captivated by your singing before everyone passed out, and they probably just want to hear more of it, so take it as a compliment. Besides, Chompy is in the back; he's the one you really have to watch out for."

As if on cue, the egg farthest away from us clacked its sharp teeth together audibly.

"Good Chompy," I cooed.

"Anyway," I continued. "If Virgil is keeping us here for a minute, I'm going to take a leak."

I began making my way toward the trees, but a hand on my shoulder stopped me.

"No, you absolutely are *not*," Jes said.

"Man, what are you, the dick police?" I asked. "It's just gonna take a second, and I gotta whiz super bad."

"It is bad form to relieve oneself while perils abound," said a voice from behind me. I turned to see that Calden had caught up with us, and he was flanked by Merra, Frida, and Dedyc.

"Wow, just great," I grumbled. "The gang's all here. Wonderful."

"Don't even think about bleeding your fuckin' worm right now, orc," Stinky said. "Unless you want a ghoul to come and snatch it away in its teeth. I'm fine with it, though. Have at."

I grimaced.

"Well, now I *can't*, Stinky," I said with a dramatic flourish. "Not with an audience. I have a shy bladder."

"Listen," Jes commanded suddenly, putting his hand up to silence us. We all stood stock-still, hands on weapons or readying other forms of attack. After a moment of deadly quiet, I heard a rustle and Virgil's face popped out from the foliage.

"We're gonna need t' go round," he drawled.

"What is it, Virgil?" Jes asked.

"Don't rightly know," the cowboy said. "There's a cave up ahead. Same one we passed on the way to the ravine. 'Cept now, it's loaded up with varmints of indeterminate origin. Grievous ones."

"How many?" Jes asked.

"Best reckoning?" Virgil asked.

"Best reckoning," the elf confirmed.

"Ten? Twelve? Damn near too many to handle," Virgil said.

"How do you know that?" I asked. "If you don't know what they are, how can you tell we can't fight them?"

"I got a 'Bility that can peruse the numbers o' creatures—their Levels. These 'uns register higher than I can view. With their multitude, we'd be deader 'n a calf in coyote country were we to wake 'em. Best to ford a different river on this."

I nodded. So, Virgil had a trait that could read at least some of the details of monsters. It sounded similar to Stinky's Ability, though Stinky could usually tell what the encountered creatures were, as well. Something didn't make sense to me, though.

"Why would something that powerful be in the second stage of this dungeon?" I asked. "I have it on good authority that this place is supposed to be survivable for someone of my Level until at least the fifth chamber. Difficult, probably. Dangerous—definitely. But not impossibly deadly."

Jes regarded me suspiciously.

"And how—pray, tell—do you know that, Loon? I was led to believe you were ignorant of this place. That is curiously specific."

Ah, shit. I revealed too much of my hand. Backpedal, backpedal, baby.

I wasn't exactly sure if I was supposed to keep Zeol's hand in my travels secret—he could fuck off, honestly—but despite the fact that I cared very little whether he was happy or not, now that I was in it, it seemed unwise to spill the beans on his involvement. My *liar brain* started working.

"It was, uh, Pontivex," I said, not sure if I was convincing enough to fool anyone. "Part of our conversation involved him giving up the details on my general likelihood of not being killed before a certain point. He's a total shithead but probably didn't lie about that."

I noticed Stinky gave me a look but didn't say anything in opposition to my bit o' fibbin'.

Jes considered my words, and then nodded.

"Very well," he said. "I was unaware of this particular development. However, I have seen nothing to counter this claim. Every harried encounter we have observed in this place has been well under our own Level by quite a lot. Save, of course, the simulacrum—but that was an anomaly and a variable we brought forth through our own ignorance. It makes sense."

I breathed a sigh of relief.

"So, that probably means we are supposed to circumvent this nest of *deadlies*," Merra offered. "They likely won't raise much of a fuss if we don't bother them, if Loon's accounts are in order. A bigger challenge for mightier heroes than ourselves."

The others nodded, and I reasoned that was the most sensible route.

"How come we didn't notice them the first time we came through?" I asked. "The time dilation?"

"Precisely," Calden said. "They may have moved in during our prolonged absence. Truly, armed with this knowledge, so much more makes sense about this area. Fortune shined brightly upon us when the two of you stumbled into our path."

Stinky snickered disbelievingly but didn't offer up anything further.

For once, I'm with you, Stinkster, I thought. *We've maybe messed everything up for them more than we've helped. I can only imagine what absolute shittery we've unlocked for this group.*

And so, we moved on. Carefully. We emerged from the jungle trees and into a large open area leading up to a yawning cave. My skin prickled as I saw dozens of dark shapes in the dim arrayed around the mouth of the fissure, possibly asleep and definitely dangerous. They were big—maybe horse-sized—and looked like massive frogs with scorpion tails.

Fuck one hundred percent of that noise. They probably leap and *sting. That prospect is fuckin' terrifying.*

We skirted by, careful not to make any sounds. I, unfortunately, was also on babysitting duty with my new DNA-donors, the possessed roe. I'd told them to be quiet before we left the safety of the obfuscating foliage, and I'd worried just the command wouldn't be enough. However, whatever force had a hold over them in this dungeon seemed to work, because the eggs shivered as they slowly moved, their senses apparently tuned in to the peril nearby. Even their mind-voices were silent. I couldn't help but draw a comparison to the way they were acting now with their cowardly display in the first chamber with the hive beasts.

Good. That makes this slightly easier. Now we just have to make sure we don't uncork any attention ourselves.

The time it took us to get safely by was painstakingly slow, but eventually, we had made it to the other side of the open stretch and found a narrow trail through the trees. We followed the telltale light from Jes's item for probably another hour before Virgil finally raised his hand again.

"Friends," he said. "We've arrived."

I let out a breath of relief and smiled.

"See? That wasn't so bad!"

I received a mixture of smirks and scathing expressions from the group from my comments. Despite that, it seemed like everyone was feeling a sense of relief, and the mood lightened. The group spread out, and in the distance I could just make out the familiar territory we'd arrived in. The Archway was there! I could see it standing tall and wedged against the only true wall we'd encountered in this place. I smiled.

I noticed the others all crouching down and beginning to dig through their packs. I looked at my own as the others dutifully pilfered their own belongings.

Should I be prepping like they are?

I didn't know what I had on hand that made any difference in my odds in going through the Arch, but I figured I should check. After a few moments, I opted to put on my Grenalyn's Gussying Gauntlets—just in case. I had a few other items that I felt wouldn't really work as well for me as they could for other members of the party, so I approached Calden and Frida.

"I, uh, have some stuff you guys might be able to use," I said, gesturing to the objects in my arms. The Guardian's Buckler and the Cincture of Suresight.

Calden examined them both quickly and then shook his head.

"Oh, as much as I delight in the idea of accepting such a generous offer of goods from you, dear orc—I must decline."

"Huh? What, are they crap or something?"

"Nah," Frida said with a smile. "But they're yoors, no' ours. Our gear's go' pluck 'nough for us to handle. Thank ye, though."

"I don't understand," I said, frowning. "So, it *is* crap?"

"Aye, for us," Frida said, her smile never faltering. "No' for ye. 'Preciate ye thinkin' 'bout us, however."

"What Frida means to say," Calden cut in, "is that these items are better suited to your own proclivities—or someone with a similar cut to their cloth. You should hold on to them, if you cannot use them yourself, and sell them for a good price. Dungeon loot is notoriously more valuable than others you may encounter out in the world."

"Really? Oh, then, on that note—I'll be taking back my gifts, gang. Sorry, but I've just discovered you're not worthy enough."

"Right-o," Frida said, standing. "But ah've go' somethin' for *you*, Loon."

The Guardian lifted her hand, and in her gauntleted palm was a small golden ring.

I suddenly got very uncomfortable.

Is she asking me to marry her?!

I took a few steps back, not knowing what to say in this scenario. Sure, she was beautiful, but I was only eighteen. Well, I suppose that was old enough from where I was from, and also—was I the same age here? I didn't really check to see what the body's age was that I'd grifted from the ethereal starter plane. For all I knew, this could be a sixty-year-old orc costume. Did I have wrinkles? It was at that moment I realized I'd never even gotten a proper look at my own face since arriving. I'd need to fix that immediately. But I had to be eighteen, right? Frida couldn't have been much older than that—maybe twenty? Twenty-five at most. *An older lady.* Is that my type? Would there be too much of a generational divide? Would we argue about the good ol' days and be referring to different periods of time? Man, I hadn't even lived on my own yet, and now I'd have to shack up with some chick I barely knew. *At least she could fight my battles for me.* I winced, realizing I'd already gone too far. I'd have to accept the proposal first. This was so conflicting.

Calden must have seen my horror and confusion, because he too stood and began to chuckle.

"Frida, my dear," he said, "I believe you have, perhaps unintentionally, rattled our friend Loon. He seems to be misunderstanding your intent. Though I am marvelously interested in seeing an orc sweat arrows over a misperceived notion, it is likely not the best time to allow this to continue further."

I straightened, blinking at Calden.

"Huh?"

"Ah'm no' proposin'," Frida said, her smile as wide as could be. "Ah'm offerin' a magical item."

I blinked again.

"Oh, heh-heh," I fumbled, laughing nervously. "I mean . . . for sure, that's obvious. The boy does the proposing."

"Is that the case in your culture?" Calden asked. "Or perhaps this is something from orc culture you've gleaned? In any case, here in the Kingdom, the interested party is the one to initiate the proposal—though gaudy rings are rarely the presumed method nowadays. So archaic and *traditional*."

"'Sides," Frida said with a wink, "if et were me proposin' to ye, ye'd know it—and ye'd be *wanting* to marry me."

"That's, uh, a lot of confidence . . . " I said.

"Ah'm confident," Frida said simply. "Ah'm a right catch."

"It is part of her allure, to be sure," Calden said. "Though perhaps we can display a bit more haste in accepting Frida's ring—necessitating implications or not. I can already feel Jesimir's aura of anger coalescing around us as we speak."

I glanced down at the ring in Frida's unmoving hand and activated Analysis.

Ring of Redoubt
Rarity: Elusive
Item Class: Ring
Durability: 70/70
Weight: N/A
Defense: +3
Bonuses: +3 *to Constitution*
Casts Fortification Spell Charges: [3] Per Day

A ring forged of High-Grade Yellow Hydris-Gold and imbued with defensive capabilities, the Ring of Redoubt is the surest method to protect you *slightly* from outside damage. Grants +3 to Defense and +3 to Constitution while the ring is worn. Additionally, this item allows the wearer to cast the Fortification Spell [3] times per day. Hope you weren't planning on a quick death! This will make your end nice and slow—so seize the day and enjoy the (final) moment!

I grinned.

"Thank you, Frida," I said. "This will likely keep me from getting killed *immediately*."

"That's the shake," she said. "Figured a bit o' bashin' could do ye some good in hardening that hide o' yoors."

"Frida!" Calden admonished scandalously. "Bashing and hardening? Was this a marriage proposal or not? I find I am very conflicted as to the nature of your offer."

Then he turned to me.

"Though her virtue is unassailable, my dear orc, her vigor is—"

Frida shoved him enough to quiet him but not enough to hurt, it seemed.

"Enough," she said, still smiling.

"Very well," Calden said. "I will speak no more on the matter and shall remain privately astonished to the untoward seductions of a lusty lass and her concubine."

"As long as whatever ye do is *silent*, ye can act as ye please," Frida said.

I pulled off the glove on my left hand and slid the perfectly smooth circle of metal over my middle finger. Surprisingly, it fit well.

"What's the Fortification Spell do?" I asked, slipping my glove back on over the ring. "Does it turn me into a powerhouse of might and strategy?"

Frida laughed.

"Aye, a bit," she said. "Et's strategic, sure. Lets ye have a bit more endurance in lastin' out a fight s' long as yoor standin' stock-still."

"Well, I will treasure this gift for the rest of my days," I said. "Which, most likely, is until I step through that Archway."

"Oh, you'll have to give us *some* credit," Calden said. "Our own force should allow you to survive for at least a moment *after* crossing the threshold of the gate."

"I'll be happy to have the extra seconds for screaming," I said.

"There you are—an incongruously positive outlook on the woes of the soon-to-be vanquished," Calden said.

"Is everyone ready to cross?" came Jes's baritone, jarring us from our jocular tomfoolery. I turned to see that he and the others were already walking toward the Archway.

"We are right behind you, O High and Fearless Party Leader," Calden shouted. "Just wrapping up Loon and Frida's nuptials."

Jes turned and cocked his head to the side, then, probably deciding it was just Calden being Calden, shook his head.

"Whatever you're referring to, I am uninterested in its content," he said. "Hurry along, lest we spend another few centuries dawdling."

"Oh, but *Jesimir*," Calden called back, sounding affronted, "have you lost your spirit of romance? You cannot rush love, and there are no shortcuts to wedded bliss. These two must have their moment under the rays of the sun and nurture their mutual affection."

I stopped walking. Everything Calden was saying was—of course—pure bullshit, but that wasn't precisely what had given me pause.

Shortcut?
A bolt of goddamn lightning went off in my brain and I grinned.
I'd almost fucking forgot!
Zeol, for all of his babbling, was annoyingly sly. Before, when he'd first been telling me about this excursion, he'd halfway mentioned a *shortcut*. A shortcut in the *second chamber*. That was here.

Ha, I know things! I'm smarter than I thought! Look at me—Mr. Big Brain. King Cranium. Captain . . . Smartypants? Eh, well, I know this *at least!*

I started to really think about how things had worked out up until this point. Zeol had known enough to give me the ability to comprehend alternate languages—which led to my fruitful interaction with Pontivex. At least, the part where I wasn't tied to him in matters of my soul. He'd given me that Spell and tried to fuck me over—but the Spell was where my curiosity lived. I pulled open my menu and re-read the description on the magic.

Discover [Doorway]
- *Arcane Cost: 10 Arcana*
- *Range: 30 feet*
- *Duration: 5 Minutes*
- *Restrictions: Utterance*
- *Wait: N/A*

A spell allowing the user to find hidden doorways, gates, and other exits or outlets within thirty feet. This spell's duration is five minutes, after which time the opening cannot be found unless the spell is cast a second time. This spell uses Utterance and, as such, must be spoken.

I could have cheered.
Maybe it was my increased brain power because of Jes's dead girlfriend's swan song, but something about that seemed important. The spell very specifically mentioned gates, and unless it was referring to the kind in a white picket fence, I had to believe it was significant phrasing. I was bad at remembering things, usually. I'd forgotten Uncle Luke's birthday every year—*even though it was also my birthday*—and I was notoriously incompetent at school or flash cards. But *this* . . . I remembered this. I had to imagine that being thrust into a world of immediate life-or-death consequences probably assisted in that, but that didn't matter at the moment. I had an idea, and I didn't get many of those unless they were terrible. So, hoping that wasn't the case in this scenario, I vaulted forward, racing ahead of the others toward the Archway. At my movement, the eggs began to follow, barreling behind me as I blazed toward my goal. I slid to a stop in front of the Archway and heard the roe collide with one

another as they mimed my actions. They scattered like billiards in their collision and I heard angry chittering.

Warn us. No like. Ouchie.

"Sorry, guys," I said, not looking at them. My eyes were locked on the Archway and the void within.

"What are you doing, orc?!" I heard Stinky shout from about a hundred feet away. I raised my hand to indicate I'd heard him but was busy, and then I opened my menu to the Discover Doorway spell.

I'd never used a spell before—that I knew of—but I had to believe the process for accessing them was similar to all my other Abilities. I mentally selected it, and suddenly, words that I'd never known before came vomiting out of my mouth.

"*Though the passages of life may be dark, I summon the art of the discovery to make clear my path.*"

Instantly, the world around me flashed, and much like I was used to with Darkvision, became muted. The verdant green of the jungle dimmed to a gray-green and the walls became a bleak slate color. However, the Archway was the outlier and instead of its usual stony hue, brightened. As if I was looking through heat vision goggles, I could suddenly see swirling tongues of energy in blue and purple, flickering from the Archway like a gigantic beacon. A message populated above the Archway, and I quickly read it over.

Hell. Yes.

I turned to the eggs.

"Jumpy. Chompy. Slappy. Clucky. Mortimer," I announced. "Papa's a motherfuckin' genius."

The roe began hopping up and down excitedly, and I played into it by waving my hands around like a conductor, swishing back and forth as though the greatest symphony ever concocted was playing out right in front of me.

"That's right, little homies! Dance! Celebrate this victory, m' babies!"

After just a moment, the others arrived, throwing me glances as though I'd just started shoveling handfuls of mud into my mouth.

"What is this?" Jes asked, giving the possessed roe a wide berth.

"One second," I singsonged, still leading the eggs in their gyration. I closed my eyes, humming tunelessly. Finally, I brought my hands up and then swiped them in opposite directions as if to cut off the flow of music.

"And . . . *fin*," I announced, opening my eyes.

"What the fuck are you doing, orc?" Stinky demanded, sidling through the eggs to poke me in the chest.

"Ow!" I exclaimed. "Easy on the titties, Stinky."

"Please explain why you're entertaining us with this grotesque display, Loon," Merra said. "You're acting as though you've gone mad."

"Ah," I said, flourishing my hands dramatically and winking at her. "I am not crazy, Merra. I've only just *solved all of our problems*."

They all stared.

"Check it out!" I announced, and gestured toward the Archway and began to explain. "I picked up a cute little spell in my journeys—"

"From the devil," Stinky interrupted, but I was undeterred.

"—that I was able to use my brilliance to—"

"Fucked around and got lucky."

"—get us a leg up—"

"Create additional fuckin' complications."

"—and whisk us farther down the path," I finished, eyeing Stinky to see if he'd continue interrupting. He didn't.

"What are ye on about, then?" Frida asked.

"Allow me," I said, and turned to the Archway again. "Ahem. This is a direct quote from a message—that only I can see—above the gateway that was conjured from a spell. You will recall that this occurred because of my gigantic brain."

"Yeah, cuz it's full of hot air, water, and concussions," Stinky said. I glowered.

"*Anyway*," I said, "as I said, my *huge and important* mind grapes have been able to reveal a method of super badass express travel."

I glanced at the message again.

You have used the Discover [Doorway] spell!

You have unearthed a secret exit! You have unearthed additional features to an established passage! This path is connected as a bridge to other areas of the Forbidden Crypt of the Dreadnaught Lord. It allows you to select which dungeon floor and chamber you would like to access. Please note: not all chambers connect to this doorway.

Please choose which floor and chamber you wish to travel to:
Floor One
Chamber 1
Chamber 3
Chamber 5
Chamber 7
Chamber 9
Floor Two
Chamber 1
Chamber 2
Chamber 4
Floor Four

Chamber 2
Chamber 3
Chamber 4
Chamber 7
Exit Dungeon

This is it, I thought. *I could just leave right now. We* all *could.*

But, as tempting as the thought was, I knew the only person who would accept that offer was likely to be Stinky. The others had their mission to bring Merra's magical zombie trinket . . . wherever it was it needed to go, and I still had to wrench Zeol's action figure out of the fifth chamber.

I explained what I'd done and what it meant—with only a *little* bit of gloating. Everyone considered the options. I almost didn't mention the exit, but . . . I didn't want to have a situation in the future where they figured out I'd omitted information—a classic trope if ever there was one. They deserved to leave this place if they wanted to—even Stinky.

"We should move to the fourth floor and the deepest chamber we can," Merra said. "That way, we at least gain back a little bit of the momentum we lost being here for so long."

"Agreed!" Dedyc said. "Give ourselves a leg up!"

"Well, in that case," I said, "I will send you guys there first. Then I can send Stinky to the exit. I, personally, have business in a different spot."

"Where would that be?" Frida asked.

"Uh. The fifth chamber on the first floor," I said. "For a Quest."

"So, we're headin' in diff'rent directions?" Frida asked. "'S'a shame. Just warmin' up to ye two."

"I suppose so," I mumbled. It didn't feel right. I was growing kind of fond of this group, too. It had been a long time since I'd had people that I'd wanted to be around longer than a few minutes. Even Stinky had grown on me—you know, despite him constantly saying he was going to slit my throat or hack my body into bits. But I needed to get Zeol's little gopher mission done so that I could get out of there and hopefully get on a course to figuring out what the fuck was going on. I was a hostage in this world, and I'd only seen a small slice of it so far.

"We're breaking up the group?" Dedyc hissed sadly—you know, however that worked.

"Yeah . . . " I said, scratching the back of my head. "Looks like it, huh?"

I'd noticed that Stinky hadn't said anything so far in relation to this new information. Instead, he had just been staring at the Archway. I figured he'd have blabbered on about how he still needed to drag me to the headsman's block or whatever. However, that would involve telling everyone our immediate backstory—and I was positive he didn't want to throw that wrench in the gears. Even *I* knew that revealing that information would cast one of us in a bad light, and it was impossible to tell which way that would go with this group. They were clearly stronger than me, and I suspected even if they were each near the same Level as Stinky, he couldn't take all of them if they decided to unite against him. Besides... something about what we'd been through in the last day made the encounter at the Redmark camp seem inconsequential. I couldn't put my finger on it, but there was something itching at the back of my mind that told me bigger things were going on. I knew I was forgetting something important, but I couldn't recall what that could possibly be. I didn't know if Stinky would stick to his guns on holding my heels to the fire over his suspicions, but somehow, I was starting to doubt it.

"Nonsense," Calden said suddenly, interrupting my train of thought.

"Eh? What is?" I asked.

"All of it," Calden clarified. "This melodramatic send-off. The idea of separating this merry amalgam is almost too much for my heart to bear. I refuse."

"Enough, Calden," Jes said. "If this alliance was temporary, then that is all it ever needed to be. There is no use attempting to wrest a longer coalition when its natural end is at hand."

Damn, baby. That's cold.

"I hate to agree with Jes," Merra said, giving the elf a wink, "but he's right. We are heading elsewhere, and we shouldn't expect our endeavors to supersede Loon and Akiva's own desires to leave as quickly as possible."

"No," Calden said, and his tone was strangely firm. "I do not accept that result. We—that is, the collective standing here—did not meet by happenstance. I believe it must have been ordained. I am a godly sort—"

Frida snickered at that.

"—and I know the impression of insistent hands of deific providence when I encounter it. It is clear beyond all reasonable doubt that we must keep this fellowship afloat. Think of the benefits, all of you. Akiva—for his robust timekeeping, strength, and insightful intellect—"

His what? I thought.

"—and Loon, for his perseverance and good humor. I cannot abide the idea that we twisted our dear orc out of death's clutches just to set him on the side of the trail and release him to the wilds like an unwanted pet."

"I agree," Frida said. "Makes no fang o' sense t' cast 'em aside now. No' 'en we've already shared the blood o' battle."

"Yes, *exactly*, Frida!" Calden exclaimed exuberantly, his finger wagging in her direction as if he was at the cusp of some brain-busting eureka moment. "And—*and* we are party members!"

"Yes," Dedyc hissed. "Party members are sacred."

"It is effort best not wasted!" Calden continued.

Jes looked between the three of them.

"That is not precisely a finite resource," he said.

"Oh, but you cannot put *friendship* in a box, Jesimir! It is that which gives meaning to life."

"We're all *friends* now, are we?" Virgil said, his voice joining the others for the first time in a while.

"Oh, but of course, Virgil," Calden continued. "Friends, companions, compeers . . . jolly good chums and bruvs."

I was . . . well, *touched*. Calden had strongly suggested that I—and I guess, Stinky—should stay with them. It was an odd feeling, the sensation of knowing I wasn't just being tolerated but actively *wanted* around. Had I really made friends with this strange group of adventurers? I hadn't been requested to join anything remotely friendly since I was a kid. Usually, if it *had* happened, it was a prank of some sort or an attempt to shove me down a flight of stairs or trap me inside of a decommissioned sewer drain.

I smiled. It was time to contribute to the discussion.

"Yeah, we are straight homies, I suppose," I said. "But that doesn't really matter if we are heading toward different goals, right? Nothing can be done about that. It sucks, but I sort of *have* to do this thing—and even though nobody cares what Stinky wants to do, he technically has a choice in the matter."

Stinky made a noncommittal grunt, which I found odd. I'd expected him to stick to his curmudgeonly distaste, but this was different. What was going on there?

"Ah," Calden said, apparently losing steam in his argument. "There is that."

"Aye," Frida said, but her face had a mischievous glint to it. "But Loon. Is ye final destination that chamber?"

"Whatcha mean?" I asked.

"Where are ye goin' *afterward*? Ye jus' goin' to keel over in there, or are ye plannin' to keep explorin' and perceivin' the world?"

"Uh, well . . . " I thought about it. It really wasn't the end of the road, I had to suppose. Surely, there would be shit I'd need to do afterward. It was a good point—at least if I understood where she was going with this.

"Ye comin' around to my way o' thinkin', then?" Frida grinned. "I knew ye were a smart 'un, orc."

"And what is the suggestion, then?" Jes asked incredulously. "We are on a timetable that requires our expedient attention. We cannot wait around for Loon to finish his errand. We have lost far too much time as it is."

"Well," Merra offered, "there is no expiration on the artifact's power. It has no restraint on the time necessary for it to work. We could wait around for another half-century and still be able to utilize it. Loon. How long do you think it would take to finish your Quest?"

I considered this question.

"Well," I said, unsure, "I'm supposed to snatch a—what's the word—talisman. It was pitched as a walk in the park . . . though all of this was supposed to be pretty easy, and I think we know how that turned out. Best estimation on my part? I'd say a few minutes—barring any unforeseen issues, that is."

"And there's no end of that with you," Stinky said.

"Hey, asshole," I said, "I'm not a *Quest doctor*. I don't know what is or isn't usual in a situation like this, so why don't you cut me some goddamn slack? I'm just making this up as I go along. But I have to believe that this will be a quick B-and-E sorta jam, y'know? In and out lickety-split."

"I do not understand this marvelous tongue of yours, Loon, but I believe I gleaned the long and short of it," Calden said, his eyes sparkling.

"Thank you," I said. "I'm honestly flattered you guys would even consider asking me to join you for the rest of your ride. Now, that being said—and if I'm picking up what Frida's puttin' down—I doubt the spell will work if I walk through the gate and leave you guys here. If I sent you guys ahead and *then* did my business, I might never find my way back to you. So, the easiest way around this is to have you guys tag along on *my* leg of the Quest, scoop up the item of importance, and then we all hitch our wagons together—that one was for you, Virgey-boy—and hit up you guys' bonanza."

"I could not have put it better myself," Calden said, then eyed Frida. "I really could not—I am not sure that most of those are genuine words."

Frida laughed.

"Aye, Loon," she said, her eyes finding me and making me feel . . . *some* type of way. "Ye did good. Tha's 'zactly what I were hintin' at. Good on ye."

"Aw, shucks," I said, pretending to fan myself. "You're gonna make me blush, Frida."

"It is an outlandish suggestion," Jes said somberly. "But if this is the course the rest of you wish to pursue, I will not stand in the way of it. I only ask that we do this task quickly."

"It'll be so speedy," I said. "You'll be like—"

I adopted a voice that couldn't even be described as vaguely resembling Jes's for comedic effect.

"'Oh, shit, bro. This was totally so fast! You're like the coolest *bloke* I've ever encountered. Here is all my money and stuff. Buy a castle or something, cuz I'm totally loaded and can easily afford that.'"

Everyone laughed, save for Jes.

"It's like there's two of you," Merra said.

"Which one is the real Jes?" Dedyc asked, rubbing his eyes for effect.

"All right," Jes relented with a sigh. "You have had your fun. I am agreeing, for what it's worth. So, you can do away with the jests at my expense."

I walked over and slapped Jes on the back. It was maybe a bit too hard, but he could handle it. Maybe. The elf winced but didn't turn me into a quivering pile of jelly, so I figured he didn't mind too much.

"However," Jes continued, "if we are going to do this, we must do it properly." He turned to Stinky.

"Akiva," he said formally, "you have not yet indicated if you are going to stay with us or if you would prefer to continue to the exit on your own. If you have designs to remain for a time, would you acquiesce to joining our party?"

"We are a lovely bunch," Dedyc offered.

"The loveliest bunch that currently walks the surface of this plane," Calden said. "Considering what we have seen elsewhere in this chamber, I can say that with confidence. Now, when we walk through the Archway, however . . ."

The blond man shrugged as a way of finishing his sentence.

I turned to look at Stinky as well with a gigantic smug grin plastered on my face. I received a venomous glare in return, and he quickly jerked his head toward the gateway.

"Fine, fine," I said, turning my back. "I'll let you have this one."

I sauntered over to the Arch. My spell had already dissipated, but considering I only had a single spell I could use, my magic—er, Arcana—was still near the top of its max. I quickly said the words again—which was super fucking weird still—and the spell activated. Then, following the prompt, I selected the fifth chamber on the first floor. I took a step back, expecting something to change or maybe to hear like a chime or something—but there was nothing.

"Well, huh," I muttered, disappointed.

Then I felt a different sensation, one I'd experienced recently. Another *presence* joined the collection of others I'd almost forgotten was there. I smiled to myself. Stinky had joined the party.

Someone moved past me, and I jumped. I hadn't expected that, and it had startled me. Calden paused, turning to look at me with a big grin.

"Oh, my dear orc," he said fondly. "We are going to go on *so* many adventures together. I am looking forward to seeing your progression."

"Don't get too excited," I said. "Like I said, I'm probably doomed the moment I walk through that gate. Remember?"

"Nonsense, Loon," he said, resting a hand on my shoulder. "You will outlive us all. Is it active?"

He nodded to the Arch.

"Yep," I said, perking up. "Next stop, Quest town."

"Marvelous," he said with a wink. "See you on the other side!"

Before I could say anything else, he stepped through the portal and disappeared into the purple light.

Dedyc was next, moving past me as well, but just smiled awkwardly with a knowing expression.

"What?" I asked.

"Nothing," he said. "Just happy."

I chuckled.

"All right, all right. Enough touchy-feely. In you go, big guy," I said.

"You're one to talk, big guy," he said, but then ducked into the gate and was gone.

Merra sidled up.

"Good to have you aboard," she said, and I nodded at her. Then she, too, disappeared into the Archway. Virgil was next and just patted me on the back as he passed, followed by Frida. She didn't say anything but offered me a wink—which I returned terribly.

Jes stepped in front of the Archway next, and though he didn't look my way, he did address me.

"Let us make this swift, shall we?" He said, then nervously looked over his shoulder. "Oh, *hell*!"

I heard bouncing and knew that the eggy-boys were hot on his heels. They'd been dogging his steps for the last few hours, and apparently, this occasion was no different. I guess there was something about him they really liked. Jes was gone before I could retort, but I saw one of the roe—Chompy, I knew somehow—collide with the stone of the archway at top speed in his efforts to give chase. He bounced into the air and I caught him on the downturn.

"Easy!" I scolded, righting him and setting him on the ground. "Y'all are gonna wanna take this slow. It might be nothing but knives and broken glass on the other side, and we don't need you guys deflating before we finish this out."

Chompy looked properly reprimanded and sadly slumped toward the gate. I heard the others approaching quickly as well and made to turn, but Mortimer appeared in my vision, bashing into me and knocking me backward.

"Goddammit—" I started, but then I fell right into the opening of the gate and felt myself nearly *sucked* through. I stumbled over what must have been a wet log as I came through, and careened. I slid in a puddle of water and then tripped over a stray rock. I landed hard on stone flagstones with an *oof*, slamming my head and chest on the ground and felt the wind knock out of me.

"Fuck..." I groaned, trying to lift myself up. I was dizzy and in immediate pain.

It figures, I thought. I lay there for a moment, trying to get my bearings. Right away, though, I noticed something was off.

The jungle depths of the last chamber had been pretty quiet, so it was weird that now everything was so *loud*. In my daze, I couldn't really distinguish what the exact difference was, and it took me a moment to figure it out. My heart dropped into my stomach and I launched myself to my feet.

I was in a large room—not as big as any of the previous chambers—but still substantial by most metrics. It wasn't as dim in there as the jungle had been, on account of flickering torches lining the gray stone walls, which helped me to make out the features of this place a bit better. In the center of this room was a humongous statue of some kind of bird-person with their winged arms outstretched. But that was irrelevant to what I was witnessing.

Carnage. Blood. Fighting.

Frida and Merra were racing toward a point with their weapons out, swinging with reckless abandon at something unseen. Frida's ax connected with the air, and I heard a metallic *clang* ring out through the chamber. Merra's sword, however, missed whatever she was aiming at, and she hurtled to the side, attempting to regain her balance. They were maybe fifty feet away from me, and yet I couldn't tell what was happening.

What is going on?! Have they gone fucking crazy?!

I glanced around, looking for the others. Then my heart sank even more. Chompy. The egg was in two bloody pieces on the ground not far from my right, his mouth still frozen in a snarl.

What the hell happened?

Red viscera coated the ground where he lay and, really, everywhere. But that didn't make sense. The roe had yellow, pus-colored blood. That meant...

Fuck! No, no, no!

I wheeled to my left and saw the crumpled body of Dedyc, his eyes open and sightless, his body torn open from neck to waist down the center of his torso. My stomach lurched, as I could see his guts had spilled out into a pile at his side. Next to him was Jes, his eyes closed and both of his arms bent in disgustingly *wrong* directions.

"What the fuck," I whispered, too horrified to even scream. I doubled over and covered my mouth with my arm. That was when I noticed that there was blood *on* me.

No! Do not let this be what I think it is!

I regained my composure for a moment, a deadened numbness flooding my body. I looked back toward the arch, a feeling of pure dread welling up within me, fighting against the dull blackness of emptiness. I spotted a shape, and all the air left my lungs. The log I had tripped over when I'd arrived was *not* a log. It was a body. And it was resting in a pool of thick blood. I shakily moved closer, afraid of what I was going to see, but *knowing* I had to confirm it. Right where I'd fallen was the rock I had thought I'd tripped on. Instead, a head lay in its place. Blond hair was matted with dark blood, and the cocky expression I associated with the face was replaced by anger and confusion. Calden's face stared back at me with its bleak, frozen rage. It would be like that forever.

Why?! I demanded in my own mind. *Why did this happen?! Who did this?! How did this happen so quickly?! I'd only been seconds behind them!*

Some of Calden's last words echoed in my mind.

You will outlive us all.

I was too stunned to think clearly. None of this made sense. Part of me believed in that moment that this was just another one of his pranks and he'd come leaping up at me, pretending to be a zombie or reveal it had been an illusion of some kind.

I turned back to where Merra and Frida were battling their unseen foe. Frida brought her ax down again, bellowing in rage as she did. The edge of her weapon connected again with a *clink*, but then whatever specter occupied the space in front of her acted. With a loud crunch, something struck her in the center of her armored torso and sent her flying backward against the far wall. Her head crashed against the stone and she slumped to the ground. In a flash, Merra appeared in her place, a tornadic frenzy of blade and shield. She sliced through air, but I heard a grunt, and a ribbon of blood traced behind her slash, as she must have made contact with whoever was battling against her.

Then Merra stopped moving, her body going limp. With a fresh new pang of terror, I saw a hole had appeared in her forehead, blood spurting from the wound as she too fell to the ground in a heap.

"No!" I roared, and gripped the blade of my haladie. I raced forward but was stopped in my tracks as I heard laughter. A man's voice cut through the sudden and deafening silence. It was a cruel sound, filled with joy. Where there had been empty air before suddenly shimmered, and I watched as a form materialized in front of me.

It was a man—that much I could tell—with long red hair and a mocking grin on his face. I would have considered him handsome if I hadn't just seen everything unfold the way it had, and as such, all I could think about was how it would feel to puncture his unblemished features with my weapon. The man moved gracefully, stepping around the body at his feet as though he were on the catwalk at a fashion show. He was wearing form-fitting leather armor that seemed to absorb the light around him, and carried a large knife, the tip of which, I realized, was coated in fresh blood.

He stabbed her in the head with that.

His eyes were locked on me as he moved, seemingly uncaring about the destruction he'd just unleashed. Casually, he continued toward me, and stopped about ten paces away.

"Hello, Loon," he said. His tone was sickeningly sweet, as if he took pleasure in what he'd just done. The numbness inside me budged for just a moment as anger tried to well up, but I was still so horrified and confused that it didn't take hold.

I didn't say anything. I *couldn't* say anything. I just stared at this fucking jackal as he smiled at me like we were old friends meeting up for coffee.

"Oh, *this*?" he said, answering a question I didn't ask. He gestured to the room with the hand holding the dagger.

"Don't you worry about it. That was for *them*. Yours is a different fate."

"W-who. Are you?" I managed, my teeth chattering.

Why did you do this? I wanted to scream, but I couldn't manage more than a whisper.

"I am Frey," he said. I didn't recognize the name. Then he continued.

"But you may know me better as . . . What did you call me?"

He pressed the tip of his dagger to his chin in thought.

"Ah, *yes*," he said, and then his smile grew so wide, I was certain it would split his face.

"I believe you called me *Ocho*."

CHAPTER THIRTY-SEVEN

COWBOY MIST

My heart was in a meat grinder. Dozens of conflicting emotions swirled inside me while my brain felt like it was on fire.

Ocho.

So, this motherfucking shitmouth had been the one who'd followed us into the dungeon? Apparently, he'd been able to listen in to my conversations as well, because he knew the nickname I'd casually tossed out to Stinky in reference to him. That meant that he'd likely been invisible the whole time too, just watching us. Why, though? What reason did he have to secretly accompany us?

"Are you a Redmark?" I hissed, gripping my haladie so hard, I thought it might snap. I had a shitload of questions brimming out of my skull, but this was the one that came out first—which surprised me.

Ocho, or Frey, or whatever his name was, simply chuckled.

"Not at all," he said. "I would not be caught in their ranks if they paid me in platinum! But that isn't a bad guess, considering the circumstances you've recently encountered. No, the Redmark are probably still trying to decipher precisely what happened to their campsite, the poor devils. Not the brightest stars in the sky, to be sure. But even *we* have use for idiots of that caliber."

"*We?*" I asked.

"There's plenty of time for further introductions later. However, now is not opportu—"

"Why?!" I shouted, interrupting him, and it actually seemed like it startled him a bit. "Why did you do this? If you were around long enough to fucking eavesdrop, then you sure as *shit* had ample opportunity to do this at any point! Why?"

Ocho shrugged noncommittally.

"I was bored."

"Bored?!" I continued, raising the haladie. "You killed them because you were *bored*?!"

He tilted his head as if he didn't understand.

"Yes," he answered in a tone that made it sound like he thought I was stupid. "I was weary of waiting around, and they presented an excellent chance to invigorate my evening."

Calm down for just a second, I scolded myself. *I need to get information before I go into a rage. I have to be smart for once. Get the details and then unleash pure murder.*

"Then why didn't you do it before, like when we were all sleeping? Why now?"

I was seething but was still hurt and confused enough to keep a lid on my trump card. If I could get him to talk, I could maybe force him into making a mistake. He'd implied he wasn't going to kill me—or, at least, not the same way he'd killed the others. So, that meant I needed to learn as much as I could before he did . . . well, whatever it was he was going to do.

"I didn't have the occasion," Ocho said, flicking some of his red hair over his shoulder. "You realize you were in that second chamber for a very long time, yes? It was dreadful—nothing at all to do except patiently wait. I went ahead right after the first chamber, since I knew this was your ultimate goal."

His eyes flickered to the gigantic statue to our right for just a moment, but it was enough of a tell. For some reason, he thought I would need to use this statue for something, and that was his clue somehow. That was weird.

Congratulations! You have raised a Skill!
Insight [E-Rank Level 2]
Delyra's Musical Mantle of Empowerment temporarily brings this Skill to [E-Rank Level 3]!

"Honestly," he continued. "I wasn't even aware you'd collected allies around you until they stepped through that Archway."

So, he wasn't watching us on the other plane. That's good. It means that even if he was able to spy on me long enough to learn some of my abilities, he didn't suss out my entire bag of tricks. But how did he know about the design of this dungeon? I thought no one had been in here forever.

He'd followed me in there, so I knew he hadn't been trapped in stasis like the others. It didn't make a lot of sense to me—so, that hadn't changed. Yet somehow, he knew enough about the layout to figure out not only where I was going but *how* to get here quicker than I did.

"Oh, I'm sorry you had to . . . what? Sit around with your thumb up your dick before you could off my whole squad? Must have been fuckin' miserable, not killin' for that long, right?"

Ocho grinned so wide, it was scary.

"See? You understand," he said. "Apology accepted."

I scowled.

Oh, no, you don't, Ass-lips. You ain't gonna rustle my jimmies. I'm the jimmy-rustler round these parts.

I breathed slow, fighting to wrangle a hold over my own desire to practically burst into flame and blast this fucker right in his pretty face. I still needed to get some info, but that was going to be difficult. My anger was overtaking every other conflicting feeling I had, but I was able to bottle it—like capping a shaken soda right before it erupted from the bottle. I cleared my throat.

"So, what the fuck is so special about me, then? Did you need someone tall to get your itchy butthole medication down from a high shelf for you?"

"Ah, here it is," Ocho said with amusement. "I was wondering when you'd actually come out to play. I've heard an endless supply of your ornery oaths and was eager to find out what it would be like on the receiving end."

The man shrugged.

"I suppose I'm not very impressed. It wasn't your best. Quite unfortunate, really. You would think that being cursed by being *you*, the gods would have seen fit to provide you with *some* redeeming quality. I suppose they weren't attentive enough the day you arrived—having clearly dragged your own face through miles of pointed rocks along the way."

An ugliness burn? Is this guy fucking serious? He could have made fun of a thousand other things. My smell, my intelligence, the fact that I can't create a long-lasting connection with anyone . . . There was a bunch of shit to draw from, and he decided that attempting to shame me for my appearance was the call?

I'm a motherfucking orc, dingledick. We're supposed to be ugly. That was weak.

"I'll tell you what, bud," I said, motioning to my scantily clad body. "First and foremost—I'm a hot piece of ass, so I don't care what you say. But even if I was *half* as foul as your swampy, leather-wrapped taint, at least I'm not creeping around stalking half-naked *children* and killing *good* people. Fuck you, you dumb son of a bitch. You're going to look even worse than me after I carve six new sphincters into your body. I'm going to *make you* ugly. Answer my fucking question."

If there was one thing I knew about people, it was that a lot of them tended to try to insult what *they* were actually insecure about. This guy was probably so vain, he thought the rest of the world cared as much as he did about being easy on the eyes.

"Ah, I see you're finding your legs and getting bold. I thought you'd take longer to recover from my merriment, but I see I misjudged you. Very well—I will tell you. I gain nothing by not informing you."

His reference to the act of *joyful* slaughter almost sent me over the edge of Slap-a-Bitch Cliff, however, I caught movement near the wall behind him. I stifled myself again and regained my composure. *Be chill. Don't look.*

"You were a bit off the mark," Ocho said, gesturing in a vague direction. "But I believe you have already been told that, so I won't ingrain it further. It is my job to see that you are shepherded back to the appropriate path. While this dungeon-delving escapade has been an interesting little detour—it has become tiresome. Now it's time to take you to your friends. That is when the real fun begins."

"My friends?" I spat. "You just killed my only friends, asshole."

"Call the beasts what you will in your pedantry," Ocho continued. "I refer to those that you arrived with from the other world."

This confirms they're alive! I thought, a sharp stab of hope piercing the horrifying dread that was overwhelming me. *Or whatever it's considered when you're transported to another reality after a long, deadly fall. This changes things.*

I had started to form something of a plan, and now I had to do what I did best: irritate someone to the point of anger.

"So, what?" I asked. "You think you can just kill my fucking party members and I will be happy to fuck off into the sunset with you? Fat chance, shit-for-brains. You must be dumb as shit if you think I'm going to spend a single second following you and your badly styled, glam-band roadie haircut around. What sort of back-alley, spaghetti-fingered crackhead did that to you, anyway? Because *that's* who you should fucking murder. I mean—*Jesus*—did they use a salad fork, or did they just see what monstrosity they were about to release into the world and kill themselves halfway through?"

"Your attempts to goad me are—"

"Goddamn," I interrupted, shaking my head. "Your hair really is just awful. It looks like an orangutan's ass pubes. Is it a wig? It's gotta be a wig, right? I mean, come on—no one grows hair that shitty naturally. Then again, I didn't think anyone would intentionally leave the house like that, so maybe it *is* real. It's probably—"

"Shut your mouth, orc," Ocho said. "I've heard just about en—"

"Holy shit!" I laughed. "You actually *like* it! Fuck, man. That's fucking depressing."

I had seen an explosion of hot anger behind his eyes during my in-person cyber-bullying, but suddenly, it was gone—as if it had just evaporated. Another cruel smirk climbed across the man's face.

Shit, he's better at restraining himself than I am. Go figure.

"That was much better than your first attempt, orc," he said, crouching down to examine the blood from his kills on the stone floor. I internally cringed.

"I'm happy to help," I said. "Brow-busting, *Mean Girl* shit is my *jam*. It's a service I usually offer free of charge, but I think you're fucking gross—so there's going to be an activation fee."

Ocho dipped a gloved finger into the blood and lifted it up to examine it before squishing it between the digit and his thumb, as if checking its properties.

"You're quite strange, you know," Ocho said, his eyes locked at the blood between his fingers. "It was why I offered to follow you in the first place. You see, all signs pointed to you being an utterly feeble-minded clod. A simpleton. Your Intelligence rating indicated as such, and your choices upon entering this place were something even a freshly weaned yearling would advise against. However, it has—for many years now—seemed to me that perhaps our Abilities aren't as precise as we like to believe. Particularly when considering mental faculties..."

He stood again and raised his fingers in the air, showing me the blood-stained leather of his gloves.

"Take this, for instance," he said. "Blood is the very essence of life but also affects so much about *who we are*. I can cut off the flow of blood and bask in the euphoria of ending a life—but there are some who can change the composition of the blood and modify a person to the point that they become wholly deranged or inert. You can stop the flow to an appendage or organ, and it will wither and die. This, too, can happen with the blood in the mind."

Where the fuck is he going with this? I guess as long as he keeps talking, it doesn't matter. The longer he's distracted, the better I can plan.

I had a lot of questions, but asking now seemed like it would be stupid—not to mention a backstage pass on changing the scenario into something less advantageous. I wanted to know how he was aware of my stats. That seemed not only super invasive but also impossible to know without me being a member of his party. I knew that wasn't that case, because I would likely be able to see his. There had to be something else, but it'd have to wait. Maybe there'd be time for a get-to-know-you once I'd pummeled his torso to the ground and was bashing him in the face with a large rock?

"Ah," Ocho said, blinking and returning his eyes to mine. "Apologies, I can be long-winded. To make a very complex issue somewhat less convoluted: I believe that some of the numerical values involved with the way our system works are flawed or incomplete."

I snorted.

"What, you don't think your Charisma is high enough? Figure you should be having an easier time relating to me on a personal level? I got news for you, buddy—"

"To a degree," Ocho interrupted, seemingly unaffected by my taunt. "But, myself disregarded from the conversation, I think that *you* are smarter than your score would suggest."

That actually gave me pause. If this was a tactic, it was one I hadn't considered. *Complimenting* me to throw me off? Damn, that was good. It wouldn't work, but it was good. I was a bit too much of a pain in the butt to let something silly like praise change the course of my actions. But maybe . . .

"About time someone else agreed with me," I said smugly. "I'm a certified brainiac, and I'm tired of the world—uh, *worlds*—not recognizing my greatness."

Ocho wasn't really listening to me, though. He continued his monologue like a 1980s movie villain while staring intently at me.

"The rules, laws, system—whatever you want to call it—seem to take a very literal interpretation of the boundaries of Ability quantification. If you are strong enough to climb a tree but too weak to say, carry a heavy crate—then it assigns a value. This is plain and simple. You raise your Strength score and you get stronger; you get stronger and it raises your Strength score. Easy enough to understand. You can also see these values with the other Abilities. How fast and agile or charming or ferocious one is. At the outset of one's entry into this world—whether natural native or transplant—"

He waved a hand toward me to indicate the latter.

"—the system dictates where you begin, and it is up to that person to forge the rest of their destiny from there."

"Yeah, I get it," I said. "You only get out of it what you put in. It's a libertarian's wet dream. What's your point?"

"My point is that the system doesn't always get it right. Some start out stronger or more robust and hearty—or more intelligent than those around them. Each individual has their proclivities, but the system . . . the laws decide what that is. However, it cannot see inside your mind. It can only affect it, to a degree. It also does not take into consideration the experiences or innate blood-borne qualities that might modulate an individual. That is why the hardest score to raise has been, and likely always will be, Intelligence."

He wiped the blood from his fingers onto his armor absently and cracked his fingers.

"I have known many folk who have intellectual abilities that differ from their Intelligence rating. A simple farmer with an Intelligence of seven, who cannot read or write but can perceive the space he stands in with the clarity of an Oracle—knowing the precise dimensions and volume at a glance. Or a master strategist born with a razor-sharp comprehension in puzzles and problem-solving but fails to understand the basics of the stars or remedial anatomy. Or . . . "

He gestured toward me again.

" . . . an assertive child with a penchant for poor planning and lack of foresight but with an astute grasp of language and guileful solutions to issues."

He smiled.

"I have been watching you for a while, Loon," he said. "You do not possess the ability to perceive the best action for any particular situation, nor do you apply your knowledge in a way that is obvious to most casual observers. But you are able to utilize your surroundings in a way that offers instant results. For instance, your deft and seemingly foolhardy application of the Titanic Strength potion, or your acquisition of . . . the Traveler's Veil. Wonderfully executed chaos on both accounts. Intelligence is specialized—and rarely, if ever, broad. However, the system in place seems to assign it with a single stroke, not knowing what truly lies within the mind of an individual."

"Yeah, yeah," I said. "Make a fish ride a bike, or whatever Einstein said. If you're trying to butter me up to get on my good side, it ain't happening. So what if I'm smarter than the great magical overlord algorithm thinks I am? I'm still stuck in here with you, and even my infinitely massive brainpower can't figure out why that's a good thing."

"Because you will have an option that others will not," Ocho said simply, taking a step forward. "You can jo—"

"Join you?!" I interrupted. "That's where you were going with that, right? Man, you really sounded insightful for a second there, but then you had to go and ruin it with your ready-made, cookie-cutter, last-ditch-effort-before-the-iceberg melodrama. I'll save you the trouble: I'm going to refuse, and you'll be all like, 'That is a pity; you could have been a great asset to our cause,' then we will fight, and spoilers—I fight dirty as hell. Like biting, hair-pulling, ball-punching—all that noise. Let's just skip to the part where you reveal your ultimate plan and I can say something cool like 'Well, plans change, asshole' before kicking you off a skyscraper while a helicopter explodes."

Ocho seemed taken aback for a moment but then smiled again.

"You're only proving my point, Loon. I—and the others in my fold—are planning to dismantle the very system I speak of. We are chained by it. Those in Regaia are bound by its whims, reluctantly toiling against the laws in place. It makes us slaves."

"Yeah, whatever you say Serj Tankian," I spat. "Here's the thing. You can offer me what? Power? Wealth? To be unshackled? News flash, dipshit: I am from a world without any of the magical woo-woo overlord stuff, and guess what? It still sucks big ol' rhinoceros rods. You can talk about freeing yourself or whatever it is you want to do, but it won't change anything for me, since I plan to get the fuck outta here as soon as possible."

"It will change *everything*," he said matter-of-factly. "The system—now that you are a part of it—will not relinquish its hold over you. While it remains, so will you."

"Guess I'm going to have to figure something else out, then," I said. "It doesn't matter what Rage Against the Machine album you grossly misinterpreted to fit your modus operandi, but I know you're not the head coach of this third-string multi-level-marketing scheme. Whatever your plans are, you ain't captain. So, that means everything tumbling out of your lotion hole is boiled horseshit. I can't figure out why you're offering this 'opportunity of a lifetime' to *me*, but I'm going to have to decline. Sorry you didn't add me to your downline. Maybe you'll hit Double Black Diamond Level next year?"

"I am offering this to you because the system, by its very nature, valued you so differently, Loon. It perceived you as waste, as irrelevant. That is why you were discarded—separated from your peers—and left to die in the mountains. That means you have an opportunity the others do *not*."

"Oh?" I asked, not caring what he was saying now. I could see more movement behind him. "I'm trash, so I can fight against the powers that be?" I continued. "Neat. I don't care. There's some nefarious purpose you and your curly-haired girlfriend have brought us here for—and guess what? I'm not going to make it easy for you. Besides, even if you had some super-sweet lucrative offer to hand me, you can't make the decision to keep me alive. You're not the boss. Puppet masters don't do lackey work. I know myself well enough that I am definitely *not* a priority to your overall fuckery. The most important people get the big guns, because the mothership always goes after the White House—and I'm like an understaffed IHOP."

Ocho gave me a pitying look—*Don't even think about judging* me, *you douchebag*—and sighed.

"Well, if you're sure," he said, taking a step toward me, knife out. "You're right that you're trash, but we need *all* the rubbish for our efforts. None can be wasted. I suppose if you're not going to come willingly—"

"*Then I shall have to take you by force*," I interrupted again. Ocho looked a bit peeved that I'd stolen the words right out of his mouth, and I couldn't help it, but I laughed.

"Bro, watch a fucking movie," I said. "It'll help you avoid those dialogue faux pas in the future. Now here's the part where you go to grab me and a *twist* happens."

Ocho scowled.

"The only twist you will experience will be—"

"Your knife in my guts? My bones under your mighty power? Please, say something original. I dare you."

Rather than say anything at all, Ocho growled and lunged. I leaped backward just in time to see him drag his knife through the air where I'd just been. If I wasn't mistaken, he'd been going for the back of my leg.

You were trying to wing-clip me, you son of a bitch? Rude!

I was aware that I was now *much* faster than I had been earlier in the day, and I reasoned that it was because of the gift from Sababo. I was still Fatigued, which would hamper my quick thinking and Stamina but bolster my physical prowess. Why did it work this way? Who knew, but I wasn't going to argue when it was currently aiding me.

Ocho seemed perplexed by my movement but shrugged.

"You got faster? That's all right; I'll just *move* faster."

He shot forward again, but I brought my haladie down to block just in time to hear the *pang* of metal versus metal as his dagger slashed at the back of my knee. He was trying to disable me! I shoved against him, but even with more strength, it was like trying to budge a dump truck, and I tumbled backward awkwardly, tripping on a stone that definitely wasn't a person's head this time. I hit the ground hard but managed to roll to my right and onto my hands and knees. I shot up and forward, hoping my momentum would bring me to my feet. It . . . sort of worked. I got too much force and moved in a motion best described as "almost falling up the stairs." I did tiny, quick steps to keep myself upright until I collided with a wall, but was able to use that to right myself. I turned around just as Ocho was soaring up behind me and flattened myself against the stone behind me to protect my juicy tendons from being slashed.

Ocho changed tactics just as he was preparing to strike and instead rammed the pommel of the dagger into my solar plexus. I heaved, trying to gasp for the air that had just been ejected from my lungs, and doubled over, my legs still flat against the wall. There was a crushing crack on the back of my head as Ocho drove the handle against my skull. I expected for everything to go black, but instead, a cloud of stars filled my vision and I collapsed to the ground. I couldn't do anything else in that moment but think of my legs and clamp my meaty hands over the backs of my knees just before I felt the hot, searing agony of a dagger slashing into them.

I roared, feeling blood trickle out from the backs of my hands. I'd protected my ability to walk for another half-moment, but what would it matter if this motherfucker nullified the use of everything else? I kicked backward against the wall, which sent me rolling forward on the ground, and I was able to stand up and, in the unknown chaos of directionless panic, flung my arms out wildly to protect myself. My hands felt useless at the moment, but I felt my left wrist connect with the side of Ocho's face. I spun to face him.

He stood, his knife still out, spitting at the ground.

"You got blood in my mouth!" he shouted, then wiped his face with the back of his arm. "I cannot tell you how disgusting that is!"

Ignoring the burning in my hands, I forced a grin onto my face.

"I told you I fight dirty, bitch."

I intended to swipe at him with my haladie but realized I'd dropped it on the ground a few feet away when I'd needed to save my leg-pits.

"Fuck," I groaned, and instead used the momentary distraction to tear ass out of there. My foot hadn't even touched the ground before I heard Ocho's quick boot falls directly behind me. I only made it two steps before I knew he was close enough to do something, and dropped to my hands and knees. His legs hit my side at a full sprint and sailed over me, crashing to the ground. I screeched in pain. He must have been mid-swipe when it happened, because his dagger sliced a line up my hip and across my lower back. Fortunately, it hadn't been deep, because of the collision, but *un*fortunately, Ocho had been able to turn his tumble into a somersault. He rotated once and was back on his feet and running at me again in an instant, faster than I could imagine possible. He must have been at least a few dozen Levels above me, which did not bode well for my survivability. The only thing keeping me alive right now was my enhanced physical attributes.

"Now would be a great time for that plot twist!" I shouted, backpedaling as he zoomed straight into my personal bubble.

Ocho struck at me, but his arm suddenly locked to his side in a green flash of light. His legs followed suit as magically constructed emerald binds appeared around him.

Yes! About time! I thought, but while Ocho's limbs had been disabled, his body kept moving, and he smashed into me full-force and sent me flying. I hit the ground again—fuck, I was sick of that—and this time, the force stunned me to the point of momentary immobility. I could still see, though.

Ocho was on the ground a few feet away, fighting hard against the Arcane snare that had him locked up like a frat boy in a hazing ritual. Just a few more feet beyond, I could see a sight that sent my heart soaring. Virgil had his hands in the air, his eyes narrowed in concentration as his spell squeezed Ocho like a stubborn tube of toothpaste.

"Fucking finally!" I shouted, finally able to lurch upward into a sitting position. "I was almost kebabbed like ten times!"

It'd taken me a moment to realize that part of my unease with the situation was the wrenching loss of my party members' connections being torn away from me. However, while Ocho had kept slobbering on about how cool he was, I'd noticed there were still some remaining lifelines in my network. One of which was Virgil. Another was . . .

I saw a glint of steel as an armored shape soared through the air, an ax raised high above her head as she descended like a titan of war, rage and hatred spewing from her lips in a terrifying snarl of murderous intent.

I'd never seen anything more beautiful in all my life.

The movement I'd seen behind Ocho earlier was Virgil moving to where Frida had hit the wall. He had to have slipped into the shadows during the fight—since most of his abilities drew from attacking from a hidden spot. I knew I needed to distract Ziggy Stardust if I wanted any help at all, but it seemed like the cattle rancher had been successful in aiding her. Now she was *pissed*.

Unfortunately, this second of relief was ruined. Just as Frida's ax head was nearing Ocho's neck, the red-haired man broke free from the magic binds and—faster than I could follow—brought both legs up to connect right with Frida's chest. I heard a loud *crack* as she struck his boots and jackknifed in midair like a gruesome game of airplane. Blood sprayed from her mouth, showering Ocho in a vibrant red mist, and she hit the ground in a heap. She'd lost the grip on her ax, and it crashed to the ground with a loud clang.

"No!" I shouted, leaping up and rushing toward her. Ocho wheeled on Virgil.

"Good of you to join in on the fun," Ocho said. "Let's see what other skills you think might work on me."

Ocho zipped toward Virgil as the cowboy raised his hands again and tried to cast some other spell, but he didn't have time. In an instant, the red-haired fiend had smacked Virgil's hands to the side and jammed his dagger right into his throat.

Oh, fuck, I groaned internally.

"I don't blame you for trying," Ocho chuckled, as Virgil stared wild-eyed at him, blood spurting from his wound. "I don't know who you all are, but you're clearly still pretty green in your Levels. I'm Level Twenty-five, unfortunately. You never had a chance."

Level Twenty-five?! What the fuck?! What the actual, hard-boiled fuck?!

There was nothing I could do against someone like that. It was only now dawning on me that anything I hoped to achieve was completely pointless.

Ocho had killed the others, and taken on Frida and Merra at the same time, and they were Levels Fifteen and Sixteen. The Guardian lay nearby, rasping, trying desperately to get a full breath as she stared off into nothingness, her connection to the party fading.

I stopped with sudden realization.

How was the party still intact? Doesn't the leader have to . . .

I looked over at Jes's inert form, his limbs twisted and broken. I could sense it. He was still alive! His lifeline was weaker even than Frida's, but it was still there. I thought about sprinting to him but knew that would be pointless. Ocho would snatch me up before I even got close and chop my knees off.

I was Level Six. I could run away—but I wasn't a coward. I could kill myself, but that would likely send me back to Pontivex. Which would likely be worse. If he was going to kidnap me anyway, I was going to make Ocho's abduction of me the worst thing that ever happened to him.

I stood.

Ocho had been laughing, but suddenly, he stopped, his face twisting into bewildered anger. I couldn't see why until I saw a colorful mist floating through the air in front of him. Virgil was . . . dissolving?

He's a sojourner! This must be what happens when we die.

"No!" Ocho shouted, ripping his dagger out of Virgil's throat and grasping at the fog uselessly. "I didn't know he was a sojourner! Fuck!"

The last thing to disappear was Virgil's face, his mouth upturned into a smug, satisfied grin. He was dead, but he'd be back.

At least one of us will get out of here. See you, mist cowboy.

Ocho turned, raising his dagger and gritting his teeth. Apparently, he didn't like missing out on a big fish, and it seemed this had transformed his devil-may-care facade into cold intensity. It was unnerving, but I didn't care. If I had to play his game, I was going to use *my* rules. I glanced at the giant statue in the center of the chamber.

Maybe I can—

I didn't even get to finish my thought. Ocho shot across the room in an instant and knocked me to the ground—again! I was on my back, and he took advantage of this by quickly climbing on top of me and pinning my arms under his knees, his body weighing me down. I pushed with all of my strength against him, but it was useless. He was too strong. He raised the dagger.

"Thought you weren't going to kill me, asshole," I shouted into his face.

"Shut up, orc," he said. "Enough of you, now. It's tiresome. I'm not killing you; that would be stupid. I won't let another sojourner escape, not after all this time and effort. However . . . "

He smiled so cruelly, I wanted to throw up.

"You don't need your arms to still be of use."

My heart was beating so hard in my chest, I could hear it reverberating off the stone.

Wait. That's not my heart.

Ping. Ping. Ping. Ping.

Another connection suddenly entered my consciousness.

Had it been cut off from the Arch?

That had to be it. Another player had entered the game, and oddly, his lifeline felt *strong*. Like, really strong. Innately, somehow, I knew why—it had to be part of the party system, I supposed. It didn't matter. Fear abandoned me. I threw my head back and laughed.

"It is good to see boldness in the face of your fate," Ocho mused.

"Oh, you are so, *so* fucked," I said in between giggles.

"Doubtful," Ocho stated, though I could see his eyes flickering around him, looking for some trick. He couldn't see the Archway, though. "As you said, I killed all of your friends."

"Yeah," I said. "You did."

But he made it very clear he isn't my friend.

"Enough," Ocho said, and slashed down at my arm with the dagger.

Blood sprayed across my face, but I wasn't worried. I was howling with laughter as Ocho's eyes bulged in confusion, the absurdity of the situation too much for my mind to handle. I seemed to process everything in slow motion as his dagger floated through the air, several of his fingers with it. Then a shaft of metal bowled into the man, sending him crashing away from me.

Stinky stood over me, his arms still extended as he held Frida's ax. The head had broken off of it—perhaps when it hit the ground—leaving only the shaft and the barbed point at the top. Earlier, I'd asked him why he sucked *so* bad at fighting, and he'd told me it was because he had a particular specialization. Now that he was in my party, I could finally see why.

Akiva zun Gara
Matau
Level 27 Spearmaster
Party Member

Stinky glowered, aiming the point of his makeshift pike at Ocho, who was struggling to stand back up. Stinky raised an eyebrow and leaned forward in the red-haired man's direction.

"Let's see how you fuckin' fare now, cockface."

CHAPTER THIRTY-EIGHT

THE RETURN OF THE SMACK

"Stinky!" I called, picking myself up from the ground. "What the fuck?! You're Level Twenty-seven?! How come I beat your ass so bad before?"

"Not the time, orc," Stinky shouted, never tearing his gaze away from Ocho—who was still staring dumbfounded at his missing fingers.

"Oh, yeah," I said, remembering where we were. "Right. My bad. Sic him, Fido!"

"We need to get the everlasting fuck out of here, orc," Stinky said. "I'll maim him while you open that Arch back up."

"Wait, wait, wait," I said, peering around at the carnage, my eyes finding Frida again. "We can't yet. We've gotta rescue Frida—and probably Jes, too, unfortunately. Seems like the right thing even though he's a bit of a dick. Oh, and we should probably bury—"

"No, orc," Stinky commanded. "You will go and open the gate, and we will abandon this place. Don't fuckin' argue; we've got—"

He was interrupted by a piercing, high-pitched peal of laughter.

It came from Ocho. The man was still half-lying on the ground, staring at his hand that was now a little lighter thanks to Stinky and cackling with hysteric glee. It gave me the super willies to hear him, and I took an unconscious step backward. His laughter rose in volume, the intensity making him seem very unhinged, and I quickly looked toward the statue.

I'm supposed to get to that thing. I know it. That has got to be where the . . . thing that Zeol wants is.

I allowed another glance at Frida, who was still weakly trying to survive, and frowned.

I can't do anything! I don't have anything that can help her. No healy magic or potions or anything. If Dedyc was alive, he could do something. If I could use Merra's amulet . . .

But even that was an impossibility. They'd wasted the good stuff on me, and apparently the only other way to utilize it would be to get it to some ghost pond in the crypt's basement to unlock its mega revive power. That was unfeasible as well. Since I couldn't help Frida, I had to get her out of there and find someone who could do something. Maybe Zeol?

If anyone can do something, it would be him. He fuckin' owes me big for this. I'm going to get his little curio, and then I'm going to punch him right in the face. Then I am going to make him save everyone. Then I'm going to punch him in the face again.

I had to stop fantasizing and start acting, though. Stinky told me to open the gate—and I would—but not before I got what I came there for. It was my bargaining chip.

With one last look at Frida, I dashed toward the statue. I could still hear Ocho laughing and wondered why Stinky didn't just attack him right then and there. He was a sitting, literal daffy duck and ripe for the bonking. He'd fucking steamroll Ocho into cream if he attacked. So, why didn't he?

I stopped, looking right at the matau. He was unmoving, holding the same position as before, his makeshift spear in a forward lunge.

"Stab him or something, dickhead!" I shouted.

Stinky didn't even react. He was frozen in place, staring at the maniacally laughing villain on the ground.

"STINKY!" I roared. "Fuckin' do some—"

Ocho's laughter suddenly stopped.

Uh-oh, I thought. *He's up to something.*

The red-haired man stood, tilting his head to the side and looking at Stinky quizzically. Then he began to slowly approach him.

"Oh," Ocho said, removing his gloves carefully and tossing them aside. "Are you unable to move? You're probably wondering why that is. Well, I've made the mistake already of speaking too flippantly, and now I'm aggravated. I suppose you'll die not knowing what spell it was that aided in your quick demise."

A spell? Well, shit, buster. You may have been trying to keep your cards close to your snatch, but you just gave me the moldy morsel of info I needed.

I sighed.

Stinky might not have been able to do anything about being frozen. But I could.

I darted back toward Ocho, *loving* how my new beefed-up speed allowed me to move quick as frick.

"Hey, motherfucker!" I roared as I got within a few feet of him and saw Ocho's eyes flick in my direction. Then a look of amusement passed over his already-too-smug face.

"Oh, this is delightful," Ocho chuckled, turning his body toward me. "Two for the price of—"

I didn't even slow down. I activated my ability and felt power gather in my throat and jowls.

"EXPECTOPATRONUM!"

The word ejected from me like a roar but muddied the words together. I didn't care. It was baller as fuck. As Blackout Warchant worked its magic, I felt the words tear from my jaws like a tangible wave of force and saw a colorless blast of air flash out in front of me, slamming into both of the men. Then I activated my trap card: I used my momentum to rocket my fist right into Ocho's throat. The blow connected a fraction of a second after the wave, and I watched as his hair seemed to blow out like a candle flame. His eyes bulged, and his face contorted as he collapsed backward, making a long hissing, gurgling noise. I'd also noticed that as the wave hit him, canceling out all magic in the radius, his face transformed—and not just from my walloping.

His entire face was different. It wasn't exactly *ugly*, but it was pretty plain in comparison to what he'd been a moment before. I noticed his hair was altered too. Gone were the long, luxurious locks of crimson, replaced by shaggy, ashen-brown tufts and a forehead that practically ended at the back of his neck.

His handsome face is some kind of illusion! And his hairline looks like someone scooped it away with a snow plow.

Congratulations! You have raised a Skill!
Unarmed Fighting has advanced to (E-Rank Level 1)

The morphed—or, rather, *de*morphed—Ocho crumpled in front of me, allowing me a moment to wheel on Stinky. However, as the matau shook off his paralysis and came back online, I saw another ripple wash over him in a sparkling wave of green light.

Uh-oh.

Akiva zun Gara
Matau
Level 12 Spearmaster
Party Member

Stinky's apparent strength had been some sort of spell as well. And I'd just disabled it.

"Oh, *shit*," I groaned, and Stinky scowled at me.

"Just fucking great, orc!"

"Goddammit, that was unintentional!" I shouted. "How was I supposed to know that was magic? I didn't know you could do that!"

"It was the Kameas that demon gave me! Now it's fuckin' gone!"

"Shit! Well, it'll be back in a second. But we don't have time to wait! He's gagging on the ground—which means he probably had some sort of shield up or something before—but it *also* means he's going to recover and then he's going to beat the greasy shit out of us. Grab Frida—and, if there's time—Jes, and run to the gate! I'll be there in two shakes!"

"Two shakes?!"

"Shut the fuck up and go!"

I didn't wait for a response; I just tore ass toward the gigantic statue. I made record time, watching as my Stamina drained with my effort. I was getting fucking *tired*, but I couldn't afford to slow my roll at all. I reached the monstrous plinth at a breakneck pace and slid to a stop in front of it, staring up at its height.

"Shit, how the fuck am I going to climb this thing?"

I snuck a glance behind me and saw that Ocho was just starting to rise again, finally having recovered from my heroic sucker punch. His hair was still short and his face looked like it hadn't reverted back to Chris Evans' hotter brother yet, so I still had a moment to put more distance between us.

"Fuck it," I said, and slid around behind the statue and out of sight of the malformed ne'er-do-well. I concentrated on being both sneaky *and* acrobatic, and hoped that was the eleven herbs and spices necessary to utilize my Skills in a way that would help me out. I had no fucking clue if that was accurate or not, but it would have to do. The statue itself was carved in great painstaking detail and covered in a web of cracks and breaks due to what I imagined was its ancient construction date. I had to figure that maybe some of the contours of the stone would be easy enough to scale. So, having no other course of action, I grabbed onto the first groove I saw and yanked myself up.

It worked!

It was slow going, but I was able to find a few more spots to wedge myself up. It was a lot easier than I thought but still an arduous climb. Hand over hand I moved up, shifting along and creeping around the statue until I'd made it halfway up the endeavor, my position nearly to the front. I looked out into the chamber, seeing Stinky struggling to carry the injured Frida under the bulk of her heavy armor.

Where are the egg boys? I suddenly wondered, and glanced around from my perch. I'd heard them bouncing through the chamber earlier, heralding Stinky's arrival, but hadn't seen any of them the whole time. I spotted a splotch of pink in the distance and my heart fell.

There they are.

The remaining four roe were clustered around the body of their fallen brother, Chompy. They were each sadly trying to prod the dead egg with their own bodies, as if attempting to wake him up. In my mind I could hear faint whimpering noises. It felt awful. A part of me could feel that sense of loss as well, as if a piece of myself had died with Chompy. Maybe part of it was because I was connected to them through resurrection, but a big portion was based on the fact that I'd grown kind of fond of the little guys, and seeing one sliced to ribbons wasn't fair at all. It hurt.

I suddenly felt a hard tug on my ankle, and anxiety and adrenaline flooded my body. I almost lost my grip as a strong hand pulled hard on me. I gripped the stone with all my might and looked down.

Ocho.

"Hello!" he called. He was scaling the statue now as well, one hand gripping the stone, the other wrapped around my foot as he tried to jerk me loose from my position. He was still in his ugly mode, but whatever had faded momentarily, allowing me to hurt him earlier, seemed to have returned to him. His eyes were full of gleeful malice, and he let out a laugh that chilled me.

No, not chill, I realized too late. *Frozen.*

Like ice settling into my veins, my body locked into position as I was subjected to the whims of whatever sneaky spell Ocho had tossed on me. I couldn't move at all, only watch as Ocho released his grip on my ankle and went to the dagger at his waist.

Fuck! Fuck! Fuck! FUCK!

What could I do? I was out of moves. He wouldn't kill me, but he was going to maul me and drag me off to whatever glue factory his crew used in their sojourner machinations.

Think! Think! I shouted in my own mind.

Think! Think! came a response.

Holy butt-paddlin' Christ!

The roe could hear me. I couldn't move, but I forced all of my concentration toward screaming my head off in my mind to try to reach them.

Guys! I need your help!

Help? Help! Guys. What?

Ocho flashed the dagger up at me, grinning ear to ear.

THIS MOTHERFUCKER KILLED CHOMPY! I howled mentally.

There was silence in my mind. I couldn't tell if they'd heard me or not. For a moment. I didn't hear a response, but I *felt* one. Anger flooded my mind. It wasn't my emotion, but I could still sense it, bubbling, boiling—a pot of venom simmering on a stovetop. This was the rabid rage of combined pain and maddening, animalistic fury of a crop of creatures who had a less-complex understanding of the world, but they knew loss. They also knew vengeance.

Arcane power enveloped Ocho again, his hair flickering back into its full, scarlet magnitude and his face shifting back into the handsome, manicured features he'd worn when I'd first seen him. Dagger poised, he tightened his grip and struck at my leg. The point pierced the muscle of my calf, and blood gushed out, sending a lightning bolt of pain up through my leg and through my body. I couldn't scream out loud, but I did so in my mind. I was trapped, unable to do anything except bear the intensity of the stab and exist in that moment of horrible agony. I wanted to shudder, to spasm, to lash out, but I could only watch as he pressed the blade deeper, slowly turning it to completely ruin any chance I had of using that leg to kick his teeth out of his face once the spell faded. This was excruciating and the worst physical pain I'd ever endured in my life. To make matters worse, Ocho was smiling the whole while, delighting in the searing torment he was inflicting on me.

Ping. Ping. Ping. Ping.

A blur of pink struck Ocho in the face. But it didn't fly away. No, it stuck there.

Slappy!

The little bastard clung to Ocho's face like a lamprey, sawing into the man's flesh with razor-sharp fangs. Three more blurs hit him in the neck, the back of the head, and the hand holding on to the rock, suctioning on, as Jumpy, Clucky, and Mortimer followed their brother into battle.

Get him, boys!

I could only see one of Ocho's eyes, as the other was obscured by Slappy's surprise lunch attack, but it was wild and crazed. Apparently, this dipshit didn't know what to do about it, because he began thrashing in place, trying to shake them off of him, as his hands were occupied. Unfortunately, this caused him to plunge the dagger farther, gouging me even deeper as blood began to gush from the wound in my leg. A notification popped up in my vision.

190/302 Health remaining!
Condition: Severe Bleeding
Will continue to lose Health while suffering from this effect at a rate of 20 per 10 seconds.

Dammit, that's not good!

There was no way I was going to survive at this rate, and I still couldn't move. Fortunately, the intensity of the bites must have gotten to ol' Number Eight, because he released his grip on the dagger so that he could swat at the eggies. However, they'd apparently figured out a few more stratagems since I tussled with their kind at the entrance, because as he did so, they released their hold all at once and fell to the ground.

Ocho relaxed for a single second, but he shouldn't have. I would have smiled if I could have, because I knew how gravity worked for this particular brand of monster.

PING. PING. PING. PING. My boys hit the stone hard, and from the height they'd fallen, it acted like a souped-up bouncy castle, and they flew back up at their foe. Now they were using pack tactics, because each and every one of those beautiful bastards targeted Ocho's free hand and latched on to his flesh. He howled with pain and began bashing them against the stone. I was worried for a moment that his strength would smash them to bits—but then I remembered that even when I'd been 'roiding out on Titan juice, I'd still only killed *some* of the roe with blunt-force trauma. This proved to be true, and my little buddies held on tightly as he pummeled them wildly against the statue's cracked face. He pulled back his fist, and I saw a spark of Arcane energy glitter from his elbow.

Shit, he's going to do something shifty.

As he punched forward—presumably to blast them to smithereens against the stone—I sent out a mental command.

Release!

Jumpy, Slappy, Clucky, and Mortimer all dropped away from his arm just as it collided with the hard surface of the statue. There was a loud, shattering crunch and a spray of blood, followed by a wailing screech as Ocho's closed fist exploded against the rock. He howled louder, pulling back his smashed stump to examine it. The pain was apparently enough to weaken the spell's hold over me, and I was ready. I wrenched the dagger out of my calf and hurled it—blade down—into his face. Unfortunately, Ocho was too quick for that, his unmarred hand snatching the blade out of air mere millimeters from his unprotected eyes. Fortunately, that was the hand holding on to the statue. He fell backward, windmilling his arms as he plummeted toward the ground far below.

"Suck it, ya doofy bitch!"

However, he twisted in midair as he dropped, landing on the ground in a roll, and stood, staggering as he did. His ankle buckled beneath him, but he caught himself. Apparently, his fall had been a little harder than he'd anticipated. I grinned despite the burning agony in my leg and turned back to the task at hand. Summoning all of my strength, I forced a three-limbed climb, hobbling my way up and to the extended arm of the statue.

Back off for now, I commanded the roe. *Wait for my cue.*

I didn't need them being needlessly slaughtered, and even with one working hand, I had no doubt that Ocho could inflict serious damage upon the little egg creatures. However, I knew it'd be harder for the gigantic prick to reach the top with one of his climbing paws out of commission.

I heard the sound of scraping and looked down.

Never mind!

Ocho, bound and determined to knab me, was quickly scaling the goddamn statue with only one hand! I'd never seen someone so deftly clamber up a vertical space before in my life. Not even on TV.

He's a goddamn spider monkey!

I'd misjudged him. But I was almost to my goal. I put some pep in my schlep and heaved myself up the last few feet to the extended arm of St. Birdman, and rolled onto my back, heaving for air.

My Stamina was low, and blood was pouring out of me faster than a vampire with diarrhea, causing my Health to plummet enough to resemble my middle school's fundraising thermometer. I was in dire straits without a life preserver. I only lay there a moment, knowing I had to move or my I'd-rather-be-fishing posture was going to be easy pickins for Captain Kidnap. I vaulted onto my hands and knees and stood. That's when I saw it.

Resting in the center of the giant stone palm was an object that instantly read as *Zeol's Talisman*. It was probably eight inches tall, made of black stone—or maybe metal—and fashioned to look like an ancient wizard's tower. It was like a piece from one of those model villages—you know, if the designer was super into *Magic: The Gathering*. It sat on a tiny platform, practically screaming that it was an item of importance.

Say no more.

I limped forward, hissing with pain with each agonizing lurch. The talisman was fifteen feet away from me, just within hobbling distance—but then I heard a shuffle and scrape behind me.

"Fuck!"

I wheeled around, expecting to see Ocho slopping into view, but there was nothing.

Invisible! I thought, jerking back, remembering his trick only a half-second before I felt another searing slash across the outside of my knee. A gash appeared as if by magic, welling up with blood. It wasn't deep, but it still hurt. Fortunately, I'd stepped back enough to avoid this dumb asshole's sneaky tendon-slice maneuver.

"Fucking *ow*!" I roared, swiping at the air with my fist. "Stop doing that, you buttmunch!"

I connected with nothing but heard a delighted chuckle to my left.

You wanna be the incredible invisi-bitch, eh? Not on my watch!

I spun to my left and felt power well up in my throat again as I activated Blackout Warchant again. I opened my jaws to scream something super badass into my red menace's face, and the world suddenly spun. I was dazed for a moment but definitely remembered the immediate and loud sound of crunching bone. Then pain filled my entire existence, rocking my whole face and head. My vision swam and I staggered. Something had happened to my face. It felt like I'd been hit with a sledgehammer. My jaw was on fire. Before I could get my bearings, I felt something connect with my chin again. More bone-crunching. More blinding pain. I stumbled backward and—worried I was going to fall to my death—had the sense to activate Enduring Perch.

It took me a second to realize what had happened. Ocho had uppercut me. Twice. Hard. Now I couldn't even open my jaw, because it was definitely one hundred percent broken.

Condition: Fractured [Mandible]
- **Will continue to lose Stamina while suffering from this effect at a rate of 1 Stamina per 5 second(s).**

Fuck!

He'd effectively, and gruesomely, nullified my ability to knock him out of invisibility—or anything else. That meant that unless there was a heavy lag time between his instances of casting it, he'd probably hit me with his Red Light Green Light stop-motion bullshit.

Another blow landed to the side of my head, but despite the jarring surge of pure torment, I was able to hold on to my Enduring Perch. I heard a grunt of frustration to my right and moved to block my head but immediately felt a spike of pain in my ribs. He wasn't even trying to stab me now! He was using me as a punching bag, taking out his rage with raining body blows.

"I hope this is what you intended by running off," Ocho declared, now behind me. I twisted to avoid another attack, but there was no indication of him, and then felt a fist smash into my right ear.

"You will be mangled and battered, but don't fret, Loon: the killing will not come."

I needed to figure out a way of leveling the playing field, but I was in an incredible amount of pain, and my thoughts were running wild.

If only I had a way to get stronger, like Stinky's cursed demon gift . . .

Well, I actually could do that—-it might just take a minute. That meant I had to risk using something I only had the foggiest daydream of an idea on what it actually did. But, based on the naming convention . . . it *could* possibly work. Maybe.

I focused on the Ring of Redoubt under my glove and could feel the tingling of latent magic inside of it. I wasn't even fully certain how I did it, but, like a lot of the things in this world, I was just able to activate the Fortification spell, as if my brain was already hardwired for the process.

Fortification
- *Arcane Cost: 50 Arcana*
- *Casting Time: Instant*
- *Range: Self*
- *Duration: 30 seconds*
- *Restrictions: Material/Imbued Object*
- *Wait: 1 minute*

A spell that casts a protective barrier on the user. While active, this spell will reinforce the user, dampening physical attacks by 30 percent. Additionally, any user-targeted magical attack effectiveness will be reduced by 10 percent. Finally, this spell will grant a temporary boost to maximum Health. Outcome for efficiency is Constitution + Strength quotient.

Yeehaw! I thought, then felt immediately ashamed that those words were the ones that popped into my head. The spell essentially allowed me to last a little bit longer as Ocho's personal whack-a-mole, as long as I didn't run out of Health. The boost to my full hitbox likely wouldn't help in this scenario, since I was already *well* into this pain party, but I'd have to keep that in mind for the future. Sure, it would have been nice to have, but my focus was on carving out a bit more time to work toward my plan, and this would definitely help.

There was another scuffle near my right, and knowing this was an obvious feint, threw my hands up to block the back of my head. It didn't work. This time, when the crimson crack whore struck me, it was exactly where the sound had come from. However, the damage dealt was considerably less painful than before, almost as if there was a layer of rubber against my skin to absorb the blow.

Don't get me wrong, it still fucking hurt, but it was negligible this go-around. I did some more hands-on intensive study of Ocho's personal fighting style for a bit longer—taking a beating that would make some boxing coach proud, I'm sure—until I finally saw my Stamina dip to almost empty. I released Enduring Perch and quickly dove into a roll toward the talisman. I made it a quarter-roll before I felt a kick that sent me flying forward and onto my stomach.

I pushed myself up but then felt an arm loop around my neck from behind, tightening in a chokehold. It pinched my lower jaw as well, sending an absolutely monumental amount of agony coursing through my body, and I roared in pain. I yanked on the arm, trying to free myself, but only received a chuckle and rock-solid resistance in response. The worst part about it was that this close, I could smell Ocho, and he had an infuriatingly good scent, and it was weirdly familiar.

Lavender.

I stopped struggling for a second, and Ocho used that opportunity to drag me up and backward into a sitting position. I'd recently encountered someone else who had an identical perfume.

His odor isn't as strong as Fawn's was, almost as if this is a lingering smell. But it is *the same one, I'm sure of it.*

Ocho *had* mentioned being impressed with using the Trespasser's Veil—and he knew its name. Had he been there the whole time? The thought would have made me feel some type of way, were I not currently allowing the man to practice his wrestling moves on me. I had some questions for this slimeball.

I gasped, trying to speak, but Ocho was too busy strangling me. I released a string of garbled hisses and gags, trying to make my point understood, but to no avail. My eyes began to roll, scanning the room that I now had a perfect view of from my vantage point. Fat lot of good it would do. I could see my Stamina bar draining again as my vision began to pepper with sparkles and dark spots that were the precursor to passing out. My thoughts got lazier as oxygen fought harder and harder to make its way into my brain.

Ah, look at that. It's Stinky.

I could just make out his shape against the dark stone of the wall far on the other side of the chamber. Not that great of a distance away was the Archway—inactive and showing blank stone within. I could see Frida's prone form there, as well as Jes.

That's nice, I thought dreamily. *Looks like Stinky had enough time to gather them. That Archway must not be the regular entrance to this room. Huh. That's neat. I hope whatever Stinky's digging around for is going to help them get out.*

The matau was pulling apart a pile of rocks hastily, searching the rubble urgently for something, but I had no idea what that could be.

Condition: Fatigue II
- **Negative 10% to Skills and Intelligence, Wisdom, and Charisma Attributes.**

The notification popped up, but I couldn't be bothered. Absently, I remembered that it was the whole reason I was trying to exhaust myself, but couldn't really recall why.

Oh, well, it was fun while it lasted.

My thoughts drifted away from me. I was definitely passing out now, and time seemed to stretch for the moment. It was odd, though; I felt the presence of another individual. Or was it two? I glanced up, and while I was definitely still on the arm of the huge, cracked statue, I was also sitting in a pool of water surrounded by mushrooms. Two massive shadows loomed over me, nearly identical in shape. Like floating shields, though I couldn't make out their finer features. It was the haze of a dream, and I seemed to be stuck in several worlds at once.

Loon, said a voice. The tone was odd, like two people speaking at once or one of those Mongolian throat singers that can hit multiple notes at the same time.

We do not have long. You must reach the talisman, the speaker said.

I smiled.

Sure thing; I'll just float over there after my ghost leaves my body.

Unlike in most scenarios, I wasn't being sarcastic. This seemed like a perfectly reasonable solution at the moment, and I was more than happy to oblige in my oxygen-deprived state.

Loon, the dual voices continued in unison. *We can assist you only once more. After this, we will be gone from you for a long, long time. We have greatly enjoyed watching your progress, but our time is at an end. We are so glad we took the opportunity to peer through the gate and follow you on this portion of your journey.*

Oh, that made sense. This was Zeol and Sababo. Nice to see them working together on this. I hadn't known either of them long, but it didn't matter. They were saying their goodbyes for some reason. I thought that maybe I didn't like them, but I couldn't remember why. It didn't matter. Sometimes, even annoying people had to give their regards.

You and your friends are trapped here, by forces even beyond those that brought you to Regaia. We, like you, are subject to the whims of these forces. This communication is the last that we can grant you. Please treasure our gifts.

Okay, see ya later! I said happily.

Loon. Listen to us. You must retrieve the talisman. Then you must escape and find the others from your world.

You got it, dudes.

You are not listening. We know that you in peril at the moment, but it is important you absorb this information. The only hope that you have of getting back to your world, and we to ours, is to destroy the system that rules over this realm. It is imperative you remember this. Once you have the talisman, everything will change. This entire plane will be hunting you, desperate to stop you. You are trapped here, but you will need to fight to escape. Do not remain a hostage.*

I tried to nod, but my neck wouldn't move. Whatever they wanted, sure, that was perfectly fine. I could see Stinky had apparently found what he was looking for and was now facing me, holding something big and unwieldy in his arms.

Words floated in front of me, obscuring the two shadows from my sight.

Because of Fatigue II, Loon's Bombastic Beatdown Aegis has temporarily reached Tier II effects.
- Strength Attribute increase [+8 multiplied by 150%]!
- Dexterity Attribute increase [+8 multiplied by 150%]!
- Constitution Attribute increase [+8 multiplied by 150%]!

Strength: 50 (Fatigue II)
Dexterity: 50 (Fatigue II)
Constitution: 96 (Fatigue II) (Ring of Redoubt)

Instantly, the hold on my throat seemed to lessen, and my Health pool stopped decreasing so rapidly. Air bubbled into my brain, and I felt high for a second as the sweet, nourishing elixir of life restored the balance to my long dormant brain cells.

Fuck. Zeol and Sababo are trying to get me to do shit? I'm being held hostage? Well, no doy, *dingledumps, that's been apparent since Jump Street. What are they talking about, though, with the whole* leaving forever *thing? I gotta—*

Here is the last thing we can offer you.

Before I could respond, images flooded my brain.

The television in my old apartment is radiating illumination into my dark bedroom, the sole light as I sit on my moth-eaten bed.

A noise.

It doesn't sound like the usual rigamarole typical of this neighborhood. I climb off the couch to investigate.

A door. Roger's room.

People inside. There's screaming.

I'm running, trying to get to the front door.

A shape looms behind me as I struggle with the deadbolt.

I'm on the ground.

There is a knife.

I am screaming.

The hairy face of a man, eyes wild with anger. Dad. Why is this happening? How did he find us?

I'm bleeding, lying on the carpet in front of the door. I'm screaming. I can still feel the knife. Dad stomps back down the hallway. He's doing it again. First Mom, now us. I am frozen with fear.

I hear the screaming still. Roger. He's going back to his room.
I can still feel the knife.
No, I don't want to see this ever again.
But I can't escape this.
I can still feel the knife.
I can still feel the knife.
I force myself to my feet.
Roger.
I'm holding the knife.
I can feel the knife.
I hear screaming. I'm screaming.
I'm so terrified.
Blood.
I'm so sad.
More blood.
I'm so FUCKING angry!

The images cleared from my vision as venomous wrath boiled in my blood. I grabbed the arm choking me and *wrenched*, hurling it forward, and saw a glimmer of distorted air as the invisible Ocho flew over my head, landing hard on the cracked stone. I couldn't see him, but I knew he was there. I could smell his putrid stink. It smelled like lavender. It smelled like a corpse.

I stood, the images having done their job. Faintly, I could hear Zeol and Sababo's voices, as if they were miles away now, fading from my awareness.

Goodbye, Loon. We must hide. Retrieve the talisman, destroy the chains holding all of us here, and most importantly—if you encounter the Drifter . . . run.

A maniacal laugh escaped from my broken jaw as the white-hot fury built up within me once more. I was only partially paying attention to them now. I didn't know who the Drifter was—though it sounded familiar—but I didn't care. I was going to destroy everything. This fucking derelict in front of me. This dungeon. The fucking forces that brought me there and refused to let me leave. Whoever the motherfucking Drifter was, I'd tear him apart if he made the mistake of encountering *me*.

I had entered my Primal Rage once more, and it felt *heavenly*. The notification was still in my vision. But it was different now. The previous numbers were higher. I recalled that Primal Rage also boosted some of those bad boys.

Good.

Strength: 83 (Fatigue II) (Primal Rage)
Dexterity: 83 (Fatigue II) (Primal Rage)
Constitution: 170 (Fatigue II) (Ring of Redoubt) (Primal Rage)

I took a step forward, not caring that my leg was still bleeding out, nor that my jaw was likely destroyed beyond any chance of fully healing. It felt fucking fantastic. My field of vision was narrow, adrenaline pounding in my veins like drums of war. I couldn't see my foe, but that filled me with joy. I heard the scrape of boots on stone, and I sucked in a deep breath and felt further power gathering in my throat.

I released Blackout Warchant with a roar mightier than thunder, more bestial than a prowling predator, more terrifying than death. My jaw crunched with the strain, and I welcomed the sweet sting. The blast flew directly in front of me, and I watched as the ugly stain on life that was my enemy appeared from the void, his hair thinning and short, his simple face frozen in surprise. I'd removed both of his pesky illusions, and now . . . now he was going to get a *real* show.

He opened his mouth to speak, but I was already moving forward. Faster, stronger, harder to kill than ever before. I was a god of wrath, a being of rage and hate—parched from my long removal from my dominion of chaos.

Now I would quench my thirst.

CHAPTER THIRTY-NINE

THE WORLD'S SEXIEST KARATE CHOP

My closed fist collided with Ocho's face with a satisfying crunch, his cheekbone crumbling under my force. He made a screeching warble, but I followed up with a chop to the throat—his second of the night. It was greedy of him to accept my offer of unyielding violence, but I was more than happy to oblige.

Congratulations! You have raised a Skill!
Unarmed Fighting has advanced to (E-Rank Level 2)

The judo slice to his Adam's apple dropped him to the ground, but he recovered quickly, executing a very acrobatic reverse somersault, and was back on his feet a moment later. But I was already going after him, bowling over and on top of him, my hands grasping the back of his head and delivering a punishing kablam to his unprotected face. I tried again, but he twisted to the side, my fingers unable to stay connected with his scalp. I was mid-follow-through and fell forward onto my face on the stone.

I felt several quick stabs to my side as his dagger needled away at me, and I roared, shooting a hand out, grabbing him by the neck, and yanking him toward me. The dagger flashed again, and suddenly my arm was seething with gashes from his riddling. I was fast, but apparently, he was still faster. No matter. I held on to his throat, gripping tight, but he slammed the pommel of the dagger against the inside of my elbow, and my hand opened on reflex. He rolled away again, dancing for a moment as he almost went over the edge of the arm. I raced forward, intending to ram him over the side, but he dove away. I, however, did not have enough time to stop and tumbled off the precipice and toward the stone floor a hundred feet below.

I screamed with rage, my thoughts clouded by my pure, instinctual desire to cause as much destruction as possible.

Fuck this ground, I thought to myself. *I will kill* it, *too!*

However, whatever may have transpired during my climactic duel with the rapidly approaching earth was not to be. The eggs had my back. They clustered together beneath me and, as I hit them, acted as a trampoline, sending me right back up from whence I'd come.

"Fuck, yeah!" I roared as I ascended through the sky like a gigantic, angry green messiah. However, gravity be a motherfucker, because, even considering the additional kinetic energy provided by the roe, I overshot by a few dozen feet, and when my inertia faded, I was forced to hurtle back to the arm at a painful speed.

I hit the stone hard, landing on my feet, but the shock sent me falling forward. I landed on my hands and knees, noticing my collision had cracked the stone arm of the statue a bit more. I didn't wait. Ocho was almost to the head of the bird statue and looked like he was planning on climbing up and out of my reach. I couldn't let *that* happen.

I stuffed my hand in my pocket, withdrew the small object within, and hurled it at him. Just before it reached him, I was able to manage to shout.

"Feather Chest: Maximize!"

The big ol' fantasy steam trunk exploded outward and slammed right into Ocho, smashing him against the stone chin of the statue.

"Fuck, yeah!" I roared again, my cognitive capabilities severely diminished while I was both Fatigued and under my hulking stupidity power. I raced after Ocho and slammed my shoulder into the chest as I reached it. I heard a loud cry of pain from the other side. I could see the back of Ocho's balding head poking out, so I reached forward and punched it. His head bounced off the rock, so I hit it again. It was like a speed bag that doubled as revenge.

Consequences! I thought.

I slid the chest back a couple of inches so that I could ram him again, but that was a mistake. Ocho dropped low and darted out from beneath it and between my kilted legs. He raked the dagger across my naked thigh as he passed, and it hurt, but my overabundance of protection mitigated the majority of the damage. So, I pivoted. Literally.

Congratulations! You have raised a Skill!
Improvised Weapon has advanced to (E-Rank Level 2)

Grabbing the gigantic chest with both hands, I swiveled my hips and swiped at Ocho's retreating form. However, there was an issue with that: I'd forgotten how light the chest actually was—though using it on Ocho had been surprisingly effective. I mean, the fact that it was called the *Feather Chest* should have kept that reminder fresh in my mind, but you'll have to remember that I was a towering battle boner of fury at the moment, so little details like that escaped me. The motion sent me spinning forward, but I activated Enduring Perch and rescued myself from a mean case of the danger dizzies. I'd lost my grip on the chest and it clattered away, cartwheeling down the arm and over the side.

I was undeterred, though. I shot up triumphantly, roaring with happy rage and focused on Ocho. He was at the other end of the arm already and was beelining straight for the talisman. But in that moment, I couldn't give a quarter shit about that item. I just wanted my just desserts paid in blood and screams.

I took off, chugging along the narrow path of the arm like a linebacker with a vendetta. Objectively, I supposed that was actually a pretty accurate description of myself. Anyway, I was halfway to my goal when Ocho reached the tiny platform Baby's First Wizard Tower was resting on. He paused for a moment, which allowed me to close the distance more, but then I saw why: his hair was reappearing. His illusion had returned.

The bastard turned to smirk at me before leaning down to snatch the talisman from its podium.

There was a magical crackle and then a dome of vibrant pink light flared into being around the talisman, ending right where Ocho's remaining hand had been. He was hurled back a few feet onto his ass, smoke curling from the exposed flesh of his hand. He squealed hoarsely in pain, and for once, I was hoping he wasn't *too* injured. That would take all of the fun out of this.

My Stamina was getting low, but I made a push and scraped by the last few feet. Ocho was facing away from me.

Fuck, yeah!

I didn't stop. I didn't slow down. I *sped up*. Then I kicked the man as hard as I could in the back. I heard a snapping noise as I connected, and the force hurled him forward again—right into the dome of hurty. He crashed against it and screamed, rebounding once more and into my open arms. I caught him and instantly slammed him against the stone again, watching as more cracks appeared. Then I kneeled down and started pummeling him again.

Punch. Punch. Punch. Punch.

I laughed maniacally as I did so, blood dripping freely from my mouth.

SHINK!

I felt hot blood spray against the back of my thigh, and looked down to see the battered and bruised face of Ocho. He was smiling. I could see blood pouring down my calves in rivulets.

He's finally done it! He's sliced apart the back of my knee.

I couldn't make sense of it at first, but Ocho took the moment of pause as an opportunity and rolled away from me and out of reach. I tried to grab at him, but he was too quick, and I only succeeded in making my leg collapse beneath me as I lunged. It was no longer able to support my weight. In this state, it was hardly relevant to me. I still had one good leg, and all I needed those for was clobbering, anyway. I vaulted forward, dragging myself along with my hands and good leg like an orangutan, swiping at Ocho when I thought I was close enough. My anger and rage kept me blind to what was happening until it was too late.

Ocho had led me along and then stopped. I tried to take advantage of this like he'd done with me, but as I flung myself at him, he sprang to the side and over my shoulder to land behind me. That was the point when I smashed head-first into the protective dome around the talisman.

I screamed as the skin of my face felt like it was being stabbed, burned, and sent through a paper shredder all at once. I felt a weight behind me and realized in a panic that Ocho must have been holding me down against it. With only one good leg, I couldn't gain enough leverage in the struggle to push back. I was, however, able to turn over to face him head-on. In a tremendous amount of torment, I managed to pivot, but my shoulders and the back of my head were still currently being abused by this bullshit-ass energy enemy. I was still crying out, pain emptying me of all but my insatiable fury, and I struck out blindly at Ocho.

"Ha!" he crowed, hopping out of range for a moment and then doubling his efforts as he lurched forward again. Then a crossbow bolt struck him right in the collarbone. He fell over, wailing, his fingers clenched around the shaft of the bolt that had pierced him. However, it was on the side with his single remaining meat paw. And with only one hand for grabbin', he couldn't get the angle well enough to pull it out.

Like a dumb, predictable turd, I looked to where I thought the attack had come from. Far below, Stinky was reloading Virgil's crossbow, and I suddenly realized what he'd been fucking around with back when I was getting asphyxiated into sleepy town.

I looked back at Ocho, and could feel my rage abating.

Shit! I gotta take advantage of this or I'm gonna be toast.

"Let me help you with that," I grunted, and slammed my palm against the end of the bolt, wedging it deeper into Ocho's screeching torso. Then I grabbed him by the ankles and hefted him over my shoulder.

Don't worry; I've done this before!

I hopped up to my one capable leg and gripped Ocho tight enough to hear a *crack*, then I whipped him forward and smashed him against the stone like I was laying down railroad spikes. Speaking of spikes, the force of the blow stuffed the crossbow bolt farther into Ocho's beauty bone.

Hammer, meet nail.

After a few of those, I swung Ocho and released him directly into the path of the dome. He hit it, and, of course, I'd forgotten that I could hardly stand. He rebounded again and flew right at me, knocking me over as he landed on top of me . . . where he immediately began frantically stabbing me in the stomach.

I'll say one thing: he may have been a total douchebag murderer with bad hair, but he did *not* have trouble acting fast when he saw an opening. I started punching him from my back, trying to dislodge him, but he didn't stop. I punched, he stabbed. We were a good team.

Even with my rage-enhanced damage mitigation, I was nearing the bad place on my Health bar, and that was when my Primal Rage finally dissipated.

Fuck, no!

I knew my physical Attributes were much higher than usual, but they weren't going to be anywhere near where they'd just been. I had to stop this fight *now*. I peered around quickly, and, having no other recourse—utilized the one trait I hadn't yet taken for a test drive. Everything I'd just endured hit me like a freight train, but I somehow managed to fight back the ensuing convulsions and focus. Fortunately, it was enough to get the information I needed. Call it adrenaline, or call it willpower; I wasn't ready to be taken to Ocho's spooky lair just yet. I was still flat on my back, but all of the man's weight was on my legs. As he reared back to stab my belly for the five hundredth time, I performed the first sit-up of my life and snatched his forearm, holding his dagger hand aloft. For good measure, I punched him right in the mangled stump of his destroyed hand—you know, just to be a dick.

Over his yowls of pain, I screamed down to Stinky below.

"Shoot him again!"

I didn't know what his handicap would be on the range, but so far, his average was one out of one, so maybe I could take Señor Shithead out with this effort. I heard the *clack* and *spring* of the crossbow firing, and I hoped to Zeol and Sababo that he didn't miss.

He didn't miss. But he also didn't hit Ocho. Instead, Stinky's shot sailed up and stuck directly in the exposed flesh on the bottom of my bare foot.

"What the fuck!?" I screamed, still holding Ocho and turning to glare down at Stinky.

The matau's eyes were wide, but when he caught my gaze, he hurriedly returned to reload the weapon.

"That fuckin' hurts! Fuck!" I screamed. Ocho tried to wrestle himself out of my grasp, but it was no use—I was roughly his equal at the moment, at least as far as knife-grappling was concerned.

"You're outmatched!" I cheered directly into his face. "Accept defeat and I'll go easy on y– URAGH!"

Ocho had headbutted me mid-sentence. I reeled back, releasing my grip on the knife.

"Oh, what the goddamn!" I shouted. Then, before he could do anything further, I rolled sideways and off the arm of the statue. I didn't know if he would come with me or disengage, but I figured either way, I was in better straits. Ocho chose to grab on to the rock and let me go on my merry way without him—which was fine by me. I'd tippy-tapped my way around this for too long, and now it was time to end it once and for all.

Famous last words, right?

As I fell, I summoned the eggs in my mind and watched as they swarmed beneath me as one. Then I shouted to my matau companion.

"Stinky!" I called. "Get my haladie!"

Stinky followed my descent with his gaze.

"Your what?!"

I released a frustrated growl.

"My double-bladed knife thingy! It's right there!" I pointed at my discarded weapon not far from where he stood. It—and my knapsack—were resting against a pile of rubble near the wall. I hit the egg trampoline and bounced back up into the air as Stinky raced to retrieve my belongings.

"AND MY BAG!"

I shot up and past the arm I'd fallen from, watching as the broken, battered, and bloody form of Ocho stood still, his one remaining hand gripping the handle of his knife.

Good. He's waiting for me. Hold tight, bitch.

I took that opportunity to grab on to the bolt in my foot and yank it out in a gout of blood. It was both a relief and an agony to do so, but I couldn't run through this next sequence with medieval bone spurs. Rather than try to land on the statue again, I just let gravity take me back down once I'd reached the highest point, and flashed back through Ocho's line of sight. I waved.

A moment before I hit my charming little minions again, I heard the cutting *whoosh* of a blade helicoptering through the air toward me. In a panic, I reached my hand out, hoping the bonded effect would work even if I hadn't been the one to throw it. Otherwise, I was going to be a matching pair with our red-haired friend. The handle of the haladie slapped against my palm just as I hit the eggs and rebounded. I glanced at Stinky; he was just now hefting my pack and racing toward me to get a better toss. Unfortunately, I'd have to get it on the next pass.

I flew by Ocho again and flipped him off this time. He didn't move much, but I did see that he was muttering something under his breath.

Probably a spell to untangle his balls from his diaper.

As I fell back down, I called out to him in my passage.

"Be right there!"

"Orc!" Stinky shouted, and I looked down to see my yellow-fleshed punishment partner lob my knapsack up at me. I almost missed it but caught it by the loop as I fell.

Yes! Now for action.

I focused my message to the eggy boys, forcing all of the seriousness I could muster into my mental tone.

All right, gang. I need a big bounce. Really big.

Big bounce, confirmed the four voices in unison.

Good boys.

When I was about twenty feet from them, they acted. As a unit, they flattened themselves and then fired up at me like slimy, pink bullets and collided with me as one. I don't know what I expected, but it wasn't this.

I slammed hard against them, my limbs and head flopping forward like a ragdoll, and suddenly slammed into reverse, rocketing up and away from them faster than I'd ever moved before. I was like those demonstrations of astronauts in g-force as I *pew-pew*'d through the air.

Once I finally caught my breath, I roared.

"FOR CHOOOOOOOOMPY!"

As I ascended higher and higher, I got worried that I might actually hit the ceiling—which wouldn't be good, because I had some finite resources I couldn't waste. However, as I slowed in my raise, I breathed a sigh of relief.

No orc pâté today!

Then I looked down at the statue far below me and the ground even farther still.

Yet.

Ocho was staring up at me, and apparently whatever incantation he'd been fellating was finished, because he waved his arm in the air and a cloud of magical light descended around him like slowly falling stars.

Aw, that's real pretty, Ocho. Too bad I'm about to wreck your whole career!

The magic mist settled in midair before flashing brightly and coalescing into a long, pointed barb. The spell's effects then drifted over to surround his dagger. The edge of the blade expanded, joining with the magic until there were a pair of blades—one overlaid on top of the other.

Neat trick; let's see how that pans out for you.

With a jolt, I realized I hadn't even started the next phase of my plan yet, so, quickly, I raised the haladie.

Here you go, you worst-haircut-award-winnin'-cumsock; I've also got two blades! Eat strategy, jizz pilot!

I hurled my weapon as I fell, watching it spin like the world's deadliest fidget spinner. Remember those? My aim was superb. The haladie flew directly toward Ocho, carving through the air and traveling directly toward his stupid perfect face.

Congratulations! You have raised a Skill!
Throwing Weapons has advanced to (F-Rank Level 9)

Ocho leaped backward out of the path of the blades, and it spun harmless by.

"Nice try! But—"

CRASH!

Just as Ocho had been about to fire off one of his trademark *super lame* comebacks, he'd been hit in the face with a bottle that shattered on impact.

You see, I'd seen precisely one episode of the anime *Naruto*, and in it, one of the wizard acrobats hid his real attack in the shadow of one of his big-ass throwing stars. I didn't really dig cartoons, but that idea had always been in the back of my mind. So, being as I was in a new world where shit like martial-arts magicians could possibly exist, I'd taken some creative liberty with that tactic and made it *better*.

"Pocket sand!" I roared.

As liquid coated Ocho's face, I smiled. Pepper's Hair Tonic was a delightful distraction for my next— *Holy shit!*

The unintended abrupt chaos of my action's consequence suddenly became apparent. Everywhere the tonic had splashed instantly began to sprout hair. Like . . . a *lot* of it. Coarse blond hair erupted from Ocho's face, his shoulders, his belt—a bunch of places. Soon, the entire front half of his body had sprouted at least three feet of follicles, immediately changing this encounter from Naruto to whatever the fuck *Bobobo-bo Bo-bobo* was.

As I was zeroing in on my perfect range, Ocho was hilariously fighting for his life as hair had entirely consumed his existence. Muffled screams emanated from beneath the majestic mane on the front half of his body, and he began ripping and pulling at it to free himself. If I'd had more time to, boy, oh, boy, would I have gloated.

Instead, it was on to Part Three: Loon's Smirking Revenge.

I slipped my pack onto my shoulder (which was super difficult while falling—guys, don't try something like that in a universe where physics exists) and readied my two nuclear-level payback devices. In my left hand was the Guardian's Buckler, and in my right was a little bad boy known—mostly by me—as the Indestructible Orb. It was a sphere of what looked like milky glass, but I'd had it on good authority—my interface—that it couldn't be destroyed. Now it was time to see if that check could be cashed.

I was approaching fast, and when Ocho finally ripped away the last bits of tangly face-pubes from his beautiful lips, his eyes grew wide. He readied his mega knife and took a few cautious steps back. He grinned.

There you go, my guy. The more you envision your success, the sweeter it's gonna be when I make you eat shit.

He backed up one more pace. But that was fine. He wasn't my target.

As I passed the invisible dome housing the talisman, I launched the Indestructible Orb from my mitt as hard as I could, angling it straight down. It struck the magical barrier encasing Zeol's bauble and fucking *smashed right through it!* It hit the platform like the baseball that killed Ashley Judd in *Simon Birch*, and *just like that movie*, goddamn obliterated the entire platform.

Motherfuck, yes!

I didn't wait to see if the godly trinket had survived the disaster, though: I had more shit to do. I aimed the buckler to the side so that the thin, rounded age was facing down.

Here goes nothing!

I ignited Grenalyn's Gussying Gauntlets' once-a-day fuck-everybody ultra power and transformed the metal shield from *pervious* to *impervious*. I was ninety percent certain I had those two words on *lock*.

Finally: my pièce de résistance. I used ol' reliable—Calden's Hang Time—and raised my empty hand in the air, positioning it where I thought it would be the most advantageous, and with my other brought the buckler down in an arc, performing a maneuver that I was confident would one day be known far and wide as the World's Sexiest Karate Chop. The edge of the buckler struck one of the cracks in the stone—but a very specific crack.

Earlier, when I'd been getting my dick punched inside-out by Ocho's *totally not painful* attacks, I'd played a hand I'd yet to utilize. I used my *other* new Ability, the one I'd been so excited about. I'd taken a risk and sacrificed both my Sabotage Ability *and* my Identify back in Chamber Two. This had created something wholly unique for the price of some Esper juice.

Eye of the Saboteur
This feature not only grants the user the ability to view detail on items and effects but to also learn its components and structural makeup. This is an

Ability forged with the scavenger in mind, as it makes material breakdown a breeze! Please use responsibly.

I'd divined that this statue *was* quite old indeed, and all those cracks had really done a number on its structural integrity. The Ability allowed me to discern not only the weakest areas of the stone plinth but also the *worst* spot to apply pressure—or say, the best place to administer I World's Sexiest Karate Chop.

Because it had worked so well, I had used it on the barrier while I was getting personally acquainted with it. Turns out, the point where it was weakest was at the top—just like Ocho.

There was a resounding *crunch* from within the statue as I hit, followed by a long, deafening silence. Too long. Nothing was happening.

Oh, fuck. Did I just fuck this up? Goddammit, I knew I shouldn't have trusted myself with—

Everything imploded all at once.

The statue crumbled so quickly, I didn't even have time to react; I just fell. Dust and debris filled my vision, and I accidentally sucked in a lungful of it and began choking and coughing. My eyes watering, I free-fell into oblivion before landing abruptly against a pile of rubble. If the statue had taken any longer to collapse, I don't think I would have been protected by the Aegis, and the outcome would have been much different. As it stood, I didn't feel a thing from my tumble—well, other than the broken bones, gashes, scrapes, magic burns, and other boo-boos I'd been saddled with from my climactic clash with Ocho.

Speaking of Ocho.

I could hear him sobbing not far from me, but it was impossible to see within the chamber's rocky vape cloud. So, hobbling along with only one good leg, I followed the sounds as best I could, stumbling over broken rocks and sections of shattered stone until a shape emerged suddenly from the mist. He was crouched, trembling atop a cluster of debris and clutching his hand to his thigh to stop the blood from pouring out of it—which he was doing a poor job of.

Nearby on the ground was my haladie, covered in the blood that undoubtedly came from his leg.

Ha! Guess I judged correctly.

I'd summoned the haladie back to me just before I'd hit, positioning my hand in his path and hoping it would, like, chop him in half or something. I'd been a little off, but this would do. That kind of injury would slow him down if it didn't straight-up kill him.

I'll just tell everyone I meant to do that.

I stepped forward and rolled a little as the ball of my foot slid on a smooth, round object. I stopped and bent down to pick it up.

The Indestructible Orb. Well, buddy, you sure lived up to your namesake.

That was when I heard the familiar *ping ping* of my approaching pink partners over the muffled mewling of Ocho's adult sobs.

Alive? Living? Alive? Hurt?

I chuckled.

I'm alive, but yes, I am hurt. Thanks for the help back there, homies. You really came in clutch.

Good! I heard in unison, as the four shapes cautiously emerged from the cloud. I noticed that Jumpy, Clucky, and Mortimer were carrying something in their mouths, and moved forward to retrieve them.

Gifts!

Jumpy was holding an oblong object about eight inches long in his teeth, but it took me a moment to recognize it for what it was. The talisman! I took it from him and patted him on his head. Clucky spat his item out at my feet, but that one I knew instantly on sight.

The Feather Chest? Who reverted its size?

Clucky, Clucky said.

How?

Copy.

Copy?

Copy, he confirmed.

So, he was somehow able to tell the chest to minimize? With his mind talk? I'm definitely going to have to test that out later when it's more . . .

I looked over at Ocho.

. . . opportune.

Lastly was Mortimer's "gift." He carefully approached me, holding his object gingerly in his mouth. When I realized what it was, I took a sharp breath.

Mortimer, you retrieved Merra's amulet?!

Yes, he responded. His tone sounded careful, as if he wasn't sure if he was going to be punished.

Why? I asked.

Need.

I didn't know what to say to that. There was a level of sophisticated understanding involved in these little guys' comprehension, and though I wasn't sure to what level, I knew without a doubt I'd be relying on these four in the future.

That is . . . amazing! I intimated, patting him on the head fondly. *That settles it! You're all getting promoted!*

There was a general feeling of joy emanating from the carton.

Slappy? Slappy questioned, looking bashful that he hadn't brought me a gift of any variety.

You too, Slapster.

He brightened, his mouth opening wide. If I didn't know any better, I'd have said it was a smile.

Well, the work isn't over, I said. *We need to—*

"How?!" a broken voice demanded behind me.

I turned toward it to see Ocho. He was still crouched, clutching his leg, but now his face was turned toward me. His *real* face. It was bloody and bruised, his nose clearly having been broken and one of his eyes swollen shut.

Guess he's outta magic—er, Arcana.

"How what?" I asked, hobbling forward, picking up my discarded haladie, and stuffing it into my waistband. "How do I make whooping your tailfeathers look this good? I want to be humble and say 'hard work and practice,' but really, this is *au naturel*, baby. You can't teach this sort of handsome skill."

"How did you know the pylon was contained within the statue?"

"The *what* what?"

"The pylon—the gate," he clarified stupidly. "Who told you of its presence?"

I was about to ask a few more questions—mostly *What the fuck are you on about?* but as the dust began to settle, a form took shape behind him where the statue's central mass once stood. It was a tall monolith, dark as night, and loomed over us, the still-floating debris giving it an ominous cast. I noticed, however, that it appeared to be missing its top section. I could see it looked fractured, and peering further, I could see the top portion lying in multiple pieces around its base. It was looking like I had fucked up something for Ocho and his crew.

"Oh," I said, realization dawning on me. "So, *that's* what was in there."

I'd seen an area of emptiness within the structure of the statue, but I had no clue there was a *python* hiding in there. Weird, it didn't look like a snake.

"I'll be honest," I said. "I didn't know what it was. Still don't. Care to share?"

"I don't believe you," Ocho hissed with conviction. "There is no other explanation why you would destroy the Statue of Vosket unless you knew what lay within! Who are you working for?"

His eyes were looking frantic now. Either because of whatever conspiracy he thought was happening, or because he was about to pass out from blood loss. I looked at my own Health and let out a low whistle.

Looks like I got out of there by the skin of my loins. I'm still pretty worse for wear, but as long as I can get out of here soon, I should be good.

"Vosket?" I asked. "Isn't the guy whose dick Stinky's always talking about?"

"Answer me," Ocho demanded, attempting to stand, but winced and seemed to decide against it, leaning back and cradling his leg.

"Listen, butt breath," I said. "You want to know why I destroyed the statue? Because it seemed like the best way to kill you. Apparently, that was a miscalculation on my part but shouldn't be an issue going forward."

Ocho continued to stare at me silently, so I sighed.

"Fine," I said. "When you were talking to me earlier, I saw that you kept stealing peeps at the thing. I thought you might know about . . . "

I paused, considering.

" . . . why I was here. But then I realized you weren't party to most of the conversations that would have been relevant to that information. So, I figured there was some other purpose. I gambled and I won. Wait—am I good at gambling? Should I find a casino and bet it all on green?"

"You destroyed the statue on . . . a *guess?*" Ocho asked, disbelieving.

"What can I say? I'm very sneaky. My motives are mysterious."

"Preposterous. You must be lying. Are you working with the Tides?"

"Pah! We're a Fabuloso family round these parts," I said. "I don't know what you're talking about, man. I don't know anything about no damn py . . . ply? Plypongs? You know what—never mind. I told you what I know. Now you tell me what you and your posse of super friends want me and my kind for. Why did you bring us here? Is it like some fucked-up human zoo? You know those are racist, right?"

"What?" Ocho asked, looking baffled.

"Is it?!" I demanded, taking a step closer. "Is it a zoo?!"

Ocho sighed.

"I suppose it doesn't matter now," he said softly. "To put it simply: we brought you here to harvest your Abilities."

"Huh? Harvest our abilities? Like put us to work and mine resources off of us? Maybe observe us together under strict conditions for research *and* entertainment? I dunno, maybe something like . . . *a human zoo?!*"

I pointed an accusatory finger at the man.

"It's not a zoo," Ocho stated dourly.

"Yeah, we'll see about that," I said.

"There are things in this world that you have no concept of, nor could you begin to fathom," Ocho continued. "We are prisoners, as I said before, and in order to escape from beneath the thumb of tyranny, we must—"

"Where are they?" I interrupted.

"What? Whom?"

"The others—er, from my world," I said. "Tell me their location."

Ocho shook his head.

"Right. They have set up a camp not far from the area where the Crypt lies."

"*How* far away exactly is this 'not far' you speak of?"

"Perhaps two or three days' travel by foot. Northeast."

That was suspiciously easy to get out of him. What's his game?

"All right, thanks!" I said, turning away and waving him off. "See you later, Ocho. Don't come after me ever again, mmkay? All right, byeeee."

I began walking away toward where I assumed Stinky and the remaining living members of the group were. That was when I heard a shuffle.

Oh, this treacherous son of a—

I wheeled around and, not realizing I still had the Orb in my hand, brought my hands up just in time to catch the magically beefed-up blade of Ocho's dagger as he soared through the air to pounce on me. The force of his attack connected with the Orb, sending a shockwave through my body, and both the magical and physical blades shattered instantly. But that wasn't the only thing that was destroyed. Ocho screamed, staring at his *other* stump where once had been his only remaining hand. He'd hit the Orb so hard that the reverberation had blasted most of his arm to smithereens.

I curled my fist around the Orb, angry now. In one swift motion, I'd closed the distance between us and leveled a blow right on the side of Ocho's head, sending him spinning away from me. Shocked, I looked down at my bum leg. The injury was healed. In fact, all of my major aches and pains had started to fade. I could see in the corner of my vision that I had a *fuckload* of notifications but ignored it. I was probably about to Level Up.

I took a deep, heaving breath and spat on the ground. Ocho was still alive—somehow—but I doubted it would be for very long.

"I was going to let you off easy, Stumpy," I said. "But now I'm pissed."

I leaned forward.

"Tell your crew to watch their backs. Because if they try to come after me again—or any of the people I came here with—I'm going to kill them. Slowly. Then I'm going after whatever dumbass powers that be and I'm going to rip them to shreds. In fact, I think I'll do that second part anyway. This place sucks."

I looked up at the ceiling and scowled.

"You hear that, you miserable pieces of shit?" I demanded to empty air. "Fucking fight me. See what happens. You better think long and hard about how important it is for you to keep me here and whether it's worth experiencing never-ending misery. I will burn this world down if that's what it takes. I will drag each and every one of you kicking and screaming to the altar of judgment and baptize you in my nightmare."

There was a moment of silence only broken after a time by Ocho's weakened, shaky voice.

"No," he said from the ground, bleeding out on the stone from his many, *many* wounds. I looked down at him.

"No?"

"No," he reiterated, struggling to lift himself up from his back until he was in a sitting position. "You are a fool, Loon. You do not know what anger you will unearth with your idiotic gnashing of teeth. The Echoes—*we* will hunt you down and strip every last inch of flesh from your bones. Then we will wrench your essence from your soul and feed you to the pylons. Your existence will churn in the bowels of this world for all that remains of eternity. Then we will move on to your friends. It will be an unyielding torment. And if we do not get to you first, the Tides will."

He wobbled to a standing position, blood drenching his form and dripping out of . . . well, everywhere.

"We will hunt you to the edges of existence. *I* will hunt you. There will be no respite, no safe haven, no stranger you can trust that will not hide my shadow. As long as there is air in my lungs, there will be nothing you can do to—"

A blur of motion carved through the smoke, and suddenly, a long shaft of metal blossomed from the center of Ocho's chest. He stopped, looking down at the new development. Then he swayed where he stood, staggered, and, with a belch of blood from his mouth, fell dead to the ground. A moment passed, and then a specter emerged from the shroud of debris and stood over Ocho's body. Then he twisted Frida's broken ax from the fallen man's torso and turned to me.

"Pity," Stinky said. "I was just fuckin' warming up to him, too."

I chuckled.

"You really have a flair for dramatic timing, don't you?" I asked.

"It's the whimsical curse that was placed on me," the matau returned seriously, and for a moment, I might have considered that he was being genuine.

At that moment, a shining yellow light appeared in the air above Ocho's lifeless body. It was an Esper Node, but I hadn't seen one in this color yet.

For defeating a [Group] opponent more than FIFTEEN Levels above your own, you have received a [Greater] Topaz Esper Node!

Accept [1] Greater Topaz Esper Node?

Yes / No

"Bitchin'," I breathed, staring up at the fluttering majesty of this new Esper Node. I let a grin creep across my face and turned to Stinky.

He bristled.

"What the fuck are you waiting for, orc? Let's scoot. Grab the fuckin' thing and let's go. We've got injured."

"Yes, sir," I said, giving him a mock salute, and then gestured toward the gateway. "After you, O Great One."

"Fuck off, orc."

EPILOGUE

I hadn't seen the sun in days. In fact, it was painful to look at, so as we moved down the long, stony tunnel toward the portal of light of the exit, I cursed the fact that I didn't have a free hand to shield my eyes.

Over each of my shoulders I carried one of our party members. Frida was unconscious—but alive. The Experience she'd earned from her battle with Ocho was more than enough to bring her over the threshold of Level Sixteen, which healed the injuries sustained from combat but not her physical or emotional exhaustion. She'd actually fallen asleep before the effect took hold, which was a strange thing to witness—and a little funny. Someone dropping into slumber on the ground right before a little flash of light enveloped their body while a merry golden marquee danced overhead declaring a Level Up.

Jes was worse off. He'd sustained fairly serious trauma from both his physical altercation and the anguish of seeing several of his closest companions ripped apart in front of him. He'd been removed from the fight almost immediately, and apparently that little bit of an encounter didn't net him enough to get him over the Level hump and heal his wounds. Fortunately, it seemed most of his ailments were from broken bones, so he wasn't in as great a danger of bleeding out. Though it was clear that a *lot* of his bones were shattered. He'd need whatever the closest thing to medical attention was. Stinky had explained that Leveling Up only worked to remove injuries within the first handful of hours after receiving them, so if we couldn't find anyone soon, he'd likely be permanently maimed. I wasn't sure if hoisting him up over my shoulder was the right move for someone in his condition, but Stinky assured me that it was better to move quickly and uncomfortably so that we'd have the best opportunity to find him help.

He was from a race of hyper-intelligent know-it-alls—if it was to be believed—so he likely had a better idea of necessity than I ever would.

Jumpy, Clucky, Slappy, and Mortimer—my captains, I decided—followed along at an easy pace behind us. I'd put them in charge of carrying various items of *vast* importance. This was mostly to make them feel like valiant heroes and instrumental to the group and not at all because I wanted easier access to certain tools or resources. What do you take me for? Among their collection that they dutifully transported in their jaws were the Feather Chest, the Guardian's Buckler, the Indestructible Orb, and—because I thought it was funny—the dented helm from Berg's corpse. All four seemed to take the job quite seriously, proudly hopping along in the possessed-roe version of marching with your chest puffed out. Every once in a while, I'd make a show of requesting one of the items, inspecting it, and then returning it to them with reverent respect and warm gratitude. The accompanying wave of pride that washed over me after each of these interactions made it all worth it.

As we stepped out into the light for the first time, I took a big breath and shook my head.

"Man," I said. "You really don't appreciate how fresh regular air is until you spend a few weeks in a grimy, farty crypt."

"Try a few fuckin' centuries, in their case," Stinky said, jabbing a thumb toward my shoulders.

"Oh, shit, yeah," I breathed. "We may want to leave them in the tunnel to make sure their lungs don't explode."

I peered out at the world around us and felt relief course through me. We were apparently pressed into the side of a mountain or maybe a big-ass hill. The tunnel looked out over a sloping valley with verdant hills and a huge swatch of lush forest. Birds fluttered off in the distance, speckling the blue sky and tweeting happy melodies of the morning. At least, it looked like morning. It was really hard to tell, as I'd hadn't actually *seen* one since arriving in this world. But it felt like morning. Smelled like it too. The air was crisp, and most of the visible grass still had glimmering patches of dew clinging to the blades.

Yeah, definitely morning.

Far below us, beyond the mouth of the tunnel, was a meandering dirt path that sloped down and away from the hillside and into the trees. From this distance, though, it would be hard to tell that it was a tunnel, let alone the exit from a dungeon. It was probably part of the reason it wasn't well known anymore. The way down to the trail was a perilous one and not easily navigable with two incomprehensibly heavy adventurers dangling from either side of your neck. So, we decided to pop a squat and rest until Frida woke up and could manage her own weight.

I was glad for the chance to relax, and it wasn't until I was mid-doze in the rays of early-morning sunshine that I realized it was truly the first time

I'd been able to do so. I was fucking exhausted, and ever since I'd arrived, I'd been screaming, or running, or fighting, or all three at once. It also struck me that other than the many, *many* times I'd either been knocked unconscious or straight-up *died*, I hadn't slept a single wink. At this point I was almost afraid that if I did try to catch some Zs, I'd wake up trapped in Pontivex's pleasure palace and have to eat my way through mysterious meats to escape. That was not a euphemism, either. That dude loved him some exotic creature tissue.

Stinky had been pretty quiet since we'd had our encounter. I wasn't sure what was going on but didn't feel like shaking the cage, for once. So, instead, I pulled some of the rations out of my pack and offered some to him.

He accepted wordlessly and began eating in a fashion I'd be tempted to liken to a starved weasel. I wasn't much more dignified with my own meal, but at least I was chewing. Stinky seemed to just be biting off big hunks of jerky and choking them down whole.

Why you got all them needle teeth if you ain't going to use them? Whoever your people's god is probably feels like they got slapped in the face.

After a while of lazing about, I finally decided to break the silence.

"Fuckin' wild, right?" I said, gesturing back at the mouth of the tunnel.

Stinky followed my gesture and then shrugged.

"It's fuckin' up there," he said, and stretched out, splaying his legs out on the ground.

"Bet it felt pretty cool to kick your Level up so high, huh?"

"It did," he said. "'Least until some frog-faced arse-sniffer blasted it away with his shouting."

"Ah, I actually think Ocho looked more like a lizard than a frog."

Stinky stared at me for a moment, as if trying to decide if I was kidding or if I was just stupid, then he shrugged.

"I can do it once per day. So, if you go pissing me off, I'll fire up the fucker again and you can see for yourself what it's like."

"Much obliged," I said, then paused. "By the way . . ."

"Nope," Stinky interjected. "Don't want to talk about it."

"Aw, come on, Stinky. I wanna know what your dark, mysterious reasoning is for being so . . . bad. Why intentionally make yourself shit? Spill the beans, buddy. The suspense is killing me."

"As long as *something* kills you, I'll be happy. It'll save me the trouble."

"Well, now you're just being rude."

"Yep," Stinky said. "I am."

I sighed, then a thought occurred to me.

"Do you know anything about what Ocho was bitching about back there? With the whole Echoes and Tides thing. Ring a bell?"

"No fuckin' clue," Stinky said, crossing his arms and dipping his head in preparation for a nap. "Probably better that we don't know. If we don't go looking for them, that makes it harder for them to look for us."

He grunted.

"I'm going to sleep. Wake me when Frida comes to, and we'll fuck off down the road to Tallrock so that the elf can piss and moan about surviving the attack."

I paused.

"Tallrock? Is that where we're going?"

"Aye, orc," Stinky mumbled. "You'd be better off tradin' your ears for something you'll use."

I stood up and peered over the ledge at the valley beyond.

"Where is it? It must be close, right?" I scanned the greenery with excitement. "Can we see it from here?"

Stinky didn't stir but simply continued mumbling, sleep clearly taking hold of him.

"The tower near the horizon. You can just make it out above the tree line."

I squinted and traced the ribbon of color where green met blue until I saw a splotch of gray poking above the treetops miles and miles away.

Tallrock.

I had business there—and money if I brought those Quest items . . .

I jerked upright and opened my menu. I'd been ignoring my notifications, but this seemed important. Before anything else, I saw the celebrational message on my ascent to a higher Level. I'd known I had, but it still surprised me.

Congratulations! You have reached LEVEL TEN.
You grow stronger and receive the benefit of [12] additional Attribute Points. 10% Health and Arcana restored. Combat conditions healed.

I quickly moved through the menu, ignoring everything else, and found the notification I was seeking. I read it over with a grin and then re-read it. Then I read it a third time.

Outstanding! You have completed a Quest!
[Faith Quest] *Into the Dungeon*
Rewards:
2,500 Experience
25 Silver
Achieved Initiate Degree in the Cult of the Capricious
Bonus Reward:
Talisman

Huh, so I get to keep that piece of shit after all that malarkey? Fine. But no takesies-backsies once I'm using it to enrich my life.

I smiled despite myself, but then I remembered my last conversation with both Zeol and Sababo. They were gone. I'd have thought I'd been happier about it, but the way it went down . . .

Forget it. Fuck them. They got in your head and showed you some fucked-up shit you were trying hard to banish from your memories. Hope wherever they're hiding out is humid and warps the wood of their masks.

I flipped back to the main menu to admire my progress and take my mind off of the more downer aspects of what had gone down.

Loon
Race: Orc*
Class: Barbarian
Level: 10
Profession: Unassigned
Health: 302/302
Arcana: 85/85
Max Stamina: 159 (-10% due to Fatigue II)
Reputation: N/A

Attributes
Remaining Points to Allocate: 12

Strength: 50
Constitution: 96
Dexterity: 50
Wisdom: 10
Intelligence: 8
Charisma: 6
Luck: 15*

Skills
(-10% due to Fatigue II)
Acrobat (E-Rank, Level 1)
Camp (F-Rank Level 1)
Hunting (F-Rank Level 1)
Improvised Weapon (E-Rank Level 2)
Improvised Shield (F-Rank Level 2)
Insight (F-Rank Level 9)

Intimidate (F-Rank Level 2)
Knowledge [Nature] (F-Rank Level 1)
Perception (F-Rank Level 4)
Simple Weapon Proficiency (F-Rank Level 6)
Simple Armor Proficiency (F-Rank Level 1)
Sneaking (B-Rank Level 4)
Survival (F-Rank Level 1)
Two-Handed Weapons (F-Rank Level 6)
Throwing Weapons (F-Rank Level 9)
Unarmed Fighting (E-Rank Level 2)

Active Abilities
Armorless Defense (E-Rank Level 6)
Battle Born I
Enduring Perch I
Eye of the Saboteur I
Darkvision I
Primal Rage (E-Rank Level 1)
Nature's Resilience (F-Rank Level 2)
Uncommon Consumption (F-Rank Level 1)
Blackout Warchant

Passive Abilities
Outsider
Unfaltering
Wildling

Perks
Adventurous Tastes *(First Perk Bonus)*
Aegis Synthesis

Aegis
Calden's Hang Time
Loon's Bombastic Beatdown

Esper Nodes
Emerald: 1
Sapphire: 1
Topaz: 1

My eyes itched. It was possibly time for me to close them for a bit and maybe see what all the hubbub was about. I envisioned finding a spot to make myself more comfortable, but before I knew it, I was out.

I woke a short while later to find a familiar face staring at me from a few feet away.

Frida looked exhausted, her eyes were bloodshot, and she seemed a bit paler than normal. I couldn't blame her.

I yawned.

"Hey," I said softly.

"Hey," she returned.

"Sleep well?"

"Like ah were dead," she said quietly, then lowered her eyes. "Thought ah were, actually. A few times. P'raps ah *did* die, an' now ah'm back. Feels like t' could be the way of et."

"Well, then," I said, clearing my throat, "as ambassador of life, I would like to cordially welcome you back to the realm of the living. Now, you've been gone for a while. So, before you get too comfortable, you'll want to know that there have been some changes."

"Oh?" She leaned forward conspiratorially. "That is quite interesting. Pray tell?"

"Nobody wears pants anymore."

I gestured to my kilt.

"That is a revelation, te be sure."

I adopted a frown and stared at her armored legs.

"Yeah, it's actually considered pretty rude now to wear them."

Frida made a show of grasping at her legs and glanced up at me.

"Well, ah don' want te offend. Should ah jus' remove 'em here? Or . . ."

She'd called my bluff, and I commended her for it. I chose to laugh awkwardly to ease the tension that was almost definitely one-sided.

"Seriously, though, glad you're still around."

"Aye," she said, nodding and glancing around. She seemed to spend a fair bit of time looking over the edge of the entrance to the tunnel, and I cleared my throat.

"Does it feel the same?"

"Eh?" she asked, glancing back at me in confusion.

"As it did before? I don't know how to gauge something like that. I've never been—you know, pulled through time. I'd imagine *some* things might be different, though."

Frida placed a finger on her chin thoughtfully.

"Hard te say," she said, surveying our little makeshift camp. "Haven't seen much o' et yet."

Then she locked her eyes on me and raised an eyebrow.

"Though things seem te be lookin' fine as far as locals."

I cleared my throat again.

She's just messing with me, to see what my reaction is. That's gotta be it.

"You wanna know something crazy?" I asked.

"Ye mean *more* mad than what we jus' survived?"

I chuckled.

"Possibly. Okay, here goes: I haven't actually seen what I look like."

"What?"

"I know, right?" I asked. "All this time running around, getting poked by the bad guys, and I never stopped to take a peep at my reflection."

"Goodness," she said. "Yoor missing out on et, then."

I frowned.

"Yeah, but I guess I haven't really come across any mirrors or ponds or anything like that. What's that about? I'm going to start a campaign to install one full-length mirror for every fifteen miles of woodland area."

Frida brightened and gestured to my side.

"Ah've an idea! Hand me pack over."

I glanced down and picked up her knapsack, sliding it across the stone to her. She yanked it open and in an instant had a silvery helmet in her hands.

"Behold."

"Eh?" I wondered. "Is that yours?"

"'Course et's mine," she said. "Don't wear et much—gets in the way a bit when ah'm tusslin'. But more 'portantly—it's shiny. Now then. Off you go."

She handed me the helmet gingerly. I accepted it and turned it around to the back and stared, suddenly gobsmacked. Not only was the reflection clear, the face that glowered back was surprising. It wasn't the face I was used to, but it was also not one I was expecting. My skin was green—that much I could have guessed—but there were other aspects that really threw me for a loop. My cheek bones were high, slightly more prominent than I'd have assumed would be normal. My jaw, no longer broken from battle, was angular and symmetrical. My nose wasn't shaped like a pig's or anything, and my teeth were only a *little* sharper than they were in the old world. I had tusks jutting out from my lower gums, and I'd felt those, but they looked much more proportional to the rest of my face. Most surprising was that I actually *liked* what I saw. I'll admit to having been a bit hesitant initially because of my preconceived notions—but this was shockingly dissimilar to the image I'd conjured in my mind this whole time.

"Holy shit! I'm *handsome!*" I exclaimed. "What the hell? I thought I was going to be ugly as fuck."

"Why would ye think that?"

"Well, mostly because the menu straight up *said* that I'd be uglier than most orcs."

"Well," Frida began thoughtfully. "P'raps it were judging ye by the standards o' most orcs?"

"What's that now?"

"Orcs value a certain look about 'em," she continued. "By human standards—and ye've led me to believe that's what ye were 'riginally—the harsher we perceive 'em, the more brassy they'd be lookin' to others o' their kind. Mayhaps the opposite's true."

"So, all the fly orc honeys would find me repulsive to behold, but the elf ladies will be wanting to break off a piece?"

"If'n I understand what ye saying—an' ah'm no' sure ah do . . . aye."

"This is fantastic news!" I chuckled. "I'm a fuckin' *morsel*."

"Donnae let et go to yoor head." Frida smirked.

"But it's already *on* my head! This is a game-changer!"

Frida beamed at me and rolled her eyes before glancing at Stinky. She nudged me and nodded his way.

"Should we wake him?"

I took a gander at the matau, who was snoring quietly with his chin pressed to his chest.

"Nah, maybe in a bit," I said with a smirk. "If we rouse him too soon, he's just gonna be cranky."

"Ain't he always cranky?"

"That's a good point," I said. "But let's chill for a bit longer without the oppressive cloud of grump hanging over our heads."

"Right-o," Frida said, then frowned. "Sorry."

"For what?"

"Merra used te always say that," she said softly. "Got use te slingin' et about meself."

"I think that's good," I said, surprising myself with my own sense of introspection. "Keeps the memory alive. I use phrases my—er, people that are gone used to use all the time. Helps to sort of feel like they're still around, you know?"

"Aye," Frida said.

"Besides," I said, trying to bring the mood back up, "we won't have to wait long."

I reached into the front pocket of the kilt and removed the glittering necklace of Merra's amulet. Frida's face brightened.

"Ach! Loon! Why dinnae ye tell me ye had that hangin' about by yoor nethers! Ah'd just gone and got meself a mantle o' heartbreak. Rude te do to a girl, that."

I grinned.

"Stinky isn't the only one who appreciates a dramatic flair."

"Him?" Frida said, gesturing toward the sleeping matau and looking aghast at the prospect. "Dramatic? Nae, lad. Get yoor head on."

"It's on, and as previously established . . . "—I winked at her—" . . . quite handsome."

"It wonnae be fer long if ye surprise me like that 'gain," Frida chuckled.

"All right, easy, killer," I said. "From now on, I'll divulge *all* of my secrets well in advance."

"Thank ye," she said, but then her smile drifted away as she took on a more serious tone. "Ye think we'll be able te make et all t' way doon there? Te the lower chamber, ye ken?"

"Not easily," I said, focusing on the tower in the distance where the unknown variable of Tallrock was located. "And not as we are now. We'll need to get stronger, gain some Levels—probably a *lot* of Levels—and still . . . not alone. We'll need more people if we're going to have any chance at making it out of this garbage-ass Shitsville alive."

"Aye," Frida said, her gaze unfocusing at a spot in front of her.

I didn't need her falling out of her good mood right then, so I optioned for optimism.

"Fortunately," I said emphatically, and clapped my hands, knocking her out of her daze, "I know a spot where *loads* of people of similar interests are. Real agreeable types, you know? We'll swing by, scoop them up, and then get our training montage going before flying back into that Crypt and reviving our friends."

"Think they're keen te help out?" Frida asked. "Might be a tad harder than yer thinkin' to bring 'em round te the idea of delving into a dungeon like that 'un."

"Oh, yeah," I said brazenly. "I'm like a king to those people—they'll be falling all over themselves to help."

"Is that right, Yer Majesty?" Frida laughed.

"*Your Highness* will do," I said.

"S'pose ye won 'em over with yer keen peoplin' skills?"

I raised an eyebrow.

"Yes," I stated matter-of-factly. "That's exactly what I did. People love me. I am a people person."

"Aye," Frida said. "S'pose ye are. Guess we'll jus' have te see, won't we?"

I nodded once.

"Yes, we certainly will."

I tucked the amulet back into the pouch.

"Until then, this bad boy is going to be danglin' near my bits for safe keeping."

"Is that truly the best spot fer et?" Frida asked. "Seems a bit unwholesome."

"Frida," I said, acting offended. "I might get blasted in the face by fire, stabbed in the legs with magic knives, have my fingers eaten off by dragon-skunks—but I always protect my bits."

I shrugged.

"Plus, it's the only place I have pockets."

"Tellin' of," Frida said, staring at my kilt, "what's that parcel ye got danglin' out of ye there?"

I looked down. The top of the miniature wizard tower that was Zeol's talisman was jutting out from my pocket at an angle, easily noticed, obviously.

Well, that won't do. I'll have to find a better method of not only keeping it secure but keeping it hidden from public view. I don't know how many people are aware of its existence, and I'd like to keep that number as close to zero as I can manage.

I removed the talisman and held it up.

"Just a trinket."

"What's et do?"

I frowned.

"You know . . . I'm not quite sure. Let me check."

I no longer had my Analysis Ability but had replaced it for a newer, improved version that I was calling *Better Analysis*. I accessed Eye of the Saboteur and then held the talisman in my gaze for a moment.

This better not be one of Zeol's sex toys or something. It would be hilarious, but also, a lot of people died so that I could get my hands on it.

When the information populated in front of me, I scowled. Unlike with the statue and the magical barrier, the talisman didn't hold any information about the materials, weakness, or really *anything* like before. In fact, the description was just two lines long. I hadn't actually absorbed it out of disappointment, but then I went back and read it. I felt my heart sink. My expression must have been *very* telling, because Frida nudged me.

"What's wrong, Loon?"

I sighed, reading it again to make sure I'd understood. That couldn't be right, could it?

Zeol's Talisman
Acquired inside the Forbidden Crypt of the Dreadnaught Lord. Contains the soul of Rexen Gravetongue – the Dreadnaught Lord.

"Ah, fuck," I hissed, staring in disbelief at the simple-seeming item. "Well, this fuckin' complicates things."

ACKNOWLEDGMENTS

I want to give a loud and obnoxious shout out to those ride-and/or-die homies who spent their extremely limited free time contributing to this book in some capacity—whether it was alpha reading, beta reading, or just offering thumbs-up emojis when I would give unsolicited progress updates in a group chat.

In particular, I'd like to thank these fine folk:

Michaela Eagen, who always said "I like it" during my reads of chapters and consistently told me whether a line was funny enough.

Reece McDuffee, for reading the first few chapters and immediately demanding spoilers.

Patrick McDuffee, who was convinced I was writing a book about something completely different and bizarrely specific despite my many attempts to clarify otherwise.

Ali McDuffee, who said the cover art was "cool."

Tomas Yanes, Billy Little, Zach Phillips, and Chase Slocum, for being excellent and patient real ones despite my tyrannical demands for criticism.

Lindsey Yanes, for supporting the book blindly and without question.

Jordan Abbe, for an off-handed statement that inspired my creativity.

Kyra Martin, for reading each chapter episodically through the medium of Snapchat.

Karl Renfro, for being an OG reader (even though you didn't invite me to your wedding).

Chris Jung, for introducing me to this ridiculous genre.

Luke Chmilenko, for patience with my deluge of inquiries and for thinking this was a tale worth telling.

Warlizard (allegedly from the Warlizard Gaming Forum), for his sage advice and acting as my pro tem literary agent.

Tim Kaiver, for being a real solid homie and tolerating my frequent absences.

Theo Hodges, whose output of whole-ass books is almost as impressive as his cover art. ;)

Sig Kusanagi, the nicest mod to ever helm r/LitRPG on Reddit.

The entire staff at Podium, who will definitely read this section before anyone else. Thanks for this opportunity.

Everyone else I can't fit on one page, including my Patrons and all of you who read each installment on Scribble Hub and Royal Road.

If you've enjoyed this story, please consider checking out the weekly *Dungeons & Dragons* 5e actual play podcast that I host and DM for, *The d20 Syndicate*. My fellow castmates are some of the wiliest comedic minds you could shake a handful of dice at. You can find us at www.d20syndicate.com, as well as on Instagram, Twitter, Twitch, or wherever podcasts are available.

Check out sethmcduffee.com for updates and other media and to join my mailing list.

ABOUT THE AUTHOR

Seth McDuffee is the bestselling author of the novel *Good Boy* and Dungeon Master for the popular *Dungeons & Dragons* 5e podcast *The d20 Syndicate*, as well as a purveyor of fine soups.

DISCOVER
STORIES UNBOUND

PodiumAudio.com

 www.ingramcontent.com/pod-product-compliance
Ingram Content Group UK Ltd.
Pitfield, Milton Keynes, MK11 3LW, UK
UKHW041304180426
11947UKWH00009B/669